Lest Darkness Fall

The Roman Empire had spread order, knowledge, and civilisation throughout the ancient world. When Rome fell, the light of reason flickered out across the Empire. The Dark Ages had begun; they would last a thousand years. Could a man from the 20th century prevent the fall of Rome?

Rogue Queen

Decades before a certain five-year voyage, L. Sprague de Camp sent a spirited crew to a strange and distant world, where their meeting with its inhabitants created chaos in local politics, upset the balance of power and generally created the most entertaining havoc.

The Tritonian Ring and Other Pusadian Tales

The gods of Poseidonis – or Atlantis – were powerful and real. Now they were determined to destroy the kingdom ruled by the father of Prince Vakar, the one man whose mind they could not read. The only way to save the kingdom was to discover that thing which the gods feared most.

D0840553

Also by L. Sprague de Camp

Science Fiction

Viagens Interplanetarias Series

Krishna

1. The Queen of Zamba (1949)
2. The Hand of Zei (1950)
3. The Hostage of Zir (1977)
4. The Prisoner of Zhamanak (1982)
5. The Virgin of Zesh (1953)
6. The Bones of Zora (1983) (with Catherine Crook de Camp)
7. The Tower of Zanid (1958)
8. The Swords of Zinjaban (1991) (with Catherine Crook de Camp)

Ormazd

9. Rogue Queen (1951)

Kukulkan

10. The Stones of Nomuru (1988) (with Catherine Crook de Camp)
11. The Venom Trees of Sunga (1992)

Other SF

Lest Darkness Fall (1941)
Divide and Rule (1948)
Genus Homo (1950) (with P. Schuyler Miller)
The Glory That Was (1960)
The Virgin & the Wheels (1976)
The Great Fetish (1978)

Fantasy

Harold Shea Series (With Fletcher Pratt)

1. The Incomplete Enchanter (1941)
2. The Castle of Iron (1950)
3. Wall of Serpents (1960)

Novarian Series

1. The Fallible Fiend (1973)

2. The Goblin Tower (1968)
3. The Clocks of Iraz (1971)
4. The Unbeheaded King (1983)
5. The Honorable Barbarian (1989)

Other Fantasy

Tales from Gavagan's Bar (1953 collection, expanded 1978) (L. Sprague de Camp and Fletcher Pratt)
The Tritonian Ring (1953)
The Incorporated Knight (1988)
The Pixilated Peeress (1991) (with Catherine Crook de Camp)
The Purple Pterodactyls (collection) (1980)
Land of Unreason (1942) (with Fletcher Pratt)
The Carnelian Cube (1948) (with Fletcher Pratt)
The Undesired Princess (1951)
Solomon's Stone (1957)
The Reluctant Shaman and Other Fantastic Tales (1970)
The Continent Makers and Other Tales of the Viagens (1953)

Non-Fiction

Dark Valley Destiny: the Life of Robert E. Howard (1983) (with Catherine Crook de Camp and Jane Whittington Griffin)
Literary Swordsmen and Sorcerers (1976)
Lovecraft: a Biography (1975)
Time and Chance: an Autobiography (1996)
Science-Fiction Handbook (1953 (revised 1975, with Catherine Crook de Camp))

L. Sprague de Camp
SF GATEWAY OMNIBUS

LEST DARKNESS FALL
ROGUE QUEEN
THE TRITONIAN RING AND OTHER
PUSADIAN TALES

GOLLANCZ
LONDON

First published in Great Britain in 2014 by
Gollancz
An imprint of the Orion Publishing Group
Orion House, 5 Upper St Martin's Lane,
London WC2H 9EA

An Hachette UK Company

A CIP catalogue record for this book is
available from the British Library

ISBN 978 0 575 10367 2

1 3 5 7 9 10 8 6 4 2

Typeset by Jouve (UK), Milton Keynes

Printed and bound by CPI Group (UK) Ltd, Croydon, CR0 4YY

The Orion Publishing Group's policy is to use papers
that are natural, renewable and recyclable products and
made from wood grown in sustainable forests. The logging
and manufacturing processes are expected to conform to
the environmental regulations of the country of origin.

www.orionbooks.co.uk
www.gollancz.co.uk

CONTENTS

ENTER THE SF GATEWAY . . .

Towards the end of 2011, in conjunction with the celebration of fifty years of coherent, continuous science fiction and fantasy publishing, Gollancz launched the SF Gateway.

Over a decade after launching the landmark SF Masterworks series, we realised that the realities of commercial publishing are such that even the Masterworks could only ever scratch the surface of an author's career. Vast troves of classic SF and fantasy were almost certainly destined never again to see print. Until very recently, this meant that anyone interested in reading any of those books would have been confined to scouring second-hand bookshops. The advent of digital publishing changed that paradigm for ever.

Embracing the future even as we honour the past, Gollancz launched the SF Gateway with a view to utilising the technology that now exists to make available, for the first time, the entire backlists of an incredibly wide range of classic and modern SF and fantasy authors. Our plan, at its simplest, was – and still is! – to use this technology to build on the success of the SF and Fantasy Masterworks series and to go even further.

The SF Gateway was designed to be the new home of classic science fiction and fantasy – the most comprehensive electronic library of classic SFF titles ever assembled. The programme has been extremely well received and we've been very happy with the results. So happy, in fact, that we've decided to complete the circle and return a selection of our titles to print, in these omnibus editions.

We hope you enjoy this selection. And we hope that you'll want to explore more of the classic SF and fantasy we have available. These are wonderful books you're holding in your hand, but you'll find much, much more ... through the SF Gateway.

www.sfgateway.com

INTRODUCTION

from The Encyclopedia of Science Fiction

L. [Lyon] Sprague de Camp (1907–2000) was a US writer, married from 1939 until her death early in 2000 to Catherine Adelaide Crook, who collaborated on a number of his books, sometimes without printed credit, though always freely acknowledged by de Camp. She had always been actively involved in his career, and the two were increasingly recognized after about 1960 to be genuine collaborators. De Camp was educated at the California Institute of Technology, where he studied aeronautical engineering, and at Stevens Institute of Technology, where he gained a master's degree in 1933. He went to work for a company dealing with patenting, and his first published work was a co-written textbook on the subject.

He then met P. Schuyler Miller, with whom he collaborated on a novel, *Genus Homo* (1950), which failed to find a publisher for several years; it is a Sleepers Awake tale whose protagonists find that, a million years hence, the human species has been supplanted by apes. De Camp's first published story was 'The Isolinguals' (September 1937 *Astounding*), which appeared before the arrival of John W. Campbell Jr as *Astounding* editor. After Campbell took over the two men proved highly compatible, and de Camp soon became a central figure of the Golden Age of SF, writing prolifically for Astounding over the next few years. His contributions included the Johnny Black series about an intelligent, uplifted bear; the best of this early work were collected in *The Best of L. Sprague de Camp* (1978).

It was, however, the appearance in 1939 of *Astounding*'s fantasy companion *Unknown* which stimulated de Camp's most notable early work, including his most famous single novel, *Lest Darkness Fall* (December 1939 *Unknown*; 1941) (see below). Other contributions to *Unknown* included 'None but Lucifer' (September 1939) with H. L. Gold; *Solomon's Stone* (June 1942); the long title story of *Divide and Rule* (1948); 'The Wheels of If' (October 1940), a Parallel Worlds story later assembled in *The Wheels of If, And Other Science-Fiction* (1948); and 'The Undesired Princess' (February 1942), later assembled in a collection, *The Undesired Princess* (1951). These works exuberantly dramatized Campbell's desire that stories in *Unknown* would treat activities normally treated as pure fantasy, like the use of Magic, as *techniques*, Fantasy was sf on vacation. De Camp's humour was consistently of this sort. *Lest Darkness Fall* remains in print, more than 70 years later.

Sprague was, unusually, an author who seemed equally comfortable solo and in collaboration. Over and above the huge influence of his wife, he was most successful in his collaborations with Fletcher Pratt, whom he met in 1939. Pratt conceived the idea behind their highly successful Incomplete Enchanter series of humorous fantasies in which the protagonist, Harold Shea, is transported into a series of Parallel Worlds based on various myths and legends. As usual with de Camp, the publication sequence is complex, but the main titles – all credited to both authors – are *The Incomplete Enchanter* (1941), *The Castle of Iron* (1950) and *Wall of Serpents* (1960). Various compilations were issued over the years; the most complete of these is *The Intrepid Enchanter* (1988), where all three original titles are properly assembled.

Other collaborations with Pratt included *The Land of Unreason* (1942), *The Carnelian Cube: A Humorous Fantasy* (1948), and the Gavagan's Bar series of Club Stories assembled in *Tales From Gavagan's Bar* (1953). After Pratt's death in 1956, De Camp returned inconclusively to the Enchanter sequence with *Sir Harold and the Gnome King* (1991) and some stories in collaboration with Christopher Stasheff assembled as *The Exotic Enchanter* (1995). Book publication of these fantasy titles, sometimes years after their release in *Unknown* and other magazines, obscures a significant interruption to De Camp's writing career.

After joining the US Naval Reserve in 1942, he spent the war working in the Philadelphia Naval Yard alongside Isaac Asimov and Robert A. Heinlein. Afterward he published a few articles, but hardly any new fiction until 'The Animal-Cracker Plot' (July 1949 *Astounding*) introduced his Viagens Interplanetarias stories, a loosely linked sf series set in a future where Brazil has become the dominant world power, the stories themselves being sited mainly on three worlds which circle the star Tau Ceti and are named after the Hindu gods Vishnu, Ganesha and Krishna – these being romantically barbarian worlds on which he could set, couched as sf, the kind of Planetary Romance he had previously written as fantasy, the market for pure fantasy having disappeared with the demise of *Unknown* in 1943. Planets circling other stars and sharing the same conceptual universe were given names like Osiris, Isis and Thoth.

Many of the short stories in the series were included in *The Continent Makers and Other Tales of the Viagens* (1953); others appeared in *Sprague de Camp's New Anthology of Science Fiction* (1953) and in *The Virgin and the Wheels* (1976). *Rogue Queen* (1951), a novel set in the Viagens Interplanetarias universe, is, with *Lest Darkness Fall*, de Camp's most highly regarded sf work (see below). The remaining novels, an internal series all set on Krishna, are *Cosmic Manhunt* (1954); *The Search for Zei* (1962) and *The Hand of Zei* (1963), both titles, which had been complicatedly edited, finally being superseded by book publication of the full original novel, *The Hand of Zei*

(1982); *The Tower of Zanid* (1958); *The Hostage of Zir* (1977); plus *The Bones of Zora* (1983) and *The Swords of Zinjaban* (1991), both written with his wife. The series as a whole contains a blend of intelligent, exotic adventure and wry humour characteristic of de Camp's better work, though the later tales in particular do not explore any too deeply either the romantic or the human-condition ironies available to aspiring authors of the Planetary Romance.

Along with the Viagens Interplanetarias series, De Camp's most notable sf writings after about 1950 were stories like *The Glory that Was* (1960) and 'A Gun for Dinosaur' (March 1956 Galaxy), the Dinosaur title story of *A Gun for Dinosaur, And Other Imaginative Tales* (1963), which also included 'Aristotle and the Gun' (February 1958 *Astounding*). The first and third of these tales use history themes, in the case of the third combined with Time Travel, in a manner similar to *Lest Darkness Fall*; the second is a straightforward time-travel story.

De Camp did not in fact write much more sf, his later career increasingly being devoted to outright fantasy and to Sword and Sorcery. He had gained an early interest in the latter category through his close study of Robert E Howard's famous Conan stories, and worked extensively on editing and adding to that series. *Tales of Conan* (1955) consists of unfinished Howard manuscripts converted into Conan stories and completed by de Camp; some later titles were essentially by De Camp alone. His nonfiction writings on the sword-and-sorcery genre were published as *The Conan Reader* (1968), *Literary Swordsmen and Sorcerers* (1976) and *Blond Barbarians and Noble Savages* (1975). He also edited several theme anthologies, beginning with *Swords and Sorcery* (1963), and co-edited the critical anthologies *The Conan Swordbook* (1969) and *The Conan Grimoire* (1972), both with George H Scithers.

De Camp's first entirely original sword-and-sorcery effort was the Pusadian sequence of tales assembled as *The Tritonian Ring and Other Pusadian Tales* (1953) (see below). He later wrote several stories set in the imaginary world of Novaria: *The Goblin Tower* (1968), which is his most substantial novel of this type, *The Clocks of Iraz* (1971), *The Fallible Fiend* (1973), *The Unbeheaded King* (1983) and *The Honorable Barbarian* (1989). The later years of De Camp's long career were dominated by his nonfiction. He had produced one of the earliest books about modern sf, *Science Fiction Handbook* (1953) with his wife; a useful compendium of information and advice for aspiring writers in its original edition, it gained little but smoothness from its subsequent revision in 1975 – indeed, the revised version omitted some material of interest. A book on Magic written with his wife, *Spirits, Stars and Spells: The Profits and Perils of Magic* (1966), was sprightly. His opinions about the nature of Fantasy, and the appropriate decorum necessary to write within the genre, were expressed in an energetic, if sometimes reactionary, fashion in his many articles.

He also wrote definitive lives of H P Lovecraft – *Lovecraft: A Biography* (1975) – and of Robert E Howard – *Dark Valley Destiny: The Life of Robert E. Howard* (1983) with his wife and Jane Whittington Griffin, the latter book having been preceded by *The Miscast Barbarian: A Biography of Robert E Howard (1906–1936)* (1975). In the 1980s, and into his own ninth decade, more and more often in explicit collaboration with his wife, he maintained a remarkable reputation for consistency of output, whatever they put their hands to. He was given the Gandalf (Grand Master) Award for 1976, the SFWA Grand Master Award for 1978, the World Fantasy Award for lifetime achievement in 1984, and the Pilgrim Award in 1998. His autobiography, *Time & Chance: An Autobiography* (1996), which won a Hugo, reflects little of the darker side of a long life lived in interesting times, and is occasionally stiff-tongued; but it valuably records much of the sf genre's early history. This last work seemed as agelessly smiling as the first Harold Shea tales sixty years earlier.

The first of the three titles presented here is perhaps the most successful child of John W Campbell's fantasy magazine, *Unknown*, which was killed by paper shortages in 1943. *Lest Darkness Fall* (December 1939 *Unknown*; 1941 in book form) follows the story of an involuntary time-traveller who ends up in sixth-century Rome, where he introduces technologies – most importantly the printing press – in an attempt to prevent the onset of the Dark Ages. There are echoes throughout of Mark Twain's *A Connecticut Yankee in King Arthur's Court* (1889), but although de Camp is not foolish enough to argue that an insertion of technological fixes will bring utopia, he is more sanguine than Twain, and some of the Darkness is indeed averted. The tale still seems fresh-minted; it is a classic vision, told with the clarity of a fine dream.

Rogue Queen (1951), a novel in the Viagens Interplanetarias series, may be less serious in its underlying argument than *Lest Darkness Fall*, but exploits the Planetary Romance – stories of adventure and discovery set on worlds whose inhabitants interact complexly, and sometimes romantically, with heroic intruders – to the full. An otherwise slightly improbable matriarchal humanoid society based on a hive structure becomes the venue for high-spirited action, intricate schemes, and a touch of sex; the novel is, with *Lest Darkness Fall*, de Camp's most highly regarded sf work.

The third title in this gathering represents De Camp's first full-blown sword-and-sorcery work, the Pusadian sequence of tales assembled as *The Tritonian Ring and Other Pusadian Tales* (coll 1953). There is still a touch of the old *Unknown* writer here, but laced through with a freedom and hilarity whose full expression the grim-visaged Campbell may have sometimes hampered. These stories are what *Unknown* may have been able to publish in the 1950s: hard-headed but at points almost wacky; full of the flavours of

Romance Unbound. They are probably De Camp's happiest works. We are very lucky to have these crafty romps still with us, so that we can smile as we read.

For a more detailed version of the above, see L. Sprague de Camp's author entry in *The Encyclopedia of Science Fiction*: http://sf-encyclopedia.com/entry/de_camp_l_sprague.

Some terms above are capitalised when they would not normally be so rendered; this indicates that the terms represent discrete entries in *The Encyclopedia of Science Fiction*.

LEST DARKNESS FALL

To Catherine

CHAPTER I

Tancredi took his hands off the wheel again and waved them. '— so I envy you, Dr Padway. Here in Rome we have still some work to do. But *pah*! It is all filling in little gaps. Nothing big, nothing new. And restoration work. Building contractor's work. Again, *pah*!'

'Professor Tancredi,' said Martin Padway patiently, 'as I said, I am not a doctor. I hope to be one soon, if I can get a thesis out of this Lebanon dig.' Being himself the most cautious of drivers, his knuckles were white from gripping the side of the little Fiat, and his right foot ached from trying to shove it through the floor boards.

Tancredi snatched the wheel in time to avoid a lordly Isotta by the thickness of a razor blade. The Isotta went its way thinking dark thoughts. 'Oh, what is the difference? Here everybody is a doctor, whether he is or not, if you understand me. And such a smart young man as you – What was I talking about?'

'That depends.' Padway closed his eyes as a pedestrian just escaped destruction. 'You were talking about Etruscan inscriptions, and then about the nature of time, and then about Roman archaeol —'

'Ah, yes, the nature of time. This is just a silly idea of mine, you understand. I was saying all these people who just disappear, they have slipped back down the suitcase.'

'The what?'

'The trunk, I mean. The trunk of the tree of time. When they stop slipping, they are back in some former time. But as soon as they do anything, they change all subsequent history.'

'Sounds like a paradox,' said Padway.

'No-o. The trunk continues to exist. But a new branch starts out where they come to rest. It has to, otherwise we would all disappear, because history would have changed and our parents might not have met.'

'That's a thought,' said Padway. 'It's bad enough knowing the sun might become a nova, but if we're also likely to vanish because somebody has gone back to the twelfth century and stirred things up —'

'No. That has never happened. We have never vanished, that is. You see, doctor? We continue to exist, but another history has been started. Perhaps there are many such, all existing somewhere. Maybe, they aren't much different from ours. Maybe the man comes to rest in the middle of the ocean. So what? The fish eat him, and things go on as before. Or they think he is mad, and shut him up or kill him. Again, not much difference. But suppose he becomes a king or a *duce*? What then?

'*Presto*, we have a new history! History is a four-dimensional web. It is a tough web. But it has weak points. The junction places – the focal points, one might say – are weak. The backslipping, if it happens, would happen at these places.'

'What do you mean by focal points?' asked Padway. It sounded to him like polysyllabic nonsense.

'Oh, places like Rome, where the world-lines of many famous events intersect. Or Istanbul. Or Babylon. You remember that archaeologist, Skrzetuski, who disappeared at Babylon in 1936?'

'I thought he was killed by some Arab holdup men.'

'Ah. They never found his body! Now, Rome may soon again be the intersection point of great events. That means the web is weakening again here.'

'I hope they don't bomb the Forum,' said Padway.

'Oh, nothing like that. There will be no more great wars; everybody knows it is too dangerous. But let us not talk politics. The web, as I say, is tough. If a man did slip back, it would take a terrible lot of work to distort it. Like a fly in a spider web that fills a room.'

'Pleasant thought,' said Padway.

'Is it not, though?' Tancredi turned to grin at him, then trod frantically on the brake. The Italian leaned out and showered a pedestrian with curses.

He turned back to Padway. 'Are you coming to my house for dinner tomorrow?'

'Wh-what? Why yes, I'll be glad to. I'm sailing next —'

'Si, *si*. I will show you the equations I have worked out. Energy must be conserved, even in changing one's time. But nothing of this to my colleagues, please. You understand.' The sallow little man took his hands off the wheel to wag both forefingers at Padway. 'It is a harmless eccentricity. But one's professional reputation must not suffer.'

'*Eek*!' said Padway.

Tancredi jammed on the brake and skidded to a stop behind a truck halted at the intersection of the Via del Mare and the Piazza Aracoeli. 'What was I talking about?' he asked.

'Harmless eccentricities,' said Padway. He felt like adding that Professor Tancredi's driving ranked among his less harmless ones. But the man had been very kind to him.

'Ah, yes. Things get out, and people talk. Archaeologists talk even worse than most people. Are you married?'

'What?' Padway felt he should have gotten used to this sort of thing by now. He hadn't. 'Why yes.'

'Good. Bring your wife along. Then you see some real Italian cooking, not this spaghetti-and-meatballs stuff.'

'She's back in Chicago.' Padway didn't feel like explaining that he and his wife had been separated for over a year.

He could see, now, that it hadn't been entirely Betty's fault. To a person of her background and tastes he must have seemed pretty impossible: a man who danced badly, refused to play bridge, and whose idea of fun was to get a few similar creatures in for an evening of heavy talk on the future of capitalism and the love life of the bullfrog. At first she had been thrilled by the idea of traveling in far places, but one taste of living in a tent and watching her husband mutter over the inscriptions on potsherds had cured that.

And he wasn't much to look at – rather small, with out-size nose and ears and a diffident manner. At college they had called him Mouse Padway. Oh, well, a man in exploratory work was a fool to marry, anyway. Just look at the divorce rate among them – anthropologists, paleontologists, and such—

'Could you drop me at the Pantheon?' he asked. 'I've never examined it closely, and it's just a couple of blocks to my hotel.'

'Yes, doctor, though I am afraid you will get wet. It looks like rain, does it not?'

'That's all right. This coat will shed water.'

Tancredi shrugged. They bucketed down the Corso Vittorio Emanuele and screeched around the corner into the Via Cestari. Padway got out at the Piazza del Pantheon, and Tancredi departed, waving both arms and shouting: 'Tomorrow at eight, then? *Si*, fine.'

Padway looked at the building for a few minutes. He had always thought it a very ugly one, with the Corinthian front stuck on the brick rotunda. Of course that great concrete dome had taken some engineering, considering when it had been erected. Then he had to jump to avoid being spattered as a man in a military uniform tore by on a motorcycle.

Padway walked over to the portico, round which clustered men engaged in the national sport of loitering. One of the things that he liked about Italy was that here he was, by comparison, a fairly tall man. Thunder rumbled behind him, and a raindrop struck his hand. He began to take long steps. Even if his trench coat would shed water, he didn't want his new twelve-thousand-lire Borsalino soaked. He liked that hat.

His reflections were cut off in their prime by the granddaddy of all lightning flashes, which struck the Piazza to his right. The pavement dropped out from under him like a trapdoor.

His feet seemed to be dangling over nothing. He could not see anything for the reddish-purple afterimages in his retinas. The thunder rolled on and on.

It was a most disconcerting feeling, hanging in the midst of nothing. There was no uprush of air as in falling down a shaft. He felt somewhat as Alice must have felt on her leisurely fall down the rabbit-hole, except that his senses gave him no clear information as to what was happening. He could not even guess how fast it was happening.

Then something hard smacked his soles. He almost fell. The impact was about as strong as that resulting from a two-foot fall. As he staggered by he hit his shin on something. He said 'Ouch!'

His retinas cleared. He was standing in the depression caused by the drop of a roughly circular piece of pavement.

The rain was coming down hard, now. He climbed out of the pit and ran under the portico of the Pantheon. It was so dark that the lights in the building ought to have been switched on. They were not.

Padway saw something curious: the red brick of the rotunda was covered by slabs of marble facing. That, he thought, was one of the restoration jobs that Tancredi had been complaining about.

Padway's eyes glided indifferently over the nearest of the loafers. They switched back again sharply. The man, instead of coat and pants, was wearing a dirty white woolen tunic.

It was odd. But if the man wanted to wear such a getup, it was none of Padway's business.

The gloom was brightening a little. Now Padway's eyes began to dance from person to person. They were all wearing tunics. Some had come under the portico to get out of the rain. These also wore tunics, sometimes with poncholike cloaks over them.

A few of them stared at Padway without much curiosity. He and they were still staring when the shower let up a few minutes later. Padway knew fear.

The tunics alone would not have frightened him. A single incongruous fact might have a rational if recondite explanation. But everywhere he looked more of these facts crowded in on him. He could not concisely notice them all at once.

The concrete sidewalk had been replaced by slabs of slate.

There were still buildings around the Piazza, but they were not the same buildings. Over the lower ones Padway could see that the Senate House and the Ministry of Communications – both fairly conspicuous objects – were missing.

The sounds were different. The honk of taxi horns was absent. There were no taxis to honk. Instead, two oxcarts creaked slowly and shrilly down the via della Minerva.

Padway sniffed. The garlic-and-gasoline aroma of modern Rome had been replaced by a barnyard-and-backhouse symphony wherein the smell of horse was the strongest and also the most mentionable motif. Another ingredient was incense, wafting from the door of the Pantheon.

The sun came out. Padway stepped out into it. Yes, the portico still bore the inscription crediting the construction of the building to M. Agrippa.

Glancing around to see that he was not watched, Padway stepped up to one of the pillars and slammed his fist into it. It hurt.

'Hell,' said Padway, looking at his bruised knuckles.

He thought, I'm not asleep. All this is too solid and consistent for a dream. There's nothing fantastic about the early afternoon sunshine and the beggars around the Piazza.

But if he was not asleep, what? He might be crazy ... But that was a hypothesis difficult to build a sensible course of action on.

There was Tancredi's theory about slipping back in time. Had he slipped back, or had something happened to him to make him imagine he had? The time-travel idea did not appeal to Padway. It sounded metaphysical, and he was a hardened empiricist.

There was the possibility of amnesia. Suppose that flash of lightning had actually hit him and suppressed his memory up to that time; then suppose something had happened to jar it loose again ... He would have a gap in his memory between the first lightning flash and his arrival in this archaistic copy of old Rome. All sorts of things might have happened in the meantime. He might have blundered into a movie set. Mussolini, having long secretly believed himself a reincarnation of Julius Caesar, might have decided to make his people adopt classical Roman costume.

It was an attractive theory. But the fact that he was wearing exactly the same clothes, and had the same things in his pockets as before the flash, exploded it.

He listened to the chatter of a couple of the loafers. Padway spoke fair, if pedantic, Italian. He could not quite get the substance of these men's talk. In the rush of syllables he would often catch a familiar sound-group, but never enough at one time. Their speech had the tantalizing pseudo familiarity of Plattdeutsch to an English-speaking person.

He thought of Latin. At once the loafers' speech became more familiar. They were not speaking classical Latin. But Padway found that if he took one of their sentences and matched it first against Italian and then against Latin, he could understand most of it.

He decided that they were speaking a late form of Vulgar Latin, rather more than halfway from the language of Cicero to that of Dante. He had never even tried to speak this hybrid. But by dredging his memory for his knowledge of sound changes, he could make a stab at it: *Omnia Gallia e devisa en parte trei, quaro una encolont Beige, alia ...*

The two loafers had observed his eavesdropping. They frowned, lowered their voices, and moved off.

No, the hypothesis of delirium might be a tough one, but it offered fewer difficulties than that of the time-slip.

If he was imagining things, was he really standing in front of the Pantheon and imagining that the people were dressed and speaking in the manner of the period 300-900 AD? Or was he lying in a hospital bed recovering from near-electrocution and imagining he was in front of the Pantheon? In the former case he ought to find a policeman and have himself taken to a hospital. In the latter this would be waste motion. For safety's sake he had better assume the former.

No doubt one of these people was really a policeman complete with shiny hat. What did he mean 'really'? Let Bertrand Russell and Alfred Korzybski worry about that. How to find …

A beggar had been whining at him for a couple of minutes. Padway gave such a perfect impression of deafness that the ragged little hunchback moved off. Now another man was speaking to him. On his left palm the man held a string of beads with a cross, all in a heap. Between his right thumb and forefinger he held the clasp of the string. He raised his right hand until the whole string hung from it, then lowered it back onto his left palm, then raised it again, talking all the while.

Whenever and however all this was, that gesture assured Padway that he was still in Italy.

Padway asked in Italian: 'Could you tell me where I could find a policeman?'

The man stopped his sales talk, shrugged, and replied, 'Non compr'endo.'

'Hey!' said Padway. The man paused. With great concentration Padway translated his request into what he hoped was Vulgar Latin.

The man thought, and said he didn't know.

Padway started to turn elsewhere. But the seller of beads called to another hawker: 'Marco! The gentleman wants to find a police agent.'

'The gentleman is brave. He is also crazy,' replied Marco.

The bead-seller laughed. So did several people. Padway grinned a little; the people were human if not very helpful. He said: 'Please, I-really-want-to-know.'

The second hawker, who had a tray full of brass knickknacks tied around his neck, shrugged. He rattled off a paragraph that Padway could not follow.

Padway slowly asked the bead-seller: 'What did he say?'

'He said he didn't know,' replied the bead-seller. 'I don't know either.'

Padway started to walk off. The bead-seller called after him: 'Mister.'

'Yes?'

'Did you mean an agent of the municipal prefect?'

'Yes.'

'Marco, where can the gentleman find an agent of the municipal prefect?'

'I don't know,' said Marco.

The bead-seller shrugged. 'Sorry, I don't know either.'

If this were twentieth-century Rome, there would be no difficulty about finding a cop. And not even Benny the Moose could make a whole city change its language. So he must be in (a) a movie set, (b) ancient Rome (the Tancredi hypothesis), or (c) a figment of his imagination.

He started walking. Talking was too much of a strain.

It was not long before any lingering hopes about a movie set were dashed by the discovery that this alleged ancient city stretched for miles in all directions, and that its street plan was quite different from that of modern Rome. Padway found his little pocket map nearly useless.

The signs on the shops were in intelligible classical Latin. The spelling had remained as in Caesar's time, if the pronunciation had not.

The streets were narrow, and for the most part not *very* crowded. The town had a drowsy, shabby-genteel, rundown personality, like that of Philadelphia.

At one relatively busy intersection, Padway watched a man on a horse direct traffic. He would hold up a hand to stop an oxcart, and beckon a sedan chair across. The man wore a gaudily striped shirt and leather trousers. He looked like a central or northern European rather than an Italian.

Padway leaned against a wall, listening. A man would say a sentence just too fast for him to catch. It was like having your hook nibbled but never taken. By terrific concentration, Padway forced himself to think in Latin. He mixed his cases and numbers, but as long as he confined himself to simple sentences he did not have too much trouble with vocabulary.

A couple of small boys were watching him. When he looked at them, they giggled and raced off.

It reminded Padway of those United States Government projects for the restoration of Colonial towns, like Williamsburg. But this looked like the real thing. No restoration included all the dirt and disease, the insults and altercations, that Padway had seen and heard in an hour's walk.

Only two hypotheses remained: delirium and time-slip. Delirium now seemed the less probable. He would act on the assumption that things were in fact what they seemed.

He couldn't stand there indefinitely. He'd have to ask questions and get himself oriented. The idea gave him gooseflesh. He had a phobia about accosting strangers. Twice he opened his mouth, but his glottis closed up tight with stage fright.

Come on, Padway, get a grip on yourself. 'I beg your pardon, but could you tell me the date?'

The man addressed, a mild-looking person with a loaf of bread under his arm, stopped and looked blank. '*Qui e'*? What is it?'

'I said, could you tell me the date?'

The man frowned. Was he going to be nasty? But all he said was, '*Non compr'endo.*' Padway tried again, speaking very slowly. The man repeated that he did not understand.

Padway fumbled for his date-book and pencil. He wrote his request on a page of the date-book, and held the thing up.

The man peered at it, moving his lips. His face cleared. 'Oh, you want to know the *date*?' said he.

'*Sic*, the date.'

The man rattled a long sentence at him. It might as well have been in Trabresh. Padway waved his hands despairingly, crying, '*Lento!*'

The man backed up and started over. 'I said I understood you, and I thought it was October 9th, but I wasn't sure because I couldn't remember whether my mother's wedding anniversary came three days ago or four.'

'What year?'

'What *year*?'

'*Sic*, what year?'

'Twelve eighty-eight *Anno Urbis Conditae.*'

It was Padway's turn to be puzzled. 'Please, what is that in the Christian era?'

'You mean, how many years since the birth of Christ?'

'*Hoc ille* – that's right.'

'Well, now – I don't know; five hundred and something. Better ask a priest, stranger.'

'I will,' said Padway. 'Thank you.'

'It's nothing,' said the man, and went about his business. Padway's knees were weak, though the man hadn't bitten him, and had answered his question in a civil enough manner. But it sounded as though Padway, who was a peaceable man, had not picked a very peaceable period.

What was he to do? Well, what would any sensible man do under the circumstances? He'd have to find a place to sleep and a method of making a living. He was a little startled when he realized how quickly he had accepted the Tancredi theory as a working hypothesis.

He strolled up an alley to be out of sight and began going through his pockets. The roll of Italian bank notes would be about as useful as a broken five-cent mousetrap. No, even less; you might be able to fix a mousetrap. A book of American Express traveler's checks, a Roman street-car transfer, an Illinois driver's license, a leather case full of keys – all ditto. His pen, pencil, and lighter would be useful as long as ink, leads, and lighter fuel held out. His pocketknife and his watch would undoubtedly fetch good prices, but he wanted to hang onto them as long as he could.

He counted the fistful of small change. There were just twenty coins, beginning with four ten-lire silver cartwheels. They added up to forty-nine lire, eight centesimi, or about five dollars. The silver and bronze should be exchangeable. As for the nickel fifty-centesimo and twenty-centesimo pieces, he'd have to see. He started walking again.

He stopped before an establishment that advertised itself as that of S. Dentatus, goldsmith and money changer. He took a deep breath and went in.

S. Dentatus had a face rather like that of a frog. Padway laid out his change and said: 'I … I should like to change this into local money, please.' As usual he had to repeat the sentence to make himself understood.

S. Dentatus blinked at the coins. He picked them up, one by one, and scratched at them a little with a pointed instrument. 'Where do these – you – come from?' he finally croaked.

'America.'

'Never heard of it.'

'It is a long way off.'

'Hm-m-m. What are these made of? Tin?' The money changer indicated the four nickel coins.

'Nickel.'

'What's that? Some funny metal they have in your country?'

'Hoc ille.'

'What's it worth?'

Padway thought for a second of trying to put a fantastically high value on the coins. While he was working up his courage, S. Dentatus interrupted his thoughts:

'It doesn't matter, because I wouldn't touch the stuff. There wouldn't be any market for it. But these other pieces – let's see —' He got out a balance and weighed the bronze coins, and then the silver coins. He pushed counters up and down the grooves of a little bronze abacus, and said: 'They're worth just under one solidus. Give you a solidus even for them.'

Padway didn't answer immediately. Eventually he'd have to take what was offered, as he hated the idea of bargaining and didn't know the values of the current money. But to save his face he had to appear to consider the offer carefully.

A man stepped up to the counter beside him. He was a heavy, ruddy man with a flaring brown mustache and his hair in a long or Ginger Rogers bob. He wore a linen blouse and long leather pants. He grinned at Padway, and reeled off: '*Ho, frijond, habais faurthei! Alai skalljans sind waidedjans.*'

Oh, Lord, another language! Padway answered: 'I … I am sorry, but I do not understand.'

The man's face fell a little; he dropped into Latin: 'Sorry, thought you were from the Chersonese, from your clothes. I couldn't stand around and watch a fellow Goth swindled without saying anything, ha, ha!'

The Goth's loud, explosive laugh made Padway jump a little; he hoped nobody noticed. 'I appreciate that. What is this stuff worth?'

'What has he offered you?' Padway told him. 'Well,' said the man, 'even I can see that you're being hornswoggled. You give him a fair rate, Sextus, or I'll make you eat your own stock. That would be funny, ha, ha!'

S. Dentatus sighed resignedly. 'Oh, very well, a solidus and a half. How am I to live, with you fellows interfering with legitimate business all the time? That would be, at the current rate of exchange, one solidus thirty-one sesterces.'

'What is this about a rate of exchange?' asked Padway.

The Goth answered: 'The gold-silver rate. Gold has been going down the last few months.'

Padway said: 'I think I will take it all in silver.'

While Dentatus sourly counted out ninety-three sesterces, the Goth asked: 'Where do you come from? Somewhere up in the Hunnish country?'

'No,' said Padway, 'a place farther than that, called America. You have never heard of it, have you?'

'No. Well now, that's interesting. I'm glad I met you, young fellow. It'll give me something to tell the wife about. She thinks I head for the nearest brothel every time I come to town, ha, ha!' He fumbled in his handbag and brought out a large gold ring and an unfaceted gem. 'Sextus, this thing came out of its setting again. Fix it up, will you? And no substitutions, mind.'

As they went out, the Goth spoke to Padway in a lowered voice. 'The real reason I'm glad to come to town is that somebody put a curse on my house.'

'A curse? What kind of a curse?'

The Goth nodded solemnly. 'A shortness-of-breath curse. When I'm home I can't breathe. I go around like this —' He gasped asthmatically. 'But as soon as I get away from home I'm all right. And I think I know who did it.'

'Who?'

'I foreclosed a couple of mortgages last year. I can't prove anything against the former owners, *but* —' He winked ponderously at Padway.

'Tell me,' said Padway, 'do you keep animals in your house?'

'Couple of dogs. There's the stock, of course, but we don't let them in the house. Though a shoat got in yesterday and ran away with one of my shoes. Had to chase it all over the damned farm. I must have been a sight, ha, ha!'

'Well,' said Padway, 'try keeping the dogs outside all the time and having your place well swept every day. That might stop your – uh – wheezing.'

'Now, that's interesting. You really think it would?'

'I do not know. Some people get the shortness of breath from dog hairs. Try it for a couple of months and see.'

'I still think it's a curse, young fellow, but I'll try your scheme. I've tried everything from a couple of Greek physicians to one of St. Ignatius' teeth, and none of them works.' He hesitated. 'If you don't mind, what were you in your own country?'

Padway thought quickly, then remembered the few acres he owned in downstate Illinois. 'I had a farm,' he said.

'That's fine,' roared the Goth, clapping Padway on the back with staggering force. 'I'm a friendly soul but I don't want to get mixed up with people too far above or below my own class, ha, ha! My name is Nevitta; Nevitta Gummund's son. If you're passing up the Falminian Way sometime, drop in. My place is about eight miles north of here.'

'Thanks. My name is Martin Padway. Where would be a good place to rent a room?'

'That depends. If I didn't want to spend too much money, I'd pick a place farther down the river. Plenty of boarding houses over toward the Viminal Hill. Say, I'm in no hurry; I'll help you look.' He whistled sharply and called: *'Hermann, hiri her!'*

Hermann, who was dressed much like his master, got up off the curb and trotted down the street leading two horses, his leather pants making a distinctive *flop-flop* as he ran.

Nevitta set out a brisk walk, Hermann leading the horses behind. Nevitta said: 'What did you say your name was?'

'Martin Padway – Martinus is good enough.' (Padway properly pronounced it Mar*tee*no.)

Padway did not want to impose on Nevitta's good nature, but he wanted the most useful information he could get. He thought a minute, then asked: 'Could you give me the names of a few people in Rome, lawyers and physicians and such, to go to when I need them?'

'Sure. If you want a lawyer specializing in cases involving foreigners, Valerius Mummius is your man. His office is alongside of the Aemilian Basilica. For a physician try my friend Leo Vekkos. He's a good fellow as Greeks go. But personally I think the relic of a good Arian saint like Asterius is as effective as all their herbs and potations.'

'It probably is at that,' said Padway. He wrote the names and addresses in his date-book. 'How about a banker?'

'I don't have much truck with them; hate the idea of getting in debt. But if you want the name of one, there's Thomasus the Syrian, near the Aemilian Bridge. Keep your eyes open if you deal with him.'

'Why, isn't he honest?'

'Thomasus? Sure he's honest. You just have to watch him, that's all. Here, this looks like a place you could stay.' Nevitta pounded on the door, which was opened by a frowsy superintendent.

This man had a room, yes. It was small and ill lighted. It smelled. But then so did all of Rome. The superintendent wanted seven sesterces a day.

'Offer him half,' said Nevitta to Padway in a stage whisper.

Padway did. The superintendent acted as bored by the ensuing haggling as Padway was. Padway got the room for five sesterces.

Nevitta squeezed Padway's hand in his large red paw. 'Don't forget, Martinus, come see me some time. I always like to hear a man who speaks Latin with a worse accent than mine, ha, ha!' He and Hermann mounted and trotted off.

Padway hated to see them go. But Nevitta had his own business to tend to. Padway watched the stocky figure round a corner, then entered the gloomy, creaking boarding house.

CHAPTER II

Padway awoke early with a bad taste in his mouth, and a stomach that seemed to have some grasshopper in its ancestry. Perhaps that was the dinner he'd eaten – not bad, but unfamiliar – consisting mainly of stew smothered in leeks. The restaurateur must have wondered when Padway made plucking motions at the table top; he was unthinkingly trying to pick up a knife and fork that weren't there.

One might very well sleep badly the first night on a bed consisting merely of a straw-stuffed mattress. And it had cost him an extra sesterce a day, too. An itch made him pull up his undershirt. Sure enough, a row of red spots on his midriff showed that he had not, after all, slept alone.

He got up and washed with the soap he had bought the previous evening. He had been pleasantly surprised to find that soap had already been invented. But when he broke a piece off the cake, which resembled a slightly decayed pumpkin pie, he found that the inside was soft and gooey because of incomplete potash-soda metathesis. Moreover, the soap was so alkaline that he thought he might as well have cleaned his hands and face by sandpapering.

Then he made a determined effort to shave with olive oil and a sixth-century razor. The process was so painful that he wondered if it mightn't be better to let nature take its course.

He was in a tight fix, he knew. His money would last about a week – with care, perhaps a little longer.

If a man knew he was going to be whisked back into the past, he would load himself down with all sorts of useful junk in preparation, an encyclopedia, texts on metallurgy, mathematics, and medicine, a slide rule, and so forth. And a gun, with plenty of ammunition.

But Padway had no gun, no encyclopedia, nothing but what an ordinary twentieth-century man carries in his pockets. Oh, a little more, because he'd been traveling at the time: such useful things as the traveler's checks, a hopelessly anachronistic street map, and his passport.

And he had his wits. He'd need them.

The problem was to find a way of using his twentieth-century knowledge that would support him without getting him into trouble. You couldn't, for example, set out to build an automobile. It would take several lifetimes to collect the necessary materials, and several more to learn how to handle them and to worry them into the proper form. Not to mention the question of fuel.

The air was fairly warm, and he thought of leaving his hat and vest in the room. But the door had the simplest kind of ward lock, with a bronze key big enough to be presented by a mayor to a visiting dignitary. Padway was sure he could pick the lock with a knife blade. So he took all his clothes along. He went back to the same restaurant for breakfast. The place had a sign over the counter reading, RELIGIOUS ARGUMENTS NOT ALLOWED. Padway asked the proprietor how to get to the address of Thomasus the Syrian.

The man said: 'You follow along Long Street down to the Arch of Constantine, and then New Street to the Julian Basilica, and then you turn left onto Tuscan Street, and —' and so on.

Padway made him repeat it twice. Even so, it took most of the morning to find his objective. His walk took him past the Forum area, full of temples, most of whose columns had been removed for use in the five big and thirty-odd little churches scattered around the city. The temples looked pathetic, like a Park Avenue doorman bereft of his pants.

At the sight of the Ulpian Library, Padway had to suppress an urge to say to hell with his present errand. He loved burrowing into libraries, and he definitely did not love the idea of bearding a strange banker in a strange land with a strange proposition. In fact, the idea scared him silly, but his was the kind of courage that shows itself best when its owner is about to collapse from blue funk. So he grimly kept on toward the Tiber.

Thomasus hung out in a shabby two-story building. The Negro at the door – probably a slave – ushered Padway into what he would have called a living room. Presently the banker appeared. Thomasus was a paunchy, bald man with a cataract on his left eye. He gathered his shabby robe about him, sat down, and said: 'Well, young man?'

'I' – Padway swallowed and started again – 'I'm interested in a loan.'

'How much?'

'I don't know yet. I want to start a business, and I'll have to investigate prices and things first.'

'You want to start a new business? In Rome? *Hmmm.*' Thomasus rubbed his hands together. 'What security can you give?'

'None at all.'

'*What?*'

'I said, none at all. You'd just have to take a chance on me.'

'But ... but, my dear sir, don't you know anybody in town?'

'I know a Gothic farmer named Nevitta Gummund's son. He sent me hither.'

'Oh, yes, Nevitta. I know him slightly. Would he go your note?'

Padway thought. Nevitta, despite his expansive gestures, had impressed him as being pretty close where money was concerned. 'No,' he said, 'I don't think he would.'

Thomasus rolled his eyes upward. 'Do You hear that, God? He comes in here, a barbarian who hardly knows Latin, and admits that he has no security and no guarantors, and still he expects me to lend him money! Did You ever hear the like?'

'I think I can make you change your mind,' said Padway.

Thomasus shook his head and made clucking noises. 'You certainly have plenty of self-confidence, young man; I admit as much. What did you say your name was?' Padway told him what he had told Nevitta. 'All right, what's your scheme?'

'As you correctly inferred,' said Padway, hoping he was showing the right mixture of dignity and cordiality, 'I'm a foreigner. I just arrived from a place called America. That's a long way off, and naturally it has a lot of customs and features different from those of Rome. Now, if you could back me in the manufacture of some of our commodities that are not known here —'

'Ai!' yelped Thomasus, throwing up his hands. 'Did You hear that, God? He doesn't want me to back him in some well-known business. Oh, no. He wants me to start some newfangled line that nobody ever heard of! I couldn't think of such a thing, Martinus. What was it you had in mind?'

'Well, we have a drink made from wine, called brandy, that ought to go well.'

'No, I couldn't consider it. Though I admit that Rome needs manufacturing establishments badly. When the capital was moved to Ravenna, all revenue from Imperial salaries was cut off, which is why the population has shrunk so the last century. The town is badly located, and hasn't any real reason for being any more. But you can't get anybody to do anything about it. King Thiudahad spends his time writing Latin verse. Poetry! But no, young man, I couldn't put money into a wild project for making some weird barbarian drink.'

Padway's knowledge of sixth-century history was beginning to come back to him. He said: 'Speaking of Thiudahad, has Queen Amalaswentha been murdered yet?'

'Why' – Thomasus looked sharply at Padway with his good eye – 'yes, she has.' That meant that Justinian, the 'Roman' emperor of Constantinople, would soon begin his disastrously successful effort to reconquer Italy for the Empire. 'But why did you put your question that way?'

Padway asked. 'Do-do you mind if I sit down?'

Thomasus said he didn't. Padway almost collapsed into a chair. His knees were weak. Up to now his adventure had seemed like a complicated and difficult masquerade party. His own question about the murder of Queen

Amalaswentha had brought home to him all at once the fearful hazards of life in this world.

Thomasus repeated: 'I asked why, young sir, you put your question that way?'

'What way?' asked Padway innocently. He saw where he'd made a slip.

'You asked whether she had been murdered *yet*. That sounds as though you had known ahead of time that she would be killed. Are you a soothsayer?'

There were no flies on Thomasus. Padway remembered Nevitta's advice to keep his eyes open.

He shrugged. 'Not exactly. I heard before I came here that there had been trouble between the two Gothic sovereigns, and that Thiudahad would put his co-ruler out of the way if he had a chance. I – uh – just wondered how it came out, that's all.'

'Yes,' said the Syrian. 'It was a shame. She was quite a woman. Good-looking, too, though she was in her forties. They caught her in her bath last summer and held her head under. Personally I think Thiudahad's wife Gudelinda put the old jellyfish up to it. He wouldn't have nerve enough by himself.'

'Maybe she was jealous,' said Padway. 'Now, about the manufacture of that barbarian drink, as you call it —'

'What? *You* are a stubborn fellow. It's absolutely out of the question, though. You have to be careful, doing business here in Rome. It's not like a growing town. Now, if this were Constantinople —' he sighed. 'You can really make money in the East. But I don't care to live there, with Justinian making life exciting for the heretics, as he calls them. What's your religion, by the way?'

'What's yours? Not that it makes any difference to me.'

'Nestorian.'

'Well,' said Padway carefully, 'I'm what we call a Congregationalist.' (It was not really true, but he guessed an agnostic would hardly be popular in this theology-mad world.) 'That's the nearest thing we have to Nestorianism in my country. But about the manufacture of brandy —'

'Nothing doing, young man. Absolutely not. How much equipment would you need to start?'

'Oh, a big copper kettle and a lot of copper tubing, and a stock of wine for the raw material. It wouldn't have to be good wine. And I could get started quicker with a couple of men to help me.'

'I'm afraid it's too much of a gamble. I'm sorry.'

'Look here, Thomasus, if I show you how you can halve the time it takes you to do your accounts, would you be interested?'

'You mean you're a mathematical genius or something?'

'No, but I have a system I can teach your clerks.'

Thomasus closed his eyes like some Levantine Buddha. 'Well – if you don't want more than fifty solidi —'

'All business is a gamble, you know.'

'That's the trouble with it. But – I'll do it, *if* your accounting system is as good as you say it is.'

'How about interest?' asked Padway.

'Three per cent.'

Padway was startled. Then he asked. 'Three per cent per what?'

'Per month, of course.'

'Too much.'

'Well, what do you expect?'

'In my country six per cent per year is considered fairly high.'

'You mean you expect *me* to lend you money at that rate? *Ai!* Did You hear that, God? Young man, you ought to go live among the wild Saxons, to teach them something about piracy. But I like you, so I'll make it twenty-five per year.'

'Still too much. I might consider seven and a half.'

'You're being ridiculous. I wouldn't consider less than twenty for a minute.'

'No. Nine per cent, perhaps.'

'I'm not even interested. Too bad; it would have been nice to do business with you. Fifteen.'

'That's out, Thomasus. Nine and a half.'

'Did You hear that, God? He wants me to make him a present of my business! Go away, Martinus. You're wasting your time here. I couldn't possibly come down any more. Twelve and a half. That's absolutely the bottom.'

'Ten.'

'Don't you understand Latin? I said that was the bottom. Good day; I'm glad to have met you.' When Padway got up, the banker sucked his breath through his teeth as though he had been wounded unto death, and rasped: 'Eleven.'

'Ten and a half.'

'Would you mind showing your teeth? My word, they are human after all. I thought maybe they were shark's teeth. Oh, very well. This sentimental generosity of mine will be my ruin yet. And now let's see that accounting system of yours.'

An hour later three chagrined clerks sat in a row and regarded Padway with expressions of, respectively, wonderment, apprehension, and active hatred. Padway had just finished doing a simple piece of long division with Arabic numerals, had barely gotten started on the interminable trial-and-error process that their system required. Padway translated his answers back into Roman, wrote it out on his tablet, and handed the tablet to Thomasus.

'There you are,' he said. 'Have one of the boys check it by multiplying the divisor by the quotient. You might as well call them off their job; they'll be at it all night.'

The middleaged clerk, the one with the hostile expression, copied down the figures and began checking grimly. When after a long time he finished, he threw down his stylus. 'That man's a sorcerer of some sort,' he growled. 'He does the operations in his head, and puts down all those silly marks just to fool us.'

'Not at all,' said Padway urbanely. 'I can teach you to do the same.'

'What? *Me* take lessons from a long-trousered barbarian? I —' he started to say more, but Thomasus cut him off by saying that he'd do as he was told, and no back talk. 'Is that so?' sneered the man. 'I'm a free Roman citizen, and I've been keeping books for twenty years. I guess I know my business. If you want a man to use that heathen system, go buy yourself some cringing Greek slave. I'm through!'

'Now see what you've done!' cried Thomasus when the clerk had taken his coat off the peg and marched out. 'I shall have to hire another man, and with this labor shortage —'

'That's all right,' soothed Padway. 'These two boys will be able to do all the work of three easily, once they learn American arithmetic. And that isn't all; we have something called double-entry bookkeeping, which enables you to tell any time how you stand financially, and to catch errors —'

'Do You hear that, God? He wants to turn the whole banking business upside down! Please, dear sir, one thing at a time; or you'll drive us mad! I'll grant your loan, I'll help you buy your equipment. Only don't spring any more of your revolutionary methods just now!' He continued more calmly: 'What's that bracelet I see you looking at from time to time?'

Padway extended his wrist. 'It's a portable sundial, of sorts. We call it a watch.'

'A *vatcha*, hm? It looks like magic. Are you sure you aren't a sorcerer after all?' He laughed nervously.

'No,' said Padway. 'It's a simple mechanical device, like a – a water clock.'

'Ah. I see. But why a pointer to show sixtieths of an hour? Surely nobody in his right mind would want to know the time as closely as that?'

'We find it useful.'

'Oh, well, other lands, other customs. How about giving my boys a lesson in your American arithmetic now? Just to assure us that it is as good as you claim.'

'All right. Give me a tablet.' Padway scratched the numerals 1 to 9 in the wax, and explained them. 'Now,' he said, 'this is the important part.' He drew a circle. 'This is our character meaning *nothing*.'

The younger clerk scratched his head. 'You mean it's a symbol without meaning? What would be the use of that?'

'I didn't say it was without meaning. It means nil, zero – what you have left when you take two away from two.'

The older clerk looked skeptical. 'It doesn't make sense to me. What is the use of a symbol for what does not exist?'

'You have a *word* for it, haven't you? Several words, in fact. And you find them useful, don't you?'

'I suppose so,' said the older clerk. 'But we don't use *nothing* in our calculations. Whoever heard of figuring the interest on a loan at no per cent? Or renting a house for no weeks?'

'Maybe,' grinned the younger clerk, 'the honorable sir can tell us how to make a profit on no sales —' Padway snapped: 'And we'll get through this explanation sooner with no interruptions. You'll learn the reason for the zero symbol soon enough.'

It took an hour to cover the elements of addition. Then Padway said the clerks had had enough for one day; they should practice addition for a while every day until they could do it faster than by Roman numerals. Actually he was worn out. He was naturally a quick speaker, and to have to plod syllable by syllable through this foul language almost drove him crazy.

'Very ingenious, Martinus,' wheezed the banker. 'And now for the details of that loan. Of course you weren't serious in setting such an absurdly low figure as ten and a half per cent —'

'What? You're damn right I was serious! And you agreed —'

'Now, Martinus. What I meant was that *after* my clerks had learned your system, if it was as good as you claimed, I'd consider lending you money at that rate. But meanwhile you can't expect me to give you my —'

Padway jumped up. 'You - you wielder of a - oh, hell, what's Latin for *chisel*? If you won't —'

'Don't be hasty, my young friend. After all, you've given my boys their start; they can go alone from there if need be. So you might as well —'

'All right, you just let them try to go on from there. I'll find another banker and teach his clerks properly. Subtraction, multiplication, div —'

'*Ai!*' yelped Thomasus. 'You can't go spreading this secret all over Rome! It wouldn't be fair to me!'

'Oh, can't I? Just watch. I could even make a pretty good living teaching it. If you think —'

'Now, now, let's not lose our tempers. Let's remember Christ's teachings about patience. I'll make a special concession because you're just starting out in business …'

Padway got his loan at ten and a half. He agreed grudgingly not to reveal his arithmetic elsewhere until the first loan was paid off.

Padway bought a copper kettle at what he would have called a junk shop. But nobody had ever heard of copper tubing. After he and Thomasus had exhausted the secondhand metal shops between the latter's house and the warehouse district at the south end of town, he started in on coppersmith's places. The coppersmiths had never heard of copper tubing, either. A couple of them offered to try to turn out some, but at astronomical prices.

'Martinus!' wailed the banker. 'We've walked at least five miles, and my feet are giving out. Wouldn't lead pipe do just as well? You can get all you want of that.'

'It would do fine except for one thing,' said Padway, 'we'd probably poison our customers. And that *might* give the business a bad name, you know.'

'Well, I don't see that you're getting anywhere as it is.'

Padway thought a minute while Thomasus and Ajax, the Negro slave, who was carrying the kettle, watched him. 'If I could hire a man who was generally handy with tools, and had some metal-working experience, I could show him how to make copper tubing. How do you go about hiring people here?'

'You don't,' said Thomasus. 'It just happens. You could buy a slave – but you haven't enough money. I shouldn't care to put up the price of a good slave into your venture. And it takes a skilled foreman to get enough work out of a slave to make him a profitable investment.'

Padway said, 'How would it be to put a sign in front of your place, stating that a position is open?'

'What?' squawked the banker. 'Do You hear that, God? First he seduces my money away from me on this wild plan. Now he wants to plaster my house with signs! Is there no limit —'

'Now, Thomasus, don't get excited. It won't be a big sign, and it'll be *very* artistic. I'll paint it myself. You want me to succeed, don't you?'

'It won't work, I tell you. Most workmen can't read. And I won't have you demean yourself by manual labor that way. It's ridiculous; I won't consider it. About how big a sign did you have in mind?'

Padway dragged himself to bed right after dinner. There was no way, as far as he knew, of getting back to his own time. Never again would he know the pleasures of the *American Journal of Archaeology*, of Mickey Mouse, of flush toilets, of speaking the simple, rich, sensitive English language …

Padway hired his man the third day after his first meeting with Thomasus the Syrian. The man was a dark, cocky little Sicilian named Hannibal Scipio.

Padway had meanwhile taken a short lease on a tumble-down house on the Quirinal, and collected such equipment and personal effects as he thought he would need. He bought a short-sleeved tunic to wear over his pants, with the idea of making himself less conspicuous. Adults seldom paid much attention to him in this motley town, but he was tired of having small boys follow him through the streets. He did, however, insist on having ample pockets sewn into the tunic, despite the tailor's shocked protests at ruining a good, stylish garment with this heathen innovation.

He whittled a mandrel out of wood and showed Hannibal Scipio how to bend the copper stripping around it. Hannibal claimed to know all that was necessary about soldering. But when Padway tried to bend the tubing into shape for his still, the seams popped open with the greatest of ease. After that Hannibal was a little less cocky – for a while.

Padway approached the great day of his first distillation with some apprehension. According to Tancredi's ideas this was a new branch of the tree of time. But mightn't the professor have been wrong, so that, as soon as Padway did anything drastic enough to affect all subsequent history, he would make the birth of Martin Padway in 1908 impossible, and disappear?

'Shouldn't there be an incantation or something?' asked Thomasus the Syrian.

'No,' said Padway. 'As I've already said three times, this isn't magic.' Looking around though, he could see how some mumbo-jumbo might have been appropriate: running his first large batch off at night in a creaky old house, illuminated by flickering oil lamps, in the presence of only Thomasus, Hannibal Scipio, and Ajax. All three looked apprehensive, and the Negro seemed all teeth and eyeballs. He stared at the still as if he expected it to start producing demons in carload lots any minute.

'It takes a long time, doesn't it?' said Thomasus, rubbing his pudgy hands together nervously. His good eye glittered at the nozzle from which drop after yellow drop slowly dripped.

'I think that's enough,' said Padway. 'We'll get mostly water if we continue the run.' He directed Hannibal to remove the kettle and poured the contents of the receiving flask into a bottle. 'I'd better try it first,' he said. He poured out a little into a cup, sniffed, and took a swallow. It was definitely not good brandy. But it would do.

'Have some?' he said to the banker.

'Give some to Ajax first.'

Ajax backed away, holding his hands in front of him, yellow palms out. 'No, please, master —'

He seemed so alarmed that Thomasus did not insist. 'Hannibal, how about you?'

'Oh, no,' said Hannibal. 'Meaning no disrespect, but I've got a delicate stomach. The least little thing upsets it. And if you're all through, I'd like to go home. I didn't sleep well last night.' He yawned theatrically. Padway let him go, and took another swallow.

'Well,' said Thomasus, 'if you're sure it won't hurt me, I might take just a little.' He took just a little, then coughed violently, spilling a few drops from the cup. 'Good God, man, what are your insides made of? That's volcano juice!' As his coughing subsided, a saintlike expression appeared. 'It does warm you up nicely inside, though, doesn't it?' He screwed up his face and his courage, and finished the cup in one gulp.

'Hey,' said Padway. 'Go easy. That isn't wine.'

'Oh, don't worry about me. Nothing makes me drunk.'

Padway got out another cup and sat down. 'Maybe you can tell me one thing that I haven't got straight yet. In my country we reckon years from the birth of Christ. When I asked a man, the day I arrived, what year it was, he said 1288 after the founding of the city. Now, can you tell me how many years before Christ Rome was founded? I've forgotten.'

Thomasus took another slug of brandy and thought. 'Seven hundred and fifty-four – no, 753. That means that this is the year of our Lord 535. That's the system the church uses. The Goths say the second year of Thiudahad's reign, and the Byzantines the first year of the consulship of Flavius Belisarius. Or the somethingth year of Justinian imperium. I can see how it might confuse you.' He drank some more. 'This is a wonderful invention, isn't it?' He held his cup up and turned it this way and that. 'Let's have some more. I think you'll make a success, Martinus.'

'Thanks. I hope so.'

'Wonderful invention. Course it'll be a success. Couldn't help being a success. A big success. Are You listening, God? Well, make sure my friend Martinus has a big success.

'I know a successful man when I see him, Martinus. Been picking them for years. That's how I'm such a success in the banking business. Success – success – let's drink to success. Beautiful success. Gorgeous success.

'I know what, Martinus. Let's go some place. Don't like drinking to success in this old ruin. You know, atmosphere. Some place where there's music. How much brandy have you got left? Good, bring the bottle along.'

The joint was in the theater district on the north side of the Capitoline. The 'music' was furnished by a young woman who twanged a harp and sang songs in Calabrian dialect, which the cash customers seemed to find very funny.

'Let's drink to —' Thomasus started to say 'success' for the thirtieth time, but changed his mind. 'Say, Martinus, we'd better buy some of this lousy wine, or he'll have us thrown out. How does this stuff mix with wine?' At Padway's expression, he said: 'Don't worry, Martinus, old friend, this is on me. Haven't made a night of it in years. You know, family man.' He winked and snapped his fingers for the waiter. When he had finally gotten through his little ceremony, he said: 'Just a minute, Martinus, old friend, I see a man who owes me money. I'll be right back.' He waddled unsteadily across the room.

A man at the next table asked Padway suddenly: 'What's that stuff you and old one-eye have been drinking, friend?'

'Oh, just a foreign drink called brandy,' said Padway uneasily.

'That's right, you're a foreigner, aren't you? I can tell by your accent.' He screwed up his face, and then said: 'I know; you're a Persian. I know a Persian accent.'

'Not exactly,' said Padway. 'Farther away than that.'

'That so? How do you like Rome?' The man had very large and very black eyebrows.

'Fine, so far,' said Padway.

'Well, you haven't seen anything,' said the man. 'It hasn't been the same since the Goths came.' He lowered his voice conspiratorially: 'Mark my words, it won't be like this always, either!'

'You don't like the Goths?'

'No! Not with the persecution we have to put up with!'

'Persecution?' Padway raised his eyebrows.

'Religious persecution. We won't stand for it forever.'

'I thought the Goths let everybody worship as they pleased.'

'That's just it! We Orthodox are forced to stand around and watch Arians and Monophysites and Nestorians and Jews going about their business unmolested, as if they owned the country. If that isn't persecution, I'd like to know what is!'

'You mean that you're persecuted because the heretics and such are not?'

'Certainly, isn't that obvious? We won't stand – What's your religion, by the way?'

'Well,' said Padway, 'I'm what in my country is called a Congregationalist. That's the nearest thing to Orthodoxy that we have.'

'Hm-m-m. We'll make a good Catholic out of you, perhaps. So long as you're not one of these Maronites or Nestorians —'

'What's that about Nestorians?' said Thomasus, who had returned unobserved. 'We who have the only logical view of the nature of the Son – that He was a man in whom the Father indwelt —'

'Nonsense!' snapped Eyebrows. 'That's what you expect of half-baked amateur theologians. Our view – that of the dual nature of the Son – has been irrefutably shown —'

'Hear that, God? As if one person could have more than one nature —'

'You're all crazy!' rumbled a tall, sad-looking man with thin yellow hair, watery blue eyes, and a heavy accent. 'We Arians abhor theological controversy, being sensible men. But if you want a sensible view of the nature of the Son —' 'You're a Goth?' barked Eyebrows tensely.

'No, I'm a Vandal, exiled from Africa. But as I was saying' – he began counting on his fingers – 'either the Son was a man, or He was a god, or He was something in between. Well, now, we admit He wasn't a man. And there's only one God, so He wasn't a god. So He must have been —'

About that time things began to happen too fast for Padway to follow them all at once. Eyebrows jumped up and began yelling like one possessed. Padway couldn't follow him, except to note that the term 'infamous heretics' occurred about once per sentence. Yellow Hair roared back at him, and other men began shouting from various parts of the room: 'Eat him up, barbarian!' 'This is an Orthodox country, and those who don't like it can go back where they —' 'Damned nonsense about dual natures! We Monophysites —' 'I'm a Jacobite, and I can lick any man in the place!' 'Let's throw all the heretics out!' 'I'm a Eunomian, and I can lick any *two* men in the place!'

Padway saw something coming and ducked; the mug missed his head by an inch and a half. When he looked up the room was a blur of action. Eyebrows was holding the self-styled Jacobite by the hair and punching his face; Yellow Hair was swinging four feet of bench around his head and howling a Vandal battle song. Padway hit one champion of Orthodoxy in the middle; his place was immediately taken by another who hit Padway in the middle. Then they were overborne by a rush of men.

As Padway struggled up through the pile of kicking, yelling humanity, like a swimmer striking for the surface, somebody got hold of his foot and tried to bite it off. As Padway was still wearing a pair of massive and practically indestructible English walking shoes, the biter got nowhere. So he shifted his attack to Padway's ankle. Padway yelped with pain, yanked his foot free, and kicked the biter in the face. The face yielded a little, and Padway wondered whether he'd broken a nose or a few teeth. He hoped he had.

The heretics seemed to be in a minority, that shrank as its members were beaten down and cast forth into darkness. Padway's eye caught the gleam of a knife blade and he thought it was well past his bedtime. Not being a religious man, he had no desire to be whittled up in the cause of the single, dual, or any other nature of Christ. He located Thomasus the Syrian under a table. When he tried to drag him out, the banker shrieked with terror and hugged the table leg as if it were a woman and he a sailor who had been six months at sea. Padway finally got him untangled.

The yellow-haired Vandal was still swinging his bench. Padway shouted at him. The man couldn't have understood in the uproar, but his attention was attracted, and when Padway pointed at the door he got the idea. In a few seconds he had cleared a path. The three stumbled out, pushed through the crowd that was beginning to gather outside, and ran. A yell behind them made them run faster, until they realized that it was Ajax, and slowed down to let him catch up.

They finally sat down on a park bench on the edge of the Field of Mars, only a few blocks from the Pantheon, where Padway had his first sight of post-

Imperial Rome. Thomasus, when he got his breath, said: 'Martinus, why did you let me drink so much of that heathen drink? Oh, my head! If I hadn't been drunk, I'd have had more sense than to start a theological argument.'

'I tried to slow you down,' said Padway mildly, 'but you —'

'I know, I know. But you should have prevented me from drinking so much, forcibly if necessary. My head! What will my wife say? I never want to see that lousy barbarian drink again! What did you do with the bottle, by the way?'

'It got lost in the scuffle. But there wasn't much left in it anyway.' Padway turned to the Vandal. 'I guess I owe you some thanks for getting us out of there so quickly.'

The man pulled his drooping mustache. 'I was glad to do it, friend. Religious argument is no occupation for decent people. Permit me; my name is Fritharik Staifan's son.' He spoke slowly, fumbling for words occasionally. 'Once I was counted a man of noble family. Now I am merely a poor wanderer. Life holds nothing for me any more.' Padway saw a tear glistening in the moonlight.

'You said you were a Vandal?'

Fritharik sighed like a vacuum cleaner. 'Yes, mine was one of the finest estates in Carthage, before the Greeks came. When King Gelimer ran away, and our army scattered, I escaped to Spain, and thence I came hither last year.'

'What are you doing now?'

'Alas, I am not doing anything now. I had a job as bodyguard to a Roman patrician until last week. Think of it – a noble Vandal serving as bodyguard! But my employer got set on the idea of converting me to Orthodoxy. That,' said Fritharik with dignity, 'I would not allow. So here I am. When my money is gone, I don't know what will become of me. Perhaps I will kill myself. Nobody would care.' He sighed some more, then said: 'You aren't looking for a good, reliable bodyguard, are you?'

'Not just now,' said Padway, 'but I may be in a few weeks. Do you think you can postpone your suicide until then?'

'I don't know. It depends on how my money holds out. I have no sense about money. Being of noble birth, I never needed any. I don't know whether you'll ever see me alive again.' He wiped his eyes on his sleeve.

'Oh, for heaven's sake,' said Thomasus, 'there are plenty of things you could do.'

'No,' said Fritharik tragically. 'You wouldn't understand, friend. There are considerations of honor. And anyway, what has life to offer me? Did you say you might be able to take me on later?' he asked Padway. Padway said yes, and gave him his address. 'Very well, friend, I shall probably be in a nameless lonely grave before two weeks have passed. But if not, I'll be around.'

CHAPTER III

At the end of the week, Padway was gratified not only by the fact that he had not vanished into thin air, and by the appearance of the row of bottles on the shelf, but by the state of his finances. Counting the five solidi for the first month's rent on the house, the six more that had gone into his apparatus, and Hannibal's wages and his own living expenses, he still had over thirty of his fifty borrowed solidi left. The first two items wouldn't recur for a couple of weeks, anyway.

'How much are you going to charge for that stuff?' asked Thomasus.

Padway thought. 'It's a luxury article, obviously. If we can get some of the better-class restaurants to stock it, I don't see why we shouldn't get two solidi per bottle. At least until somebody discovers our secret and begins competing with us.'

Thomasus rubbed his hands together. 'At that rate, you could practically pay back your loan with the proceeds of the first week's sales. But I'm in no hurry; it might be better to reinvest them in the business. We'll see how things turn out. I think I know the restaurant we should start with.'

Padway experienced a twinge of dread at the idea of trying to sell the restaurateur the idea. He was not a born salesman, and he knew it.

He asked: 'How should I go about getting him to buy some of the stuff? I'm not very familiar with your Roman business methods.'

'That's all right. He won't refuse, because he owes me money, and he's behind in his interest payments. I'll introduce you.'

It came about as the banker had said. The restaurant owner, a puffy man named Gaius Attalus, glowered a bit at first. The entrepreneur fed him a little brandy by way of a sample, and he warmed up. Thomasus had to ask God whether He was listening only twice before Attalus agreed to Padway's price for half a dozen bottles.

Padway, who had been suffering from one of his periodic fits of depression all morning, glowed visibly as they emerged from the restaurant, his pockets pleasantly heavy with gold.

'I think,' said Thomasus, 'you had better hire that Vandal chap, if you're going to have money around the house. And I'd spend some of it on a good strong box.'

So when Hannibal Scipio told Padway 'There's a tall, gloomy-looking bird outside who says you said to come see you,' he had the Vandal sent in and hired him almost at once.

When Padway asked Fritharik what he proposed to do his bodyguarding with, Fritharik looked embarrassed, chewed his mustache, and finally said: 'I had a fine sword, but I hocked it to keep alive. It was all that stood between me and a nameless grave. Perhaps I shall end in one yet,' he sighed.

'Stop thinking about graves for a while,' snapped Padway, 'and tell me how much you need to get your sword back.'

'Forty solidi.'

'*Whew!* Is it made of solid gold, or what?'

'No. But it's good Damascus steel, and has gems in the handle. It was all that I saved from my beautiful estate in Africa. You have no idea what a fine place I had —'

'Now, now!' said Padway. 'For heaven's sake don't start crying! Here's five solidi; go buy yourself the best sword you can with that. I'm taking it out of your salary. If you want to save up to get this bejeweled cheese knife of yours back, that's your business.' So Fritharik departed, and shortly thereafter reappeared with a secondhand sword clanking at his side.

'It's the best I could do for the money,' he explained. 'The dealer claimed it was Damascus work, but you can tell that the Damascus marks on the blade are fakes. This local steel is soft, but I suppose it will have to do. When I had my beautiful estate in Africa, the finest steel was none too good.' He sighed gustily.

Padway examined the sword, which was a typical sixth-century *spatha* with a broad single-edged thirty-inch blade. It was, in fact, much like a Scotch broadsword without the fancy knuckle-guard. He also noticed that Fritharik Staifan's son, though as mournful as ever, stood straighter and walked with a more determined stride when wearing the sword. He must, Padway thought, feel practically naked without it.

'Can you cook?' Padway asked Fritharik.

'You hired me as a bodyguard, not as a housemaid, my lord Martinus. I have my dignity.'

'Oh, nonsense, old man. I've been doing my own cooking, but it takes too much of my time. If I don't mind, you shouldn't. Now, can you cook?'

Fritharik pulled his mustache. 'Well – yes.'

'What, for instance?'

'I can do a steak. I can fry bacon.'

'What else?'

'Nothing else. That is all I ever had occasion to do. Good red meat is the food for a warrior. I can't stomach these greens the Italians eat.'

Padway sighed. He resigned himself to living on an unbalanced diet until – well, why not? He could at least inquire into the costs of domestic help.

Thomasus found a serving-wench for him who would cook, clean house, and make beds for an absurdly low wage. The wench was named Julia. She came from Apulia and talked dialect. She was about twenty, dark, stocky, and gave promise of developing tremendous heft in later years. She wore a single shapeless garment and padded about the house on large bare feet. Now and then she cracked a joke too rapidly for Padway to follow and shook with peals of laughter. She worked hard, but Padway had to teach her his ideas from the ground up. The first time he fumigated his house he almost frightened her out of her wits. The smell of sulphur dioxide sent her racing out the door shrieking that Satanas had come.

Padway decided to knock off on his fifth Sunday in Rome. For almost a month he had been working all day and most of the night, helping Hannibal to run the still, clean it, and unload casks of wine; and seeing restaurateurs who had received inquiries from their customers about this remarkable new drink.

In an economy of scarcity, he reflected, you didn't have to turn handsprings finding customers, once your commodity caught on. He was meditating striking Thomasus for a loan to build another still. This time he'd build a set of rolls and roll his own copper sheeting out of round stock, instead of trying to patch together this irregular hand-hammered stun.

Just now, though, he was heartily sick of the business. He wanted fun, which to him meant the Ulpian Library. As he looked in the mirror, he thought he hadn't changed much inside. He disliked barging in on strangers and bargaining as much as ever. But outside none of his former friends would have known him. He had grown a short reddish beard. This was partly because he had never in his other life shaved with a guardless razor, and it gave him the jitters to do so; and partly because he had always secretly coveted a beard, to balance his oversized nose.

He wore another new tunic, a Byzantine-style thing with ballooning sleeves. The trousers of his tweed suit gave an incongruous effect, but he didn't fancy the short pants of the country, with winter coming on. He also wore a cloak, which was nothing but a big square blanket with a hole in the middle to put his head through. He had hired an old woman to make him socks and underwear.

Altogether he was pretty well pleased with himself. He admitted he had been lucky in finding Thomasus; the Syrian had been an enormous help to him.

He approached the library with much the same visceral tingle that a lover gets from the imminence of a meeting with his beloved. Nor was he disappointed. He felt like shouting when a brief nosing about the shelves showed him Berosus' *Chaldean History*, the complete works of Livius, Tacitus' *History of the Conquest of Britain*, and Cassiodorus' recently published *Gothic History* complete. Here was stuff for which more than one twentieth-century historian or archaeologist would cheerfully commit murder.

For a few minutes he simply dithered, like the proverbial ass between two haystacks. Then he decided that Cassiodorus would have the most valuable information to impart, as it dealt with an environment in which he himself was living. So he lugged the big volumes out and set to work. It was hard work, too, even for a man who knew Latin. The books were written in a semi-cursive minuscule hand with all the words run together. The incredibly wordy and affected style of the writer didn't bother him as it would have if he had been reading English; he was after facts.

'Excuse me, sir,' said the librarian, 'but is that tall barbarian with the yellow mustache your man?'

'I suppose so,' said Padway. 'What is it?'

'He's gone to sleep in the Oriental section, and he's snoring so that the readers are complaining.'

'I'll tend to him,' said Padway.

He went over and awakened Fritharik. 'Can't you read?' he asked.

'No,' said Fritharik quite simply. 'Why should I? When I had my beautiful estate in Africa, there was no occasion —'

'Yes, I know all about your beautiful estate, old man. But you'll have to learn to read, or else do your snoring outside.'

Fritharik went out somewhat huffily, muttering in his own East-German dialect. Padway's guess was that he was calling reading a sissy accomplishment.

When Padway got back to his table, he found an elderly Italian dressed with simple elegance going through his Cassiodorus. The man looked up and said: 'I'm sorry; were you reading these?'

'That's all right,' said Padway. 'I wasn't reading all of them. If you're not using the first volume …'

'Certainly, certainly, my dear young man. I ought to warn you, though, to be careful to put it back in its proper place. Scylla cheated of her prey by Jason has no fury like that of our esteemed librarian when people misplace his books. And what, may I ask, do you think of the work of our illustrious pretorian prefect?'

'That depends,' said Padway judiciously. 'He has a lot of facts you can't get elsewhere. But I prefer my facts straight.'

'How do you mean?'

'I mean with less flowery rhetoric.'

'Oh, but my dear, dear young man! Here we moderns have at last produced a historian to rank with the great Livius, and you say you don't like —' He glanced up, lowered his voice, and leaned forward. 'Just consider the delicate imagery, the glorious erudition! Such style! Such wit!'

'That's just the trouble. You can't give me Polybius, or even Julius Caesar —'

'Julius Caesar! Why everybody knows *he* couldn't write! They use his *Gallic War* as an elementary Latin text for foreigners! All very well for the skin-clad barbarian, who through the gloomy fastnesses of the northern forests pursues the sanguinary boar and horrid bear. But for cultivated men like ourselves – I ask you, my dear young man! Oh' – he looked embarrassed – 'you will understand that in my remarks on foreigners I meant nothing personal. I perceive that you are an outlander, despite your obvious breeding and erudition. Are you by any chance from the fabled land of Hind, with its pearl-decked maidens and its elephants?'

'No, farther away than that,' said Padway. He knew he had flushed a literary Roman patrician, of the sort who couldn't ask you to pass the butter without wrapping the request in three puns, four mythological illusions, and a dissertation on the manufacture of butter in ancient Crete. 'A place called America. I doubt whether I should ever return, though.'

'Ah, how right you are! Why should one live anywhere but in Rome if one can? But perhaps you can tell me of the wonders of far-off China, with its gold-paved streets!'

'I can tell you a little about it,' said Padway cautiously. 'For one thing, the streets aren't gold-paved. In fact they're mostly not paved at all.'

'How disappointing! But I daresay that a truthful traveler returning from heaven would pronounce its wonders grossly overrated. We must get together, my excellent young sir. I am Cornelius Anicius.'

Evidently, Padway thought, he was expected to know who Cornelius Anicius was. He introduced himself. Ah, he thought, enter romance. A pretty slim dark girl approached, addressed Anicius as 'Father,' and said that she had not been able to find the Sabellian edition of Persius Flaccus.

'Somebody is using it, no doubt,' said Anicius. 'Martinus, this is my daughter Dorothea. A veritable pearl from King Khusrau's headdress of a daughter, though I as her father may be prejudiced.' The girl smiled sweetly at Padway and excused herself.

Anicius asked: 'And now, my dear young man, what is your occupation?'

Without thinking, Padway said he was in business.

'Indeed? What sort of business?'

Padway told him. The patrician froze up as he digested the information. He was still polite and smiling, but with a smile of a different sort.

'Well, well, that's interesting. Very interesting. I daresay you'll make a good financial success of your business.' He spoke the sentence with a slight difficulty, like a YMCA secretary talking about the facts of life. 'I suppose we aren't to blame for the callings wherein God stations us. But it's too bad you haven't tried the public service. That is the only way to rise above one's class, and an intelligent young man like you deserves to do so. And now, if you'll excuse me, I'll do some reading.'

Padway had been hoping for an invitation to Anicius' house. But now that Anicius knew him to be a mere vulgar manufacturer, no invitation would be forthcoming. Padway looked at his watch; it was nearly lunch time. He went out and awoke Fritharik.

The Vandal yawned. 'Find all the books you wanted, Martinus? I was just dreaming of my beautiful estate —'

'To hell with —' barked Padway, then shut his mouth.

'What?' said Fritharik. 'Can't I even dream about the time I was rich and respected? That's not very —'

'Nothing, nothing. I didn't mean you.'

'I'm glad of that. My one consolation nowadays is my memories. But what are you so angry at, Martinus? You look as if you could bite nails in two.' When there was no answer, he went on: 'It must have been something in those books. I'm glad I never learned to read. You get all worked up over things that happened long ago. I'd rather dream about my beaut – *oop*! I'm sorry, boss; I won't mention it again.'

Padway and Thomasus the Syrian sat, along with several hundred naked Romans, in the steam room of the Baths of Diocletian. The banker looked around and leered: 'I hear that in the old days they let the women into these baths, too. Right mixed in with the men. Of course that was in pagan times; there's nothing like that now.'

'Christian morality, no doubt,' said Padway dryly.

'Yes,' chuckled Thomasus. 'We moderns are *such* a moral people. You know what the Empress Theodora used to complain about?'

'Yes,' said Padway, and told Thomasus what the empress used to complain about.

'Damn it!' cried Thomasus. 'Every time I have a dirty story, either you've heard it, or you know a better one.'

Padway didn't see fit to tell the banker that he had read that bit of dirt in a book that hadn't yet been written, namely, the *Anecdotes* by Procopius of Cæsarea.

Thomasus went on: 'I've got a letter from my cousin Antiochus in Naples. He's in the shipping business. He has news from Constantinople.' He paused impressively. 'War.'

'Between us and the Empire?'

'Between the Goths and the Empire, anyway. They've been carrying on mysterious dickerings ever since Amalaswentha was killed. Thiudahad has tried to duck responsibility for the murder, but I think our old poet-king has come to the end of his rope.'

Padway said: 'Watch Dalmatia and Sicily. Before the end of the year —' He stopped.

'Doing a bit of soothsaying?'

'No, just an opinion.'

The good eye sparkled at Padway through the steam, very black and very intelligent. 'Martinus, just who are you?'

'What do you mean?'

'Oh, there's something about you – I don't know how to put it – not just your funny way of putting things. You produce the most astonishing bits of knowledge, like a magician pulling rabbits out of his cap. And when I try to pump you about your own country or how you came hither, you change the subject.'

'Well —' said Padway, wondering just how big a lie to risk. Then he thought of the perfect answer – a truthful one that Thomasus would be sure to misconstrue. 'You see, I left my own country in a great hurry.'

'Oh. For reasons of health, eh? I don't blame you for being cagy in that case.' Thomasus winked.

When they were walking up Long Street toward Padway's house, Thomasus asked how the business was. Padway told him: 'Pretty good. The new still will be ready next week. And I sold some copper strip to a merchant leaving for Spain. Right now I'm waiting for the murder.'

'The *murder*?'

'Yes, Fritharik and Hannibal Scipio didn't get along. Hannibal's been cockier than ever since he's had a couple of men under him. He rides Fritharik.'

'*Rides* him?'

'American vernacular, literally translated. Meaning that he subjects him to constant and subtle ridicule and insult. By the way, I'm going to pay off your loan when we get home.'

'Entirely?'

'That's right. The money's in the strong box waiting for you.'

'Splendid, my dear Martinus! But won't you need another?'

'I'm not sure,' said Padway, who was sure that he would. 'I was thinking of expanding my distillery.'

'That's a great idea. Of course now that you're established we'll put our loans on a business basis —'

'Meaning?' said Padway.

'Meaning that the rate of interest will have to be adjusted. The normal rate, you know, is much higher —'

'Ha, ha,' said Padway. 'That's what I thought you had in mind. But now that you know the business is a sure one, you can afford to give me a lower rate.'

'Ai, Martinus, that's absurd! Is that any way to treat me after all I've done for you?'

'You don't have to lend it if you don't want to. There are other bankers who'd be glad to learn American arithmetic —'

'Listen to him, God! It's robbery! It's extortion! I'll never give in! Go to your other bankers, see if I care!'

Three blocks of argument brought the interest rate down to ten per cent, which Thomasus said was cutting his own heart out and burning it on the altar of friendship.

When Padway had spoken of an impending murder, he had neither been passing off hindsight as foresight, nor trying to be literally prophetic. He was more astonished than Thomasus, when they entered his big workshop, to find Fritharik and Hannibal glaring like a couple of dogs who dislike each other's smell. Hannibal's two assistants were looking on with their backs to the door; thus nobody saw the newcomers.

Hannibal snarled: 'What do you mean, you big cottonhead? You lie around all day, too lazy to turn over, and then you dare criticize me —'

'All I said,' growled the Vandal in his clumsy, deliberate Latin, 'was that the next time I caught you, I'd report it. Well I did, and I'm going to.'

'I'll slit your lousy throat if you do!' yelled Hannibal.

Fritharik cast a short but pungent aspersion on the Sicilian's sex life. Hannibal whipped out a dagger and lunged at Fritharik. He moved with rattlesnake speed, but he used the instinctive but tactically unsound overhand stab. Fritharik, who was unarmed, caught his wrist with a smack of flesh on flesh, then lost it as Hannibal dug his point into the Vandal's forearm.

When Hannibal swung his arm up for another stab, Padway arrived and caught his arm. He hauled the little man away from his opponent, and immediately had to hang on for dear life to keep from being stabbed himself. Hannibal was shrieking in Sicilian patois and foaming a little at the mouth. Padway saw that he wanted to kill him. He jerked his face back as the dirty fingernails of Hannibal's left hand raked his nose, which was a target hard to miss.

Then there was a thump, and Hannibal collapsed, dropping his dagger. Padway let him slide to the floor, and saw that Nerva, the older of the two assistants, was holding a stool by one leg. It had all happened so quickly that Fritharik was just bending over to pick up a short piece of board for a weapon, and Thomasus and Carbo, the other workman, were still standing just inside the door.

Padway said to Nerva: 'I think you're the man for my next foreman. What's this about, Fritharik?'

Fritharik didn't answer, he stalked toward the unconscious Hannibal with plain and fancy murder in his face.

'That's enough, Fritharik!' said Padway sharply. 'No more rough stuff, or you're fired, too!' He planted himself in front of the intended victim. 'What was he doing?'

The Vandal came to himself. 'He was stealing bits of copper from stock and selling them. I tried to get him to stop without telling you; you know how it is if your fellow employees think you're spying on them. Please, boss, let me have one whack at him. I may be a poor exile, but no little Greek catamite —'

Padway refused permission. Thomasus suggested swearing out a complaint and having Hannibal arrested; Padway said no, he didn't want to get mixed up with the law. He did allow Fritharik to send Hannibal, when the Sicilian came to, out the front door with a mighty kick in the fundament. Exit villain, sneering, thought Padway as he watched the ex-foreman slink off.

Fritharik said: 'I think that was a mistake, Martinus. I could have sunk his body in the Tiber without anybody's knowing. He'll make trouble for us.'

Padway suspected that the last statement was correct. But he merely said: 'We'd better bind your arm up. Your whole sleeve is blood-soaked. Julia, get a strip of linen and boil it. Yes, *boil* it!'

CHAPTER IV

Padway had resolved not to let anything distract him from the task of assuring himself a livelihood. Until that was accomplished, he didn't intend to stick his neck out by springing gunpowder or the law of gravitation on the unsuspecting Romans.

But the bankers war talk reminded him that he was, after all, living in a political and cultural as well as an economic world. He had never, in his other life, paid more attention to current events than he had to. And in post-Imperial Rome, with no newspapers or electrical communication, it was even easier to forget about things outside one's immediate orbit.

He was living in the twilight of western classical civilization. The Age of Faith, better known as the Dark Ages, was closing down. Europe would be in darkness, from a scientific and technological aspect, for nearly a thousand years. That aspect was, to Padway's naturally prejudiced mind, the most, if not the only, important aspect of a civilization. Of course, the people among whom he was living had no conception of what was happening to them. The process was too slow to observe directly, even over the span of a lifetime. They took their environment for granted, and even bragged about their modernity.

So what? Could one man change the course of history to the extent of preventing this interregnum? One man had changed the course of history before. Maybe. A Carlylean would say yes. A Tolstoyan or Marxist would say no; the environment fixes the pattern of a man's accomplishments and throws up the man to fit that pattern. Tancredi had expressed it differently by calling history a tough web, which would take a huge effort to distort.

How would one man go about it? Invention was the mainspring of technological development. But even in his own time, the lot of the professional inventor had been hard, without the handicap of a powerful and suspicious ecclesiasticism. And now much could he accomplish by simply 'inventing,' even if he escaped the unwelcome attentions of the pious? The arts of distilling and metal rolling were launched, no doubt, and so were Arabic numerals. But there was so much to be done, and only one lifetime to do it in.

What then? Business? He was already in it; the upper classes were contemptuous of it; and he was not naturally a businessman, though he could hold his own well enough in competition with these sixth-century yaps. Politics? In an age when victory went to the sharpest knife, and no moral rules of conduct were observable? *Br-r-r!*

How to prevent darkness from falling?

The Empire might have been together longer if it had had better means of communication. But the Empire, at least in the west, was hopelessly smashed, with Italy, Gaul, and Spain under the muscular thumbs of their barbarian 'garrisons.'

The answer was *Rapid communication and the multiple record* – that is, printing. Not even the most diligently destructive barbarian can extirpate the written word from a culture wherein the *minimum* edition of most books is fifteen hundred copies. There are just too many books.

So he would be a printer. The web might be tough, but maybe it had never been attacked by a Martin Padway.

'Good morning, my dear Martinus,' said Thomasus. 'How is the copper-rolling business?'

'So-so. The local smiths are pretty well stocked with strip, and not many of the shippers are interested in paying my prices for such a heavy commodity. But I think I'll clean up that last note in a few weeks.'

'I'm glad to hear that. What will you do then?'

'That's what I came to see you about. Who's publishing books in Rome now?'

'Books? Books? Nobody, unless you count the copyists who replace worn-out copies for the libraries. There are a couple of bookstores down in the Agiletum, but their stock is all imported. The last man who tried to run a publishing business in Rome went broke years ago. Not enough demand, and not enough good authors. You're not thinking of going into it, I hope?'

'Yes, I am. I'll make money at it, too.'

'What? You're crazy, Martinus. Don't consider it. I don't want to see you go broke after making such a fine start.'

'I shan't go broke. But I'll need some capital to start.'

'What? Another loan? But I've just told you that nobody can make money publishing in Rome. It's a proven fact. I won't lend you an as on such a hare-brained scheme. How much do you think you'd need?'

'About five hundred solidi.'

'*Ai, ai!* You've gone mad, my boy! What would you need such a lot for? All you have to do is buy or hire a couple of scribes —'

Padway grinned. 'Oh, no. That's the point. It takes a scribe months to copy out a work like Cassiodorus' *Gothic History* by hand, and that's only one copy. No wonder a work like that costs fifty solidi per copy! I can build a machine that will turn out five hundred or a thousand copies in a few weeks, to retail for five or ten solidi. But it will take time and money to build the machine and teach an operator how to run it.'

'But that's real money! God, are You listening? Well, please make my misguided young friend listen to reason! For the last time, Martinus, I won't consider it! How does the machine work?'

If Padway had known the travail that was in store for him, he might have been less confident about the possibilities of starting a printshop in a world that knew neither printing presses, type, printer's ink, nor paper. Writing ink was available, and so was papyrus. But it didn't take Padway long to decide that these would be impractical for his purposes.

His press, seemingly the most formidable job, proved the easiest. A carpenter down in the warehouse district promised to knock one together for him in a few weeks, though he manifested a not unnatural curiosity as to what Padway proposed to do with the contraption. Padway wouldn't tell him.

'It's not like any press I ever saw,' said the man. 'It doesn't look like a felt press. I know! You're the city's new executioner, and this is a newfangled torture instrument! Why didn't you want to tell me, boss? It's a perfectly respectable trade! But say, how about giving me a pass to the torture chamber the first time you use it? I want to be sure my work holds up, you know!'

For a bed they used a piece sawn off the top of a section of a broken marble column and mounted on wheels. All Padway's instincts revolted at this use of a monument of antiquity, but he consoled himself with the thought that one column mattered less than the art of printing.

For type, he contracted with a seal cutter to cut him a set of brass types. He had, at first, been appalled to discover that he would need ten to twelve thousand of the little things, since he could hardly build a type-casting machine, and would therefore have to print directly from the types. He had hoped to be able to print in Greek and Gothic as well as in Latin, but the Latin types alone set him back a round two hundred solidi. And the first sample set that the seal cutter ran off had the letters facing the wrong way and had to be melted up again. The type was what a twentieth-century printer would have called fourteen-point Gothic, and an engraver would have called sanserif. With such big type he would not be able to get much copy on a page, but it would at least, he hoped, be legible.

Padway shrank from the idea of making his own paper. He had only a hazy idea of how it was done, except that it was a complicated process. Papyrus was too glossy and brittle, and the supply in Rome was meager and uncertain.

There remained vellum. Padway found that one of the tanneries across the Tiber turned out small quantities as a side line. It was made from the skins of sheep and goats by extensive scraping, washing, stretching, and paring. The price seemed reasonable. Padway rather staggered the owner of the tannery by ordering a thousand sheets at one crack.

He was fortunate in knowing that printer's ink was based on linseed oil and lampblack. It was no great trick to buy a bag of flaxseed and run it through a set of rolls like those he used for copper rolling, and to rig up a contraption consisting of an oil lamp, a waterfilled bowl suspended and revolved over it, and a scraper for removing the lampblack. The only thing wrong with the resulting ink was that it wouldn't print. That is, it either made no impression or came off the type in shapeless gobs.

Padway was getting nervous about his finances; his five hundred solidi were getting low, and this seemed a cruel joke. His air of discouragement became so obvious that he caught his workers remarking on it behind their hands. But he grimly set out to experiment on his ink. Sure enough, he found that with a little soap in it, it would work fairly well.

In the middle of February Nevitta Grummund's son wandered in through the raw drizzle. When Fritharik showed him in, the Goth slapped Padway on the back so hard as to send him halfway across the room. 'Well, well!' he bellowed. 'Somebody gave me some of that terrific drink you've been selling, and I remembered your name. So I thought I'd look you up. Say, you got yourself well established in record time, for a stranger. Pretty smart young man, eh? Ha, ha!'

'Would you like to look around?' invited Padway. 'Only I'll have to ask you to keep my methods confidential. There's no law here protecting ideas, so I have to keep my things secret until I'm ready to make them public property.'

'Sure, you can trust me. I wouldn't understand how your devices work anyhow.'

In the machine shop Nevitta was fascinated by a crude wire-drawing machine that Padway had rigged up. 'Isn't that pretty?' he said, picking up the roll of brass wire. 'I'd like to buy some for my wife. It would make nice bracelets and earrings.'

Padway hadn't anticipated that use of his products, but said he would have some ready in a week.

'Where do you get your power?' asked Nevitta.

Padway showed him the workhorse in the back yard walking around a shaft in the rain.

'Shouldn't think a horse would be efficient,' said the Goth. 'You could get a lot more power out of a couple of husky slaves. That is, if your driver knew his whip. Ha, ha!'

'Oh, no,' said Padway. 'Not this horse. Notice anything peculiar about his harness?'

'Well, yes, it *is* peculiar. But I don't know what's wrong with it.'

'It's that collar over his neck. You people make your horses pull against a strap around the throat. Every time he pulls, the strap cuts into his windpipe and shuts off the poor animal's breath. That collar puts the load on his shoulders. If you were going to pull a load, you wouldn't hitch a rope around your neck to pull it with, would you?'

'Well,' said Nevitta dubiously, 'maybe you're right. I've been using my kind of harness for a long time, and I don't know that I'd care to change.'

Padway shrugged. 'Any time you want one of these outfits, you can get it from Metellus the Saddler on the Appian Way. He made this to my specifications. I'm not making them myself; I have too much else to do.'

Here Padway leaned against the doorframe and closed his eyes.

'Aren't you feeling well?' asked Nevitta in alarm.

'No. My head weighs as much as the dome of the Pantheon. I think I'm going to bed.'

'Oh, my word, I'll help you. Where's that man of mine? *Hermann!*' When Hermann appeared, Nevitta rattled a sentence of Gothic at him wherein Padway caught the name of Leo Vekkos.

Padway protested: 'I don't want a physician —'

'Nonsense, my boy, it's no trouble. You were right about keeping the dogs outside. It cured my wheezes. So I'm glad to help you.'

Padway feared the ministrations of a sixth-century physician more than he feared the grippe with which he was coming down. He did not know how to refuse gracefully. Nevitta and Fritharik got him to bed with rough efficiency.

Fritharik said: 'It looks to me like a clear case of elf-shot.'

'What?' croaked Padway.

'Elf-shot. The elves have shot you. I know, because I had it once in Africa. A Vandal physician cured me by drawing out the invisible darts of the elves. When they become visible they are little arrowheads made of chipped flint.'

'Look,' said Padway, 'I know what's wrong with me. If everybody will let me alone, I'll get well in a week or ten days.'

'We couldn't think of that!' cried Nevitta and Fritharik together. While they were arguing, Hermann arrived with a sallow, black-beared, sensitive-looking man.

Leo Vekkos opened his bag. Padway got a glimpse into the bag, and shuddered. It contained a couple of books, an assortment of weeds, and several small bottles holding organs of what had probably been small mammals.

'Now then, excellent Martinus,' said Vekkos, 'let me see your tongue. Say ah.' The physician felt Padway's forehead, poked his chest and stomach, and asked him intelligent-sounding questions about his condition.

'This is a common condition in winter,' said Vekkos in a didactic tone. 'It is something of a mystery. Some hold it to be an excess of blood in the head, which causes that stuffy feeling whereof you complain. Others assert that it is an excess of black bile. I hold the view that it is caused by the conflict of the natural spirits of the liver with the animal spirits of the nervous system. The defeat of the animal spirits naturally reacts on the respiratory system —'

'Its nothing but a bad cold —' said Padway.

Vekkos ignored him. '— since the lungs and throat are under their control. The best cure for you is to rouse the vital spirits of the heart to put the natural spirits in their place.' He began fishing weeds out of the bag.

'How about elf-shot?' asked Fritharik.

'What?'

Fritharik explained the medical doctrine of his people.

Vekkos smiled. 'My good man, there is nothing in Galen about elf-shot. Nor in Celsus. Nor in Asclepiades. So I cannot take you seriously —'

'Then you don't know much about doctoring,' growled Fritharik.

'Really,' snapped Vekkos. 'Who is the physician?'

'Stop squabbling, or you'll make me worse,' grumbled Padway. 'What are you going to do to me?'

Vekkos held up a bunch of weeds. 'Have these herbs stewed and drink a cupful every three hours. They include a mild purgative, to draw off the black bile through the bowels in case there should be an excess.'

'Which is the purgative?' asked Padway.

Vekkos pulled it out. Padway's thin arm shot out and grabbed the weed. 'I just want to keep this separate from the rest, if you don't mind.'

Vekkos humored him, told him to keep warm and stay in bed, and departed. Nevitta and Hermann went with him.

'Calls himself a physician,' grumbled Fritharik, 'and never heard of elf-shot.'

'Get Julia,' said Padway.

When the girl came, she set up a great to-do: 'Oh, generous master, whatever is wrong with you? I'll get Father Narcissus —'

'No, you won't,' said Padway. He broke off a small part of the purgative weed and handed it to her. 'Boil this in a kettle of water, and bring me a cup of the water.' He handed her the rest of the bunch of greenery. 'And throw these out. Somewhere where the medicine man won't see them.'

A slight laxative should be just the thing, he thought. If they would only leave him alone …

Next morning his head was less thick, but he felt very tired. He slept until eleven, when he was wakened by Julia. With Julia was a dignified man wearing an ordinary civilian cloak over a long white tunic with tight sleeves. Padway guessed that he was Father Narcissus by his tonsure.

'My son,' said the priest. 'I am sorry to see hat the Devil had set his henchmen on you. This virtuous young woman besought my spiritual aid …'

Padway resisted a desire to tell Father Narcissus where to go. His one constant principle was to avoid trouble with the Church.

'I have not seen you at the Church of the Angel Gabriel,' continued Father Narcissus. 'You are one of us, though, I hope?'

'American rite,' mumbled Padway.

The priest was puzzled by this. But he went on. 'I know that you have consulted the physician Vekkos. How much better it is to put your trust in God, compared to whose power these bleeders and stewers of herbs are impotent! We shall start with a few prayers …'

Padway lived through it. Then Julia appeared stirring something.

'Don't be alarmed,' said the priest. 'This is one cure that never fails. Dust from the tomb of St. Nereus, mixed with water.'

There was nothing obviously lethal about the combination, so Padway drank it. Father Narcissus asked conversationally: 'You are not, then, from Padua?'

Fritharik put his head in. 'That so-called physician is here again.'

'Tell him just a moment,' said Padway. God, he was tired. 'Thanks a lot, Father. It's nice to have seen you.'

The priest went out, shaking his head over the blindness of mortals who trusted in *materia medica*.

Vekkos came in with an accusing look. Padway said: 'Don't blame me. The girl brought him.'

Vekkos sighed. 'We physicians spend our lives in hard scientific study, and then we have to compete with these alleged miracle-workers. Well, how's my patient today?'

While he was still examining Padway, Thomasus the Syrian appeared. The banker waited around nervously until the Greek left. Then Thomasus said: 'I came as soon as I heard you were sick, Martinus. Prayers and medicines are all very well, but we don't want to miss any bets. My colleague, Ebenezer the Jew, knows a man, one of his own sect named Jeconias of Naples, who is pretty good at curative magic. A lot of these magicians are frauds; I don't believe in them for a minute. But this man has done some remarkable —'

'I don't want him,' groaned Padway. 'I'll be all right if everybody will stop trying to cure me …'

'I brought him along, Martinus. Now do be reasonable. He won't hurt you. And I couldn't afford to have you die with those notes outstanding – of course that's not the only consideration; I'm fond of you personally …'

Padway felt like one in the grip of a nightmare. The more he protested, the more quacks they sicked on him.

Jeconias of Naples was a little fat man with a bouncing manner, more like a high-pressure salesman than the conventional picture of a magician.

He chanted: 'Now, just leave everything to me, excellent Martinus. Here's a little cantrip that'll scare off the weaker spirits.' He pulled out a piece of papyrus and read off something in an unknown language. 'There, that didn't hurt, did it? Just leave it all to old Jeconias. He knows what he's doing. Now we'll put this charm under the bed, so-o-o! There, don't you feel better already? Now we'll cast your horoscope. If you'll give me the date and hour of your birth ...'

How the hell, thought Padway, could he explain to this damned little quack that he was going to be born 1,373 years hence? He threw his reserve to the winds. He heaved himself up in bed and shouted feebly: 'Presumptuous slave, know you not that I am one of the hereditary custodians of the Seal of Solomon? That I can shuffle your silly planets around the sky with a word, and put out the sun with a sentence? And you talk of casting *my* horoscope?'

The magician's eyes were popping. 'I – I'm sorry, sir, I didn't know ...'

'Shemkhamphoras!' yelled Padway. 'Ashtaroth! Baâl-Marduk! St. Frigidaire! Tippecanoe and Tyler too! Begone, worm! One word from you of my true identity, and I'll strike you down with the foulest form of leprosy! Your eyeballs will rot, your fingers will drop off joint by joint —' But Jeconias was already out the door. Padway could hear him negotiate the first half of the stairway three steps at a time, roll head over heels the rest of the way, and race out of the front door.

Padway chuckled. He told Fritharik, who had been attracted by the noise: 'You park yourself at the door with your sword, and say that Vekkos has given orders to let nobody see me. And I mean *nobody*. Even if the Holy Ghost shows up, keep him out.'

Fritharik did as ordered. Then he craned his neck around the doorframe. 'Excellent boss! I found a Goth who knows the theory of elf-shot. Shall I have him come up and —'

Padway pulled the covers over his head.

It was now April 536. Sicily had fallen to General Belisarius in December. Padway had heard this weeks after it happened. Except for business errands, he had hardly been outside his house in four months in his desperate anxiety to get his press going. And except for his workers and his business contacts he knew practically nobody in Rome, though he had a speaking acquaintance with the librarians and two of Thomasus' banker friends, Ebenezer the Jew and Vardan the Armenian.

The day the press was finally ready he called his workers together and said: 'I suppose you know that this is likely to be an important day for us. Fritharik will give each of you a small bottle of brandy to take home when you leave. And the first man who drops a hammer or anything on those little brass letters gets fired. I hope none of you do, because you've done a good job and I'm proud of you. That's all.'

'Well, well,' said Thomasus, 'that's splendid. I always knew you'd get your machine to run. Said so right from the start. What are you going to print? The *Gothic History*? That would flatter the pretorian prefect, no doubt.'

'No. That would take months to run off, especially as my men are new at the job. I'm starting off with a little alphabet book. You know, A is for *asinus* (ass), B is for *braccae* (breeches), and so on.'

'That sounds like a good idea. But, Martinus, can't you let your men handle it, and take a rest? You look as if you haven't had a good night's sleep in months.'

'I haven't, to tell the truth. But I can't leave; every time something goes wrong I have to be there to fix it. And I've got to find outlets for this first book. Schoolmasters and such people. I have to do everything myself, sooner or later. Also, I have an idea for another kind of publication.'

'What? Don't tell me you're going to start another wild scheme —'

'Now, now, don't get excited, Thomasus. This is a weekly booklet of news.'

'Listen, Martinus, don't overreach yourself. You'll get the scribes' guild down on you. As it is, I wish you'd tell me more about yourself. You're the town's great mystery, you know. Everybody asks about you.'

'You just tell them I'm the most uninteresting bore you ever met in your life.'

There were only a little over a hundred freelance scribes in Rome. Padway disarmed any hostility they might have had for him by the curious expedient of enlisting them as reporters. He made a standing offer of a couple of sesterces per story for acceptable accounts of news items.

When he came to assemble the copy for his first issue, he found that some drastic censorship was necessary. For instance, one story read:

Our depraved and licentious city governor, Count Honorius, was seen early Wednesday morning being pursued down Broad Way by a young woman with a butcher's cleaver. Because this cowardly wretch was not encumbered by a decent minimum of clothing, he outdistanced his pursuer. This is the fourth time in a month that the wicked and corrupt count has created a scandal by his conduct with women. It is rumored that King Thiudahad will be petitioned to remove him by a committee of the outraged fathers of daughters whom he has dishonored. It is to be hoped that the next time the diabolical count is chased with a cleaver, his pursuer will catch him.

Somebody, thought Padway, doesn't *like* our illustrious count. He didn't know Honorius, but whether the story was true or not, there was no free-press clause in the Italian constitutions between Padway and the city's torture chambers.

So the first eight-page issue said nothing about young women with cleavers. It had a lot of relatively innocuous news items, one short poem contributed by a scribe who fancied himself a second Ovid, an editorial by Padway in which he said briefly that he hoped the Romans would find his paper useful, and a short article – also by Padway – on the nature and habits of the elephant.

Padway turned the crackling sheepskin pages of the proof copy, was proud of himself and his men, a pride not much diminished by the immediate discovery of a number of glaring typographical errors. One of these, in a story about a Roman mortally wounded by robbers on High Path a few nights back, had the unfortunate effect of turning a harmless word into an obscene one. Oh, well, with only two hundred and fifty copies he could have somebody go through them and correct the error with pen and ink.

Still, he could not help being a little awed by the importance of Martin Padway in this world. But for pure good luck, it might have been he who had been fatally stabbed on High Path – and behold, no printing press, none of the inventions he might yet introduce, until the slow natural process of technical development prepared the way for them. Not that he deserved too much credit – Gutenberg ought to have some for the press, for instance.

Padway called his paper *Tempora Romae* and offered it at ten sesterces, about the equivalent of fifty cents. He was surprised when not only did the first issue sell out, but Fritharik was busy for three days turning away from his door people who wanted copies that were not to be had.

A few scribes dropped in every day with more news items. One of them, a plump cheerful-looking fellow about Padway's age, handed in a story beginning:

The blood of an innocent man has been sacrificed to the lusts of our vile monster of a city governor, Count Honorius.

Reliable sources have revealed that Q. Aurelius Galba, crucified on a charge of murder last week, was the husband of a wife who had long been adulterously coveted by our villainous count. At Galba's trial there was much comment among the spectators on the flimsiness of the evidence …

'Hey!' said Padway. 'Aren't you the man who handed in that other story about Honorius and a cleaver?'

'That's right,' said the scribe. 'I wondered why you didn't publish it.'

'How long do you think I'd be allowed to run my paper without interference if I did?'

'Oh, I never thought of that.'

'Well, remember next time. I can't use this story either. But don't let it discourage you. It's well done; a lead sentence and everything. How do you get all this information?'

The man grinned. 'I hear things. And what I don't hear, my wife does. She has women friends who get together for games of backgammon, and they talk.'

'It's too bad I don't dare run a gossip column,' said Padway. 'But you would seem to have the makings of a newspaper man. What's your name?'

'George Menandrus.'

'That's Greek, isn't it?'

'My parents were Greek; I am Roman.'

'All right, George, keep in touch with me. Some day I may want to hire an assistant to help run the thing.'

Padway confidently visited the tanner to place another order for vellum.

'When will you want it?' said the tanner. Padway told him in four days.

'That's impossible. I might have fifty sheets for you in that time. They'll cost you five times as much apiece as the first ones.'

Padway gasped. 'In God's name, why?'

'You practically cleaned out Rome's supply with that first order,' said the tanner. 'All of our stock, and all the rest that was floating around, which I went out and bought up for you. There aren't enough skins left in the whole city to make a hundred sheets. And making vellum takes time, you know. If you buy up the last fifty sheets, it will be weeks before I can prepare another large batch.'

Padway asked: 'If you expanded your plant, do you suppose you could eventually get up to a capacity of two thousand a week?'

The tanner shook his head. 'I should not want to spend the money to expand in such a risky business. And, if I did, there wouldn't be enough animals in Central Italy to supply the demand.'

Padway recognized when he was licked. Vellum was essentially a by-product of the sheep-and-goat industry. Therefore a sudden increase in demand would skyrocket the price without much increasing the output. Though the Romans knew next to nothing of economics, the law of supply and demand worked here just the same.

It would have to be paper after all. And his second edition was going to be very, very late.

For paper, he got hold of a felter and told him that he wanted him to chop up a few pounds of white cloth and make them into the thinnest felt that anybody had ever heard of. The felter dutifully produced a sheet of what looked like exceptionally thick and fuzzy blotting paper. Padway patiently insisted on finer breaking up of the cloth, on a brief boiling before felting, and on pressing after. As he went out of the shop he saw the felter tap his forehead significantly. But after many trials the man presented him with a paper not much worse for writing than a twentieth-century paper towel.

Then came the heartbreaking part. A drop of ink applied to this paper spread out with the alacrity of a picnic party that has discovered a rattlesnake in their midst. So Padway told the felter to make up ten more sheets, and into the mush from which each was made to introduce one common substance – soap, olive oil, and so forth. At this point the felter threatened to quit, and had to be appeased by a raise in price. Padway was vastly relieved to discover that a little clay mixed with the pulp made all the difference between a fair writing paper and an impossible one.

By the time Padway's second issue had been sold out, he had ceased to worry about the possibility of running out of paper. But another thought moved into the vacated worrying compartment in his mind: What should he do when the Gothic War really got going? In his own history it had raged for twenty years up and down Italy. Nearly every important town had been besieged or captured at least once. Rome itself would be practically depopulated by sieges, famine, and pestilence. If he lived long enough he might see the Lombard invasion and the near-extinction of Italian civilization. All this would interfere dreadfully with his plans.

He tried to shake off the mood. Probably the weather was responsible; it had rained steadily for two days. Everything in the house was dank. The only way to cure that would be to build a fire, and the air was too warm for that already. So Padway sat and looked out at the leaden landscape.

He was surprised when Fritharik brought in Thomasus' colleague, Ebenezer the Jew. Ebenezer was a frail-looking, kindly oldster with a long white beard. Padway found him distressingly pious; when he ate with the other bankers he did not eat at all, to put it Irishly, for fear of transgressing one of the innumerable rules of his sect.

Ebenezer took his cloak off over his head and asked: 'Where can I put this where it won't drip, excellent Martinus? Ah. Thank you. I was this way on business, and I thought I'd look your place over, if I may. It must be interesting, from Thomasus' accounts.' He wrung the water from his beard.

Padway was glad of something to take his mind off the ominous future. He showed the old man around.

Ebenezer looked at him from under bushy white eyebrows. 'Ah. Now I can believe that you are from a far country. From another world, almost. Take that system of arithmetic of yours; it has changed our whole concept of banking —'

'What?' cried Padway. 'What do you know about it?'

'Why,' said Ebenezer, 'Thomasus sold the secret to Vardan and me. I thought you knew that.'

'He *did*? How much?'

'A hundred and fifty solidi apiece. Didn't you —'

Padway growled a resounding Latin oath, grabbed his hat and cloak, and started for the door.

'Where are you going, Martinus?' said Ebenezer in alarm.

'I'm going to tell that cutthroat what I think of him!' snapped Padway. 'And then I'm going to —'

'Did Thomasus promise you not to reveal the secret? I cannot believe that he violated —'

Padway stopped with his hand on the door handle. Now that he thought, the Syrian had never agreed not to tell anybody about Arabic numerals. Padway had taken it for granted that he would not want to do so. But if Thomasus got pressed for ready cash, there was no legal impediment to his selling or giving the knowledge to whom he pleased.

As Padway got his anger under control, he saw that he had not really lost anything, since his original intention had been to spread Arabic numerals far and wide. What really peeved him was that Thomasus should chisel such a handsome sum out of the science without even offering Padway a cut. It was like Thomasus. He was all right, but as Nevitta had said you had to watch him.

When Padway did appear at Thomasus' house, later that day, he had Fritharik with him. Fritharik was carrying a strong box. The box was nicely heavy with gold.

'Martinus,' cried Thomasus, a little appalled, 'do you really want to pay off all your loans? Where did you get all this money?'

'You heard me,' grinned Padway. 'Here's an accounting of principal and interest. I'm tired of paying ten per cent when I can get the same for seven and a half.'

'What? Where can you get any such absurd rate?'

'From your esteemed colleague, Ebenezer. Here's a copy of the new note.'

'Well, I must say I wouldn't have expected that of Ebenezer. If all this is true, I suppose I could meet his rate.'

'You'll have to better it, after what you made from selling my arithmetic.'

'Now, Martinus, what I did was strictly legal —'

'Didn't say it wasn't.'

'Oh, very well. I suppose God planned it this way. I'll give you seven and four tenths.'

Padway laughed scornfully.

'Seven, then. But that's the lowest, absolutely, positively, finally.'

When Padway had received his old notes, a receipt for the old loans, and a copy of the new note, Thomasus asked him, 'How did you get Ebenezer to offer you such an unheard-of figure?'

Padway smiled. 'I told him that he could have had the secret of the new arithmetic from me for the asking.'

Padway's next effort was a clock. He was going to begin with the simplest design possible: a weight on the end of a rope, a ratchet, a train of gears, the hand and dial from a battered old clepsydra or water clock he picked up secondhand, a pendulum, and an escapement. One by one he assembled these parts – all but the last.

He had not supposed there was anything so difficult about making an escapement. He could take the back cover off his wristwatch and see the escapement-wheel there, jerking its merry way around. He did not want to take his watch apart for fear of never getting it together again. Besides, the parts thereof were too small to reproduce accurately.

But he could *see* the damned thing; why couldn't he make a large one? The workmen turned out several wheels, and the little tongs to go with them. Padway filed and scraped and bent. But they would not work. The tongs caught the teeth of the wheels and stuck fast. Or they did not catch at all, so that the shaft on which the rope was wound unwound itself all at once. Padway at last got one of the contraptions adjusted so that if you swung the pendulum with your hand, the tongs would let me escapement-wheel revolve one tooth at a time. Fine. But the clock would not run under its own power. Take your hand off the pendulum, and it made a couple of half-hearted swings and stopped.

Padway said to hell with it. He'd come back to it some day when he had more time and better tools and instruments. He stowed the mess of cog-wheels in a corner of his cellar. Perhaps, he thought, this failure had been a good thing, to keep him from getting an exaggerated idea of his own cleverness.

Nevitta popped in again. 'All over your sickness, Martinus? Fine; I knew you had a sound constitution. How about coming out to the Flaminian race-track with me now and losing a few solidi? Then come on up to the farm overnight.'

'I'd like to a lot. But I have to put the *Times* to bed this afternoon.'

'Put to bed?' queried Nevitta.

Padway explained.

Nevitta said: 'I see. Ha, ha, I thought you had a girl friend named Tempora. Tomorrow for supper, then.'

'How shall I get there?'

'You haven't a saddle horse? I'll send Hermann down with one tomorrow afternoon. But mind, I don't want to get him back with wings growing out of his shoulders!'

'It might attract attention,' said Padway solemnly. 'And you'd have a hell of a time catching him if he didn't want to be bridled.'

So the next afternoon Padway, in a new pair of rawhide Byzantine jack boots, set out with Hermann up the Flaminian Way. The Roman Campagna, he noted, was still fairly prosperous farming country. He wondered how long it would take for it to become the desolate, malarial plain of the Middle Ages.

'How were the races?' he asked.

Hermann, it seemed, knew very little Latin, though that little was still better than Padway's Gothic. 'Oh, my boss ... he terrible angry. He talk ... you know ... hot sport. But hate lose money. Lose fifty sesterces on horse. Make noise like ... you know ... lion with gut ache.'

At the farmhouse Padway met Nevitta's wife, a pleasant, plump woman who spoke no Latin, and her eldest son, Dagalaif, a Gothic *scaio*, or marshal, home on vacation. Supper fully bore out the stories that Padway had heard about Gothic appetites. He was agreeably surprised to drink some fairly good beer, after the bilgewater that went by that name in Rome.

'I've got some wine, if you prefer it,' said Nevitta.

'Thanks, but I'm getting a little tired of Italian wine. The Roman writers talk a lot about their different kinds, but it all tastes alike to me.'

'That's the way I feel. If you really *want* some, I have some perfumed Greek wine.'

Padway shuddered.

Nevitta grinned. 'That's the way I feel. Any man who'd put perfume in his liquor probably swishes when he walks. I only keep the stuff for my Greek friends, like Leo Vekkos. Reminds me, I must tell him about your cure for my wheezes by having me put my dogs out. He'll figure out some fancy theory full of long words to explain it.'

Dagalaif spoke up: 'Say, Martinus, maybe you have inside information on how the war will go.'

Padway shrugged. 'All I know is what everybody else knows. I haven't a private wire – I mean a private channel of information to heaven. If you want a guess, I'd say that Belisarius would invade Bruttium this summer and besiege Naples by August. He won't have a large force, but he'll be infernally hard to beat.'

Dagalaif said: 'Huh! We'll let him up all right. A handful of Greeks won't get very far against the united Gothic nation.'

'That's what the Vandals thought,' answered Padway dryly.

'*Aiw*,' said Dagalaif. 'But we won't make the mistakes the Vandals made.'

'I don't know, son,' said Nevitta. 'It seems to me we are making them already – or others just as bad. This king of ours – all he's good for is hornswoggling his neighbors out of land and writing Latin poetry. And digging around in libraries. It would be better if we had an illiterate one, like Theoderik. Of course,' he added apologetically, 'I admit I can read and write. My old man came from Pannonia with Theoderik, and he was always talking about the sacred duty of the Goths to preserve Roman civilization from savages like the Franks. He was determined that I would have a Latin education if it killed me. I admit I've found my education useful. But in the next few months it'll be more important for our leader to know how to lead a charge than to say *amo-amas-amat*.'

CHAPTER V

Padway returned to Rome in the best of humor. Nevitta was the first person, besides Thomasus the Syrian, who had asked him to his house. And Padway, despite his somewhat cool exterior, was a sociable fellow at heart. He was, in fact, so elated that after he dismounted he handed the reins of the borrowed horse to Hermann without noticing the three tough-looking parties leaning against the new fence in front of the old house on Long Street.

When Padway headed for the gate, the largest of the three, a black-bearded man, stepped in front of him. The man was holding a sheet of paper – real paper, no doubt from the felter to whom Padway had taught the art – and reading out loud to himself: – 'medium height, brown hair and eyes, large nose, short beard. Speaks with an accent.' He looked up sharply. 'Are you Martinus Paduei?'

'*Sic. Quis est?*'

'You're under arrest. Will you come along quietly?'

'*What?* Who – What for —'

'Order of the municipal Prefect. Charge of Sorcery.'

'But … but – *Hey!* You can't —'

'I said *quietly.*'

The other two men had moved up on each side of Padway, and each took an arm and started to walk him along the street. When he resisted, a short bludgeon appeared in the hand of one. Padway looked around frantically. Hermann was already out of sight. Fritharik was not to be seen; no doubt he was snoring as usual. Padway filled his lungs to shout; the man on his right tightened his grip and raised the bludgeon threateningly. Padway didn't shout.

They marched him down the Argiletum to the old jail below the Record Office on the Capitoline. He was still in somewhat of a daze as the clerk demanded his name, age, and address. All he could think of was that he had heard somewhere that you were entitled to telephone your lawyer before being locked up. And that information seemed hardly useful under the present circumstances.

A small, snapping Italian who had been lounging on a bench got up. 'What's this, a sorcery case involving a foreigner? Sounds like a national case to me.'

'Oh, no, it isn't,' said the clerk. 'You national officers have authority in

Rome only in mixed Roman-Gothic cases. This man isn't a Goth; says he's an American, whatever that is.'

'Yes, it is! Read your regulations. The pretorian prefect's office has jurisdiction in all capital cases involving foreigners. If you have a sorcery complaint, you turn it and the prisoner over to us. Come on, now.' The little man moved possessively toward Padway who paled at the term 'capital cases.'

The clerk continued arguing with the policeman: 'Don't be a fool. Think you're going to drag him clear up to Ravenna for interrogation? We've got a perfectly good torture chamber here.'

'I'm only doing my duty,' snapped the state policeman. He grabbed Padway's arm and started to haul him toward the door. 'Come along now, sorcerer. We'll show you some real, up-to-date torture at Ravenna. These Roman cops don't know anything.'

'*Christus!* Are you crazy?' yelled the clerk. He jumped up and grabbed Padway's other arm, as did the black-bearded man who had arrested him. As the state policemen pulled, so did the other two.

'Hey!' yelled Padway. But the assorted functionaries were too engrossed in their tug-of-war to notice their prisoner's complaint.

The state policeman shouted in a penetrating voice: 'Justinius, run and tell the adjutant prefect that these municipal scum are trying to withhold a prisoner from us!' As the man ran out the door, another door opened, and a fat, sleepy-looking man came in. 'What's this?' he squeaked.

For a moment the clerk and the municipal policeman stood at attention, releasing Padway. Then, as the state policeman resumed hauling him toward the door, the local cops abandoned their etiquette and grabbed Padway again. They all shouted at once at the fat man who Padway inferred was the municipal *commentariensius*, or police chief.

At that two more municipal policemen came in with a thin, ragged prisoner. They entered into the dispute with true Italian fervor, which meant using both hands. The ragged prisoner promptly darted out the door and his captors didn't notice his absence for a full minute.

They then began shouting at each other. 'What did you let him go for?' 'You brass-bound idiot, you're the one who let him go!'

Just then the man called Justinius came back with an elegant person who announced himself as the *corniculatis*, or adjutant prefect. This individual waved a perfumed handkerchief at the noisy, struggling group and said: 'Let him go, you chaps. Yes, you, too, Sulla. There won't be anything left of him to interrogate if you keep this up.'

From the speed with which the others in the nowcrowded room quieted, Padway guessed that the adjutant prefect was a pretty big shot.

The adjutant prefect asked a few questions, then said: 'I'm sorry, my dear old *commentariensius*, but I'm afraid he's our man.'

'Not yet he isn't,' squeaked the police chief. 'You fellows can't just walk in here and grab a prisoner any time you feel like it. It would cost me my job to let you have him.'

The adjutant prefect yawned. 'Dear, dear, you're *such* a bore. You forget that I represent the pretorian prefect, who represents the king, and if I order you to hand the prisoner over, you hand him over and that's the end of it. I so order you, now.'

'Go ahead and order. You'll have to take him by force, and I've got more force than you have.' The chief beamed Billiken-like and twiddled his thumbs. 'Clodianus, go fetch our illustrious city governor, if he's not too busy. We'll see whether we have authority over our own jail.' The clerk departed. 'Of course,' the chief continued, 'we *might* use Solomon's method.'

'You mean cut him in two?' asked the adjutant prefect with a grin.

'Lord Jesus, that would be funny, wouldn't it? Ho, ho, ho!' The chief laughed shrilly until the tears ran down his face. 'Would you prefer the head end or the legs? Ho, ho, ho, ho, ho!' He rocked on his seat.

As the other municipal officers laughed dutifully, the adjutant prefect permitted himself a wan, bored smile. Padway thought the chief's humor in questionable taste.

Eventually the clerk returned with the city governor. Count Honorius wore a tunic with the two purple stripes of a Roman senator, and walked with such a carefully measured tread that Padway wondered if his footsteps hadn't been laid out ahead of time with chalk marks. He had a square jaw and all the warmth of expression of a snapping turtle.

'What,' he asked in a voice like a steel file, 'is this all about? Quick, now, I'm a busy man.' As he spoke, the little wattle under his jaw wobbled in a way that reminded Padway more than ever of a snapper.

The chief and the adjutant prefect gave their versions. The clerk dragged out a couple of law books; the three executive officers put their heads together and talked in low tones, turning pages rapidly and pointing to passages.

Finally the adjutant prefect gave in. He yawned elaborately. 'Oh, well, it would be a dreadful bore to have to drag him up to Ravenna, anyway. Especially as the mosquito season will be starting there shortly. Glad to have seen you, my lord count.' He bowed to Honorius, nodded casually to the chief, and departed.

Honorius said: 'Now that we have him, what's to be done with him? Let's see that complaint.'

The clerk dug out a paper and gave it to the count who read aloud.

'*Hm.* "— and furthermore, the said Martinus Paduei did most wickedly and feloniously consort with the Evil One, who taught him the diabolical arts of magic wherewith he has been jeopardizing the welfare of the citizens of the city of Rome – signed, Hannibal Scipio of Palermo."' The count paused to study Padway, then he said: 'Wasn't this Hannibal Scipio a former associate of yours or something?'

'Yes, my lord count,' said Padway, who stated the circumstances of his parting with his foreman. 'If it's my printing press that he's referring to, I can easily show that it's a simple mechanical device, no more magical than one of your water clocks.'

'*Hm-m-m*,' said Honorius, 'that may or may not be true.' He looked through narrowed eyes at Padway. 'These new enterprises of yours have prospered pretty well, haven't they?' His faint smile reminded Padway of a fox dreaming of unguarded henroosts.

'Yes and no, my lord. I have made a little money, but I've put most of it back in the business, so I have no more cash than I need for day-to-day expenses.'

'Too bad,' said Honorius. 'It looks as though we'd have to let the case go through.'

Padway was getting more and more nervous under that penetrating scrutiny, but he put up a bold front. 'My lord, I don't think you have a sound case. It would be most unfortunate for your dignity to let the case come to trial.'

'So? I'm afraid my good man, that you don't know our expert interrogators. You'll have admitted all sorts of things by the time they finish … ah … questioning you.'

'Um-m-m. My lord, I said I didn't have much *cash*. But I have an idea that might interest you.'

'That's better. Lutetius, may I use your private office?'

Without waiting for an answer, Honorius marched to the office, jerking his head to Padway to follow. The chief looked after them sourly, obviously resenting the loss of his share of the swag.

In the chief's office, Honorius turned to Padway. 'You weren't proposing to bribe your governor by any chance, were you?' he asked coldly.

'Well … uh … not exactly —'

The count shot his head forward. 'How much?' he snapped. 'And what's it in jewels?'

Padway sighed with relief. 'Please, my lord, not so fast. It'll take a bit of explaining.'

'Your explanation had better be good, foreigner.'

'It's this way, my lord: I'm just a poor stranger in Rome, and naturally I have to depend on my wits for a living. The only really valuable thing I have is those wits. But, with reasonably kind treatment, they can be made to pay a handsome return.'

'Get to the point, young man.'

'You have a law against limited-liability corporations in other than public enterprises, have you not?'

Honorius rubbed his chin. 'We did have once. I don't know what its status is, now that the senate's authority is limited to the city. I don't think the Goths have made any regulations on that subject. Why?'

'Well if you can get the senate to pass an amendment to the old law – I don't think it would be necessary, but it would look better – I could show you how you and a few other deserving senators could benefit handsomely from the organization and operation of such a company.'

Honorius stiffened. 'Young man, that's a miserable sort of offer. You ought to know that the dignity of a patrician forbids him to engage in trade.'

'You wouldn't engage in trade, my lord. You'd be the owner of the stockholders.'

'We'd be the what?'

Padway explained the operation of a stock corporation.

Honorius rubbed his chin again. 'Yes, I see where something might be made of that plan. What sort of company did you have in mind?'

'A company for the transmission of information over long distances much more rapidly than a messenger can travel. In my country they'd call it a semaphore telegraph. The company gets its revenue from tolls on private messages. Of course, it wouldn't hurt if you could get a subsidy from the royal treasury, on the ground that such an institution was invaluable for national defense.'

Honorius thought awhile. Then he said: 'I won't commit myself now; I shall have to think about the matter and sound out my friends. In the meantime, you will, of course, remain in Lutetius' custody here.'

Padway grinned. 'My lord count, your daughter is getting married next week, isn't she?'

'What of it?'

'You will want a nice write-up of the wedding in my paper. A list of distinguished guests, a woodcut picture of the bride, and so forth.'

'Hm-m-m. I shouldn't mind that; no.'

'Well, then, you better not hold me, or I shan't be able to get the paper out. It would be a pity if such a gala event missed the news because the publisher was in jail at the time.'

Honorius rubbed his chin and smiled thinly. 'For a barbarian, you're not as stupid as one would expect. I shall have you released.'

'Many thanks, my lord. I might add that I shall be able to write more glowing paragraphs after that complaint has been dismissed. We creative workers, you know —'

When Padway was out of earshot of the jail, he indulged in a long 'Whew!' He was sweating, and not with the heat, either. It was fortunate that none of the officials noticed how near he had been to collapse from sheer terror. The prospect of a stand-up fight wouldn't have bothered him more than most young men. But torture …

As soon as he had put his workshop in order, he went into a huddle with Thomasus. He was properly prepared when at last, a procession of five sedan chairs, bearing Honorius and four other senators, crawled up the avenue to his place. The senators seemed not only willing but eager to lay their money on the line, especially after they saw the beautiful stock certificates that Padway had printed. But they didn't seem to have quite Padway's idea of how to run a corporation.

One of them poked him in the ribs and grinned. 'My dear Martinus, you're not *really* going to put up those silly signal towers and things?'

'Well,' said Padway cautiously, 'that was the idea.'

The senator winked. 'Oh, I understand that you'll have to put up a couple to fool the middle class, so we can sell our stock at a profit. But *we* know it's all a fake, don't we? You couldn't make anything with your signaling scheme in a thousand years.'

Padway didn't bother to argue with him. He also didn't bother to explain the true object of having Thomasus the Syrian, Ebenezer the Jew, and Vardan the Armenian each take eighteen per cent of the stock. The senators might have been interested in knowing that these three bankers had agreed ahead of time to hold their stock and vote as Padway instructed, thereby giving him, with fifty-four per cent of the stock, complete control of the corporation.

Padway had every intention of making his telegraph company a success, starting with a line of towers from Naples to Rome to Ravenna, and tying its operation in with that of his paper. He soon ran into an elementary difficulty: If he wanted to keep his expenses down to somewhere within sight of income, he needed telescopes, to make possible a wide spacing of the towers. Telescopes meant lenses. Where in the world was there a lens or a man who could make one? True, there was a story about Nero's emerald lorgnette …

Padway went to see Sextus Dentatus, the froglike goldsmith who had changed his lire to sesterces. Dentatus croaked directions to the establishment of one Florianus the Glazier.

Florianus was a light-haired man with a drooping mustache and a nasal accent. He came to the front of his dark little shop smelling strongly of wine. Yes, he had owned his own glass factory once, at Cologne. But business was bad for the Rhineland glass industry: the uncertainties of life under the Franks, you know, my sir. He had gone broke. Now he made a precarious living mending windows and such.

Padway explained what he wanted, paid a little on account, and left him. When he went back on the promised day, Florianus flapped his hands as if he were trying to take off. 'A thousand pardons, my sir! It has been hard to buy up the necessary cullet. But a few days more, I pray you. And if I could have a little more money on account – times are hard – I am poor —'

On Padway's third visit he found Florianus drunk. When Padway shook him, all the man could do was mumble Gallo-romance at him, which Padway did not understand. Padway went to the back of the shop. There was no sign of tools or materials for making lenses.

Padway left in disgust. The nearest real glass industry was at Puteoli, near Naples. It would take forever to get anything done by correspondence.

Padway called in George Menandrus and hired him as editor of the paper. For several days he talked himself hoarse and Menandrus deaf on How to Be an Editor. Then, with a sinking heart, he left for Naples. He experienced the famous canal-boat ride celebrated by Horace, and found it quite as bad as alleged.

Vesuvius was not smoking. But Puteoli, on the little strip of level ground between the extinct crater of Solfatara and the sea, was. Padway and Fritharik sought out the place recommended by Dentatus. This was one of the largest and smokiest of the glass factories.

Padway asked the doorman for Andronicus, the proprietor. Andronicus was a short, brawny man covered with soot. When Padway told who he was, Andronicus cried: 'Ah! Fine! Come, gentlemen, I have just the thing.'

They followed him into his private inferno. The vestibule, which was also the office, was lined with shelves. The shelves were covered with glassware. Andronicus picked up a vase. 'Ah! Look! Such clearness! You couldn't get whiter glass from Alexandria! Only two solidi!'

Padway said: 'I didn't come for a vase, my dear sir. I want —'

'No vase? No vase? Ah! Here is the thing.' He picked up another vase. 'Look! The shape! Such purity of line! It reminds you —'

'I said I didn't want to buy a vase. I want —'

'It reminds you of a beautiful woman! Of love!' Andronicus kissed his fingertips.

'I want some small pieces of glass, made specially —'

'Beads? Of course, gentlemen. Look.' The glass manufacturer scooped up a handful of beads. 'Look at the color! Emerald, turquoise, everything!' He picked up another bunch. 'See here, the faces of the twelve apostles, one on each bead —'

'Not beads —'

'A beaker, then! Here is one. Look, it has the Holy Family in high relief —'

'Jesus!' yelled Padway. 'Will you listen?'

When Andronicus let Padway explain what he wanted, the Neapolitan said: 'Of course! Fine! I've seen ornaments shaped like that. I'll rough them out tonight, and have them ready day after tomorrow —'

'That won't quite do,' said Padway. 'These have to have an exactly spherical surface. You grind a concave against a convex with – what's your word for *emery*? The stuff you use in rough grinding? Some *naxium* to true them off ...'

Padway and Fritharik went on to Naples and put up at the house of Thomasus' cousin, Antiochus the Shipper. Their welcome was less than cordial. It transpired that Antiochus was fanatically Orthodox. He loathed his cousin's Nestorianism. His pointed remarks about heretics made his guests so uncomfortable that they moved out on the third day. They took lodgings at an inn whose lack of sanitation distressed Padway's cleanly soul.

Each morning they rode out to Puteoli to see how the lenses were coming. Andronicus invariably tried to sell them a ton of glass junk.

When they left for Rome, Padway had a dozen lenses, half plano-convex and half plano-concave. He was skeptical about the possibility of making a telescope by holding a pair of lenses in line with his eye and judging the distances. It worked, though.

The most practical combination proved to be a concave lens for the eyepiece with a convex one about thirty inches in front of it. The glass had bubbles, and the image was somewhat distorted. But Padway's telescope, crude as it was, would make a two-to-one difference in the number of signal towers required.

About then, the paper ran its first advertisement. Thomasus had had to turn the screw on one of his debtors to make him buy space. The ad read:

DO YOU WANT A GLAMOROUS FUNERAL?

Go to meet your Maker in style! With one of our funerals to look forward to, you will hardly mind dying!
Don't imperil your chances of salvation with a bungled burial!
Our experts have handled some of the noblest corpses in Rome.
Arrangements made with the priesthood of any sect. Special rates for heretics. Appropriately doleful music furnished at slight extra cost.

JOHN THE EGYPTIAN, GENTEEL UNDERTAKER
NEAR THE VIMINAL GATE

CHAPTER VI

Junianus, construction manager of the Roman Telegraph Co., panted into Padway's office. He said: 'Work' – stopped to get his breath, and started again – 'work on the third tower on the Naples line was stopped this morning by a squad of soldiers from the Rome garrison. I asked them what the devil was up, and they said they didn't know; they just had orders to stop construction. What, most excellent boss, are you going to do about it?'

So the Goths objected? That meant seeing their higher-ups. Padway winced at the idea of getting involved any further in politics. He sighed. 'I'll see Liuderis, I suppose.'

The commander of the Rome garrison was a big, portly Goth with the bushiest white whiskers Padway had ever seen. His Latin was fair. But now and then he cocked a blue eye at the ceiling and moved his lips silently, as if praying; actually he was running through a declension or a conjugation for the right ending.

He said: 'My good Martinus, there is a war on. You start erecting these … ah … mysterious towers without asking our permission. Some of your backers are patricians … ah … notorious for their pro-Greek sentiments. What are we to think? You should consider yourself lucky to have escaped arrest.'

Padway protested: 'I was hoping the army would find them useful for transmitting military information.'

Liuderis shrugged. 'I am merely a simple soldier doing my duty. I do not understand these … ah … devices. Perhaps they will work as you say. But I could not take the … ah … responsibility for permitting them.'

'Then you won't withdraw your order?'

'No. If you want permission, you will have to see the king.'

'But, my dear sir, I can't spare the time to go running up to Ravenna —'

Another shrug. 'All one to me, my good Martinus. I know my duty.'

Padway tried guile. 'You certainly do, it seems. If I were the king, I couldn't ask for a more faithful soldier.'

'You flatterer!' But Liuderis grinned, pleased. 'I regret that I cannot grant your little request.'

'What's the latest war news?'

Liuderis frowned. 'Not very – But then I should be careful what I say. You are a more dangerous person than you look, I am sure.'

'You can trust me. I'm pro-Gothic.'

'Yes?' Liuderis was silent while the wheels turned. Then: 'What is your religion?'

Padway was expecting that. 'Congregationalist. That's the nearest thing to Arianism we have in my country.'

'Ah, then perhaps you are as you say. The news is not good, what little there is. There is nobody in Bruttium but a small force under the king's son-in-law, Evermuth. And our good king —' He shrugged again, this time hopelessly.

'Now look here, most excellent Liuderis, won't you withdraw that order? I'll write Thiudahad at once asking his permission.'

'No, my good Martinus, I cannot. You get the permission first. And you had better go in person, if you want action.'

Thus it came about that Padway found himself, quite against his wishes, trotting an elderly saddle horse across the Apennines toward the Adriatic. Fritharik had been delighted at first to get any kind of a horse between his knees. Before they had gone very far his tone changed.

'Boss,' he grumbled, 'I'm not an educated man. But I know horseflesh. I always claimed that a good horse was a good investment.' He added darkly: 'If we are attacked by brigands, we'll have no chance with those poor old wrecks. Not that I fear death, or brigands either. But it would be sad for a Vandal knight to end in a nameless grave in one of these lonely valleys. When I was a noble in Africa —'

'We aren't running a racing stable,' snapped Padway. At Fritharik's hurt look he was sorry he had spoken sharply. 'Never mind, old man, we'll be able to afford good horses some day. Only right now I feel as if I had a pantsful of ants.'

Brazilian army ants, he added to himself. He had done almost no riding since his arrival in old Rome, and not a great deal in his former life. By the time they reached Spoleto he felt as if he could neither sit nor stand, but would have to spend the rest of his life in a sort of semi-squat, like a rheumatic chimpanzee.

They approached Ravenna at dusk on the fourth day. The City in the Mist sat dimly astride the thirty-mile causeway that divided the Adriatic from the vast marshy lagoons to the west. A faint sunbeam lighted the gilded church domes. The church bells bonged, and the frogs in the lagoons fell silent; then resumed their croaking. Padway thought that anyone who visited this strange city would always be haunted by the bong of the bells, the croak of the frogs, and the thin, merciless song of the mosquitoes.

Padway decided that the chief usher, like Poo-Bah, had been born sneering. 'My good man,' said this being, 'I couldn't possibly give you an audience with our lord king for three weeks at least.'

Three weeks! In that time half of Padway's assorted machines would have broken down, and his men would be running in useless circles trying to fix them. Menandrus, who was inclined to be reckless with money, especially other people's, would have run the paper into bankruptcy. This impasse required thought. Padway straightened his aching legs and started to leave.

The Italian immediately lost some of his top-loftiness. 'But,' he cried in honest amazement, 'didn't you bring any *money*?'

Of course, Padway thought, he should have known that the man hadn't meant what he'd said. 'What's your schedule of rates?'

The usher, quite seriously, began counting on his fingers. 'Well, for twenty solidi I could give you your audience tomorrow. For the day after tomorrow, ten solidi is my usual rate; but that's Sunday, so I'm offering interviews on Monday at seven and a half. For one week in advance, two solidi. For two weeks —'

Padway interrupted to offer a five-solidi bribe for a Monday interview, and finally got it at that price plus a small bottle of brandy. The usher said: 'You'll be expected to have a present for the king, too, you know.'

'I know,' said Padway wearily. He showed the usher a small leather case. 'I'll present it personally.'

Thiudahad Tharasmund's son, King of the Ostrogoths and Italians; Commander in Chief of the Armies of Italy, Illyria, and Southern Gaul; Premier Prince of the Amal Clan; Count of Tuscany; Illustrious Patrician; ex officio President of the Circus; et cetera, et cetera, was about Padway's height, thin to gauntness, and had a small gray beard. He peered at his caller with watery gray eyes, and said in a reedy voice: 'Come in, come in, my good man. What's *your* business? Oh, yes, Martinus Paduei. You're the publisher chap aren't you? Eh?' He spoke upper-class Latin without a trace of accent.

Padway bowed ceremoniously. 'I am, my lord king. Before we discuss the business, I have —'

'Great thing, that book-making machine of yours. I've heard of it. Great thing for scholarship. You must see my man Cassiodorus. I'm sure he'd like you to publish his *Gothic History*. Great work. Deserves a wide circulation.'

Padway waited patiently. 'I have a small gift for you, my lord. A rather unusual —'

'Eh? Gift? By all means. Let's see it.'

Padway took out the case and opened it.

Thiudahad piped: 'Eh? What the devil is that?'

Padway explained the function of a magnifying glass. He didn't dwell on Thiudahad's notorious nearsightedness.

Thiudahad picked up a book and tried the glass on it. He squealed with delight. 'Fine, my good Martinus. Shall I be able to read all I want without getting headaches?'

'I hope so, my lord. At least it should help. Now, about my business here —'

'Oh, yes, you want to see me about publishing Cassiodorus. I'll fetch him for you.'

'No, my lord. It's about something else.' He went on quickly before Thiudahad could interrupt again, telling him of his difficulty with liuderis.

'Eh? I never bother my local military commanders. They know their business.'

'But, my lord —' and Padway gave the king a little sales talk on the importance of the telegraph company.

'Eh? A money-making scheme, you say? If it's as good as all that, why wasn't I let in on it at the start?'

That rather jarred Padway. He said something vague about there not having been time. King Thiudahad wagged his head. 'Still, that wasn't considerate of you, Martinus. It wasn't loyal. And if people aren't loyal to their king, where are we? If you deprive your king of an opportunity to make a little honest profit, I don't see why I should interfere with Liuderis on your account.'

'Well, ahem, my lord, I did have an idea —'

'Not considerate at all. What were you saying? Come to the point, my good man, come to the point.'

Padway resisted an impulse to strangle this exasperating little man. He beckoned Fritharik, who was standing statuesquely in the background. Fritharik produced a telescope, and Padway explained *its* functions ...

'Yes, Yes? Very interesting, I'm sure. Thank you, Martinus. I will say that you bring your king original presents.'

Padway gasped; he hadn't intended giving Thiudahad his best telescope. But it was too late now. He said: 'I thought that if my lord king saw fit to ... ah ... ease matters with your excellent Liuderis, I could insure your undying fame in the world of scholarship.'

'Eh? What's that? What do you know about scholarship? Oh, I forgot; you're a publisher. Something about Cassiodorus?'

Padway repressed a sigh. 'No, my lord. *Not* Cassiodorus. How would you like the credit for revolutionizing men's idea about the solar system?'

'I don't believe in interfering with my local commanders, Martinus. Liuderis is an excellent man. Eh? What were you saying. Something about the solar system? What's that got to do with Liuderis?'

'Nothing, my lord.' Padway repeated what he had said.

'Well, maybe I'd consider it. What is this theory of yours?'

Little by little Padway wormed from Thiudahad a promise of a free hand for the telegraph company, in return for bits of information about the Copernican hypothesis, instructions for the use of the telescope to see the moons of Jupiter, and a promise to publish a treatise on astronomy in Thiudahad's name.

At the end of an hour he grinned and said, 'Well, my lord, we seem to be in agreement. There's just one more thing. This telescope would be a valuable instrument of warfare. If you wanted to equip your officers with them —'

'Eh? Warfare? You'll have to see Wittigis about that. He's my head general.'

'Where's he?'

'Where? Oh, dear me, I don't know. Somewhere up north, I think. There's been a little invasion by the Allemans or somebody.'

'When will he be back?'

'How should I know, my good Martinus? When he's driven out these Allemans or Burgunds or whoever they are.'

'But, most excellent lord, if you'll pardon me, the war with the Imperialists is definitely on. I think it's important to get these telescopes into the hands of the army as soon as possible. We'd be prepared to supply them at a reasonable —'

'Now, Martinus,' snapped the king peevishly, 'don't try to tell me how to run my kingdom. You're as bad as my Royal Council. Always "Why don't you do this?' Why don't you do that?" I trust my commanders; don't bother myself with details. I say you'll have to see Wittigis, and that settles it.'

Thiudahad was obviously prepared to be mulish, so Padway said a few polite nothings, bowed, and withdrew.

CHAPTER VII

When Padway got back to Rome, his primary concern was to see how his paper was coming. The first issue that had been put out since his departure was all right. About the second, which had just been printed, Menandrus was mysteriously elated, hinting that he had a splendid surprise for his employer. He had. Padway glanced at a proof sheet, and his heart almost stopped. On the front page was a detailed account of the bribe which the new Pope, Silverius, had paid King Thiudahad to secure his election.

'Hell's bells!' cried Padway. 'Haven't you any better sense than to print this, George?'

'Why?' asked Menandrus, crestfallen. 'It's true, isn't it?'

'Of course, it's true! But you don't want us all hanged or burned at the stake, do you? The Church is already suspicious of us. Even if you find that a bishop is keeping twenty concubines, you're not to print a word of it.'

Menandrus sniffled a little; he wiped away a tear and blew his nose on his tunic. 'I'm sorry, excellent boss. I tried to please you; you have no idea how much trouble I went to to get the facts about that bribe. There *is* a bishop, too – not *twenty* concubines, but —'

'But we don't consider that news, for reasons of health. Thank heaven, no copies of this issue have gone out yet.'

'Oh, but they have.'

'*What?*' Padway's yell made a couple of workmen from the machine shop look in.

'Why, yes, John the Bookseller took the first hundred copies out just a minute ago.'

John the Bookseller got the scare of his life when Padway, still dirty from days of travel, galloped down the street after him, dove off his horse, and grabbed his arm. Somebody set up a cry of 'Thieves! Robbers! Help! Murder!' Padway found himself trying to explain to forty truculent citizens that everything was all right.

A Gothic soldier pushed through the crowd and asked what was going on here. A citizen pointed at Padway and shouted: 'It's the fellow with the boots. I heard him say he'd cut the other man's throat if he didn't hand over his money!' So the Goth arrested Padway.

Padway kept his clutch on John the Bookseller, who was too frightened to speak. He went along quietly with the Goth until they were out of earshot of the crowd. Then he asked the soldier into a wineshop, treated him and John, and explained. The Goth was noncommittal, despite John's corroboration, until Padway tipped him liberally. Padway got his freedom and his precious papers. Then all he had to worry about was the fact that somebody had stolen his horse while he was in the Goth's custody.

Padway trudged back to his house with the papers under his arm. His household was properly sympathetic about the loss of the horse. Fritharik said: 'There, illustrious boss, that piece of crow bait wasn't worth much anyhow.'

Padway felt much better when he learned that the first leg of the telegraph ought to be completed in a week or ten days. He poured himself a stiff drink before dinner. After his strenuous day it made his head swim a little. He got Fritharik to join him in one of the latter's barbarian warsongs:

> *The black earth shakes*
> *As the heroes ride,*
> *And the raven's blood—*
> *Red sun will hide!*
> *The lances dip*
> *In a glittering wave,*
> *And the coward turns*
> *His gore to save ...*

When Julia was late with the food, Padway gave her a playful spank. He was a little surprised at himself.

After dinner he was sleepy. He said to hell with the accounts and went upstairs to bed, leaving Fritharik already snoring on his mattress in front of the door. Padway would not have laid any long bets on Fritharik's ability to wake up when a burglar entered.

He had just started to undress when a knock startled him. He could not imagine ...

'Fritharik?' he called.

'No. It's me.'

He frowned and opened the door. The lamplight showed Julia from Apulia. She walked in with a swaying motion.

'What do you want, Julia?' asked Padway.

The stocky, black-haired girl looked at him in some surprise. 'Why – uh – my lord wouldn't want me to say right out loud? That wouldn't be nice!'

'Huh?'

She giggled.

'Sorry,' said Padway. 'Wrong station. Off you go.'

She looked baffled. 'My – my master doesn't want me?'

'That's right. Not for that anyway.'

Her mouth turned down. Two large tears appeared. 'You don't like me? You don't think I'm nice?'

'I think you're a fine cook and a nice girl. Now out with you. Good night.'

She stood solidly and began to sniffle. Then she sobbed. Her voice rose to a shrill wail: 'Just because I'm from the country – you never looked at me – you never asked for me all this time – then tonight you were nice – I thought – I thought – boo-oo-oo ...'

'Now, now ... for heaven's sake stop crying! Here, sit down. I'll get you a drink.'

She smacked her lips over the first swallow of diluted brandy. She wiped off the remaining tears. 'Nice,' she said. Everything was nice – *bonus, bona,* or *bonum,* as the case might be. 'You are nice. Love is nice. Every man should have some love. Love – ah!' She made a serpentine movement remarkable in a person of her build.

Padway gulped. 'Give me that drink,' he said. 'I need some too.'

After a while. 'Now,' she said, 'we make love?'

'Well – pretty soon. Yes, I guess we do.' Padway hiccuped.

Padway frowned at Julia's large bare feet. 'Just – *hic* – just a minute, my bounding hamadryad. Let's see those feet.' The soles were black. 'That won't do. Oh, it absolutely won't do, my lusty Amazon. The feet present an insur-insurmountable psychological obstacle.'

'Huh?'

'They interpose a psychic barrier to the – *hic* – appropriately devout worship of Ashtaroth. We must have the pedal extremities —'

'I don't understand.'

'Skip it; neither do I. What I mean is that we're going to wash your feet first.'

'Is that a religion?'

'You might put it that way. Damn!' He knocked the ewer on its base, miraculously catching it on the way down. 'Here we go, my Tritoness from the winedark, fish-swarming sea ...'

She giggled. 'You are the nicest man. You are a real gentleman. No man ever did *that* for me before ...'

Padway blinked his eyes open. It all came back to him quickly enough. He tightened his muscles serratus. He felt fine. He prodded his conscience experimentally. It reacted not at all.

He moved carefully, for Julia was taking up two-thirds of his none-too-wide bed. He heaved himself on one elbow and looked at her. The movement uncovered her large breasts. Between them was a bit of iron, tied around her neck. This, she had told him, was a nail from the cross of St. Andrew. And she would not put it off.

He smiled. To the list of mechanical inventions he meant to introduce he added a couple of items. But for the present, should he …

A small gray thing with six legs, not much larger than a pinhead, emerged from the hair under her armpit. Pale against her olive-brown skin, it crept with glacial slowness …

Padway shot out of bed. Face writhing with revulsion, he pulled his clothes on without taking time to wash. The room smelled. Rome must have blunted his sense of smell, or he'd have noticed it before.

Julia awoke as he was finishing. He threw a muttered good morning at her and tramped out.

He spent two hours in the public baths that day. The next night Julia's knock brought a harsh order to get away from his room and stay away. She began to wail. Padway snatched the door open. 'One more squawk and you're fired!' he snapped, and slammed the door.

She was obedient but sulky. During the next few days he caught venomous glances from her; she was no actress.

The following Sunday he returned from the Ulpian Library to find a small crowd of men in front of his house. They were just standing and looking. Padway looked at the house and could see nothing out of order.

He asked a man: 'What's funny about my house, stranger?'

The man looked at him silently. They all looked at him silently. They moved off in twos and threes. They began to walk fast, sometimes glancing back.

Monday morning two of the workmen failed to report. Nerva came to Padway and, after much clearing of the throat, said: 'I thought you'd like to know, lordly Martinus. I went to mass at the Church of the Angel Gabriel yesterday as usual.'

'Yes?' That Church was on Long Street four blocks from Padway's house.

'Father Narcissus preached a homily against sorcery. He talked about people who hired demons from Satanas and work strange devices. It was a very strong sermon. He sounded as if he might be thinking of you.'

Padway worried. It might be coincidence, but he was pretty sure that Julia had gone to confessional and spilled the beans about fornicating with a magician. One sermon had sent the crowd to stare at the wizard's lair. A few more like that …

Padway feared a mob of religious enthusiasts more than anything on earth, no doubt because their mental processes were so utterly alien to his own.

He called Menandrus in and asked for information on Father Narcissus.

The information was discouraging from Padway's point of view. Father Narcissus was one of the most respected priests in Rome. He was upright, charitable, humane, and fearless. He was in deadly earnest twenty-four hours a day. And there was no breath of scandal about him, which fact by itself made him a distinguished cleric.

'George,' said Padway, 'didn't you once mention a bishop with concubines?'

Menandrus grinned slyly. 'It's the Bishop of Bologna, sir. He's one of the Pope's cronies; spends more time at the Vatican than at his see. He has two women – at least, two that we know of. I have their names and everything. Everybody knows that a lot of bishops have one concubine, but two! I thought it would make a good story for the paper.'

'It may yet. Write me up a story, George, about the Bishop of Bologna and his loves. Make it sensational, but accurate. Set it up and pull three or four galley proofs; then put the type away in a safe place.'

It took Padway a week to gain an audience with the Bishop of Bologna, who was providentially in Rome. The bishop was a gorgeously dressed person with a beautiful, bloodless face. Padway suspected a highly convoluted brain behind that sweet, ascetic smile.

Padway kissed the bishop's hand, and they murmured pleasant nothings. Padway talked of the Church's wonderful work, and how he tried in his humble way to further it at every opportunity.

'For instance,' he said, '— do you know of my weekly paper, reverend sir?'

'Yes, I read it with pleasure.'

'Well, you know I have to keep a close watch on my boys, who are prone to err in their enthusiasm for news. I have tried to make the paper a clean sheet fit to enter any home, without scandal or libel. Though that sometimes meant I had to write most of an issue myself.' He sighed. 'Ah, sinful men! Would you believe it, reverend sir, that I have had to suppress stories of foul libel against members of the Holy Church? The most shocking of all came in recently.' He took out one of the galley proofs. 'I hardly dare show it to you, sir, lest your justified wrath at this filthy product of a disordered imagination should damn me to eternal flames.'

The bishop squared his thin shoulders. 'Let me see it, my son. A priest sees many dreadful things in his career. It takes a strong spirit to serve the Lord in these times.'

Padway handed over the sheet. The bishop read it. A sad expression came over his angelic face. 'Ah, poor weak mortals! They know not that they hurt themselves far more than the object of their calumny. It shows that we must have God's help at every turn lest we fall into sin. If you will tell me who wrote this, I will pray for him.'

'A man named Marcus,' said Padway. 'I discharged him immediately, of course. I want nobody who is not prepared to cooperate with the Church to the full.'

The bishop cleared his throat delicately. 'I appreciate your righteous efforts,' he said. 'If there is some favor within my power —'

Padway told him about the good Father Narcissus, who was showing such a lamentable misunderstanding of Padway's enterprises ...

Padway went to mass next Sunday. He sat well down in front, determined to face the thing out if Father Narcissus proved obdurate. He sang with the rest:

> *Imminet, imminet,*
> *Recta remuneret.*
> *Aethera donet,*
> *Ille supremus!*

He reflected that there was this good in Christianity: By its concepts of the Millennium and Judgment Day it accustomed people to looking forward in a way that the older religions did not, and so prepared their minds for the conceptions of organic evolution and scientific progress.

Father Narcisus began his sermon where he had left off a week before. Sorcery was the most damnable of crimes; they should not suffer a witch to live, etc. Padway stiffened.

But, continued the good priest with a sour glance at Padway, we should not in our holy enthusiasm confuse the practitioner of black arts and the familiar of devils with the honest artisan who by his ingenious devices ameliorates our journey through this vale of tears. After all, Adam invented the plow and Noah the ocean-going ship. And this new art of machine writing would make it possible to spread the word of God among the heathen more effectively ...

When Padway got home, he called in Julia and told her he would not need her any more. Julia from Apulia began to weep, softly at first, then more and more violently. 'What kind of man are you? I give you love. I give you everything. But no, you think I am just a little country girl you can do anything you want and then you get tired ...' The patois came with such machine-gun rapidity that Padway could no longer follow. When she began to shriek and tear her dress, Padway ungallantly threatened to have Fritharik throw her out bodily forthwith. She quieted.

The day after she left, Padway gave his house a personal going over to see whether anything had been stolen or broken. Under his bed he found a curious object: a bundle of chicken feathers tied with horse-hair around what appeared to be a long-defunct mouse; the whole thing stiff with dried blood. Fritharik did not know what it was. But George Menandrus did; he turned a little pale and muttered: 'A curse!'

He reluctantly informed Padway that this was a bad-luck charm peddled by one of the local wizards; the discharged housekeeper had undoubtedly left it there to bring Padway to an early and gruesome death. Menandrus himself wasn't too sure he wanted to keep on with his job. 'Not that I really believe in curses, excellent sir, but with my family to support I can't take chances ...'

A raise in pay disposed of Menandrus' qualms. Menandrus was disappointed that Padway didn't use the occasion to have Julia arrested and hanged for witchcraft. 'Just think,' he said, 'it would put us on the right side of the Church, and it would make a wonderful story for the paper!'

Padway hired another housekeeper. This one was gray-haired, rather frail-looking, and depressingly virginal. That was why Padway took her.

He learned that Julia had gone to work for Ebenezer the Jew. He hoped that Julia would not try any of her specialties on Ebenezer. The old banker did not look as if he could stand much of them.

Padway told Thomasus: 'We ought to get the first message from Naples over the telegraph any time now.'

Thomasus rubbed his hands together: 'You are a wonder, Martinus. Only I'm worried that you'll over-reach yourself. The messengers of the Italian civil service are complaining that this invention will destroy their livelihood. Unfair competition, they say.'

Padway shrugged. 'We'll see. Maybe there'll be some war news.'

Thomasus frowned. 'That's another thing that's worrying me. Thiudahad hasn't done a thing about the defense of Italy. I'd hate to see the war carried as far north as Rome.'

'I'll make you a bet,' said Padway. 'The king's son-in-law, Evermuth the Vandal, will desert to the Imperialists. One solidus.'

'Done!' Almost at that moment Junianus, who had been put in charge of operations, came in with a paper. It was the first message, and it carried the news that Belisarius had landed at Reggio; that Evermuth had gone over to him; that the Imperialists were marching on Naples.

Padway grinned at the banker, whose jaw was sagging. 'Sorry, old man, but I need that solidus. I'm saving up for a new horse.'

'Do You hear that, God? Martinus, the next time I lay a bet with a magician, you can have me declared incompetent and a guardian appointed.'

Two days later a messenger came in and told Padway that the king was in Rome, staying at the Palace of Tiberius, and that Padway's presence was desired. Padway thought that perhaps Thiudahad had reconsidered the telescope proposal. But no.

'My good Martinus,' said Thiudahad, 'I must ask you to discontinue the operation of your telegraph. At once.'

'What? Why, my lord king?'

'You know what happened? Eh? That thing of yours spread the news of my son-in-law's good fort – his treachery all over Rome a few hours after it happened. Bad for morale. Encourages the pro-Greek element, and brings criticism on me. *Me.* So you'll please not operate it any more, at least during the war.'

'But, my lord, I thought that your army would find it useful for —'

'Not another word about it, Martinus. I forbid it. Now, let me see. Dear me, there was something else I wanted to see you about. Oh, yes, my man Cassiodorus would like to meet you. You'll stay for lunch, won't you? Great scholar, Cassiodorus.'

So Padway presently found himself bowing to the pretorian prefect, an elderly, rather saintly Italian. They were immediately deep in a discussion of historiography, literature, and the hazards of the publishing business. Padway to his annoyance found that he was enjoying himself. He knew that he was abetting these spineless old dodderers in their criminal disregard of their country's defense. But – upsetting thought – he had enough of the unworldly intellectual in his own nature so that he couldn't help sympathizing with them. And he hadn't gone on an intellectual debauch of this kind since he'd arrived in old Rome.

'Illustrious Cassiodorus,' he said, 'perhaps you've noticed that in my paper I've been trying to teach the typesetter to distinguish between U and V, and also between I and J. That's a reform that's long been needed, don't you think?'

'Yes, yes, my excellent Martinus. The Emperor Claudius tried something of the sort. But which letter do you use for which sound in each case?'

Padway explained. He also told Cassiodorus of his plans for printing the paper, or at least part of it, in Vulgar Latin. At that Cassiodorus held up his hands in mild horror.

'Excellent Martinus! These wretched dialects that pass for Latin nowadays? What would Ovid say if he heard them? What would Virgil say? What would any of the ancient masters say?'

'As they were a bit before our time,' grinned Padway, 'I'm afraid we shall never know. But I will assert that even in their day the final s's and m's had been dropped from ordinary pronunciation. And in any event, the pronunciation and grammar have changed too far from the classical models ever to be changed back again. So if we want our new instrument for the dissemination of literature to be useful, we shall have to adopt a spelling that more or less agrees with the spoken language. Otherwise people won't bother to learn it. To begin with, we shall have to add a half dozen new letters to the alphabet. For instance —'

When Padway left, hours later, he had at least made an effort to bring the conversation around to measures for prosecuting the war. It had been useless, but his conscience was salved.

Padway was surprised, though he shouldn't have been, at the effect of the news of his acquaintance with the king and the prefect. Well-born Romans called on him, and he was even asked to a couple of very dull dinners that began at four p.m. and lasted most of the night.

As he listened to the windy conversation and the windier speeches, he thought that a twentieth-century after-dinner speaker could have taken lessons in high-flown, meaningless rhetoric from these people. From the slightly nervous way that his hosts introduced him around, he gathered that they still regarded him as something of a monster, but a well-behaved monster whom it might be useful to know.

Even Cornelius Anicius looked him up and issued the long-coveted invitation to his house. He did not apologize for the slight snub in the library, but his deferential manner suggested that he remembered it.

Padway swallowed his pride and accepted. He thought it foolish to judge Anicius by his own standards. And he wanted another look at the pretty brunette.

When the time came, he got up from his desk, washed his hands, and told Fritharik to come along.

Fritharik said, scandalized: 'You are going to *walk* to this Roman gentleman's house?'

'Sure. It's only a couple of miles. Do us good.'

'Oh, most respectable boss, you can't! It isn't done! I know; I worked for such a patrician once. You should have a sedan chair, or at least a horse.'

'Nonsense. Anyway, we've got only one saddle-horse. You don't want to walk while I ride, do you?'

'N-no-not that I mind walking; but it would look funny for a gentleman's free retainer like me to go afoot like a slave on a formal occasion.'

Damn this etiquette, thought Padway.

Fritharik said hopefully: 'Of course there's the workhorse. He's a good-looking animal; one might almost mistake him for a heavy cavalry horse.'

'But I don't want the boys in the shop to lose a couple of hours' production just because of some damned piece of facesaving —'

Padway rode the workhorse. Fritharik rode the remaining bony saddle horse.

Padway was shown into a big room whose ornamentation reminded him of the late Victorian gewgaw culture. Through a closed door he could hear Anicius' voice coming through in rolling pentameters:

Rome, the warrior-goddess, her seat had taken, With breast uncovered, a mural crown on her head. Behind, from under her spacious helmet escaping, The hair of her plumed head flowed over her back. Modest her mien, but sternness her beauty makes awesome.

Of purple hue is her robe, with fanglike clasp; Under her bosom a jewel her mantle gathers. A vast and glowing shield her side supports, Whereon, in stout metal cast, the cave of Rhea—

The servant had sneaked through the door and whispered. Anicius broke off his declamation and popped out with a book under his arm. He cried: 'My dear Martinus! I crave your pardon; I was rehearsing a speech I am to give tomorrow.' He tapped the book under his arm and smiled guiltily. 'It will not be a strictly original speech; but you won't betray me, will you?'

'Of course not. I heard some of it through the door.'

'You did? What did you think of it?'

'I thought your delivery was excellent.' Padway resisted a temptation to add: 'But what does it *mean*?' Such a question about a piece of post-Roman rhetoric would, he realized, be both futile and tactless.

'You did?' cried Anicius. 'Splendid! I am greatly gratified! I shall be as nervous tomorrow as Cadmus when the dragon's teeth began to sprout, but the approval of one competent critic in advance will fortify me. And now I'll leave you to Dorothea's mercy while I finish this. You will not take offense, I hope? Splendid! Oh, daughter!'

Dorothea appeared and exchanged courtesies. She took Padway out in the garden while Anicius went back to his plagiarism of Sidonius.

Dorothea said: 'You should hear father some time. He takes you back to the time when Rome really was the mistress of the world. If restoring the power of Rome could be done by fine talk, father and his friends would have restored it long ago.'

It was hot in the garden, with the heat of an Italian June. Bees buzzed.

Padway said: 'What kind of flower do you call that?'

She told him. He was hot. And he was tired of strain and responsibility and ruthless effort. He wanted to be young and foolish for a change.

He asked her more questions about flowers – trivial questions about unimportant matters.

She answered prettily, bending over the flowers to remove a bug now and then. She was hot too. There were little beads of sweat on her upper lip. Her thin dress stuck to her in places. Padway admired the places. She was standing close to him, talking with grave good humor about flowers and about the bugs and blights that beset them. To kiss her, all he had to do was reach and lean forward a bit. He could hear his blood in his ears. The way she smiled up at him might almost be considered an invitation.

But Padway made no move. While he hesitated his mind clicked off reasons: (a) He didn't know how she'd take it, and shouldn't presume on the strength of a mere friendly smile; (b) if she resented it, as she very likely would, there might be repercussions of incalculable scope; (c) if he made love to her, what would she think he was after? He didn't want a mistress – not that Dorothea Anicius would be willing to become such – and he was not, as far as he knew, in need of a wife: (d) he was in a sense already married ...

So, he thought, you wanted to be young and foolish a few minutes ago, eh,

Martin, my boy? You can't; it's too late; you'll always stop to figure things out rationally, as you've been doing just now. Might as well resign yourself to being a calculating adult, especially as you can't do anything about it.

But it made him a little sad that he would never be one of those impetuous fellows – usually described as tall and handsome – who take one look at a girl, know her to be their destined mate, and sweep her into their arms. He let Dorothea do most of the talking as they wandered back into the house to dinner with Cornelius Anicius and Anicius' oratory. Padway, watching Dorothea as she preceded him, felt slightly disgusted with himself for having let Julia invade his bed.

They sat down – or rather stretched themselves out on the couches, as Anicius insisted on eating in the good old Roman style, to Padway's acute discomfort. Anicius had a look in his eye that Padway found vaguely familiar.

Padway learned that the look was that of a man who is writing or is about to write a book. Anicius explained: 'Ah, the degenerate times we live in, excellent Martinus! The lyre of Orpheus sounds but faintly; Calliope veils her face; blithe Thalia is mute; the hymns of our Holy Church have drowned Euterpe's sweet strains. Yet a few of us strive to hold high the torch of poetry while swimming the Hellespont of barbarism and hoeing the garden of culture.'

'Quite a feat,' said Padway, squirming in a vain effort to find a comfortable position.

'Yes, we persist despite Herculean discouragements. For instance, you will not consider me forward in submitting to your publisher's eagle-bright scrutiny a little book of verses.' He produced a sheaf of papyrus. 'Some of them are not really bad, though I their unworthy author say so.'

'I should be very much interested,' said Padway, smiling with effort. 'As for publication, however, I should warn you that I'm contracted for three books by your excellent colleagues already. And between the paper and my schoolbook, it will be some weeks before I can print them.'

'Oh,' said Anicius with a drooping inflection.

'The Illustrious Trajanus Herodius, the Distinguished John Leontius, and the Respectable Felix Avitus. All epic poems. Because of market conditions these gentlemen have undertaken the financial responsibility of publication.'

'Meaning – ah?'

'Meaning that they pay cash in advance, and get the whole price of their books when sold, subject to bookseller's discounts. Of course, distinguished sir, if the book is really good, the author doesn't have to worry about getting back his cost of publication.'

'Yes, yes, excellent Martinus, I see. What chances do you think my little creation would have?'

'I'd have to see it first.'

'So you would. I'll read some of it now, to give you the idea.' Anicius sat up. He held the papyrus in one hand and made noble gestures with the other:

Mars with his thunderous trumpet his lord acclaims,
The youthful Jupiter, new to his throne ascended,
Above the stars by all-wise Nature placed.
The lesser deities their sire worship,
To ancient sovereignty with pomp succeeding—

'Father,' interrupted Dorothea, 'your food's getting cold.'

'What? Oh, so it is, child.'

'And,' continued Dorothea, 'I think you ought to write some good Christian sentiment some time, instead of all that pagan superstition.'

Anicius sighed. 'If you ever have a daughter, Martinus, marry her off early, before she develops the critical faculty.'

In August Naples fell to General Belisarius. Thiudahad had done nothing to help the town except seize the families of the small Gothic garrison to insure their fidelity. The only vigorous defense of the city was made by the Neapolitan Jews. These, having heard of Justinian's religious complexes, knew what treatment to expect under Imperial rule.

Padway heard the news with a sick feeling. There was so much that he could do for them if they'd only let him alone. And it would take such a little accident to snuff him out – one of the normal accidents of warfare, like that which happened to Archimedes. In this age civilians who got in the way of belligerent armies would be given the good old rough and ruthless treatment to which the military of his own twentieth century, after a brief hundred and fifty years of relatively humane forbearance, had seemed to be returning.

Fritharik announced that a party of Goths wanted to look Padway's place over. He added in his sepulchral voice: 'Thiudegiskel's with them. You know, the king's son. Watch out for him, excellent boss. He makes trouble.'

There were six of them, all young, and they tramped into the house wearing swords, which was not good manners by the standards of the times. Thiudegiskel was a handsome, blond young man who had inherited his father's high-pitched voice.

He stared at Padway, like something in a zoo, and said: 'I've wanted to see your place ever since I heard you and the old man were mumbling over manuscripts together. I'm a curious chap, you know, active-minded. What the devil are all these silly machines for?'

Padway did some explaining, while the prince's companions made remarks about his personal appearance in Gothic, under the mistaken impression that he couldn't understand them.

'Ah, yes,' said Thiudegiskel, interrupting one of the explanations. 'I think that's all I'm interested in here. Now, let's see that bookmaking machine.'

Padway showed him the presses.

'Oh, yes, I understand. Really a simple thing, isn't it? I could have invented it myself. All very well for those who like it. Though I can read and write and all that. Better than most people, in fact. But I never cared for it. Dull business, not suited to a healthy man like me.'

'No doubt, no doubt, my lord,' said Padway. He hoped that the red rage he was feeling didn't show in his face.

'Say, Willimer,' said Thiudegiskel, 'you remember that tradesman we had fun with last winter? He looked something like this Martinus person. Same big nose.'

Willimer roared with laughter. 'Do I remember it! *Guths in himinam!* I'll never forget the way he looked when we told him we were going to baptize him in the Tiber, with rocks tied to him so the angels couldn't carry him off! But the funniest thing was when some soldiers from the garrison arrested us for assault!'

Thiudegiskel said to Padway, between guffaws: 'You ought to have been there, Martinus. You should have seen old Liuderis' face when he found out who we were! We made him grovel, I can tell you. I've always regretted that I missed the flogging of those soldiers who pinched us. That's one thing about me; I can appreciate the humor of things like that.'

'Would you like to see anything more, my lord?' asked Padway, his face wooden.

'Oh, I don't know – Say, what are all those packing cases for?'

'Some stuff just arrived for our machines, my lord, and we haven't gotten around to burning the cases,' Padway lied.

Thiudegiskel grinned good-naturedly. 'Trying to fool me, huh? I know what you're up to. You're going to sneak your stuff out of Rome before Belisarius gets here, aren't you? That's one thing about me; I can see through little tricks like that. Well, can't say I blame you. Though it sounds as though you had inside information on how the war will go.' He examined a new brass telescope on a workbench. 'This is an interesting little device. I'll take it along, if you don't mind.'

That was too much even for Padway's monumental prudence. 'No, my lord, I'm sorry, but I need that in my business.'

Thiudegiskel's eyes were round with astonishment. 'Huh? You mean I can't have it?'

'That, my lord, is it.'

'Well … uh … uh … if you're going to take that attitude, I'll pay for it.'

'It isn't for sale.'

Thiudegiskel's neck turned slowly pink with embarrassment and anger. His five friends moved up behind him, their left hands resting on their sword hilts.

The one called Willimer said in a low tone: 'I *think*, gentlemen, that our king's son has been insulted.'

Thiudegiskel had laid the telescope on the bench. He reached out for it; Padway snatched it up and smacked the end of the tube meaningfully against his left palm. He knew that, even if he got out of this situation in one piece, he'd curse himself for a double-dyed knight-erranting idiot. But at the moment he was too furious to care.

The uncomfortable silence was broken by the shuffle of feet behind Padway; he saw the Goths' eyes shift from him. He glanced around. In the doorway was Fritharik, with his sword belt hitched around so the scabbard was in front, and Nerva, holding a three-foot length of bronze bar-stock. Behind them came the other workmen with an assortment of blunt instruments.

'It seems,' said Thiudegiskel, 'that these people have no manners whatever. We should give them a lesson. But I promised my old man to lay off fighting. That's one thing about me; I always keep my promises. Come along boys.' They went.

'*Whew!*' said Padway. 'You boys certainly saved my bacon. Thanks.'

'Oh, it was nothing,' said George Menandrus airily. 'I'm rather sorry they didn't stay to fight it out. I'd have enjoyed smacking their thick skulls.'

'You? *Honh!*' snorted Fritharik. 'Boss, the first thing I saw when I started to round the men up was this fellow sneaking out the back door. You know how I changed his mind? I said I'd hang him with a rope made of his own guts if he didn't stick! And the others, I threatened to cut their heads off and stick them on the fence palings in front of the house.' He contemplated infinite calamities for a few seconds, then added: 'But it won't do any good, excellent Martinus. Those fellows will have it in for us, and they're pretty influential, naturally. They can get away with anything. We'll all end in nameless graves yet.'

Padway struggled mightily to get the movable parts of his equipment packed for shipment to Florence. As far as he could remember his Procopius, Florence had not been besieged or sacked in Justinian's Gothic War, at least in the early part.

But the job was not half done when eight soldiers from the garrison descended on him and told him he was under arrest. He was getting rather used to arrest by now, so he calmly gave his foremen and editor orders about getting the equipment moved and set up, and about seeing Thomasus and trying to get in touch with him. Then he went along.

On the way he offered to stand the Goths drinks. They accepted quickly. In the wineshop he got the commander aside to suggest a little bribe to let him go. The Goth seemed to accept, and pocketed a solidus. Then when Padway, his mind full of plans for shaving his beard, getting a horse, and galloping off to Florence, broached the subject of his release, the Goth looked at him with an air of pained surprise.

'Why, most distinguished Martinus, I couldn't think of letting you go! Our commander-in-chief, the noble Liuderis, is a man of stern and rigid principles. If my men talked, he'd hear about it, and he'd break me sure. Of course I appreciate your little *gift*, and I'll try to put in a good word for you.'

Padway said nothing, but he made a resolve that it would be a long day before he put in a good word for this officer.

CHAPTER VIII

Liuderis blew out his snowy whiskers and explained: 'I am sorry you deceived me, Martinus. I never thought a true Arian would stoop to … ah … conniving with these pro-Greek Italians to let a swarm of Orthodox fanatics into Italy.'

'Who says so?' asked Padway, more annoyed than apprehensive.

'No less a person than the … ah … noble Thiudegiskel. He told how when he visited your house, you not only insulted and reviled him, but boasted of your connections with the Imperialists. His companions corroborated him. They said you had inside information about a plan for betraying Rome, and that you were planning to move your effects elsewhere to escape any disturbances. When my men arrested you, they found that you were in fact about to move.'

'My dear sir!' said Padway in exasperation. 'Don't you think I have *any* brains? If I were in on some plot of some sort, do you think I would go around telling the world about it?'

Liuderis shrugged. 'I would not know. I am only doing my duty, which is to hold you for questioning about this secret plan. Take him away, Sigifrith.'

Padway hid a shudder at the word 'questioning.' If this honest blockhead got set on an idea, he'd have a swell chance of talking the fellow out of it.

The Goths had set up a prison camp at the north end of the city, between the Flaminian Way and the Tiber. Two sides of the camp were formed by a hastily erected fence, and the remaining two by the Wall of Aurelian. Padway found that two Roman patricians had preceded him in custody; both said they had been arrested on suspicion of complicity in an Imperialist plot. Several more Romans arrived within a few hours.

The camp was no escape-proof masterpiece, but the Goths made the best of it. They kept a heavy guard around the fence and along the wall. They even had a squad camped across the Tiber, in case a prisoner got over the wall and tried to swim the river.

For three days Padway rusticated. He walked from one end of the camp to the other, and back, and forward, and back. When he got tired of walking he sat. When he got tired of sitting he walked. He talked a little with his fellow prisoners, but in a moody and abstracted manner.

He'd been a fool – well, at least he'd been badly mistaken – in supposing that he could carry out his plans with as little difficulty as in Chicago. This was a harsh, convulsive world; you had to take it into account, or you'd get caught in the gears sooner or later. Even the experts at political intrigue and uniformed banditry often came to a bad end. What chance would such a hopelessly unwarlike and unpolitical alien as himself have?

Well, what chance did he have anyway? He'd kept out of public affairs as much as possible, and here he was in a horrifying predicament as a result of a petty squabble over a brass telescope. He might just as well have gone adventuring up to the hilt. If he ever got out, he *would* go adventuring. He'd show 'em!

The fourth day failed to settle Padway's gnawing anxiety about his interrogation. The guards seemed excited about something. Padway tried to question them, but they rebuffed him. Listening to their muttering talk, he caught the word *folkmote*. That meant that the great meeting was about to be held near Terracina, at which the Goths would consider what to do about the loss of Naples.

Padway got into talk with one of the patrician prisoners.

'Bet you a solidus,' he said, 'that they depose Thiudahad and elect Wittigis king in his place.'

The patrician, poor man, took him on.

Thomasus the Syrian arrived. He explained: 'Nerva tried to get in to see you, but he couldn't afford a high enough bribe. How do they treat you?'

'Not badly. The food's not exactly good, but they give us plenty of it. What worries me is that Liuderis thinks I know all about some alleged conspiracy to betray Rome, and he may use drastic methods to try to get information out of me.'

'Oh, that. There's a conspiracy afoot, all right. But I think you'll be safe for a few days anyway. Liuderis has gone off to a convention, and the Goths' affairs are all in confusion.' He went on to report on the state of Padway's business. 'We got the last case off this morning. Ebenezer the Jew is going up to Florence in a couple of weeks. He'll look in and see that your foremen haven't run off with all your property.'

'You mean to see *whether* they've run off with it. Any war news?'

'None, except that Naples suffered pretty badly. Belisarius' Huns got out of hand when the town was captured. But I suppose you know that. You can't tell me that you haven't some magical knowledge of the future.'

'Maybe. Which side do you favor, Thomasus?'

'Me? Why – I haven't thought about it much, but I suppose I favor the Goths. These Italians haven't any more fight than a lot of rabbits, so the country can't be really independent. And if we have to be ruled by outsiders, the Goths have been a lot easier on us than Justinian's tax gathers would be. Only my Orthodox friends can't be made to see it that way. Like my cousin, Antiochus, for instance. They become completely irrational when they get off on the subject of Arian heretics.'

When Thomasus was ready to go, he asked Padway: 'Is there anything I can bring you? I don't know what the guards will allow, but if there's something —'

Padway thought. 'Yes,' he said. 'I'd like some painting equipment.'

'Painting? You mean you're going to whitewash the Wall of Aurelian?'

'No; stuff for painting pictures. *You* know.' Padway made motions.

'Oh, *that* kind of painting. Sure. It'll pass the time.'

Padway wanted to get on top of the wall, to give the camp a proper looking-over for ways of escape. So when Thomasus brought his painting supplies he applied to the commander of the guards, a surly fellow named Hrotheigs, for permission. Hrotheigs took one look, and spoke one word: '*Ni!*'

Padway masked his annoyance and retired to ponder on How to Win Friends. He spent the better part of the day experimenting with his equipment, which was a bit puzzling to one unaccustomed to it. A fellow prisoner explained that you coated one of the thin boards with wax, painted in water color on this surface, and then warmed the board until the wax became soft enough to absorb the pigment. It was ticklish business; if you overheated the board, the wax melted and the colors ran.

Padway was not a professional artist by any means. But an archeologist has to know something about drawing and painting in the exercise of his profession. So the next day Padway felt confident enough to ask Hrotheigs if he would like his portrait painted.

The Goth for the first time looked almost pleased. '*Could* you make a picture of me? I mean, one for me to keep?'

'Try to, excellent captain. I don't know how good it'll be. You may end up looking like Satanas with a gut ache.'

'Huh? Like whom? Oh, I see! Haw! Haw! Haw! You *are* a funny fellow.'

So Padway painted a picture. As far as he could see, it looked as much like any black-bearded ruffian as it did like Hrotheigs. But the Goth was delighted, asserting that it was his spit and image. The second time he made no objections to Padway's climbing the wall to paint landscapes from the top, merely detailing a guard to keep close to him at all times.

Saying that he had to pick the best vantage point for painting, Padway walked up and down the wall the length of the camp. At the north end, where the wall turned east toward the Flaminian Gate, the ground outside sloped down for a few yards to a recess in the river bank – a small pool full of water lilies.

He was digesting this information when his attention was attracted to the camp. A couple of guards were bringing in a prisoner in rich Gothic clothes who was not cooperating. Padway recognized Thiudegiskel, the king's precious son. This was too interesting. Padway went down the ladder.

'*Hails,*' he said. 'Hello.'

Thiudegiskel was squatting disconsolately by himself. He was somewhat disheveled, and his face had been badly bruised. Both eyes would soon be swollen shut. The Roman patricians were grinning unsympathetically at him.

He looked up. 'Oh, it's you,' he said. Most of the arrogance seemed to have been let out of him, like air out of a punctured balloon.

'I didn't expect to run into you here,' said Padway. 'You look like you had a hard time of it.'

'*Unh*.' Thiudegiskel moved his joints painfully. 'A couple of those soldiers we had flogged for arresting us got hold of me.' Surprisingly, he grinned, showing a broken front tooth. 'Can't say I blame them much. That's one thing about me; I can always see the other fellow's point of view.'

'What are you in for?'

'Hadn't you heard? I'm not the king's son any more. Or rather my old man isn't king. The convention deposed him and elected that fathead Wittigis. So Fathead has me locked up so I can't make trouble.'

'*Tsk, tsk*. Too bad.'

Thiudegiskel grinned painfully again. 'Don't try to tell me *you're* sorry for me. I'm not that stupid. But say, maybe you can tell me what sort of treatment to expect, and whom to bribe, and so on.'

Padway gave the young man a few pointers on getting on with the guards, then asked: 'Where's Thiudahad now?'

'I don't know. The last I'd heard he'd gone up to Tivoli to get away from the heat. But he was supposed to come back down here this week. Some piece of literary research he's working on.'

Between what Padway remembered of the history of the time and the information he had recently picked up, he had a good picture of the course of events. Thiudahad had been kicked out. The new king, Wittigis, would put up a loyal and determined resistance. The result would be worse than no resistance at all as far as Italy was concerned. He could not beat the Imperialists, having no brains to speak of. He would begin his campaign with the fatal mistake of marching off to Ravenna, leaving Rome with only its normal garrison.

Neither could the Imperialists beat him with their slender forces except by years of destructive campaigning. Anything, from Padway's point of view, was preferable to a long war. If the Imperialists did win, their conquest would prove ephemeral. Justinian should not be blamed too much; he would require supernatural foresight to foresee all this. That was the point: Padway *did* have such foresight. So wasn't it up to him to do something about it?

Padway had no violent prejudices in favor either of Gothic or of Imperial rule. Neither side had a political setup for which he could feel enthusiasm. Liberal capitalism and socialist democracy both had good points, but he did not think there was the remotest chance of establishing either one definitively in the sixth-century world.

If the Goths were lazy and ignorant, the Greeks were rapacious and venal. Yet these two were the best rulers available. The sixth-century Italian was too hopelessly unmilitary to stand on his own feet, and he was supinely aware of the fact.

On the whole the Gothic regime had not had an ill effect. The Goths enforced tolerance on a people whose idea of religious liberty was freedom to hang, drown, or burn all members of sects other than their own. And the Goths looked on the peninsula as a pleasant home to be protected and preserved. This was a more benign attitude than could be expected of a savage like the Meroving monarch, Theudebert of Austrasia, or an insatiable grafter like Justinian's quartermaster-general, John of Cappadocia.

Suppose, then, he decided to work for a quick victory by the Goths instead of a quick victory for the Imperialists. How could the Gothic regime be succored? It would do no good for him to try to persuade the Goths to get rid of Wittigis. If the Gothic king, whoever he was, could be induced to take Padway's advice, something might be done. But old Thiudahad, worthless as he was by himself, *might* be managed.

A plan began to form in Padway's mind. He wished he'd told Thomasus to hurry back sooner. To keep darkness from falling—

When Thomasus did appear, Padway told him: 'I want a couple of pounds of sulphur, mixed with olive oil to form a paste, and some candles. And forty feet of light rope, strong enough to support a man. Believe it or not, I got the idea from the voluptuous Julia. Remember how she acted when I fumigated the house?'

'Look here, Martinus, you're perfectly safe for the time being, so why don't you stay here instead of trying some crazy scheme of escaping?'

'Oh, I have reasons. The convention should break up today or tomorrow, from what I hear, and I've got to get out before it does.'

'Listen to him! Just listen! Here I am, the best friend he has in Rome, and does he pay attention to my advice? No! He wants to break out of the camp, and maybe get an arrow through the kidney for his pains, and then go get mixed up with Gothic politics. Did you ever hear the like? Martinus, you haven't some wild idea of getting yourself elected king of the Goths, have you? Because it won't work. You have to be —'

'I know,' grinned Padway. 'You have to be a Goth of the noble family of the Amalings. That's why I'm in such a hurry to get out. You want the business saved so you'll get your loans back, don't you?'

'But how on earth am I going to smuggle those things in? The guards watch pretty closely.'

'Bring the sulphur paste in a container at the bottom of a food basket. If they open it, say it's something my physician ordered. Better coach Vekkos to corroborate. And for the rope – let's see – I know, go to my tailor and get a green cloak like mine. Have him fasten the rope inside around the edges, lightly, so it can be ripped out quickly. Then, when you come in, lay your cloak alongside mine, and pick mine up when you go.'

'Martinus, that's a crazy plan. I'll get caught sure, and what will become of my family? No, you'd better do as I say. I can't risk innocent persons' futures. What time would you want me to come around with the rope and things?'

Padway sat on the Wall of Aurelian in the bright morning sunshine. He affected to be much interested in the Tomb of Hadrian down river on the other side. The guard who was detailed to him, one Aiulf, looked over his shoulder. Padway appreciated Aiulf's interest, but he sometimes wished the Goth's beard was less long and bristly. It was a disconcerting thing to have crawling over your shoulder and down your shirt front when you were trying to get the color just right.

'You see,' he explained in halting Gothic, 'I hold the brush out and look past it at the thing I am painting, and mark its apparent length and height off on the brush with my thumb. That is how I keep everything in proper proportion.'

'I see,' said Aiulf in equally bad Latin – both were having a little language practice. 'But suppose you want to paint a small picture – how would you say – with a lot of things in it just the same? The measurements on the brush would all be too large, would they not?' Aiulf, for a camp guard, was not at all stupid.

Padway's attention was actually on things other than the Tomb. He was covertly watching all the guards, and his little pile of belongings. All the prisoners did that, for obvious reasons. But Padway's interest was special. He was wondering when the candle concealed in the food basket would burn down to the sulphur paste. He had apparently had a lot of trouble that morning getting his brazier going; actually he had been setting up his little infernal machine. He also couldn't help stealing an occasional nervous glance at the soldiers across the river, and at the lily-covered pool behind him.

Aiulf grew tired of watching and retired a few steps. The guard sat down on his little stool, took up his flutelike instrument and started to play faint moaning notes. The thing sounded like a banshee lost in a rain barrel, and never failed to give Padway the slithering creeps. But he valued Aiulf's good will too much to protest.

He worked and worked, and still his contraption showed no signs of life. The candle must have gone out; it would surely have burned down to the sulphur by now. Or the sulphur had failed to light. It would soon be time for lunch. If they called him down off the wall, it would arouse suspicion for him to say he wasn't hungry. Perhaps.

Aiulf stopped his moaning for an instant. 'What is the matter with your ear, Martinus? You keep rubbing it.'

'Just an itch,' replied Padway. He didn't say that fingering his ear lobe was a symptom of shrieking nervousness. He kept on painting. One result of his attempt, he thought, would be the lousiest picture of a tomb ever painted by an amateur artist.

As he gave up hope, his nerves steadied. The sulphur hadn't lit, and that was that. He'd try again tomorrow ...

Below, in the camp, a prisoner coughed; then another. Then they were all coughing. Fragments of talk floated up: 'What the devil —' 'Must be the tanneries —' 'Can't be, they're two or three miles from here —' 'That's burning sulphur, by all the saints —' 'Maybe the Devil is paying us a call —' People moved around; the coughing increased; the guards trailed into the camp. Somebody located the source of the fumes and kicked Padway's pile. Instantly a square yard was covered with yellow mush over which little blue flames danced. There were strangled shouts. A thin wisp of blue smoke crawled up through the still air. The guards on the wall, including Aiulf, hurried to the ladder and down.

Padway had planned his course so carefully in his mind that he went through it almost unconscious of the individual acts. Over his brazier were two little pots of molten wax, both already pigmented. He plunged his hands into the scalding stuff and smeared his face and beard with dark green wax. It hardened almost instantly. With his fingers he then smeared three large circles of yellow wax from the other pot over the green.

Then, as if he were just strolling, he walked up to the angle of the wall, squatted down out of sight of those in the camp, ripped the rope out of the lining of his cloak, and slipped a bight over a projection at the corner of the wall. A last glance across the river showed that the soldiers over there had not, apparently, noticed anything, though they could have heard the commotion inside the wall if they had listened. Padway lowered himself down the north face of the wall, hand over hand.

He flipped the rope down after him. As he did so, a flash of sunlight on his wrist made him curse silently. His watch would be ruined by prolonged soaking; he should have thought to give it to Thomasus. He saw a loose stone in the wall. He pulled it out, wrapped the watch in his handkerchief, put it in the hole, and replaced the stone. It took only a few seconds, but he knew he was being insanely foolish to risk the loss of time for the sake of the watch. On the other hand, being the kind of person he was, he just could not ruin the watch knowingly.

He trotted down the slope to the pond. He did not throw himself in, but walked carefully out to where it was a couple of feet deep. He sat down in the dark water, like a man getting into an over-hot tub bath, and stretched out on his back among the pond lilies until only his nose and eyes were above water. He moved the water plants around until they hid him pretty thoroughly. For the rest, he had to rely on the green of his cloak and his bizarre facial camouflage for concealment. He waited, listening to his own heart and the murmur from over the wall.

He did not have long to wait. There were shouts, the blowing of whistles, the pounding of large Gothic feet on the top of the wall. The guards waved to the soldiers across the river. Padway didn't dare turn his head far enough to see, but he could imagine a row-boat's being put out.

'*Ailôe!* The fiend seems to have vanished into thin air —'

'He's hiding somewhere, you idiot! Search, search! Get the horses out!'

Padway lay still while guards searched around the base of the wall and poked swords into bushes barely big enough to hide a Sealyham. He lay still while a small fish maddeningly investigated his left ear. He lay still, his eyes almost closed, while a couple of Goths walked around the pond and stared hard at it and him, hardly thirty feet from them. He lay still while a Goth on a horse rode splashing through the pond, actually passing within fifteen feet of him. He lay still through the whole long afternoon, while the sounds of search and pursuit rose and ebbed, and finally faded away completely.

Nevitta Gummund's son was justifiably startled when a man rose from the shadows of the bushes that lined the driveway to his house and called him by name. He had just ridden up to the farm. Hermann, in tow as usual, had his sword halfway out before Martin Padway identified himself.

He explained: 'I got here a couple of hours ago, and wanted to borrow a horse. Your people said you were away at the convention, but that you'd be back sometime tonight. So I've been waiting.' He went on to tell briefly of his imprisonment and escape.

The Goth bellowed. 'Ha! Ha! You mean to say, ha! ha! that you lay in the pond all day, right under the noses of the guards, with your face painted up like a damned flower? Ha! ha! Christ, that's the best thing I ever heard!' He dismounted. 'Come on in the house and tell me more about it. *Whew*, you certainly look like a frog pond, old *friend!*' Later, he said more seriously: 'I'd like to trust you, Martinus. By all accounts, you're a pretty reliable young man, in spite of your funny foreign ways. But how do I *know* that Liuderis wasn't right? There *is* something queer about you, you know. People say you can foresee the future, but try to hide the fact. And, some of those machines of yours do smell a little bit of magic.'

'I'll tell you,' said Padway thoughtfully. 'I can see a little bit in the future. Don't blame me; I just happen to have that power. Satanas has nothing to do with it. That is, I can sometimes see what will happen *if* people are allowed to do what they intend to. If I use my knowledge to intervene, that changes the future, so my vision isn't true any more.

'In this case, I know that Wittigis will lose the war. And will lose in the worst possible way – at the end of years of fighting which will completely devastate Italy. Not his fault. He's simply built that way. The last thing I want is to see the country ruined; it would spoil a lot of plans I have. So I propose to intervene and change the natural course of events. The results may be better; they could hardly be worse.'

Nevitta frowned. 'You mean you're going to try to defeat the Goths quickly. I don't think I could agree to such —'

'No. I propose to win your war for you. If I can.'

CHAPTER IX

Padway wasn't mistaken, and if Procopius' history had not lied, Thiudahad ought to pass along the Flaminian Way within the next twenty-four hours in his panicky flight to Vienna. All the way, Padway had asked people whether the king had passed that way. All said no.

Now, on the outskirts of Narnia, he was as far north as he dared go. The Flaminian Way forked at this point, and he had no way of knowing whether Thiudahad would take the new road or the old. So he and Hermann made themselves easy by the side of the road and listened to their horses cropping grass. Padway looked at his companion with a bilious eye. Hermann had taken much too much beer aboard at Ocriculum.

To Padway's questions and his instructions about taking turns at watching the road, he merely grinned idiotically and said, '*Ja, ja!*' He had finally gone to sleep in the middle of a sentence, and no amount of shaking would arouse him.

Padway walked up and down in the shade, listening to Hermann's snores and trying to think. He had not slept since the previous day, and here that whiskery slob was taking the ease that he, Padway, needed badly. Maybe he should have grabbed a couple of hours at Nevitta's – but if he'd once gotten to sleep nothing short of an earthquake would have gotten him up. His stomach was jumpy; he had no appetite; and this accursed sixth-century world didn't even have coffee to lighten the weights that dragged down the eyelids.

Suppose Thiudahad didn't show up? Or suppose he went roundabout, by the Salarian Way? Or suppose he'd already passed? Time after time he'd tensed himself as dust appeared down the road, only to have it materialize as a farmer driving an oxcart, or a trader slouching along on a mule, or a small half-naked boy driving goats.

Could his, Padway's, influence have changed Thiudahad's plans so that his course of action would be different from what it should have been? Padway saw his influence as a set of ripples spreading over a pool. By the mere fact of having known him, the lives of people like Thomasus and Fritharik had already been changed radically from what they would have been if he'd never appeared in Rome.

But Thiudahad had only seen him twice, and nothing very drastic had happened either time. Thiudahad's course in time and space might have been altered, but only very slightly. The other higher-up Goths, such as King Wittigis, ought not to have been affected at all. Some of them might have read his paper. But few of them were literary and many were plain illiterate.

Tancredi had been right about the fact that this was an entirely new branch of the tree of time, as he called it. The things that Padway had done so far, while only a fraction of what he hoped to do, couldn't help but change history somewhat. Yet he had not vanished into thin air, as he should have if this was the same history that had produced him in the year AD 1908.

He glanced at his wrist, and remembered that his watch was cached in the Wall of Aurelian. He hoped he'd get a chance to recover it some day, and that it would be in running order when he did.

That new bit of dust down the road was probably another damned cow or flock of sheep. No, it was a man on a horse. Probably some fat Narnian burgher. He was in a hurry, whoever he was. Padway's ears caught the blowing of a hard-ridden mount; then he recognized Thiudahad.

'Hermann!' he yelled.

'Akhkhkhkhkhkhkhg,' snored Hermann. Padway ran over and hit the Goth with his boot. Hermann said: 'Akhkhkhkhg Akhkhkhkhg. Meina luibs – guhhg. Akhkhkhg.'

Padway gave up; the ex-king would be up to them in an instant. He swung aboard his horse and trotted out into the road with his arm up. 'Hai, Thiudahad! My lord!'

Thiudahad kicked his horse and hauled on the reins at the same time, apparently undecided whether to stop, try to run with Padway, or turn around the way he had come. The exhausted animal thereupon put his head down and bucked.

Waters of the Nar showed blue between Thiudahad and his horse for a second; he came down on the saddle with a thump and clutched it frantically. His face was white with terror and covered with dust.

Padway leaned over and gathered up the reins. 'Calm yourself, my lord,' he said.

'Who … who … what – Oh, it's the publisher. What's your name? Don't tell me; I know it. Why are you stopping – We've got to get to Ravenna … Ravenna —'

'Calm yourself. You'd never reach Ravenna alive.'

'What do you mean? Are you out to murder me, too?'

'Not at all. But, as you may have heard, I have some small talent reading the future.'

'Oh, dear, yes, I've heard. What's … what's my future? Don't tell me I'm going to be killed! Please don't tell me that, excellent Martinus. I don't want to die. If they'll just let me live I won't bother anybody again, ever.' The little gray-bearded man fairly gibbered with fright.

'If you'll keep still for a few minutes, I'll tell you what I can. Do you remember when, for a consideration, you swindled a noble Goth out of a beautiful heiress who had been promised to him in marriage?'

'Oh, dear me. That would be Optaris Winithar's son, wouldn't it? Only don't say 'swindled,' excellent Martinus. Merely … ah … exerted my influence on the side of the man. But why?'

'Wittigis gave Optaris a commission to hunt you down and kill you. He's following you now, riding day and night. If you continue toward Ravenna, this Optaris will catch up with you before you get there, pull you off your horse, and cut your throat – like this, *khh!*' Padway clutched his own throat with one hand, tilted up his chin, and drew a finger across his Adam's apple.

Thiudahad covered his face with his hands. 'What'll I do? What'll I do? If I could get to Ravenna, I have friends there —'

'That's what *you* think. I know better.'

'But isn't there anything? I mean, is Optaris fated to kill me no matter what I do? Can't we hide?'

'Perhaps. My prophecy is good only if you try to carry out your original plan.'

'Well, we'll hide, then.'

'All right, just as soon as I get this fellow awake.' Padway indicated Hermann.

'Why wait for him? Why not just leave him?'

'He works for a friend of mine. He was supposed to take care of me, but it's turned out the other way around.' They dismounted, and Padway resumed his efforts to arouse Hermann.

Thiudahad sat down on the grass and moaned: 'Such ingratitude! And I was such a good king —'

'Sure,' said Padway acidly, 'except for breaking your oath to Amalaswentha not to interfere in public affairs, and then having her murdered —'

'But you don't understand, excellent Martinus. She had our noblest patriot, Count Tulum, murdered, along with those other two friends of her son Atha-larik —'

'— and intervening – for a consideration, again – in the last Papal election; offering to sell Italy to Justinian in return for an estate near Constantinople and an annuity —'

'*What?* How did you know – I mean it's a lie!'

'I know lots of things. To continue: neglecting the defense of Italy; failing to relieve Naples —'

'Oh, dear me. You don't understand, I tell you. I hate all this military business. I admit I'm no soldier; I'm a scholar. So I leave it to my generals. That's only sensible, isn't it?'

'As events have proved – no.'

'Oh, dear. Nobody understands me,' moaned Thiudahad. 'I'll tell you,

Martinus, why I did nothing about Naples. I knew it was no use. I had gone to a Jewish magician, Jeconias of Naples, who has a great reputation for successful prophecy. Everybody knows the Jews are good at that. This man took thirty hogs, and put ten in each of three pens. One pen was labeled "Goths," one "Italians," and one "Imperialists." He starved them for weeks. We found that all the "Goths" had died; that the "Italians" were some of the dead, and the rest had lost their hair; but the "Imperialists" were doing fine. So we knew the Goths were bound to lose. In that case, why sacrifice a lot of brave boys' lives to no effect?'

'Bunk,' said Padway. 'My prophecies are as good as that fat faker's any day. Ask my friends. But any prophecy is good only as long as you follow your original plans. If you follow yours, you'll get your throat cut like one of your magical hogs. If you want to live, you'll do as I say and like it.'

'What? Now, look here, Martinus, even if I'm not king anymore, I'm of noble birth, and I won't be dictated to —'

'Suit yourself.' Padway rose and walked toward his horse. 'I'll ride down the road a way. When I meet Optaris, I'll tell him where to find you.'

'Eek! Don't do that! I'll do what you say! I'll do anything, only don't let that awful man catch me!'

'All right. If you obey orders, I may even be able to get you back your kingship. But it'll be purely nominal this time, understand.' Padway didn't miss the crafty gleam in Thiudahad's eyes. Then the eyes shifted past Padway.

'Here he comes! It's the murderer, Optaris!' he squealed.

Padway spun around. Sure enough, a burly Goth was poking up the road toward them. This was a fine state of affairs, thought Padway. He'd wasted so much time talking that the pursuer had caught up with them. He should have had a few hours' leeway still; but there the man was. What to do; what to do?

He had no weapon but a knife designed for cutting steaks rather than human throats. Thiudahad had no sword, either.

To Padway, brought up in a world of Thompson submachine-guns, swords seemed silly weapons, always catching you between the knees. So it had never occurred to him to form the habit of toting one. He realized his error as his eye caught one flash of Optaris' blade. The Goth leaned forward and kicked his horse straight at them.

Thiudahad stood rooted to the spot, trembling violently and making little meowing sounds of terror. He wet his dry lips and squealed one word over and over: 'Armaio! Mercy!' Optaris grinned through his beard and swung his right arm up.

At the last instant Padway dived at the ex-king and tackled him, rolling him out of the way of Optaris' horse. He scrambled up as Optaris reined in furiously, the animal's hoofs kicking dust forward as they braked. Thiudahad got up, too, and bolted for the shelter of the trees. With a yell of rage Optaris jumped to the ground and took after him. Meantime, Padway had had a rush of brains to the head. He bent over Hermann, who was beginning to revive, tore Hermann's sword out of the scabbard, and sprinted to cut off Optaris. It wasn't necessary. Optaris saw him coming and started for him, evidently preferring to settle with Padway before the latter could take him in flank.

Now Padway cursed himself for all kinds of a fool. He had only the crudest theoretical knowledge of fencing, and no tactical experience whatever. The heavy Gothic broadsword was unfamiliar and uncomfortable in his sweaty hand. He could see the whites of Optaris' eyes as the Goth trotted up to him, took his measure, shifted his weight, and whipped his sword arm up for a back-hand slash.

Padway's parry was more instinctive than designed. The blades met with a great clang, and Padway's borrowed sword went sailing away, end over end, into the woods. Quick as a flash Optaris struck again, but met only air and swung himself halfway around. If Padway was an incompetent fencer, there was nothing the matter with his legs. He sprinted after his sword, found it, and kept right on running with Optaris panting heavily after him. He'd been a minor quarter-mile star in college; if he could run the legs off Optaris maybe the odds would be nearer even when they finally – *umph!* He tripped over a root and sprawled on his face.

Somehow he rolled over and got to his feet before Optaris came up to him. And, somehow, he got himself between Optaris and a pair of big oaks that grew too close together to be squeezed between. So there was nothing for him to do but stand and take it. As the Goth chumped forward and swung his sword over his head, Padway, in a last despairing gesture, thrust as far as he could at Optaris' exposed chest, more with the idea of keeping the man off than of hurting him.

Now, Optaris was an able fighter. But the sword-play of his age was entirely with the edge. Nobody had ever worked a simple stop thrust on him. So it was no fault of his that in his effort to get within cutting distance of Padway he spitted himself neatly on the outthrust blade. His own slash faltered and ended against one of the oaks, The Goth gasped, tried to breathe, and his thick legs slowly sagged. He fell, pulling the sword out of his body. His hands clawed at the dirt, and a great river of blood ran from his mouth.

When Thiudahad and Hermann came up they found Padway vomiting quietly against a tree trunk. He barely heard their congratulations.

He was reacting to his first homicide with a combination of humane revulsion and buck fever. He was too sensible to blame himself much, but he was still no mere thoughtless adventurer to take a killing lightly. To save Thiudahad's worthless neck, he had killed one who was probably a better man, who had a legitimate grudge against the ex-king, and who had never harmed Pad-way. If he could only have talked to Optaris, or have wounded him slightly ... But that was water over the dam; the man was as dead as one of John the Egyptian's customers. The living presented a more immediate problem.

He said to Thiudahad: 'We'd better disguise you. If you're recognized, Wit-tigis will send another of your friends around to call. Better take that beard off first. It's too bad you already have your hair cut short, Roman style.'

'Maybe,' said Hermann, 'could cut him off nose. Then nobody recognize.'

'Oh!' cried Thiudahad, clutching the member indicated. 'Oh, dear me! You wouldn't *really* disfigure me that way, most excellent, most noble Martinus?'

'Not if you behave yourself, my lord. And your clothes are entirely too fancy. Hermann, could I trust you to go into Narnia and buy an Italian peas-ant's Sunday-go-to-church outfit?'

'Ja, ja, you give me *silubr*. I go.'

'What?' squeaked Thiudahad. 'I will not get myself up in such an absurd costume! A prince of the Amalings has his dignity —'

Padway looked at him narrowly and felt the edge of Hermann's sword. He said silkily: 'Then, my lord, you *do* prefer the loss of your nose? No? I thought not. Give Hermann a couple of solidi. We'll make a prosperous farmer of you. How are you on Umbrian dialect?'

CHAPTER X

Liuderis Oskar's son, commander of the garrison of the city of Rome, looked out of his office window gloomily at the gray September skies. The world had been turning upside down too often for this simple, loyal soul. First Thiudahad is deposed and Wittigis elected king. Then Wittigis, by some mysterious process, convinces himself and the other Gothic leaders that the way to deal with the redoubtable Belisarius is to run off to Ravenna, leaving an inadequate garrison in Rome. And now it transpires that the citizens are becoming dissatisfied; worse, that his troops are afraid to try to hold the city against the Greeks; worse yet, that Pope Silverius, blandly violating his oaths to Wittigis on the ground that the king is a heretic, has been corresponding with Belisarius with the object of arranging a bloodless surrender of the city.

But all these shocks were mild compared to that which he got when the two callers announced by his orderly turned out to be Martin Padway and ex-King Thiudahad, whom he recognized immediately despite his clean-shaven state. He simply sat, stared, and blew out his whiskers. 'You!' he said. 'You!'

'Yes, us,' said Padway mildly. 'You know Thiudahad, King of the Ostrogoths and Italians, I believe. And you know me. I'm the king's new quæstor, by the way.' (That meant he was a combination of secretary, legal draftsman, and ghost writer.)

'But ... but we have another king! You two are supposed to have prices on your heads or something.'

'Oh, that,' smiled Padway negligently. 'The Royal council was a little hasty in its action as we hope to show them in time. We'll explain —'

'But where have you been? And how did you escape from my camp? And what are you doing here?'

'One thing at a time, please, excellent Liuderis. First, we've been up at Florence collecting a few supplies for the campaign. Second —'

'What campaign?'

'— second, I have ways of getting out of camps denied to ordinary men. Third, we're here to lead your troops against the Greeks and destroy them.'

'You are mad, both of you! I shall have you locked up until —'

'Now, now, wait until you hear us. Do you know of my ... ah ... little gifts for seeing the future results of men's actions?'

'Unh, I *have* heard things. But if you think you can seduce me away from my duty by some wild tale —'

'Exactly, my dear sir. The king will tell you how I foresaw Optaris' unfortunate attempt on his life, and how I used my knowledge to thwart Optaris' plans. If you insist, I can produce more evidence.

'For instance, I can tell you that you'll get no help from Ravenna. That Belisarius will march up the Latin Way in November. That the Pope will persuade your garrison to march away before they arrive. And that *you* will remain at your post, and be captured and sent to Constantinople.'

Liuderis gasped. 'Are you in league with Satanas? Or perhaps you are the Devil himself? I have not told a soul of my determination to stay if my garrison leaves, and yet you know of it.'

Padway smiled. 'No such luck, excellent Liuderis. Just an ordinary flesh-and-blood man who happens to have a few special gifts. Moreover, Wittigis will eventually lose his war, though only after years of destructive fighting. That is, all these things will happen unless you change your plans.'

It took an hour of talk to wear Liuderis down to the point where he asked: 'Well, what plans for operations against the Greeks did you have in mind?'

Padway replied: 'We know they'll come by the Latin Way, so there's no point in leaving Terracina garrisoned. And we know about when they'll come. Counting the Terracina garrison, about how many men could you collect by the end of next month?'

Liuderis blew out his whiskers and thought. 'If I called in the men from Formia – six thousand, perhaps seven. About half and half archers and lancers. That is, assuming that King Wittigis did not hear of it and interfere. But news travels slowly.'

'If I could show you how you'd have a pretty good chance against the Greeks, would you lead them out?'

'I do not know. I should have to think. Perhaps. If as you say our king – excuse me, noble Thiudahad, I mean the *other* king – is bound to be defeated, it might be worth taking a chance on. What would you do?'

'Belisarius has about ten thousand men,' replied Padway. 'He'll leave two thousand to garrison Naples and other southern towns. He'll still out-number us a little. I notice that your brave Wittigis ran off when he had twenty thousand available.'

Liuderis shrugged and looked embarrassed. 'It is true, that was not a wise move. But he expects many thousands more from Gaul and Dalmatia.'

'Have your men had any practice at night attacks?' asked Padway.

'Night attacks? You mean to assault the enemy at *night*? No. I never heard of such a proceeding. Battles are always fought in the daytime. A night attack does not sound very practical to me. How would you keep control of your men?'

'That's just the point. Nobody ever heard of the Goths making a night attack, so it ought to have some chance of success. But it'll require special training. First, you'll have to throw out patrols on the roads leading north, to turn back people who might carry the news to Ravenna. And I need a couple of good catapult engineers. I don't want to depend entirely on the books in the libraries for my artillery. If none of your troops know anything about catapults, we ought to be able to dredge up a Roman or two who does. And you might appoint me to your staff – you don't have staffs? Then it's time you started – at a reasonable salary —'

Padway lay on a hilltop near Fregellae and watched the Imperialists through a telescope. He was surprised that Belisarius, as the foremost soldier in his age, hadn't thrown scouts out farther, but, then this was 536. His advance party consisted of a few hundred mounted Huns and Moors, who galloped about, pushing up side roads a few hundred yards and racing back. Then came two thousand of the famous *cataphracti* or cuirassiers, trotting in orderly formation. The low, cold sun glittered on the scales of their armor. Their standard was a blown-up leather serpent writhing from the top of a long pole, like a balloon from Macy's Thanksgiving Day parade.

These were the best and certainly the most versatile soldiers in the world, and everybody was afraid of them. Padway, watching their cloaks and scarves flutter behind them, didn't feel too confident himself. Then came three thousand Isaurian archers marching afoot, and finally two thousand more cuirassiers.

Liuderis, at Padway's elbow, said: 'That is some sort of signal. *Ja*, I believe they are going to camp there. How did you know they would pick that spot, Martinus?'

'Simple. You remember that little device I had on the wheel of that wagon? That measures distance. I measured the distances along the road. Knowing their normal day's march and the point they started from, the rest was easy.'

'*Tsk, tsk*, wonderful. How do you think of all those things?' Liuderis' big, trustful eyes reminded Padway of those of a St. Bernard. 'Shall I have the engineers set up Brunhilde now?'

'Not yet. When the sun sets, we'll measure the distance to the camp.'

'How will you do that without being seen?'

'I'll show you when the time comes. Meanwhile make sure that the boys keep quiet and out of sight.'

Liuderis frowned. 'They will not like having to eat a cold supper. If we do not watch them, somebody will surely start a fire.'

Padway sighed. He'd had plenty of sad experience with the temperamental and undisciplined Goths. One minute they were as excited as small boys over the plans of Mysterious Martinus, as they called him; the next day they were growling on the edge of mutiny about the enforcement of some petty regulation. Since Padway felt that it wouldn't do for him to order them around directly, poor Liuderis had to take it.

The Byzantines set up their camp with orderly promptitude. Those, Padway thought, were real soldiers. You could accomplish something with men like that to command. It would be a long time before the Goths attained such a smooth perfection of movement. The Goths were still obsessed with childish, slam-bang ideas of warfare.

Witness the grumbling that had greeted Padway's requisition of a squad for engineers. Running catapults was a sissy job, inconsistent with knightly honor. And well-born lancers fight on foot like a lot or serfs? Perish the thought! Padway had seduced them away from their beloved horses by an ingenious method: He, or rather Liuderis at his suggestion, formed a company of pikemen, loudly announcing that only the best men would be admitted, and that furthermore candidates would be made to *pay* for admission. Padway explained that there was no type of troop wherein morale and discipline were as vital as in heavy infantry, because one man flinching from a cavalry charge might break the line of spears and let the enemy in.

It was getting too dark for his telescope to be useful. He could make out the general's standard in front of a big tent. Perhaps Belisarius was one of those little figures around it. If he had a machine-gun – but he didn't have, and never would. You need machines to make a machine-gun, and machines to make those machines, and so on. If he ever got a workable muzzle-loading musket he'd be doing well.

The standard no doubt bore the letters S. P. Q. R. – the Senate and the People of Rome. An army of Hunnish, Moorish, and Anatolian mercenaries, commanded by a Thracian Slav who worked for a Dalmatian autocrat who reigned in Constantinople and didn't even rule the city of Rome, called himself the Army of the Roman Republic and saw nothing funny in the act.

Padway got up, grunting at the weight of his shirt of scale mail. He wished a lot of things, such as that he'd had time to train some mounted archers. They were the only troops who could really deal on even terms with the deadly Byzantine cuirassiers. But he'd have to hope that darkness would nullify the Imperialists' advantage in missile fire.

He superintended the driving of a stake into the ground and paced off the base of a triangle. With a little geometry he figured the quarter-mile distance that was Brunhilde's range, and ordered the big catapult set up. The thing required eleven wagon-loads of lumber, even though it was not of record size. Padway hovered around his engineers nervously, jumping and hissing reprimands when somebody dropped a piece of wood.

Snatches of song came from the camp. Apparently Padway's scheme of leaving a wagon-load of brandy where foragers would be sure to find it had had results, despite Belisarius' well-known strictness with drunken soldiers.

The bags of sulphur paste were brought out. Padway looked at his watch, which he had recovered from the hole in the wall. It was nearly midnight, though he'd have sworn the job hadn't taken over an hour.

'All ready?' he asked. 'Light the first bag.' The oil-soaked rags were lit. The bag was placed in the sling. Padway himself pulled the lanyard. *Wht-bam!* said Brunhilde. The bag did a fiery parabola. Padway raced up the little knoll that masked his position. He missed seeing the bag land in the camp. But the drunken songs ended, instead there was a growing buzz as of a nest of irritated hornets. Behind him whips cracked and ropes creaked in the dark, as the horses heaved on the block-and-tackle he'd rigged up for quick recocking. *Wht-bam!* The fuse came out of the second bag in midair, so that it continued its course to the camp unseen and harmless. Never mind, another would follow in a few seconds. Another did. The buzz was louder, and broken by clear, high-pitched commands. *Wht-bam!*

'Liuderis!' Padway called. 'Give your signal!'

Over in the camp the horse lines began to scream. The horses didn't like the sulphur dioxide. Good; maybe the Imperialist cavalry would be immobilized. Under the other noises Padway heard the clank and shuffle of the Goths, getting under way. Something in the camp was burning brightly. Its light showed a company of Goths on Padway's right picking their way over the broken, weed-covered ground. Their big round shields were painted white for recognition, and every man had a wet rag tied over his nose. Padway thought they ought to be able to frighten the Imperialists if they couldn't do anything else. On all sides the night was alive with the little orange twinkle of firelight on helmets, scale skirts, and sword blades.

As the Goths closed in, the noise increased tenfold, with the addition of organized battle yells, the flat snap of bowstrings, and finally the blacksmith's symphony of metal on metal. Padway could see 'his' men, black against the fires, grow smaller and then drop out of sight into the camp ditch. Then there was only a confused blur of movement and a great din as the attackers scrambled up the other side – invisible until they popped up into the firelight again – and mixed in with the defenders.

One of the engineers called to say that that was all the sulphur bags, and what should they do now? 'Stand by for further orders,' replied Padway.

'But, Captain, can't we go fight? We're missing all the fun!'

'*Ni*, you can't! You're the only engineer corps west of the Adriatic that's worth a damn, and I won't have you getting yourselves killed off!'

'Huh!' said a voice in the dark. 'This is a cowardly way of doing, standing back here. Let's go, boys. To hell with Mysterious Martinus!' And before Padway could do anything, the twenty-odd catapult men trotted off toward the fires.

Padway angrily called for his horse and rode off to find Liuderis. The commander was sitting his horse in front of a solid mass of lancers. The fire-light picked out their helms and faces and shoulders, and the forest of vertical lances. They looked like something out of a Wagnerian opera.

Padway asked: 'Has there been any sign of a sortie yet?'

'No.'

'There will be, if I know Belisarius. Who's going to lead this troop?'

'I am,' said Liuderis.

'Oh, lord! I thought I explained why the commander should —'

'I know, Martinus,' said Liuderis firmly. 'You have lots of ideas. But you're young. I'm an old soldier, you know. Honor requires that I lead my men. Look, isn't something doing in the camp?'

True enough, the Imperial cavalry was coming out. Belisarius had, despite his difficulties, managed to collect a body of manageable horses and cuirassiers to ride them. As they watched, this group thundered out the main gate, the Gothic infantry scattering in all directions before them. Liuderis shouted, and the mass of Gothic knights clattered off, picking up speed as they went. Padway saw the Imperialists swing widely to take the attacking foe in the rear, and then Liuderis' men hid them. He heard the crash as the forces met, and then everything was dark confusion for a few minutes.

Little by little the noise died. Padway wondered just what had happened. He felt silly, sitting alone on his horse a quarter mile from all the action. Theoretically, he was where the staff, the reserves, and the artillery ought to be. But there were no reserves, their one catapult stood deserted off in the dark somewhere, and the artillerists and staff were exchanging sword strokes with the Imperialists up front.

With a few wordless disparagements of sixth-century ideas of warfare, Padway trotted toward the camp. He came across a Goth peacefully tying up his shin with a cloth torn from his tunic, another who clutched his stomach and moaned, and a corpse. Then he came upon a considerable body of dis-mounted Imperial cuirassiers standing weaponless.

'What are you doing?' Padway asked.

One replied: 'We're prisoners. There were some Goths supposed to be guarding us, but they got angry at missing the looting, so they went off to the camp.'

'What became of Belisarius?'

'Here he is.' The prisoner indicated a man sitting on the ground with his head in his hands. 'A Goth hit him on the head and stunned him. He's just coming to. Do you know what will be done with us, noble sir?'

'Nothing very drastic, I imagine. You fellows wait here until I send some-body for you.' Padway rode on toward the camp. Soldiers were strange people, he thought. With Belisarius to lead them and a fair chance to use their famous bow-plus-lance tactics, the *cataphracti* could lick thrice their number of another troop. Now, because their leader had been conked on the head, they were as meek as lambs.

There were more corpses and wounded near the camp, and a few riderless horses calmly grazing. In the camp itself Imperial soldiers, Isaurians and Moors and Huns, stood around in little clumps, holding bits of clothing to their noses against the reek of sulphur fumes. Goths ran hither and thither among them looking for movable property worth stealing.

Padway dismounted and asked a couple of the looters where Liuderis was. They said they had no idea, and went on about their business. He found an officer he knew, Gaina by name. Gaina was squatting by a corpse and weeping. He turned a streaked, bearded face up to Padway.

'Liuderis is dead,' he said between sobs. 'He was killed in the mêlée when we struck the Greek cavalry.'

'Who's that?' Padway indicated the corpse.

'My younger brother.'

'I'm sorry. But won't you come with me and get things organized? There are a hundred cuirassiers out there with nobody guarding them. If they come to their senses they'll make a break —'

'No, I will stay with my little brother. You go on, Martinus. You can take care of things.' Gaina dissolved in fresh tears.

Padway hunted until he found another officer, Gudareths, who seemed to have some sort of wits about him. At least, he was making frantic efforts to round up a few troopers to guard the surrendered Imperialists. The minute he turned his back on his men, they melted off into the general confusion of the camp.

Padway grabbed him. 'Forget them,' he snapped.

'Liuderis is dead, I hear, but Belisarius is alive. If we don't nab him —'

So they took a handful of Goths in tow and marched back to where the Imperial general still sat among his men. They moved the lesser prisoners away, and set several men to guard Belisarius. Then they spent a solid hour rounding up troopers and prisoners and getting them into some sort of order.

Gudareths, a small, cheerful man, talked continually: 'That was some charge, some charge. Never saw a better, even in the battle against the Gepids on the Danube. We took them in flank, neatest thing you ever saw. The Greek general fought like a wild man, until I hit him over the head. Broke my sword, it did. Best stroke I ever made, by God. Even harder than the time I cut off that Bulgarian Hun's head, five years ago. Oh, yes, I've killed hundreds of enemies in my time. Thousands, even. I'm sorry for the poor devils. I'm not really a bloodthirsty fellow, but they will try to stand up against me. Say, where were you during the charge?' He looked sharply at Padway, like an accusatory chipmunk before rambling on.

'I was supposed to be running the artillery. But my men ran off to join the fight. And by the time I arrived it was all over.'

Another chatterbox broke in: '*Aiw*, no doubt, no doubt. Like one time when I was in a battle with the Burgunds. My orders kept me out of the thick until the fighting was nearly over. Of course, when I arrived I must have killed at least twenty —'

At last troops and prisoners headed north on the Latin Way. Padway, still a little bewildered to find himself in command of the Gothic army, simply by virtue of having taken over Liuderis' responsibilities on the night of confusion, rode near the front. The best are always the first to go, he thought sadly, remembering the simple, honest old Santa Claus who lay dead in one of the wagons in the rear, and thinking of the mean and treacherous little king whom he would have to manage when he got back to Rome.

Belisarius, jogging along beside him, was even less cheerful. The Imperial general was a surprisingly young man, in his middle thirties, tall and a bit stout, with gray eyes and curly brown beard. His Slavic ancestry was highlighted by his wide cheekbones.

He said gravely: 'Excellent Martinus, I ought to thank you for the consideration you showed my wife. You went out of your way to make her comfortable on this sad journey.'

'Quite all right, illustrious Belisarius. Maybe you'll capture me some day.'

'That seems hardly likely, after this fiasco. By the way, if I may ask, just what are you? I hear you called Mysterious Martinus! You're no Goth, nor yet an Italian, by your speech.'

Padway stated his impressively vague connection to America.

'Really? They must be a people skilled in war, these Americans. I knew when the fight started that I was not dealing with any barbarian commander. The timing was much too good, especially on that cavalry charge. *Phew!* I can still smell that damnable sulphur!'

Padway saw no point in explaining that his previous military experience consisted of one year of ROTC in a Chicago high school. Instead he asked: 'How would you like the idea of coming over to our side? We need a good general, and as Thiudahad's quæstor, I'll have my hands full now.'

Belisarius frowned. 'No, I swore an oath to Justinian.'

'So you did. But as you'll probably hear, I can sometimes see a little into the future. And I can tell you that the more faithful you are to Justinian, the meaner and more ungrateful he'll be to you. He'll —'

'I said no!' said Belisarius sternly. 'You can do what you like with me. But the word of Belisarius is not to be questioned.'

Padway argued some more. But, remembering his Procopius, he had little hope of shaking the Thracian's stern rectitude. Belisarius was a fine fellow, but his rigid virtue made him a slightly uncomfortable companion. He asked: 'Where's your secretary, Procopius of Cæsarea?'

'I do not know. He was in southern Italy, and should be on his way to join us.'

'Good. We shall need a competent historian.'

Belisarius' eyes widened. 'How do you know about the histories for which he's collecting notes? I thought he'd told nobody but me.'

Padway smiled. 'Oh, I have my private ways. That's why they call me Mysterious Martinus.'

At dawn they marched into Rome by the Latin Gate, north past the Circus Maximus and the Colosseum, and up the Quirinal Valley to the Old Viminal Gate and the Pretorian Camp.

Here Padway gave orders to encamp the prisoners, and told Gudareths to set a guard over them. That done, Padway found himself in the midst of a crowd of weary officers who looked at him expectantly. He could not think what orders to give next.

He rubbed his ear lobe for a few seconds, then took the captive Belisarius aside, 'Say, illustrious general,' he said in a low voice, 'what in hell should I do next? This military business isn't my proper trade.'

There was a hint of amusement in Belisarius' broad and usually solemn face. He answered: 'Call out your paymaster and have him settle the men's wages. Better give them a little bonus for winning the battle. Detail an officer to round up some physicians to tend the wounded; at least I don't suppose a barbarian army like this has its own medical corps. Choose a man whose duty it is to check the rolls. I hear the commander of the Rome garrison was killed. Appoint a man in his place, and have the garrison returned to barracks. Tell the commanders of the other contingents to find what lodging they can for their men. If they are to board at private houses, say the owners will be compensated at standard rates. You can settle with them later. But first you ought to make a speech.'

'*I* make a speech?' hissed Padway in horror. 'My Gothic is lousy —'

'That's part of a captain's business, you know. Tell your men what good soldiers they are. Make it short. They won't listen very closely anyway.'

CHAPTER XI

After some searching Padway located Thiudahad in the Arian Library. The little man was barricaded behind a huge load of books. Four bodyguards sprawled on a table, a bench, and the floor, snoring thunderously. The librarian was staring at them with a look compounded of hydrofluoric acid and cobra venom, but did not dare protest.

Thiudahad looked up blearily. 'Oh, yes, it's the publisher fellow. Martinus, isn't it?'

'That's right, my lord. I might add that I'm your new quæstor.'

'What? What? Who told you so?'

'You did. You appointed me.'

'Oh, dear me, so I did. Silly of me. When I get engrossed in books I really don't know what's going on. Let's see, you and Liuderis were going to fight the Imperialists, weren't you?'

'*Hoc ille*, my lord. It's all over.'

'Hmm. I suppose you sold out to Belisarius, didn't you? I hope you arranged for an estate and an annuity from Justinian for me.'

'It wasn't necessary, my lord. We won.'

'*What?*'

Padway gave a résumé of the last three days' events. 'And you'd better get to bed early tonight, my lord. We're leaving in the morning for Florence.'

'Florence? Why, in heaven's name?'

'We're on our way to intercept your generals, Asinar and Grippas. They're coming back from Dalmatia, having been ordered out by the Imperial general, Constantianus. If we can catch them before they get to Ravenna and learn about Wittigis, we might be able to get your crown back.'

Thiudahad sighed. 'Yes, I suppose we ought to. But how did you know that Asinar and Gippas were coming home?'

'Trade secret, my lord. I've also sent a force of two thousand to reoccupy Naples. It's held by General Herodianus with a mere three hundred, so there shouldn't be much trouble.'

Thiudahad narrowed his watery eyes. 'You do get things done, Martinus. If you can deliver that vile usurper Wittigis into my hands – *aaah*! I'll send clear to Constantinople for a torturer, if I can't find one ingenious enough in Italy!'

Padway did not answer that one, having his own plans for Wittigis. He said instead: 'I have a pleasant surprise for you. The pay chests of the Imperial army —'

'Yes?' Thiudahad's eyes gleamed. 'They're mine, of course, Very considerate of you, excellent Martinus.'

'Well, I did have to dip into them a little to pay our troops and clear up the army's bills. But you'll find the rest an agreeable addition to the royal purse. I'll be waiting for you at home.'

Padway neglected to state that he had sequestered over half the remainder and deposited the money with Thomasus. Who owns the pay chests of a captured army, especially when the captor is a volunteer theoretically serving one of two rival kings, was a question that the legal science of the time was hardly equipped to decide. In any event Padway was sure he could make better use of the money than Thiudahad. I'm becoming quite a hardened criminal, he thought with pride.

Padway rode up to Cornelius Anicius' home. Its rhetorical owner was out at the baths, but Dorothea came out. Padway had to admit that it made him feel pretty good to sit on a powerful horse in a (to him) romantic get-up, with cloak and boots and all, and report to one of the prettier girls of Rome on his success.

She said: 'You know, Martinus, father was silly at first about your social standing. But after all you've done he's forgotten about that. Of course he is not enthusiastic about Gothic rule. But he much prefers Thiudahad, who *is* a scholar, to that savage Wittigis.'

'I'm glad of that. I like your old man.'

'Everybody's talking about you now. They call you "Mysterious Martinus."'

'I know. Absurd, isn't it?'

'Yes. You never seemed very mysterious to me, in spite of your foreign background.'

'That's great. You're not afraid of me, are you?'

'Not in the least. If you made a deal with Satanas as some people hint, I'm sure the Devil got the worst of it.' They laughed. She added: 'It's nearly dinner time. Won't you stay? Father will be back any time.'

'I'm sorry, but I can't possibly. We're off to the wars again tomorrow.'

As he rode off, he thought: If I *should change* my mind about the expediency of marriage, I'd know where to begin. She's attractive and pleasant, and has what passes for a good education here …

Padway made one more attempt to shake Belisarius, but without success. He did, however, enlist five hundred of the Imperial cuirassiers as a personal guard. His share of the Imperialist loot would suffice to pay them for some weeks. After that he'd see.

The trip to Florence was anything but pleasant. It rained most of the way, with intermittent snow squalls as they climbed toward the City of Flowers. Being in a hurry, Padway took only cavalry.

In Florence he sent his officers around to buy warmer clothes for the troops, and looked in on his business. It seemed to be surviving, though Fritharik said: 'I don't trust any of them, excellent boss. I'm sure the foreman and this George Menandrus have been stealing, though I can't prove it. I don't understand all this writing and figuring. If you leave them alone long enough they'll steal everything, and then where'll we be? Out in the cold, headed for a pair of nameless graves.'

'We'll see,' said Padway. He called in the treasurer, Proclus Proclus, and asked to see the books. Proclus Proclus instantly looked apprehensive, but he got the books. Padway waded into the figures. They were all nice and neat, since he himself had taught the treasurer double-entry bookkeeping. All his employees were astounded to hear Padway burst into a shout of laughter.

'What ... what is it, noble sir?' asked Proclus Proclus.

'Why, you poor fool, didn't you realize that with my system of bookkeeping, your little thefts would stick up in the accounts like a sore toe? Look here: thirty solidi last month, and nine solidi and some sesterces only last week. You might just as well have left a signed receipt every time you stole something!'

'What ... what are you going to do to me?'

'Well – I *ought* to have you jailed and flogged.' Padway was silent for a while and watched Proclus Proclus squirm. 'But I hate to have your family suffer. And I certainly oughtn't to keep you on, after this. But I'm pretty busy, and I can't take the time to train a new treasurer to keep books in a civilized manner. So I'll just take a third of your salary until these little *borrowings* of yours are paid back.'

'Thank you, thank you kindly, sir. But just to be fair – George Menandrus ought to pay a share of it, too. He —'

'Liar!' shouted the editor.

'Liar yourself! Look, I can prove it. Here's an item for one solidus, November 10th. And on November 11th George shows up with a pair of new shoes and a bracelet. I know where he bought them. On the 15th —'

'How about it, George?' asked Padway.

Menandrus finally confessed, though he insisted that the thefts were merely temporary borrowings to tide him over until pay day.

Padway divided the total liability between the two of them. He warned them sternly against recidivism. Then he left a set of plans with the foreman for new machines and metal-working processes, including plans for a machine for spinning copper plate into bowls. The intelligent Nerva caught on immediately.

As Padway was leaving, Fritharik asked him: 'Can't I go with you, excellent Martinus? It's very dull here in Florence. And you need somebody to take care of you. I've saved up almost enough to get my jeweled sword back, and if you'll let —'

'No, old man. I'm sorry, but I've got to have *one* person I can trust here. When this damned war and politics is over, we'll see.'

Fritharik sighed gustily. 'Oh, very well, if you insist. But I hate to think of your going around unprotected with all these treacherous Greeks and Italians and Goths. You'll end in an unmarked grave yet, I fear.'

They shivered and skidded across the icy Apennines to Bologna. Padway resolved to have his men's horses shod if he could ever get a few days to spare – stirrups had been invented but not horseshoes. From Bologna to Padua – still largely in ruins from its destruction by Attila's Huns – the road was no longer the splendid stone-paved affair they had earlier traveled on, but a mere track in the mud. However, the weather turned almost springlike, which was something.

At Padua they found they had missed the Dalmatian force by one day. Thiudahad wanted to halt. 'Martinus,' he whined, 'you've dragged my old bones all over northern Italy, and nearly frozen me to death. That's not considerate. You do owe your king some consideration, don't you?'

Padway repressed his irritation with some effort. 'My lord, *do* you or *don't* you want your crown back?'

So poor Thiudahad had to go along. By hard riding they caught up with the Dalmatian army halfway to Atria. They heaved past thousands and thousands of Goths, afoot and on horses. There must have been well over fifty thousand of them. All these big, tough-looking men had skedaddled at the mere thought that Count Constantianus was approaching.

The count had had only a small force, but Padway was the only one present who knew that, and his source of information was not strictly kosher. The Goths cheered Thiudahad and Padway's Gothic lancers, and stared and muttered at the five hundred cuirassiers. Padway had made his guard don Gothic helmets and Italian military cloaks in lieu of the spiked steel helmets and burnooselike mantles they had worn. But still their lean chins, tight pants, and high yellow boots made them sufficiently different to arouse suspicion.

Padway found the two commanders near the head of the column. Asinar was tall and Grippas was short, but otherwise both were just a couple of middle-aged and bewhiskered barbarians. They respectfully saluted Thiudahad, who seemed to move slightly from so much latent force. Thiudahad introduced Padway as his new prefect – no, he meant his new quæstor.

Asinar whispered to Padway: 'In Padua we heard a rumor that war and usurpation had been going on in Italy. Just what is the news, anyway?'

Padway was for once thankful that his telegraph hadn't been operating that far north. He laughed scornfully. 'Oh, our lord General Wittigis had a brainstorm a couple of weeks ago. He put himself up in Ravenna, where the Greeks couldn't kill him, and had himself proclaimed king. We've cleaned up the Greeks, and are on our way to settle with Wittigis now. These boys will be a help.' All of which was rather unjust to Wittigis.

Padway wondered whether there'd be anything left of his character after a few years in this mendacious atmosphere. The two Gothic generals accepted his statement without comment. Padway decided quickly that neither of them could be called very bright.

They marched into Ravenna at noon two days later. The mists were so thick about the northern causeway that a man had to precede the leading horsemen on foot to keep them from spattering off into the marsh.

There was some alarm in Ravenna when the force appeared in the fog. Padway and Thiudahad prudently kept quiet as Asinar and Grippas identified themselves. As a result, most of the huge force was in the city before anybody noticed the little gray man with Padway. Immediately there were shouts and running to and fro.

Presently a Goth in a rich red cloak dashed out to the head of the column. He shouted: 'What the devil's going on here? Have you captured Thiudahad, or is it the other way around?'

Asinar and Grippas sat their horses and muttered: 'Uh … well.. that is —'

Padway spurred up front and asked the Goth: 'Who are you, my dear sir?'

'It it's any of your business, I'm Unilas Wiljarith's son, general of our lord Wittigis, King of the Goths and Italians. Now who are *you?*'

Padway grinned and replied smoothly: 'I'm delighted to know you, General Unilas. I'm Martin Paduei, quæstor to old lord Thiudahad, King of the Goths and Italians. Now that we know each other —'

'But, you fool, there isn't any King Thiudahad! He was deposed! We've got a new king! Or hadn't you heard about it?'

'Oh, I've heard lots of things. But, my excellent Unilas, before you make any more rude remarks, consider that we – that is to say King Thiudahad – have over sixty thousand troops in Ravenna, whereas you have about twelve thousand. You don't want any unnecessary unpleasantness, do you?'

'Why, you impudent … you … uh … did you say *sixty* thousand?'

'Maybe seventy; I haven't counted them.'

'Oh. That's different.'

'I thought you'd see it that way.'

'What are you going to do?'

'Well, if you can tell where *General* Wittigis is, I thought we might pay him a visit.'

'He's getting married today. I think he ought to be on his way to St. Vitalis' Church about now.'

'You mean he hasn't married Mathaswentha yet?'

'No. There was some delay in getting his divorce.'

'Quick, how do we get to St. Vitalis' Church?'

Padway hadn't hoped to be in time to interfere with Wittigis' attempt to engraft himself on the Amal family tree by a forcible marriage with the late Queen Amalaswentha's daughter. But this was too good an opportunity to let it slip.

Unilas pointed out a dome flanked by two towers. Padway shouted to his guard and kicked his horse into a canter. The five hundred men galloped after him, spattering unfortunate pedestrians with mud. They thundered across a bridge over one of Ravenna's canals, the stench from which fully lived up to its reputation, and reached the door of St. Vitalis' Church.

There were a score of guards at the door, through which organ music wafted faintly. The guards brought their spears up to 'poise.'

Padway reined in and turned to the commander of his guard, a Macedonian named Achilleus. 'Cover them,' he snapped.

There was a quick, concerted movement among the cuirassiers, who had been sorting themselves into a semicircle in front of the church door. The next instant the guards were looking at a hundred stiff Byzantine bows drawn to the cheek. '*Nu*,' said Padway in Gothic, 'if you boys will put your stickers down and your hands up, we have an appointment – oh, that's better. Much better.' He slid off his horse. 'Achilleus, give me a troop. Then surround the church, and keep those inside in and those outside out until I finish with Wittigis.'

Padway marched into St. Vitalis' Church with a hundred cuirassiers at his heels. The organ music died with a wail, and people turned to stare at him. It took his eyes a few seconds to become accustomed to the gloom.

In the center of the huge octagon towered a pickle-faced Arian bishop, before whom stood three people. One was a big man in a long, rich robe, wearing a crown on his dark, graying hair: King Wittigis. Another was a tall girl with a strawberries-and-cream complexion and hair plated in thick golden braids: the princess Mathaswentha. The third was an ordinary Gothic soldier, somewhat cleaned up, who stood beside the bride and held her arm behind her back. The audience was a handful of Gothic nobles and their ladies.

Padway walked purposefully down the aisle, as people squirmed, rustled in their seats, and murmured: 'The Greeks! The Greeks have come to Ravenna!'

The bishop addressed Padway: 'Young man, what is the meaning of this intrusion?'

'You'll soon learn, my lord bishop. Since when has the Arian faith countenanced the taking of a woman to wife against her will?'

'What's that? Who is being taken against her will? What business is this wedding of yours? Who are you, young man, who dares to interrupt —'

Padway laughed his most irritating laugh. 'One question at a time, please. I am Martinus Paduei, quæstor to King Thiudahad. Ravenna is in our hands, and prudent persons will comport themselves accordingly. As for the wedding, it is not usually necessary to assign a man to twist the bride's arm to make sure she gives the right answers. You do not want to marry this man, do you, my lady?'

Mathaswentha jerked her arm away from the soldier, who had been relaxing his grip. She made a fist and punched him in the nose with enough force to rock his head back on its hinges. Then she swung at Wittigis, who dodged back. 'You beast!' she cried. 'I'll claw your eyes —'

The bishop grabbed her arm. 'Calm yourself, my daughter! Please! This is a house of God —'

King Wittigis had been blinking at Padway, gradually soaking in the news. Mathaswentha's attack had shocked him out of his lethargy. He growled: 'You're trying to tell me that the miserable pen pusher, Thiudahad, has taken the town? *My* town?'

'That, my lord, is true. I fear you'll have to abandon your idea of becoming an Amaling and ruling the Goths. But we'll —'

Wittigis' face had been turning darker and darker red. Now he burst into a shocking roar. 'You swine!' he yelled. 'You think I'll hand over my crown and my bride peaceably? By Jesus, I'll see you in the hottest hell first!' As he spoke he whipped out his sword and ran heavily at Padway, his gold-embroidered robe flapping.

Padway was not entirely taken by surprise. He got his own sword out and parried Wittigis' terrific downward cut easily enough, though the force of the blow almost disarmed him. Then he found himself chest to chest with the Goth, hugging the barrel torso and chewing Wittigis' pepper-and-salt beard. He tried to shout up to his men, but it was like trying to talk with a mouth full of shredded wheat.

He spat out, it seemed, half a bale of the stuff. 'Grab … *gffth* … *pffth* … grab him, boys! Don't hurt him!'

That was easier said than done. Wittigis struggled like a captive gorilla, even when five men were hanging onto him, and he bellowed and foamed all the while. The Gothic gentlemen were standing, some with hands on their sword hilts, but in a hopeless minority. None seemed anxious to die for his king just then. Wittigis began to sob between roars.

'Tie him up until he cools off,' said Padway unfeelingly. 'My lord bishop, may I trouble you for pen and paper?'

The bishop looked bleakly at Padway, and called a sexton, who led Padway to a room off the vestibule. Here he sat down and wrote:

Martinus Paduei to Thomasus the Syrian. Greetings:
My dear Thomasus: I am sending you with this letter the person of Wittigis, former King of the Goths and Italians. His escort has orders to deliver him to your house secretly, so forgive me for any alarm they cause you if they get you out of bed.

As I remember, we have a telegraph tower under construction on the Flaminian Way near Helvillum. Please arrange to have a chamber constructed in the earth underneath this tower and fitted up as an apartment forthwith. Incarcerate Wittigis therein with an adequate guard. Have him made as comfortable as possible, as I judge him a man of moody temperament, and I do not wish him to harm himself.

The utmost secrecy is to be observed at all times. That should not be too difficult, as this tower is in a wild stretch of country. It would be advisable to have Wittigis delivered to the tower by guards other than those who take him to Rome, and to have him guarded by men who speak neither Latin nor Gothic. They shall release their prisoner only on my order, delivered either in person or via the telegraph, or without orders in the event of my imprisonment or death.

With best regards,

MARTINUS PADUEI

Padway said to Wittigis: 'I'm sorry to have to treat you so roughly, my lord. I would not have interfered if I hadn't known it was necessary to save Italy.'

Wittigis had relapsed into morose taciturnity. He glared silently.

Padway continued: 'I'm really doing you a favor, you know. If Thiudahad got hold of you, you would die – slowly.'

There was still no reply.

'Oh, well, take him away boys. Wrap him up so the people won't recognize him, and use the back streets.'

Thiudahad peered moistly at Padway. 'Marvelous, marvelous, my dear Martinus. The Royal Council accepted the inevitable. The only trouble is that the evil usurper had my crown altered to fit his big head; I'll have to alter it back. Now I can devote my time to some real scholarly research. Let's see – there was something else I wanted to ask you. Oh, yes, what did you do with Wittigis?'

Padway put on a benign smile. 'He's out of your reach, my lord king.'

'You mean you killed him? Now, that's too bad! Most inconsiderate of you, Martinus. I told you I'd promised myself a nice long session with him in the torture chambers —'

'No, he's alive. Very much so.'

'What? What? Then produce him, at once!'

Padway shook his head. 'He's where you'll never find him. You see, I figured it would be foolish to waste a good spare king. If anything happened to you, I might need one in a hurry.'

'You're insubordinate, young man! I won't stand for it! You'll do as your king orders you, or else —'

Padway grinned, shaking his head. 'No, my lord. Nobody shall hurt Wittigis. And you'd better not get rough with me, either. His guards have orders to release him if anything happens to me. He doesn't like you any better than you like him. You can figure the rest out for yourself.'

'You devil!' spat the king venomously. 'Why, oh, why did I ever let you save my life? I haven't had a moment's peace since. You might have a little consideration for an old man,' he whined. 'Let's see, what was I talking about?'

'Perhaps,' said Padway, 'about the new book we're going to get out in our joint names. It has a perfectly splendid theory, about the mutual attraction of masses. Accounts for the movements of the heavenly bodies, and all sorts of things. It's called the law of gravitation.'

'Really? Now, that's most interesting, Martinus, most interesting. It would spread my fame as a philosopher to the ends of the earth, wouldn't it?'

Padway asked Unilas if Wittigis' nephew Urias was in Ravenna. Unilas said yes, and sent a man to hunt him up.

Urias was big and dark like his uncle. He arrived scowling defiance. 'Well, Mysterious Martinus, now that you've overthrown my uncle by trickery, what are you going to do with me?'

'Not a thing,' said Padway. 'Unless you force me to.'

'Aren't you having a purge of my uncle's family?'

'No. I'm not even purging your uncle. In strict confidence, I'm hiding Wittigis to keep Thiudahad from harming him.'

'Really? Can I believe that?'

'Sure. I'll even get a letter from him, testifying to the good treatment he's getting.'

'Letters can be produced by torture.'

'Not with Wittigis. For all your uncle's faults, I think you will agree that he's a stubborn chap.'

Urias relaxed visibly. 'That's something. Yes, if that's true, perhaps you have some decency, after all.'

'Now to get down to business. How do you feel about working for us – that is, nominally for Thiudahad but actually for me?'

Urias stiffened. 'Out of the question. I'm resigning my commission, of course. I won't take any action disloyal to my uncle.'

'I'm sorry to hear that. I need a good man to command the reoccupation of Dalmatia.'

Urias shook his head stubbornly. 'It's a question of loyalty. I've never gone back on my plighted word yet.'

Padway sighed. 'You're as bad as Belisarius. The few trustworthy and able men in the world won't work with me because of previous obligations. So I have to struggle along with crooks and dimwits.'

Darkness seemed to want to fall by mere inertia—

CHAPTER XII

Little by little Ravenna's nonce population flowed away, like trickles of water from a wet sponge on a tile floor. A big trickle flowed north, as fifty thousand Goths marched back toward Dalmatia. Padway prayed that Asinar, who seemed to have little more glimmering of intelligence than Grippas, would not have another brainstorm and come rushing back to Italy before he'd accomplished anything.

Padway did not dare leave Italy long enough to take command of the campaign himself. He did what he could by sending some of his personal guard along to teach the Goths horse-archery tactics. Asinar might decide to ignore this newfangled nonsense as soon as he was out of sight. Or the cuirassiers might desert to Count Constantianus. Or – but there was no point in anticipating calamities.

Padway finally found time to pay his respects to Mathaswentha. He told himself that he was merely being polite and making a useful contact. But he knew that actually he didn't want to leave Ravenna without another look at the luscious wench.

The Gothic princess received him graciously. She spoke excellent Latin, in a rich contralto vibrant with good health. 'I thank you, excellent Martinus, for saving me from that beast. I shall never be able to repay you properly.'

They walked into her living room. Padway found that it was no effort at all to keep in step with her. But then, she was almost as tall as he was.

'It was very little, my lady,' he said. 'We just happened to arrive at an opportune time.'

'Don't deprecate yourself, Martinus. I know a lot about you. It takes a real man to accomplish all you have. Especially when one considers that you arrived in Italy, a stranger, only a little over a year ago.'

'I do what I must, princess. It may seem impressive to others, but to me it's more as if I had been forced into each action by circumstances, regardless of my intentions.'

'A fatalistic doctrine, Martinus. I could almost believe that you're a pagan. Not that I'd mind.'

Padway laughed. 'Hardly. I understand that you can still find pagans if you hunt around the Italian hills.'

'No doubt. I should like to visit some of the little villages some day. With a good guide, of course.'

'I ought to be a pretty good guide, after the amount of running around I've done in the last couple of months.'

'Would you take me? Be careful; I'll hold you to it, you know.'

'That doesn't worry me any, princess. But it would have to be some day. At the present rate, God knows when I'll get time for anything but war and politics, neither of which is my proper trade.'

'What is, then?'

'I was a gatherer of facts; a kind of historian of periods that had no history. I suppose you could call me a historical philosopher.'

'You're a fascinating person, Martinus. I can see why they call you Mysterious. But if you don't like war and politics, why do you engage in them?'

'That would be hard to explain, my lady. In the course of my work in my own country, I had occasion to study the rise and fall of many civilizations. In looking around me here, I see many symptoms of a fall.'

'Really? That's a strange thing to say. Of course, my own people, and barbarians like the Franks, have occupied most of the Western Empire. But they're not a danger to civilization. They protect it from the real wild men like the Bulgarian Huns and the Slavs. I can't think of a time when our western culture was more secure.'

'You're entitled to your opinion, my lady,' said Padway. 'I merely put together such facts as I have, and draw what conclusions I can. Facts such as the decline in the population of Italy, despite the Gothic immigrations. And such things as the volume of shipping.'

'Shipping? I never thought of measuring civilization *that* way. But in any event, that doesn't answer my question.'

'*Triggws*, to use one of your own Gothic words. Well, I want to prevent the darkness of barbarism from falling over western Europe. It sounds conceited, the idea that one man could do anything like that. But I can try. One of the weaknesses of our present setup is slow communication. So I promote the telegraph company. And because my backers are Roman patricians suspected of Græcophile leanings, I find myself in politics up to my neck. One thing leads to another, until today I'm practically running Italy.'

Mathaswentha looked thoughtful. 'I suppose the trouble with slow communication is that a general can revolt or an invader overrun the border weeks before the central government hears about it.'

'Right. I can see you're your mother's daughter. If I wanted to patronize you, I should say that you had a man's mind.'

She smiled. 'On the contrary, I should be very much pleased. At least, if you mean a man like yourself. Most of the men around here – bah! Squalling infants, without one idea among them. When I marry, it must be to a man – shall we say both of thought and action?'

Padway met her eyes, and was aware that his heart had stepped up several beats per minute. 'I hope you find him, princess.'

'I may yet.' She sat up straight and looked at him directly, almost defiantly, quite unconcerned with the inner confusion she was causing him. He noticed that sitting up straight didn't make her look any less desirable. On the contrary.

She continued: 'That's one reason I'm so grateful to you for saving me from the beast. Of all these thick-headed ninnies, he had the thickest head. What became of him, by the way? Don't pretend innocence, Martinus. Everybody knows your guards took him into the vestibule of the church, and then he apparently vanished.'

'He's safe, I hope, both from our point of view and his.'

'You mean you hid him? Death would have been safer yet.'

'I had reasons for not wanting him killed.'

'You did? I give you fair warning that if he ever falls into my hands, I shall not have such reasons.'

'Aren't you a bit hard on poor old Wittigis? He was merely trying, in his own muddle-headed way, to defend the kingdom.'

'Perhaps. But after that performance in the church, I hate him.' The gray eyes were cold as ice. 'And when I hate, I don't do it halfway.'

'So I see,' said Padway dryly, jarred out of the pink fog, for the moment. But then Mathaswentha smiled again, all curvesome and desirable woman. 'You'll stay to dinner, of course? There will only be a few people, and they'll leave early.'

'Why —' There were piles of work to be done that evening. And he needed to catch up on his sleep – a chronic condition with him. 'Thank you, my lady, I shall be delighted.'

By the third visit to Mathaswentha, Padway was saying to himself: There's a real woman. Ravishing good looks, forceful character, keen brain. The man who gets her will have one in a million. Why shouldn't I be the one? She seems to like me. With her to back me up, there's nothing I couldn't accomplish. Of course, she *is* a bit bloodthirsty. You wouldn't exactly describe her as a 'sweet' girl. But that's the fault of the times, not of her. She'll settle down when she has a man of her own to do her fighting for her.

In other words, Padway was as thoroughly in love as such a rational and prudent man can ever be.

But how did one go about marrying a Gothic princess? You certainly didn't take her out in an automobile and kiss her lipstick off by way of a starter. Nor did you begin by knowing her in high school, the way he had known Betty. She was an orphan, so you couldn't approach her old man. He supposed that the only thing to do was to bring the subject up a little at a time and see how she reacted.

He asked: 'Mathaswentha, my dear, when you spoke of the kind of man you'd like to marry, did you have any other specifications in mind?'

She smiled at him, whereat the room swam slightly. 'Curious, Martinus? I didn't have many, aside from those I mentioned. Of course he shouldn't be *too* much older than I, as Wittigis was.'

'You wouldn't mind if he wasn't much taller than you?'

'No, unless he were a mere shrimp.'

'You haven't any objections to large noses?'

She laughed a rich, throaty laugh. 'Martinus, you *are* the funniest man. I suppose it's that you and I are different. I go directly for what I want, whether it's love, or revenge, or anything else.'

'What do I do?'

'You walk all around it, and peer at it from every angle, and spend a week figuring out whether you want it badly enough to risk taking it.' She added quickly. 'Don't think I mind. I like you for it.'

'I'm glad of that. But about noses —'

'Of *course* I don't mind! I think yours, for instance, is artistocratic-looking. Nor do I mind little red beards or wavy brown hair or any of the other features of an amazing young man named Martinus Paduei. That's what you were getting at, wasn't it?'

Padway knew a great relief. This marvelous woman went out of her way to ease your difficulties! 'As a matter of fact it was, princess.'

'You needn't be so frightfully respectful, Martinus. Anybody would know you are a foreigner, the way you meticulously use all the proper titles and epithets.'

Padway grinned. 'I don't like to take chances, as you know. Well, you see, now, it's this way. I – uh – was wondering – uh – if you don't dislike these – uh – characteristics, whether you couldn't learn to – uh – uh —'

'You don't by any chance mean love, do you?'

'Yes!' said Padway loudly.

'With practice I might.'

'*Whew!*' said Padway mopping his forehead.

'I'd need teaching,' said Mathaswentha. 'I've lived a sheltered life, and know little of the world.'

'I looked up the law,' said Padway quickly, 'and while there's an ordinance against marriage of Goths to Italians, there's nothing about Americans. So —'

Mathaswentha interrupted: 'I could hear you better, dear Martinus, if you came closer.'

Padway went over and sat down beside her. He began again: 'The Edicts of Theoderik —'

She said softly: 'I know the laws, Martinus. That is not what I need instruction in.'

Padway suppressed his tendency to talk frantically of impersonal matters to cover emotional turmoil. He said, 'My love, your first lesson will be this.' He kissed her hand.

Her eyes were half closed, her mouth slightly open, and her breath was quick and shallow. She whispered: 'Do the Americans, then, practice the art of kissing as we do?'

He gathered her in and applied the second lesson.

Mathaswentha opened her eyes, blinked, and shook her head. 'That was a foolish question, my dear Martinus. The Americans are way ahead of us. What ideas you put in an innocent girl's head!' She laughed joyfully. Padway laughed too.

Padway said: 'You've made me very happy, princess.'

'You've made me happy, too, my prince. I thought I should never find anyone like you.' She swayed into his arms again.

Mathaswentha sat up and straightened her hair. She said in a brisk, businesslike manner: 'There are a lot of questions to settle before we decide anything finally. Wittigis, for instance.'

'What about him?' Padway's happiness suddenly wasn't quite so complete.'

'He'll have to be killed, naturally.'

'Oh?'

'Don't 'oh' me, my dear. I warned you that I am no halfhearted hater. And Thiudahad, too.'

'Why him?'

She straightened up, frowning. 'He murdered my mother, didn't he? What more reason do you want? And eventually you will want to become king yourself —'

'No, I won't,' said Padway.

'Not want to be king? Why, Martinus!'

'Not for me, my dear. Anyhow, I'm not an Amaling.'

'As my husband you will be considered one.'

'I still don't want —'

'Now, darling, you just *think* you don't. You will change your mind. While we are about it, there is that former serving-wench of yours, Julia I think her name is —'

'What about – what do you know about her?'

'Enough. We women hear everything sooner or later.'

The little cold spot in Padway's stomach spread and spread. 'But – but —'

'Now, Martinus, it's a small favor that your betrothed is asking. And don't think that a person like me would be jealous of a mere house-servant. But it would be a humiliation to me if she were living after our marriage. It needn't be a painful death – some quick poison ...'

Padway's face turned as blank as that of a renting agent at the mention of cockroaches. His mind was whirling. There seemed to be no end to Mathaswentha's lethal little plans. His underwear was damp with cold sweat.

He knew now that he was not in the least in love with Mathaswentha. Let some roaring Goth have this fierce blond Valkyr! He preferred a girl with less direct ideas of getting what she wanted. And no insurance man would give a policy on a member of the Amal clan, considering their dark and bloody past.

'Well?' said Mathaswentha.

He was thinking, frantically, how to get out of this fix.

'I just remembered,' he said slowly, 'I have a wife back in America.'

'Oh. A fine time to think of *that*,' she answered coldly.

'I haven't seen her for a long time.'

'Well, then, there's a divorce, isn't there?'

'Not in my religion. We Congregationalists believe there's a special compartment in hell for frying divorced persons.'

'Martinus!' Her eyes were a pair of gray blow-torches. 'You're trying to back out. No man shall ever do that to me and live to tell —'

'No, no, not at all!' cried Padway. 'Nothing of the sort, my dear! I'd wade through rivers of blood to reach your side.'

'*Hmmm.* A very pretty speech, Martinus Paduei. Do you use it on all the girls?'

'I mean it. I'm mad about you.'

'Then why don't you act as if —'

'I'm devoted to you. It was stupid of me not to think of this obstacle sooner.'

'Do you really love me?' She softened a little.

'Of course I do! I've never known anyone like you.' The last sentence was truthful. 'But facts are facts.'

Mathaswentha rubbed her forehead, obviously struggling with conflicting emotions. She asked: 'If you haven't seen her for so long, how do you know she's alive?'

'I don't. But I don't know that she isn't. You know how strict your laws are about bigamy. Edicts of Atha-larik, Paragraph Six. I looked it up.'

'You would,' she said with some bitterness. 'Does anyone else in Italy know about this American bitch of yours?'

'N-no – but —'

'Then aren't you being a bit silly, Martinus? What difference does it make, if she's on the other side of the earth?'

'Religion.'

'Oh, the devil fly away with the priests! I'll handle the Arians when we're in power. For the Catholics, you have influence with the Bishop of Bologna, I hear, and that means with the Pope.'

'I don't mean the churches. I mean my personal convictions.'

'A practical fellow like you? Nonsense. You're using them as an excuse —'

Padway, seeing the fires about to flare up again, interrupted: 'Now, Mathas-wentha, you don't want to start a religious argument, do you? You let my creed alone and I'll say nothing against yours. Oh, I just thought of a solution.'

'What?'

'I'll send a messenger to America to find out whether my wife is still alive.'

'How long will that take?'

'Weeks. Months, perhaps. If you really love me, you won't mind waiting.'

'I'd wait,' she said without enthusiasm. She looked up sharply. 'Suppose your messenger finds the woman alive?'

'We'll worry about that when the time comes.'

'Oh, no, we won't. We'll settle this now.'

'Look, darling, don't you trust your future husband? Then —'

'Don't evade, Martinus. You're as slippery as a Byzantine lawyer.'

'In that case, I suppose I'd take a chance on my immortal —'

'Oh, but, Martinus!' she cried cheerfully. 'How stupid of me not to see the answer before! You shall instruct your messenger, if he finds her alive, to poison her! Such things can always be managed discreetly.'

'That *is* an idea.'

'It's the obvious idea! I'd prefer it to a mere divorce anyway, for the sake of my good name. Now all our worries are over.' She hugged him with discon-certing violence.

'I suppose they are,' said Padway with an utter lack of conviction. 'Let's continue our lessons, dearest.' He kissed her again, trying for a record this time.

She smiled up at him and sighed happily. 'You shall never kiss anyone else, my love.'

'I wouldn't think of it, princess.'

'You'd better not,' she said 'You will forgive me, dear boy, for getting a little upset just now. I am but an innocent young girl, with no knowledge of the world and no will of her own.'

At least, thought Padway, he was not the only liar present. He stood up and pulled her to her feet. 'I must go now. I'll send the messenger off the first thing. And tomorrow I leave for Rome.'

'Oh, Martinus! You surely don't have to go. You just *think* you do —'

'No, really. State business, you know. I'll think of you all the way.' He kissed her again. 'Be brave, my dear. Smile, now.'

She smiled a trifle tearfully and squeezed the breath out of him.

When Padway got back to his quarters, he hauled his orderly, an Arme-nian cuirassier, out of bed. 'Put on your right boot,' he ordered.

The man rubbed his eyes. 'My *right* boot? Do I understand you, noble sir?'

'You do. Quickly, now.' When the yellow rawhide boot was on, Padway turned his back to the orderly and bent over. He said over is shoulder, 'You will give me a swift kick in the fundament, my good Tirdat.'

Tirdat's mouth fell open. '*Kick my commander?*'

'You heard me the first time. Go ahead. Now.'

Tirdat shuffled uneasily, but at Padway's glare he finally hauled off and let fly. The kick almost sent Padway sprawling. He straightened up, rubbing the spot. 'Thank you, Tirdat. You may go back to bed.' He started for the wash bowl to brush his teeth with a willow twig. (Must start the manufacture of real toothbrushes one of these days, he thought.) He felt much better.

But Padway did not set off for Rome the next day, or even the day after that. He began to learn that the position of king's quæstor was not just a nice well-paying job that let you order people around and do as you pleased. First Wakkis Thurumund's son, a Gothic noble of the Royal Council, came around with a rough draft of a proposed amendment to the law against horse stealing.

He explained: 'Wittigis agreed to this revision of the law, but the counter-revolution took place before he had a chance to change it. So, excellent Martinus, it's up to you to discuss the matter with Thiudahad, put the amendment in proper legal language, and *try* to hold the king's attention long enough to get his signature.' Wakkis grinned. 'And may the saints help you if he's in a stubborn mood, my lad!'

Padway wondered what the devil to do; then he dug up Cassiodorus, who as head of the Italian Civil Service ought to know the ropes. The old scholar proved a great help, though Padway saw fit to edit some of the unnecessarily flowery phrases of the prefect's draft.

He asked Urias around for lunch. Urias came and was friendly enough, though still somewhat bitter about the treatment of his uncle Wittigis. Padway liked him. He thought, I can't hold out on Mathaswentha indefinitely. And I shan't dare take up with another girl while she looks on me as a suitor. But this fellow is big and good-looking, and he seems intelligent. If I could engineer a match—

He asked Urias whether he was married. Urias raised eyebrows. 'No. Why?'

'I just wondered. What do you intend to do with yourself now?'

'I don't know. Go rusticate on my land in Picenum, I suppose. It'll be a dull life, after the soldiering I've been doing the past few years.'

Padway asked casually: 'Have you ever met the Princess Mathaswentha?'

'Not formally. I arrived in Ravenna only a few days ago for the wedding. I saw her in the church, of course, when you barged in. She's attractive, isn't she?'

'Quite so. She's a person worth knowing. If you like, I'll try to arrange a meeting.'

Padway, as soon as Urias had gone, rushed around to Mathaswentha's house. He contrived to make his arrival look as unpremeditated as possible. He started to explain: 'I've been delayed, my dear. I may not get off to Rome *ubb* —' Mathaswentha had slid her arms around his neck and stopped his little speech in the most effective manner. Padway didn't dare seem tepid, but that wasn't at all difficult. The only trouble was that it made coherent thought impossible at a time when he wanted all his craft. And the passionate wench seemed satisfied to stand in the vestibule and kiss him all afternoon.

She finally said: 'Now, what were you saying, my dearest?'

Padway finished his statement. 'So I thought I'd drop in for a moment.' He laughed. 'It's just as well I'm going to Rome; I shall never get any work done as long as I'm in the city with you. Do you know Wittigis' nephew Urias by the way?'

'No. And I'm not sure I want to. When we kill Wittigis, we shall naturally have to consider killing his nephews, too. I have a silly prejudice against murdering people I know socially.'

'Oh, my dear, I think that's a mistake. He's a splendid young man; you'd really like him. He's one Goth with both brains and character; probably the only one.'

'Well, I don't know —'

'And I need him in my business, only he's got scruples against working for me. I thought maybe you could work your flashing smile on him, to soften him up a bit.'

'If you think I could really help you, perhaps —'

Thus the Gothic princess had Padway and Urias for company at dinner that night. Mathaswentha was pretty cool to Urias at first. But they drank a good deal of wine, and she unbent. Urias was good company. Presently they were all laughing uproariously at his imitation of a drunken Hun, and at Padway's hastily translated off-color stories. Padway taught the other two a Greek popular song that Tirdat, his orderly, had brought from Constantinople. If Padway hadn't been conscious of a small gnawing anxiety for the success of his various plots, he'd have said he was having the best time of his life.

CHAPTER XIII

Back in Rome, Padway went to see his captive Imperial generals. They were comfortably housed and seemed well enough pleased with their situation, though Belisarius was moody and abstracted. Enforced inactivity didn't sit well with the former commander-in-chief.

Padway asked him: 'As you can learn easily enough, we shall soon have a powerful state here. Have you changed your mind about joining us?'

'No, my lord quæstor, I have not. An oath is an oath.'

'Have you ever broken an oath in your life?'

'Not to my knowledge.'

'If for any reason you should swear an oath to me, I suppose, you'd consider yourself as firmly bound by it as by the others, wouldn't you?'

'Naturally. But that's a ridiculous supposition.'

'Perhaps. How would it be if I offered you parole and transportation back to Constantinople, on condition that you would never again bear arms against the kingdom of the Goths and Italians?'

'You're a crafty and resourceful man, Martinus. I thank you for the offer, but I couldn't square it with my oath to Justinian. Therefore I must decline.'

Padway repeated his offer to the other generals. Constantianus, Perianus, and Bessas accepted at once. Padway's reasoning was as follows: these three were just fair-to-middling commanders. Justinian could get plenty more of this kind, so there was not much point in keeping them. Of course they'd violate their oaths as soon as they were out of his reach. But Belisarius was a real military genius; he mustn't be allowed to fight against the kingdom again. Either he'd have to come over, or give his parole – which he alone would keep – or be kept in detention.

On the other hand, Justinian's clever but slightly warped mind was unreasonably jealous of Belisarius' success and his somewhat stuffy virtue. When he learned that Belisarius had stayed behind in Rome rather than give a parole that he'd be expected to break, the emperor *might* be sufficiently annoyed to do something interesting.

Padway wrote:

King Thiudahad to the Emperor Justinian, Greetings.
Your serene highness: We send you with this letter the persons of your generals Constantianus, Perianus, and Bessas, under parole not to bear

arms against us again, A similar parole was offered your general Belisarius, but he declined to accept it on grounds of his personal honor.

As continuation of this war seems unlikely to achieve any constructive result, we take the opportunity of stating the terms that we should consider reasonable for the establishment of enduring peace between us.

1. Imperial troops shall evacuate Sicily and Dalmatia forthwith.
2. An indemnity of one hundred thousand solidi in gold shall be paid us for damages done by your invading armies.
3. We shall agree never again to make war, one upon the other, without mutual consultation in advance. Details can be settled in due course.
4. We shall agree not to assist any third parties, by men, money, or munitions, which hereafter shall make war upon either of us.
5. We shall agree upon a commercial treaty to facilitate the exchange of goods between our respective realms.

This is of course a very rough outline, details of which would have to be settled by conference between our representatives. We think you will agree that these terms, or others very similar in intent, are the least that we could reasonably ask under the circumstances.

We shall anticipate the gracious favor of a reply at your serenity's earliest convenience.

by MARTINUS PADUEI, Quæstor

When he saw who his visitor was, Thomasus got up with a grunt and waddled toward him, good eye sparkling and hand outstretched. 'Martinus! It's good to see you again. How does it feel to be important?'

'Wearisome,' said Padway, shaking hands vigorously. 'What's the news?'

'News? News? Listen to that! He's been making most of the news in Italy for the past two months, and he wants to know what the news is!'

'I mean about our little bird in a cage.'

'Huh? Oh, you mean' – Thomasus looked around cautiously – 'ex-King Wittigis? He was doing fine at last reports, though nobody's been able to get a civil word out of him. Listen, Martinus, of all the lousy tricks I ever heard of, springing the job of hiding him on me without warning was the worst. I'm sure God agrees with me, too. Those soldiers dragged me out of bed, and then I had them and their prisoner around the house for several days.'

'I'm sorry, Thomasus. But you were the only man in Rome I felt I could trust absolutely.'

'Oh, well, if you put it that way. But Wittigis was the worst grouch I ever saw. Nothing suited him.'

'How's the telegraph company coming?'

'That's another thing. The Naples line is working regularly. But the lines to Ravenna and Florence won't be finished for a month, and until they are there's no chance of a profit. *And* the minority stockholders have discovered that they're a minority. You should have heard them howl! They're after your blood. At first Count Honorius was with them. He threatened to jail Vardan and Ebenezer and me if we didn't sell him – give him, practically – a controlling interest. But we learned he needed money worse than he needed the stock, and bought his from him. So the other patricians have to be satisfied with snubbing us when they pass us in the street.'

'I'm going to start another paper as soon as I get time,' said Padway. 'There'll be two, one in Rome and one in Florence.'

'Why one in Florence?'

'That's where our new capital's going to be.'

'*What?*'

'Yes. It's better located than Rome with regard to roads and such, and it has a much better climate than Ravenna. In fact I can't think of a place that *hasn't* a better climate than Ravenna, hell included. I sold the idea to Cassiodorus, and between us we got Thiudahad to agree to move the administrative offices thither. If Thiudahad wants to hold court in the City of Fogs, Bogs, and Frogs, that's his lookout. I'll be just as glad not to have him in my hair.'

'In your hair? Oh, ho-ho-ho, you *are the* funniest fellow, Martinus. I wish I could say things the way you do. But all this activity takes my breath away. What else of revolutionary nature are you planning?'

'I'm going to try to start a school. We have a flock of teachers on the public payroll now, but all they know is grammar and rhetoric. I'm going to have things taught that really matter: mathematics, and the sciences, and medicine. I see where I shall have to write all the textbooks myself.'

'Just one question, Martinus. When do you find time to sleep?'

Padway grinned wanly. 'Mostly I don't. But if I can ever get out of all this political and military activity, I hope to catch up. I don't really like it, but it's a necessary means to an end. The end is things like the telegraph and the presses. My politicking and soldiering may not make any difference a hundred years from now, but the other things will, I hope.'

Padway started to go, then said: 'Is Julia from Apulia still working for Ebenezer the Jew?'

'The last I heard she was. Why? Do you want her back?'

'God forbid. She's got to disappear from Rome.'

'Why?'

'For her own safety. I can't tell you about it yet.'

'But I thought you disliked her —'

'That doesn't mean I want her murdered. And my own hide may be in danger, too, unless we get her out of town.'

'Oh, God, why didst Thou let me get involved with a politician? I don't know, Martinus; she's a free citizen ...'

'How about your cousin in Naples, Antiochus? I'd make it worth his while to hire her at higher wages.'

'Well, I —'

'Have her go to work for Antiochus under another name. Fix it up quietly, old man. If the news leaks out, we'll all be in the soup.'

'Soup? Ha, ha. Very funny. I'll do what I can. Now, about that old six-month note of yours ...'

Oh, dear, thought Padway, now it would begin again. Thomasus was easy enough to get on with most of the time. But he could not or would not conduct the simplest financial transactions without three hours of frantic haggling. Perhaps he enjoyed it. Padway did not.

Jogging along the road to Florence again, Padway regretted that he had not seen Dorothea while he was in Rome. He had not dared. That was one more reason for getting Mathaswentha married off quickly. Dorothea would be a much more suitable if less spectacular girl for *him*. Not that he was in love with her. Though he probably would be if he saw enough of her, he thought somewhat cold-bloodedly.

He had too much else to do now. If he could only get time to relax, to catch up on his sleep, to investigate the things that really interested him, to have a little fun! He liked fun as much as the next man, even if the next man would consider his ideas of fun peculiar.

But his sharp, conscientious mind goaded him on. He knew that his job rested on the unstable foundation of his influence over a senile, unpopular king. As long as Padway pleased them, the Goths would not interfere, as they were accustomed to leaving civil administration in the hands of non-Goths. But when Thiudahad went? Padway had lots of hay to gather, and there were plenty of thunderheads forming over the barn.

In Florence Padway leased office space in the name of the government, and looked in on his own business. This time there were no irregularities in the accounts. Either there had been no more stealing, or the boys were getting cleverer at concealing it.

Fritharik renewed his plea to be allowed to come along, showing with much pride his jeweled sword, which he had redeemed and sent up from Rome. The sword disappointed Padway, though he did not say so. The gems were merely polished, not cut; faceting had not been invented. But wearing it seemed to add inches to Fritharik's already imposing stature. Padway, somewhat against his better judgment, gave in. He appointed the competent and apparently honest Nerva his general manager.

They were snowed in by a late storm for two days crossing the mountains, and arrived in Ravenna still shivering. The town with its clammy atmosphere and its currents of intrigue depressed him, and the Mathaswentha problem made him nervous. He called on her and made some insincere love to her, and grew all the more anxious to get away. But there was lots of public business to be handled.

Urias announced that he was ready and willing to enter Padway's service. 'Mathaswentha talked me into it,' he said. 'She's a wonderful woman, isn't she?'

'Certainly is,' replied Padway. He thought he detected a faintly guilty and furtive air about the straightforward Urias when he spoke of the princess. He smiled to himself. 'What I had in mind was setting up a regular military school for the Gothic officers, somewhat on the Byzantine model, with you in charge.'

'What? Oh, my word, I hoped you'd have a command on the frontiers for me.'

So, thought Padway, he wasn't the only one who disliked Ravenna. 'No, my dear sir. This job has to be done for the sake of the kingdom. And I can't do it myself, because the Goths don't think any non-Goth knows anything about soldiering. On the other hand, I need a literate and intelligent man to run the school, and you're the only one in sight.'

'But, most excellent Martinus, have you ever tried to teach a Gothic officer anything? I admit that an academy is needed, but —'

'I know. I know. Most of them can't read or write and look down on those who do. That's why I picked *you* for the job. You're respected, and if anybody can put sense into their heads you can.' He grinned sympathetically. 'I wouldn't have tried so hard to enlist your services if I'd had just an easy, everyday job in mind.'

'Thanks. I see you know how to get people to do things for you.'

Padway went on to tell Urias some of his ideas. How the Goths' great weakness was the lack of coordination between their mounted lancers and their foot archers; how they needed both reliable foot spearmen and mounted archers to have a well-rounded force. He also described the crossbow, the calthorp, and other military devices.

He said: 'It takes five years to make a good longbowman, whereas a recruit can learn to handle a crossbow in a few weeks.

'And if I can get some good steel workers. I'll show you a suit of plate armor that weighs only half as much as one of those scale-mail shirts, but gives better protection and allows fully as much freedom of action.' He grinned. 'You may expect grumbling at all these newfangled ideas from the more conservative Goths. So you'd better introduce them gradually. And remember, they're your ideas; I won't try to deprive you of the credit for them.'

'I understand,' grinned Urias. 'So if anybody gets hanged for them, it'll be me and not you. Like that book on astronomy that came out in Thiudahad's name. It has every churchman from here to Persia sizzling. Poor old Thiuda-had gets the blame, but I know you furnished the ideas and put him up to it. Very well, my mysterious friend, I'm game.'

Padway himself was surprised when Urias appeared with a very respectable crossbow a few days later. Although the device was simple enough, and he'd furnished an adequate set of drawings for it, he knew from sad experience that to get a sixth-century artisan to make something he'd never seen before, you had to stand over him while he botched six attempts, and then make it yourself.

They spent an afternoon in the great pine wood east of the city shooting at marks. Fritharik proved uncannily accurate, though he affected to despise missile weapons as unworthy of a noble Vandal knight. 'But,' he said, 'it is a remarkably easy thing to aim.'

'Yes,' replied Padway. 'Among my people there's a legend about a crossbow-man who offended a government official, and was compelled as punishment to shoot an apple off his son's head. He did so, without harming the boy.'

When he got back, Padway learned that he had an appointment the next day with an envoy from the Franks. The envoy, one count Hlodovik, was a tall, lantern-jawed man. Like most Franks he was cleanshaven except for the mustache. He was quite gorgeous in a red silk tunic, gold chains and bracelets, and a jeweled baldric. Padway privately thought that the knobby bare legs below his short pants detracted from his impressiveness. Moreover, Hlodovik was rather obviously suffering from a hangover. 'Mother of God, I'm thirsty,' he said. 'Will you please do something about that, friend quæstor, before we discuss business?' So Padway had some wine sent in. Hlodovik drank in deep gulps. 'Ah! That's better. Now, friend quæstor, I may say that I don't think I've been very well treated here. The king would only see me for a wink of the eye; said you handle the business. Is that the proper reception for the envoy of King Theudebert, King Hildebert, and King Hlotokar? Not just *one* king, mind you; *three*.'

'That's a lot of kings,' said Padway, smiling pleasantly. 'I am greatly impressed. But you mustn't take offense, my lord count. Our king is an old man, and he finds the press of public business hard to bear.'

'So, *hrrmp*. We'll forget about it, then. But we shall not find the reason for my coming hither so easy to forget. Briefly, what became of that hundred and fifty thousand solidi that Wittigis promised my masters, King Theudebert, King Hildebert, and King Hlotokar if they wouldn't attack him while he was involved with me Greeks? Moreover, he ceded Provence to my masters, King Theudebert, King Hildebert, and King Hlotokar. Yet your general Sisigis has not evacuated Provence. When my masters sent a force to occupy it a few weeks ago, they were driven back and several were killed. You should know that the Franks, who are the bravest and proudest people on earth, will never submit to such treatment. What are you going to do about it?'

Padway answered: '*You*, my lord Hlodovik, should know that the acts of an unsuccessful usurper cannot bind the legitimate government. We intend to hold what we have. So you may inform your masters, King Theudebert, King Hildebert, and King Hlotokar, that there will be no payment and no evacuation.'

'Do you really mean that?' Hlodovik seemed astonished. 'Don't you know, young man, that the armies of the Franks could sweep the length of Italy, burning and ravaging, any time they wished? My masters, King Theudebert, King Hildebert, and King Hlotokar, are showing great forbearance and humanity by offering you a way out. Think carefully before you invite disaster.'

'I have thought, my lord,' replied Padway. 'And I respectfully suggest that you and your masters do the same. Especially about a little military device that we are introducing. Would you like to see it demonstrated? The parade ground is only a step from here.'

Padway had made the proper preparations in advance. When they arrived at the parade ground, Hlodovik weaving slightly all the way, they found Urias, Fritharik, the crossbow, and a supply of bolts. Padway's idea was to have Fritharik take a few demonstration shots at a target. But Fritharik and Urias had other ideas. The latter walked off fifty feet, turned, and placed an apple on his head. Fritharik cocked the crossbow, put a bolt in the groove, and raised the bow to his shoulder.

Padway was frozen speechless with horror. He didn't dare shout at the two idiots to desist for fear of losing face before the Frank. Yet if Urias was killed, he hated to think of the damage that would be done to his plans.

The crossbow snapped. There was a short *splash*, and fragments of apple flew about. Urias, grinning, picked pieces of apple out of his hair and walked back.

'Do you find the demonstration impressive, my lord?' Padway asked.

'Yes, quite,' said Hlodovik. 'Let's see that device. *Hm-m-m*. Of course, the brave Franks don't believe that any battle was ever won by a lot of silly arrows. But for hunting, now, this mightn't be bad. How does it work? I see; you pull the string back to here —'

While Fritharik was demonstrating the crossbow, Padway took Urias aside and told him, in a low tone, just what he thought of such a fool stunt. Urias tried to look serious, but couldn't help a faint, small-boy grin. Then there was another snap, and something whizzed between them, not a foot from Padway's face. They jumped and spun around. Hlodovik was holding the crossbow, a foolish look on his long face. 'I didn't know it went off so easily,' he said.

Fritharik lost his temper. 'What are you trying to do, you drunken fool? Kill somebody?'

'What's that? *You* call me a fool? Why —' and the Frank's sword came halfway out of the scabbard.

Fritharik jumped back and grabbed his own sword hilt. Padway and Urias pounced on the two and held their elbows.

'Calm yourself, my lord!' cried Padway. 'It's nothing to start a fight over. I'll apologize personally.'

The Frank merely got angrier and tried to shake off Padway. 'I'll teach that low-born bastard! My honor is insulted!' he shouted. Several Gothic soldiers loafing around the field looked up and trotted over. Hlodovik saw them coming and sheathed his sword, growling: 'This is fine treatment for the representatives of King Theudebert, King Hildebert, and King Hlotokar. Just wait till they hear of this.'

Padway tried to mollify him, but Hlodovik merely grumped, and soon left Ravenna. Padway dispatched a warning to Sisigis to be on the lookout for a Frankish attack. His conscience bothered him a good deal. In a way he thought he ought to have tried to appease the Franks, as he hated the idea of being responsible for war. But he knew that such a fierce and treacherous tribe would only take each concession as a sign of weakness.

Then another envoy arrived, this time from the Kutrigurs or Bulgarian Huns. The usher told Padway: 'He's very dignified; doesn't speak any Latin or Gothic, so he uses an interpreter. Says he's a boyar, whatever that is.'

'Show him in.'

The Bulgarian envoy was a stocky, bowlegged man with high cheek bones, a fiercely upswept mustache, and a nose even bigger than Padway's, He wore a handsome furlined coat, baggy trousers, and a silk turban wound about his shaven skull, from the rear of which two black pigtails jutted absurdly. Despite the finery, Padway found reason to suspect that the man had never had a bath in his life. The interpreter was a small, nervous Thracian who hovered a pace to the Bulgar's left and rear.

The Bulgar clumped in, bowed stiffly, and did not offer to shake hands. Probably not done among the Huns, thought Padway. He bowed back and indicated a chair. He regretted having done so a moment later, when the Bulgar hiked his boots up on the upholstery and sat cross-legged. Then he began to speak, in a strangely musical tongue which Padway surmised was related to Turkish. He stopped every three or four words for the interpreter to translate. It ran something like this:

Envoy: (Twitter, twitter.)
Interpreter: I am the Boyar Karojan—
Envoy: (Twitter, twitter.)
Interpreter: The son of Chakir—
Envoy: (Twitter, twitter.)
Interpreter. Who was the son of Tardu—

Envoy: (Twitter, twitter.)
Interpreter: Envoy of Kardam—
Envoy: (Twitter, twitter.)
Interpreter: The son of Kapagan—
Envoy: (Twitter, twitter.)
Interpreter: And Great Khan of the Kutrigurs.

It was distracting to listen to, but not without a certain poetic grandeur. The Bulgar paused impassively at that point. Padway identified himself, and the duo began again:
'My master, the Great Khan —'
'Has received an offer from Justinian, Emperor of the Romans —'
'Of fifty thousand solidi —'
'To refrain from invading his dominions.'
'If Thiudahad, King of the Goths —'
'Will make us a better offer —'
'We will ravage Thrace —'
'And leave the Gothic realm alone.'
'If he does not —'
'We will take Justinian's gold —'
'And invade the Gothic territories —'
'Of Pannonia and Noricum.'
Padway cleared his throat and began his reply, pausing for translation. This method had its advantages, he found. It gave him time to think.
'My master, Thiudahad, King of the Goths and Italians —'
'Authorizes me to say —'
'That he has better use for his money —'
'Than to bribe people not to attack him —'
'And that if the Kutrigurs think —'
'That they can invade our territory —'
'They are welcome to try —'
'But that we cannot guarantee them —'
'A very hospitable reception.'
The envoy replied:
'Think man, on what you say.'
'For the armies of the Kutrigurs —'
'Cover the Sarmatian steppe like locusts.'
'The hoofbeats of their horses —'
'Are a mighty thunder.'
'The flight of their arrows —'
'Darkens the sun.'
'Where they have passed —'

'Not even grass will grow.'

Padway replied:

'Most excellent Karojan —'

'What you say may be true.'

'But in spite of their thundering and sundarkening —'

'The last time the Kutrigurs —'

'Assailed our land, a few years ago —'

'They got the pants beat off them.'

As this was translated, the Bulgar looked puzzled for a moment. Then he turned red. Padway thought he was angry, but it soon appeared that he was trying to keep from laughing. He said between sputters:

'This time, man, it will be different.'

'If any pants are lost —'

'They will be yours.'

'How would this be?'

'You pay us sixty thousand —'

'In three installments —'

'Of twenty thousand each?'

But Padway was immovable. The Bulgar finished:

'I shall inform my master —'

'Kardam, the Great Khan of the Kutrigurs —'

'Of your obduracy.'

'For a reasonable bribe —'

'I am prepared to tell him —'

'Of the might of the Gothic arms —'

'In terms that shall dissuade him —'

'From his projected invasion.'

Padway beat the Bulgar down to half the bribe he originally asked, and they parted on the best of terms. When he went around to his quarters, he found Fritharik trying to wind a towel around his head.

The Vandal looked up with guilty embarrassment. 'I was trying, excellent boss, to make a headgear like that of the Hunnish gentleman. It has style.'

Padway had long since decided that Thiudahad was a pathological case. But lately the little king was showing more definite signs of mental failure. For instance, when Padway went to see about a new inheritance law, Thiudahad gravely listened to him explain the reasons that the Royal Council and Cassiodorus had agreed upon bringing the Gothic law more into line with the Roman.

Then he said: 'When are you going to put out another book in my name, Martinus? Your name *is* Martinus, isn't it? Martinus Paduei, Martinus Paduei. Didn't I appoint you prefect or something? Dear me, I can't seem to remember anything. Now, what's this you want to see me about? Always business, business, business. I hate business. Scholarship is more important. Silly state papers. What is it, an order for an execution? I hope you're going to torture the rascal as he deserves. I can't understand this absurd prejudice of yours against torture. The people aren't happy unless they're terrified of their government. Let's see, what was I talking about?'

It was convenient in one way, as Thiudahad didn't bother him much. But it was awkward when the king simply refused to listen to him or to sign anything for a day at a time.

Then he found himself in a hot dispute with the paymaster-general of the Gothic army. The latter refused to put the Imperialist mercenaries whom Padway had captured on the rolls. Padway argued that the men were first-rate soldiers who seemed glad enough to serve the Italo-Gothic state, and that it would cost little more to enlist them than to continue to feed them as prisoners. The paymaster-general replied that national defense had been a prerogative of the Goths since the time of Theoderik, and the men in question were not, with some few exceptions, Goths. Q.E.D.

Each stubbornly maintained his point, so the dispute was carried to Thiudahad. The king listened to the argument with a specious air of wisdom.

Then he sent the paymaster-general away and told Padway: 'Lots to be said on both sides, dear sir, lots to be said on both sides: Now, if I decide in your favor, I shall expect a suitable command for my son, Thiudegiskel.'

Padway was horrified, though he tried not to show it. 'But, my lord king, what military experience has Thiudegiskel had?'

'None; that's just the trouble. Spends all his time drinking and wenching with his wild young friends. He needs a bit of responsibility. Something good, consistent with the dignity of his birth.'

Padway argued some more. But he didn't say that he couldn't imagine a worse commander than this self-conceited and arrogant puppy. Thiudahad was obstinate. 'After all, Martinus, I'm king, am I not? You can't browbeat me and you can't frighten me with your Wittigis. Heh, heh. I'll have a surprise for you one of these days. What was I talking about? Oh, yes. You do, I think, owe Thiudegiskel something for putting him in that horrid prison camp —'

'But *I* didn't put him in jail —'

'Don't interrupt, Martinus. It isn't considerate. Either you give him a command, or I decide in favor of the other man, what's-his-name. That is my final royal word.'

So Padway gave in. Thiudegiskel was put in command of the Gothic forces in Calabria, where, Padway hoped, he wouldn't be able to do much harm. Later he had occasion to remember that hope.

Padway may seem rash to have incorporated such an alien element as the ex-Imperialists in the Italo-Gothic army. But in this age there was no such thing as nationalism in the modern sense. The ties that counted were those of religion and personal loyalty to a commander. Many of the Imperialists were Thracian Goths who had remained in the Balkans at the time of the migration under Theoderik. And some Italian Goths had served the Empire as mercenaries. They mixed with little prejudice on either side.

Then three things happened. General Sisigis sent word of suspicious activity among the Franks.

Padway got a letter from Thomasus, which told of an attempt on the life of ex-King Wittigis. The assassin had inexplicably sneaked into the dugout, where Wittigis, though slightly wounded in the process, had killed him with his bare hands. Nobody knew who the assassin was until Wittigis had declared, with many a bloodcurdling curse, that he recognized the man as an old-time secret agent of Thiudahad. Padway knew what that meant. Thiudahad had discovered Wittigis' whereabouts, and meant to put his rival out of the way. If he succeeded, he'd be prepared to defy Padway's management, or even to heave him out of his office. Or worse.

Finally Padway got a letter from Justinian. It read:

Flavius Anicius Justinian, Emperor of the Romans, to King Thiudahad, Greetings.

Our serenity's attention has been called to the terms which you propose for termination of the war between us.

We find these terms so absurd and unreasonable that our deigning to reply at all is an act of great condescension on our part. Our holy endeavor to recover for the Empire the provinces of western Europe, which belonged to our forebears and rightfully belong to us, will be carried through to a victorious conclusion.

As for our former general, Flavius Belisarius, his refusal of parole is an act of gross disloyalty, which we shall fittingly punish in due course. Meanwhile the illustrious Belisarius may consider himself free of all obligations to us. Nay more, we order him to place himself unreservedly under the orders of that infamous heretic and agent of the Evil One who calls himself Martinus of Padua, of whom we have heard.

We are confident that, between the incompetence and cowardice of Belisarius and the heavenly wrath that will attach to those who submit to the unclean touch of the diabolical Martinus, the doom of the Gothic kingdom will not be long delayed.

Padway realized, with a slightly sick feeling, that he had a lot to learn about diplomacy. His defiance of Justinian, and of the Frankish kings, and of the Bulgars, had each been justified, considered by itself. But he shouldn't have committed himself to taking them on all at once.

The thunderheads were piling up fast.

CHAPTER XIV

Padway dashed back to Rome and showed Justinian's letter to Belisarius. He thought he had seldom seen a more unhappy man than the stalwart Thracian.

'I don't know,' was all Belisarius would say in answer to his questions. 'I shall have to think.'

Padway got an interview with Belisarius' wife, Antonina. He got along fine with this slim, vigorous redhead.

She said: 'I told him repeatedly that he'd get nothing but ingratitude from Justinian. But you know how he is – reasonable about everything except what concerns his honor. The only thing that would make me hesitate is my friendship with the Empress Theodora. That's not a connection to be thrown over lightly. But after this letter – I'll do what I can, excellent Martinus.'

Belisarius, to Padway's unconcealed delight, finally capitulated.

The immediate danger point seemed to be Provence. Padway's runner-collecting service had gathered a story of another bribe paid by Justinian to the Franks to attack the Goths. So Padway did some shuffling. Asinar, who had sat at Senia for months without the gumption to move against the Imperialists in Spalato, was ordered home, Sisigis, who if no genius was not obviously incompetent, was transferred to command of Asinar's Dalmatian army. And Belisarius was given command of Sisigis' forces in Gaul. Belisarius, before leaving for the North, asked Padway for all the information available about the Franks.

Padway explained: 'Brave, treacherous, and stupid. They have nothing but unarmored infantry, who fight in a single deep column. They come whooping along, hurl a volley of throwing-axes and javelins, and close with the sword. If you can stop them by a line of reliable pikemen, or by cavalry charges, they're suckers for mounted archers. They're very numerous, but such a huge mass of infantry can't forage enough territory to keep themselves fed. So they have to keep moving or starve.

'Moreover, they're so primitive that their soldiers are not paid at all. They're expected to make their living by looting. If you can hold them in one spot long enough, they melt away by desertion. But don't underestimate their numbers and ferocity.

'Try to send agents into Burgundy to rouse the Burgunds against the

Franks, who conquered them only a few years ago.' He explained that the Burgunds were of East-German origin, like the Goths and Lombards, spoke a language much like theirs, and like them were primarily stock-raisers. Hence they did not get on with the West-German Franks, who were agriculturists when they were not devastating their neighbors' territory.

If there was going to be more war, Padway knew one invention that would settle it definitely in the Italo-Goths' favor. Gunpowder was made of sulphur, charcoal, and saltpeter. Padway had learned that in the sixth grade. The first two were available without question.

He supposed that potassium nitrate could be obtained somewhere as a mineral. But he did not know where, or what it would look like. He could not synthesize it with the equipment at hand, even had he known enough chemistry. But he remembered reading that it occurred at the bottom of manure piles. And he remembered an enormous pile in Nevitta's yard.

He called on Nevitta and asked for permission to dig. He whooped with joy when, sure enough, there were the crystals, looking like maple sugar. Nevitta asked him if he was crazy.

'Sure,' grinned Padway. 'Didn't you know? I've been that way for years.'

His old house on Long Street was as full of activity as ever, despite the move to Florence. It was used as Rome headquarters by the Telegraph Company. Padway was having another press set up. And now the remaining space downstairs became a chemical laboratory. Padway did not know what proportions of the three ingredients made good gunpowder, and the only way to find out was by experiment.

He gave orders, in the government's name, for casting and boring a cannon. The brass foundry that took the job was not co-operative. They had never seen such a contraption and were not sure they could make it. What did he want this tube for, a flower pot?

It took them an interminable time to get the pattern and core made, despite the simplicity of the thing. The first one they delivered looked all right, until Padway examined the breach end closely. The metal here was spongy and pitted. The gun would have blown up the first time it was fired.

The trouble was that it had been cast muzzle down. The solution was to add a foot to the length of the barrel, cast it muzzle up, and saw off the last foot of flawed brass.

His efforts to produce gunpowder got nowhere. Lots of proportions of the ingredients would burn beautifully when ignited. But they did not explode. He tried all proportions; he varied his method of mixing. Still all he got was a lively sizzle, a big yellow flame, and a stench. He tried packing the stuff into improvised firecrackers. They went *fuff*. They would not go *bang*.

Perhaps he had to touch off a large quantity at once, more tightly compressed yet. He pestered the foundary daily until the second cannon appeared.

Early next morning he and Fritharik and a couple of helpers mounted the cannon on a crude carriage of planks in a vacant space near the Viminal Gate. The helpers had previously piled up a sandhill for a target, thirty feet from the gun.

Padway rammed several pounds of powder down the barrel, and a cast-iron ball after it. He filled the touch-hole.

He said in a low voice: 'Fritharik, give me that candle. Now get back everybody. Way over there, and lie down. You too, Fritharik.'

'Never!' said Fritharik indignantly. 'Desert my lord in the hour of danger? I should say not!'

'All right, if you want to chance being blown to bits. Here goes.'

Padway touched the candle flame to the touch-hole.

The powder sizzled and sparkled.

The gun went *pfoomp*! The cannonball hopped from the muzzle, thumped to earth a yard away, rolled another yard, and stopped.

Back went the beautiful shiny new gun to Padway's house, to be put in the cellar with the clock.

In the early spring, Urias appeared in Rome. He explained that he'd left the military academy in the hands of subordinates, and was coming down to see about raising a military force of Romans, which had been another of Padway's ideas. But he had an unhappy, hangdog air that made Padway suspect that that wasn't the real reason.

To Padway's leading questions he finally burst out: 'Excellent Martinus, you'll simply have to give me a command somewhere away from Ravenna. I can't stand it any longer.'

Padway put his arm around Urias' shoulders. 'Come on, old man, tell me what is bothering you. Maybe I can help.'

Urias looked at the ground. 'Uh ... well ... that is – Look here, just what *is* the arrangement between you and Mathaswentha?'

'I thought that was it. You've been seeing her, haven't you?'

'Yes, I have. And if you send me back there, I shall see her some more in spite of myself. Are you and she betrothed, or what?'

'I did have some such idea once.' Padway put on the air of one about to make a great sacrifice. 'But, my friend, I wouldn't stand in the way of anybody's happiness. I'm sure you're much better suited to her than I. My work keeps me too busy to make a good husband. So if you want to sue for her hand, go to it, with my blessing.'

'You *mean* that?' Urias jumped up and began pacing the floor, fairly beaming. 'I … I don't know now to thank you … it's the greatest thing you could do for me … I'm your friend for life —'

'Don't mention it; I'm glad to help you out. But now that you're down here, you might as well finish the job you came to do.'

'Oh,' said Urias soberly. 'I suppose I ought to, at that. But how shall I press my suit, then?'

'Write her.'

'But how can I? I don't know the pretty phrases. In fact, I've never written a love letter in my life.'

'I'll help you out with that, too. Here, we can start right now.' Padway got out writing materials, and they were presently concocting a letter to the princess. 'Let's see,' said Padway reflectively, 'we ought to tell her what her eyes are like.'

'They're just like eyes, aren't they?'

'Of course, but in this business you compare them to the stars and things.'

Urias thought. 'They're about the color of a glacier I once saw in the alps.'

'No, that wouldn't do. It would imply that they were as cold as ice.'

'They also remind you of a polished sword blade.'

'Similar objection. How about the northern seas?'

'*Hm-m-m.* Yes, I think that would do, Martinus. Gray as the northern seas.'

'It has a fine poetic ring to it.'

'So it has. Northern seas it shall be, then.' Urias wrote slowly and awkwardly.

Padway said: 'Hey, don't bear down so hard with that pen. You'll poke a hole in the paper.'

As Urias was finishing the letter, Padway clapped on his hat and made for the door.

'*Hai,*' said Urias, 'what's your hurry?'

Padway grinned. 'I'm just going to see some friends; a family named Anicius. Nice people. I'll introduce you to them some day when you're safely sewed up.'

Padway's original idea had been to introduce a mild form of selective conscription, beginning with the city of Rome and requiring the draftees to report for weekly drill. The Senate, which at this time was a mere municipal council, balked. Some of them disliked or distrusted Padway. Some wanted to be bribed.

Padway did not want to give in to them until he had tried everything else. He had Urias announce drills on a voluntary basis, at current wages. Results were disappointing.

Padway's thoughts were abruptly snatched from the remilitarization of the Italians when Junianus came in with a telegraph message. It read simply:

WITTIGIS ESCAPED FROM DETENTION LAST NIGHT. NO TRACE OF
HIM HAS BEEN FOUND.

(SIGNED)

ATURPAD THE PERSIAN,

COMMANDING

For a minute Padway simply stared at the message. Then he jumped up and
yelled: 'Fritharik! Get our horses!'

They clattered over to Urias' headquarters. Urias looked grave. 'This puts
me in an awkward position, Martinus. My uncle will undoubtedly try to
regain his crown. He's a stubborn man, you know.'

'I know. But you know how important it is to keep things going the way
they are.'

'Ja. I won't go back on you. But you couldn't expect me to try to harm my
uncle. I like him, even if he is a thick-headed old grouch.'

'You stick with me and I promise you I'll do my best to see that he isn't
harmed. But just now I'm concerned with keeping him from harming us.'

'How do you suppose he got out? Bribery?'

'I know as much as you do. I doubt the bribery; at least Aturpad is considered an honorable man. What do you think Wittigis will do?'

'If it were me, I'd hide out for a while and gather my partisans. That would
be logical. But my uncle never was very logical. And he hates Thiudahad
worse than anything on earth. Especially after Thiudahad's attempt to have
him murdered. My guess is that he'll head straight for Ravenna and try to do
Thiudahad in personally.'

'All right, then, we'll collect some fast cavalry and head that way ourselves.'

Padway thought he was pretty well hardened to long-distance riding. But
it was all he could do to stand the pace that Urias set. When they reached
Ravenna in the early morning he was reeling, redeyed, in the saddle.

They asked no questions, but galloped straight for the palace. The town
seemed normal enough. Most of the citizens were at breakfast. But at the palace the normal guard was not to be seen.

'That looks bad,' said Urias. They and their men dismounted, drew their
swords, and marched in six abreast. A guard appeared at the head of the
stairs. He grabbed at his sword, then recognized Urias and Padway.

'Oh, it's you,' he said noncommittally.

'Yes, it's us,' replied Padway. 'What's up?'

'Well … uh … you'd better go see for yourselves, noble sirs. Excuse me.'
And the Goth whisked out of sight.

They tramped on through the empty halls. Doors shut before they came to
them, and there was whispering behind them. Padway wondered if they were
walking into a trap. He sent back a squad to hold the front door.

At the entrance to the royal apartments they found a clump of guards. A couple of these brought their spears up, but the rest simply stood uncertainly. Padway said calmly, 'Stand back, boys,' and went in.

'Oh, merciful Christ!' said Urias softly.

There were several people standing around a body on the floor. Padway asked them to stand aside, which they did meekly. The body was that of Wittigis. His tunic was ripped by a dozen sword and spear wounds. The rug under him was sopping.

The chief usher looked amazedly at Padway. 'This just happened, my lord. Yet you have come all the way from Rome because of it. How did you know?'

'I have ways,' said Padway. 'How did it happen?'

'Wittigis was let into the palace by a guard friendly to him. He would have killed our noble king, but he was seen, and other guards hurried to the rescue. The guards killed him,' he added unnecessarily. Anybody could see that.

A sound from the corner made Padway look. There crouched Thiudahad, half dressed, Nobody seemed to be paying much attention. Thiudahad's ashy face peered at Padway.

'Dear me, it's my new prefect, isn't it? Your name is Cassiodorus. But how much younger you look, my dear sir. Ah, me, we all grow old sometime. Heh-heh. Let's publish a book, my dear Cassiodorus. Heigh-ho, yes, indeed, a lovely new book with purple covers. Heh-heh. We'll serve it for dinner, with pepper and gravy. That's the way to eat a fowl. Yes, three hundred pages at least. By the way, have you seen that rascally general of mine, Wittigis? I heard he was coming to call. Dreadful bore; no scholar at all. Heigh-ho, dear me, I feel like dancing. Do you dance, my dear Wittigis? La-la-la, la-la-la, dum de-um de-um.'

Padway told the king's house physician: 'Take care of him, and don't let him out. The rest of you, go back to work as if nothing has happened. Somebody take charge of the body. Replace this rug, and make the preparations for a dignified but modest funeral. Urias, maybe you'd better tend to that.' Urias was weeping. 'Come on, old man, you can do your grieving later. I sympathize, but we've got things to do.' He whispered something to him, whereat Urias cheered up.

CHAPTER XV

The members of the Gothic Royal Council appeared at Padway's office with a variety of scowls. They were men of substance and leisure, and did not like being practically dragged away from their breakfast tables, especially by a mere civil functionary.

Padway acquainted them with the circumstances. His news shocked them to temporary silence. He continued: 'As you know, my lords, under the unwritten constitution of the Gothic nation, an insane king must be replaced as soon as possible. Permit me to suggest that present circumstances make the replacement of the unfortunate Thiudahad an urgent matter.'

Wakkis growled: 'That's partly *your* doing, young man. We could have bought off the Franks —'

'Yes, my lord. I know all that. The trouble is that the Franks won't stay bought, as you very well know. In any event, what's done is done. Neither the Franks nor Justinian have moved against us yet. If we can run the election of a new king off quickly, we shall not be any worse off than we are.'

Wakkis replied: 'We shall have to call another convention of the electors, I suppose.'

Another councilor, Mannfrith, spoke up: 'Apparently our young friend is right, much as I hate to take advice from outsiders. When and where shall the convention be?'

There were a lot of uncertain throaty noises from the Goths. Padway said: 'If my lords please, I have a suggestion. Our new civil capital is to be at Florence, and what more fitting way of inaugurating it is there than holding our election there?'

There was more growling, but nobody produced a better idea. Padway knew perfectly well that they didn't like following his directions, but that, on the other hand, they were glad to shirk thought and responsibility themselves.

Wakkis said: 'We shall have to give time for the messages to go out, and for the electors to reach Florence —'

Just then Urias came in. Padway took him aside and whispered: 'What did she say?'

'She says she will.'

'When?'

'Oh, in about ten days, I think. It don't look very nice so soon after my uncle's death.'

'Never mind that. It's now or never.'

Mannfrith asked. 'Who shall the candidates be? I'd like to run myself, only my rheumatism has been bothering me so.'

Somebody said: 'Thiudegiskel will be one. He's Thiudahad's logical successor.'

Padway said: 'I think you'll be pleased to hear that our esteemed General Urias will be a candidate.'

'What?' cried Wakkis. 'He's a fine young man, I admit, but he's ineligible. He's not an Amaling.'

Padway broke into a triumphant grin. 'Not now, my lords, but he will be by the time the election is called.' The Goths looked startled. 'And, my lords, I hope you'll all give us the pleasure of your company at the wedding.'

During the wedding rehearsal, Mathaswentha got Padway aside. She said: 'Really, Martinus, you've been most noble about this. I hope you won't grieve too much.'

Padway tried his best to look noble. 'My dear, your happiness is mine. And if you love this young man, I think you're doing just the right thing.'

'I *do* love him,' replied Mathaswentha. 'Promise me you won't sit around and mope, but will go out and find some nice girl who is suited to you.'

Padway sighed convincingly. 'It'll be hard to forget, my dear. But since you ask it, I'll promise. Now, now, don't cry. What will Urias think? You want to make *him* happy, don't you? There, that's a sensible girl.'

The wedding itself was quite a gorgeous affair in a semibarbaric way. Padway discovered an unsuspected taste for stage management, and introduced a wrinkle he'd seen in pictures of United States Military Academy weddings: that of having Urias' friends make an arch of swords under which the bride and groom walked on their way down the church steps. Padway himself looked as dignified as his moderate stature and nondescript features permitted. Inwardly he was holding on tight to repress a snicker. It had just occurred to him that Urias' long robe looked amazingly like a bathrobe he, Padway, had once owned, except that Padway's robe hadn't had pictures of saints embroidered on it in gold thread.

As the happy couple departed, Padway ducked out of sight around a pillar. Mathaswentha, if she saw him out of the tail of her eye, may have thought that he was shedding a final tear. But actually he was allowing himself the luxury of a long-drawn *'Whew!'* of relief. Before he reappeared, he heard a couple of Goths talking on the other side of the pillar:

'He'd make a good king, eh, Albehrts?'

'Maybe. *He* would, by himself. But I fear he'll be under the influence of this

Martinus person. Not that I have anything specifically against Mysterious Martin, you understand. But – you know how it is.'

'*Ja, ja.* Oh, well, one can always flip a sesterce to decide which to vote for.'

Padway had every intention of keeping Urias under his influence. It seemed possible. Urias disliked and was impatient with matters of civil administration. He was a competent soldier, and at the same time was receptive to Padway's ideas. Padway thought somberly that if anything happened to *this* king he'd hunt a long time before finding another as satisfactory.

Padway had the news of the impending election sent out over the telegraph, thereby saving the week that would normally be necessary for messengers to travel the length and breadth of Italy, and incidentally convincing some of the Goths of the value of his contraptions. Padway also sent out another message, ordering all the higher military commanders to remain at their posts. He sold Urias the idea by arguing military necessity. His real reason was a determination to keep Thiudegiskel in Calabria during the election. Knowing Urias, he didn't dare explain this plan to him, for fear Urias would have an attack of knightly honor and, as ranking general, countermand the order.

The Goths had never seen an election conducted on time-honored American principles. Padway showed them. The electors arrived in Florence to find the town covered with enormous banners and posters reading:

VOTE FOR URIAS
THE PEOPLE'S
CHOICE!

Lower taxes! Bigger public works!
Security for the aged!
Efficient government!

And so forth. They also found a complete system of ward-heelers to take them in tow, show them the town – not that Florence was much to see in those days – and butter them up generally.

Three days before the election was due, Padway held a barbecue. He threw himself into debt for the fixings. Well, not exactly; he threw poor Urias into debt, being much too prudent to acquire any more liabilities in his own name than he could help.

While he kept modestly in the background, Urias made a speech. Padway later heard comments to the effect that nobody had known Urias could make such good speeches. He grinned to himself. He had written the speech and had spent all his evenings for a week teaching Urias to deliver it. Privately

Padway thought that his candidate's delivery still stank. But if the electors didn't mind, there was no reason why he should.

Padway and Urias relaxed afterward over a bottle of brandy. Padway said that the election looked like a pushover, and then had to explain what a push-over was. Of the two opposing candidates, one had withdrawn, and the other, Harjis Austrowald's son, was an elderly man with only the remotest connection with the Amal family.

Then one of the ward-heelers came in breathless. It seemed to Padway that people were always coming to see him breathless.

The man barked: 'Thiudegiskel's here.'

Padway wasted no time. He found where Thiudegiskel was staying, rounded up a few Gothic soldiers, and set out to arrest the young man. He found that Thiudegiskel had, with a gang of his own friends, taken over one of the better inns in town, pitching the previous guests and their belongings out in the street.

The gang were gorging themselves downstairs in plain sight. They hadn't yet changed their traveling clothes, and they looked tired but trough. Padway marched in. Thiudegiskel looked up. 'Oh, it's *you* again. What do you want?'

Padway announced: 'I have a warrant for your arrest on grounds of insub-ordination and deserting your post, signed by Ur —'

The high-pitched voice interrupted: '*Ja, ja,* I know all about that, my dear *Sineigs*. Maybe you thought I'd stay away from Florence while you ran off an election without me, eh? *But* I'm not like that, Martinus. Not one little bit. I'm here, I'm a candidate, and anything you try now I'll remember when I'm king. That's one thing about me; I've got an infernally long memory.'

Padway turned to his soldiers: 'Arrest him!'

There was a great scraping of chairs as the gang rose to its feet and grasped its collective sword hilts. Padway looked for his soldiers; they hadn't moved.

'Well?' he snapped.

The oldest of them, a kind of sergeant, cleared his throat. 'Well, sir, it's this way. Now we know you're our superior and all that. But things are kind of uncertain, with this election and all, and we don't know whom we'll be taking orders from in a couple of days. Suppose we arrest this young man, and then he gets elected king? That wouldn't be so good for us, now would it, sir?'

'Why – you —' raged Padway.

But the only effect was that the soldiers began to slide out the door. The young Gothic noble named Willimer was whispering to Thiudegiskel, sliding his sword a few inches out of the scabbard and back.

Thiudegiskel shook his head and said to Padway: 'My friend here doesn't seem to like you, Martinus. He swears he'll pay you a visit as soon as the election is over. So it might be healthier if you left Italy for a little trip. In fact, it's all I can do to keep him from paying his visit right now.'

The soldiers were mostly gone now. Padway realized that he'd better go too, if he didn't want these well-born thugs to make hamburger of him.

He mustered what dignity he could. 'You know the law against dueling.'

Thiudegiskel's invincibly good-natured arrogance wasn't even dented. 'Sure, I know it. But remember. *I'll* be the one enforcing it. I'm just giving you fair warning, Martinus. That's one thing about —'

But Padway didn't wait to hear Thiudegiskel's next contribution to the inexhaustible subject of himself. He went, full of rage and humiliation. By the time he finished cursing his own stupidity and thought to round up his eastern troops – the few who weren't up north with Belisarius – and make a second attempt, it was too late. Thiudegiskel had collected a large crowd of partisans in and around the hotel, and it would take a battle to dislodge them. The ex-Imperialists seemed far from enthusiastic over the prospect, and Urias muttered something about its being only honorable to let the late king's son have a fair try for the crown.

The next day Thomasus the Syrian arrived. He came in wheezing. 'How are you, Martinus? I didn't want to miss all the excitement, so I came up from Rome. Brought my family along.'

That meant something, Padway knew, for Thomasus' family consisted not only of his wife and four children, but an aged uncle, a nephew, two nieces, and his black house slave Ajax and *his* wife and children.

He answered: 'I'm fine, thanks. Or I shall be when I catch up on my sleep. How are you?'

'Fine, thanks. Business has been good for a change.'

'And how is your friend God?' Padway asked with a straight face.

'He's fine too – why, you blasphemous young scoundrel! That will cost you an extra interest on your next loan. How's the election?'

Padway told him. 'It won't be as easy as I thought. Thiudegiskel has developed a lot of support among the conservative Goths, who don't care for self-made men like Wittigis and Urias. The upper crust prefer an Amaling by birth —'

'Upper crust? Oh, I see! Ha, ha, ha! I hope God listens to you. It might put Him in a good humor the next time He considers sending a plague or a quake.'

Padway continued: 'And Thiudegiskel is not as stupid as one might expect. He'd hardly arrived before he'd sent out friends to tear down my posters and put up some of his own. His weren't much to look at, but I was surprised that he thought of using any. There were fistfights and one stabbing, not fatal, fortunately, so – you know Dagalaif Nevitta's son?'

'The marshal? By name only.'

'He's not eligible to vote. Well, the town watch is too scared of the Goths to keep order, and I don't dare use my own guards for fear of rousing all the

Goths against the 'foreigners.' I blackmailed the city fathers into hiring Dagalaif to deputize the other marshals who are not electors as election police. As Nevitta is on our side, I don't know how impartial my friend Dagalaif will be. But it'll save us from a pitched battle, I hope.'

'Wonderful, wonderful, Martinus. Don't overreach yourself; some of the Goths call your electioneering methods newfangled and undignified. I'll ask God to keep a special watch over you and your candidate.'

The day before the election, Thiudegiskel showed his political astuteness by throwing a barbecue even bigger than Padway's. Padway, having some mercy on Urias' modest purse, had limited his party to the electors. Thiudegiskel, with the wealth of Thiudahad's immense Tuscan estates to draw upon, shot the works. He invited all the electors and their families and friends also.

Padway and Urias and Thomasus, with the former's ward-heelers, the latter's family, and a sizable guard, arrived at the field outside Florence after the festivities had begun. The field was covered with thousands of Goths of all ages, sizes, and sexes, and was noisy with East-German gutturals, the clank of scabbards, and the *flop-flop* leather pants.

A Goth bustled up to them with beer suds in his whiskers. 'Here, here, what are you people doing? You weren't invited.'

'*Ni ogs, frijond*,' said Padway.

'What? You're telling *me* not to be afraid?' The Goth bristled.

'We aren't even trying to come to your party. We're just having a little pic- . nic of our own. There's no law against picnics, is there?'

'Well – then why all the armament? *Looks* to me as though you were planning a kidnapping.'

'There, there,' soothed Padway. 'You're wearing a sword, aren't you?'

'But I'm official. I'm one of Willimer's men.'

'So are these people our men. Don't worry about us. We'll stay on the other side of the road, if it'll make you happy. Now run along and enjoy your beer.'

'Well, don't try anything. We'll be ready for you if you do.' The Goth departed, muttering over Padway's logic.

Padway's party made themselves comfortable across the road, ignoring the hostile glares from Thiudegiskel's partisans. Padway himself sprawled on the grass, eating little and watching the barbecue through narrowed eyes.

Thomasus said: 'Most excellent General Urias, that look tells me our friend Martinus is planning something particularly hellish.'

Thiudegiskel and some of his gang mounted the speakers' stand. Willimer introduced the candidate with commendable brevity. Then Thiudegiskel began to speak. Padway hushed his own party and strained his ears. Even so, with so many people, few of them completely silent, between him and the speaker, he missed a lot of Thiudegiskel's shrill Gothic. Thiudegiskel appeared to be bragging as usual about his own wonderful character. But, to Padway's consternation, his audience ate it up. And they howled with laughter at the speaker's rough and ready humor.

'— and did you know, friends, that General Urias was twelve years old before his poor mother could train him not to wet his bed? It's a fact. That's one thing about me; I never exaggerate. Of course you *couldn't* exaggerate Urias' peculiarities. For instance, the first time he called on a girl —'

Urias was seldom angry, but Padway could see the young general was rapidly approaching incandescence. He'd have to think of something quickly, or there *would* be a battle.

His eye fell on Ajax and Ajax's family. The slave's eldest child was a chocolate-colored, frizzy-haired boy of ten.

Padway asked: 'Does anybody know whether Thiudegiskel's married?'

'Yes,' replied Urias. 'The swine was married just before he left for Calabria. Nice girl, too; a cousin of Willimer.'

'*Hm-m-m.* Say, Ajax, does that oldest boy of yours speak any Gothic?'

'Why no, my lord, why should he?'

'What's his name?'

'Priam.'

'Priam, would you like to earn a couple of sesterces, all your own?'

The boy jumped up and bowed. Padway found such a servile gesture in a child vaguely repulsive. Must do something about slavery some day, he thought. 'Yes, my lord,' squeaked the boy.

'Can you say the word "*atta*"? That's Gothic for "father".'

Priam dutifully said: '*Atta.* Now where are my sesterces, my lord?'

'Not so fast, Priam. That's just the beginning of the job. You practice saying "*atta*" for a while.'

Padway stood up and peered at the field. He called softly: '*Hai*, Dagalaif!'

The marshal detached himself from the crowd and came over. '*Hails*, Martinus! What can I do for you?'

Padway whispered his instructions.

Then he said to Priam: 'You see the man in the red cloak on the stand, the one who is talking? Well, you're to go over there and climb up on the stand, and say '*atta*' to him. Loudly, so everybody can hear. Say it a lot of times, until something happens. Then you run back here.'

Priam frowned in concentration. 'But the man isn't my father! This is my father!' He pointed to Ajax.

'I know. But you do as I say if you want your money. Can you remember your instructions?'

So Priam trailed off through the crowd of Goths with Dagalaif at his heels. They were lost to Padway's sight for a few minutes, while Thiudegiskel shrilled on. Then the little Negro's form appeared on the stand, boosted up by Dagalaif's strong arms. Padway clearly heard the childish cry of 'Atta!'

Thiudegiskel stopped in the middle of a sentence. Priam repeated: 'Atta! Atta!'

'He seems to know you!' shouted a voice down front.

Thiudegiskel stood silent, scowling and turning red. A low mutter of laughter ran through the Goths and swelled to a roar.

Priam called 'Atta!' once more, louder.

Thiudegiskel grabbed his sword hilt and started for the boy. Padway's heart missed a beat.

But Priam leaped off the stand into Dagalaif's arms, leaving Thiudegiskel to shout and wave his sword. He was apparently yelling, 'It's a lie!' over and over. Padway could see his mouth move, but his words were lost in the thunder of the Gothic nation's Wagnerian laughter.

Dagalaif and Priam appeared, running toward them. The Goth was staggering slightly and holding his midriff. Padway was alarmed until he saw Dagalaif was suffering from a laughing and coughing spell.

He slapped him on the back until the coughs and gasps moderated. Then he said: 'If we hang around here, Thiudegiskel will recover his wits, and he'll be angry enough to set his partisans on us with cold steel. In my country we had a word "scram" that is, I think, applicable. Let's go.'

'Hey, my lord,' squealed Priam, 'where's my two sesterces? Oh, thank you, my lord. Do you want me to call anybody else "father," my lord?'

CHAPTER XVI

Padway told Urias: 'It looks like a sure thing now. Thiudegiskel will never live this afternoon's episode down. We Americans have some methods for making elections come out the right way, such as stuffing ballot boxes, and the use of floaters. But I don't think it'll be necessary to use any of them.'

'What on earth is a floater, Martinus? You mean a float such as one uses in fishing?'

'No; I'll explain sometime. I don't want to corrupt the Gothic electoral system more than is absolutely necessary.'

'Look here, if anybody investigates, they'll learn that Thiudegiskel was the innocent victim of a joke this afternoon. Then won't the effect be lost?'

'No, my dear Urias, that's not how the minds of electors work. Even if he's proved innocent, he's been made such an utter fool of that nobody will take him seriously, regardless of his personal merits, if any.'

Just then a ward-heeler came in breathless. He gasped: 'Thiu-Thiudegiskel —'

Padway complained: 'I am going to make it a rule that people who want to see me have to wait outside until they get their breath. What is it, Roderik?'

Roderik finally got it out. 'Thiudegiskel has left Florence, distinguished Martinus. Nobody knows whither. Willimer and some of his other friends went with him.'

Padway immediately sent out over the telegraph Urias' order depriving Thiudegiskel of his colonel's rank – or its rough equivalent in the vague and amorphous Gothic system of command. Then he sat and stewed and waited for news.

It came the next morning during the voting. But it did not concern Thiudegiskel. It was that a large Imperialist army had crossed over from Sicily and landed, not at Scylla on the toe of the Italian boot where one would expect, but up the coast of Bruttium at Vibo.

Padway told Urias immediately, and urged: 'Don't say anything for a few hours. This election is in the bag – I mean it's certain – and we don't want to disturb it.'

But rumors began to circulate. Telegraph systems are run by human beings, and few groups of more than a dozen human beings have kept a secret for long. By the time Urias' election by a two-to-one majority was announced, the Goths were staging an impromptu demonstration in the streets of Florence, demanding to be led against the invader.

Then more details came in. The Imperialists' army was commanded by Bloody John, and numbered a good fifty thousand men. Evidently Justinian, furious about Padway's letter, had been shipping adequate force into Sicily in relays.

Padway and Urias figured that they could, without recalling troops from Provence and Dalmatia, assemble perhaps half again as many troops as Bloody John had. But further news soon reduced this estimate. That able, ferocious, and unprincipled solider sent a detachment across the Sila Mountains by a secondary road from Vibo to Scyllacium, while he advanced with his main body down the Popilian Way to Reggio. The Reggio garrison of fifteen thousand men, trapped at the end of the toe of the boot, struck a few blows for the sake of their honor and surrendered. Bloody John reunited his forces and started north toward the ankle.

Padway saw Urias off in Rome with many misgivings. The army looked impressive, surely, with its new corps of horse archers and its batteries of mobile catapults. But Padway knew that the new units were inexperienced in their novel ways of fighting, and that the organization was likely to prove brittle in practice.

Once Urias and the army had left, there was no more point in worrying. Padway resumed his experiments with gunpowder. Perhaps he should try charcoal from different woods. But this meant time, a commodity of which Padway had precious little. He soon learned that he had none at all.

By piecing together the contradictory information that came in by telegraph, Padway figured out that this had happened: Thiudegiskel had reached his force in Calabria without interference. He had refused to recognize the telegraphic order depriving him of his command, and had talked his men into doing likewise. Padway guessed that the words of an able and self-confident speaker like Thiudegiskel would carry more weight with the mostly illiterate Goths than a brief, cold message arriving over a mysterious contraption.

Bloody John had moved cautiously; he had only reached Consentia when Urias arrived to face him. That might have been arranged beforehand with Thiudegiskel, to draw Urias far enough south to trap him.

But, while Urias and Bloody John sparred for openings along the river Crathis, Thiudegiskel arrived in Urias' rear-on the Imperialist side. Though he had only five thousand lancers, their unexpected charge broke the main Gothic army's morale. In fifteen minutes the Crathis Valley was full of thousands of Goths – lancers, horse archers, foot archers, and pikemen – streaming off in every direction. Thousands were ridden down by Bloody John's cuirassiers and the large force of Gepid and Lombard horse he had with him. Other thousands surrendered. The rest ran off into the hills, where the rapidly gathering dusk hid them.

Urias managed to hold his lifeguard regiment together, and attacked Thiudegiskel's force of deserters. The story was that Urias had personally killed
Thiudegiskel. Padway, knowing the fondness of soldiers for myths of this
sort, had his doubts. But it was agreed that Thiudegiskel had been killed, and
that Urias and his men had disappeared into the Imperial host in one final,
desperate charge, and had been seen no more by those on the Gothic side
who escaped from the field.

For hours Padway sat at his desk, staring at the pile of telegraph messages
and at a large and painfully inaccurate map of Italy.

'Can I get you anything, excellent boss?' asked Fritharik.

Padway shook his head.

Junianus shook his head. 'I fear that our Martinus' mind has become
unhinged by disaster.'

Fritharik snorted. 'That just shows you don't know him. He gets that way
when he's planning something. Just wait. He'll have a devilish clever scheme
for upsetting the Greeks yet.'

Junianus put his head in the door. 'Some more messages, my lord.'

'What are they?'

'Bloody John is halfway to Salerno. The natives are welcoming him.
Belisarius reports he has defeated a large force of Franks.'

'Come here, Junianus. Would you two boys mind stepping out for a minute? Now, Junianus, you're a native of Lucania, aren't you?'

'Yes, my lord.'

'You were a serf, weren't you?'

'Well … uh … my lord … you see —' The husky young man suddenly
looked fearful.

'Don't worry; I wouldn't let you be dragged back to your landlord's estate
for anything.'

'Well – yes, my lord.'

'When the messages speak of the "natives" welcoming the Imperialists,
doesn't that mean the Italian landlords more than anybody else?'

'Yes, my lord. The serfs don't care one way or the other. One landlord is as
oppressive as the next, so why should they get themselves killed fighting for
any set of masters, Greek or Italian or Gothic as the case may be?'

'If they were offered their holdings as free proprietors, with no landlords
to worry about, do you think they'd fight for that?'

'Why?' – Junianus took a deep breath – 'I think they would. Yes. Only it's
such an extraordinary idea, if you don't mind my saying so.'

'Even on the side of Arian heretics?'

'I don't think that would matter. The curials and the city folk may take
their Orthodoxy seriously. But a lot of the peasants are half pagan anyway.
And they worship their land more than any alleged heavenly powers.'

'That's about what I thought,' said Padway. 'Here are some messages to send out. The first is an edict, issued by me in Urias' name, emancipating the serfs of Bruttium, Lucania, Calabria, Apulia, Campania, and Samnium. The second is an order to General Belisarius to leave a screening force in Provence to fight a delaying action in case the Franks attack again and return south with his main body at once. Oh, Fritharik! Will you get Gudareths for me? And I want to see the foreman of the printshop.'

When Gudareths arrived, Padway explained his plans to him. The little Gothic officer whistled. 'My, my, that *is* a desperate measure, respectable Martinus. I'm not sure the Royal Council will approve. If you free all these low-born peasants, how shall we get them back into serfdom again?'

'We won't,' snapped Padway. 'As for the Royal Council, most of them were with Urias.'

'But, Martinus, you can't make a fighting force out of them in a week or two. Take the word of an old soldier who has killed hundreds of foes with his own right arm. Yes, thousands, by God!'

'I know all that,' said Padway wearily.

'What then? These Italians are no good for fighting. No spirit. You'd better rely on what Gothic forces we can scrape together. Real fighters, like me.'

Padway said: 'I don't expect to lick Bloody John with raw recruits. But we can give him a hostile country to advance through. You tend to those pikes, and dig up some more retired officers.'

Padway got his army together and set out from Rome on a bright spring morning. It was not much of an army to look at: elderly Goths who had supposed themselves retired from active service, and young sprigs whose voices had not finished changing.

As they cluttered down Patrician Street from the Pretorian Camp, Padway had an idea. He told his staff to keep on; he'd catch up with them. And off he cantered, *poddle-op, poddle-op*, up the Suburban Slope toward the Esquiline.

Dorothea came out of Anicius' house. 'Martinus!' she cried. 'Are you off somewhere again?'

'That's right.'

'You haven't paid us a real call in months! Every time I see you, you have only a minute before you must jump on your horse and gallop off somewhere.'

Padway made a helpless gesture. 'It'll be different when I've retired from all this damned war and politics. Is your excellent father in?'

'No; he's at the library. He'll be disappointed not to have seen you.'

'Give him my best.'

'Is there going to be more war? I've heard Bloody John is in Italy.'

'It looks that way.'

'Will you be in the fighting?'

'Probably.'

'Oh, Martinus. Wait just a moment.' She ran into the house.

She returned with a little leather bag on a loop of string. 'This will keep you safe if anything will.'

'What is it?'

'A fragment of St. Polycarp's skull.'

Padway's eyebrows went up. 'Do you believe in its effectiveness?'

'Oh, certainly. My mother paid enough for it, there's no doubt that it's genuine.' She slipped the loop over his head and tucked the bag through the neck opening in his cloak.

It had not occurred to Padway that a well-educated girl would accept the superstitions of her age. At the same time he was touched. He said: 'Thank you, Dorothea, from the bottom of my heart, But there's something that I think will be a more effective charm yet.'

'What?'

'This.' He kissed her mouth lightly, and threw himself aboard his horse. Dorothea stood with a surprised but not displeased look. Padway swung the animal around and sent it back down the avenue, *poddleop, poddle-op.* He turned in the saddle to wave back and was almost pitched off. The horse plunged and skidded into the nigh ox of a team that had just pulled a wagon out of a side street.

The driver shouted: '*Carus-dominus, Jesus-Christus, Maria-mater-Dei,* why don't you look where you're going? *San'tus-Petrus-Paulusque-Joann-esque-Lucasque …*'

By the time the driver had run out of apostles Padway had ascertained that there was no damage. Dorothea was not in sight. He hoped that she had not witnessed the ruin of his pretty gesture.

CHAPTER XVII

It was the latter part of May, 537, when Padway entered Benevento with his army. Little by little the force had grown as the remnants of Urias' army trickled north. Only that morning a forage-cutting party had found three of these Goths who had settled down comfortably in a local farmhouse over the owner's protests, and prepared to sit out the rest of the war in comfort. These joined up, too, though not willingly.

Instead of coming straight down the Tyrrhenian or western coast to Naples, Padway had marched across Italy to the Adriatic, and had come down that coast to Teate. Then he had cut inland to Lucera and Benevento. As there was no telegraph line yet on the east coast, Padway kept in touch with Bloody John's movements by sending messengers across the Apennines to the telegraph stations that were till out of the enemy's hands. He timed his movements to reach Benevento after John had captured Salerno on the other side of the peninsula, had left a detachment masking Naples, and had started for Rome by the Latin Way.

Padway hoped to come down on his rear in the neighborhood of Capua, while Belisarius, if he got his orders straight, would come directly from Rome and attack the Imperialists in front.

Somewhere between Padway and the Adriatic was Gudareths, profanely shepherding a train of wagons full of pikes and of handbills bearing Padway's emancipation proclamation. The pikes had been dug out of attics and improvised out of fence palings and such things. The Gothic arsenals at Pavia, Verona, and other northern cities had been too far away to be of help in time.

The news of the emancipation had spread like a gasoline fire. The peasants had risen all over southern Italy. But they seemed more interested in sacking and burning their landlords' villas than in joining the army.

A small fraction of them had joined up; this meant several thousand men. Padway, when he rode back to the rear of his column and watched this great disorderly rabble swarming along the road, chattering like magpies and taking time out to snooze when they felt like it, wondered how much of an asset they would be. Here and there one wore great-grandfathers legionary helmet and loricated cuirass, which had been hanging on the wall of his cottage for most of a century.

Benevento is on a small hill at the confluence of the Calore and Sabbato Rivers. As they plodded into the town, Padway saw several Goths sitting against one of the houses. One of these looked familiar. Padway rode up to him, and cried: 'Dagalaif!'

The marshal looked up. *'Hails'*, he said in a toneless, weary voice. There was a bandage around his head, stained with black blood where his left ear should have been. 'We heard you were coming this way, so we waited.'

'Where's Nevitta?'

'My father is dead.'

'What? Oh.' Padway was silent for seconds. Then he said: 'Oh, hell. He was one of the few real friends I had.'

'I know. He died like a true Goth.'

Padway sighed and went about his business of getting his force settled. Dagalaif continued sitting against the wall, looking at nothing in particular.

They lay in Benevento for a day. Padway learned that Bloody John had almost passed the road junction at Calatia on his way north. There was no news from Belisarius, so that the best Padway could hope for was to fight a delaying action, and hold John in southern Italy until more forces arrived.

Padway left his infantry in Benevento and rode down to Calatia with his cavalry. But this time he had a fairly respectable force of mounted archers. They were not as good as the Imperialist cuirassiers, but they would have to do.

Fritharik, riding beside him, said: 'Aren't the flowers pretty, excellent boss? They remind me of the gardens in my beautiful estate in Carthage. Ah, that was something to see —'

Padway turned a haggard face. He could still grin, though it hurt. 'Getting poetical, Fritharik?'

'Me a poet? *Honh!* Just because I like to have some pleasant memories for my last earthly ride —'

'What do you mean, your last?'

'I mean my last, and you can't tell me anything different. Bloody John outnumbers us three to one, they say. It won't be a nameless grave for us, because they won't bother to bury us. Last night I had a prophetic dream …'

As they approached Calatia, where Trajan's Way athwart Italy joined the Latin Way from Salerno to Rome, their scouts reported that the tail of Bloody John's army had just pulled out of town. Padway snapped his orders. A squadron of lancers trotted out in front, and a force of mounted archers followed them. They disappeared down the road. Padway rode up to the top of a knoll to watch them. They got smaller and smaller, disappearing and reappearing over humps in the road, he could hear the faint murmur of John's army, out of sight over the olive groves.

Then there was shouting and clattering, tiny with distance, like a battle between gnats and mosquitoes. Padway fretted with impatience. His telescope was no help, not being able to see around corners. The little sounds went on, and on, and on. Faint columns of smoke began to rise over the olive trees. Good; that meant that his men had set fire to Bloody John's wagon train. His first worry had been that they'd insist on plundering it in spite of orders.

Then a little dark cluster, toppled by rested lances that looked as thin as hairs, appeared on the road. Padway squinted through his telescope to make sure they were his men. He trotted down the knoll and gave some more orders. Half his horse archers spread themselves out in a long crescent on either side of the road, and a body of lancers grouped themselves behind it.

Time passed, and the men sweated in their scalemail shirts. Then the advance guard appeared, riding hard. They were grinning, and some waved bits of forbidden plunder. They clattered down the road between the waiting bowmen.

Their commander rode up to Padway. 'Worked like a charm!' he shouted. 'We came down on their wagons, chased off the wagon guards, and set them on fire. Then they came back at us. We did like you said; spread the bowmen out and filled them full of quills as they charged; then hit them with the lance when they were all nice and confused. They came back for more, twice. Then John himself came down on us with his whole damned army. So we cleared out. They'll be along any minute.'

'Fine,' replied Padway. 'You know your orders. Wait for us at Mt. Tifata pass.'

So they departed, and Padway waited. But not for long. A column of Imperial cuirassiers appeared, riding hell-for-leather. Padway knew this meant Bloody John was sacrificing order to speed in his pursuit, as troops couldn't travel through the fields and groves alongside the road at any such rate. Even if he'd deployed it would take his wings some time to come up.

The Imperialists grew bigger and bigger, and their hoofs made a great pounding on the stone-paved road. They looked very splendid, with their cloaks and plumes on their officers' helmets streaming out behind. Their commander, in gilded armor, saw what he was coming to and gave an order. Lances were slung over shoulders and bows were strung. By that time they were well within range of the crescent, and the Goths opened fire. The quick, flat snap of the bowstrings and the whiz of the arrows added themselves to the clamor of the Byzantines' approach. The commander's horse, a splendid white animal, reared up and was bowled over by another horse that charged into it. The head of the Imperialist column crumpled up into a mass of milling horses and men.

Padway looked at the commander of his body of lancers; swung his arm around his head twice and pointed at the Imperialists. The line of horse archers opened up, and the Gothic knights charged through. As usual they went slowly at first, but by the time they reached the Imperialists their heavy horses had picked up irresistible momentum. Back went the cuirassiers with a great clatter, defending themselves desperately at close quarters, but pulling out and getting their bows into action as soon as they could.

Out of the corner of his eye, Padway saw a group of horsemen ride over a nearby hilltop. That meant that Bloody John's wings were coming up. He had his trumpeter signal the retreat. But the knights kept on pressing the Imperialist column back. They had the advantage in weight of men and horses, and they knew it. Padway kicked his horse into a gallop down the road after them. If he didn't stop the damned fools they'd be swallowed up by the Imperialist army.

An arrow went by Padway uncomfortably close. He found the peculiar screech that it made much harder on the nerves than he'd expected. He caught up with his Goths, dragged their commander out of the press by main force, and shouted in his ear that it was time to withdraw.

The men yelled back at him: 'Nil Nist! Good fighting!' and tore out of Padway's grip to plunge back in.

While Padway wondered what to do, an Imperialist broke through the Goths and rode straight at him. Padway had not thought to get his sword out. He drew it now, then had to throw himself to one side to avoid the other's lance point. He lost a stirrup, lost his reins, and almost lost his sword and his horse. By the time he had pulled himself back upright, the Imperialist was out of sight. Padway in his haste had nicked his own horse with his sword. The animal began to dance around angrily. Padway dug his left fingers into its mane and hung on.

The Goths now began to stream back down the road. In a few seconds they were all galloping off except a few surrounded by the Imperialists. Padway wondered miserably if he'd be left on this uncontrollable nag to face the Byzantines alone, when the horse of its own accord set off after its fellows.

In theory it was a strategic retreat. But from the look of the Gothic knights, Padway wondered if it would be possible to stop them this side of the Alps.

Padway's horse tossed its reins up to where Padway could grab them. Padway had just begun to get the animal under control when he sighted a man on foot, bareheaded but gaudy in gilded armor. It was the commander of the Imperialist column. Padway rode at him. The man started to run. Padway started to swing his sword, then realized that he had no sword to swing. He had no recollection of dropping it, but he must have done so when he grabbed the reins. He leaned over and grabbed a fistful of hair. The man yelled, and came along in great bucking jumps.

A glance back showed that the Imperialists had disposed of the Goths who had not been able to extricate themselves, and were getting their pursuit under way.

Padway handed his prisoner over to a Goth. The Goth leaned and pulled the Imperialist officer up over his pommel, face down, so that half of him hung on each side. Padway saw him ride off, happily spanking the unfortunate Easterner with the flat of his sword.

According to plan, the horse archers fell in behind the lancers and galloped after them, the rearmost ones shooting backward.

It was nine miles to the pass, most of it uphill. Padway hoped never to have such a ride again. He was sure that at the next jounce his guts would burst from his abdomen and spill abroad. By the time they were within sight of the pass, the horses of both the pursued and the pursuers were so blown that both were walking. Some men had even dismounted to lead their horses. Padway remembered the story of the day in Texas that was so hot that a coyote was seen chasing a jackrabbit with both walking. He translated the story into Gothic, making a coyote a fox, and told it to the nearest soldier. It ran slowly down the line.

The bluffs were yellow in a late afternoon sun when the Gothic column finally stumbled through the pass. They had lost few men, but any really vigorous pursuer could have ridden them down and rolled them out of their saddles with ease. Fortunately the Imperialists were just about as tired. But they came on nevertheless.

Padway heard one officer's shout, echoing up the walls of the pass: 'You'll rest when I tell you to, you lazy swine!'

Padway looked around, and saw with satisfaction that the force he had sent up ahead were waiting quietly in their places. These were the men who had not been used at all yet. The gang who had burned the wagons were drawn up behind them, and those who had just sprawled on the ground still farther up the pass.

On came the Imperialists. Padway could see men's heads turn as they looked nervously up the slopes. But Bloody John had apparently not yet admitted that his foe might be conducting an intelligent campaign. The Imperialist column clattered echoing into the narrowest part of the pass, the slanting rays of the sun shooting after them.

Then there was a great thumping roar as boulders and tree trunks came bounding down the slopes. A horse shrieked quite horribly, and the Imperialists scuttled around like ants whose nest had been disturbed. Padway signaled a squadron of lancers to charge.

There was room for only six horses abreast, and even so it was a tight fit. The rocks and logs hadn't done much damage to the Imperialists, except to form a heap cutting their leading column in two. And now the Gothic knights struck the fragment that had passed the point of the break. The cuirassiers, unable to maneuver or even to use their bows, were jammed back against the barrier by their heavier opponents. The fight ended when the surviving

Imperialists slid off their horses and scrambled back to safety on foot. The Goths rounded up the abandoned horses and led them back whooping.

Bloody John withdrew a couple of bowshots. Then he sent a small group of cuirassiers forward to lay down a barrage of arrows. Padway moved some dismounted Gothic archers into the pass. These, shooting from behind the barrier, caused the Imperialists so much trouble that the cuirassiers were soon withdrawn.

Bloody John now sent some Lombard lancers forward to sweep the archers out of the way. But the barrier stopped their charge dead. While they were picking their way, a step at a time, among the boulders, the Goths filled them full of arrows at close range. By the time the bodies of a dozen horses and an equal number of Lombards had bee added to the barrier, the Lombards had had enough.

By this time it would have been obvious to a much stupider general than Bloody John that in those confined quarters horses were about as useful as green parrots. The fact that the Imperialists could hold their end of the pass as easily as Padway held his could not have been much comfort, because they were trying to get through it and Padway was not. Bloody John dismounted some Lombards and Gepids and sent them forward on foot. Padway meanwhile had moved some dismounted lancers up behind the barrier, so that their spears made a thick cluster. The archers moved back and up the walls to shoot over the knights' heads.

The Lombards and Gepids came on at a slow dogtrot. They were equipped with regular Imperialist mail shirts, but they were still strange-looking men, with the back of their heads shaven and their front hair hanging down on each side of their faces in two long, butter-greased braids. They carried swords, and some had immense two-handed battleaxes. As they got closer they began to scream insults at the Goths, who understood their East-German dialects well enough and yelled back.

The attackers poured howling over the barrier and began hacking at the edge of spears which were too close together to slip between easily. More attackers, coming from behind, pushed the leaders into the spear points. Some were stuck. Others wedged their bodies in between the spear shafts and got at spearmen. Presently the front ranks were a tangle of grunting, snarling men packed too closely to use their weapons, while those behind them tried to reach over their heads.

The archers shot and shot. Arrows bounced off helmets and stuck quivering in big wooden shields. Men who were pierced could neither fall nor withdraw.

An archer skipped back among the rocks to get more arrows. Gothic heads turned to look at him. A couple more archers followed, though the quivers of these had not been emptied. Some of the rearmost knights started to follow them.

Padway saw a rout in the making. He grabbed one man and took his sword away from him. Then he climbed up to the rock vacated by the first archer, yelling something unclear even to himself. The men turned their eyes on him.

The sword was a huge one. Padway gripped it in both hands, hoisted it over his head, and swung at the nearest enemy, whose head was on a level with his waist. The sword came down on the man's helmet with a clang, squashing it over his eyes. Padway struck again and again. That Imperialist disappeared; Padway hit at another. He hit at helmets and shields and bare heads and arms and shoulders. He never could tell when his blows were effective, because by the time he recovered from each whack the picture had changed.

Then there were no heads but Gothic ones within reach. The Imperialists were crawling back over the barrier, lugging wounded men with blood-soaked clothes and arrows sticking in them.

At a glance there seemed to be about a dozen Goths down. Padway for a moment wondered angrily why the enemy had left fewer bodies than that. It occurred to him that some of these dozen were only moderately wounded, and that the enemy had carried off most of their casualties.

Fritharik and his orderly Tirdat and others were clustering around Padway, telling him what a demon fighter he was. He couldn't see it; all he had done was climb up on a rock, reach over the heads of a couple of his own men, and take a few swipes at an enemy who was having troubles of his own and could not hit back. There had been no more science to it than to using a pickax.

The sun had set, and Bloody John's army retired down the valley to set up its tents and cook its supper. Padway's Goths did likewise. The smell of cooking-fires drifted up and down pleasantly. Anybody would have thought that here were two gangs of pleasure-seeking campers, but for the pile of dead men and horses at the barrier.

Padway had no time for introspection. There were injured men, and he had no confidence in their ability to give themselves first aid. He raised no objections to their prayers and charms and potations of dust from a saint's tomb stirred in water. But he saw to it that bandages were boiled – which of course was a bit of the magic of Mysterious Martinus – and applied rationally.

One man had lost an eye, but was still full of fight. Another had three fingers gone, and was weeping about it. A third was cheerful with a stab in the abdomen. Padway knew this one would die of peritonitis before long, and that nothing could be done about it.

Padway, not underestimating his opponent, threw out a very wide and close-meshed system of outposts. He was justified; an hour before dawn his sentries began to drift in. Bloody John, it transpired, was working two large bodies of Anatolian foot archers over the hills on either side of them. Padway saw that his position would soon be untenable. So his Goths, yawning and grumbling, were roused out of their blankets and started for Benevento.

When the sun came up and he had a good look at his men, Padway became seriously concerned for their morale. They grumbled and looked almost as discouraged as Fritharik did regularly. They did not understand strategic retreats. Padway wondered how long it would be before they began to run away in real earnest.

At Benevento there was only one bridge over the Sabbato, a fairly swift stream. Padway thought he could hold this bridge for some time, and that Bloody John would be forced to attack him because of the loss of his provisions and the hostility of the peasantry.

When they came out on the plain around the confluence of the two little rivers, Padway found a horrifying surprise. A swarm of his peasant recruits was crossing the bridge toward him. Several thousand had already crossed. He had to be able to get his own force over the bridge quickly, and he knew what would happen if that bottleneck became jammed with retreating troops.

Gudareths rode out to meet him. 'I followed your orders!' he shouted. 'I tried to hold them back. But they got the idea they could lick the Greeks themselves, and started out regardless. I told you they were no good!'

Padway looked back. The Imperialists were in plain sight, and as he watched they began to deploy. It looked like the end of the adventure. He heard Fritharik make a remark about graves, and Tirdat ask if there wasn't a message he could take – preferably to a far-off place.

The Italian serfs had meanwhile seen the Gothic cavalry galloping up with the Imperialists in pursuit, and had formed their own idea that the battle was lost. Ripples of movement ran through their disorderly array, and its motion was presently reversed. Soon the road up to the town was white with running Italians. Those who had crossed the bridge were jammed together in a clawing mob trying to get back over.

Padway yelled in a cracked voice, to Gudareths: 'Get back over the river somehow! Send mounted men out on the roads to stop the runaways! Let those on this side get back over. I'll try to hold the Greeks here.'

He dismounted most of his troops. He arranged the lancers six deep in a semicircle in front of the bridgehead, around the caterwauling peasants, with lances outward. Along the river bank he posted the archers in two bodies, one on each flank, and beyond them his remaining lancers, mounted. If anything would hold Bloody John, that would.

The Imperialists stood for perhaps ten minutes. Then a big body of Lombards and Gepids trotted out, cantered, galloped straight at his line of spears. Padway, standing afoot behind the line, watched them grow larger and larger. The sound of their hoofs was like that of a huge orchestra of kettledrums, louder and louder. Watching these big, long-haired barbarians loom up out of the dust their horses raised, Padway sympathized with the peasant recruits. If he hadn't had his pride and his responsibility, he'd have run himself until his legs gave out.

On came the Imperialists. They looked as though they could ride over any body of men on earth. Then the bowstrings began to snap. Here a horse reared or buckled; there a man fell on with a musical clash of scale-mail. The charge slowed perceptibly. But they came on. To Padway they looked twenty feet tall. And then they were right on the line of spears. Padway could see the spearmen's tight lips and white faces. If they held – They did. The Imperialist horses reared, screaming, when the lancers pricked them. Some of them stopped so suddenly that their riders were pitched out of the saddle. And then the whole mass was streaming off to right and left, and back to the main army. It wasn't the horses' war, and they had no intention of spitting themselves on the unpleasant-looking lances.

Padway drew his first real breath in almost a minute. He'd been lecturing his men to the effect that no cavalry could break a really solid line of spearmen, but he hadn't believed it himself until now.

Then an awful thing happened. A lot of his lancers, seeing the Imperialists in flight, broke away from the line and started after their foes on foot. Padway screeched at them to come back, but they kept on running, or rather trotting heavily in their armor, like at Senlac, thought Padway. With similar results. The alert John sent a regiment of cuirassiers out after the clumsily running mob of Goths, and in a twinkling the Goths were scattering all over the field and being speared like so many boars. Padway raved with fury and chagrin; this was his first serious loss. He grabbed Tirdat by the collar, almost strangling him.

He shouted: 'Find Gudareths! Tell him to round up a few hundred of those Italians! I'm going to put them in the line!'

Padway's line was now perilously thin, and he couldn't contract it without isolating his archers and horsemen. But this time John hurled his cavalry against the flanking archers. The archers dropped back down the riverbank, where the horses couldn't get at them, and Padway's own cavalry charged the Imperialists, driving them off in a dusty chaos of whirling blades.

Presently the desired peasantry appeared, shepherded along by dirty and profane Gothic officers. The bridge was carpeted with pikes dropped in flight; the recruits were armed with these and put in the front line. They filled the gap nicely. Just to encourage them, Padway posted Goths behind them, holding sword points against their kidneys.

Now, if Bloody John would let him alone for a while, he could set about the delicate operation of getting his whole force back across the bridge without exposing any part of it to slaughter.

But Bloody John had no such intention. One came two big bodies of horse, aimed at the flanking Gothic cavalry.

Padway couldn't see what was happening, exactly, between the dust and the ranks of heads and shoulders in the way. But by the diminishing clatter he judged his men were being drawn off. Then came some cuirassiers galloping at the archers, forcing them off the top of the bank again. The cuirassiers strung their bows, and for a few seconds Goths and Imperialists twanged arrows at each other. Then the Goths began slipping off up and down the river, and swimming across.

Finally, on came the Gepids and Lombards, roaring like lions. This time there wouldn't be any arrow fire to slow them up. Bigger and bigger loomed the onrushing mass of longhaired giants on their huge horses, waving their huge axes.

Padway felt the way a violin string must the moment before it snaps.

There was a violent commotion in his own ranks right in front of him. The backs of the Goths were replaced by the brown faces of the peasants. These had dropped their pikes and clawed their way back through the ranks, sword points or no sword points. Padway had a glimpse of their popping eyes, their mouths gaping in screams of terror, and he was bowled over by the wave. They stepped all over him. He squirmed and kicked like a newt on a hook, wondering when the bare feet of the Italians would be succeeded by the hoofs of the hostile cavalry. The Italo-Gothic kingdom was done for, and all his work for nothing ...

The pressure and the pounding let up. A battered Padway untangled himself from those who had tripped over him. His whole line had begun to give way, but then had been frozen in the act, staring – all but a Goth in front of him who was killing an Italian.

The Imperialist heavy cavalry was not to be seen. The dust was so thick that nothing much could be seen. From beyond the pall in front of Padway's position came tramplings and shoutings and clatterings.

'What's happened?' yelled Padway. Nobody answered. There was nothing to be seen in front of them but dust, dust, dust. A couple of riderless horses ran dimly past them through it, seeming to drift by like fish in a muddy aquarium tank.

Then a man appeared, running on foot. As he slowed down and walked up to the line of spears, Padway saw that he was a Lombard.

While Padway was wondering if this was some lunatic out to tackle his army single-handed, the man shouted: *'Armaio! Mercy!'* The Goths exchanged startled glances.

Then a couple of more barbarians appeared, one of them leading a horse. They yelled. '*Armaio, timrja!* Mercy, comrade! *Armaio, frijond!* Mercy, friend!'

A plumed Imperial cuirassier rode up behind them, shouting in Latin: '*Amicus!*' Then appeared whole companies of Imperialists, horse and foot, German, Slav, Hun, and Anatolian mixed, bawling, 'Mercy, friend!' in a score of languages.

A solid group of horsemen with a Gothic standard in their midst rode through the Imperialists. Padway recognized a tall, brown-bearded figure in their midst. He croaked: 'Belisarius!'

The Thracian came up, leaned over, and shook hands. 'Martinus! I didn't know you with all that dust on your face. I was afraid I'd be too late. We've been riding hard since dawn. We hit them in the rear, and that was all there was to it. We've got Bloody John, and your King Urias is safe. What shall we do with all these prisoners? There must be twenty or thirty thousand of them at least.'

Padway rocked a little on his feet. 'Oh, round them up and put them in a camp or something. I don't really care. I'm going to sleep on my feet in another minute.'

CHAPTER XVIII

Back in Rome, Urias said slowly: 'Yes, I see your point. Men won't fight for a government they have no stake in. But do you think we can afford to compensate all the loyal landlords whose serfs you propose to free?'

'We'll manage,' said Padway. 'It'll be over a period of years. And this new tax on slaves will help.' Padway did not explain that he hoped, by gradually boosting the tax on slaves, to make slavery an altogether unprofitable institution. Such an idea would have been too bewilderingly radical for even Urias' flexible mind.

Urias continued: 'I don't mind the limitations on the king's power in this new constitution of yours. For myself, that is. I'm a soldier, and I'm just as glad to leave the conduct of civil affairs to others. But I don't know about the Royal Council.'

'They'll agree. I have them more or less eating out of my hand right now. I've shown them how without the telegraph we could never have kept such good track of Bloody John's movements, and without the printing press we could never have roused the serfs so effectively.'

'What else is there?'

'We've got to write the kings of the Franks, explaining politely that it's not our fault if the Burgunds prefer our rule to theirs, but that we certainly don't propose to give them back to their Meroving majesties.

'We've also got to make arrangements with the king of Visigoths for fitting out our ships at Lisbon for their trip to the lands across the Atlantic. He's named you his successor, by the way, so when he dies the east and west Goths will be united again. Reminds me, I have to make a trip to Naples. The shipbuilder down there says he never saw such a crazy design as mine, which is for what we Americans would call a Grand Banks schooner. Procopius'll have to go with me, to discuss details of his history course at our new university.'

'Why are you so set on this Atlantic expedition, Martinus?'

'I'll tell you. In my country we amused ourselves by sucking the smoke of a weed called tobacco. It's a fairly harmless little vice if you don't overdo it. Ever since I arrived here I've been wishing for some tobacco, and the land across the Atlantic is the nearest place you can get any.'

Urias laughed his big, booming laughs. 'I've got to be off. I'd like to see the draft of your letter to Justinian before you send it.'

'Okay, as we say in America. I'll have it for you tomorrow, and also the appointment of Thomasus the Syrian as minister of finance for you to sign. He arranged to get those skilled ironworkers from Damascus through his private business connections, so I shan't have to ask Justinian for them.'

Urias asked: 'Are you sure your friend Thomasus is honest?'

'Sure he's honest. You just have to watch him. Give my regards to Mathaswentha. How is she?'

'She's fine. She's calmed down a lot since all the people she most feared have died, or gone mad. We're expecting a little Amaling, you know.'

'I didn't know! Congratulations.'

'Thanks. When are you going to find a girl, Martinus?'

Padway stretched and grinned. 'Oh, just as soon as I catch up on my sleep.'

Padway watched Urias go with a twinge of envy. He was at the age when bachelors get wistful about their friends' family life. Not that he wanted a repetition of his fiasco with Betty, or a stick of female dynamite like Mathaswentha. He hoped Urias would keep his queen pregnant practically from now on. It might keep her out of mischief.

Padway wrote:

Urias, King of the Goths and Italians, to his Radiant Clemency Flavius Anicius Justinian, Emperor of the Romans, Greetings.

Now that the army sent by your Serene Highness to Italy, under John, the nephew of Vitalianus, better known as Bloody John, is no longer an obstacle to our reconciliation, we resume discussion for terms for the honorable termination of the cruel and unprofitable war between us.

The terms proposed in our previous letter stand, with this exception: Our previously asked indemnity of a hundred thousand solidi is doubled, to compensate our citizens for damages caused by Bloody John's invasion.

There remains the question of the disposal of your general, Bloody John. Though we have never seriously contemplated the collection of Imperial generals as a hobby, your Serenity's actions have forced us into a policy that looks much like it. As we do not wish to cause the Empire a serious loss, we shall release the said John on payment of a modest ransom of fifty thousand solidi.

We earnestly urge your Serenity to consider this course favorably. As you know, the Kingdom of Persia is ruled by King Khusrau, a young man of great force and ability. We have reason to believe that Khusrau will soon attempt another invasion of Syria. You will then need the ablest generals you can find.

Further, our slight ability to foresee the future informs us that in about thirty years there will be born in Arabia a man named Mohammed, who, preaching a heretical religion, will, unless stopped, instigate a great wave of barbarian conquest, subverting the rule both of the Persian Kingdom and the East Roman Empire. We respectfully urge the desirability of securing control of the Arabian Peninsula forthwith, that this calamity shall be stopped at the source.

Please accept this warning as evidence of our friendliest sentiments. We await the gracious favor of an early reply.

by MARTINUS PADUEI, Quæstor

Padway leaned back and looked at the letter. There were other things to attend to: the threat of invasion of Noricum by the Bavarians, and the offer by the Khan of the Avars of an alliance to exterminate the Bulgarian Huns. The alliance would be courteously refused. The Avars would make no pleasanter neighbors than the Bulgars.

Let's see: There was a wandering fanatical monk who was kicking up another row about sorcery. Should he try to smother the man in cream, as by giving him a job? Better see the Bishop of Bologna first; if he had influence in that direction, Padway knew how to make use of it. And it was time he cottoned up to that old rascal Silverius ...

And should he go on with his gunpowder experiments? Padway was not sure that this was desirable. The world had enough means of inflicting death and destruction already. On the other hand his own interests were tied up with those on the Italo-Gothic State, which must therefore be saved at all costs ...

To hell with it, thought Padway. He swept all the papers into a drawer in his desk, took his hat off the peg, and got his horse. He set out for Anicius' house. How could he expect to cut any ice with Dorothea if he didn't even look her up for days after his return to Rome?

Dorothea came out to meet him. He thought how pretty she was.

But there was nothing of hail-the-conquering-hero about her manner. Before he could get a word out, she began: 'You beast! You slimy thing! We befriended you, and you ruin us! My poor old father's heart is broken! And now you've come around to gloat, I suppose!'

'What?'

'Don't pretend you don't know! I know all about that illegal order you issued, freeing the serfs on our estates in Campania. They burned our house, and stole the things I've kept since I was a little girl —' She began to weep.

Padway tried to say something sympathetic, but she flared up again. 'Get out! I never want to see you again! It'll take a squad of your barbarian soldiers to get you into our house. *Get out!*'

Padway got, slowly and dispiritedly. It was a complex world. Almost anything big you did was bound to hurt somebody.

Then his back straightened. It was nothing to feel sorry for oneself about. Dorothea was a nice girl, yes, pretty, and reasonably bright. But she was not extraordinary in these respects; there were plenty of others equally attractive. To be frank, Dorothea was a pretty average young woman. And being Italian, she'd probably be fat at thirty-five.

Government compensation for their losses would do a lot to mend the broken hearts of the Anicii. If they tried to apologize for treating him roughly, he'd be polite and all, but he didn't think he'd go back.

Girls were okay, and he'd probably fall one of these days. But he had more important things to worry over. His success so far in the business of civilization outweighed any little failures in personal relationship.

His job wasn't over. It never would be – until disease or old age or the dagger of some local enemy ended it. There was so much to do, and only a few decades to do it in; compasses and steam engines and microscopes and the writ of habeas corpus.

He'd teetered along for over a year and a half, grabbing a little power here, placating a possible enemy there, keeping far enough out of the bad graces of the various churches, starting some little art such as spinning of sheet copper. Not bad for Mouse Padway! Maybe he could keep it up for years.

And if he couldn't – if enough people finally got fed up with the innovations of Mysterious Martinus – well, there was a semaphore telegraph system running the length and breadth of Italy, some day to be replaced by a true electric telegraph, if he could find time for the necessary experiments. There was a public letter post about to be set up. There were presses in Florence and Rome and Naples pouring out books and pamphlets and newspapers. Whatever happened to him, these things would go on. They'd become too well rooted to be destroyed by accident.

History had, without question, been changed.

Darkness would not fall.

ROGUE QUEEN

To Willy Ley

AUTHOR'S NOTE

While the reader may pronounce the Ormazdian words in this story as he pleases, I offer the following suggestions: *i, e, a, o*, and *u* as in 'police', 'let', 'calm', 'more', and 'rule', respectively; *y* when followed by a vowel as in 'yet', when followed by *r* as in 'myrtle', and otherwise as in 'cyst'. Vowels (other than *y*) have the same values in combination as singly; hence, *Gliid* is 'glee-eed'; *Yaedh* 'yah-edh'. *Dh* represents the *th* in 'the'; *lh* the voiceless *l* (Welsh *ll*); *rh* the voiceless *r* (Welsh *rh*); *kh* the velar fricative (German *ch*). As the last three sounds do not occur in English, they may be rendered as ordinary *l, r,* and *k*. *Viagens* (a Portuguese word) rhymes approximately with 'Leah paints', with the *g* as in 'beige'. A glossary of Ormazdian words and names is appended to the book, but is not necessary to the understanding of the story. The quotation by Bloch in *Chapter IX* is from 'The Oracles' from *Last Poems* by A. E. Housman. Copyright, 1922, 1950. Used by permission of Henry Holt and Company, Inc.

I

The Community

The messenger rose from her chariot seat and sharply cracked her whip. The ueg, its big hands gripping the shafts, craned its long neck around, grunted its indignation, and slightly speeded up the slap-slap of its big flat feet. Many-jointed creeping things scuttled across the wet sand of the beach and slipped with small splashes into the Scarlet Sea.

As soon as the rhythm of the ueg's two feet showed signs of slowing, Rhodh of Elham cracked her whip again. This ueg was an old bluffer, adept at appealing to its driver's sympathy. But with the hills behind them and only a half-hour's drive ahead, Rhodh (who was not given to squandering senti-ment on dumb beasts anyway) had no sympathy to spare. For the news she bore was more important to the Community than the life of an ueg, or even of a worker like herself.

The chariot lurched and canted as the ueg cut in from the beach where the road took up again to cross the base of Khinad Point. Rhodh hardly glanced at the ruined towers of Khinam thrusting jaggedly up from the jagged rocks, though one of her fellow workers, Iroedh, had tried to interest her in the ancient artifacts to be found in the ruins. Such interest was all very well for drones, who had nothing better to do with their time between assignations than to make silly rhythmic noises, or even for Iroedh, who was a queer crea-ture anyway.

But she, Rhodh, could never feel any fascination for the pastimes of her remote ancestors. No creatures with the bestial customs of her forebears, like those described in the *Lay of Idhios*, could produce anything worth the inter-est of a dutiful worker. Besides, her destiny lay higher than the collection of useless knowledge. Someday she'd sit on the Council and do something about round dances and other forms of time wastage. General Rhodh? For-eign Officer Rhodh? With her efficiency rating and moral superiority, there was nothing she could not do.

Rhodh cracked her whip again, this time against the ueg's leathery hide. The animal squawked and leaned forward in a run. This news must go to the highest officer at Elham; if the Council could not grasp the situation, then to the queen herself.

The sun was low in the hazy sky when Rhodh drew up at the outer wall of the Community. The guards, knowing Rhodh, let her through without formal identification. She drove on toward the cluster of interconnected domes that rose from the middle of the intramural park.

In front of the entrance she called '*Branio!*' to the ueg, hitched the beast, and walked stiffly up to the portal. Two workers stood guard on either side of the door, their freshly polished brazen cuirasses, studded kilts, greaves, and crested helmets blazing in the low sun. Their spears stood straight and their faces showed nothing but corpse-like calm.

Rhodh knew them. The one on the left was young Tydh, a sound regulation-minded worker; the other was the woolly-minded antiquarian Iroedh.

A few minutes before, these guards had been standing at ease while Tydh chattered and Iroedh ate a ripe vremoel and half listened, half daydreamed.

'... and you'd think any fool would know better than to change queens with the war cry of the Arsuuni practically ringing in our ears. I know Intar's rate of laying is down, but so what? It's high enough for the purposes of the Community, but when the Council get an idea in their heads ...'

Between bites Iroedh said: 'We don't know that queens will be changed.'

'Intar cannot refuse the challenge ... Or do you think she will kill Princess Estir? Not likely; she's fat and wheezy, while Estir moves like a noag on the hunt and handles a spear like a soldier of Tvaarm. Of course there are those who say Intar's lucky. But for the conflict with the Arsuuni we need, not a lively young queen who can lean her own height and best an old one in the Royal Duel, but an old and crafty one who—'

Iroedh sighted Rhodh, finished her vremoel in one big bite, threw the pit into the shrubbery, and said: 'Attention! A chariot's coming.'

Tydh snapped upright but continued to talk. 'That's Rhodh, who went to Thidhem on that project to plant a colony in Gliid. She's always rushing about on some mission or other; they say she'll make the Council yet. She was to get a quit-claim from Queen Maiur on the valley—'

'Belay the talk.'

'But she's one of our own—'

'I said belay it.'

As junior, Tydh perforce shut up while the chariot drew near and stopped. Iroedh watched Rhodh stamp up the steps in an umbrella hat, laced boots, and a traveling cloak of long-stapel suroel which because of the warmth was thrown back over both shoulders. Her only other item of wear was a sheath knife hanging from a light baldric. Her spear she had left in its boot in the chariot.

Iroedh watched her approach with mixed feelings. Once she had liked Rhodh, thinking she shared her own enthusiasm for the lost arts of antiquity. However, they had both been very young at the time, and later Rhodh's interest in Iroedh's hobbies had faded into the grim devotion to duty of the ideal

Avtiny worker. For a while Iroedh had almost hated Rhodh in her disappointment, but then this feeling too had subsided into a vague regret for the loss of early promise.

Rhodh exclaimed in a voice high with tension: 'Sisters, who is the highest officer of the Council at Elham now? I must see her at once!'

'Great Eunmar!' said Tydh. 'What on Niond is the matter, Rhodh? Has another Community declared war upon us?'

'Never mind. Quick, who is she?'

'I'll check the list,' said Iroedh. 'The general is of course with the scouting force on the frontier of Tvaarm. The commissary officer has gone to Thidhem for the eight-day. The upbringing officer is sick. The foreign officer is with the general; the royal officer's at the queen's laying ... By Gwyyr, not one officer of the Council is available!'

'That is impossible! The law requires at least one to be on duty at all times.'

'The upbringing officer was supposed to be, but was taken with cramps. Meanwhile—'

'Then I must see the queen!'

'What?' cried Iroedh and Tydh together.

'Queen Intar of Elham, herself, at once!'

'Are you mad?' said Iroedh. 'She's laying!'

'That cannot be helped. This news is more important than one egg more or less.'

'Impossible, unless Queen Omvyr's soldiers have already attacked.'

'This is even more momentous than that. At least we know all about the Arsuuni.'

Tydh looked at Iroedh, who as senior would have the final say. 'We dare not, Iroedh. The regulations are explicit. We should be punished.'

Iroedh said: 'Tell us your story, Rhodh, and I will judge.'

Rhodh fanned herself with her wide-brimmed hat. 'Stupid, stupid ... But I suppose I must. Hmp. When the representative of Queen Maiur of Thidhem and I went to Gliid to rough out the bounds of the proposed colony, we arrived just as a – what would you call it? – an airship or sky ship alighted, bringing beings from the stars who call themselves *men*.'

Iroedh and Tydh exchanged glances of puzzlement shading into consternation. The latter said:

'Impossible, Rhodh dear! It's been proved that the stars must be too hot to support life. Or is this a new version of one of those old legends Iroedh collects, about the gods' coming to earth?'

'I assure you,' snapped Rhodh, 'that I saw the creatures myself and talked to them. And nobody has ever accused me of lying. It seems that many stars are circled by worlds like ours, and many of these worlds support life. There is even a sort of interstellar government called the Interplanetary Council.

These men are among the most advanced of the civilized species on these other worlds (or at least advanced in the natural sciences) and have sent their sky ship to discover us, as we might send a galley to look over an island in the remote regions of the Scarlet Sea.'

As Rhodh paused for breath, Tydh said: 'It's just as the Oracle of Ledhwid said:

> 'When the stars fall down and the waters rise
> Then flowers of bronze shall grow on the dome;
> And a drone shall be deemed uncommonly wise
> When he seeks a new home.'

Rhodh said: 'I suppose you mean that when the sky ship comes all our drones will turn rogue. We'll see to *that!*'

'But what do these men look like? Are they many-legged like a dhwyg or all jelly like a huusg?'

'They are really quite human-looking, with certain differences.'

'Such as?' said Tydh.

'Oh, they're a little shorter than we are, with skins of yellow and brown instead of red like ours; they have five digits on each hand and foot instead of four; their ears are large and wrinkled around the edge; their eyes have round pupils instead of slit pupils like ours; they have hair all over the tops of their heads instead of a single strip running from the scalp down the back as with us; and – well, that gives you an idea. What is more important is that they have no caste of workers!'

Iroedh spoke: 'Then who built and manned this sky ship?'

'Their drones and queens. The ship's company consists mainly of drones, with two or three queens. When I asked where their workers were it took them a while to understand the question, and then the one who learned our language assured me they had none – all were functional males and females.'

'What!' cried Iroedh.

'And you call them civilized?' said Tydh. 'When they reproduce like animals?'

'I do not care to argue the point,' said Rhodh. 'I am trying to convince you that this arrival has enormous possibilities for good or evil to the Community, and it therefore behooves you to take me to the queen at once!'

Tydh said: 'If you'll wait an hour, the queen will have laid and the royal officer will have certified the egg and placed it in the incubator—'

'No,' said Iroedh, 'I agree that the matter requires immediate attention. We will go to the queen—'

'But the regulations!' wailed Tydh. 'We shall be punished—'

'I'll take responsibility,' said Iroedh. 'You stay here, Tydh.'

Iroedh led the way through the corridors to the central dome. Outside the anteroom to the queen's chambers stood extra guards, for Princess Estir was practically of age and there must be no risk of a chance encounter before the formal fight for succession. In the anteroom sat a massive drone with a cheerful air. As Iroedh clanked across he said:

'Hello, beautiful!'

'Hail, Antis,' said Iroedh. 'You're on tonight?'

Antis grinned. 'Right. She'd have me out of turn if she dared. And tomorrow, if I can – you know. How about it?'

'I have to work. Scrubbing.'

'Sad; all work and no play will make Iroedh a dull girl, don't you think? Let me know when you get a day off.'

Iroedh became aware that Rhodh was staring sternly at her. Just then the inner door opened and Iroedh told the worker who opened it:

'Guard Iroedh to see the queen, with Messenger Rhodh.'

'She's laying this very minute! I cannot—'

'This is an emergency. The minute the egg is laid, inform me. I take responsibility.'

The worker ducked back into the inner chambers and presently returned, saying: 'It's been laid, and she'll see you. But she says your news had better be important.'

Queen Intar's lounge chair overflowed with her sagging bulk. A worker operated on the queen's huge mammae with a breast pump. The egg lay in the sandbox, where the royal officer was marking code symbols upon it in crayon.

'Well?' snapped the queen. 'Don't tell me you broke in upon my laying period just to inform me that old Maiur won't give up her nonexistent claims on Gliid! I've had workers whipped for less.'

Iroedh said: 'Many eggs, Queen. I take responsibility for this interruption. Pray let Rhodh speak.'

Rhodh repeated her story with further details. Queen Intar leaned forward when she described the men's sexual organization, and asked:

'Could these self-styled functional males be mere male neuters, a caste of male workers corresponding to our neuter females?'

'No; at least they said such was not the case. We could not very well demand proof.'

'Then does this discrepancy in numbers mean that their males much outnumber the females?'

'Again, no. In numbers they are about equal, but as the female is smaller and viviparous they seldom go in for anything so strenuous as exploration.'

'A fine lot of females! Are they mammals like us, or do they feed their young on this and that?'

'They are mammals; the functional females had fully developed glands – though not so fine as yours, Queen.'

Trust Rhodh, Iroedh thought, always to work in some little bootlicking compliment to her superiors. The queen asked:

'How are they fertilized?'

'I was not able to examine their organs, but—'

'I don't mean that; I mean what social code governs the act? Do they go about it catch-as-catch-can, like the beasts?'

'On the contrary, they are governed by an elaborate code. During their long journey from their star, not one of all those males—'

'What star *is* that?'

'We cannot see it from here, but they pointed to the constellation Huusg. They call it Sol or Sun and their planet Terra or Yrth, depending upon the language.'

'What are their intentions?' asked the queen.

'They say they wish merely to study our planet and to try to trace part of an earlier expedition which disappeared on Niond. At least they say it did.'

'I've never heard of such a thing. Do you believe their peaceful protestations?'

Rhodh shrugged. 'One cannot, without proof, believe the statements of beings not merely from another Community or of another race, but of another world. They may be truthful and harmless; Ledhwid only knows. Personally I am always suspicious of people who profess to be motivated by a passion for knowledge for its own sake, regardless of its utility.'

She shot a sharp look at Iroedh as she said this. Queen Intar persisted in her questions:

'What did they think of us?'

'At first they seemed a little afraid of us, as indeed we were of them. After they learned we had no weapons but spears they became friendly enough, and appeared quite as amused by our account of our ways and achievements as we were astonished by them. This interpreter, called *Blos* or *Blok*, told me our caste system reminded him of a small flying creature called a *bii*, domesticated on his home world for its sweet secretions.'

'I trust you didn't give them information that would be useful to an enemy!'

'No, no, I was careful ...'

At length the queen said: 'I can certainly see those possibilities for good and evil. The omens have been hinting at some portentous development. If we could somehow use them against the Arsuuni ... If, for instance, we could capture one and hold him as a hostage to compel the others—'

'Queen, I have tried to make clear that their powers are so far beyond ours that any violence would be sheer madness.'

'Poof! What powers?'

'Could we build a ship like that?'

'N-no, but what of it? How can they harm anybody with their magical ship, save by dropping it on them? And if it's anything like a normal water-ship it would break like an egg if they tried it.'

'They have other powers. I have seen one stand up to a charging vakhnag and point a little hollow metal rod at it, and *bang*! the beast fell dead with a hole through it you could put your head into.'

'Did they tell you how this device worked?'

'No. When I asked, they became evasive.'

'Clever rascals, it seems. What other devils' tricks have they to hand?'

'That is hard to say. I heard they had a device that tells whether a person is lying. There was so much new about them I couldn't absorb it all at once. I will make notes as I remember and write a report for the Council.'

'Good.' Intar turned. 'My good Iroedh, you did well to bring Rhodh in without waiting to untangle the threads of protocol. Resume your watch, and, as I shall probably have further orders for you, don't leave Elham. By the way, on your way out tell that drone I shan't want him. I have other matters on my mind.'

As Iroedh passed through the anteroom on her way out, she saw Antis pacing the floor and gave him the message.

'My luck!' Antis scowled, then brightened. 'In that case, why shouldn't we take our supper over to the ruins? Ythidh guards the dronery tonight, and if I can neither elude nor bribe her my name's not Antis of Elham.'

'Fine,' said Iroedh. 'But Antis dear, let me warn you again not to drop hints of our unsupervised amusements in front of others.'

'I don't.'

'You did before Rhodh just now.'

'That stupid creature?'

'She's not so stupid she didn't understand what you were talking about. If she complains to the Council it could be unpleasant. She would, too.'

'What do they think I'm going to do to you? What *can* I do besides eat supper and help you look for antiques?' He laughed heartily, showing a fine set of blue teeth. 'Anybody'd think you were a functional female!'

Iroedh sniffed. 'Sometimes I find your peculiar sense of humor positively revolting.'

He waved a hand. 'Forget it, beautiful. I shall see you at Khinam at sunset.'

Iroedh had been back on watch for an hour and was beginning to look for her relief when Rhodh appeared, saying:

'Queen Intar has decided to send a party back to this sky ship to establish closer relations with the men. As senior member I shall head the party, the foreign officer being unavailable. The others will be Iinoedh, Avpandh, Vardh, and you.'

Iroedh's face lit up. She was especially pleased that Vardh was coming, for Vardh had always looked up to Iroedh.

'What wonderful luck! Thank you, Rhodh dear!'

'Hmp! Don't thank me. I would never have chosen you, and I don't know why the queen did. This would never have happened if the Council had been functioning, but you know Queen Intar. The agricultural officer must have put in a word for you; we all know you're a pet of hers.'

Iroedh listened first in astonishment and then in anger to this tirade. She flared:

'What have you got against me? I've traveled before, and my efficiency rating is well above the mean.'

'It is not that, but these tales of your fraternizing with a drone, sneaking off on picnics with him and Ledhwid knows what else. He practically confirmed the rumor with his own words today.'

'And what business is that of yours?'

'None, but you asked me why I didn't think you an ideal choice for this mission. Workers who associate with drones fall into dronish habits. They waste time, fool around, and take their pleasure when there is work to be done. They dance and plant flowers and that sort of nonsense. However, the next Cleanup will take care of that!'

Iroedh, who had reason to hate the word 'Cleanup,' made her face blank and replied coldly: 'I suggest you defer judgment on my fitness for the mission until it's over. When do I report?'

'Tomorrow after brunch, in full campaign gear. Good night.'

Iroedh watched Antis peck with his flint and pyrites until he had a small fire going, then slipped around to windward so as not to have to endure the smell of cooking meat. It was a measure of their affection that they were willing to eat together, the pleasure they got from each other's company outweighing the disgust that the diet of each aroused in the other.

Out on the Scarlet Sea a great flying fish flapped and wheeled in circles, looking for smaller sea creatures to snap up, and silhouetted blackly against a blood-colored setting sun. Around them rose the ruins of Khinam, whose shattered spires and hypnotic mosaics the modern Avtini did not even try to imitate, let alone surpass. Near at hand rose the Memorial Pillar of Khinam, celebrating some forgotten hero or victory. Although the statue that crowned it had been eroded down to a mere pitted torso, the pillar itself, being of solid masonry, had survived better than most of the city's structures.

Antis, looking up from his fire making to watch the flying fish, remarked: 'That's an omen of change.'

'What is?'

'When a flying fish circles withershins.'

'Oh, silly! You see omens in everything, and changes are always occurring.'

Iroedh fell into a reverie as she absently munched her own meager meal of biscuits and vegetables while turning over her loot in the fading light.

'What,' she said, 'do you suppose this is? It's too frail for a weapon, and doesn't look like an ornament. A staff of office, perhaps?'

Antis looked up from the haunch of leipag he was roasting. 'That's a telh, with which the ancients used to make music.'

'How does it work?'

'You blow into that hole at the end and twiddle your fingers over the other holes. Remember that picture on the wall of the Throne Hall?'

Iroedh blew without result.

'Come to think,' said Antis, 'you don't blow into the hole, but across it – like that!' Iroedh's shift in position was rewarded by a wail from the flute. 'Here, let me try it.'

'Your hands are greasy!' said Iroedh.

'Very well, after I finish this. What's that book among the junk?'

Iroedh picked up an ancient volume from the litter. Its pages of vakhwil bark were cracked and crumbly, and the ink so faded that the text could not be read in the waning light. Above each line of writing ran a strip of fine parallel lines dotted with little black spots.

'A songbook!' cried Antis. 'What luck!'

'I suppose those little black spots show what hole you close with your fingers?'

'Or more likely which you leave open. Try it.'

Iroedh began blowing and fingering. Despite her inexpertness, a certain tune became recognizable.

'I think I know that one,' said Antis. 'When I was first admitted to the dronery there was an old drone named Baorthus who'd been let live through several Cleanups after his time because he was so skilled at his task. He used to hum a tune like that. I suppose I ought to have memorized it, but I was too occupied with my new function, and at the next Cleanup Baorthus got it. I'd forgotten all about it till now.'

He wiped his hands on a weed and came to look over Iroedh's shoulder. 'By Eunmar! With more light we could read the song and the notes at the same time, don't you think? Let me feed the fire.'

He went out, leaving Iroedh to tweedle mournfully. There was a sound of breaking sticks and back he came with a bundle of fuel.

'Now,' he said when the fire was blazing, 'let's start at the beginning. You play, I sing.' He scowled at the faint spidery letters. 'A plague on this archaic spelling! Let's go:

'Love does not torment forever.
Came it on me like a fire,
Like the lava of Mount Wisgad,
Or the blaze that sears a forest.
When my love is not far distant,
Do not think my sleep is easy;
All the night I lie in torment,
Preyed upon by love in secret ...'

Their performance was hampered by the fact that every line or two one or the other would get off the tune, and it finally broke up in a fit of mutual laughter.

When she could get her breath Iroedh asked: 'What's this 'loved one' the fellow keeps talking about?'

'A friend, I suppose; a fellow member of the Community.'

'I can't imagine losing sleep over a fellow worker; or even over you, my best friend.'

Antis shrugged. 'Ask the Oracle of Ledhwid. The ancients had some funny ideas. Maybe their lack of dietary control had something to do with it.'

Iroedh mused: 'The only time I ever saw an Avtin so stirred was when that foreigner, Ithodh of Yeym, learned that her Community had been annihilated by the Arsuuni. She killed herself, even though the Council offered to admit her to Elham as a member.'

'Well, no doubt we should be upset if we heard Elham had been wiped out. It may be yet, you know.'

'Let's not think of anything so horrible before we must!'

'All right, my dear. Let me borrow the telh and the book, will you?'

'Certainly, but why?' said Iroedh.

'I thought I should have fun with my fellow drones. If you hear strange sounds from the dronery, it'll be Kutanas and I teaching them the ancient art of singing.'

'I hope it won't cause the trouble the *Lay of Idhios* did!'

'And who taught me the *Idhios*?'

'I did, but only to keep it from dying out. I didn't expect a poetic orgy —'

'Just so; and neither shall these songs be let perish. After all, I shan't be around too much longer to cherish them.'

'What do you mean?' she asked, knowing very well what he meant, but hoping against hope.

'One of these days there'll be a Cleanup, and I'm one of the oldest drones.'

'Oh, Antis!' She seized his arm. 'How dreadful! Has the queen been complaining?'

'Not so far as I know, and I've certainly been giving her upstanding service. But a Cleanup has been overdue for some time.'

'But you're not really old! You're hardly older than I, and should be able to perform your duty for many years.'

'I know, but that's not the Council's view. Maybe they're afraid we shall turn rogue if let live until we're old and crafty.'

'You wouldn't ever, would you?'

'I hadn't thought about it. I suppose if you learned I was planning to escape and join the rogues you'd turn me in like a dutiful worker?'

'Of course. I mean I suppose so. It would be a dreadful decision to make. But don't plan anything so anti-Communitarian! Hold on as long as you can. You don't – I—'

Her voice choked off in a sob.

'Why, Iroedh!' said Antis, putting an arm around her. 'You sound like one of those ancients with their "burning love."'

Iroedh pulled herself together. 'I'm foolish. And I'm no ancient, but a neuter worker and proud of it. Still, life would be so utterly empty without you.'

'Thanks.' He gave her a friendly squeeze.

'Nobody else in Elham shares my love for antiques. Sometimes I feel as a solitary rogue must feel, wandering the woods and looking in on the domes of the Communities he can never enter again.'

Antis grinned in the gathering dark. 'I can reassure you on one point, darling: If I should ever plan to go rogue, I won't confide in anybody who might spoil my plan.'

She shivered. 'Br-r-r. We should have brought clothing with us. Let's go back.'

II

The Sky Ship

'Remember,' said Rhodh, 'we have two objectives: to use these men and their knowledge against Tvaarm, and to keep them from learning anything they might use against us.'

Her ueg trotted beside that of Iroedh along the stretch where the road to Thidhem became one with the beach of the Scarlet Sea. The chariots of Iinoedh, Avpandh, and Vardh bumped along behind.

Rhodh continued: 'So keep your eyes and ears open and your mouth, as far as possible, shut. There is so much new about these men that none of us can grasp it all at once. Flatter them, get them to brag, anything to loosen their tongues. But don't encourage them to visit us, tell them where Elham is, or reveal our political situation or methods of warfare. I am speaking particularly to you, Iroedh, because I know your weaknesses. They are interested not only in us but also in our history, and would like nothing better than to be guided to Khinam to look for relics. Then all they would have to do is to climb one of the towers to see the domes of Elham.'

'I'll be careful,' said Iroedh, bored almost to the screaming point because Rhodh had been through all this before. She wanted Rhodh to leave her alone so that she could get back to her golden daydreams of ancient times.

'Your task will be to cultivate Blok, who speaks Avtinyk after a fashion and, like you, is interested in many different philosophies. If you apply yourself diligently to your task you will forget all about that drone you so imprudently befriended.'

'Why should I?' said Iroedh in a louder voice than she intended. There went her good resolution not to let Rhodh bait her!

'Don't shout. You had better begin soon, because he will no longer be around on our return.'

'You mean—'

Rhodh turned a cruel smile toward Iroedh. 'Didn't you know? The Council collected a quorum this morning just before we left and fixed the date for the next Cleanup. It was decided to kill the three senior drones: Antis, Kutanas, and Dyos, to make room for the next crop, some time this eightday. They were of course confined to balk escape.'

Iroedh's rose-red skin paled a shade. Eunmar blast them! So that was why Antis hadn't said goodbye. First she had thought he must be angry; then she wondered if he'd forgotten (which was unlike him); then she speculated as to whether he was trying to protect her by minimizing their attachment. When all the while ...

'*Weu!*' she said in a choked voice. 'You might have told me sooner.'

'And have you throw an emotional scene or balk at your orders, and hold up our departure? I'm not so stupid. You will live to thank me yet.'

'Why was such an early date chosen for the Cleanup?'

'Because of that prophecy Tydh cited, about a drone's seeking a new home. It was feared that if the drones heard of it they would desert in a mass. And it is not really an early date; one has been due for some time. Antis will certainly be no loss; there is no place in a well-run Community for his japes and scrapes.'

Iroedh subsided, her mind in turmoil. She even thought of wheeling her chariot around and dashing back to Elham, but lifelong discipline and ingrained devotion to the Community stopped her. Besides, what would she accomplish except to get herself punished?

What to do? Though a mature worker, Iroedh had not yet settled into fatalistic acceptance of the tragedies of life. There must be something ...

Why should Rhodh gloat? Iroedh could think of no reason for Rhodh to hate her. She had done nothing except be herself. That must be it; Rhodh, outwardly contemptuous of Iroedh's interest in the ancient arts, secretly envied her it. Or perhaps Rhodh was simply one with a passion for uniformity, to whom Iroedh's heterodoxy represented a social eyesore to be extirpated.

Iroedh's mind went back into its little revolving cage: How to save Antis? There must be something. No, nothing. But there must be. If she could only be clever enough to think of it. What, then? If I could only think of it. How do you know there is anything to think of? There simply must be. But that's wretched logic; things don't exist because you wish they did ...

She pondered the matter for hours while they drove past the place where the beasts had devoured the unfortunate Queen Rhuar, and over the Lhanwaed Hills where forgotten legends told of an egg the size of a royal dome waiting to hatch out – what, nobody knew. Iroedh had come to no conclusion when they reached the frontier of Thidhem.

Here they were stopped by a pair of guards whose armor bore the symbol of Queen Maiur. Rhodh identified herself to the senior of these guards, Gogledh.

'I know you, Rhodh,' said Gogledh in the dialect of Thidhem. 'I met you when you came here about the Gliid colony. Is this a surveying party, or what? When will the first colonists go out?'

Rhodh replied: 'No, we are investigating the sky ship. What is Thidhem doing about it?'

'Nothing. Queen Maiur feels that contact with visitors having customs so different from ours might unsettle our social structure. She is even trying to stop all discussion of the event – which you know as well as I can't be done.'

'Has your Council no say?'

'In theory, yes, but in practice Maiur usually gets her way. How about your colony?'

'No colony until the war with Tvaarm has been settled. If it comes we shall need every worker who can wield a spear.'

Gogledh said: 'You have a princess near her majority, whom you were going to send to Gliid, haven't you?'

'Yes: Estir. She matures in about another eight-day.'

'And if you don't send her out with the new colony, there will have to be a Royal Duel, won't there?' Gogledh added eagerly. 'And maybe there'll be passes for visitors from Thidhem?'

'I don't know; that will be up to the Council.'

'Oh. Well, have the Arsuuni moved yet?'

'Not the last I heard. Our general's on the frontier watching.'

'Poor Elham! I wish, just once, an Avtiny Community would overcome one of the Arsuuni.'

Rhodh sighed. 'We will do our best, but what can we accomplish against a caste of soldiers half again our size? We should need not only luck but also a great superiority in numbers, which we do not have.'

'How many adult workers have you?'

'About four hundred and fifty. There would have been more but for last year's plague.'

Gogledh said: 'It's too bad there is no method by which our workers and yours could both fight the Arsuuni at once.'

'Yes, isn't it? But that is the way of things. They are too shrewd to attack both our Communities at the same time.'

On the afternoon of the third day, after Gogledh had left them, the five Elhamny workers entered the valley of Gliid.

Iinoedh cried: 'Oh, look!'

Down near the center of the valley, dull-gleaming in the sunshine, rose a cylindrical object that could only be the sky ship, standing upon its base like the Memorial Pillar of Khinam, and tapering to a blunt point at the upper end.

Even Rhodh, normally a stranger to such emotions, seemed stirred. She said: 'Let's hurry!' and cracked her whip.

The five vehicles filed down the winding road into the valley. Vardh said:

'I'm so excited; I've never been to Gliid! What's that strange-looking pinnacle springing out from the cliffs?'

She pointed. Iroedh explained:

'That's Survivors' Point.'

'What does the name mean?'

'It refers to the last survivors among the bisexual Avtini, two thousand years ago.'

'You mean when Queen Danoakor rationalized the diet of the race?'

'Yes,' said Iroedh.

Iinoedh asked: 'What became of the survivors?'

'They were besieged sixty-fours of days. One account says that when Danoakor's army reached the Point, the bisexuals were all dead of starvation; another asserts that they leaped off the cliff to their deaths.'

'How dreadful!' said Vardh.

'Served them right,' snapped Rhodh over her shoulder. 'We should forget about those bestial savage days. If I had my way I would destroy every historical record. If it weren't for dronish sentimentalists like Iroedh, we should have done away with all that rubbish long ago.'

The three younger workers subsided, as prudent juniors do when a quarrel impends among their seniors. Iroedh for her part said nothing because her mind was too full of reveries about the survivors and their tragic fate, of speculations about the impending meeting with the men, and the ever-present nagging worry over the doom of Antis.

As the sky ship loomed nearer, Iroedh was struck by the vast size of the thing. You could crowd a whole Community into it, assuming it was all hollow and not filled with the magical machinery of the men.

Things moved around the base of the sky ship. Evidently, Iroedh thought, those within had seen the column of chariots from afar. Rhodh, with Queen Intar's guidon whipping at the head of her spear, drove along the over-grown road to the open space where the thing had alighted. This space looked as though it had been cleared by the landing itself, for trees and shrubs were burned to ashes in a wide circle around the object.

One of the men stood where the burned circle touched the edge of the road. Iroedh looked it over as Rhodh, with a clang, jumped down from her chariot and the rest followed suit. Iinoedh gathered up the reins of the five uegs while the rest crowded forward.

The man was about Iroedh's height, quite Avtiny-looking despite its other-worldly origin. It was of slim build like a worker or princess, not burly like a drone or fat like a queen. It was covered with a substance that Iroedh at first thought to be a queer loose skin, but which closer scrutiny showed to be clothes, cut and stitched in various intricate ways to hug the body: boots not unlike those of the Avtini, but higher; a garment like a tunic with short sleeves; and another garment which Iroedh could only have called a leg tunic, or forked kilt, covering the creature from waist to calf where the legs of the garment disappeared into the boots. The whole was held together by an assortment of buttons and belts so complicated to Iroedh's eye that she wondered how the man had any time left after putting on and taking off these intricate vestments.

Though Rhodh had spoken of the men as having 'hair all over the tops of their heads,' this one had no hair on top at all, but a bare pink scalp with a fringe of brownish hair around the sides and back and another smaller fringe on the upper lip. Iroedh found the blue of its eyes startling, since most of the eyes she was familiar with were yellow.

In the crook of one arm it held an object something like a large version of the flute she had found in Khinam: a wooden stock or handle whence a dark metal rod or tube projected, the whole thing about as long as the man's arm, with mysterious knobs and projections. Then Iroedh remembered: This must be one of the men's magical weapons. She hoped the man would not be seized with an urge to point it at her and cause it to make a hole in her one could stick one's head into.

The man's cheeks drew back, exposing teeth of a surprising yellow-white. Rhodh, Iroedh thankfully remembered, had warned her not to be alarmed by this gesture. It meant, not that the man was going to bite, but that it was pleased; the act was in fact the Terran equivalent of a smile, which among the Avtini was of course made by rounding the mouth into an O.

The man spoke: 'Hello, Rhodh! I did not expect you back so soon. Another worker was just here, from a place called Ledhwid. I see you have brought company.'

It spoke Avtinyk slowly, with a thick accent and many mistakes. Iroedh was a little puzzled by the statement about 'bringing company,' which anybody could see for herself. Perhaps such a meaningless statement was a ceremonial gesture, of which the men employed many. Just as a worker meeting a queen said: 'Many eggs!'

Rhodh said: 'This is my next junior, Iroedh,' and went on to introduce the rest.

The man said: 'I am Bloch – Winston Bloch, and I am surely pleased to know you.'

Vardh spoke: 'Do you mean Winston *of* Blok? Is Blok your Community?'

'No; it is my – uh – one of my names.'

'You mean you have more than one?'

'Yes. Three, in fact.'

'Why?' asked Vardh.

'Too complicated to explain now.'

'At least tell us the proper manner of addressing you.'

'On Terra they call me Dr Bloch. What can we do for you?'

'Iroedh will tell you,' said Rhodh. 'The rest of us will set up a camp nearby, if you have no objections.'

'None at all,' said Bloch with a wary air. 'My dear Iroedh, would you care to – uh – step into our ship?'

'Thank you. I should like to see the whole ship,' said Iroedh, not knowing quite how to handle the situation but plunging ahead anyway.

Bloch gave its head a shake. 'I fear that is impossible. We are overhauling for the return trip, and you would get – uh – what do you call *grease?* – dirt all over your pretty pink skin. But come on; we will have a cup of coffee.'

'*Kothi?*' said Iroedh, walking beside him toward the ship.

'Coffee, with a *ff*. You shall see.'

'Has your ship a name?'

'Sure; do you see those letters? They spell *Paris*, the name of one of our – ah – Communities.'

'Are you really a functional male?'

Bloch looked at her with a curious expression. 'Of course!'

'And yet you *work?*'

'Certainly. Our males are not at all like your drones, who exist for one purpose only. Though I dare say there are those among us who would not find that such a bad deal.' He tilted his head back and shouted in his own tongue: 'Ahoy! Let down the hoist!'

Though she did not understand the words, Iroedh was taken with a desire to run away, for it had just occurred to her that these creatures might seize her for a hostage, or for a specimen to take apart. It would be just her luck. Yet Rhodh and her squad were over on the far side of the clearing. Having taken off their armor and the loose wrap-around tunics they wore under it to keep it from chafing, they were setting up their camp in apparent unconcern. And here came a thing like an oversized bucket dangling down on the end of a chain of gray metal. No doubt Iroedh was serving her Community by risking her life in the clutches of the men, but …

Bloch swung his legs over the side of the bucket, saying: 'Hop in!'

Oh well, thought Iroedh, what did anything matter if Antis would be dead when she returned? She climbed in. The hoist rose.

Iroedh glanced over the side, then seized the edge of the car in a frenzy of panic. Her eyes bulged. She tried to speak but could only croak. Her stomach heaved so that she thought she would lose her hours-old brunch. With a little moan she curled up on the floor of the vehicle, hands over eyes.

She had never before been dangled in mid-air without a tree trunk or other support in plain sight, and found the experience terrifying beyond all recollection. As the hoist rose, the hum of the hoisting machinery came louder and louder to her ears.

'Cheer up,' said Bloch's voice; 'the chain has never broken yet. Here we are.'

Iroedh, feeling a little ashamed, forced herself to rise. Clutching the hand-rail with a deathly grip and refraining from looking down, she climbed after Bloch onto the platform against which the bucket now hung.

She went through the entrance, observing that the ship was built of the same gray metal as the hoist. She asked:

'What is the ship made of, Daktablak?'

'We call it *steel* – or rather *iron*. It is the common metal that is harder than copper and its – what would you call a mixture?'

'Alloys? We know no metal harder than cold-worked bronze. We have gold and silver, but they have only a few special uses.'

She fell silent as they ducked through passageways into the little wardroom. It was crowded with other men, both male and female. Iroedh recognized the females by their smaller size and their breasts, despite the fact that, like the males, they were clothed.

She now realized that Bloch must be tall for his kind, for all the others were shorter than he. Their colors ranged from pale yellow-pink through various tans and bronzes to a brown that was almost black. Perhaps, she thought, different races were represented on the ship, though how they associated without trying to exterminate one another, as did the races on Niond, she did not understand.

Bloch introduced her, beginning with a dark brown man almost as tall as he but much fatter, wearing brass buttons on his tunic: 'Captain Subbarau; Miss Dulac, my assistant; Mr O'Mara, our photographer ...'

He went on through other names until they ceased to register in Iroedh's mind: 'Norden, Markowicz, elJandala, Kang, Lobos, Cody ...' Most of them she could not have pronounced even if she could have remembered them.

At last they were all gone but Captain Subbarau, O'Mara, Miss Dulac, and Bloch. The photographer was shorter and thicker than Bloch (though not so stout as Subbarau) with wavy black hair and blunt features. Subbarau looked at him and said:

'O'Mara!'

The man gave the others what Iroedh interpreted as a sour look and went. Bloch and the Dulac female stared at his back, and Iroedh caught an impression of tension.

'Now,' said Subbarau, 'we shall have a spot of coffee and cake. I trust, my dear Iroedh, they won't poison you. They didn't hurt your friend Rhodh when she was here before. Take off your helmet if you like.'

Bloch translated, and the conversation proceeded creepingly with much fumbling for words. Iroedh was glad to take off her helmet, as she was tired of bumping the crest against the overhead.

Bloch said: 'Captain, when I asked them what we could do for them by way of making conversation, their leader said Iroedh would tell us.'

Subbarau gave a thin version of the startling Terran smile. 'I take it they want something. How different from the rest of the Galaxy! Say your say, Madame Iroedh.'

Iroedh told of the war with the Arsuuni, feeling her way nervously. For all she knew, these strangers might be the sort who always sided with the stronger party.

'So,' she concluded, pausing between phrases for Bloch to translate, 'if you could destroy Tvaarm with your magical weapons, we should be everlastingly grateful and would promise to support your interests among the Communities on Niond.'

The men exchanged glances. Iroedh, feeling that this was not going too well, faltered:

'We could pay you. We have large stores of cereal grains, and of the suroel fibers we make our cloaks from. We even have a fair supply of the gold and silver from which we make our queens' regalia and other ornaments.'

Subbarau and Bloch conversed briefly and then the latter turned to Iroedh. Though she could not interpret his expression, he sounded sympathetic.

'It is not a matter of payment, Iroedh. If we could we would do it for nothing – that is, if conditions are as you describe them. But while we do not wish to injure your feelings, your grain and gold would be of no value to us unless we were marooned here by a failure of the ship. Our real reason for refusal is that our orders strictly forbid us to interfere in the local affairs of any planet, regardless of our sympathies.'

'Even to help a peaceful Community defend itself against wrongful and unprovoked aggression?'

'Even that. Why are the Arsuuni attacking you?'

'It's their regular method of providing for their natural increase. Instead of building themselves new Communities, they seize ours and occupy them, and make slaves of such of our workers as survive the fighting.'

'Well, you perceive how it is. Not that I doubt your story, but every combatant always has an adequate justification for his position. When we land on a strange planet, the first people we meet are likely to have hereditary enemies over the hill and to give us a dozen excellent reasons for helping them to exterminate these foes. If we yield to the temptation we are likely to discover that we have destroyed the side with the better cause, at least according to our way of thinking, or that we have antagonized half the inhabitants of the planet. The only sure method of avoiding such *gaffes* is a rigid rule against interference.'

Iroedh cautiously sipped her coffee. It seemed like a bitter beverage to drink for pleasure, but if it hadn't poisoned Rhodh it probably would not kill her. She must keep trying to hook the space travelers into some kind of commitment. Not only was the life of the Community at stake, but also she had vague hopes of using diplomatic success as a lever to free Antis.

'Then,' she said, 'why not give us some of your magical weapons? A few – even one – might turn the scale.'

Subbarau whistled.

'It need not be a permanent gift,' said Iroedh, not knowing the meaning of the strange sound but suspecting it to be an unfavorable indication, 'but a mere loan. You need not fear we should try to use it against you.'

Bloch said: 'You do not understand, my dear Iroedh. This is a ship of the *Viagens Interplanetarias*, the Terran space authority. Off Terra it is subject to the rules of the Interplanetary Council. One of this Council's regulations forbids introducing to – uh – backward planets inventions or technical knowledge these planets do not already possess.'

'What do they mean by "backward"?'

'Planets that have not attained a certain standard of development in science, law, ethics, and politics.'

'What is the purpose of this rule?' asked Iroedh.

'That is a long story, but the gist of it is that they do not wish to arm some warlike race that might then irrupt out of its home planet and cause trouble elsewhere.'

'Why doesn't our world qualify as civilized? We have an advanced culture, with writing, metalworking, large buildings, and a high degree of social organization. What more do you wish?'

'One of the first requirements is a single government for the entire planet. You do not have that, do you?'

'Great Gwyyr, no! Whoever heard of such a thing?'

'And you have not abolished the institution of war, have you?'

'Nobody has even thought of getting rid of it. It is part of the nature of things.'

'There you are. Speaking of which, why does not your Community combine with some of its neighbors like Thidhem and smash the Arsuuni before they destroy you piecemeal?'

'Now it's you who don't understand, Daktablak. One Community could never combine with another, because the general of one would have to admit that the queen of another was equal or superior in authority to her own. And as the nominal supremacy of each queen in her own Community is the first principle of our society, such a course is out of the question.'

'What do you mean by nominal supremacy?' asked Bloch.

'The actual governing is done by the Council, elected by the workers. The queen reigns but does not rule.'

'Strict constitutional monarchy,' said Bloch to Subbarau; then, to Iroedh:

'I am sorry, my dear, but that is the best advice we can give you. If some irrational rule of your society prevents, so much the worse for your society. Now then, what is interesting around here? As a xenologist—'

'As a what?' queried Iroedh.

'A xenologist; an expert on worlds other than my own. Anything is grist to my mill: geology, climate, plants, animals, people, science, history, art – practically anything you could mention. We have already secured a good collection of the plants and animals of this locale, however. Nearly all your land animals seem to be bipeds with no hair except occasional ornamental patches, like that crest on top of your head. Is that the case with the other continents?'

'As far as they are known to us, yes. Why shouldn't it be? Are things different on other worlds?'

'They certainly are. On our planet most animals walk on all fours and have hair all over, and on Vishnu most land life has six limbs.'

'Why?' said Iroedh.

'Various reasons. For instance, the type of planetary motion and the distribution of land and water on our planet give it a more variable and extreme climate than yours, so the animals had to develop hair to keep warm during the cold seasons. But to get back: Are there any Communities hereabouts that we could see?'

'I don't think any Communities would admit you until they knew you better – unless you forced your way in, and I hope you won't do that.'

'Then must we fly off to some other continent where the people are more approachable? We can give each continent only a limited time on a preliminary reconnaissance like this.'

'The Avtini aren't unfriendly, but we can't take chances until we know more about you.' When they looked at her silently she rushed on: 'There are other things I'm sure will interest you. For instance, there are the ruins on Survivors' Point, in plain sight of this sky ship.'

'Survivors' Point?' said Bloch.

Iroedh told them the story of the last bisexual Avtini, adding: 'The remains of their fortress are still up there, if you can climb.'

'How much of a climb is it? We can climb, but not vertically up the cliff face.'

'You wouldn't have to. The old trail that leads up the side of the valley is still usable though somewhat over-grown.'

'What is up there?' asked Bloch.

'You'll find many relics of former times. The fort was rebuilt fifty-odd years ago, when a band of rogue drones used it as a base.'

'Not a bad idea,' said Bloch. 'Would you guide some of us up tomorrow?'

'Gladly. What time will be convenient?'

'A couple of hours after sunrise, let us say.'

'That will be fine. Let's each of us bring her own food, as we might not find each other's fare palatable.'

After Iroedh had left the *Paris*, Bloch asked Captain Subbarau: 'How do you like our little redskin this time?'

'Better than the other one,' replied Subbarau thoughtfully. 'It gives one a curious sensation, like talking to an intelligent ant or bee in quasi-human form.'

'They're not, really; it's just their familial organization. You mustn't press the parallel too far. They're intelligent, not instinctive like those fellows on Sirius Nine. And bees don't have democratically elected councils.'

'True. If one filled her—Should I refer to Iroedh as "her" or "it"?'

'I think of her as "her." After all, you call a girl baby "her" even though she's no more sexually developed than Iroedh.'

'Well, if you filled her out a little here' – Subbarau made motions with his cupped hands in front of his chest – 'and put a wig of real hair on her head instead of that feathery Iroquois crest, she wouldn't make a bad-looking human female. If your taste runs to pink sixfooters with cats' eyes. Are they as backward as they seem? They don't appear to have iron, let alone machinery.'

'Funny about that. From all I can gather, they had a progressive culture up to two thousand of their years ago, when they adopted this sex-caste system. Since then they've not only stagnated, they've actually retrogressed.'

'Perhaps they adopted a materialistic view, like the Earthly West, and it stultified their spiritual development?'

'Don't start that again, boss! Their sciences have stopped too. As for their religion, it's all gone except for petty superstitions and curses. They're great ones for omens and oracles, but the emotions that used to find a religious outlet are now devoted to their Communities.'

'You mean hives,' said Subbarau.

Rhodh told Iroedh: 'Perhaps I was mistaken in sending you to deal with them. As far as I can see, all you accomplished was to shirk your share of the work of setting up the camp.'

'I had nothing to do with their refusal,' said Iroedh with heat. 'I told you, they're bound by the rules of their own government.'

'In any case, I had better deal with them tomorrow. What have you planned?'

Iroedh told of the projected expedition to Survivors' Point, adding: 'I pray you let me guide them. If another takes my place tomorrow, they'll wonder if we've fallen out. Besides, I have much more in the way of common interests with Daktablak than you.'

'I do not think—'

'Give me one more day,' said Iroedh, forcing herself to adopt a wheedling tone. 'Anyway, it's a two hours' climb, and I know the way. Have you ever been there?'

'I waste the Community's time visiting worthless ancient rubbish? Hmp! Go ahead, then, with your silly men. Truth to tell, I'm just as glad not to spend time on this trip that could be put to better use in ordering the camp so that it reflects credit on Elham.'

That night Iroedh hardly slept at all.

III

Survivors' Point

Next morning as Iroedh walked toward the *Paris*, Bloch stood awaiting her. With him were the female man named Dulac and the male one called O'Mara, the latter with a rectangular leather case slung from one shoulder. Bloch again bore his mysterious weapon.

'Camera,' said O'Mara in answer to Iroedh's question, which left her no wiser.

Bloch explained: 'A magical picture-making machine. He comes on all these expeditions to make them.'

'And what are those? Ornaments?' Iroedh pointed to a row of brass clips in Bloch's belt, each clip holding a number of little brass cylindrical things.

'They're for this.' Bloch indicated the tube of dark metal, which Iroedh had learned was called a *gon* or *gyn*.

'What's that you're saying, Baldy?' said O'Mara. 'Don't go blackguarding me to the young lady, now, just because I don't speak the heathen dialect of her.'

Iroedh, not understanding this speech, led the party along the road by which the Avtini had entered the valley. O'Mara made a peculiar shrill noise with his mouth, like that which Subbarau had made the previous day.

'What's that?' asked Iroedh.

'We call it whistling,' said Bloch, and tried to show her how. But though she puckered and blew, nothing came out but air.

She gave up and said: 'Daktablak, you've asked many questions about our sex castes. Perhaps you'd tell me how your Terran sex system works?'

When Bloch had given her a brief account of Terran monogamy, she said: 'Does it make you men happier than we?'

'How should I know? One cannot measure happiness with a meter, and anyway I am not intimately enough acquainted with your people to judge. Among men, some esteem the system highly while others find it extremely distressing.'

'How so?'

'Take Subbarau. He is unhappy because his female refused any longer to hibernate in a trance while he was away on his space trips, which take many years each, and left him for another male. And he comes from a country called India, where they take a serious view of such actions.'

'Then you must age greatly during such a trip!'

'No, because of the Lorenz-Fitzgerald effect, which slows down time when you go almost as fast as light so that to those on the ship the trip seems to consume only a fraction of the time it actually does.'

'I don't understand.'

'Confidentially, neither do I, but it does operate that way. Of course this is hard on the mates of the ship people who are left home, so they usually take a medicine that puts them into a profound sleep, in which they do not age appreciably, while their partners are gone.'

'How about you? Have you such a mate, and if so, is she on the ship or back on Terra?'

'I am single, unmated, and quite satisfied with my state.'

'Like a rogue drone?'

'I suppose so, though I do not rob people as I understand they do.'

'How about the Dylak?' asked Iroedh, glancing back to where Barbe Dulac plodded beside O'Mara, each looking frozenly forward. The longer legs of Iroedh and Bloch had enabled them to draw ahead of their companions.

'Oh, she is unhappy also.'

'How?'

'She and O' – the man walking beside her – how would you say "fell in love"?'

There followed several minutes of a search for synonyms, at the end of which Iroedh exclaimed: 'I know what you mean! It's our word *oedhurh*, which now means devotion to one's Community, but which was used by the ancients in the sense of that violent emotion you describe. I've come across it in that sense in some of the old songs and poems. But how can you "fall into" a condition like that? One "falls into" a hole in the ground …'

When Bloch had straightened her out on English figures of speech, she asked: 'Are all men subject to this passion?'

'Some more than others. In the culture of my people, for instance, it plays a substantial part, whereas Subbarau's countrymen take a more detached view of it.'

'But you said it made him unhappy.'

'I think that was more hurt pride than love.'

'And what happened to those two people behind us?'

'They got en – they entered into a contract to mate permanently, such as I told you about.'

'Something like when a drone is initiated into adulthood and swears to serve his queen?'

'Yes. They got engaged, as we say, but then Barbe found her man was not what she had thought. He is what we call a roughneck—'

'A rough neck? You mean he has bumps on the skin of his neck, like the creeping thing called an umdhag?'

'A manner of speaking. He is a domineering fellow with a frightful temper, and she would not have fallen for him—'

'You mean she fell out of a window or something to please him? A strange custom—'

'Would not have fallen in love with him, I mean, if they had not been cooped up together so long on the ship. So she broke the engagement, and he has been in a rage ever since. He only insisted on coming along today to make things unpleasant for the rest of us.'

'Because he's unhappy, then, he wants everybody else to be unhappy too?'

'That is about it.'

'We sometimes have workers like that,' said Iroedh, thinking of Rhodh.

'And he is frightfully jealous of me,' continued Bloch, 'because she works with me all the time, preparing my specimens and transcribing my notes.'

'Why, are you in love with her?'

'I – uh – what?' Bloch looked at her with a startled expression, then said: 'No, no, nothing of the sort,' and cast a furtive glance at the two following. 'But he thinks I am.'

To Iroedh his protestations sounded too vehement to be altogether convincing. She asked:

'Could it be that you really are, Daktablak, but dislike to admit it because you fear the wrath of that strong man?'

'Ridiculous, young lady. Let us talk of something else.'

'If you wish, though I fear I shall never understand you mysterious men. And your kind of love can't be worth much if it makes everybody so unhappy. Here we turn off.'

She led them along a trail that ran from the road across the floor of the valley. Bloch said:

'Iroedh, have you ever heard of another space ship's landing here, before the *Paris?*'

'No. We have ancient myths of gods coming down from the sky, but nobody believes them any more.'

'This was only a few years ago, comparatively speaking. A mixed Osirian-Thothian expedition—'

'What sort of expedition?'

'One manned by people from the planets Osiris and Thoth, in the Procyonic system. Procyon is the second brightest star in the sky from here.'

'You mean Ho-olhed?'

'Whatever you call it. The Osirians are something like your uegs, but with scales all over, while the Thothians are only about so high' – he held out a hand at waist level – 'and are covered with hair. Their ship alighted on what I think is this same continent, judging from their descriptions and photographs. But after they had been here only a few days a party they had sent out to reconnoiter was attacked. When the only survivor got back to their ship—'

'Who attacked them?' asked Iroedh.

'Avtini, from the account; probably a band of those rogue drones you tell about. Anyway, the survivor told such a wild tale that the captain, an Osirian named Fafashen, got panicky and ordered them to take off for their own system at once. Osirians are really too impulsive and emotional for space exploration.'

'I haven't heard of any such thing; but then it might have happened many sixty-fours of borbi from here, and such news wouldn't travel far because one Community normally neither knows nor cares what goes on in the territory of another. The few people like me who are interested in the race as a whole are looked upon as queer.'

'I have heard that before too,' said Bloch.

The trail now wound slantwise up the slope. Knowing what she faced, Iroedh had worn nothing but her boots and a shoulder strap supporting her lunch bag and a bronze hatchet. When she began hacking at the brush that had overgrown the trail, Bloch said:

'Here, let me!'

He drew from his gear an object the like of which Iroedh had never seen: a thing like a knife, but several times as large, with a straight back edge and a curved cutting edge that made the blade widest about a third of the distance from the point to the hilt. A single slash of this tool sent a swath of plants tumbling.

Iroedh started to exclaim in wonderment, then checked herself. She could not afford to risk the slightest advantage by impulsiveness. Her agile mind had instantly seen the possibilities of the thing as a weapon; in fact she wondered why none of the Avtini had thought of it. Bloch seemed to take it for granted that she was familiar with such a device, but if she made a fuss over it he would guess that she was not and invoke his precious regulations to keep her from learning more about it.

'What's your name for that?' she asked casually.

'A machete.'

'*A matselh,*' she said, unconsciously giving the word the Avtinyk ending for tools and other artifacts.

'What would you call it?'

'A *valh,*' she replied, giving the Avtinyk for 'knife.' 'Do you use them as weapons?'

Bloch paused before answering. 'One could, though it's a little point-heavy for the purpose. Centuries ago we fought with implements like this, called 'swords.' The best shape for that use would be somewhat lighter and tapering to a narrow point. Now, however, we employ these.' He touched the gun. 'Or we should if we still had wars. How about your people?' he asked with a trace of suspicion.

'Oh, some Communities use them,' Iroedh lied, 'though the Avtini prefer the spear. May I try it?'

'Do not cut yourself,' he warned, handing over the machete hilt-first.

Iroedh took a few awkward swipes at the brush before she got the hang of the tool. She gave an Avtiny smile as she imagined the next stalk to be the neck of an Arsuun of Tvaarm. *Swish!*

'Come on, come on,' said O'Mara, who, with Barbe Dulac, had caught up with Bloch and Iroedh during the discussion. 'Let a man be showing you how a trail is cleared.'

And he waded into the brush with his own machete, sending great masses of vegetation flying.

Thereafter they took turns, all but Barbe Dulac, who was too small. Sweat darkened the shirts of the three men until the two male ones pulled theirs off. Iroedh thereupon became fascinated by a Terran characteristic:

'Daktablak, how is it that though you say you're a functional male, you and O'Mara have rudimentary breasts like an Avtiny worker? Save that yours are even more rudimentary than ours.'

'Your drones do not possess them?'

'No. Are you *sure* you're males?'

Bloch gave the barking Terran laugh. 'I have always believed so.'

She persisted: 'And why doesn't the little Bardylak take off her tunic too? I should like to study her.'

'It is against our custom.'

At the request of Barbe Dulac, Bloch translated the last bit of conversation. Iroedh could not understand why Barbe turned red and O'Mara laughed loudly.

'These heathens have no shame at all,' said the photographer, pausing to wipe the sweat from his forehead with the back of one hairy arm. 'Here, Baldy,' he said to Bloch, 'take over.'

Though Iroedh could catch only an occasional word, Bloch's manner told her he did not like to be so addressed. The xenologist went to work on the overgrowth in grim silence.

Iroedh dropped back to talk to Barbe Dulac, a process that entailed the usual difficulty when each knows but a few words of the other's language, though by pointing at things and making inquiring noises each soon expanded her vocabulary. The process was further complicated by the fact that the English spoken by the others was not Barbe's native tongue, for she came from a place she called Helvetia and the others Switzerland.

'We have the same sort of inconsistency,' said Iroedh. 'The Arsuuni call themselves *Arshuul*, but, as we have no *sh* sound and a different system of word endings, we call them *Arsuuni*.'

Then Iroedh took her turn at trail cutting, and the grade became too steep for conversation. They hoisted themselves over outcrops from which they could look far across the valley. For a time the trail wound along an almost sheer slope to which a few weeds clung precariously. Although the trail had been adequate when made, time and weather had piled debris on the cliffward side and worn away the outer edge so that they walked nervously along a reverse bank that almost spilled them over the edge when the gravel rolled and slid away under their feet.

Iroedh pointed. 'There's the ruin.'

'If we live to see it,' said O'Mara, mopping his forehead with his wadded-up shirt.

Another half hour brought them to the base of the shoulder on which the fortress stood, and from there it was an easy walk out. Bloch indicated the great blocks of Cyclopean masonry, weighing tons apiece, and asked:

'However did they transport their stones up here?'

Iroedh shrugged. 'We don't know, unless they cut them from the cliff. The ancients did many things we can't duplicate.'

'And when will we be eating?' said O'Mara.

'Any time,' said Bloch.

They got out their lunch. Iroedh, munching her biscuits, asked about the various items of human food.

'Do you mean,' she exclaimed, 'that your males eat plant food and your females meat?'

'Yes, and the other way round,' said Bloch. 'Why don't you try a bite of meat?'

'Impossible! Not only is it against our laws, but when a worker has eaten nothing but plant food all her life a bite of meat would poison her. It's a painful death. Though it is said that thousands of years ago, before the reforms, people lived on such mixed diets, nowadays we should consider it a mark of savagery.'

O'Mara produced a bottle filled with a yellow-brown liquid, which he unstoppered and drank from.

'Where'd you get that?' asked Bloch.

O'Mara grinned. 'Out of Doc Markowicz's stores when the lad wasn't looking. Have a swallow.'

He held out the bottle to Bloch, who hesitantly took it and drank.

'Weesky?' said Barbe Dulac. 'Let me have some, please!'

'How about the native girl?' said O'Mara. 'That's one human custom the darling should try.'

'Be careful,' said Bloch. 'Just a sip. It might not agree with you.'

Iroedh tipped her head back as she had seen the others do. Unaccustomed to drinking from such a vessel, she got a whole mouthful. She felt as if she had swallowed a bucket of live coals, and coughed violently, spraying half the mouthful on the ground.

'I – I'm poisoned!' she gasped between coughs.

'Let us hope not,' said Bloch, thumping her back. When Iroedh's equilibrium was restored he said: 'Now let us prowl the ruins.'

O'Mara replied: 'You prowl, Baldy, while I take a bit of a snooze. The pictures wouldn't be no damn good with the sun so high anyway.'

'I, too, should like to rest,' said Barbe Dulac.

'How about you, Iroedh?' said Bloch.

Iroedh yawned, 'Would you mind if I took a small nap also? I can hardly keep my eyes open.'

'Do not tell me that half a swallow of whisky has had that much effect already!'

'I don't think it was that but the fact that I hardly slept last night.'

'That is the coffee you drank yesterday. You nap, then, and I shall rouse you after a while.'

O'Mara was taking another big swig and arranging his pack as a pillow. Barbe Dulac spoke to him:

'John, won't you get the sunburn, going to sleep with your chest bare?'

'Sure, and these stinking little red dwarf stars don't put out enough ultraviolet to matter.'

Iroedh asked for a translation, then inquired: 'Is your sun, then, different from ours?'

'Very much so,' said Barbe Dulac, 'It looks about half as big and four times as bright. To us this one looks like a big orange – one of our fruits – in the sky.'

'What do you call our sun?'

'Lalande 21185. That's just a number in a star catalogue.'

Iroedh was about to ask what a star catalogue was when she saw that Barbe had dropped off. Accustomed to the simplest of sleeping accommodations, Iroedh dozed off herself, sprawled on the shattered pavement of the fort with her head pillowed on a stone.

Later the voices of the other two aroused her. While she struggled to remain asleep, she was brought sharply out of the twilight zone by a loud smack, as of an open hand striking bare flesh.

She opened her eyes to see Barbe Dulac stumble backward, half fall, and recover. A grille of red stripes across the female man's cheek implied that the sound *had* been that of a slap. Barbe screamed and O'Mara roared:

'That'll learn you to trifle with an honest man!'

He advanced with a curiously unsteady gait. Iroedh, gathering herself to rise, saw the bottle lying empty on the stones.

This conflict left Iroedh at a loss. She was sure it was wrong, but as a member of another species she did not think it incumbent on her to intervene. At that moment, however, Bloch stepped around from behind a section of wall and walked toward O'Mara, saying:

'What's this? Look here, you can't—'

' 'Tis your doing!' cried O'Mara. 'No bald-headed old omadhaun is going to steal my girl!'

Bloch halted in hesitation, his bodily attitude bespeaking fear of the other man's violence. He looked toward Barbe, who said something Iroedh could not catch. However, it seemed to stiffen his sinews, for he took another step toward O'Mara.

Smack! O'Mara's big fist shot out and struck the side of Bloch's face. Bloch's head snapped back and he fell supine upon the stones.

'Now,' said O'Mara, 'will you get up and fight like a man, or must I—'

Bloch got to his feet, moving at first slowly and jerkily, then with more agility. Iroedh, watching with horrified fascination, wondered why neither tried to pick up the gun or the machetes piled against the wall with the other gear. Such a method of settling differences was utterly foreign to the discipline of an Avtiny Community, where violence (except in war, the Royal Duel, and the Cleanup) was unknown.

With a roar O'Mara lowered his head and charged like a bull vakhnag. Bloch stood a fraction of a second holding futile fists before him, then threw himself to one side, leaving one long leg thrust out to trip his assailant. O'Mara tripped, staggered on in a half-falling run, and fetched up against the knee-high parapet that ran along a section of the cliffward side of the stronghold.

Iroedh had a glimpse of O'Mara's boots in the air, then – no O'Mara.

A long dwindling scream came up, cut off by the sound of a body striking a ledge. Sounds followed of the body striking again and again, and there was a rattle of loosened rocks.

'*Tonnerre de Dieu!*' said Barbe Dulac.

The three survivors hurried to the parapet and looked over. After they had searched for some seconds, Iroedh, catching a glimpse of contrasting color, said:

'Isn't that he in the branches of that khal tree?'

They looked where she pointed. Bloch got out a small black object with shiny glass eyes and looked through it.

'That is he,' he said. 'Dead, all right.'

He handed the glasses to Iroedh. She almost dropped them with astonishment as the pink-and-olive speck at the foot of the cliff leaped almost to within arms' length. After one long look she handed the glasses back.

'I'm sure he's very dead indeed,' she said.

*

'I fear,' said Iroedh, 'I don't understand your Terran customs yet. Did the O'Mara leap off the cliff because of his love for Bardylak, or was that some sort of ceremonial execution?'

She stopped her questions when she saw the other two were paying no attention. They were jabbering at each other in their own tongue and Barbe Dulac was making strangled sounds while tears ran down her face. Iroedh understood this to be a Terran gesture symbolizing grief, but found it hard to understand. The female man had come to dislike O'Mara, who had certainly abused her. Why, then, such a display of emotion? Unless, of course, O'Mara was so important to the Terran Community that his death jeopardized its existence.

She caught an occasional word she knew, like 'terrible' and 'love.' Presently the men put their arms around each other and pressed their mouths together, whereupon Barbe Dulac shed more tears than ever.

At last Bloch said to Iroedh: 'You saw what occurred, did you not?'

'Yes, though I still don't understand it. Did O'Mara kill himself?'

'No. He was trying to kill me, or something close to it, and when I tripped him he fell over accidentally. Now, among us when one kills another for his own private purposes—'

'You mean as when we kill off surplus drones or defective workers for the good of the Community?'

'No; as if an Avtiny worker killed another merely because she disliked her, or because the other worker had something—'

'Such a thing could never happen!' Iroedh exclaimed.

'Your rogue drones attack workers to steal food and supplies, do they not?'

'That's different. A worker *never* attacks a fellow worker from the same Community, unless in carrying out the orders of the Council.'

'It is different with us. The act is called "murder" and is punished by death or long imprisonment.'

'By "long imprisonment" do you mean they starve the culprit to death? That's a strange—'

'No, they feed and house them, though not in fancy style.'

'Then where's the punishment? Some of our lazier workers would like nothing better—'

Bloch made motions of tugging at his vanished hair. 'We keep getting off the subject! Just permit me to talk, please. If I go back to the ship and narrate this incident as it happened, some will say I murdered O'Mara because of our rivalry over Barbe. And while I do not believe I should be convicted, since Barbe can testify it was an accident and self-defense, it would cause a great stench and ruin my reputation back on Terra—'

'If the death was justified according to your laws, why should anyone blame you?'

'Never mind; take it from me that my career would be jeopardized. Therefore Barbe and I will not mention any fight or slapping. We will simply say that he got intoxicated on the medicinal whisky and tried to show off by walking on the parapet, and fell over.'

'You mean to *lie* to your own Community?'

'Not exactly; just to withhold part of the truth. He did get drunk and fall over the parapet, after all.'

'A strange race, the men. What do you wish of me?'

'Not to spoil our story. Keep silent about the fight.'

Iroedh pondered. 'Would it be right?'

'We think so. I do not see what good would be accomplished by having an inquest and perhaps a trial when we were only defending ourselves.'

'Very well, I'll say nothing. As I'm awake now, shall I explain the ruins to you?'

'Good God, no! We have to get back down, report O'Mara's fall, and endeavor to recover his body.'

'Why? His clothes and equipment would be ruined by the fall.'

'It is custom,' said Bloch, starting to collect the gear.

'Do you eat the bodies of your dead? Or do you make soap of them as we do?'

Barbe Dulac squawked, and Bloch said: 'Not ordinarily; we bury them ceremonially.'

Iroedh sighed. 'What people! Shall I carry his gear?'

Bloch gave Iroedh O'Mara's camera and container of photographic material and machete to carry, and led the way homeward. They wound down the trail, faster this time because it was mostly downhill and the worst brush had been cleared on the way up.

As she picked her way down with O'Mara's equipment banging against her skin as it swung from its straps, Iroedh wondered on the predicament of her companions. While she liked them as individuals, as one might like a friendly ueg or other tame beast, her first loyalty still lay toward her Community. She would therefore not hesitate to turn their troubles to her own advantage if occasion offered.

She remembered the forgotten epic, the *Lay of Idhios*, which in its last canto told how the drone Idhios had used his knowledge of the liaison of Queen Vinir with the drone Santius to force the queen to steal the Treasure of Inimdhad and give it to him. That was back in the bad barbarous days when workers laid eggs and queens had but a single drone apiece, called the king, who presumed to dictate to the queen whom she should be fertilized by.

Evidently, in dealing with creatures of primitive social organization like the men or her own remote ancestors, one could sometimes extort goods and services from one by threatening to reveal something to her discredit. Could she force Bloch to help Elham against Tvaarm by threatening to tell Subbarau on him? For an instant she thought she had an answer to her Community's problem, and imagined Bloch mowing down the Arsuuny giants with his magical gun.

But then second thoughts dampened her enthusiasm. Bloch was not the head man in his Community. She could not use her knowledge to force the whole complement of the *Paris* to help Elham, because their leader was Subbarau, over whom she had no hold.

She might try to force Bloch to come back to Elham alone to fight for the Avtini – but that might not work either. Accustomed to a highly organized and disciplined Community, Iroedh realized that Bloch could probably not wander off at his own sweet will.

Another thought struck her. 'Bardylak!'

'Yes?' said Barbe Dulac.

'Have you, in the sky ship, one of those machines that tells when a man is lying?'

'I understand we do. Nobody has to submit to it, but if an accused refuses, it makes the officers all the more suspicious.'

So it wouldn't be necessary for Subbarau to find evidence of irregularities, but merely to have his suspicions aroused, and the true story of O'Mara's death would come out.

Then could she make Bloch reveal some bit of technical knowledge that would give the Avtini the advantage they needed? If, for example, he'd lend her the gun ... A dubious expedient. The gun was a complicated mechanism, and if not used right might blow a hole in the user instead of the target. To tell the truth, Iroedh was definitely afraid of it. Besides, one needed a supply of the little brass things that went with it.

But something simpler, now, like the machete whose scabbard was slapping against her thigh. Anybody could understand that.

Then she remembered how the *Idhios* continued. As the triumphant Idhios turned away, his eyes upon the treasure in his hands, Queen Vinir had driven a knife into his back and slain him. She explained that Idhios had tried to fertilize her without her consent – an impossible situation under modern Community organization, but one that in ancient days, apparently, occurred often and was deemed a serious crime.

The lesson was that when you try to force a being of primitive social organization to do something for you by threatening to disclose her secret, take care she does not kill you to close your mouth forever.

However, if the *Lay* contained this warning, it also pointed the way out. For it transpired that Idhios had written an account of the relationship of Queen Vinir with Santius and left it with his friend Gunes with instructions to deliver it to King Aithles, the queen's one official drone, if anything happened to Idhios. So Gunes had given the tablet to the king, and the epic ended with King Aithles' minions holding Queen Vinir and her lover with their necks across the windowsill of the palace while the king hewed off their heads with a hatchet so that the heads fell into the moat.

Though as a result of her studies Iroedh was more broadminded than most Avtiny workers, even she could not visualize the slaying of a queen by a drone without a shudder. No wonder all the Avtiny Communities forbade the *Lay of Idhios!*

Would any such elaborate maneuver be necessary in her case, however?

They had nearly reached the floor of the valley of Gliid. Where the trail grew wider Bloch and Barbe Dulac walked side by side holding hands and paying Iroedh no heed.

While Iroedh had at first been a little irked at being ignored, she now began to calculate how to turn their absorption in each other to her advantage. She hefted the machete. Perhaps in the excitement of telling their story and organizing the search for O'Mara's body they'd never miss it.

She said: 'Daktablak! If you like, I'll run ahead to our camp and ask our leader to assign some of us to help you recover the corpse.'

'That will be splendid; thank you, Iroedh,' said Bloch vaguely, and turned his attention back to Barbe.

Iroedh jogged off toward the main road, taking O'Mara's possessions with her.

IV

The Helicopter

At the Avtiny camp the only worker in sight was Vardh. Iroedh asked her:

'Where's Rhodh?'

Vardh pointed toward the towering bulk of the *Paris*. 'Over there, prowling around in hope of picking up something useful. What sort of time have you had? Iinoedh thought they'd surely devour you—'

'Go fetch Rhodh, please, dear,' said Iroedh.

Vardh went obediently. Iroedh walked over to her chariot, climbed up, and pulled up the seat cover, which was hinged and served as the top of a chest in which she stored her cloak and other gear. She wrapped the machete in the cloak and laid the bundle back in the recess, then closed the top and placed the camera and other things upon it.

'Well?' snapped Rhodh from the ground. 'Will they fight on our side?'

Iroedh gave a jump; she had not expected Rhodh to slip up on her like that. Rhodh had removed her cuirass and kilt (though she still wore the hip-length haqueton-tunic) and so had been able to come close without clanking. Now was the time, before Bloch arrived, to show her the machete and explain her plans for duplicating it in bronze to use in battle.

'Not exactly,' said Iroedh. 'But I have—'

'What do you mean, not exactly? Will they fight for us or not?'

'No, but—'

'Failed again! I should have known better than to let you try. Another precious day wasted, with the Arsuuni due to march! I suppose that in your dreamy way you forgot all about our mission and spent your time discussing that rubbish on the Point! Of all the stupid, incompetent—Anyway, I won't let it happen again. Tomorrow you can spend policing the camp while I take charge of Blok.'

Rhodh marched off, leaving Iroedh to bite her lips. Forbidden thoughts of physical assault seeped into her mind, no doubt, she guessed, inspired by the lawless violence she had witnessed on Survivors' Point.

She called: 'Rhodh!'

'What is it now?'

'I was trying to tell you one of the men fell off the cliff and was killed, and they'll want to fetch his body. You could ingratiate yourself with them by sending a party to help.'

Rhodh glowered back. 'Let the men tend to their own ridiculous customs and I'll tend to mine.'

'Then I'll go—'

'You shall not! You shall clean the tethering area of the uegs and fetch them a fresh supply of greens. Get to work.'

'Then you'd better return these to the men.' Iroedh held up O'Mara's gear, all but the hidden machete. 'They belong to the dead man, and the others will be looking for them.'

'Hmp. Let me see them.'

Rhodh took the articles and walked off, turning them over and pulling and poking at them. She walked toward the *Paris*, the low sun shining redly on the brass of her helmet.

Now, thought Iroedh, if the men start looking for the missing machete, O'Mara's goods will have passed through so many hands they'll never be able to establish responsibility for it.

Iroedh got out the shovel and went to work on the camp's least popular chore. Now she'd be cursed to the hell the ancient poems spoke of before she'd show Rhodh the machete. She would keep it hidden until she could find her own use for it.

'Iroedh darling!' said the voice of young Vardh. 'Don't feel badly about Rhodh's harsh words. I'm sure you did the best you could, but she's in one of her worst humors. She's had a bad day too.'

'What's happened?'

'This morning after brunch she decided to see the leader of the men. First she put on her armor, though the day was hot and the men don't seem to stand on much ceremony. But she told us to shut up; that she knew the right way for one leader to call upon another, and that men disapproved of nudity on formal occasions.

'Then she went over and tried to get the first man she saw to take her to that Sub – you know, the fat brown one, the leader. When the man didn't understand her she seemed to think she could make him understand by saying the same thing louder. Soon they were shouting, and the noise brought out the leader, who came down in the bucket to ask what was up. When he arrived Rhodh tried the same routine on him, with no more success. He indicated by sign language and his few words of Avtinyk that he was busy and she couldn't enter the ship because it was being cleaned or something, and back he went in the bucket.

'For a while she hung around watching the men. Some were scraping and painting the ship, which she could understand, but others were doing things that made no sense to her. Some were putting together that large magical device over there, the one with three petals sticking out from its top like a ripe pomuial. When she asked them what it was, one of them said something in his own language and flapped his arms like an ueg stallion in rut. So Rhodh thinks the device must have something to do with sex.

'Others brought out a round thing about so big' – Vardh held her hands about two feet apart – 'and very light – so light that when one of them tossed it into the air it flew up into the sky while another man looked at it through a magical device. Others pulled up weeds, or turned over stones to catch the creeping things under them, which Rhodh says is a silly way for adults to act, though Avpandh thinks they may be short of food.

'One of them – the one with the almost-black skin and kinky hair – squatted in front of a box and turned little knobs on it, paying Rhodh no attention even when she spoke to him. After the third time with no response she prodded him in the buttocks with her spear. He leaped into the air with a yell and pointed a small *gon* at her, shouting in his own language. She gathered that he did not wish to be disturbed, and gave up trying to understand such unreasonable folk. She said the Terrans must have loaded all their crazy people into this ship and sent them off to get rid of them.'

'She needn't take out her irritation on me,' said Iroedh, proceeding determinedly with her work. She tried to make the sound Bloch had called whistling, but without success.

'Oh, you're right of course, darling,' said Vardh. 'Here, let me help you. Isn't it exciting, though? Like that oracular verse about

'*When the gods descend from heaven's height*
Shall the seed be sown.

'You could call these sky folk the gods, and their magical knowledge the seed. If we could only persuade them to sow it!'

Iroedh said: 'You're always quoting those things. As I remember, the quatrain begins with the line: 'When the Rogue Queen wears a crown of light,' which is utter nonsense. Whoever heard of a rogue queen? It's a contradiction in terms.'

'Oh, I don't know. That little Terran female might be considered as such, since she seems to have no harem of drones of her own.'

A noise around the *Paris* attracted their attention. Bloch and Barbe Dulac had returned. There was a mutter of Terran speech and much coming and going in the hoist. Rhodh's helmet towered amidst the crowd. Soon a group set out purposefully along the road toward Survivors' Point.

Iroedh finished her work and helped her juniors to prepare supper. Rhodh joined them for the meal. Nobody spoke much; Iroedh guessed that while the juniors sympathized with her, they did not dare show their feelings for fear of Rhodh's wrath. Vardh, however, made hers plain by sitting close to Iroedh and passing her everything before she was even asked to.

As they were washing up, the party that had set out for O'Mara's body returned with it. The three juniors dropped their jobs to rush across the camp to see.

Rhodh said in a low voice: 'I'm sorry I spoke so harshly to you. Not but that you deserved chiding, but I let my petty emotions influence me. However, I still think it best if I deal with Blok tomorrow.'

'It's nothing,' said Iroedh, far from completely mollified. While Rhodh's sense of duty would force her to admit a patent mistake, that was not enough to make people like her. Rhodh continued:

'I do not mean to be hard on you, for at times you display a glimmering of the qualities of a proper worker. If you would only model yourself on me, you might rise in the Community as I am doing.'

'Thank you, but I'll continue to get along in my own inefficient way.'

Iroedh stacked the last dish and walked off, knowing that by rejecting Rhodh's overture she had made an implacable enemy. But she could not force herself to truckle to one she now so disliked, as Rhodh would have done in her place.

Iroedh lay awake under her net, looking up at the stars through the meshes. Her mind roved in unaccustomed channels: If this was all the appreciation she got, why should she break her neck for her Community? Why not use her power to free Antis? Of course she would then have to do what she could for Elham, but Antis should come first. If that was anti-Communitarianism, let them make the most of it.

Now, what could Bloch do for Antis? He couldn't fly the *Paris* to Elham – at least not without the others' knowledge – and if she took him in her chariot he would be gone at least five days, which wouldn't do either. And when he got there, what? Not being even so strong as she, he could certainly not leap over the Community wall or batter down the stout gate. Perhaps he could blast it with his gun – but that would mean killing Elhamni, which Iroedh could not bring herself to contemplate.

For that matter, Bloch impressed her as a somewhat timorous creature – wise and likable, but no second Idhios. In fact, her early estimation of the Terrans as super-beings, impervious to the bodily ills and weaknesses of character that beset common mortals like herself, had been revised drastically downward as a result of the trip to the Point. Why, despite their science, they were in some respects even less godlike than the Avtini!

Half unconsciously she puckered her lips in one more effort to whistle. To her astonishment the sharp little sound rang out. She had to repeat it before she was sure it came from her own mouth.

She experimented. By moving her tongue back and forth, as Bloch had told her to do, she found she could vary the pitch. She tried to reproduce one of the few tunes she knew, that of the *Song of Geyliad*, which she had puzzled out from one of those manuscripts with the little black dots. The result might not have been recognized by the composer, but it pleased Iroedh.

'What's that funny noise?' came the sleepy voice of Avpandh.

'Some creeping thing,' said the deeper tones of Rhodh. 'Go to sleep.'

Next morning Iroedh policed the camp until hardly a grass blade was out of place, then went to her chariot. From the chest containing the machete she took her writing tablet of vakhwil bark and wrote a concise account of the death of John O'Mara. She tore off and folded the top sheet, then sought out Vardh, who was gawking at the antics of the Terrans. Some of these were repairing pieces of machinery with magical devices that sparkled and shone.

'Come with me,' said Iroedh. 'Can you keep a secret, Vardh dearest?'

'For you? Certainly!'

'Even from Rhodh?'

Vardh looked around nervously, but Rhodh was off somewhere with Bloch. 'Especially from her. Though she's our leader, I don't really like her!'

'Even from the Council?'

Vardh's eyes widened and her slit pupils dilated. 'O-oh, this must be something simply awful! But for you I would.'

'Even from the queen?'

Vardh hesitated. 'N – yes, I would. Not one of them is so nice as you. I love you almost as well as I do the Community.'

Iroedh handed her the folded sheet. 'This is what you must do: Hide this message, without looking at it, in your chariot. Should anything happen to me, like death or imprisonment, see it gets into the hands of Captain Subbarau. That is, if the sky ship is still here, or if I haven't asked for the sheet back. And not a word to anybody!'

'I understand, darling,' said Vardh.

She hurried off. Iroedh approached the ship, where several men were putting the finishing touches on the machine with the 'petals' that Rhodh had observed. Barbe Dulac stood there, alternately looking at the machine and at something on her finger.

'May I see that?' said Iroedh.

Barbe held up her left hand. For the first time Iroedh became really conscious of the fact that men had one more digit on each extremity than the Avtini. On the third finger sparkled a faceted gem, like those the ancients used to make, held in place by a slender ring of gray metal.

'Winston gave it to me,' said Barbe.

'What?'

They struggled with each other's languages until Iroedh understood and replied: 'That was kind of him, wasn't it?'

'Oh, more than that! It means we are engaged to be married!'

'You mean one of those Terran mating contracts?'

Barbe sighed. 'Yes. The silly darling brought it all the way from Earth, but did not dare say anything because he was afraid of John O'Mara. He is a timid old rabbit, that one, but I love him even if he has no hair.'

'That is nice.'

'You have no idea! It is too bad you people do not have the love as we know it.'

'Thank you, but if your kind of love makes people throw each other off cliffs, I'm satisfied with ours. By the way, when will you be fertilized? I should like to know how it is done.'

Barbe emitted a sound of strangulation, followed by coughs and gasps, meanwhile turning almost as red as an Avtin. Iroedh, not knowing what she could have done to cause such a reaction, assumed Barbe had gotten something in her windpipe.

Barbe straightened up and said: 'Look! Kang is almost ready to take off!'

'To take off what? His clothes?'

'No, the helicopter.'

'The hil – hiila—I meant to ask you, what is that thing for?'

'It flies.'

'It what?'

'Flies through the air.' Barbe made motions.

'Oh, now I see why Rhodh thought it was concerned with sex! Can all of you men drive it?'

'No. Kang will not let anybody but himself and Winston fly it.'

The little black-haired man with the flat yellow face got into the machine, and the men who had been working on it scattered.

Iroedh said: 'Daktablak flies it?'

'He is a good flier, him.'

'He must be brave after all.'

'In some ways. The flying machines and the high places and the savage animals do not bother him, but any man who shouts at him can make him fold up. I shall have to supply the spine he lacks.'

'The poor man has bones missing? He seems very active for a cripple—'

Before Barbe could straighten out Iroedh again, the helicopter coughed and whirred. The petals spun faster and faster until their down draft blew clouds of dust radially outward into the faces of the spectators. Iroedh and Barbe backed up until they were out of the sandstorm. They stood watching the rotors, while Kang made his interminable adjustments, and struggled with the speech barrier. Iroedh found that, while Terran grammar and vocabulary came easily enough, she could not exactly imitate the men's pronunciation, because her vocal organs differed from theirs.

'What,' said Iroedh, 'do you call this world?'

'We have named it "Ormazd," and the two uninhabited planets of this system "Mithras" and "Ahriman" after the gods of an ancient Terran religion.'

'Why don't you use our own name?'

'What is it?' asked Barbe.

'We call it "Niond."'

'Does that mean "earth" or "soil"?'

'Why yes! How did you know?'

'That is usually the case. Do all Communities call it by the same name?'

'No. With the Arsuuni it is "Sveik."'

'Well, there you are. We might as well pick a name of our own as try to decide among those in use here.'

The burbling whistle of the blades speeded up. The wind increased and the helicopter rose gently. Kang hovered a bit, then climbed until he was a mere speck and set off on a circuit of the valley.

Iroedh asked: 'How fast does that thing go?'

Barbe shrugged. 'Perhaps two hundred kilometers an hour. I do not know what that would be in your measurements, but it is ten or twenty times the speed you can run.'

'Can it carry more than one?' Iroedh tried to calculate how long the round trip to Elham would take.

'It has room for three, and can lift an even greater weight.'

'Do you think I could ride in it?'

Barbe looked wide-eyed at her companion. 'You would not have fear?'

'If it can carry you men it will carry me; and anyway I feel lucky. Could I?'

'I should have to ask. They do not let Kang take us on what they call joy rides, because the fuel is limited. But you as a native of this world might be a special case. There is Lobos, the executive officer; I will ask him.'

Iroedh watched, impassive outside but excited within, as her little human friend conversed with a small dark man, and both went to speak to Subbarau, who had likewise been a spectator.

Barbe reported: 'They say it will be all right if Kang thinks it safe.'

Kang grew from a speck into a whirligig and thence into a helicopter settling down on his take-off spot. When he shut off the engine Barbe ran over to the machine and spoke to him; then beckoned Iroedh.

The flat face grinned invitingly through the open door. Iroedh climbed in and settled herself as he directed her, but fumbled with her safety belt till he fastened it for her.

Up they went. Iroedh, seeing the ground fall away, gripped her armrests until her knuckles faded from red to pale pink, the same terrible fear sweeping over her as in the hoist. She set her jaws, determined not to lose her brunch or otherwise disgrace her race before these formidable aliens.

'You like?' said Kang.

Iroedh forced herself to open her eyes and look out through the transparent covering of the machine. Little by little the heart-stopping fear subsided. She found herself looking down upon the shiny nose of the *Paris*, the whole sky ship appearing no bigger than one of the pins used in *uintakh*. Fear surged back with the thought that Kang might, with the unpredictability of Terrans, throw her out of the machine. But her good sense fought down the idea. If they had wanted to kill her they could have done so more easily. She stretched her lips in a smile – not her own kind, but the Terran tooth display that reminded her of a noag about to bite.

'I – I – like,' she said.

The ground now looked like a relief map, the people mere specks. The fear went away. Mount Wisgad smoked quietly in the distance.

She asked in her fumbling English: 'Can you down – lower – string – rope – for man up climb?'

'Sure thing. Can haul three, four men up at once. Very strong machine. Made by Vought – damn good company.'

Little by little a plan for rescuing Antis took form.

Iroedh spent the afternoon studying an English primer Bloch had left with Barbe to give to her. Rhodh returned well before supper in an even worse humor than before, refusing to speak to anyone. The sun was setting when Iroedh slipped out of the Avtiny camp and went purposefully over to the *Paris*.

Bloch was pacing about the base of the space ship, holding a curious object in his teeth, something like a small spoon with a deep scoop-shaped bowl. A curl of smoke rose from the bowl.

Iroedh said: 'Hail, Daktablak! Do you then breathe fire like the monster worm Igog in the *Tale of Mantes?*'

'No.' He explained the uses of tobacco.

'Have you quarreled with Rhodh? She's in a remarkable rage, even for her.'

'Not exactly. She and I are not – how would you say it? – congenial. We experienced the same difficulty when she was here previously.'

'What happened today?'

'Well, first she talked too rapidly for me to comprehend her, and took it as an insult when I requested her to slow down. Then she proposed a deal to me: If I would intervene in your fool war, she would try to arrange for us to visit her Community, if her Council would assent. Did you tell her I had tendered such a proposal?'

'No,' said Iroedh.

'She seemed to think I had, and when I endeavored to explain why I could not she lectured me, waving her spear in my face, until I politely informed her I had my own work to do. And when I tried to collect some information from her she became uncommunicative. Well, it was altogether a pretty sticky day.'

'I'm told you can drive the flying machine.'

'That is correct.'

'And that the machine can lift several people from the ground by means of a rope.'

'Yes. In fact there is a rope ladder coiled up in a compartment in the bottom for rescue work. You push a lever and it falls out.'

'It would be bad for you if Captain Subbarau heard the complete story of the death of O'Mara, wouldn't it?'

'Ssh! I thought we weren't going to mention that?'

'Not if you do what I ask.'

'What is this? Blackmail?'

'If that's what you call it. I don't wish to do it, but I must to save my friend Antis.'

'Who is that? A drone, from his name.'

Iroedh told about Antis, adding: 'And don't think to make away with me, because I've written an account of the fight and arranged for it to be shown Subbarau should anything befall me.'

'Bless my soul! And I thought you Ormazdians were too primitive and innocent to think of angles like that! You do not really mean this?'

'I certainly do.'

There followed a long argument. Bloch appealed to all Iroedh's sentiments – honor, friendship, and so on – without budging her. When she felt herself weakening she thought of Antis being speared like a fish at the next Cleanup.

'One would think,' said Bloch bitterly, 'you were in love with this Antis, in our Terran sense.'

'What a revolting idea! Love between workers and other beings has nothing to do with sex.'

'What do you wish me to do?'

'Are you on guard tonight?'

'Until midnight,' he said.

'Then I wish you to take me in the flying machine to Elham and rescue the imprisoned drones by means of that rope ladder. If the machine is as fast as it's said to be we can be back by midnight.'

'How am I supposed to deliver them if they're in some subterranean prison cell?'

'Ah, but they're not! The cell where imprisoned drones are kept is in the top of the queen's dome, with a walkway running around it for the guard.'

'How do you gain access to the cell from there?'

'There's a window, small, but big enough to squeeze through, covered by bronze bars. I've hauled my spear and buckler around the walkway often enough to know it.'

'Well, that settles it. You could not expect me to gnaw through the bars with my teeth, could you?'

'You men have magical cutting devices that cut through metal as though it were water. I saw the men using them today.'

'You seem to think of everything. How can we locate the place at night? It will not look at all familiar.'

'We shall follow the coast of the Scarlet Sea to Khinad Point. I know that coast well.'

'How about the guard?'

'Leave her to me. In another hour everybody will be asleep and it will be dark. I'll meet you here, and you shall have with you one of those magical cutting devices. Farewell for the nonce, Daktablak.'

'Damn you, Iroedh,' he muttered at her retreating back.

V

The Queen's Dome

As the helicopter soared over Khinad Point, Iroedh pointed inland to where the pale domes of Elham, like a cluster of eggs, showed among the fields and woods.

'That's where we go,' she said.

'You have remarkable night vision,' said Bloch. 'I cannot see the thing at all. It must be those split pupils.'

He swung the machine toward their objective. After a few minutes Iroedh could make out the wall of the Community, like the rim of a wheel whose hub was the cluster of domes.

Under Iroedh's guidance he spiraled down upon the domes. She pointed:

'That big one in the middle is the queen's dome. Do you see that circle near its top? That's the guard's walkway. That dark spot just above the circle is the window of the condemned drones' cell. Do you see it?'

'Yes.'

'Then lower your ladder and I'll climb down it.'

'Get your legs out of the way. There, up on the crossbar. And watch your landing; it's a windy night.'

Bloch pushed a knob. There was a mechanical sound beneath them, audible over the purr of the motor and the swish of the blades, and a trap door dropped open where Iroedh had been resting her feet. Leaning forward she could see down through the trap door into empty space, in which the top two or three rungs of the rope ladder could be perceived jerking about in the air stream.

With a prayer to Gwyyr, Iroedh thrust a leg down into the opening and felt for the fixed rung; then the other leg. At last she located the topmost ladder rung and lowered her weight down upon it. Before she knew it she was altogether below the helicopter, clutching the swaying support, her cloak whipping and swirling about her as the helicopter rocked in the gusts.

Fear of falling gripped her so that she could hardly make herself look down, or let go a rung to shift her grip to the next. As she mastered her feelings she saw that the machine was descending rapidly toward the top of the queen's dome, at such an angle that the path of the lower end of the ladder would be tangent to the circular walkway.

Iroedh quickly lowered herself the rest of the length of the ladder. Over the noise of the helicopter she heard the tweedle of flute music and a voice:

'Ho there! Who are you?'

The guard was standing on the walkway a few feet from where Iroedh would strike it, her spear at ready, her helmeted head tilted back. Although it was too dark to recognize her by starlight, Iroedh knew that the guard's face must wear an astonished expression.

While reason told her it was but a matter of seconds, it seemed a year before the hovering helicopter brought her into position. She swung off the ladder, fell a couple of feet, and landed lightly in a crouch. Her hands flew to her throat to untie the cord that held her cloak in place.

For this cloak was her only weapon. Not wishing Bloch to know she possessed O'Mara's machete, and not wishing to add murder to her other offenses against the Community, she intended to attack the guard by the *rumdrekh*. As the spear darted out, one whipped one's cloak around it and jerked it out of the hands of the foe, dropped the cloak, reversed the spear, and went into action in the normal manner.

'Who goes there?' cried the guard over the sound of the wind.

As Iroedh rose to her feet without answering, holding her cloak in her hands, the guard's spear fist went up and back for the overhand stabbing thrust. The spearhead shot out. Iroedh whirled her cloak and felt the point of the spear foul itself in the folds. She tried to give that extra flip and jerk that guaranteed success, at the same time reaching with her free hand for the spear shaft ...

But this guard was no tyro, and one of the biggest workers of the whole Community of Elham. With dismay Iroedh felt the cloak jerked entirely from her grasp as the guard pulled her spear back. Another jerk sent the cloak flying away on the wind. The guard took a long step forward, her burnished greaves glistening faintly in the starlight, and drew back her arm for another thrust. This one would not miss.

In theory an agile worker, so attacked, had a remote chance of seizing the spear shaft and wresting it from her assailant. Iroedh, now entirely unencumbered except for the magical cutting device strapped to her side, had whatever meager advantage that fact gave her. In practice, however, she realized that her luck had now run out. If one snatched the spear too soon, one caught the head and severed the tendons of one's fingers on its edges; if too late, the spear point would already have reached one's vitals.

At least, she thought in the last flash, once you were dead nothing hurt any more. And since her mission had obviously failed, Antis would die, and life without him would hardly be worth the bother. She winced, closing her eyes, as the spear head darted forward.

But no point tore into her viscera. When she opened her eyes it was to see the guard drop her spear with a clatter and turn to run. The noise and wind of the helicopter had greatly increased, so that the down-wash tore at Iroedh's bare body as if it would hurl her from the walkway down the slippery slope of the dome.

Gwyyr must have heard; Bloch, bless his alien hearts, had brought his machine around in a tight circle and swooped so close to the dome that the alighting gear almost touched the combatants.

Clang! went the shield of the guard on the stones: one of the big bronze bucklers used for guard mount, ornamental, but too heavy for field use. The guard headed for the stair that spiraled down the lower half of the dome from the walkway.

'Hurry up!' called Bloch from the open window of his aircraft.

Iroedh sprinted around the walkway, her bare feet making no sound against the noise of the helicopter and the clatter of the guard descending the stairs. Meanwhile her hand sought the cutting device at her waist.

A quarter of the way around she came to the window of the drones' cell. 'Antis!' she called softly.

'For the love of Dhiis, is that you, Iroedh?' came the familiar voice. 'What on Niond is going on, and how did you get here? I thought you were at Gliid!'

'No time to explain. Are you and the others ready to escape?'

'We should love to – but how?'

'Leave that to me. Stand back!'

Iroedh felt the cutting device until she found the stud that actuated it. She pressed the button and a thin line of light appeared along the edge near the end. She touched this edge to one of the bars at its upper end. With a shower of sparks the instrument sheared through the thick bronze as if it had been tarhail mush.

Bloch had warned her not to touch the edge to her own person, lest she be similarly sectioned. An 'electronic knife,' he had called it, which meant nothing to her.

Below, she could hear the voice of the guard shouting the alarm. *Zzip!* went another bar, and then the third. Iroedh withdrew the instrument and applied it to the lower ends of the bars. *Zzip! Zzip! Zzip!* Two of the bars tumbled in through the slanting window to fall with a clatter to the floor of the cell. The third struck with a soft thump, followed by an outburst of dronish bad language: '… the fertilizing thing landed on my toe!'

Iroedh put the instrument back in its case and said: 'Can you climb out now?'

'Don't know,' said Antis. 'One of us will have to boost another up.'

With much male grunting, Antis' head and shoulders appeared in the opening.

'Give me a hand, beautiful,' he said.

Iroedh pulled, and out he came asprawl on the walkway. As he rose to his feet, the forepart of Kutanas appeared, to be helped out likewise.

Below in the courts Iroedh could hear the clink of arms and the voice of the guard talking excitedly with unseen persons. Any minute a party would come storming up the stair.

Kutanas and Antis reached back into the darkness of the cell to seize the wrists of Dyos and pull him up. When he was half out of the window he got stuck.

'The stumps of those bars are disemboweling me!' he complained.

'Shall we leave him?' said Iroedh, who did not care much what happened to Dyos so long as Antis was saved.

'I should say not!' said Antis. 'We drones have to stick together. Brace your foot, Kutanas, and heave!'

'I told him not to eat so much,' grunted Kutanas. 'Ready?'

They heaved, and Dyos came like a tooth being plucked from its socket.

'Ow! Ow!' lamented Dyos, rubbing the scraped parts. 'I shan't be able to sit for days.'

From below came the unmistakable sound of a party of armed workers, and their officer's voice: 'One at a time, and hold your spears at ready ...'

'Daktablak!' called Iroedh loudly into the darkness.

'Here,' said Bloch, swinging the helicopter back toward the window.

Dyos flinched as the machine swooped close, and seemed about to run. Antis exclaimed:

'What in the name of Tiwinos is that?'

'Never mind. When I climb the rope ladder that hangs down from it, you do likewise. I shall climb into the machine, but you three hold your places on the ladder while the machine lifts you over the wall and sets you down outside.'

'I'm afraid!' wailed Dyos.

'Stay behind and be butchered then,' snapped Iroedh. She caught the lashing ladder on the third try and began her climb.

The clatter of the guards came clearly over the sounds of the wind and the helicopter. From her height Iroedh could see them coming up the stair, spears ready. Directly below her, Antis scrambled up, and below him the other two. She reached the machine, too excited to feel fear, and swung into the swaying cabin.

'Go!' she said to Bloch.

Bloch did things with his levers and the aircraft rose. A chorus of exclamations came up from the guards as they rushed to the spot from which Dyos had just been lifted. A couple threw their spears at him, but he was already too high. The spears fell back upon the stonework and went rolling and rattling down the sides of the dome.

As Iroedh settled into her seat, Antis thrust his crest up through the trap door. 'What now?'

She replied: 'We'll drop you in the tarhail field outside the wall. When you get to the woods north of this field, you'll have cover almost all the way to the Lhanwaed Hills. Watch the road from Thidhem, and when I get back from Gliid I'll meet you at Khinam. I shall make this sound—'

She whistled a bar of the refrain of the *Song of Geyliad*.

'How do you do that?' he asked.

'I'll teach you when we have time. We're past the wall; get ready to drop.'

Antis spoke to Kutanas below him as the helicopter sank toward the field. It occurred to Iroedh that the agricultural officer would have a fit when she found that a great swath had been trampled in her ripe grain.

Dyos dropped off, but stupidly failed to get out from under Kutanas, so that the latter came down on top of him and both rolled in the dirt. Antis landed on his feet, called up: 'Farewell, beautiful!' and ran for the woods at the north side of the field, crying for the others to follow.

'Now,' said Iroedh, 'take me home ... Oh, *prutha!*'

'What is it?'

'I left my cloak on the dome where the guards will surely find it.'

'Has it got your name on it?'

'No, though I should know it anywhere by the tears I've mended. But when I return to the camp without a cloak, and the word gets around that an unclaimed one was found at the scene of the rescue, some busybody will put the facts together. Still, we dare not go back for it; that would be pressing our luck too far.'

'Tell them you gave it to Barbe in exchange for one of her feminine doodads. I will see that she gives you one.'

Rhodh asked: 'Last night I am sure I heard the flying machine of the men go up and come down again later. Do you know anything about it, Iroedh?'

'Not a thing, Leader,' said Iroedh, patting her biscuits into shape.

'Well, I am not satisfied with the situation. You are all confined to the camp for the day; I do not wish you to become involved with these dangerous and immoral creatures.'

Iroedh and the three juniors exchanged wordless looks. Rhodh strapped on her kilt and cuirass, wriggled her head into her helmet, took up her spear, and walked off toward the *Paris*.

Iroedh went back to her chores, but presently looked up to see Barbe Dulac bearing down upon her. The female man held a small gold-colored box in her extended hand, and said in a voice evidently meant for all within earshot:

'Here you are, Iroedh dear. And thank you again for the lovely cloak.'

'What's that?' said Vardh.

'Oh,' said Barbe, 'Iroedh and I are exchanging gifts, products of our respective worlds.'

'That little thing for a cloak?' said Iinoedh in wonderment. 'What does it *do*?'

'We Terran females use it to give ourselves the beauty,' said Barbe.

'How?' inquired Avpandh.

Barbe opened the little box. 'First, here is a – how would you say mirror?'

While this was being cleared up the Avtini crowded around to look at their reflections. Iroedh, though familiar with the mirror of polished brass used by the queen to prepare herself for the visits of her drones, was astonished by the fidelity of the image in the compact. It was like looking through a tiny window into another world.

'Now there is this,' said Barbe, pulling out a small furry disk. 'It is called a powder puff. Among us a shiny nose is considered ugly. Hold still, Iroedh.'

Barbe applied the furry disk with small dabs to Iroedh's nose. Iroedh inhaled a breath of powder and sneezed.

Barbe said: 'Now comes the lipstick. Make your mouth like so ... You really need a darker shade, because your skins are almost as red as this already.'

Barbe stood back from her handiwork. The three juniors looked at Iroedh and whooped with mirth.

Barbe screwed up her face at the sound and asked: 'What is that noise? It sounds like a Terran creature called an owl.'

The young Avtini explained that the hooting sound was merely their version of laughter, and insisted that Barbe do likewise by them. Vardh said:

'What's it supposed to do, to color our faces like this? Do you prepare for some ceremonial in this manner?'

'You might say so,' said Barbe. 'This is how one catches a male.'

'You mean as when we round up surplus drones to kill them at the Cleanups?'

'No; a much more agreeable ceremony.'

As the juniors straggled off to resume their tasks, Barbe said to Iroedh in a lower voice: 'Winston told me about your expedition last night. That was naughty of you, Iroedh.'

'I know, but what could I do? Is he still angry with me?'

'He was at first, that you should have made him risk his life on something that was none of his affair. But I thought I should do the same if he were in prison, and that he should have had enough romance in his soul to take the risk without having to be blackmailed into it. I told him he was a spineless old rabbit with no sentiment, caring nothing for anything but his scientific records and the good opinions of his superiors in the government department he works for. So now he is all subdued, that one.'

'What is this "romance" and "sentiment" you talk about? Has it something to do with your special Terran kind of love?'

'A great deal. It is hard to explain, but—I know; can you read English?'

'A little. I know what sounds the letters stand for, and I can puzzle out simple passages.'

'It is good the English speakers reformed their spelling not many years ago, because before then it was so irregular you could never have mastered it. What I am getting at is that I will give you a Terran book I brought to Ormazd.'

'You're much too kind!' cried Iroedh.

'No, no, I have finished it. They do not like one to take bound books on the ship anyway, because of the weight. Their library is all photographed down small on little cards that one reads with an enlarging machine, but I like to read in bed and one cannot hold the machine on one's lap in the bunk, so I brought a real book.'

'What's in this book?'

'No scientific information, but it will tell you what we mean by the "romance" and the "sentiment."'

'What is it called?'

'*A Girl of the Limberlost*, by an American writer named Porter. It was first published hundreds of years ago, but for some reason was reprinted recently, and I happened to come upon a used copy in a bookstall in Genève. As it is the most sentimental story I have ever read, I think you will find it interesting.'

Later in the day Rhodh returned, took one look, and cried: 'What in the name of Eunmar have you been doing to your faces?'

When Vardh stammered an explanation, Rhodh said: 'That is enough! Wash off that filth! I see you cannot be trusted anywhere near these men, who will corrupt you with their degenerate customs. We leave for Elham at once.'

'What!' cried Iroedh. 'But we haven't finished with the men – or they with us—'

'We have indeed finished with them. I interviewed them again this morning and found them absolutely adamant against helping us.'

'But they wish to learn about our world—'

'For what purpose? So they can conquer it more easily? You always were a credulous fool, Iroedh. In any case, they can learn from some other Community; we are all needed back home to help in the war with Tvaarm. Strike the camp and pack your gear right away.'

Iroedh got to work folding the stove and hitching up the uegs. In less than an hour they were lined up.

'Ready?' barked Rhodh.

She cracked her whip and they got into motion, the uegs pulling on the shafts with their big knobby hands. As they reached the main road through the valley of Gliid, Iroedh turned right toward the *Paris* instead of left toward Thidhem.

'Ho there!' shouted Rhodh. 'You have mistaken your turn, Iroedh!'

Iroedh called back: 'No, I'm going to speak to one of the men. Go on; I shall catch up.'

'Come back here!' screamed Rhodh. 'You shall do no such thing!'

Iroedh, as if she had not heard, kept right on.

A quarter-hour later she caught up with the tail of the procession, happy in the knowledge that the Terran book lay snug at the bottom of her chariot chest along with O'Mara's machete. Rhodh, leading the column, kept her helmeted head rigidly to the front, as if she were unaware of Iroedh's presence.

When they came to a wide stretch Vardh reined back alongside Iroedh and told her softly: 'You know, Iroedh darling, I don't think she's leaving because of the attitude of the men at all. We might have accomplished much in a few more days.'

'What, then?'

'She's made a fool of herself by antagonizing them, so she cannot bear the scene of her mistakes. And she can't let you represent us any more because if you succeeded you'd get the credit.'

Iroedh said: 'I was always taught to put the good of the Community before my own glory. Rhodh used to be as pleasant as any other worker before she became consumed with ambition.'

'Isn't it true? They say she plans to run for foreign officer at the next election. Why don't you run against her? We'd all vote for you.'

'By Gwyyr, such a thought never occurred to me! You want these bustling characters, interested in every petty detail, on the Council, not an impractical antiquarian dreamer like me.'

The five members of the mission to Gliid drove back to Elham in an all-day rain. Iroedh, when her ueg had been turned back to the Community stables, went to her quarters. In the recreation room of her section she found some of her friends and asked them if Tvaarm had begun its expected invasion yet.

'Not yet,' said Tydh, resting after a night of guard duty. 'But it's been just as exciting as if they had.'

'How so?'

'Haven't you heard of the disappearance of the condemned drones? But of course, you've been out of touch with Elham. During the night a great black flying thing came down upon the queen's dome, tore open the bars of their cell, snatched them out, and flew away with them. The guard on dome duty told how she attacked the monster with her spear, but it knocked her halfway down the stair with a flick of its legs.'

Iroedh noticed that the guard's account made no mention of a human adversary. No doubt the poor guard had not cared to confess her flight.

'And the funniest thing was,' continued Tydh, 'that the cloak of an Avtin was found on the dome alongside the walkway. The guards who rushed up the dome just as the monster flew away all swear they weren't wearing any, and the drones had no clothing in their cell. It's a great mystery.'

Iroedh's hearts pounded. Tydh went on:

'It's just like the old legends in which gods like Tiwinos and Dhiis came down to Niond to right wrongs and fertilize mortals. In fact, some of the workers are talking of reviving the ancient religion.'

'That sounds like fun. What does the Council say?'

'Oh, they tell us not to be silly. And another thing: The Council has set the Royal Duel for five days from today!'

'Really?'

'Yes. I'm offering three to one on Estir, if you care to lay a bet. Eiudh is trying to wangle a mission to Ledhwid so she can ask the Oracle to predict the outcome and clean the rest of us out, while Gruvadh is going through all the prophetic quatrains to find one that fits the case, and Ythidh spends all her liberty upon the domes watching the flight of flying things for omens.'

'How does Intar take it?'

'The queen is furious. She says it's a conspiracy to get rid of her, and that if her fertility is down it's only because of the poor quality of the drones the Council has furnished her.'

Iroedh grew cold inside. She was sure she could somehow combine her possession of the machete with the impending accession of Estir to her own advantage, but could not think how. She would have to act quickly, because when Rhodh learned about the mysterious abandoned cloak she would probably remember the flight of the helicopter on the night the drones disappeared, and draw the natural inference.

Tydh said: 'How about a game of uintakh?'

'No, thank you. The Terrans lent me a book which I'm mad with curiosity about.'

Iroedh excused herself and went to her private cell for the book. As she did not have to report for work until the following morning she settled herself comfortably in the recreation room for a good long read, evading the pleas of her friends to join them in practicing the figures of round dances to be danced at the forthcoming Queens' Conference.

She found the book hard going, for despite the exceptional linguistic talent for which she was known in the Community her knowledge of English was not so good as she had thought. While some unfamiliar words she could guess from context or infer from the primer Bloch had given her, others, like 'daffy' or 'calico,' left her baffled. Still, the general story line of *A Girl of the Limberlost* was reasonably clear, making allowance for the strangeness of Terran culture and customs.

She was deeply immersed in the adventures of Elnora Comstock when a voice said: 'Oh, Iroedh dear!'

Iroedh looked up to see the agricultural officer standing over her.

'I have bad news for you,' continued the councilman.

Iroedh's hearts skipped a beat. Had they discovered her guilt in the matter of the disappearing drones already? She sat as if paralyzed.

The agricultural officer said: 'Rhodh presented her report to us as soon as she got in. Well, you know Rhodh. She made much of the difficulties she worked under, and of the coldly unfriendly attitude of the men, and of the incompetence and insubordination of her juniors – especially one Iroedh. In fact, she demanded that your efficiency rating be reduced.

'Of course we know Rhodh is simply eaten with ambition to be the next foreign officer, and is trying to cover up her failure to get help from the men. At least I know it, though I couldn't make the rest of the Council see it. She has friends in high places, it seems, and one must admit she works herself to a frazzle for the good of the Community. Anyway, they commended her and docked your rating by five points. I'm so sorry, my dear!'

Iroedh let out her breath. So *that* was all! Ordinarily she would have been furious at such unjust treatment, but now the agricultural officer's words came as a relief.

'I've survived worse things,' she said. 'But thank you for what you tried to do.'

Tired of reading, she went back to her cell to plan her next move. She wanted to see Antis and show him the machete, now hidden under her pallet. She had brought it into her cell wrapped in her net. She could of course wrap it in her net again, but if anyone saw her going out with a net under her arm they might well wonder why she was going to spend the night outside the Community. What she most urgently needed was a new cloak.

She filled out a requisition for a new cloak from stores, all but the signature, and took the bark sheet and the Terran make-up kit Barbe Dulac had given her to the queen's apartments. As it was not yet laying time she had no difficulty getting in. She presented the compact to the queen and explained its use.

'For me?' said Intar. 'Thank you, my good Iroedh. Do you know, you're the only member of that group that went to Gliid who remembered to bring me a present?'

'It's nothing, Queen. However, there is one small matter. I traded my cloak for that kit, and should like you to initial this requisition for a new one.'

'Certainly.' Queen Intar scrawled her initials on the bottom of the sheet and handed it back. 'Of course I'm not supposed to have opinions about such matters, my dear, but I think it was a shame that the Council commended Rhodh and disciplined you.'

*

Iroedh took the requisition to stores and drew a new cloak. Toward sunset she got a take-out meal from the section mess and set out afoot for Khinam, the machete wrapped in the cloak and the cloak under her arm.

She settled herself in the section of the ruins where she and Antis had so often picnicked. While she was setting out her supper she whistled the *Song of Geyliad*.

'Here we are, beautiful!' cried a voice, and Antis dropped laughing from the top of the ruined wall.

Iroedh jumped up with a little shriek of startlement. They threw their arms around each other and squeezed, then held each other at arms' length. Iroedh noted that Antis had lost weight and had acquired a hollow-eyed look; also that he was wearing an Avtiny worker's cloak and boots.

'Where did you get those?' she asked.

'Ask me no questions and I'll tell you no lies. You didn't by chance bring any *meat*, did you?'

'No. I thought of it, but if I went to the royal mess and asked for it they'd wonder what I wanted it for.'

'I suppose so,' he said in a less enthusiastic tone. 'What couldn't I do to a nice juicy leipag steak!'

'Haven't you eaten since the rescue?'

'Practically nothing. You forgot you dropped us in that field as naked as the day we were hatched, without even boots. My feet are somewhat hardened from coming out with you, but Dyos and Kutanas have had a rough time.'

'Couldn't you make yourself a bow and arrows to hunt your meat with?'

'What with? You need a tool of some sort. I left Kutanas back in the woods trying to scrape a sapling into a spear with a sharp stone, but at the present rate we shall all be dead before he finishes it. We tried to get into the leipag enclosure to steal one, but no luck; it was too well guarded. Yesterday I caught a hudig with my bare hands, but that gave us only one good bite apiece.'

'You poor fellows! Take this, then,' she said, handing over her knife. 'You can at least carve bows and spears with it.'

'Thanks. This isn't really good hunting territory, because the workers of Elham and Thidhem have killed off or driven away most of the game so that rogues like us shall have no source of food save dhwygs and other creeping things.' He looked hungrily at Iroedh as she ate her biscuits and vegetables. 'I'd even eat that mess of yours if I didn't mind dying in convulsions.'

'Would you like to get back into the Community?'

'If it could be done without our being speared at the next Cleanup, yes. I'm afraid we're failures as rogues. This wild life doesn't suit us: I miss my food, I miss you, and I miss my proper task.'

Iroedh wrinkled her nose to indicate lack of sympathy with his desires. She said:

'I have something here to show you, and a plan that may get you back on your own terms.'

She unwrapped the machete and drew it from its scabbard. Antis stared wonderingly, took the implement, and, with a slowly dawning light of understanding in his eyes, hefted and swished it.

'Now this is something!' he cried. 'Did you get this from the men?'

'Yes. They call it something like matselh.' She told him the history of O'Mara and his machete. 'But you may not have that!' she said.

'Why not? There's an old rogue in the Lhanwaed Hills who has learned smithery and who could duplicate this thing—'

'I have a better use for it. Did you know the Royal Duel takes place in five days?'

'No, I didn't. What about it?'

'If I offered this to Estir as a sure method of winning, don't you think she might agree to issue a pardon on her accession, and to use her influence with the Council to exempt you three permanently from the Cleanups?'

'Hmm – maybe. It's a tempting idea. But how well do you know Estir?'

'Not at all well; I've merely met her a few times at social functions. They say she has a violent temper.'

'Why would you trust her?'

'A princess wouldn't lie!'

'Let's hope. I still wish I could have this thing; it makes one feel a lot less vulnerable to the whims of fortune.'

'You wouldn't find it very useful for hunting. What you need are some stout bows and spears. I'll watch for a chance to steal you some.'

VI

The Royal Duel

The dome of Princess Estir of Elham was heavily guarded, lest the queen, wandering in that way, make a sudden attempt at assassination. With a pass from the agricultural officer, however, Iroedh soon got her audience.

'Many eggs, Princess,' she said. 'Candidly, what do you think of your chances?'

Estir balanced on the balls of her feet as if sighting for a spear thrust. She was as slim and active as a worker, though her breasts were fully developed.

'I don't know,' she said in a lazy voice that reminded Iroedh of the drawl of the Arsuuni. 'Better than even, I should think. Of course there's always a factor of luck, but I'm in good form and my omens have been favorable.'

'Maybe I could guarantee you your victory.'

Estir looked sharply at Iroedh, her slit pupils widening. 'You could?'

'Perhaps.'

'You mean you'd want something in return, eh?'

'Right,' said Iroedh.

'Say on.'

'You know the three drones who disappeared?'

'Who doesn't? What about them?'

'They'd like to return to the Community.'

'So? If they don't mind the little detail of being speared to death we should be glad to have them.'

'But, Princess, that's just it. They want pardons and permanent exemption from the Cleanups.'

'How do you know? Have you been fraternizing with them? That's a serious offense, you know.'

Iroedh smiled. 'Ask me no questions and I'll tell you no lies. That's what they want.'

'Well?'

'If you'll see they get what they ask, I will see that you win your duel.'

Estir looked puzzled. 'You might almost as well ask for the Treasure of Inimdhad! That would bend our system pretty far. When you consider how many drone babies we kill to keep the population in balance, they should thank Gwyyr they've been allowed to live this long.'

'It's no doubt wrong of them to wish to prolong their lives, but such is the case.'

'Why should you be acting for them? A loyal worker should try to see that they're hunted down and killed.'

'Princess, I won't argue the rights and wrongs of the question. If you wish to win your fight, promise the other matter. Otherwise I'll go to the queen.'

Estir thought a bit. 'Very well then. Show me your trick, or special prayer to Gwyyr, or whatever it is, and if I win my duel with it I promise to get your drones pardoned and exempted from future Cleanups. Do you really mean you want them allowed to live even after they're too old to perform their function?'

'Yes.'

'All right. This may set a troublesome precedent, but I haven't much choice.'

Iroedh unwrapped the machete and explained its use.

Estir's yellow eyes glowed. 'This will do it! A dagger in the right hand for parrying spear thrusts, then get in close and slash—'

'It can also be used for thrusting,' said Iroedh, 'though it's a little heavy at the point for that purpose.'

'It's too bad I haven't a longer time to practice, but poor old Intar will never have seen such a thing! I'll write out the pardons and postdate them to take effect the minute Intar dies. I'll also get in touch with the Council. Tell your drones to come to the duel; they shan't be molested.'

'Thank you, Princess.' Iroedh headed back to her cell and *A Girl of the Limberlost.*

On the day of the duel Iroedh helped all morning to carry seats out to the exercise ground. Other workers cleared away the parallel bars and other gymnastic equipment with zest, for a Royal Duel was one of their few holidays.

A guard said: 'Iroedh!'

'Yes?'

'Two of the escaped drones are out at the main gate. They say they've been promised immunity, and want a document to show before they will come in.'

Iroedh dropped her task to hunt up the agricultural officer, who provided her with the necessary pass. She then hurried out to the front gate, where she found Antis and Kutanas waiting, both wearing stolen workers' cloaks. She escorted them past the glowering guards, who hefted their spears significantly.

'Where's Dyos?' she asked.

Antis answered: 'He didn't come; doesn't trust Estir. To tell the truth, I don't either, but I wouldn't give her the satisfaction of knowing I was afraid of her.'

'How are you making out, dear?'

'Not too badly. We killed a wild leipag and had a feast.'

'You look fit,' she said.

'Fit if not beautiful.' He laughed and slapped his belly, now nearly flat instead of the normal drone paunch. 'This life certainly does things to one's shape, don't you think? I don't know if the queen will like it, whoever *is* queen tonight. I'm all excited about the duel; I wasn't yet hatched when Intar slew Queen Pligayr. What will happen if Intar should win after all?'

'This safe-conduct is good until sundown in any case.'

'And then we light out for the timber again. Oh, well.'

They came to the exercise ground where most of the workers of Elham had already gathered. Others were pouring in from the domes of the Community and from the fields around it. A group of workers headed by Gogledh arrived from Thidhem, having been rewarded for industry and efficiency by passes to the combat. The ushers struggled to range the crowd around the four sides of the field, a row of workers squatting on the ground in front, then one of workers seated, then one of workers standing. A picked group was performing a military dance in the open space:

'I've never seen a duel either,' said Kutanas, 'and I wish the dancers would stop their dancing and spearwaving and let us get on to the main event. Do they fight in armor or what?'

'No,' said Iroedh. 'According to the rules they must fight naked, with no shields or other defenses. The object is a quick clean victory, preferably with the victor unhurt. They may use any offensive weapons other than missile weapons. Sometimes they carry a spear in both hands, and sometimes a spear in one hand and a hatchet or dagger in the other.'

The dancers finished and filed off, and a pair of workers under the direction of the grounds officer pushed a roller over the trampled sand.

An usher said: 'Iroedh, these drones with you will have to sit in the drones' section—Oh!'

'Yes, they are those that escaped, but they have a safe-conduct,' said Iroedh, waving the document under the usher's nose. 'As they have the status of visitors I think they should stay with me.'

'Here they come,' said Antis.

A murmur of the crowd presaged the appearance of Intar and Estir at opposite ends of the field, each with her seconds. Intar's efforts to train down for the fight had not been very successful. Estir, on the other hand, moved with the deadly grace of a beast of prey.

Kutanas said: 'Everybody's betting on Estir, but the old queen has some tricks the other never heard of.'

'You should know,' said Antis.

The foreign officer (who, with the general still absent, was the senior Council member) read the traditional proclamation setting forth the reason for the duel and the qualities of the combatants. She droned on until the workers were all fidgeting.

'… so, for the good of Elham, you will enter upon this sacred fray resolved to prosecute it to the death, and may the best queen win! Begin!'

Intar lumbered down from her end, her rolls of fat jouncing, while Estir trotted lightly from hers. The queen carried a standard guard's spear in both hands; the princess a dagger in one hand and O'Mara's machete in the other. The crowd muttered its surprise at the sight of the latter weapon. Iroedh caught phrases:

'What's that thing?' '… unfair; the Council shouldn't allow …' 'Why don't we use those in war?' 'I wish to withdraw my bet on Intar!'

'Iroedh darling!' said Vardh. 'I feel just sure Intar will win. Remember the Oracle of Ledhwid:

'*When the female ueg with curving claw*
Shall lop the head of a pomuial bloom,
She shall stand on her head on a vremoel raw
Or fall to her doom.'

'You applied that same stanza to the plague last year,' Iroedh reminded her.

The queen braced herself, hands wide apart on the spear shaft, and thrust at Estir as the princess came on. Estir threw herself to one side with lightning quickness and swung the machete. Intar parried with the spearhead; there was a clang of metal.

The females circled warily, now and then making a short rush or feint. Queen Intar thrust with her point, then quickly reversed the spear and swung the butt end at Estir's ankles in an effort to trip her. Estir leaped over the shaft and made a downward cut at Intar's head. Intar whipped up the spear shaft and the machete blade bit into the wood.

'I think,' said Antis, 'Estir's going slowly, to tire out Intar before closing.'

The fighters were circling again, with long periods of feinting and footwork at a distance and then an occasional quick flurry of blows and thrusts.

'Ah-h!' went the crowd.

Estir had not been quick enough in recovering after delivering a cut, and the spearhead jabbed her shoulder. As it was the right, the one that held the dagger, she seemed none the worse, though blood trickled down in a red rill and fell in slow drops from her fingers.

Advance, retreat, feint, parry, thrust, recover. On and on they went. Intar suddenly rushed in and thrust with surprising agility. Estir parried with the machete and thrust out with her dagger. The point pricked Intar's sagging left breast. Blood trickled there too.

Vardh said to Iroedh: 'Darling, I'm so sure Intar's going to win I've bet my year's clothing allowance on her. I've been saying a special prayer to Eunmar; did you know I believe in the old gods? If you try hard enough, I've found, you can believe anything.'

After another pause Intar pressed the fight again, driving Estir before her with quick jabs. As the princess parried one at her face with the dagger, Intar jerked the pike back and thrust again, low. The point struck Estir in the thigh – not squarely, but glancing, opening another small wound.

As Intar withdrew the spear for another thrust, Estir dropped her dagger and caught the spear shaft just back of the head. She pulled it toward herself and struck with the machete at the queen's right hand. The blade bit into the hand.

With a yell the queen released her hold on the shaft with that hand. She stepped back, blood spraying the sand, and tugged at the shaft with her good hand. Estir resisted for a second, then pushed. Intar stumbled backward and sat down.

Estir, leaping forward, brought the machete down in a full overhand slash. The blade sank deep into Intar's left shoulder. Her left arm went limp and Estir tore the spear out of her grasp and threw it away.

Intar took a last look at the opponent towering over her, then closed her eyes and bowed her head. The machete whistled through the air and sheared through the queen's thick neck. Spouting blood, the body collapsed and lay kicking and twitching.

Estir walked toward the table where the foreign officer sat, kicked the dead queen's head aside as she went, and cried: 'I, Estir of Elham, being a fertile and functional female of pure Elhamny descent, and having slain my predecessor Intar in fair fight in accordance with the laws and customs of Elham, do hereby proclaim myself Queen of Elham!'

The foreign officer cried: 'Homage to the new Queen of Elham!'

All the workers and drones dropped to their knees, shouting: 'Hail to the queen! *Kwa Estir!* Long life and many eggs!'

Vardh said to Iroedh: 'Isn't she just the most beautiful thing, like one of the prophecies come to life? I can forgive her for making me lose my bets.'

Iroedh had to admit that, even with blood still trickling down her skin from her wounds, Estir made a magnificent picture. It was too bad, she thought, that there were no artists nowadays like those of yore who could do justice to the scene.

Vardh continued: 'Let's try to arrange to be in her escort to the next Queens' Conference, darling. The round dances will be ever such fun.'

Before Iroedh could answer (the noise having somewhat abated) Estir cried: 'As the first act of my reign, I revoke the safe-conduct pass given to the rogue drones Antis and Kutanas. Slay them, guards, and arrest the worker Iroedh for treason!'

Iroedh looked blankly at the new queen, at the foreign officer, and at her drones, who looked equally thunderstruck. She shouted back:

'But, Queen, you promised—'

'I promised nothing! Guards, obey my commands!'

Even as the guards poised their spears and started toward them, Antis and Kutanas moved. Out from under their cloaks came two more machetes – near copies of the one wielded by Estir, but red-brown bronze instead of gray steel, and more crudely made.

'Stand back!' roared Antis, swinging his machete.

The unarmed workers scattered. Antis pulled a third machete from the belt he wore under his cloak and thrust the hilt at Iroedh.

'Take it!' he said.

'But—'

'*Take it!*'

Though unaccustomed to being ordered around by a drone, Iroedh took the machete just in time to knock aside the point of a spear.

'Make for the main gate!' said Antis, swinging wildly.

One of his blows knocked the helmet from the head of a guard; another cut through the shaft of a spear; another laid open a guard's arm and sent her back, bleeding. Kutanas was likewise busy; a guard went down under his blows with her guts spilling onto the sand.

Iroedh took a few swipes and heard her blade clank against the brass of the guards' defenses. Then all at once the way lay open before the fugitives. Antis seized Iroedh's free hand with his and ran for the gate, right through the flower beds. Behind them they could hear the screams of Queen Estir above the general uproar.

'Open up!' bellowed Antis as they neared the gate. 'Emergency!'

Whatever the guards at the gate thought, they stood staring in silent incomprehension as the fugitives threw back the bolt and pushed open the gate. Then one of them said:

'Come back here! There's something irregular about this. Why are those people chasing you?'

'Ask them!' said Antis and dragged Iroedh out.

They ran toward the field of tarhail into which Iroedh had dropped the drones from the helicopter. Behind them came the sound of the pursuit, slowed by the fact that none of the unarmed workers seemed anxious to run on ahead of the guards, while the guards, weighted down with shields and cuirasses, could not run so fast as an unencumbered Avtin.

They panted across the field and into the woods on the far side. Now, thought Iroedh, the agricultural officer would have another trampled swath to fume about; it was a shame to do such a thing to her best friend on the Council. But since through force of circumstances she was becoming a hardened anti-Communitarian, she did not give the matter much thought.

Antis led her this way and that along trails through the woods.

'Old game trails,' he said. 'We can rest now. It'll take them hours to find us in this maze.'

When Iroedh got her breath she asked: 'Where's Kutanas?'

'Dead. Didn't you see the guards get him?'

'No. I was too busy fighting on my own account.'

'He looked like a spiny dhug by the time they finished shoving their spears into him. Too bad, because he'd have made a better rogue than that fat fool Dyos, who is always complaining and afraid of his own shadow.'

'And the fat fool lives, while the worthy Kutanas lies dead. *Weu!* I feel terrible about having fought my fellow workers. Maybe I even slew one. And to have Estir act in that treacherous manner! If one cannot trust one's own queen, whom can one trust?'

'Oneself. Cheer up; such is life.'

'Where did you get the matselhi?'

'That old smith I told you about, Umwys, made them from my description. We hauled that statue of Dhiis playing a telh that we found in Khinam all the way to his hideout to supply the metal.'

'You didn't!' cried Iroedh.

'Of course we did! What of it?'

'But that's a priceless relic—'

'Maybe it is, but without that bronze we should all be dead. Since we had nothing to pay Umwys with, we had to give him the bronze left over from the making of the matselhi. He's been working day and night on those things ever since I saw you at Khinam. Are you rested enough to go on?'

'I think so.'

'Let's go to our rendezvous with Dyos, then.'

He led her on and on until Iroedh was completely lost, for as she had not had hunting duty for several years, she no longer knew the woods beyond the Community's fields and pastures very well. At last he came to a little hilltop.

'*Prutha!*' he cried. 'The rascal's run away and taken with him that bow-and-arrow set I was making!'

'What luck! What shall we do, then?'

'Go on to Umwys' hide-out, I suppose. If he has some spare food we may get a supper of sorts.'

He led the way again. The going became more and more rugged as they climbed into the Lhanwaed Hills. Iroedh was staggering with fatigue when

Antis put his hands to his mouth and gave a peculiar call. When it was answered he led Iroedh to a place where the brush was almost impassable.

Antis pushed a mass of vegetation aside and ducked into a hole that led right into the hillside. The tunnel did a sharp turn, and Iroedh found herself able to stand upright again in an illuminated chamber hollowed out of the hill. Wooden props supported a ceiling of hewn boards. Other openings led in other directions.

A wrinkled old drone faced them. When he saw Iroedh he gave a gasp, whipped up a spear he was holding, and hurled it right at her.

The point was headed straight for her midriff when Antis knocked it up with his machete. The spear stuck quivering in the ceiling.

'What's the matter, you old fool?' roared Antis.

'I thought you'd betrayed me to the workers,' said Umwys in his whining northern accent. 'Every worker's hand is against me, and mine is against every worker.'

'Iroedh is no longer a worker, but a rogue like you and me. Now apologize for trying to kill her!'

'I never heard of a rogue worker,' said Umwys sullenly. 'But if he says you are, I suppose you are. It'll be your fault, Antis, if she brings the whole Community of Elham down upon our necks. What d'you want with me, eh? To buy somewhat more of weapons?'

'No. I want to know what's become of Dyos. He failed to meet us as promised, and I think he's run off.'

'He may have at that. He was asking about the rogue bands to the north.'

'Then we're stuck again. Can you put us up for the night?'

'You may sleep here, and I can furnish you with a little meat. If she wants a meal she'll have to get her own, for I have no worker fodder. There be some khal trees with edible seeds on the hillside.'

Iroedh slipped out to forage; an unrewarding job, taking till sundown to collect enough nuts to half fill her stomach. Umwys, however, had lost some of his hostility in the meantime.

'You don't seem like a worker, lass,' he said. 'Why, you're nice!'

Not knowing quite how to take this, Iroedh munched her seeds in silence.

'If I were in your fix,' said Umwys, sucking marrow, 'I'd head north to Ledhwid and ask the Oracle for advice.'

'What?' said Iroedh. 'You sound like my mystical friend Vardh. All the responses from Ledhwid I ever heard could be taken in any of sixteen different ways.'

'No, aside from those daft verses, the Oracle sometimes offers canny advice. Nothing mystical, just logical inferences from the news its priestesses bring it. At least that's the best course I can think of. You can't live off this land; there's not enough game or wild vegetable food, and if you raid the

Communities, with but the two of ye against hundreds of them, they'll hunt you down.'

Antis asked: 'Why shouldn't we join one of the rogue bands to the north?'

'You could, but they'd slay her on sight. The rogues' attitude toward workers is to strike first and inquire afterwards.'

'That seems unreasonable,' said Iroedh.

'Eh, yes, but they feel they've been used unreasonably too. Now the band of Wythias is growing so great it could even attack a fortified Community, the way the Arsuuni do. I have enough orders from Wythias for spearheads to keep me busy half a year.'

Iroedh asked: 'If the rogue bands help the Arsuuni to destroy all the Avtiny Communities, what would then become of the drones? The whole race would perish.'

'You'd better ask Wythias about that; or, better yet, the Oracle, for Wythias wouldn't let you live long enough to get the question out. If the Oracle can't think of anything better for you to do, you might be able to take service with it.'

'With the Oracle?' said Iroedh.

'Aye. It employs somewhat of – ah – orphaned workers like yourself.'

'I know. I've seen the so-called priestesses. But what would happen to Antis?'

'How should I know? I don't think the Oracle employs drones, so he might have to join a rogue band after all.'

'We won't be separated!' said Antis.

Umwys shrugged. 'It's your lives, billies. Maybe he could leave his band to come see you once an eight-day, eh? Though where you two get that unnatural attachment for each other I can't think.'

'Ledhwid shall it be then,' said Antis.

'You'll need a cloak for her,' said Umwys. 'If you have to sleep in the open she'll get somewhat cold without clothing. And you'd better collect some vegetable food for her. Several of the plants have edible roots and berries and things, but having nought to do with workers I don't know which is which.'

Next day Antis said: 'We'll get you a cloak the same way I got mine. Come along.'

They hiked back toward Elham. After some hours Antis motioned for caution as they neared the cultivated fields.

'Down there,' he whispered.

'Down there' a small group of workers was mowing a field of tarhail – the very field, in fact, they had fled through the previous afternoon. Evidently the agricultural officer was determined not to wait for any more of her crop to be trampled.

At one side of the field a worker stood guard over the cloaks, food, water, and other gear. The guard was armed with spear, shield, and helmet, but no body armor, as this was normally not a hazardous job.

'What do we do now?' said Iroedh.

'Wait.'

'How long?'

'All day if need be. You have no idea of the patience required to be a successful thief.'

And wait for hours they did, lying on their bellies under the shrubs at the crest of the hill. At long last the guard yawned and sat down with her back to a tree.

Antis grinned. 'It's the boredom that gets them. Now watch.'

For another hour they watched. The guard chewed a grass stem, yawned some more, and turned over a stone to look at the creeping things under it.

'There she goes,' said Antis.

The guard slid down further and pulled the helmet over her face. From where Iroedh lay the guard looked like some bifurcated pink vegetable with a nutshell covering one end.

Antis rose to a crouch, beckoned, and stole down the game trail to the border of the field. On the way he picked up a dead branch as long as himself. This he maneuvered with exquisite care among the trees. When they got to where Iroedh could again see the red of the guard's skin through the green of the foliage, Antis held up a hand to halt her. He slid behind a big tree and reached around it with the stick, holding it out like a spear at full lunge. Gently he poked the point of the stick under the collar of one of the cloaks.

The guard stirred and muttered in her sleep.

Antis froze, then moved again. He raised the cloak off the branch stub that served as a peg, then drew back branch and cloak. He leaned the branch against his big tree, rolled up the cloak, and flashed a grin at Iroedh.

Iroedh glanced around to pick the route of retreat, and, as she did so, something caught her eye. Something bulky hanging from a tree.

With a vaguely reassuring motion to Antis she stepped lightly around the intervening trunks. The object proved to be a big bag, hanging like the cloaks from the stub of a branch. She lifted it down. Inside was a mass of biscuit flour and a sheet of vakhwil bark with writing on it.

She stalked back to where she had left Antis, holding the bag, and together they stole away from the clearing. When they were safely over the hill he said:

'What's that?'

Iroedh dug in and brought out the sheet. On it was a note reading:

From one who stays behind to one who has gone away:

    Here, dearest, is something that may come in handy in the strenuous days to come, as you will have trouble finding proper nourishment among the meat-eating rogues. Think kindly of one who loves and admires you. I still think you would have made a wonderful foreign officer. And whether the old gods exist or not, I pray to them to watch over you. If you get down-hearted, remember what the Oracle of Ledhwid said about the twoheaded queen riding the blue vakhnag.

'Vardh!' said Iroedh. 'The dear child!'

Though the note was unsigned she had no difficulty guessing the identity of the sender. Her throat closed up and she gave a slight sob.

Antis said: 'There's no luck like a true friend, as the Oracle once said. Now we're fixed for the journey.'

Hand in hand they started off for the cave of Umwys, Gliid, and Ledhwid, with Iroedh whistling the *Song of Geyliad*.

VII
The Rogue Drones

As they neared the *Paris*, five days later, Antis showed increasing signs of unease.

'Are you sure?' he said, 'these creatures won't eat us, or the sky ship won't fall over and crush us? It looks very unstable.'

'Quite sure,' said Iroedh. 'What's the matter with my hero, my second Idhios, who has so lightly eluded the search parties from Elham, and who has driven off a prowling noag with a piece of firewood? Has your courage all oozed away?'

'Avtiny workers and noags I know about,' he retorted in a sharp tone, 'but only fools rush into unknown dangers.'

While he spoke, Iroedh had been preparing a second and sharper gibe, but withheld it rather than foment a quarrel. Certainly he had shown enough courage and force of character during their perilous journey afoot to Gliid for three normal drones. In fact, she found herself depending upon him instead of the other way round, as an Avtin would normally expect.

Presently they came upon the clearing around the *Paris*. Iroedh was surprised to see a row of chariots parked in the place where Rhodh's party had camped, and a herd of uegs of about equal numbers tethered nearby. A man was feeding the beasts.

Iroedh, followed by a hesitant Antis, went up to the man and asked in English: 'Where is Dr Bloch to be found, please?' As her lisping Avtiny accent made the sentence into 'Hwerydh Daktablak tubi thaund, pliidh?' it took her some time to make herself clear.

'Over there, on the other side of the ship,' said the man.

They continued on until they found Bloch, with Barbe Dulac and another man, working on the ground beyond the ship. The Terrans had spread a dead leipag out on the ground and taken the beast thoroughly apart. The hide had already come off and was stretched out, with the inside up, while the other man did mysterious things to it. Meanwhile Bloch was removing all the muscles and organs from the skeleton, which had by now been nearly freed of them. Every few seconds he stopped to dictate notes to Barbe, or to tell her to draw a sketch or point a camera at the remains, or he would pop an organ into a jar full of some colorless but strong-smelling liquid. The male men were covered with blood and stank.

After Iroedh had watched for a while, Bloch looked up and said: 'Hello. It is – it's Iroedh of Elham, is it not?'

'Certainly,' said Iroedh, a little surprised that he should have trouble remembering her. 'This is Antis, also of Elham.'

'Excuse my not shaking hands,' said Bloch, twiddling his gory fingers. 'But—'

'What does he mean?' said Antis.

'Our form of greeting,' continued Bloch, his Avtinyk more fluent than on the previous visit. 'And what is a drone doing so far from his dronery? Oh, I know! You're one of the drones we hoisted out of the prison cell! What happened after that?'

'I owe you more than thanks,' said Antis with dignity. 'Any time I can do you a good turn, speak up.'

When Iroedh had finished her story she said: 'And so we are bound for Ledhwid and the Oracle. Have you thought of going there? I'm sure it would interest you.'

'Now that,' said Bloch, 'is a remarkable – how would you say "coincidence"? For only yesterday a worker named Yaedh of Yeym arrived here, saying she came from this Oracle and inviting us to call.'

Iroedh said: 'She'd be one of the Oracle's priestesses. Yeym was destroyed by the Arsuuni, and she would also be one of the few left alive from that Community. Do you plan to go?'

'Yes. We haven't obtained access to a single Community yet, and we cannot remain here much longer—'

'Why not? Where are you going?'

'The *Paris* is going to sample every continent on your planet, which means ten or twelve stops. As I was saying, Barbe would like a – how would you say "honeymoon trip"?'

After some explanation, Iroedh said: 'Oh, you're now her official drone! I should like to ask some questions about that—'

'Not just now, please,' said Bloch. 'So, since she's accustomed to roughing it also, we thought that would make an agreeable one. The only difficulty is we cannot spare enough men from the *Paris* to make up a party of safe size. Hence your coming is very convenient, and I suppose you would rather ride than walk, wouldn't you?'

'Certainly,' said Iroedh. 'Is this Yaedh of Yeym here at Gliid, and is she coming with us?'

'Yes. She's around somewhere.'

'Have any other Avtini visited your sky ship since our departure?'

'Several. A delegation arrived from Khwiem to request us to arbitrate some dispute with a neighboring Community. We had to turn them down—'

'Turn them down? You mean throw them down? Why—'

'No; I meant refuse their request. A couple of others put in an appearance just to see what they could observe. And then a great tall creature, one of the Arshuul – you call them Arsuuni, don't you? – came with a warning from Queen Omförs of Tvaar (which I take it is your Omvyr of Tvaarm) that if we dared to interfere in their program of conquest they would fill us full of spears.'

Bloch seemed amused by this threat, which fact puzzled Iroedh (who had a healthy fear of the Arsuuni) until she remembered the awesome powers of the men. If she could only somehow arrange for the Arsuuni to attack the Terran expedition …

She asked: 'How are you going to Ledhwid?'

'The same way you travel – in ueg chariots. Didn't you see those we have bought from Thidhem?'

'Why should you go that way when you can fly there in a few hours?'

'Two reasons: We don't know if there is a proper landing place for the helicopter at Ledhwid, and we can see much more of the planet by crawling around on its surface than by flying over it. Moreover, if we go in the chariots we can get acquainted with the people, whereas if they see us flying they're likely to run for cover and stay hidden until we've gone. We've been through all this on other planets.'

'What if you get into some serious danger or difficulty?'

'We shall keep in communication with the *Paris* so that if necessary Kang can fly out and rescue us.'

Iroedh asked: 'How can you talk with the ship when you're sixteens of borbi away?'

Bloch smiled. 'Terran magic. By the way, do you know who or what the Oracle is? Yaedh won't tell.'

'No. It's a living creature, but aside from that I don't know if it's queen, worker, or drone; or even whether it's Avtin or Arsuun. It never meets its clients face to face. When do we start?'

'Tomorrow morning, now that you're here. Can Antis drive one of these things?'

Iroedh exchanged looks with Antis, who said: 'I'm not really good, since drones aren't normally expected to learn that art, but Iroedh has taught me enough to manage. If you don't fear the results, I don't.'

Next morning they hitched up five of the uegs before sunrise.

Yaedh of Yeym had shown up the previous evening with a bagful of fungi of kinds that the uegs particularly liked, and which she had been out gathering when Iroedh arrived. As a result of Yaedh's pampering the beasts adored her and obeyed her every command. She was a lean and elderly worker with wrinkles on her face and her crest faded from scarlet to pale pink, who said but little.

The road ran down the floor of the valley toward the outlet, winding among the great boulders scattered around the defile at the northern or lower end. The day was uneventful. They stopped and set up camp toward sunset. Bloch took a thing like a little flat box out of his pocket, twisted some knobs, and spoke into it.

Iroedh asked: 'What on Niond are you doing, Daktablak?'

'Reporting to the *Paris*.'

'You can actually talk to the sky ship with that little thing?'

'Certainly. Would you care to say hello to Subbarau?'

Iroedh looked doubtfully at the little box. 'Hail, Captain Subbarau,' she said in a weak voice.

'How are you, Madame Iroedh?' came back Subbarau's nasal tones.

Iroedh hastily handed the box back to Bloch. After they had eaten and Bloch was puffing on his pipe and Antis practicing with his telh, Iroedh said to Barbe:

'Bardylak dear, I should like to ask some questions about you and Daktablak. First—'

'Hey!' said Bloch when he heard the first question. 'That's a Kinsey.'

'What's a kyndhi?'

'A type of interrogation named for a man who invented it long ago. You can't ask just anybody that; it's against our customs.'

'Then how do you learn what you must know in order to—'

'You may ask me the questions in private.'

Barbe spoke up: 'Not to change the subject or anything, but what became of that book I gave you, Iroedh?'

'I read more than halfway through before I had to flee. That's one reason I wish to get back into the Community.'

'How far did you get?'

'To where the two females, Elnora and Edith, each wants the drone Philip to fertilize her. At least I think that's what it means, though it's hard to be sure, because in matters of propagation Terrans never say anything right out, but use subtle hints.'

'I can tell you—' began Barbe, but Iroedh cut her off:

'Oh, please don't! I still hope to recover the book some day.'

Bloch asked: 'What book is this?' and when told, exploded: 'My God! With Tolstoy and Lewis and Balzac, and Conrad and Silberstein and Hemingway and McNaughton and a hundred other *good* novelists to choose from, you introduce her to the glories of Terran literature with one of the worst pieces of sentimental slush ever written!'

'It is not!' said Barbe. 'It's just that you're such an introvert, you, that you don't appreciate how other human beings—'

'What is "slush"?' said Iroedh.

Nobody heeded her. Barbe, getting excited, switched to French, which left Iroedh completely at a loss, especially since Bloch replied in the same language. The men waved their arms and blabbered at a furious rate, and ended up apologizing and hugging each other and making that curious mouth-touching gesture. They returned to English, in which Iroedh caught frequent use of the word 'love.'

'This love of yours,' she said, 'seems to play a large part in Barbe's book. From all I gather, love of individuals is more important among you than love of your Community. If that's the case, how can your Communities be well run?'

'Mostly they aren't,' said Bloch, relighting his pipe. 'But we have a lot of fun.'

'Oh, come now,' said Barbe, 'we love our Communities too. Besides Winston I also love my home city of Genève, me, and my country of Helvetia …'

'That's not the same sort of thing,' said Bloch. 'It's a matter of the language. Barbe's language has only one word, *aimer*, to represent all grades of affection. In English we confine 'love' to the more profound emotion, like that which Barbe and I feel for each other, and use 'like' for the milder and more superficial—'

Barbe interrupted: 'Now don't tell me you only *like* your country and your home region! I have heard your rhapsodies on the United States of America and on Bucks County, Pennsylvania, in particular—'

'Oh, all right, I suppose I do,' said Bloch, puffing. 'What we really require, I suppose, is about six words to represent all grades of love. At the top we should put love for one's mate, then love for one's parents and children, then for other close friends and relatives, then for one's locale and one's work, and so on.'

Barbe said: 'Do not claim you merely *like* your work either, Winston darling! I often think you love it better than me—'

'Not the same sort of thing at all,' said Bloch. 'Iroedh, I suppose that with you the Community comes at the top?'

'Normally, yes.'

Bloch said: 'We once had a sect or cult on Terra called Communists, who believed as you do that love of the Community should take precedence over all others. But their collectivistic love seemed to involve such fanatical hatred of everybody else and such implacable determination to impose their system on the world that we had to exterminate them. However, I suppose you are a somewhat special case because of your estrangement from your Community.'

'Yes,' said Iroedh. 'I'm so confused I don't know if I love my Community or Antis the better.'

Antis spoke up: 'I have no doubts at all; I love Iroedh the best of anything, and say a plague upon the Community! Since leaving it I've been a real person instead of a mere stud animal.'

'Thank you, Antis,' said Iroedh. 'Of course I don't think we could ever have a love in the strongest sense in which the men use the term, because that seems to be connected with sex.'

'And it is impossible for you, that there?' said Barbe.

'Certainly. I'm a neuter. But even if I never go back to Elham, I shall manage, so long as I can love Antis and perhaps my antiquities.'

Bloch said: 'You must love your antiques in the same way I love my work.' He asked Antis: 'Did you never feel this most violent grade of love for the queen when you – ah—'

'When I tupped her? By Eunmar, that was just work! Though I won't say I disliked old Intar, who was not a bad sort. When she—' The drone stopped. 'Anyhow, it is perhaps just as well that the question of sex cannot arise between Iroedh and myself. The more I hear of you men, the more I think our love will be better without that element.'

'That's what *you* think,' said Barbe. 'Me, I can tell you a different story; but since you are of another species it would not mean anything to you.' She turned to Yaedh. 'You have said nothing, sister. What or whom do you love, and why?'

Yaedh drew patterns in the dirt. 'Like any normal worker, I loved my Community,' she said, throwing a severe glance toward Iroedh. 'When that was destroyed I had nothing left. Nothing. All I can love now is animals; that's why I feed delicacies to the uegs and keep a neinog at Ledhwid.'

'How about your fellow priestesses?' asked Iroedh.

Yaedh shrugged. 'They are from many Communities, but do not themselves constitute a Community. While I like most of them well enough, there is no comparison with one's feeling for one's own Community. It's the difference between those Terran words 'like' and 'love' Daktablak was telling us about.'

Bloch said: 'How about the Oracle himself – or herself? Does he, she, or it inspire love?'

'We are not allowed to discuss the Oracle. I can however tell you that it is neither male nor female in the sense we know.' After a pause she resumed: 'My only advice to all of you would be to love as much and as many things and people as possible, so you shan't be so empty-hearted when you lose one of them. *My* only comfort is the oracular quatrain that goes:

> '*When the last sun sets and the stars grow cold*
> *And the one-eyed queen has laid her last,*
> *Then a new birth shall on Niond unfold*
> *When the old has passed.*'

'Cold comfort,' said Bloch. 'Like most oracular verse, full of vague ominous intimations of nothing in particular. But who am I to spoil your one pleasure?'

When Iroedh and Antis had gone to bed on the air mattresses provided by the *Viagens Interplanetarias*, wrapped in their cloaks and each other's arms for warmth, Bloch came and stood over them.

'Well,' he said, 'perhaps you overgrown children are physically unable to experience our kind of love, but you seem to do all right.'

For three days the journey northward progressed with little event except an occasional rain. Iroedh, feeling herself no longer bound by her Community's commands, passed on to Bloch her considerable knowledge of Avtiny history and culture. Barbe listened attentively, taking it all down in shorthand.

Bloch said: 'I should like to inspect that ruined city of Khinam. Do you suppose the Elhamni would try to chase us off if we paid it a visit before we left?'

'They know about your guns,' said Iroedh. 'They might not like it, but I don't think they would try anything drastic.'

'Then we will try to work in a visit—Hello, what's this ahead?'

'This' was a waist-high pile of logs and rocks across the road. Iroedh's eye caught a flash of brass.

'Rogues!' she cried. 'Get your gun ready, Daktablak!'

Bloch cried '*Branio!*' to his ueg, which obediently halted. He looked around nervously while unslinging the gun from his shoulder, saying:

'Do you think – uh – perhaps we could get the chariots turned around and run for it?'

'Too late,' said Antis, whipping out his bronze machete. 'Look back there!'

A group of Avtiny drones had debouched on to the road behind them and were running toward them, all but one of them, who paused to aim a bow. There were two or three shields and helmets in the group, and one cuirass, but otherwise they were naked and carried only spears and the one bow.

Antis grinned at Iroedh, swishing his blade through the air. 'If Daktablak could kill those with the armor, we could take it from them—'

Yaedh of Yeym called loudly: 'Priestess of the Oracle of Ledhwid! I claim immun—'

Whssht! went the arrow released by the archer. Yaedh and Antis cut off their speeches to duck.

'Up ahead!' exclaimed Yaedh.

A similar group of irregulars had come around the road block in front.

'Get back here, Antis!' said Iroedh, drawing her own blade. 'Let's keep together and let the men deal with them at a distance. Then if they get close —'

Crack! Iroedh's eardrums shook painfully to the discharge of Barbe's pistol. The little female man had run to the tail of the column and fired past Yaedh's chariot. The leading drone among the attackers spun around and fell in the roadway.

Barbe screamed: 'You shoot those in front, while I—'

Tactactactac! went Bloch's gun, echoed by another crack of the pistol. Then both weapons crashed together. One of the uegs upset its chariot in its terror. The racket made Iroedh wince and shut her eyes. Though she was a qualified soldier of her Community, this was as unnerving as her first helicopter flight had been.

Tactactac! Crack!

When Iroedh opened her eyes, the rogues to the rear were scattering to the shelter of the woods, leaving two of their number lying in the road. In front they were likewise running away or scrambling over the barrier. Three lay sprawled in that direction. The last to climb the barricade paused at the top to look back. Bloch raised the gun and with a single shot sent the drone flying into the road beyond.

The frightened uegs had tried to bolt, but Yaedh was calming them down by talking to them. Iroedh shook her head to get the ringing out of her ears.

'A short fight,' said Antis. 'I never got a chance to show what I could do.'

'The fiends!' said Yaedh. 'I can understand their attacking the rest of you, but to assault a priestess of the Oracle is unheard-of. This must be the band of Wythias; he's the only rogue leader ruthless enough to commit such an atrocity.'

'Are you hurt, darling?' said Barbe to her husband.

'N-no, just a little shaken,' said Bloch, doing things with his gun. Sweat stood out on his face as though he had been running. 'This must be what happened to the party from the Osirian ship.'

'Great Eunmar!' said Antis, who had walked over to look at a dead drone. 'The magic weapon certainly smashes them up. This one has hardly any head left!'

Bloch said: 'Let's right this chariot and clear the junk out of the road.'

'As soon as I collect some armor,' said Antis, tugging at the chin strap of the helmet on one of the corpses. 'Help me, Iroedh.' He got the helmet off and wiggled his own head into it. 'A little loose, but with extra padding it'll do. It's a good piece; I recognize the work of Umwys. It's too bad Bardylak made a hole in this breastplate, but I can hammer the points back in place with a stone and later have a smith patch it.'

Iroedh said: 'Why bother with those heavy things when the Terran weapons go right through them as if they were vakhwil bark?'

'We may not always have Terrans on our side. Try this helmet. Now, don't I look like a proper warrior out of the old epics?'

Antis stood up proudly in his cuirass and buckler and helmet and leaned on one of the dead drones' spears. Iroedh thought he certainly did look impressive. Barbe, however, made an odd sniffing noise and covered her mouth with her hands.

'Yes?' said Antis.

Barbe said: 'Me, I got some fluff up my nose. You look magnificent, Antis; but shouldn't it cover – I mean, should there not be one of those things to protect you below the cuirass?'

'A military kilt?' said Antis gravely. 'So there should be, except that none of our late enemies was wearing one. I shall get one eventually.'

He turned to help Bloch right the upset chariot and remove the barricade. Iroedh was astonished at the ease with which he picked up logs and hurled them into the brush.

'How strong you've become!' she said.

'The simple life.' Grinning, Antis heaved a stone that Iroedh thought no two workers could have lifted, jerked it to chest height with his great arm muscles standing out, and tossed it into the woods.

'Don't show off or you'll injure yourself,' said Bloch.

Antis turned and appeared about to launch a tart reply when there was another *whssht!* and an arrow streaked by inches from Barbe's face.

'They're attacking again!' she cried, jerking out her pistol. 'Iroedh, did you see where that came from?'

Barbe pointed the pistol this way and that at the silent forest.

'No, I didn't,' said Iroedh. 'Daktablak, come back here and cover us with your gun. I'll help Antis.'

'But – that's not female work,' blithered Bloch.

'Do as she says!' said Barbe. 'She has better sense than you!'

'Oh, all right – all right.' Bloch, looking harassed, climbed back on to his chariot and began sweeping the woods with his gun sights, first one side and then the other. Iroedh grunted and strained over the last logs.

Whssht! went another arrow, and struck Bloch full in the chest with a loud thump.

Bloch staggered, almost fell out of his chariot, and fired a burst into the section of woods from which the arrow had come. Antis and Iroedh had just carried the last log off the road and dropped it. They turned at the sound of a high scream from Barbe. The female man fired her pistol several times at random toward the woods, then leaped up to seize Bloch.

Iroedh ran back. Bloch stood upright in his vehicle and seemed to be wrestling with Barbe, though the arrow still protruded from his chest.

'No, no, I'm all right I tell you!' he protested. 'Get back in your buggy and let's get the hell out of here!'

'Aren't you dead? Aren't you hurt?' said Barbe.

'Not a scratch! Shall we go on or back? I'm for turning back—'

'When we're three quarters of the way there?' said Barbe. 'You are getting soft in the head, my old. Of course we shall go on!'

'Well, let's go either way, only quickly! You two, get aboard!'

Iroedh and Antis leaped into their chariots and cracked their whips. The uegs, impatient from the wait and nervous from the shooting, raced away with long strides, the chariots bouncing and bumping behind, and lurching to dangerous angles as they rolled over the corpses, which nobody had thought to remove from the road. Iroedh thought she heard shouts from the woods around the road block, but if so the shouters were soon left.

Yaedh called up from the rear of the line: 'You had better make good time, because that Wythias is a very persistent fellow. He may follow us.'

'How about you?' said Iroedh to Bloch. 'Are men invulnerable, or have you armor under your tunic?'

Bloch wrenched out the arrow and threw it away. 'Hit my damned radio. If it's broken, as I expect, the results may be almost as serious … I didn't know you Avtini went in for archery.'

'Ordinarily we use it only for hunting,' said Iroedh, 'because arrows won't pierce armor. Seeing us unarmored, the drones thought to use their hunting bows on us.'

Barbe said: 'I'm sure a strong Terran bow could penetrate this thin brass, at least at close range.'

'Maybe they haven't the right kind of wood,' said Bloch, 'at least on this continent.'

Iroedh went into a daydream wherein she arranged with the Community of Khwiem, which specialized in marine trade, to get a cargo of some superior bow wood from another continent for the benefit of Elham.

Then she remembered that the Arsuuny war would be over long before she could effect any such transaction, and that, furthermore, she was now an outcast from Elham – an 'orphan' like Yaedh. The thought of having no Community made her feel woebegone. Of course she had Antis, but one couldn't dedicate oneself to a single drone, however admirable, with the wholehearted devotion one gave a Community. If one were a Terran one could choose a mate of the opposite sex and apply one's *oedhurh* to this person, but as a neuter she was denied even this outlet …

They passed the junction of the road to Khwiem and the distant smoking cone of Mount Wisgad. The sky had clouded over and the uegs were puffing and staggering when they drew up, well after sunset. Bloch insisted on camping well off the road, so they plowed around in the brush and trees until they found an open space on the side of a stony hill whence they had a good view of their surroundings but could not be easily seen from the road.

Bloch pulled the radio out of his breast pocket, opened it up, looked it over by the light of another Terran device (a little cylinder with a light in its end) and threw it away.

'Hopeless,' he said. 'It will be all right, though, because when they don't receive my report this evening Subbarau will send Kang out to search for us.

He can't overlook us on that road. Hey, Antis! Belay the music!' For Antis had just played a run on his flute. Bloch turned to Yaedh. 'Don't you think we are far enough in advance of them to be safe?'

'I am not sure,' said Yaedh. 'There is a short cut over Mount Wisgad which, if they marched all night, might bring them up to us by morning.'

'Then we'll depart before morning. How much farther to Ledhwid?'

'If we leave early and drive hard we should reach it by tomorrow's nightfall.'

'Would this tough character Wythias go so far as to attack the Oracle itself?'

Yaedh hesitated. 'Had you asked me that yesterday I should have said the idea was absurd. All folk hold the Oracle in reverence, or at least respect it for its practical benefits. Workers of all Communities, even those at war with one another, meet freely and peacefully there, even Arsuuni. They exchange news and negotiate treaties. Now, however, that Wythias (if it indeed be he) has failed to respect my immunity, I am not sure what he will do.'

Bloch said: 'In any case, we'll set up a double watch.' He was fastening a tubular thing to his gun. 'Barbe and I will take turns with the rifle and with one of you Avtini.'

Iroedh asked: 'What's that thing on your *gon?*'

'It enables us to see as well at night as one of you. Now help me arrange our gear in a circle, and then we'll turn in.'

Iroedh had one of the later watches with Barbe, who said: 'Your nights are all so dark here! I don't think I should care to live on Ormazd, without a moon.'

It was dark, even Iroedh admitted, though never having seen a moon she could not compare her own world's nights with those of another. There was no sound except the regular snores of Winston Bloch and the chirp and buzz of nocturnal creeping things.

Then Iroedh stopped pacing and froze, moving her head this way and that to let her little round ears pick up the faintest sound. She could have sworn by Gwyyr that she had heard the faint noise of metal striking metal.

'Iroedh?' said Barbe. 'What is it?'

'Quiet. Somebody's coming.'

'Let's wake the others—' began Barbe, but then a voice cried:

'*Kwa, Wythias!*'

And the cry was taken up all around: 'Kwa, Wythias! Kwa, Wythias!' Heavy bodies moved through the brush.

Barbe stopped halfway to where Bloch lay and brought the gun to her shoulder. Iroedh drew her machete.

'There they come!' said Iroedh, pointing to where her dilated pupils made out a mass of moving figures.

Tactactacta! went the gun. In the lull following the uproar Iroedh heard sounds from the other direction and whirled. Three rogue drones were rushing upon the camp from that direction, spears poised. Iroedh stepped forward, bracing herself to meet the attack, though with such odds she was sure the moment would be her last.

Crack! went the pistol from where Bloch lay, and again. Bloch jumped up, grabbed the gun from Barbe, and fired another burst in yet a third direction. By the flashes Iroedh had a fleeting impression of bodies falling and others scampering back.

Bloch put one of the brass clips into the gun; then, eye to the night-seeing attachment, swept the device this way and that.

'They learn fast about taking cover,' he said. 'All out of sight but the stiffs.'

From around the camp there now came a buzz and clatter of many people moving without trying to conceal the fact. Snatches of speech could be heard, and somewhere somebody moaned in pain.

Antis and Yaedh were up now, the former with his machete out. They all huddled in the midst of the crude barricade of baggage.

'I don't think they will try that again,' said Bloch.

'Wythias is stubborn,' said Yaedh. 'His men fear him worse than they do your magic weapons.'

'Yes, but can he make them attack if they won't? What's that?'

Something was happening down near the base of the slope, though Iroedh could not quite make out what. There were thumps and jinglings and footsteps.

Yaedh cried: 'They're harnessing up the uegs! They will drive them off with our chariots!'

'Bless my soul!' said Bloch. 'What shall we do?'

Antis said: 'You could shoot in the general direction of the tethering place; that should get a few.' He was sharpening his blade with a whetstone, *wheep-wheep.*

'But that would kill the uegs, and we should be almost as badly off as if they took them!'

'Then you could go down there with your gun and attack them at close range.'

'Uh? I don't – I can't see as well in the dark, and there must be hundreds of them—'

'Are you afraid? Then I'll go after them with nothing but my matselh! I'll show—'

'There they go!' said Yaedh.

There was a cracking of whips and a shouting, and the sounds of receding chariotry.

'Too late,' groaned Bloch. 'Now we *are* in a fix! Our spare ammunition and food was in those chariots.'

'And my biscuit flour,' said Iroedh.

'And my notes,' said Barbe.

Bloch said: 'Yaedh, you speak their dialect. Ask them what they want.'

Yaedh raised her head and called: 'Wythias of Hawardem!'

After a few repetitions a voice called back: 'I am speaking.'

'What do you wish of us?'

'We wish the magical weapons of the Terrans. If they will give them up we will let you go.'

When this had been translated, Bloch asked: 'How reliable is this Wythias?'

'Not at all, seeing that he raises irreverent hands against a priestess of the Oracle.'

Bloch hesitated, nervously cracking his knuckles. At last he said: 'Tell him no. I couldn't face Subbarau if I let this fellow steal our guns.'

Yaedh told Wythias no. There were more movements in the dark and then the hateful whistle of an arrow.

Bloch said: 'Lie down inside your baggage, everybody!'

More arrows whistled; one struck the baggage with a sharp rap.

'Can't you see any of them in your magical viewer?' said Antis.

Bloch, who had been trying to do just that, replied: 'Not enough for a shot. The archers are staying out of sight over the curvature of the hill and lofting them at us.'

Iroedh said: 'In that case they may not hit us.'

'Maybe,' said Bloch. 'Keep down.'

Antis said: 'Why don't you creep out of here and attack them? If you got among them with that weapon you could slaughter them.'

'I don't know … How many are there, Yaedh?'

'If the whole band is here, over two hundred,' said the priestess.

The arrows continued to fall.

Bloch said: 'Since they got our chariots I calculate I have between eighty and a hundred rounds for the rifle, plus twenty or thirty for Barbe's pistol. With full-automatic fire you could shoot all that off in a matter of seconds, so we shall have to make every shot count. And you can see there are many more than I have cartridges.'

It seemed to Iroedh that Bloch was trying to think up excuses for not getting any closer to the rogues. Antis persisted:

'If you killed a few, the rest would run. I'll go with you with my matselh —'

Yaedh gave a little shriek and a gasp. Iroedh, her shield slung across her back for protection, crept over to where the priestess lay with an arrow through her ribs. Yaedh sighed:

'If I could only have had a real love again in my life …'

Her head lolled. Iroedh said:

'She's dead, poor thing. Daktablak, I agree with Antis that there's no point in lying here the rest of the night under this arrow rain.'

'Well?' said Bloch.

'I doubt if they have organized a tight circle around us yet. If we gathered up what we absolutely need and moved quietly we might burst through their line without their knowing it.'

'I don't know—' said Bloch.

'She has reason,' said Barbe.

'I hate to run away—' began Antis, but Barbe continued:

'We can go away from the road, which is the direction they won't expect, make a big semicircle and come back to the road several kilometers north of here, which should be near Ledhwid.'

Arrows continued to fall.

'All right,' said Bloch at last. 'Everybody make a bundle of what he most needs. I suppose Barbe and I shall have to walk ahead with the guns, so you two Avtini will have to carry all the gear —'

'No,' said Antis 'If you shoot those things the noise will tell the others what's happened. You carry the gear; Iroedh and I will walk ahead and—' He made a slashing motion.

Iroedh, fumbling in the dark, found she had comparatively few possessions. The only thing she really regretted was the biscuit flour, without which she foresaw a hungry time. She put her belongings into her cloak and tied the corners together as Antis was doing.

'Ready, everybody?' said Bloch. 'Proceed quietly now!'

Crouching low and feeling their way along in single file, they issued from the remains of the baggage barricade and headed away from the road.

VIII
Royal Jelly

Antis led the way, shield before him and machete ready. Iroedh followed, look-ing over his shoulder. Behind them arrows continued to fall upon the deserted camp. Around them the creeping things kept up their symphony of night noises, and in the distance the rogues could be heard talking and moving.

They walked away from the road up the hill. Iroedh could hear the heavy breathing of the Terrans behind her; considering their loads it was not surprising.

Antis turned his head and made a tiny hiss. Iroedh crouched lower and moved more cautiously, fingering the hilt of her weapon.

A voice spoke in front of them: 'Who is—'

As the dark shape materialized before them, Antis bounded forward and struck. Iroedh sprang after him, at an angle to bring her beside him, and swung too. She felt her blade bite into the unseen target.

The dark shape collapsed. When Bloch arrived, gun ready, the rogue lay dead.

'Come on,' murmured Antis.

They went over the crest of the hill and down the other side. Here the trees began again, so they had to move with creeping slowness to avoid entanglement.

Bloch said: 'Antis, can you see your way? How do you know you're not conducting us in a circle?'

'I don't know. I try to keep the sounds of the drones behind us.'

'Suppose,' said Bloch, 'we open out to where I can barely perceive you. I'll sight on the girls and tell you whether you are bearing to one side or the other.'

They tried this system, but without much success, because under the trees the darkness was too profound to see more than a few meters. After a while they adopted a more complicated scheme in which Bloch stood squinting through his infrared viewer while the others went ahead of him, obeying his instructions, and then they in turn stood still until he caught up with them. Where the brush was heavy Iroedh or Antis would go ahead to cut a way with a machete, all others staying well clear of the blade. Iroedh soon learned that her bronze replica of the implement did not hold an edge nearly so well as the steel original. In fact, after a couple of hours it was not much more effective than beating at the bushes with a bludgeon.

They were still struggling wearily ahead when the cloud canopy over the treetops lightened. Iroedh could never remember having been more tired; the tasks of a Community, while sometimes strenuous, were so organized as not to push the workers to exhaustion.

In the gray dawn they straggled out of the trees where a hillside rose in a bank of bare rock ledges. They climbed up these, ledge by ledge, until they were nearly at the top, then sat down to rest with their feet dangling.

Bloch said: 'Have we anything to eat?'

Antis untied the corners of his cloak. 'Of that stuff we brought from the chariots last night, only three containers were not opened. I brought them along. I think they're that soft oily meat you eat.'

He held up three cans of tuna fish.

Barbe said: 'How about the poor Iroedh?'

Bloch shrugged. 'If she wants to take a chance on Terran fish, okay. Otherwise—Is there no wild food in these woods?'

He opened one of the cans. Antis said:

'You can't easily live off this country. If I had your gun and knew how to use it, I might kill an occasional beast; but for her I don't know what there is.'

'I've been looking,' said Iroedh, 'and the few edible berries and seeds found around Elham don't seem to grow this far north. No, I won't have any tunafyth, thank you. If we can get back to the road I'm sure I can hold out till we reach Ledhwid.'

'If we can find the road again,' said Barbe. 'Winston, get out your map and compass.'

Bloch got the map from his knapsack and unfolded it, then began hunting for his compass. He went through the knapsack, then through his pockets, his face registering deeper and deeper dismay.

'I'm sure I have it,' he muttered.

Antis said: 'That little round shiny thing you were looking at last night when you consulted the map? You laid it on the ground; perhaps you forgot to pick it up again.'

Bloch went through everything again, then exclaimed: 'That tears it! Barbe, why didn't you remind me? It's your business to see I don't forget things—'

'It is not! The last time I reminded you of such a thing you shut me up.' Barbe turned to Iroedh. 'It is a curious feature of Terran culture that when the men do something of a stupidity they always blame their wives.'

'Huh,' said Bloch. 'Now we *are* in a predicament. If we had the sun I could tell north by my watch, and if we had the radio I could erect a directional loop and ascertain the direction of the *Paris*. As it is I haven't the faintest idea where we are or which way to proceed.'

Iroedh said: 'You have the map, haven't you?'

'Yes, but look at it!' He held it up. 'It's a strip map of the route from Gliid to Ledhwid, made from a series of aerial photographs by Kang. All it shows is roads, streams, and a couple of Communities; the rest is forest. And since there aren't any signposts to tell us where we are on the map, all I know is we're somewhere to the east of the main road.'

Antis said: 'If we found a stream we could follow it down, don't you think?'

'Look!' said Barbe sharply.

Across the valley they faced, figures had appeared on the crest of the opposite hill. They were scattered over a wide front and popped in and out of sight as they moved through the vegetation. Although they were too far for features to be discerned, Iroedh saw that they carried spears.

Antis said: 'Let's run for it.'

'No!' said Bloch. 'Sit absolutely still. If we don't move they may not observe us.'

They sat frozen while the first group of drones disappeared into the heavier cover of the lower slope and more came into view on the crest.

Barbe said: 'At this rate the first ones will have come up to us before the last ones have come over the hilltop.'

'Oh!' said Iroedh. 'I think they see us.'

There was a scurry of motion among the approaching drones, with much shouting and pointing. Those in sight broke into a run.

Bloch groaned. 'Off we go! Don't cut any brush, Antis; it'll give them a trail to follow.'

They got to their feet and scrambled up the slope and into the woods again.

'I wonder,' panted Barbe, 'how they – found us – this time?'

Antis answered: 'They do much hunting – and some – are expert trackers. And we did – cut a lot – of brush.'

Iroedh saved her breath for hiking, feeling weak from lack of food. They ran when the terrain permitted, otherwise walked as fast as they could. On and on, without any particular attention to direction. Sometimes Bloch led, sometimes Antis. Anything to put distance between themselves and the band.

Iroedh discarded her helmet and buckler (obtained from the dead drones the previous day) to the annoyance of Antis, who, during his sojourn with Umwys, seemed to have become a connoisseur of arms and armor, and hence resented having to give up a good piece.

At last Barbe said: 'It must that I – stop for a minute.'

As they stood panting, the hallooing of the pursuit came faintly. Off they went again.

Bloch said: 'Yaedh was correct; that Wythias lusts after these guns in the worst way.'

'Naturally,' said Antis. 'He could rule the planet with them.'

'Not without ammunition, but perhaps he doesn't know that. Can you go now, Barbe?'

On and on. To Iroedh the flight became a nightmare of running, walking, climbing over logs and rocks, stumbling, falling down, getting up again, and stumbling on some more. All day they hiked, and most of the night.

In the afternoon of the next day they came to a stream. Bloch said:

'If we wade up or down this we may throw them off our trail.'

They splashed along the stream bed for half a borb until the stream began to curve around in the direction from which they had come. Bloch, leading, turned his head back to say:

'I think we should take the woods again—*Wup!*'

His legs had suddenly sunk into the stream bed up to the knees, and the rest of him seemed to be following.

'Quicksand!' he yelled. 'Somebody shove me a pole!' He peeled off his knapsack and threw it ashore. 'Barbe, catch the gun!'

Iroedh was so exhausted that she could only stand and stare stupidly while Antis stumbled ashore and began looking for a sapling to cut. It seemed, however, that all the trees in this section were old forest giants. While Antis was still searching, Barbe got down on hands and knees and crawled out over the sand of the bottom toward where Bloch was already in up to his waist.

'Catch this!' she said, swinging her jacket toward him, holding it by one sleeve. After a couple of tries he caught it.

Iroedh pulled herself together and hurried to grasp Barbe's ankles to keep her from going in too. Little by little, holding first the jacket and then Barbe's hand, Bloch wallowed shoreward. By the time Antis showed up with a pole Bloch was safe, and a few seconds later was sitting on a rock digging the mud out of his ears while Barbe kissed him and told him how wonderful he was.

Iroedh, though she listened, could hear no sounds of pursuit. Bloch said:

'We may have eluded them. If we can find another pool further down, we might get cleaned up a little before taking to the woods again.'

They continued on down, avoiding the quicksand, and soon came to another pool in which they removed the mud from their clothes and persons. Iroedh noted that the curious exposure tabu of the Terrans seemed to be in abeyance, or perhaps it did not apply to mated persons. One Terran stood guard while the other washed. Iroedh stared at them with frank physiological interest, noting resemblances and differences between man and Avtin and speculating about their significance. As the resemblances outweighed the differences, she guessed that biological fundamentals must be much the same in the two species.

Then off into the woods they went again. By nightfall they agreed that they had probably lost their pursuers. The only trouble was that they had also lost themselves in the process, even more thoroughly than before.

'If we could only get some sun,' said Bloch, 'we could hike north a few borbi, then west again, and pick up the road in a couple of days … Oh-oh, rain!'

A pattering on the leaves overhead made itself heard. Bloch asked:

'How long is a rain likely to last hereabouts?'

Antis shrugged. 'Perhaps an hour, perhaps three or four days.'

'Everything happens to us,' said Bloch. 'All we need now is for one of your noags to try to devour us.'

'Don't say that!' said Antis. 'There are those who believe that saying such a thing makes it come true. Besides, in these northern woods the noags grow to much greater size than around Elham.'

'Anyway, we might bestir ourselves to construct a shelter,' said Bloch. 'Iroedh, if you'll cut some poles …'

Iroedh tried to get to her feet, but to her consternation found she could not.

'I can't get up,' she said. 'I'm too weak.'

'Running all that distance on an empty stomach, it's no wonder,' said Barbe.

Bloch said: 'Lend me your machete, then,' and went off with Antis. Iroedh could hear them blundering about and slashing, but was too far gone to care whether she acquired shelter from the rain or not.

'This becomes serious, my little,' said Barbe. 'Even if the rain stops it will take us two or three days to get back to the road, and how will you manage without food?'

'I – I think I could get up now,' said Iroedh. 'I shall be better when I've rested.'

The shelter took gradual form, though so much water dripped through the greenery that served as a thatch that Iroedh found it but little improvement on no shelter. Bloch, Barbe, and Antis divided the remaining tuna. Not wishing to show a light, they forewent a fire and prepared to make the best of a dank and miserable night. Antis produced his telh and began tweedling, whereupon Bloch exclaimed:

'Do you mean to say that when we were fleeing for our lives we were hauling *that* piece of junk?'

Antis replied with hauteur: 'Daktablak, I made no objections when you brought along your mouth furnace and a goodly supply of the weed you burn in it.'

Bloch looked at his freshly lit pipe and changed the subject.

The rain continued another day and another night, and yet another day and another night. Then it ceased as a brisk cool wind soughed through the tree-tops and blew away the cloud cover. Bloch hurried over to the first patch of sunlight, performed magical rites with his watch and a knife blade, and triumphantly announced:

'That's north! Let's go!'

Iroedh found that her two days' rest had given her some strength to go on – at least for a time. But the going proved harder, for now that he knew his direction, Bloch insisted upon the party's sticking close to it, even though it forced them to scramble over steep hogbacks and splash through black bogs where small creeping and flying things bit and stung, instead of following the line of least resistance as they had been doing. They marched all day, camped, and next day marched again.

During the morning they climbed out of one swamp hole and up the face of a steep hill. Presently they surmounted a ledge projecting from the side of the hill. Above the ledge the rock overhung to make a cave which, while shallow, was quite big enough to accommodate the four of them. By common consent they all sank down upon the ledge to rest. Antis, as usual, took advantage of the pause to whet his and Iroedh's machetes, while Bloch swept the sky with his binoculars for a sight of Kang.

Bloch, on whose lower face a growth of yellow-brown hair was sprouting, said: 'This would have been a much more comfortable place to spend those two rainy days, but I suppose—What's that?'

An animal had come out of the woods: a bipedal herbivore like an ueg but bigger. It was peacefully breaking off the branches of trees with its hands and eating the leaves.

Antis said: 'That's a pandre-eg, a wild relative of the ueg. Kill it, quickly!'

'Is it dangerous?' whispered Barbe.

'No, but I'm starved.'

Bang! Iroedh leaped with fright. When the ringing in her ears subsided she saw that the pandre-eg had fallen to the ground, kicking and thrashing. Bloch leaped down the slope. As he neared the beast it stopped moving.

'Dinner!' he called.

The other three trooped down to where the animal lay. Bloch said:

'I should like to save it as a specimen, of course, but I'm afraid—'

'Oh, you!' said Barbe. 'You're as bad with your specimens as Antis with his armor.'

'Can you butcher this thing, Antis?' said Bloch.

'With pleasure. I learned how from Umwys. However, it will save time if you'll lend me that knife of Terran metal. Oh, Iroedh!'

'Yes?'

'How does that hunter's dance go when you wish to change your luck?'

'You set a game animal's head on a stake and dance naked eight times around it sunwise, facing backwards. If you fall down or see a khal tree it spoils it and you have to start over.'

'There don't seem to be any khal trees,' said Antis, 'so take off your boots. We're going to try it.'

Antis began sawing on the beast's neck while Iroedh unlaced her boots, finding that it took all her strength to do so. The prospect of dancing eight times around anything appalled her, especially as she doubted whether it would actually work. On the other hand, she was a little afraid of offending Antis.

Bloch had spread a cloth on the ledge and taken his gun apart, laying the parts out in careful order and cleaning and oiling each one. Barbe went for water, using Antis' helmet as a bucket.

'There!' said Antis, forcing the pandre-eg's head down upon the point of the stake he had whittled. Blood trickled down the stake.

Bloch said: 'It seems to me your magical rite is a trifle confused. Presumably it's to transform a hunter's bad luck to good – that is, to let him kill game. But if it has to be performed with a game animal's head, that means his luck has already turned.'

'You don't understand these matters, Daktablak,' said Antis. 'It always works for us. Are you ready, beautiful?'

Iroedh got up slowly. 'I'm so tired, Antis ...'

'It will only take a minute. Come on, you stand on that side while I stand on this. Ready?'

He began clapping his hands together and hopping backwards. Iroedh, staggering, did likewise. On the third time around she tripped and sat down.

'Iroedh!' cried Antis with unconcealed exasperation. 'Now we shall have to begin over. Try to keep glancing back over your shoulder, won't you? That's a brave worker.'

They got up to six circuits of the head when two pistol shots cracked. Barbe appeared, running, and behind her came a noag – a monster of its species, half again as tall as a person. Its long neck arched, its jaws gaped, its clawed hands reached out, and its long tail stuck up behind like a guidon.

'Run!' screamed Barbe, coming toward them.

Bloch jumped to his feet on the ledge, holding his useless gun barrel.

'Up here!' he bawled. 'We can hold it off!'

Iroedh summoned her last ounce of strength to scramble up the short slope to the ledge. Antis dashed ahead of her; then, seeing her falter, caught her arm and hauled her after him.

A despairing scream from Barbe made Iroedh look back. The female man had almost reached the foot of the slope when she had tripped and fallen prone. The pistol, which she had been carrying in her hand, bounced along the ground ahead of her. The noag came on in great bounding strides.

Something went past Iroedh in a brown blur. It was Bloch, holding the machete Antis had left on the ledge over his head and uttering a Terran war cry that sounded like '*Sanavabyts! Sanavabyts!*'

The noag, stooping to seize Barbe, looked up and backed away with a startled snarl as this new antagonist hurled himself at it. The machete whirled in circles of light; the noag screamed as the blade sheared off two clawed fingers and bit into the fanged muzzle. Antis, seeing what was up, picked up Iroedh's machete from the ground and started toward the scene of the fight. Before he arrived, the noag, slashed and bloody, had turned to run. With a last cut Bloch took off the tip of its tail. The noag disappeared, its howls coming back fainter and fainter until they could no longer be heard.

Then Bloch and Barbe were embracing and uttering Terran endearments. Antis, watching, said to Iroedh:

'I misjudged Daktablak, thinking he lacked courage. That took nerve and quick wit, don't you think?'

Iroedh herself admitted that in the conflicts with the drones Bloch had acted rather uncertain, disorganized, and timid. She said:

'It must be that Terran love of theirs. Remember the quicksand? Whatever troubles it may cause, that kind of love makes them run risks for each other they wouldn't for anybody else.'

When Bloch, Barbe, and Antis had eaten their fill of pandre-eg steak, Bloch said: 'Shall we rest in the cave for a while to get our strength back, or go on right now and cover as much ground as we can before dark?'

Antis was for pushing on; Barbe for resting some more. When they turned to Iroedh she said:

'It makes no difference to me because I cannot go on in any case.'

'Why not?' said Bloch.

Barbe said: 'The poor thing is weak from the starvation, that's why not. Look at her ribs. She's had nothing to eat for six days, most of it climbing around this terrible country.'

Iroedh said: 'I'm ashamed to admit it, but that is the truth. The rest of you go on whenever you like; I'm done for.'

'Nonsense!' said Barbe. 'Do you think we would leave you here to die?'

'There is no point in your dying too. Go on.'

'I wouldn't leave you, beautiful,' said Antis. 'You are all I love.'

'If you love me you will save yourself. I can't go on, and that's that.'

'We could carry you,' said Antis.

'No, you couldn't in this rough country. I should probably be dead before you reached the road, and what good would it do to burden yourselves? Think of me as dead already, as if the noag had slain me, and make our parting as painless as possible.'

Antis said: 'Even if I knew you were going to die, I'd stay with you to the end.'

'And have the rogue drones catch you? Don't be irrational. I'll kill myself before I let you do that.'

'We'll see that you have nothing sharp.'

'There are other ways. And what's the sense of it? You didn't make such a fuss over poor Yaedh.'

'That was different,' said Barbe. 'She was dead already, and we never felt toward her as we do toward you. You are like one of us – one of our Terran kind, I mean.'

Bloch spoke up: 'I think we're interring Iroedh before there's any necessity. All she requires is a few good meals.'

'And where shall I find those?' said Iroedh, with barely the strength to talk.

Bloch gestured toward the eviscerated remains of the pandre-eg.

'You know I cannot eat meat,' said Iroedh. 'It would poison me.'

'Have you ever eaten it?' asked Bloch.

'No.'

'Have you ever known an Avtiny worker who had?'

'No. They wouldn't have been alive for me to know them.'

'Well, if you think you're going to perish anyway, why not try it? At worst it can only kill you a little sooner, and at best it might give you the strength to persevere.'

'But it's such a painful death!'

'I'll make an agreement with you. You eat a steak, and if I see you dying in convulsions I'll blow your brains out with the pistol. You'll never know what struck you.'

As Iroedh hesitated, turning this drastic proposal over in her mind, Bloch continued: 'Come on, what have you to lose? Either way it's better than waiting for one of those Jabberwocks to devour you—'

'Those what?'

'Jabberwock, a monster out of Terran folklore. I thought the noag looked a little like one. What about a steak?'

Antis said: 'I don't know. I favor her trying the meat, but I couldn't stand by and watch you slay her in cold blood.'

'No, Antis,' said Iroedh weakly. 'The Terran is right. Cook me up a piece and I will try it.'

A few minutes later Iroedh picked up a slab of steak, blew on her fingers as it scorched them, and turned it over warily.

'Go on,' said Bloch. 'A nice big bite.'

Iroedh opened her mouth, then lost her courage and closed it again. She gathered her forces, drew a long breath, shut her eyes, and sank her teeth into the meat.

A lifetime of conditioning caused her to gag and retch, but her shrunken stomach contained nothing to vomit. She clamped her jaws firmly shut until her gorge subsided, then forced herself to chew.

At first she thought it tasted vile. Then she was not sure whether she liked it or not. It was so *different* from anything she had ever eaten. She got her first bite down and took a second.

'Good for you!' said Bloch. 'No pains?'

'No, but they wouldn't have started yet. It is not so bad as I thought.'

They watched her in silence as she finished the piece.

'Do you know,' she said, 'I think I could eat another. Not that I really like it, but I'm still hungry, and I might as well die on a full stomach.'

'Wait a while,' said Bloch. 'Too much after a fast like yours *would* upset you. And it's so late now we might as well spend the night here.'

They made what camp they could and did a more thorough job on the pandre-eg, burying the guts and mounting the more edible parts on stakes. Antis, indicating the head which still grinned gruesomely at them from its stake, said:

'We never did finish our good-luck dance. Iroedh …?'

Iroedh put up a firm hand. 'My love, if it were a matter of saving our whole race from extinction I couldn't dance one step. If you must dance, why not ask the Terrans?'

'Oh, very well. How about it, Barbe?'

'How about what?'

Antis explained about the good-luck dance. Barbe first burst out laughing, to the obvious perplexity of Antis. Then she said:

'Well – I should like to, me, but I don't know …'

She cast a questioning look at Bloch, who said: 'Go right ahead, my dear. It's part of our job to participate in Ormazdian activities when opportunity offers. Besides, with his cultural attitudes I doubt if Antis would know what a *voyeur* was.'

'What a what was?' said Antis.

'A Terran organism noted for its keenness of vision. Go on, his dancing can't be worse than mine.'

Barbe caught her bare heels and sat down twice in the course of the good-luck dance, which made the wearily watching Iroedh feel somehow better.

At sunset they ate again. Iroedh, whose mind had been nervously exploring her viscera ever since her heretical meal, said:

'There's no sign of trouble yet. There must be something wrong with me, or I should be writhing in my death throes.'

'Or something wrong with your system of tabus,' said Bloch. 'Have some more?'

'By Gwyyr, I will!'

Next morning they impaled all the meat they could carry on a long pole, which Bloch and Antis carried slung between them over their shoulders.

They started down the slope into the woods. Iroedh, marching ahead of them, felt much stronger in body but bewildered in mind. Could all workers eat meat with impunity? Then why on Niond had such a rule or belief been set up in the first place?

She was thinking along these lines when a cry and the sound of a fall made her turn. Barbe lay at the base of the slope, holding her ankle. Her face was pale.

'Sprained it,' she said.

Bloch hurried back and helped his mate take off her boot. He felt the ankle while Barbe went 'Ow!'

Bloch sighed. 'I presume we shall spend another day here at least; she can't walk now. Next time we're ready to start, no doubt Antis will cut himself open with his own machete, or I shall get careless and shoot off my big toe. So much for your good-luck ritual, Antis.'

'You can't tell,' said Antis. 'Without the dance who knows what might have happened? She might have broken her leg instead of merely wrenching it.'

'Merely wrenching it!' said Barbe between clenched teeth.

'An unanswerable sophistry, my friend,' said Bloch. 'Take her other arm.'

They helped Barbe back on to the ledge and settled down again. To put the time to good use Bloch interrogated Iroedh some more about her native world. Barbe took notes in her notebook, and when she ran out of paper Antis found a vakhwil tree and peeled off enough bark to keep Barbe supplied for several days with writing material. Iroedh, eating regularly again, got stronger fast.

Barbe's sprain, however, proved more serious than they had thought. Her ankle swelled to twice its normal size and turned an assortment of greens and purples. Bloch said:

'We may be here for a week, so I'd better hunt some more food. That pandre-eg will soon begin to stink.'

And off he went with Antis.

Six days later Iroedh sat on the ledge and watched Barbe try her ankle in gingerly fashion. The males were off hunting again. Iroedh felt in need of advice but did not quite know how to go about getting it. The personnel officer of Elham, who normally handled personal problems, was many borbi away. Moreover, one of the things bothering Iroedh was that her dreams had been taking such strange forms that she was embarrassed to submit them. For instance there was the dream about the memorial pillar in the ruins of Khinam that behaved as no normal pillar should. Then there was the curious feeling of anger that possessed her when Antis artlessly bragged about his proficiency in fulfilling his function as Queen Intar's drone. Finally, she seemed to be undergoing other changes almost too bizarre for belief.

Barbe said: 'I think if I give it a little of the exercise today I may be able to hike tomorrow, or the next day at the latest.'

'The swelling is nearly gone,' said Iroedh. 'And speaking of swelling—'

'Yes, my dear?'

'It's hard to know where to begin, but as another female I thought you might understand.'

'Understand what?'

'Ever since I started eating meat I have had the oddest sensations.'

'Such as?'

'Well – for instance, there's a feeling of tightness in the skins of my chest. And when I look down I could swear my breasts are getting larger, like those of a functional female. Is it my imagination?'

Barbe gave Iroedh's figure a sharp look. 'No, it isn't. You definitely bulge.'

'And I have peculiar internal feelings, too, as if other organs were growing.'

Barbe said: 'Turn around. I can't see inside you, of course, but your hips do look wider.'

'But what shall I *do?*'

'What do you mean? You are doing all right, aren't you?'

'I can't turn into a functional female!'

'And why not?' said Barbe.

'It's unheard of! I should be a monstrosity!'

'Well, if you are bound to become a monstrosity, why not relax and enjoy the role?'

'It must be the meat. But if I stop eating it I shall die!'

'And there wouldn't be any fun to that, would there?'

'You just go right ahead, dear little monster. We shall love you in all cases.'

When Bloch and Antis came back to the cave with a leipag the former had shot, Barbe made the announcement.

Bloch said: 'Bless my soul! That's the best thing since Antis sat on the dhug and we had to pull the spines out of his podex.'

'You know, darling,' said Antis, 'I *thought* something was happening to you. What's the cause of this change, Daktablak?'

Bloch lighted his pipe before answering. 'You wouldn't know about hormones, but they are substances in your blood that make you grow up and develop in various directions. At least I suppose you have them just as we do, since your body chemistry seems to be similar to ours.

'Now, one set of hormones controls development of sexual characteristics, and apparently among the Avtini the glands that secrete these hormones require meat in the diet to function. So the workers feed meat to drones and queens and deny it to those they intend to develop into workers. It's like the bees on Terra who feed certain larvae' – he had to stop to explain what bees and larvae were – 'who feed certain larvae a special food called "royal jelly" that causes them to develop into queens.'

Antis said: 'Does that mean a drone fed on an all-plant diet would also become a neuter worker?'

'I don't know,' said Bloch, but Barbe put in:

'Don't you remember that visitor from Khwiem, who told us of the Community of Arsuuni who prefer neutermale Avtiny slaves to the usual neuter-female ones? We thought she meant they make eunuchs of them, but it may be they simply rear drone children on a diet without meat.'

'Conceivably,' said Bloch.

Antis asked: 'Then *must* drones and queens be reared on a completely meat diet? Or could they live on a mixed diet as you do?'

'You could ascertain that by trying plant food, though I wouldn't guarantee results. My own surmise is that, considering the abnormally high egg-laying capacity of your queens, they're oversexed as a result of an unmixed meat diet. The males I wouldn't even guess about.'

Iroedh wailed: 'But what will happen to me?'

Bloch blew a smoke ring. 'Well, my dear, I don't see that you'll be any worse off than you are, and you may enjoy some new experiences.'

'There won't be any place for me on Niond. Would Captain Subbarau employ Antis and me in his crew?'

'No. It's against I.C. policy to transport natives of Class H planets off their own worlds. But you'll make out, I'm certain. Funny; I once read about a young lady named Alice who became a queen by jumping over a brook, but this is the first time I ever heard of one's becoming a queen by eating steak three times a day!'

IX

The Oracle

Once again on their way, they camped by a small stream and devoured a portion of the meat they had brought from the cave. Bloch said:

'I've been wondering how a band as large as that of Wythias manages. The hunting doesn't seem good enough in these parts to feed so many in one area.'

'I've heard,' said Antis, 'that northwest of Ledhwid Wythias has land of his own where he raises the food he needs.'

'It would require a hell of a big ranch to provide steaks for all those brigands. I wonder if perhaps they don't subsist on a mixed diet despite your tabus?'

'What makes you think that?'

'Because you can get a lot more calories from a given area by using vegetable crops directly than by feeding them to animals and eating the animals ...'

Iroedh, finishing her steak, hardly heard the discussion, which wandered off into the technicalities of dietetics. She was more concerned with her own problems.

For one thing, her change of shape did not altogether suit her. Her new mammae bounced and jiggled in a ridiculous manner when she ran, and she was sure the thickening of her body through the pelvic region was making her less agile. At first she had thought this thickening a mere deposit of fat, but now it seemed that the actual bone structure was spreading as well. The Avtiny neuter-female worker's body was built to an admirably functional design, with a minimum of vulnerable projections; but this awkward thing ...

Then there was the strange attitude of Antis. On one hand he had taken to staring at her in a curiously intent fashion when he thought she was not looking. Time and again she caught him at it, and he would at once look away and pretend he had been observing something else all the time. On the other hand he developed an odd standoffishness, refusing to sleep with her any more on the mumbled pretext that he was not getting enough actual sleep.

What on Niond was bothering the dear fellow? Iroedh for her part loved him more than ever and wanted to be close to him as much as possible. She found herself, in fact, developing a possessive, sentimental, and exclusive tenderness toward him like that attributed to the females in *A Girl of the Limberlost* toward their drones.

It was very puzzling. Why had all this happened to her? In the old days, according to her researches, one blamed a jealous or capricious god for one's undeserved misfortunes, but nobody had taken the gods seriously for generations. It was, thinkers agreed, a case of the mysterious operations of luck. Emotionally, however, blind chance was a poor substitute for a god when you wanted something on which to turn your resentment at the hard treatment accorded you by fate ...

'Hey, Iroedh!' said Bloch. 'Turn in! You have third watch.'

Iroedh pulled herself together. 'Antis ...?'

Antis scowled. 'If you don't mind,' he said, indicating the far side of the open space.

'But why? I shall be cold and lonesome. Are you angry? What have I done?'

'On the contrary ...' Antis seemed torn by indecision, then burst out: 'You forget you're now a queen, Iroedh dearest.'

'Oh, but not yet!'

'Well then, a princess. A functional female. In fact we ought to call you "Iroer," except that we're used to the old name.'

'What of it? Do you love me less because of it?'

'Not at all. But I'm a functional male, do you see? And if I may not act like one ...'

'Why can't you?' she asked innocently.

'You mean – you mean with *you?*'

'Of course, stupid. You certainly boast enough about yourself and that bloated old Intar. Am I less attractive than she?'

'Oh, darling, there's no comparison. But – you see, then I was acting under orders. I shouldn't know how to take the initiative in such a case. I don't know what to do. If you were just any old queen, I'd—But you're Iroedh, whom I've always looked up to like one of the old goddesses. You're so much more intelligent than I—'

'I'm not really —'

'Don't contradict!' he roared.

Iroedh was surprised, first by his vehemence, second by the fact that she did not mind being bossed so much as she would have before her change. (That cursed diet again!)

Antis, looking at her sharply, continued: 'Does this mean you're planning to collect yourself a harem of drones like other queens?'

'I don't know. I hadn't thought. I suppose so. Why, have you any objections?'

'I certainly have! You're mine by right of discovery or something, and I've had my fill of sharing my queen with a dozen others. If I catch another drone so much as looking at you, I'll serve him as King Aithles used Idhios in the *Lay*.'

'Are you sure you can minister to the needs of a whole functional female all by yourself, when the task is normally divided among twelve or sixteen drones?'

'Certainly. I could take care, not only of you, but of two or three functional females at once. If I had a couple here—'

'I like that! You wish me to have no drones but you, yet you reserve the right to fertilize any queen who falls into your clutches.'

'Don't you think I should?'

'I don't know whether you should or not, but it would make me just as unhappy as my entertaining other drones would make you.'

Antis stared at the fire, chewing a stick for some seconds, then said: 'I suppose we need some definite agreement, like that which we drones enter into when we reach our majority. Now, the Terrans have worked out a system of male-plus-female units, based upon their long experience, which seems to work for them. According to what you tell me, our remote ancestors had such a system before the reforms of Danoakor and the rest. But that's gone and forgotten, so that we should have to start practically from nothing. I think we might ask the advice of our Terran friends.'

'I was about to suggest the same thing! Oh, Daktablak!'

'Yes?'

Antis and Iroedh, speaking alternate paragraphs, explained their predicament.

Bloch ran his fingers through his stubble of beard. 'Bless my soul! Don't tell me you two are in love in the full, ghastly, sentimental Terran sense?'

'It looks that way,' said Antis, 'as far as we can judge. To me it's like being on fire.'

'It's got you,' said Bloch. 'If Mrs Porter could only know the revolutionary effect of her sentimental potboiler on the culture of a planet eight light-years away and nearly three centuries after her time—'

'But what shall we *do?*' pleaded Iroedh.

'Why, of course you – that is—How should I know? What do you desire to do?'

Iroedh spoke: 'We should like to be like you and Barbe.'

'Well, what hinders you? I suppose you know the mechanics of—'

Antis said: 'Daktablak, you don't understand. With you Terrans mating is not a mere animal act, but an institution. Now, we have no such institution on Niond, but we should like one. If we're starting a new way of life we wish to start it right, and therefore we pick the best model we know: your system.'

'Your confidence in Terran institutions touches me, my dear friends, and I hope it is not too badly misplaced. Apparently you wish me to devise, off-hand, an institution of marriage for your whole race: a task to daunt the boldest. Have you considered that you belong to a species different from ours; that your cultural background differs greatly from ours; and that there-fore a system that worked passably well for us might not function so well with you?'

Iroedh said: 'We have to start somewhere, and if we make mistakes we can correct them as they arise.'

'Wouldn't it be better to wait a few days until we consult the Oracle? You will have a clearer idea of your destinies—'

Barbe broke in: 'Stop making excuses, Winston darling. You know you don't take this old Oracle seriously. Besides, we may all be dead in a few days.'

'I just wanted to be sure they realized—'

'*Ils y ont mûrement réfléchi.* Go ahead, marry them.'

Bloch sighed, 'Apparently I'm elected Justice of the Peace for the planet Ormazd. It may be legally invalid and sociologically imprudent, but you're three to one against me. Antis, what do you Avtini swear by when you testify to the truth of an assertion?'

'One swears by one's Community, but we have no—'

'Wait,' said Iroedh. 'There is an old form of oath, now obsolete, by the gods Dhiis and Tiwinos and Eunmar and Gwyyr and the rest. It was used up to a few years ago in some conservative Communities, even though the swearers no longer believed in the gods.'

'We'll employ that, then,' said Bloch. 'Now on Terra the agreement is exclu-sive and (at least nominally) for life, though in some cases provision is made—'

'Oh. we want it for life!' said Antis. 'Don't you, beautiful?'

'Y-yes,' said Iroedh, 'though it does seem to me that some provision should be made in case the drone's fertility and other powers decline—'

'Listen,' said Bloch, 'I'm taking a big chance in devising a marriage system for you, and I'm damned if I will also commit myself to the task of formulat-ing a divorce law. You let that work itself out. Barbe, what can you remember of that service Subbarau tied us with?'

Iroedh subsided, not without some inner reservations. In time they got the wordings straightened out, and Bloch said: 'Repeat after me: I, Antis of Elham, a functional male, take you, Iroedh of Elham, a functional female, to be my permanent and exclusive mate, to have and to hold ...'

'... and the curious thing is,' said Iroedh to Barbe, 'that whereas I used to be the dominant one of the pair, Antis now makes all the decisions. Of course I know more of the world than he, and he knows I do, so we play a little game. I make a suggestion – very tentatively, so as not to sound as if I were com-manding him – and he grunts and says he'll think about it. Then next day he bursts out: "Beautiful, I've just had the most wonderful idea!" and goes on to repeat my suggestion in the very words I used. Isn't it amazing?'

'Not so amazing to me as it seems to you,' replied Barbe. 'On the whole do you like our one-mate system?'

Iroedh did a couple of steps from a round dance. 'Like it! It is wonderful! I've given up even the thought of a harem of drones, for while it's too early to tell about Antis' fertility, I'm sure no mate could give me more pleasure.'

'Winston would say that was not a scientific attitude, but sometimes an unscientific attitude is better.'

'Of course,' continued Iroedh, 'now that I'm getting to know Antis really well I realize he has faults along with his virtues. He's headstrong, irritable, sometimes inconsiderate, and often pompous where his own dignity is concerned. But he's honest and brave and jolly, so I still adore him.'

'Oh, they all have faults. My man, for instance, is clever as anything, but he is basically weak, that one, and has moods of depression in which he's no good for sex or anything else.'

'Really? I hadn't noticed.'

'You wouldn't. They try to hide these failings from everybody except their wives. But if we wait around for the perfect mate we shall be in a deep hole before we find him. *Allô*, what is this?'

They had come out on to the road to Ledhwid about a day later than they expected, and had now been marching north on this road for some hours, with their remaining belongings in bundles on the ends of sticks they bore on their shoulders. Although the road was rough, it seemed easy to Iroedh after the endless cross-country scramble she had experienced. The hills were getting steeper and less densely wooded; right now the road was heading into a great gorge, which Iroedh knew by repute as the Gorge of Hwead. Ledhwid could not be much farther.

The cause of Barbe's exclamation was a corpse – or rather skeleton – lying by the road. A little further on lay another, and she saw still others scattered among the bushes and boulders. They had lain there long enough for the scavenger beasts to have picked the bones fairly clean, so that the stench of death had almost disappeared, but not so long but that occasional scraps of skin and cloth lingered among the remains.

'Iroedh!' cried Bloch. 'Come here and identify these for me!'

He bounded up among the rocks to where a cuirass and helmet, dulled but not yet badly corroded, lay among a litter of bones.

Iroedh climbed up after him and said: 'Let me see the teeth. That's an Avtiny worker; from the device on the helmet she would have been from Khwiem.' She went from skeleton to skeleton. 'All seem to be workers from the northern Communities. No, here's a drone, also an Avtin. I thought this might be a massacre by a war party of Arsuuni, but to judge from the remains and the weapons it was an attack on a party of workers from several Communities by a band of rogue Avtiny drones. Probably the band of Wythias.

The news of this slaughter had not yet reached Elham when I left there, but news travels slowly.'

Bloch said: 'It's that tightly compartmented society of yours. I wish I could take some of these stiffs along; I've been wanting an Avtiny skeleton in the worst way.'

'You're not going to collect a series now!' cried Barbe.

'N-no, though I would if we had transport. I'll merely take this one skull along to study on the way.'

He hopped from rock to rock back to the road, precariously balancing the round white object on the palm of one hand. The journey resumed.

Iroedh said: 'What on Niond do you want with a lot of old bones?'

'To learn how the life forms on Niond are built, and how they evolved,' said Bloch.

'How they *what?*'

'Evolved.' Bloch gave a short account of the evolutionary process.

'By Gwyyr, that's not what I learned in the filiary! We were taught that the world was hatched from an egg.'

'You may think as you please,' said Bloch. 'However, do you know of any place where bones are found imbedded in rock or earth?'

'Yes; in Thidhem there's a cliff, worn away by wind and weather, where such bones are exposed. Do you wish such things?'

'I certainly do. We need such bones, called "fossils," to learn how a race of egg-laying mammals evolved into organisms much like ourselves.'

Barbe remarked: 'It is not so strange; much the same thing happened on Krishna, and we have the platypus on Earth … This road seems very little used; we've seen nobody except that one cart that passed us an hour ago.'

'It's Wythias' band,' explained Antis. 'While they're out, all the Communities in their path keep their workers at home.'

They were now well into the Gorge of Hwead. Bloch looked nervously up at the towering walls and said:

'This would be a fine place to drop rocks on people below.' Later he added: 'What's that noise? Like bells.'

Iroedh listened too. 'It is bells; the bells of Ledhwid. They're hung from the branches of the sacred grove and are rung by the wind, and the Oracle interprets the sounds.'

Bloch murmured a Terran poem:

> "*'Tis mute, the word they went to hear on high Dodona Mountain*
> *When winds were in the oakenshaws and all the cauldrons tolled …*'*

*

The Gorge of Hwead opened out and there stood the Hill of Ledhwid, crowned by the sacred grove of trees of immense size and antiquity. Before the grove, at the top of the path that wound up the steep hillside, stood the temple, of translucent blue stone, massive and graceful at the same time.

'Bless my soul!' said Bloch. 'Whoever built that structure knew his business. I wish we hadn't donated our camera to Wythias.'

'The ancients built such things,' said Iroedh. 'Perhaps if Antis and I can start some people living as they did, we shall be able to do as well again.'

They straggled up the path to the irregular chiming of the bells. The slope made them puff. Iroedh looked down distastefully at her shape and for an instant resented her new weight; then remembered that without all this she and Antis would never have been united. That was worth hauling any number of bothersome female organs!

They passed through a gate in the stone wall that ran around the whole top of the hill. In front of the temple stood a single Avtiny worker-guard in such finery as Iroedh had never seen, even on a queen. Her cuirass and helmet seemed to be of gold, and the latter bore a rim of jewels with a big glittering stone in front, faceted like that in Barbe's engagement ring.

'Good afternoon, sister,' said Bloch. 'I wonder if—'

'You are expected,' said the guard. 'Oh, Garnedh! Conduct these two visitors of another race to the Oracle at once. You two' – she indicated the Avtini – 'will have to send in your question in the usual form.'

'But they're with me—' began Bloch.

'I'm sorry, but I have my orders. Garnedh will take care of you.'

The other guard, who had stepped out of the shadows inside the temple, led Bloch and Barbe away. Iroedh, feeling lost, sat down on the steps. Antis relaxed against a pillar and blew on his flute a bar of an ancient Terran song Bloch had taught them, one that began:

'Main aidh av siin dhe glory av dhe kamyng av dhe Lord ...'

'Antis,' said Iroedh, 'what's this 'usual form' in which they wish questions submitted?'

'I can tell you that,' said the guard. 'Write your question on this pad, giving your name and Community, and send it in with your offering.'

'Offering?'

'Certainly. You don't suppose an institution like this runs on air, do you?'

Iroedh looked at Antis. 'I have nothing to offer, darling.'

'Neither have I—'

'How about some of that handsome armor of yours?' Iroedh turned to the guard. 'Would his helmet be acceptable?'

'Quite,' said the guard.

'Hey!' cried Antis. 'I won't give up my armor! We may yet have a battle on our hands.'

274

'But then how shall we submit a question?'

'We needn't. We know what's good for us as well as the Oracle does.'

The guard said: 'There is one other course: to submit a report on your Community. If you will write several thousand words on everything that has happened there recently, as well as any other news you have picked up along the way, the Master may consider that an acceptable substitute.' The guard's voice became confidential. 'My dear, I hope you won't consider me inquisitive, but you're a queen, aren't you?'

'You might say so.'

'Well, this is something I have never seen in all my years of service here! Are you fleeing the destruction of your Community by the Arsuuni, or what?'

'No. I'm an ex-worker.'

'Impossible! Or should I say a miracle? May I make your acquaintance, Queen? I am Ystalverdh of Thidhem.'

'I'm Iroedh of Elham – or was. And this is Antis of Elham.'

'How did you become a functional female? And what are these strangers from Gliid, the gods returned to Niond? And where's Yaedh?'

Iroedh started to tell about the death of Yaedh when another priestess raced up the road in a chariot. Up the path her ueg toiled and out of sight around toward the rear of the temple. A few seconds later the priestess panted back around the corner.

'Ystalverdh!' she cried. 'Tell the Master at once. Wythias is marching on Ledhwid, searching for two strangers of another race.'

'That must be the pair just arrived,' said Ystalverdh, 'whom Yaedh was sent to fetch. Oh, Garnedh!'

The other guard was already approaching. When the newly arrived priestess had given her message, Garnedh said:

'The Master says for the two Avtini to come in also.'

'One surprise after another!' said Ystalverdh. 'It *never* lets common visitors see its face. But go on – go on.'

Garnedh led the way into an anteroom, then into the temple, with golden statues of the old gods around the sides and a smoking altar in the middle. Thence she conducted them through a curtained portal on the far side. As she neared the curtain Iroedh's nose caught the familiar scent of Bloch's pipe-tobacco.

The air in the chamber was stiflingly hot. Bloch sat on a cushion on the floor with his back to the portal, and at the sound of footsteps rose to his feet. Barbe remained upon her cushion, as did the third occupant of the room.

The third occupant was a roly-poly creature which if it had stood up would have come waist-high. It was covered all over with grizzled fur, and twiddled all fourteen digits of its seven-fingered hands. Iroedh would have thought it a mere pet had she not known it must be the Oracle.

The Oracle said, in fluent Avtinyk delivered in a high squeaky voice: 'Come in and make yourselves comfortable, Iroedh and Antis. You shouldn't have been held up outside had I known the whole story. What is it, Lhuidh?'

The priestess who had just arrived in the chariot gave her report.

When she had finished, the Oracle said: 'By Dhiis, nothing is ever simple! Here I've promised myself another sight of my native world, and this complication comes up. I get along with most drone bands well enough, but this Wythias is impossible.'

He gave the two priestesses a rapid series of orders to put the temple in condition for defense and to round up all the other priestesses in the neighborhood. During this harangue Bloch showed increasing signs of agitation and finally burst out:

'Gildakk, old man, don't you think it would be better to run for it? With a few hours' start we could lose ourselves in these hills—'

'And have them track us down in the open, when we have here one of the best natural defenses this side of Tvaar? Anyway, I'm too old and fat for racing up and down hills. We have a good stout wall and supplies for a long siege; my only worry is that I may not be able to round up more than twenty or thirty of my sisters. The rest are away on missions, but your guns should make up the difference.'

Bloch said: 'I have only about seventy rounds left, counting the pistol.'

The Oracle twiddled its many fingers. 'I should have liked more, but if you make every one count we may be able to hold them.'

Antis said: 'Why not get out the temple's chariots, head for Gliid, and shoot our way through the host?'

'Oh no!' cried Bloch, paling. 'They'd block the road, or ambush us in the Gorge of Hwead and roll down rocks—'

'I fear my Terran colleague is right,' said Gildakk, 'considering my own age and infirmity, though if conditions were a little more favorable I'd chance it.'

'Excuse me,' said Iroedh.

'To be sure, you don't know me. My name is Gildakk, from the planet Thoth in the Procyonic system. I had just started to tell these Terrans how I became Oracle. When the party from my ship was held up by the road block, I drove right over it, but the next in line stopped and the rogues got the lot. When I arrived here I saw that the building was a public structure of some sort, so I hitched my ueg out of sight and hung around a couple of days, nearly starved, until I found what was going on. Then I walked up to the guard and demanded to see the high priest or whatever they had inside. I figured it was an even chance whether they sacrificed me to some god or made a god of me.'

'Thothians,' Bloch put in, 'are notoriously the worst gamblers in the Galaxy.'

'Thank you. As it happened, the Oracle was a neutermale named Enroys who'd been stolen as a child by the Arsuuni of Denüp and reared on a meatless diet as a slave. He'd escaped to Ledhwid, become an assistant to the previous Oracle, and taken the latter's place when she died.

'As for me, since I spoke no Avtinyk, the guards took me for somebody's pet. When I could get nothing from them save a pat on the head, I went back to my chariot. As it happened, my vehicle carried the party's load of signal pyrotechnics and little else. So I fetched a mine back up the hill, set it in front of the temple, and touched it off. The noise and the colored lights scared the wits out of the guards, and by the time they stopped running I was inside talking sign-language with Enroys. In due course I became his assistant and succeeded him. And I've put the Oracle on a business basis. I've made the priestesses into the best spy corps you ever saw, and I've filed and crossindexed the prophecies properly. You should have seen them! All mixed up and written on leaves and potsherds and things.'

Bloch, who had been looking around uneasily, said: 'Shouldn't we – ah—'

'No, no, I've already done what needs doing. Unless that helicopter of yours shows up, in which case we'll use it.'

Bloch said: 'I have about given Kang up. I've watched for him every day, and I have a signal mirror, but no sign of him. Maybe he's crashed, or maybe they've given us up, or maybe they've flown away without us.'

'Winston!' cried Barbe. 'What a horrible idea!'

'Cheer up,' said Gildakk. 'If that's so, you may have to run the Oracle after I die. Since there's a pair of you, you won't find it so lonesome as I have. I admit I should like to see the gray seas of Thoth again. This insipid weather bores me.'

'You should see its planet,' said Bloch to Iroedh. 'Practically one continuous hurricane. That's why it has all those fingers, to keep from being blown away.'

'Excuse me, Gildakk,' said Iroedh, 'but are you a he or a she?'

'Both.'

'You mean a neuter worker?'

'No; I'm a functional male and female at the same time. I both beget and bear – that is, when there's another Thothian to share the task. We are viviparous but not mammalian. Bloch was telling me about your metamorphosis, by the way. Enroys also discovered a meat diet, but too late in life to do him any good. He never did develop, poor fellow.'

'Is it true that Wythias feeds his band on a mixed diet?'

'That's a secret I was holding out to make him behave, but yes, he does. He had ideas of conquering the planet that way, but now he knows of Bloch's guns I suppose he thinks that would be even quicker—' Gildakk snapped several fingers at once. 'That gives me an idea! Instead of sitting here while Wythias besieges us, why not take the offensive?'

'How?' said Antis eagerly.

'If we could use Iroedh here, and some of the prophecies I have on file – if we could use them right we might take Wythias' band away from him. Then you could march through Avtinid knocking queens off their little thrones and setting up bisexual Communities—'

Iroedh protested: 'But I don't want to be a conqueror! I just wish to settle down with Antis and lay his eggs and collect antiques! If anybody wishes to join us voluntarily—'

'You haven't much choice,' said Gildakk. 'It's the only way to beat Wythias, and then you'll find that who rides the noag cannot dismount. Besides, it will enable your race to resume their progress in the civilized arts.'

'There is that, but—'

'Of course,' said the Thothian. 'All this fuss about sex seems silly to me, who am a whole complete individual and not a mere half-person like you onesex beings; but I'm trying to be helpful. Here, let's see which pronouncement would work best ...'

The Thothian rolled to its feet and limped over to a set of drawers. It pulled one out and began fingering through a file of bark cards, humming to itself.

'Here's one,' it said:

'*The High Queen rides in a chariot bright*
With a Princess Royal between the shafts,
While the Arsuuny soldiers in panic flight
Abandon their rafts.'

'What does it mean?' asked Iroedh, looking over Gildakk's shoulder.

'Oh, it doesn't *mean* anything! Or, rather, it means whatever the hearer wishes it to mean. I issued that one a few years ago to the envoys from Yeym, when the Arsuuni were attacking that Community.'

'But Yeym was destroyed!'

'Of course it was; but I saw no harm in encouraging the poor things when they were fighting for their lives.'

'Why rafts?'

'Because it rhymes and fits the meter. Here's another:

'*When the Rogue Queen wears a crown of light*
The Golden Couch shall be overthrown;
When the gods descend from heaven's height
Shall the seed be sown.

'See? You're the rogue queen; the golden couch is the present sex-caste system with its oversexed queens and neuter workers; Bloch and the other Terrans are the gods; and the seed is that of these drones we're trying to win over. It couldn't be better if I had composed it specially for the occasion. Of course I've already applied it to other events a couple of times, but nobody will remember that.'

Iroedh asked: 'How about the crown of light?'

'Hmm, crown of light, crown of light. Garnedh! Get one of the sisters to help you drag Chest Number Four from the cellar, will you?'

Iroedh said: 'Then it's all just an imposture? There's no real prophetic knowledge? The Oracle doesn't go into a mystic trance and interpret the sound of the bells?'

'Of course it's a fake! Since I hope to leave here soon, I have no reason to deceive you. The sooner you and Antis learn to rely upon yourselves alone, and not on any of this mummery, the better off you'll be. Ah, thank you, sisters. Now. let's see ...'

Gildakk opened the chest, in which lay a litter of unfamiliar-looking tubular objects.

'Signal flares,' he said. 'I hope they haven't deteriorated too much in all these years.'

X

The Temple Grove

Toward evening, looking south from the portico of the temple, Iroedh saw dust rising from the Gorge of Hwead. Preparations for defense speeded up. From the temple came the sounds of a grindstone sharpening spearheads, and a general hammering and sawing mingled with the ever-present sound of the bells of Ledhwid.

Some of the priestesses had piled logs on the slope just above the gate, behind a pair of stakes driven into the ground, so that if the stakes were removed the logs would roll down and pile up in a heap against the inner side of the gate to lend it additional strength. Others stacked arrows and spears, or erected wicker mantlets to protect the defenders against arrow fire. For the twentieth time Iroedh felt the edge of her machete. It was as sharp as whetting could make it, and with the handsome armor provided by the temple she should make an effective warrior.

Still, there was no blinking the fact that Gildakk had been able to round up only eighteen priestesses, of which two or three were too old to be of real use in fighting. With the addition of her party, therefore, they had at most twenty effectives. No doubt the Terrans' gunfire would account for the first attackers and discourage the rest, but if Wythias pushed his attack regardless of losses …

It seemed to Iroedh that of the three alternatives they had discussed – to flee, to shoot their way through the host, or to stand their ground – they had chosen the worst. Why hadn't she put up an argument? She had become so wrapped up in her love for Antis that she was getting into the habit of blindly following his lead.

The band of Wythias was now in sight, crawling up the road from the gorge like creeping things after a sweet. As they came nearer, Iroedh's dilating pupils could see several ueg chariots at the head of the column. No doubt they were those the band had stolen from Bloch's party.

The drones came nearer and nearer, then spread out around the base of the Hill of Ledhwid like a trickle of water that meets an obstacle. A trumpet sounded back in the temple, and Iroedh went to her assigned place near the gate.

A drone in full panoply marched up the path to the gate, threw back his head, and bawled: 'O Oracle!'

'Yes?' squeaked Gildakk, peering beadily over the gate with a shawl around his head.

'Are you indeed the Oracle of Ledhwid?' asked the herald, eyes bulging.

'Absolutely. Don't you remember the prophecy:

> 'When knaves to Ledhwid Temple shall come
> With impious hands to plunder her,
> They'll be scattered like chaff by an Oracle small
> And covered with fur'?

'I did not know that one,' said the herald. 'But to get down to business: Our leader demands that you give up to him the people from the sky ship who have taken refuge with you, together with their magical weapons.'

'What people?'

'There's no use lying, Oracle. A worker of Khwiem passed them on the road this morning, and told us about it before we slew her; and a scout we left to watch the Gorge of Hwead told us a party answering the same description passed through the gorge around noon and entered the temple grounds. So render them up or take the consequences.'

'How am I supposed to do that?'

'How do you mean?'

'These strangers have godlike powers. They can blast you with lightning and thunder as easily as they can look at you.'

'We know.'

'Then how shall I coerce them, even if I were willing?'

'That's your problem,' said the herald.

'Then you will have to catch them yourselves. I can do nothing.'

'Will you and your people leave the temple grounds while we come in after the sky folk?'

Iroedh had a bad moment; it would be easy for Gildakk to sell them out in exchange for his personal safety.

'No,' said the Thothian. 'This sacred enclosure shall not be profaned by armed invasion.'

'Then you and yours shall perish, I warn you.'

'Wait, herald,' said Gildakk. 'If Wythias would care to parley, I have a counteroffer—'

'No proposals! My leader knows how clever you are and will not be drawn into negotiations. You shall either give us the fugitives, or get out of the way while we get them.'

'We defy you. Your leader shall find that trying to take this place with a mob of brigands is like a new-hatched babe trying to crack a dairtel nut with its gums.'

The herald went away. Those in the enclosure braced themselves.

The red sun sank below the ridges. Iroedh knew now that there was no hope of help from the *Paris*, for Bloch had assured her that it was against the Terrans' policy to try to land the helicopter in strange places at night.

Though there were over two hundred drones in the band, they had to spread themselves out in a pretty thin line to surround the Hill of Ledhwid. At the sound of the trumpet they started forward. When some of them broke into a run their officers called them back. As the rogues came closer and their circle contracted, their line became denser, though at the base of the hill there was still some arms' lengths between individuals. Up they came, first walking, then half crawling as the slope became steeper.

The trumpet sounded from the temple. Priestesses picked up great round stones from the poles behind the wall and heaved them over.

'Iroedh, throw your stones!' said a voice behind her.

Iroedh pulled herself together and hurled a stone as big as her head. It ricocheted down the slope, bounding clear over the head of an advancing drone. A second flew between two of them. Crash! One had struck a drone off to Iroedh's right. As the attacker's body rolled back down the slope, other drones stopped to watch. The line became disordered. Another drone went down under the bombardment. The officers ordered the line forward; some obeyed.

In front of Iroedh a little group of rogues struggled up the slope. She poised a stone and hurled it. Two spear lengths' away they paused and looked as the stone came at them, then flinched aside. The stone struck with a smack into the midst of them; there were bodies flying and bodies rolling and bodies running. When the confusion abated one drone lay still on the slope, another dragged himself along the ground, and the rest ran back down to the base of the hill.

The drones' trumpet sounded recall. The rest of the drones ran back down the slope in great bounds.

'How's it going, Iroedh?' said Bloch behind her. He was prowling up and down with the gun under his arm.

'Have we won?'

'Not by a jugful! They'll be back. I wish they had got close enough to warrant shooting; the gun becomes less effective as it gets darker, in spite of this infrared viewer. I wish I had your night vision.'

'This wall doesn't look like much protection.'

Bloch shook his head. 'In most places it's only breasthigh; they can boost each other over it. Gildakk tells me the builders never meant it for a defense, but merely to keep wild animals out of the grove and the tame animals in.'

The rogues' trumpet sounded again, this time to call them together. They formed a solid black mass on the plain below, the mutter of their leaders' instructions wafting up to Iroedh at her post.

They organized themselves into a rectangular phalanx and, at another trumpet blast, headed up the slope toward the gate, all two hundred of them. Those behind the front rank held their shields over their heads so that the mass looked like a scale-backed creeping thing.

Iroedh called: 'Daktablak! Bring your gun! The rest of you fetch more stones!'

The scaly monster swept up the slope, slower as it became steeper. Inside the enclosure priestesses grunted as they staggered along the wall with stones in their arms.

Then the stones began to fall again. One bounded over the entire testudo; others clanged against the shields. A few drones went down, but the rest closed up and came on. Some priestesses began shooting arrows into the mass. A great stone crashed into the front rank and its impact swept a whole file of drones sprawling, but the others untangled themselves and struggled on.

'Daktablak!' cried Iroedh. 'They'll gain the wall!'

She hurled a last stone and reached for her machete. Then the gun went off deafeningly: *bang-bang-bang*, shooting out bright orange flashes into the dusk. The drone advance came to a halt, then the whole mass dissolved into its component drones running for safety.

Bloch, putting another clip into the gun, said: 'I can kill two or three with one shot when they're bunched like that. How many did I get?'

'There are over twenty lying there, but I don't know how many are yours,' said Iroedh. 'Where's Antis?'

'On the other side of the grove. It would surprise me if Wythias can drive his people to another attack.' Bloch filled and lit his pipe.

The rogues had called another conference on the plain. Voices could be heard, raised in loud debate. After a long wait they got into motion again. They trickled off around both sides of the hill, as on the first attack. This time, however, instead of forming a single line, they organized themselves into a dozen or more small groups. At the signal these came bounding up the slope with almost as much *élan* as the first time.

'Bless my soul!' said Bloch. 'Those fellows have nerve, to come back after the last strafing. Not many Terran primitives would do that.'

'Perhaps they're more afraid of Wythias than of you,' grunted Iroedh, lifting a stone to hurl.

In the fading light it was hard to tell how effective the missiles were. From elsewhere on the perimeter came the cry:

'Daktablak! Daktablak! Come quickly!'

Iroedh had a glimpse of Bloch's bald head bobbing away toward the sound; then in a few seconds came the crash of the rifle. Then from another section of the wall:

'Daktablak! Come!'

From Iroedh's left there came the clash and grind of weapons. She looked along the wall toward a dark knot of struggling figures, drew her machete, and started toward them. Before she arrived she heard the high voice of Barbe:

'Stand back, you stupids!'

The group opened out and the little Terran figure stepped into the opening. Her pistol cracked several times, and the rogues who had gained the inside of the wall slumped to the ground.

A priestess looking toward Iroedh cried: 'Look out!'

Iroedh turned to see the head of a drone rising over the wall beside her. She whirled and struck backhand at the neck; felt the blade bite. The head toppled out of sight and the spouting torso followed it. Somewhere across the enclosure the big gun was firing again, and among the giant trees a drone who had gained the enclosure fought priestesses. Iroedh started toward the sound, but by the time she arrived the drone was down.

Then all noises ceased save the footsteps of running drones. Bloch and Antis appeared, the former doing things to his gun and the latter wiping a slight wound on his cheek. Bloch said:

'I hope that's the last. While we've only suffered three or four casualties, we have a total of six rounds left for the rifle and two for the pistol. We're even running low on stones.'

The rogues slowly gathered themselves together again upon the plain. Antis said:

'Wythias must have lost a fifth of his band. He can't do this many times more.'

'Once more is all that will be required,' said Bloch gloomily. 'Why did I ever go in for xenological exploration? I should have stayed home and been a professor.'

Below, argument raged again among the assembled drones. Injured rogues dragged themselves from where they had fallen toward the main mass. Some of the drones lit campfires and torches.

At last one rogue mounted the path to the gate, holding a torch over his head. Iroedh recognized the herald, who called:

'O Oracle!'

'Had enough?' squealed Gildakk from the wall.

'We have not given up, if that is what you mean. Though you defy our direct assault, we can still starve you out.'

'That will take a long time.'

'We can wait. However, as all of us have other business, my leader generously offers you a parley, to see what proposal you could possibly make that would interest him as much as getting the sky peoples' weapons.'

'Very well,' said the Thothian. 'On my side there will be myself, the sky folk, and the two who came with them. Wythias may bring not more than four officers with him, unarmed, and must stand two spears' lengths below us. We shall stand just outside the gate.'

'We don't care about the Avtini; leave them out of it.'

'No; the proposal concerns them.'

'Very well, bring them. But your party must also be unarmed; especially the sky folk must not have their magical weapons.'

'We agree,' said Gildakk. 'And since the proposal also concerns your band as a whole, it is only proper that they should hear. Let them gather with torches on the slope below Wythias, but not closer than three spears' lengths from him ...'

After some more dickering about distances, to guard against treachery, the herald agreed and departed. Gildakk said to Iroedh:

'Quick, take off your armor and tunic and put on your cloak!'

When the drones had gathered upon the slope with torches fluttering, and the logs had been dragged away from the inner side of the gate, Iroedh filed out of the gate with the others: Gildakk, Bloch, Barbe, and Antis. Iroedh, wrapped in her cloak, felt qualms at leaving her machete inside the wall and had to control a tendency to glance back at the gate every few seconds to make sure it still stood open. Antis was likewise unarmed, and Bloch and Barbe held up their hands to show they were empty. Barbe had even left her pistol holster behind.

A pair of priestesses carried lighted oil lamps out through the gate and set them on the path to provide additional illumination. Iroedh looked into the torchlit confusion below. A little group of drones, muffled in their cloaks, was ascending the hill. In front came one huge drone whose matted crest rose above a pair of fierce eyes.

Gildakk, standing beside Antis, said: 'Ask which is Wythias.' It had been arranged that Antis, having the loudest voice, should do the talking.

'I am Wythias,' said the giant. 'Speak.'

At least, thought Iroedh, it was lucky the drones used only bows and spears, for neither could readily be hidden under a cloak.

Gildakk squeaked to Antis, phrase by phrase, and Antis repeated the phrases in his piercing bellow. This gave the speech a somewhat jerky effect, though Iroedh found it all the more impressive for its pauses.

'Wythias, officers, and men of the band of Wythias!' began Gildakk and Antis. 'You think you wish the magical weapons of the sky people to conquer the world, do you not?'

'Yes!' replied Wythias, and this was echoed by several of his drones.

'But that is not what you really desire. You may think you lead a good life; you have food and drink and games and ornaments and excitement. But there is one thing you do *not* have. You know what I mean?'

'Yes!' roared the drones.

Wythias said: 'What do you expect to do? Provide us each with a queen, or some such fantastic idea?'

'Not fantastic, my dear Wythias. If you listen to us, every one of you can have – not some fat old queen who bosses you and whom you share with sixteen other drones – but a handsome and congenial functional female of your own. Your very own! To love and live with all your life, as the ancients used to do. Who will lay your eggs, which will hatch into children that you, and you alone, may rear up as you wish. What do you think of *that?*'

A murmur went through the drones. Wythias said: 'A likely story! Next you'll offer us the Treasure of Inimdhad. Where is your proof?'

'I have proof. Iroedh, show them.'

Iroedh stepped forward, threw off her cloak, and stood naked before them in the torchlight.

'There!' continued Antis-Gildakk. 'A perfect functional female, once a neuter like all workers. I can change workers into functional females!'

A drone stood up. 'How do we know she's been changed? How do we know she's not merely some runaway princess?'

'Is there any drone here from Elham?'

'I am,' said a voice.

'Dyos, you scoundrel!' roared Antis. 'You knew Iroedh of Elham, who hauled you out of the prison cell, didn't you?'

'Y-yes.'

'Then step forward and identify her.'

Dyos came up hesitantly, looked, and said: 'That's Iroedh. Just a minute to make sure those things aren't glued on …'

'Ouch!' said Iroedh. 'You—'

'Yes, she's turned functional. It's true, fellows.'

'But,' said Wythias, 'how do we know workers would accept this arrangement, assuming you transformed them?'

'Iroedh did. She is united to Antis by such a contract now, aren't you, Iroedh?'

'Yes,' said Iroedh, 'and I love it.'

'Of course,' continued Antis and Gildakk, 'there will have to be some changes. If you go ahead with this project you must accept our leadership; you will have to stop killing workers. Every worker, remember, is a potential female! Waste not, want not. You must—'

'Ridiculous!' shouted Wythias. 'I won't give up my leadership to anybody! And this is all a hoax of some kind to get these sky folk out of my hands, and we shall be left holding an empty sack.'

'I'm not finished, please!' Antis and Gildakk went on to rhapsodize on the beauties of married life, then said:

'But most of all we urge you to join us because this revolution was foretold long ago by the divine prescience of the never-failing Oracle of Ledhwid. In the incumbency of my predecessor Enroys, of sacred memory, the divine afflatus issued the following promise:

> *'When the Rogue Queen wears a crown of light*
> *The Golden Couch shall be overthrown;*
> *When the gods descend from heaven's height*
> *Shall the seed be sown.*

'Which is interpreted as follows: The Rogue Queen is obviously Iroedh. The Golden Couch is the present sexcaste system with its queens. The sky folk are the gods; the seed is yours. And as for the crown of light—'

Gildakk squeaked over his shoulder: 'Light up!'

There were faint noises from inside the wall and a whisper: 'The first one won't light!'

'Then try the next!'

The audience squirmed and rustled at the length of the pause.

'As for the crown of light—' repeated Antis.

Then it came: a sputter, a flare, a loud foomp, something soaring into the sky, a sharp pop, and a blinding magenta light drifting slowly overhead in the evening air. Then another went off, soared, exploded in a dazzling spray of green sparks, and finished with a vivid flash and an ear-shattering *bang.*

'There you are,' said Antis. 'Down with Queen Danoakor's so-called reforms! Back to the happy customs of the Golden Age! Let's overturn the Golden Couch, as prophesied by the Oracle!'

The fireworks had brought cries of astonishment and alarm from the drones. One shouted:

'It's the fire-breathing Igog!'

At the last explosion many near the edges of the crowd had started to run away. Gildakk said:

'Your music, quickly!'

Antis put the flute to his lips, and Iroedh joined Bloch and Barbe in singing the Terran song: '*Main aidh av siin dhe glory ...*'

The audience calmed down, and those who had started to flee wandered back. A drone called:

'I know you, Antis! You're no drone but the god Dhiis come back to Niond. I know you by that ancient instrument you play!'

Gildakk and Antis concluded: 'Who's with us? Who wants to try it?'

Iroedh, somewhat shaken by the pyrotechnics, could see the faces of the rogues turning and hear the murmur of voices. One drone raised his hand:

'Count me in!' 'And me!' 'And me!' '*Kwa* Queen Iroedh!'

Hands rose all over the assemblage. Wythias glaring, shouted:

'It's a trick! A cowardly, treacherous, dastardly, stinking trick! You call a parley and instead make lying speeches and sing songs to turn my own men against me!'

'Not at all; you'd be just as welcome as—'

'I'll stop your lies about every worker a queen and a queen for every drone!'

Wythias threw back his cloak, revealing that in one hand he held a spear cut to half length so that it could be hidden. His arm darted back, then forward. The spear whizzed up the slope.

Iroedh, with a little shriek, reached for the machete that was not there. Out of the corner of her eye she saw Barbe's hand dart inside her shirt.

The spear struck Gildakk in the belly and went on until the point, now green with Thothian blood, came out its back. Barbe's hand reappeared with her pistol. Gildakk fell backwards, twitching. The pistol barked and spat a sheet of flame: once, twice.

Wythias staggered back a step, then folded slowly into a heap.

While Iroedh braced herself to spring for the gate, Barbe, holding the pistol steady, called in a high voice: 'Don't start anything, any of you! You have all seen that treacherous murder. Calm yourselves, my littles, and give consideration to your situation. Your bad leader, he is gone and our offer is still open. Join us and forget the unhappy past. As the Oracle told you, the change is bound to come. Will you work with it or be crushed by it? If you wish time to consider—'

'I have considered,' said a drone. 'I'm with you.'

'So am I,' said another. 'Wythias would have had us all killed to further his ambitions.'

The others joined in assent, all but a very few who straggled off into the night. Iroedh heard Barbe murmur to Bloch:

'Hold me up, Winston darling. I think I'm going to faint. Those were my last bullets.'

'Really, Barbe,' said Bloch, 'you shouldn't have brought that gun. We promised—'

'Oh, what stupidity! He had the spear, didn't he?'

Iroedh leaned over Gildakk. The Thothian's beady eyes looked up at her and its voice squeaked faintly.

'Iroedh!'

'Yes? What can I do for you?'

'Nothing; I'm finished. I wanted to see the gray seas again, but no such luck. I have one piece of advice.'

'Yes?'

'If your revolution breaks down the – present Community pattern, revive the old religion.'

'Why? I don't really believe in it, and I'm sure you don't.'

'Without the present Communities – the Avtini will need – an emotional outlet – to take their place. And a unifying force – so you can fight the Arsuuni – and ...'

The voice trailed off and the bright eyes closed. Gildakk the Thothian was dead.

XI

The Battle

Next morning Kang dropped out of the sky in his helicopter. 'Was up on practice flight last night,' he said. 'Saw flares.'

He went on to explain in his truncated English that he had had a slight accident, bending the alighting gear of the machine, so that it had been laid up for several days. Then it was grounded further by bad weather, and when he finally took off to search for the party (lack of radio reports from whom had aroused alarm on the *Paris*) he could find no sign of them along the road to Ledhwid. A well-armed ground party was now searching for them.

Bloch told Antis and Iroedh: 'Well, this is nearly the end of the road for us, though for you it's just a beginning. What are you going to do next?'

Iroedh looked with some consternation at Antis, who returned her stare. It struck her for the first time that she would soon no longer have these wise and potent Terrans to rely on. As Gildakk had said, she and Antis would have to learn to depend upon themselves, no matter how puzzling or perilous their course.

She said: 'I suppose we shall get in touch with the other rogue drone bands and try to persuade them to join us. Then we'll start a campaign to win over the neighboring Communities, either as wholes or by seducing away individual workers.'

Bloch suggested: 'You might write messages, wrap them around arrows, and shoot them over the walls.'

'Splendid! And then we shall—But who is that approaching?'

A chariot was smoking up the road from the Gorge of Hwead. As it came closer Iroedh saw that it was driven by a priestess of the Oracle. As the driver neared, she pulled in her ueg at the sight of the drones encamped upon the plain and started to turn her vehicle around.

Iroedh, calling reassurance, ran toward the chariot. The driver hesitated on the verge of flight until Iroedh came up and tried to brief her on the situation in one short sentence.

'But where,' said the priestess, 'is our Master?'

'Dead. Wythias killed it and then was slain himself.'

'Great Eunmar! Whom then did it choose as successor?'

'Nobody; it had no time. Won't you come in?'

'If I can do so safely. Wythias' drones kill on sight.'

'No more. You can see some of your fellow priestesses moving among them unmolested.'

The priestess came timorously, saying: 'I have important news for the Master, but since he's dead I don't know whom to give it to.'

'Tell me, why don't you? Since I find myself in a somewhat authoritative position around here—'

'Oh, it wouldn't interest you, Queen. The Arsuuni of Tvaarm have routed the advanced force of the Elhamni and are now invading Elham's territory—'

'*What?* Oh, Antis!'

'Yes?' When told the news Antis looked shaken, then put on his firm face. 'So what? What did they ever do for us except try to kill us and drive us out? Let the Arsuuni have them.'

'Antis, think! We shall have to face the problem of the Arsuuni. If we don't destroy them they'll exterminate us sooner or later. Our only hope is to unite all the Communities, or whatever takes the place of the Communities under the new system, to crush the Arsuuny Communities one by one. And how can we start better than with our own? If we let it be destroyed we shall not only lose part of our eventual force, but others will say: They care only for their own power, so why should we trust them?'

'Hmmp,' said Antis. 'I'll think it over—'

'Not this time,' said Iroedh, knowing that meant that he would come out with the suggestion as his own idea the following day. 'Every day is vital.'

'What do you propose?'

'Go to Elham myself and put the case to them: If they wish to survive, join forces with your drones to fight the Arsuuni.'

'They'd kill you before you could open your mouth.'

'You forget I'm now a queen!' Iroedh proudly threw out her breasts. 'A functional female may not be attacked by a worker under any circumstances, but only by another functional female. When Queen Rhuar went mad and began killing the workers of Elham, and they had no princess of age to send against her, not even then did they harm her. They seized her with bare hands (though several died in the doing), carried her gently outside the walls, and left her.'

'What happened to her?'

'They found her remains half eaten, though whether the beasts slew her or whether she died first of starvation they never learned.'

'It sounds good, but you can't go yet.'

'Why not?'

'Because it will take me days to get my people organized, and there's no sense in your getting to Elham much ahead of me. The Arsuuni might kill you. When you walk into that gate I want to be close behind with my drones.'

No argument would shake Antis from that resolution, though he finally admitted with a shamefaced grin: 'To tell the truth, my reasons aren't entirely tactical.'

'What then?'

'If you must know, I can't bear to be separated from you longer than necessary, do you see?'

'Why, Antis! To put your petty personal feelings ahead of the future of the race—'

'Don't sneer at personal feelings. It was because of them that you rescued me from the cell and started all these events!'

When told of their plans, Bloch said: 'Don't be surprised to find me breathing down your neck from the helicopter, especially if there's a battle. Subbarau would postpone his flying date a week for some good action movies.'

'Wouldn't you help us?'

'No. Sorry, but I've explained that. Ready, Barbe?'

Barbe kissed Iroedh, shook the hand of Antis (who seemed puzzled by the gesture), and climbed into the helicopter. They smiled, waved, and rose.

A rogue drone, leaning on his spear, remarked: 'They *are* the gods! I shall tell my offspring, if I ever have any, how I saw them with my own eyes.'

Nearly two eight-days later, Iroedh and her escort approached Elham. Although she had promised Antis not to get too far ahead of his army, she could not help speeding up a little as she neared her Community. She more than half expected to find it laid waste by the Arsuuni, though when she passed the *Paris* at Gliid her friends there assured her that they had not heard of any such catastrophe.

Bloch told her surreptitiously: 'I shouldn't say this because it might be deemed intervention, but I flew over your city yesterday on a visit to Khinam and saw no sign of the enemy.'

She continued on her way, bearing the Terrans' assurances of moral if not material support. Iroedh thought moral support all very nice, but she would much have preferred the loan of a gun.

As she drove, the leader of the escort, a former officer of Wythias named Tregaros, waxed garrulous about the fights he had been in:

'... now, Queen, see that crag? Well, one time when Wythias sent us through here to pick up an order of spearheads from Umwys the smith, the Thidhemni tried to ambush us. But I had a point out, as Wythias taught me. Eh, he was a tyrant, old Wythias, but as smart a soldier as you'll find the length and breadth of Avtinid. And I also remembered the prophecy:

> '*When the noag for prey shall lie in wait*
> *And leap for the leipag with golden eyes,*

> *The leipag shall with a vakhnag mate*
> *As the noag dies.*

'So when I saw that crag I said to myself, Tregaros, wouldn't that be a fine place for an ambush? Slow down, boys; we want to look into this. And, sure enough, up the road came the point, beating his beast for all he was worth, with the Thidhemni after him. The silly creatures hadn't had the sense to let him go through and attack our main body. So we ambushed them instead of the other way round.'

Iroedh tried dutifully to listen, but found her mind wandering off into fantasies of her hoped-for reunion with Antis. She knew what he would want first.

At the frontier of Elham the guards of Queen Maiur and Queen Estir all stared as the party drew up. The Thidhemny guard said:

'We got word to let you through, though why we cannot understand. So pass on.'

Iroedh could have told her the reason was an ultimatum from Antis, informing Queen Maiur's government that he proposed to pass through the territory of Thidhem in full force, and *if* not hindered would restrain his drones from doing harm. The guards on the other side were even more nonplused when Iroedh said:

'I am Queen Iroedh, on my way for a formal visit to Elham, and these drones are my escort.'

'Are you the Iroedh who used to be a worker of Elham?'

'That is right.'

'Great Eunmar! I didn't know you with those bulges!'

'I'm glad you do now. How's the Community making out under Estir?'

The Elhamni looked at one another, evidently uncertain whether to discuss intramural matters with one who had become an outsider. One of the Thidhemni spoke:

'Oh, they're having a terrible time. Estir has proved more difficult and domineering even than our own Maiur. We had the Queens' Conference at Thidhem last eightday, you know, and instead of behaving with such modesty as becomes a new queen, and trying to learn something of her business from the older ones, Estir spent her time telling them how to reign, as if they hadn't been doing so for years. She practically insulted the Queen of Hawardem, and you can be sure they crossed Estir off their social lists in a hurry.'

One of the Elhamny guards spoke up: 'Since you will find out anyway, Iroedh, I'll admit they're right. Estir has been a trial. And many of us sympathized with you over your expulsion. Not that we don't think you were at fault too, but Estir tried to deal treacherously with you. And a queen's honor is that of her Community.'

The other said: 'It doesn't matter, with the Arsuuni coming down upon us any day. Did I hear you name yourself queen?'

'So you did.'

'But how – what are you queen *of?*'

'Of King Antis, if you must know.'

'How is that possible? Antis was a drone of Elham who escaped a Cleanup; unless this is another of the same name. And "king" is an obsolete term—'

'I haven't time to explain, sisters, and I think you had better let us through. Don't be alarmed when a whole army of drones appears behind me.'

The outnumbered guards dubiously let Iroedh and her drones pass. They drove over the Lhanwaed Hills, along the beach of the Scarlet Sea, past Khinad Point, and up the main highway to Elham itself. Iroedh felt an odd lump in her throat as the well-remembered wall and domes materialized out of the trees. Still, she wished that Antis were with her; whatever his faults, lack of courage was not among them. She told Tregaros:

'Wait here out of sight of the main gate. In case of trouble, try to get word to Antis.'

She drove on. As soon as she came in sight of the fields there was a running about of the double guards posted there. The alarm of the workers subsided when they saw it was not the Arsuuni but only a single Avtin in a chariot.

At the main gate Iroedh received an argument like that at the frontier, with much the same result. While one guard ran ahead to inform the officers, others escorted Iroedh in.

When she drove up to the main portal of the Community, workers were gathering from all parts of the complex. The crowd buzzed excitedly as it opened to let Iroedh pass. On the front steps the officers of the Council were gathering with their insignia around their necks. From the crowd came the harsh voice of Rhodh:

'It is Iroedh the traitor! I always knew she would come to a shameful end!'

Rhodh had evidently not changed. Iroedh held up a hand and began:

'Greetings, workers of Elham. Know that I am Queen Iroedh, whom you formerly knew as Worker Iroedh, the mate of King Antis, formerly Drone Antis. We rule, not a patch of land, but an army of stout-hearted and strong-muscled drones, formerly rogue drones—'

'Why aren't they still rogues?' asked the general.

'Because we are starting them on a new way of life. To make you understand I shall have to tell you some personal history ...'

Iroedh had started to narrate the story of her introduction to a meat diet when there was another stir in the crowd and Queen Estir burst through, wearing by her side the original steel machete that Iroedh had stolen from the Terrans.

'What's this?' she cried. 'Another queen in my Community? She shan't live ten seconds—'

'Please, Queen, let her finish,' said the foreign officer. 'This is important.'

Iroedh resumed her story, including her union with Antis. The foreign officer interrupted:

'What, specifically, do you propose?'

'First, to form an alliance between Elham and my army against the Arsuuni. For one thing we can furnish you all with matselhi, which for close combat are more effective—'

'Never!' cried Estir. 'I have declared the matselh a royal weapon, to be used by none but queens!'

'I don't think we want newfangled things like that anyway,' said the general. 'The spear has stood us in good stead since time immemorial, and that thing of yours looks like an uncivilized and inhumane weapon. But go on.'

'Then, assuming we can defeat the Arsuuni, those of you who wish to join us, become functional females, and mate with our drones may do so.'

'But, Queen Iroedh,' began the agricultural officer, 'what will happen if—'

'Queen Iroedh!' shrieked Estir. 'You are Iroedh, the runaway worker! The one who delivered the condemned drones from their cell!'

'Yes, as I was explaining when—'

'You mean you not only dare invade my Community without permission; you propose to seduce away my workers with your monstrous, perverted, unnatural proposal! To destroy the very basis of my society! If every worker became a queen, what distinction would there be to being a queen? Guards, slay me this revolting monstrosity at once!'

As some of the guards (among whom Iroedh recognized her old friend Vardh) raised their spears, Iroedh called: 'Wait! After all, I'm a queen, and none of you may raise a hand against me!'

The guards drew back, exchanging baffled looks. Another ueg chariot came through the main gate at a run. The worker driving it leaped down from her vehicle before it had stopped and ran up.

'Queen Estir—'

'Quiet! I'm occupied.'

'But—'

'I said quiet! Get out! Now then, guards, why don't you kill this obscene travesty of a queen? You heard me, didn't you?'

'Yes, Queen, but she *is* a functional female,' said one, 'and the basic law says —'

'Then I'll show you!' screeched Estir, drawing her machete and rushing toward Iroedh's chariot.

Iroedh had not counted upon a duel with Estir, having in fact forgotten all about the original machete until the sight of it on Estir's hip recalled it to her mind. Now she had no time to don armor. As she leaped down from the chariot her main thought was that Antis would be furious at her having run such a risk. She was not really afraid of Estir, who was also nude, for Iroedh's many days of roughing it and clearing trails had hardened her.

Clang! Clang! went the blades as Estir struck overhand, forehand, and backhand. Iroedh parried and got in a cut of her own, which Estir knocked easily aside and struck again with lightning speed. Iroedh now remembered with a touch of horror what an exercise-fanatic Estir had been as princess. She must have kept herself in prime condition.

They circled, advancing, retreating, slashing, parrying, dodging, and feinting. Iroedh realized that the steel blade was much superior, being at once lighter, stronger, and sharper. Her own blade was acquiring visible bends and almost enough notches to make a saw out of it, while that of Estir seemed undamaged.

Iroedh tried to remember some of the things Bloch had told her about swords; how Terrans had once used them for thrusting … She shifted her grip to prepare for a thrust at Estir's advanced knee.

Then Estir struck Iroedh's blade with all her might. The machete flew out of Iroedh's tingling hand and fell on the greensward sixteen paces away.

'Now!' cried Estir, poising on the balls of her feet.

Iroedh knew she was finished. Estir could run like a streak, and if Iroedh turned to flee or to run for the machete, Estir would have the steel blade into her back before she had taken three steps.

Estir advanced, swinging the machete, poised for a dash. Iroedh backed away, visualizing her head bouncing along the ground as poor Queen Intar's had done. Up came the blade as Estir leaped. The flash of sunlight on steel held Iroedh's gaze as in a vise. Poor Antis …

There was a heavy thud as a red-smeared bronze point appeared, projecting a hand's breadth from Estir's chest just below her right breast. Instead of completing her rush upon Iroedh, Estir fell forward to hands and knees with a spear-shaft sticking out of her back like a mast. Her arms gave way beneath her and she crumpled to the gravel of the driveway. Blood ran from her mouth.

Iroedh looked to see who had thrown the spear. The workers were all backing away with exclamations of horror from one who stood in the armor of a guard but without her spear. Under the helmet Iroedh recognized Vardh.

'Vardh!' she exclaimed. 'You saved my life.'

The crowd continued to point and murmur: 'She killed a queen!' 'She killed a queen!' 'Slay her!' 'Burn her!' 'Tear her to pieces!'

'You shall do nothing of the sort!' said Iroedh. 'Let her alone, do you hear?'

Vardh said shakily: 'I know it was wrong, Iroedh darling, but I still love you better than anyone, and I couldn't stand by while she killed you. *Weu!* Now I suppose I shall have to kill myself too.'

'Nonsense! I suppose I am now Queen of Elham.'

'Oh no!' said the general. 'You didn't slay Estir in fair fight!'

'But I'm of pure Elhamny blood even if the duel wasn't fought according to regulations …. What is it?'

The worker who had driven up in the chariot had been trying to attract Iroedh's attention. This newcomer now said:

'Queen Iroedh, the Arsuuni are approaching! They surrounded the remains of the scouting force and slew them all so that only I escaped!'

'Good Gwyyr!' Iroedh looked around; a swarm of workers was pouring in through the main gate from the fields. She told the general:

'We'll argue the future of Elham later; you'd better get ready for battle.'

While hundreds of workers ran madly about under the general's orders, Iroedh buckled on the armor she had been given at Ledhwid, walked down to the gate, and climbed one of the gate towers. She could not see Tregaros and his squad, and wondered if she should try to join him. On the other hand, he might already have left to seek Antis' army, and her desertion of the Community at this point would ruin her standing with them and lower their morale.

A noise caused her to look in the other direction, and there was the helicopter from the *Paris*, hovering over the spot where the road to the southeast ran through the vremoel orchard. That would be Bloch with his picturemaking machine. But what was that dust rising from the orchard? Sun flashed on brass, and Iroedh realized that Bloch, in his subtle way, was trying to help her by hovering squarely over the advancing Arsuuni.

Iroedh went back to the main portal and picked up the steel machete. She told the general about the approach of the enemy, and asked: 'Where can I sharpen this? It's not—'

'But you cannot fight! You're a queen!'

'A minute ago you were saying I couldn't be queen of Elham!'

'You're still a functional female, and the workers insist that the decencies be preserved. Go to the royal dome and await the outcome of the battle.'

'Ridiculous!' Iroedh marched off to hunt a grindstone for herself. She found one and stood in line while the workers ahead of her sharpened their spearheads.

An uproar from outside the wall drew her attention. Armored workers were running back and forth along the wall, and beyond them Iroedh could see the tops of dozens of scaling ladders placed against the wall by the Arsuuni, who were wasting no time in beginning their assault. Next among the little figures on the wall appeared the much bigger forms of Arsuuny soldiers, climbing up their ladders and trying to force their way over the wall. The workers who had been sharpening their weapons ran to take their places in the defense.

The Arsuuni had carried to its next logical step the sex-caste system imposed upon the Avtini by Queen Danoakor. In fact, before that the Arsuuni had been another race of the same species, little different from the Avtini. They had, however, found it possible through dietary control to produce not only a caste of neuter-female workers, but also a subcaste of neuter-female soldiers afflicted with a form of acromegalic giantism. Over a head taller than a normal worker, they impressed the Avtini, with their great knobby hands and huge jaws, as hideous monsters. In the Arsuuny hierarchy the queen was at the top; below her were the soldiers (who really ran the Community) and below them the workers, and below *them* the large body of Avtiny slaves who did most of the actual labor.

After a hasty sharpening of her blade, Iroedh ran after the workers to a point on the wall that seemed to be under heavy pressure. As she arrived below the wall one of the defenders pitched backward, thrust through the face by an Arsuuny spear. The Avtin was dead when she struck the ground with a clang of brass. Iroedh ran up the nearest steps to the top of the wall and looked over the parapet.

The Arsuuni had forehandedly brought along great carts full of scaling ladders, drawn by tame vakhnags, and they had rushed sixteens of these ladders against the wall. The Avtini had pushed some of them over backwards. Several Arsuuni who had fallen with the ladders lay writhing on the ground, for because of their size they could not stand so much of a fall as an Avtin.

On the ground outside, a giant in gold-plated armor walked up and down giving orders; this would be General Omvem of Tvaarm. Overhead the helicopter still whistled.

Now would be the time for Antis to appear with his drones, to take the Arsuuni in the rear. But there was no sign of him; not even a telltale cloud of dust on the road from Khinam.

'This way! This way!' cried voices on Iroedh's right, and the Avtini hurried toward the scene of the latest attack. A swarm of scaling ladders had been reared against the wall in that thinly held region, and up came the giants, shouting, '*Künnef! Künnef!*'

Iroedh made for one ladder that did not seem to have anybody watching it and started to push it away from the wall; then instinctively jerked back as a huge spearhead darted past her face. Before she could attack the ladder again the head and shoulders of an Arsuun appeared over the wall.

The long-jawed giant shifted her grip on her spear and braced herself for another stab at Iroedh. Iroedh rushed in, knocked the spearhead aside with her shield, and tried to hit the Arsuun in the face with the edge of the shield. The Arsuun brought up her own shield and for a second the shields ground together as each fighter tried to out-maneuver the other. Sensing the immense strength of her foe, Iroedh felt as if she were assailing a colossal bronze statue.

Then she caught a glimpse of the face as the shields separated, and thrust for the eyes with her machete. She felt the point go through tissue and bone, then jerked the blade out as the head of the giant pulled backward. Iroedh hacked again and again at the hateful face; then all at once there was no Arsuun there, and a great crash as the armored body struck the ground.

'Come, Queen!' shouted a worker. 'Don't you hear the recall?'

Iroedh had been too busy with the Arsuuny soldier to heed the notes of the trumpet. Now she saw that everywhere the Avtini were leaping and tumbling down from the wall and running for the plaza in front of the main portal. The Arsuuni had already broken through the defense in one section and gained the wall, and the general was withdrawing her troops before they were cut up and destroyed piecemeal.

Iroedh ran down the steps with the rest, while behind her the Arsuuni swarmed over the wall with roars of 'Künnef!'

The general, seeing Iroedh approach, cried: 'I thought I told you not to fight! Don't you know that even queens have to obey me in warfare? Now get in the middle of the square. You can't accomplish anything with that overgrown fruit-knife, but we need you as a symbol.'

'Oh, can't I?' protested Iroedh, waving her bloody blade, but the general caught her by the shoulders and pushed her into place. She was forming the Avtini into a massive hollow square, with spears and shields in double array around the outside to make a hedge that even the Arsuuni might have trouble piercing. A stream of workers rushed out of the domes with furniture and utensils which they piled in a crude barricade around the square.

'We still outnumber them,' Iroedh heard the general say. Iroedh, however, knew that one Arsuun was worth two Avtini on a simple basis of size.

Iroedh looked over the ranks of the workers, between the helmeted heads. General Omvem of Tvaarm arrived in leisurely fashion and marshaled her soldiers for the final attack. It took the form of a wedge.

The deep Arsuuny trumpet groaned. The wedge thundered forward and struck the square with a deafening crash of clashing shields and snapping spears. Iroedh saw the point soldier of the wedge trip in climbing the barricade and fall, pierced by a dozen spears, and in her fall bowl over two Avtini. But those behind her pushed ahead, stabbing and trampling. The square gradually lost its shape and became a mere mass wrapped around the blunted point of the wedge. Those behind the front ranks tried to reach over the tangle of dead, wounded, and interlocked spear-shafts to get at their opponents.

The superior size of the Arsuuni told; beside Iroedh an Arsuuny spearpoint struck down the general. Iroedh herself was buffeted by the crowd this way and that; elbows jabbed her in the face and heels stamped on her toes. An Arsuun towered over her, swinging a broken spear-shaft as a club. Iroedh caught a blow on her shield and felt as if her arm had been broken.

Then the pressure eased and the noise became even louder. When Iroedh could see around her again, a swarm of armored drones was rushing down from the wall to form a phalanx advancing upon the Arsuuni from the rear. Before she could get her breath the drones struck the Arsuuni. Their front rank was armed entirely with machetes; these rushed in under the spears and slashed at the giants' legs where a hand's breadth of thigh showed between kilt and greave. Crash! Crash! Crash! Down went the Arsuuni like felled trees. Down went General Omvem, assailed by four drones at once.

The leaderless and surrounded Arsuuni milled around, trying to fight their way out, but the instant one separated from her fellows she was thrust through the legs from behind and fell. Crash! Crash!

And then there were no more giants on their feet: only a couple of hundred lying about the plaza, while the Avtini went around cutting the throats of those that still moved.

Iroedh was cutting one such throat when a pair of bloody hands hauled her to her feet. Antis hoisted her into the air, hugged the breath out of her, then gave her a stinging slap on the behind. From him it felt good.

'I told you not to get so far ahead!' he said. 'We ran our legs off trying to catch up with you, and as it was we nearly arrived too late. We had three pieces of good luck to thank Gwyyr for. First we came across another rogue drone band who joined us. Second when we got to the Lhanwaed Hills we found that old Umwys had been forging matselhi ever since we left him; he had nearly a hundred. I bought the lot, and so armed more of my people with them than I had dared hope. Lastly the Arsuuni kindly left their ladders against the walls, so we came right up and over them. How have you made out?'

Iroedh found that, counting the defeats before the main battle, less than half the workers of Elham survived. Rhodh, for instance, had died fighting furiously; so had Tydh and Iinoedh and many of her other acquaintances. Only two officers, the royal officer and the grounds officer, lived. While the drones' losses had been negligible, the Arsuuni had been wiped out to the last giantess.

Iroedh told Antis what had happened, adding: 'Now that Estir and the more conservative officers are gone, I hope they'll adopt our program for mating them with the drones.'

'They'd better! After being filled to the ears with talk on the glories of married life, every rogue is mad with impatience to seize a worker and start stoking her with steak. And speaking of which …'

Antis gave her a piercing look whose meaning she had come to know well. However, the helicopter landed, to the intense curiosity of the Avtini who had not yet seen it, and Bloch got out.

'Congratulations on your victory!' he said.

'No thanks to you,' said Antis sourly.

Iroedh said: 'You forgot this, Antis.' She swung her machete.

Bloch exclaimed: 'You mean you never had anything like that before we came? And you copied it from us?'

'Yes.'

'Oh, lord, now I'm in trouble! Didn't you tell me—'

'Yes, I fear I stretched the truth, but to save my people. We'll say nothing to the other Terrans and perhaps they will never know.'

Bloch shook his head. 'Let's hope they won't. I should have remembered what the swords of the Spanish conquistadores did to the poor Amerinds ... But you wouldn't know about that. May I take some pictures, and remove a couple of dead Arsuuni? They'll be invaluable as specimens.'

'Go right ahead,' said Iroedh, shedding her bloody accouterments. 'Oh, there's Vardh!'

Vardh was having a wounded arm tied up. The royal officer said to Iroedh: 'The others won't let Vardh live among them even if they adopt your scheme. Their horror of harming a queen is too great.'

Vardh looked up. 'I heard you. Since Iroedh now has Antis she doesn't need me any more, so I'll make things easy for all ...'

She picked up a spear, held it horizontally in front of her so that the point touched her chest, and started to run toward the portal.

'Stop her!' cried Iroedh.

Antis, after one puzzled look, sprang after Vardh, caught her by the crest, and wrenched the spear away from her.

'Little fool!' he growled. 'As if your Community hadn't lost enough of its people!'

Iroedh said: 'There's no need to take your life, Vardh dear. I have a better program for you.'

'What? To become a bulgy functional female like you and submit to the horrid embraces of some drooling drone? No thank you!'

'How would you like to be the new Oracle of Ledhwid?'

'Me, an Oracle?'

'Yes. As the old one died without appointing a successor, the post is practically open to the first comer. I think it would suit you.'

'I'll think it over,' said Vardh. 'Excuse my discourtesy, darling. I still love you, but everything's so confused.'

Tregaros said: 'Queen Iroedh, you should organize an immediate attack on Tvaarm. They'll have but a handful of soldiers and won't expect it, and their Avtiny slaves won't help them. A quick march and a night attack, eh? We can use their own ladders ...'

The fellow was probably right, thought Iroedh, but she had seen about all the bloodshed she could stand for one day. She did not want Antis mixed up in such a project, because with his foolhardy bravery he would probably get himself killed. She said to the royal officer:

'Do the surviving members of the Council accept my program now?'

'Queen, we're so bewildered we don't know what to say. Let me speak to the grounds officer.'

Presently the two officers came back to Iroedh. The royal officer said: 'Queen Iroedh, we accept you and agree to legalize your mixed-diet program if you promise not to take away any of our constitutional liberties. Does that suit you?'

'Certainly.'

The officer went off to organize burial squads, as there were far too many corpses for the soapworks to use. The surviving workers went about their task somberly, having, despite their spectacular victory, lost too many friends to cheer. While the dead were being disposed of Bloch said:

'Hey, Iroedh! Antis! I forgot to tell you that Subbarau has a position available for you.'

'What?' said Antis.

'He can't transport you to Terra, but he can appoint you representatives of the *Viagens Interplanetarias* for the planet Ormazd. We always try to obtain a reliable native as an intermediary. To begin, you would accompany us on our tour of the other continents to familiarize yourselves with their cultures and languages.'

'It sounds fascinating,' said Iroedh, 'but I must consult Antis.' When she got him aside she said: 'What do you think? I'm all for it.'

Antis looked dubious. 'We have a good prospect here as king and queen of a new united bisexual Community, don't you think? What do you want to go flying off to the ends of nowhere for?'

'And what's a king or queen under the new dispensation? They used to need a queen to lay eggs, but if all workers become functional females, what use is a queen? We should have no political power, especially as they've warned me against tampering with their constitution.'

'I don't know ...' said Antis.

Iroedh said gently: 'Are you afraid of the sky ship?'

'Me?' His expression changed at once. 'I should say not! So if we stayed here we should be mere ornaments, deferred to but not allowed to *do* anything?'

'Exactly. While if we accept the Terran offer—'

'We shall never have a dull moment. As I've said all along, our destiny lies with the Terrans. Let's tell Daktablak quickly, before he changes his mind.'

The royal officer was at Iroedh's elbow again. 'Tregaros wants to organize a joint expedition to Tvaarm, and if you have no objections we'll set forth tomorrow. We have agreed, however, that you and Antis must stay here; we can't have you exposing yourselves in combat again.'

'Suit yourselves,' said Iroedh. 'The sky folk have offered us a much bigger job than reigning over one Community.'

'What's this?'

Iroedh told the officer about the Terran offer. Antis added: 'She's quite right; after spending most of my life cooped up in the dronery, not even a continent is big enough for me.'

'Great Eunmar!' said the royal officer. 'This is a surprise. I hope we may continue to call you "Queen" as an honorary title.'

'Certainly. I'll even wear the regalia when I visit you, but you must have a set made for Antis too.'

'We will. We need things to appeal to our sentiments, to keep us loyal to each other and to the Community—'

'Sentiment!' cried Iroedh. 'That reminds me! I never did learn what happened to Elnora.'

'Who or what is Elnora?' asked the royal officer.

'A character in a book which Daktablak's mate gave me. If I don't take another thing from Elham I want that book. But I wonder what became of it after I was driven out.'

Vardh spoke up: 'I took it from your cell and hid it in my own, thinking you might return someday for it. You'll find it under my pallet.'

'Thank you, darling! I shall be right back.'

She dashed into the portal. Antis said: 'Wait, beautiful! I'm coming too!' and ran after her.

GLOSSARY OF ORMAZDIAN
NAMES AND WORDS

Aithles – the king in the *Lay of Idhios.*
Antis – a drone of Elham and a close friend of Iroedh.
Arsuuni – a race hostile to the Avtini (in their own language, *Arshuul*).
Arsuunyk – the language of the Arsuuni.
Avpandh – a worker of Elham.
Avtini – the most civilized race of Ormazd (sing. *Avtin*).
Avtinid – the land of the Avtini.
Avtiny – adj., pertaining to the Avtini.
Avtinyk – the language of the Avtini.

Baorthus – a drone of Elham.
borb – a unit of distance comparable to a mile.
branio – 'stop' in Avtinyk.

dairtel – a plant bearing a kind of nut.
Danoakor – an ancient reforming queen of the Avtini.
Denüp – a community of the Arsuuni.
Dhiis – a god of the ancient Avtiny religion.
dhug – a small spiny animal.
dhwyg – a many-legged creeping organism.
Dyos – a drone of Elham.

Eiudh – a worker of Elham.
Elham – the heroine's community of Avtini.
Elhamni – the inhabitants of Elham.
Enroys – a former Oracle of Ledhwid.
Estir – Crown Princess of Elham.
Eunmar – a goddess of the ancient Avtiny religion.

Garnedh – a priestess of Ledhwid.
Geyliad – a locale in the *Song of Geyliad.*
Gliid – an uninhabited valley near Thidhem.
Gogledh – a worker of Thidhem.
Gruvadh – a worker of Elham.

Gunes – a drone in the *Lay of Idhios*.
Gwyyr – the ancient Avtiny goddess of luck.

Hawardem – a northern Avtiny community.
Ho-olhed – the star Procyon.
hudig – a small edible hervibore.
huusg – a jellyfish-like marine organism (also a constellation).
Hwead – a gorge near Ledhwid.

Idhios – hero of the *Lay of Idhios*.
Igog – a fire-breathing monster in the *Tale of Mantes*.
Iinoedh – a worker of Elham.
Inimdhad – a place mentioned in the *Lay of Idhios*.
Intar – Queen of Elham.
Iroedh – a worker of Elham, and the heroine.
Ithodh – a worker of Yeym.

khal – a tree with edible seeds.
Khinad Point – a place near Elham.
Khinam – a ruined city on Khinad Point.
Khwiem – an Avtiny community.
künnef – the war cry of the Arsuuni.
Kutanas – a drone of Elham.
kwa – 'Hurrah!' in Avtinyk.

Ledhwid – site of a famous oracle.
leipag – a medium-sized edible herbivore.
Lhanwaed – a range of hills near Elham.
Lhuidh – a priestess of Ledhwid.

Maiur – Queen of Thidhem.
Mantes – hero of the *Tale of Mantes*.
matselh – Avtinyk for 'machete.'

neiriog – a small animal tamed as a pet.
Niond – Avtinyk for 'earth,' 'soil,' or 'world.'
noag – a large carnivore.

oedhurh – Avtinyk for 'love.'
Omvem – general of Tvaarm.
Omvyr – Queen of Tvaarm (in her own language, *Omförs*).

pandre-eg – a large wild herbivore related to the ueg.
Pligayr – Intar's predecessor as Queen of Elham.
pomuial – a flowering plant.
prutha – an exclamation of annoyance.

Rhodh – a worker of Elham.
Rhuar – a former queen of Elham.
rumdrekh – a system of self-defense.

Santius – a drone in the *Lay of Idhios*.
suroel – a plant whose fibers are used for textiles.
Sveik – Arsuunyk for 'earth.'

tarhail – a domesticated cereal grass.
telh – a flute.
Thidhem – a neighboring Avtiny community.
Tiwinos – a god of the ancient Avtiny religion.
Tregaros – a drone, an officer of Wythias.
Tvaarm – an Arsuuny community (in their own language, *Tvaar*).
Tydh – a worker of Elham.

ueg – a large bipedal domesticated draft animal.
uintakh – a game similar to tenpins.
umdhag – a small animal.
Umwys – a rogue drone, a smith.

vakhnag – a very large quadruped herbivore.
vakhwil – a tree whose bark is used for writing material.
valh – Avtinyk for 'knife.'
Vardh – a worker of Elham, a close friend of Iroedh.
Vinir – the queen in the *Lay of Idhios*.
vremoel – a fruit.

weu – an exclamation of sorrow.
Wisgad – a volcano near Gliid.
Wythias – leader of a band of rogue drones.

Yaedh – a priestess of Ledhwid.
Yeym – an Avtiny community destroyed by the Arsuuni.
Ystalverdh – a priestess of Ledhwid.
Ythidh – a worker of Elham.

THE TRITONIAN RING
AND OTHER PUSADIAN TALES

AUTHOR'S NOTE

Alert readers will note resemblances between some of the names in these stories and the names of persons and places in ancient history and mythology. Thus my 'Euskeria' is cognate both with Scheria, the land of the Phaeacians or kingdom of Alkinoös in the *Odyssey*, and with *Euskara*, the Basques' name for their anomalous language. The stories, however, have nothing to do with my serious opinions on such subjects as lost continents, human prehistory, and the origins of civilization, for which see Willy Ley's and my *Lands Beyond* and my various articles on these subjects.

Pronounce these names as you please. The letters *ö* and (pre-consonantal) *y* are meant for vowels like German *ö* and *ü* (or French *eu* and *u*), but may be rendered by the vowels of 'up' and 'it' respectively, rhyming *Söl* and *Ryn* with 'hull' and 'in.' The characters *â, ê,* and *ô* stand for long *ah, eh,* and *oh* sounds as in French. *Awoqqas* may be rhymed with 'caucus.' The *X* in *Ximenon* is meant for a *ks* sound as in 'box,' but you may simplify it to *z* or *s* if you prefer.

L. Sprague de Camp

THE TRITONIAN RING

I

The Gorgon God

When the gods of the West were gathered in their place of assembly, Drax, the Tritonian god of war, said in his ophidian hiss:

'Events will take a deadly turn for us in the next century unless we change this pattern.'

The assembled gods shuddered, and the vibration of their trembling ran through the universe. Entigta, the sea-god of Gorgonia (a kingdom so ancient that it had withered to mere myth when Imhotep built the first pyramid for King Zoser) spoke in his bubbly voice out of the midst of his tentacles:

'Can you not tell us the true nature of this danger?'

'No. The only further clue my science gives is that the trouble centers in the continent of Poseidonis, in the kingdom of Lorsk. There is something about its being caused by a member of the royal family of Lorsk. I believe my own folk are also involved, but I cannot be sure. Since King Ximenon got that accursed ring I can no longer get through to them.'

Entigta turned to Okma, the god of wisdom of Poseidonis, or Pusâd to use the more ancient form. 'That, colleague, would be in your department. Who are the royal family of Lorsk?'

Okma replied: 'There are King Zhabutir and his sons Kuros and Vakar, and the infant children of the former. I suspect Prince Vakar, whose spiritual obtuseness is such that I cannot speak directly to him.'

Entigta's tentacles writhed. 'If we cannot communicate with this mortal, how shall we deflect him from his intended path?'

'We might pray to *our* gods for guidance,' said the small bat-eared god of the Coranians, whereupon all the gods laughed, being hardened skeptics.

Drax hissed: 'There is another way. Set other mortals upon him.'

Okma said: 'I object! Vakar of Lorsk, despite his defect, has been a faithful votary of mine, burning many fat bullocks upon my altars. Besides it might be true that such patterns of event are laid down by an inflexible fate, not to be altered even by a god.'

'I have never subscribed to that servile philosophy,' said Drax, his forked tongue flicking. He turned his wedge-shaped head towards Entigta. 'Colleague, of all of us here, you command the most warlike worshippers. Send them to destroy the royal family of Lorsk and all of Lorsk if need be!'

'Wait!' said Okma. 'The other gods of Poseidonis —' (he looked around, noting Tandyla with all three of her eyes shut and Lyr scratching his barnacles) '— and I ought to be consulted before such devastation is loosed upon our own —'

The rest of the gods (or at least those not of Poseidonian provenance) shouted Okma down. Drax concluded:

'Waste no time, squid-headed one, for the peril is imminent!'

In Sederado, the capital of Ogugia in the Hesperides, Queen Porfia sat in her chambers with emeralds in her night-black hair and eyes as green as the emeralds, consulting with her minister Garal. The minister, a short stout bald man who deceptively appeared to radiate bluff good humor and sterling worth, rolled up a sheet of papyrus and said:

'Come, come, madam. You are not consulting your best interests in refusing to marry the king of Zhysk. Why should you boggle at the mere detail of his present three queens and fourteen concubines when —'

'Mere detail!' cried Queen Porfia, looking too young for a widow. 'While Vancho was no god, at least while he lived I had that fat slob to myself. I do not care to wed one-seventeenth of any man, however royal.'

'One-eighteenth,' corrected Garal. 'But —'

'Besides, who would run Ogugia whilst I languished in gilded durance in Amferé?'

'Perhaps you could spend most of your time here, where young Thiegos could comfort you.'

'And how long before King Shvo found out and slew us both? Moreover, despite his fair promises to respect our independence, he would soon send some grasping Zhyskan governor to squeeze you dry as bones.'

Garal gave a slight start, but said calmly: 'You must remarry some time. Even your supporters murmur over the lack of a man at the head of the state. They would take even Thiegos ...'

'I do not see it. The island flourishes, and Thiegos, while amusing as a lover, would be quite impossible as king.'

'My thought also. But since you must eventually have a consort, you could hardly ask for one better situated than Shvo of Zhysk. Or is there some other man ...?'

'Not unless you count ...'

'Whom?' Garal leaned forward, eyes bright with interest.

'Just a foolish idea. When I went to Amferé as a girl ten years ago for that wedding of Shvo's daughter, one young princeling took my fancy: Vakar of Lorsk. Though no great beauty or mighty athlete, there was something about him – an irreverent wit, a soaring fancy, a keenness of insight, unlike most of his lumpish compatriots – Oh, well, he will no doubt have collected a dozen women by now and have forgotten the awkward Porfia. Now about this rise in harbor dues …'

Zeluud, king of the Gorgon Isles, slept after his midday meal, lying on his back upon his ivory-legged couch. With each inhalation his paunch rose, and with each exhalation the paunch sank while the silken handkerchief that covered his face rose in its turn with the force of the king's breath, which issued from his hidden features with a mighty snore. A Negro dwarf, kidnapped years ago from Tartaros by Zeluud's corsairs, tiptoed about the chamber with a flyswatter of reed and shredded palm-frond lest any noxious insect disturb the king's rest. And the king of ancient Gorgonia dreamed.

King Zeluud dreamed that he stood before the wet black basalt throne of Entigta, the squid-headed sea-god of the Gorgons. The king knew from Entigta's dark coloration that the god was in no affable mood, and from the rapidity with which the color-patterns chased each other over Entigta's mottled hide Zeluud further inferred that the god was in a state of ungodly agitation.

Entigta leaned forward on his sable throne, his slimy hands gripping the arm-rests carven in the likeness of sea-dragons, and fixed King Zeluud with his cold wet eyes. His voice bubbled out of the parrot-beak in the midst of the octet of tentacles that served Entigta for a face, like the gaseous products of decay bubbling up through the slime of one of the somber swamps of Blackland. Entigta said:

'King, do you obey me?'

'As always, God,' said Zeluud, beginning to shake in his sandals, for he was sure that Entigta was about to impose some outrageous demand upon him.

'Well, trouble comes upon us from the North, and it is your place to deal with it. Trouble not merely for the Gorgades, but also for the entire race of the gods.'

'What trouble, Lord?'

'The exact nature thereof we know not. I can but tell you it centers in the royal family of Lorsk in Poseidonis.'

The king replied: 'And what, God, shall I do? Lorsk lies far from here, with its capital well inland, so that it is not vulnerable to a sudden raid from my corsairs.'

Entigta's tentacles writhed impatiently. 'You shall follow two courses. First you shall send my priest Qasigan to deal with these princes in person. He is well qualified, being hardy and discreet, widely travelled, and devoted to my interests. Moreover he has two able non-human helpers.'

'And the other course?'

'You shall prepare to conquer Poseidonis.'

Zeluud, aghast, took a step back. 'God! The Gorgades are but three small islands, whereas Poseidonis is a great land whose people outnumber ours fifty to one and are famed for their athletic prowess. Moreover bronze is so common there that they even use it for arrowheads. How in the seven hells do you expect ...'

Zeluud fell silent as Entigta turned an ominous black.

'Is your faith then so fragile?' gurgled the squid-god. 'By whose help have you long raided with impunity the coasts of Poseidonis and the mainland, and the rich commerce of the Hesperides?'

'Well then – what am I to do?'

'Seize Lorsk and the rest will fall, for Lorsk is the strongest of the Pusadian states, among whom there is no unity but only mutual hatred and suspicion. Your warriors are the world's mightiest, and even if they were not, my priests have the world's deadliest weapon: their captive medusas. With your warlike people and the mineral wealth of Lorsk you can conquer the world! And I,' murmured Entigta, 'shall be sea-god not merely of the Gorgades ...'

'Still —' began Zeluud doubtfully, but Entigta said:

'There is another point of attack against Lorsk. King Zhabutir has twin sons, Vakar and Kuros. Vakar, being the younger by a quarter-hour, is heir according to their old system of ultimogeniture. Now Kuros, who mortally hates his brother, might serve your interest in return for a promise of the throne, even as a tributary of yours. And once in control you can slay all three of them.'

'How can I deal with this Kuros? He is too far for messengers, and the Pusadian sea-god would not let you communicate with one of his votaries.'

'I can handle Lyr. There is a Gorgonian fisherman on the west coast of Poseidonis, in the Bay of Kort. In accord with the pact between Lyr and myself, I visit this fisherman in dreams as if he were back in Gorgonia. You can therefore speak to Kuros through this man.'

'Mightiest of gods though you be, not even gods know all, or you would know more of the doom overhanging you. What if we fail?'

'Then the reign of the gods is ended, unless Poseidonis be sunk beneath the sea.'

'What?'

'Know you not the continent settles, the water round its shores having risen three feet in the last century? We can speed this process so that in a few centuries nought would show above the waves save the tallest peaks.' The god's slit-pupilled eyes stared into space. 'The outlines of land and water would be altered from the swamps of Blackland to the snows of Thulê. Nor would this be all. Without the copper of Poseidonis, men might even forget the metal-working art and return to stone. But even that is preferrable to the other doom, for without the gods to guide you, how could you poor weak mortals survive? Return to the waking world, then, and set about your allotted tasks.'

Entigta dissolved into a swirl of slime. The king awoke, threw the handkerchief off his sweating swarthy face, and sat up on his gold-knobbed couch. He shouted:

'Khashel! Go to the temple of Entigta and tell the priest Qasigan to come to me at once!'

II

The Sinking Land

On an early spring evening months later, thirteen hundred miles north of the Gorgades, on the continent of Poseidonis, in the kingdom of Lorsk, in the capital city of Mneset, the king of Lorsk held council. A cold wind roared through the streets of Mneset, whipping tatters of scud across the pocked face of the moon and rattling the shutters of the houses. Inside the castle of King Zhabutir, the wind swayed the wall-hangings and made cressets flare and lamps flutter. Outside in the castle courtyard the pigs huddled together to keep warm.

In the king's council room the light of the central hearth-fire flickered upon the walls of massive cyclopean stonework and the ceiling of rough-hewn oaken beams. Four men, wrapped in cloaks against the drafts, sat around the council-table listening to a fifth: Söl the spy, a thickset commonplace-looking fellow with quick-shifting eyes.

As these eyes flickered across the table they first passed over, on the left, Ryn the magician, peering vaguely through watery eyes over a stained beard like an elderly and absent-minded billygoat. A hunched back added to the grotesqueness of his appearance. Next sat the king's elder son Kuros, square-jawed and broad-shouldered, nibbling on a wedge of cheese. Then came King Zhabutir himself, in the chair of pretence at the head of the table, looking with his high-bridged nose and flowing white beard like the serene embodiment of justice and wisdom, though his nickname of 'the Indecisive' belied his looks. His golden crown glowed redly in the firelight, and little gleams from his uncut stones, polished by the black craftsmen of Tartaros, chased each other about the walls when he moved his head. A great shaggy wolfhound lay across his feet.

On the king's left sat his younger son Vakar, the twin (but not the identical twin) brother of Kuros, looking a bit vacuous (for age and experience had not yet stamped his features with character) and a bit foppish. The jewels on his fingers shone as he nervously cracked his knuckle-joints. He had a narrow hatchet-face which swept back from a long forward-jutting nose that had been straight until a fall from a horse had put a slight dog-leg in it. Instead of the normal Pusadian kilt he wore the checkered trews of the barbarians, and (another fad) copied the barbarian custom of shaving all the face but the upper lip. He was small for a Lorskan, a mere five-ten, with the swarthy skin and thick black hair of most Pusadians. Deepset dark eyes looked out of his narrow face from under heavy brow-ridges and thick black brows into those of Söl, who said:

'I couldn't get to the Gorgades myself, for their system of public messes serves to check all adult men, and they'd soon see through any disguise. Since the land lives by robbery, the ships of other nations have no peaceful occasion to touch there. I did however spend a month in Kernê and there learned that the Gorgons are preparing a great expedition somewhither.'

Kuros said: 'Pff. The Gorgons' ferocity has been exaggerated by distance and the envy of their neighbors. If we knew them at first hand we should find their intentions as peaceful as anybody's.'

Prince Vakar shifted his gaze from the smoking wood-fire to the pocked face of the spy. His tight-drawn lips betrayed his inner tension as he spoke:

'Certainly their intentions are peaceful, like those of the lion for the lamb. The lion wishes only to be allowed to devour the lamb in peace. But, Master Söl, if the Gorgons have no peaceful contacts with other nations, how could such news reach Kernê?'

'The Gorgons' isolation isn't so perfect as they pretend. They carry on a small secret trade with certain merchants in Kernê for things they can neither make, grow, nor steal. Though the Kerneans hang or head any man they catch in this traffic, such are the profits that there's always someone to take the chance. A Kernean would brave the seven hells for a profit.'

Ryn the wizard blew his nose on his robe and spoke: 'Was there any indication of the Gorgons' direction?'

The wind blew a gout of smoke into Söl's face as if trying to stop him from replying. When the spy got over coughing and wiping his eyes he answered:

'Nothing definite, but the shadow of the echo of a whisper that said "Lorsk".'

'No more?'

'No more, sir. I had it from a harlot of the town who said she'd learned it from a sailor who worked for a trader who'd heard … and so on.'

Kuros swallowed the last of his cheese, dusted the crumbs off his fingers, and said: 'That's all, Söl.'

Vakar wished to hear more, but before he could protest, Söl had glided out and Kuros said:

'Very interesting, but let's not work ourselves into a sweat over the shadow of an echo of a whisper —'

'Is that so?' said Vakar sharply. 'With due respect, my brother wishes us to take the attitude of the man in the story who went to sleep on the skerry thinking he had a spell that would hold back the tides. You remember:

'Shoreward they shouldered   with crests ever-curling,
The waxing waves   washed higher and higher —'

'For Lyr's sake don't start one of those!' said Kuros.

Vakar shot a dagger-glance at his brother and continued: 'Where there's shadow there's more often than not a substance to cast it. And the words of so reliable a spy as Master Sōl should not lightly be thrown aside. The Gorgons —'

'You have Gorgons on the brain,' said Kuros. 'Suppose they did sail against us? They must pass Tartaros and Dzen, sail west through the Hesperides, land upon the coast of Zhysk, and march through that land to come to grips with us. We should have ample warning, and one Lorksan's worth three Gorgons —'

'As I was saying when the yapping of a mongrel interrupted me,' said Vakar. 'The Gorgons don't even fight fair. I've been reading —'

'As if any real man ever learned anything from marks on papyrus,' put in Kuros.

'Those who can't read can't judge —'

King Zhabutir said: 'Boys! Boys! I forbid this dreadful quarreling. Go on, Vakar.'

'You know how we fight: in loose groups, each led by a lord or champion followed by his kinsmen and liegemen and friends. We usually start out with challenges to single combat from our champions to the foe's, and sometimes the whole day is occupied with such duels. Moreover our men go equipped as they like: with swords, spears, axes, halberds, berdiches, war-clubs, and so on.'

'What other way of fighting is there?' said Kuros.

'The Gorgons equip all their men alike, with helmets, shields, and weapons of the same pattern. They align their men in a solid mass, every man having a fixed place despite rank or kinship. They waste no time in challenges, but at a signal all move upon the foe, every man keeping his place in the whole. Such a mass goes through an army like ours like a plow through sand.'

'Fairy-tales,' said Kuros. 'No true warriors would submit to be so forced into a single rigid mold ...'

As usual the argument went round and round, with Vakar (whose disposition it was to take a gloomy view of things) arguing against Kuros while the other two remained mute. Kuros began to press the king:

'You agree, don't you, Father?'

Zhabutir the Indecisive smiled weakly. 'I know not ... I cannot decide ... What thinks Master Ryn?'

'Sir?' said the magician. 'Before sending my opinions forth across the chasm of surmise, I prefer to wait until they're provided with a more solid bridge of fact. With your permission I'll call upon witch Gra for counsel.'

'That old puzzel!' cried Kuros. 'We should have hanged her ...'

Ryn began his preparations. From his bag he produced a small bronze tripod which he unfolded and set over the guttering fire. The fire threw a streamer of smoke at him as if to keep him off, but at the mutter of a cantrip it drew in upon itself. At the first syllable the wolfhound jumped up, gave a faint howl, and trotted out with its tail between its legs, its claws clicking on the stone.

Ryn poked the fire and added sticks until it blazed up again. With a piece of charcoal he drew a circle around the hearth and added lines and glyphs whose meaning Vakar did not know. Ryn rose to his feet and prowled around the room extinguishing the wobbling flames in the little oil-lamps. His hunched shadow reminded Vakar of that of a great scuttling spider – for all that Vakar esteemed the man had tutored him as a boy. Ryn then went back to the hearth and into the miniature cauldron at the apex of the tripod he sprinkled powders whose smell made the others cough.

He resumed his stool facing the fire and spoke in a language so ancient that even the scholarly Vakar (who could read over a thousand pictographs) could not understand a word, all the while moving his hands in stiffly geo-metrical gestures.

Vakar told himself that it was mere illusion that the room became even darker. A plume of smoke arose from the cauldron, and although the wind still sent drafts whistling through the chamber, the air within the circle seemed quite still. For instead of diffusing and dispersing as it rose, the col-umn of smoke held together and twined itself snakelike into knots at the top of the column. Vakar (who would have nourished magical ambitions himself but for his peculiar disability) held his breath, his heart pounding.

The smoke thickened and solidified and became a simulacrum of a tall heavy woman clad in a wolf-skin tied over one shoulder and belted around her thick waist with a thong. She was seated, half-turned so that she seemed to be looking past the four men without seeing them. In one hand she clutched a bone from which she was gnawing the meat. Vakar realized that it was not the woman herself, for the substance of which she was made was still smoky-gray in the semi-darkness and he could see the tripod and the fire beneath it through her massive legs and feet.

'Gra!' called Ryn.

The woman stopped gnawing and looked at the men. She tossed the bone aside, and as it left her hand it vanished. She wiped her fingers on the wolf-hide and scratched under her exposed breast. Her voice came in a far-off whisper:

'What wish the lords of Lorsk with me?'

Ryn said: 'Word has come of threatening movements by the Gorgons. We are divided as to what to do. Advise us.'

The witch stared at the ground in front of her so long that Kuros squirmed and muttered until Ryn hissed him to silence. At last Gra spoke:

'Send Prince Vakar to seek the thing the gods most fear.'

'Is that all?'

'That is all.'

Ryn spoke again in his archaic speech, and the phantom of the witch turned to mere smoke which wafted about, making the spectators sneeze. Ryan took a burning stick from the fire and relighted the lamps.

Vakar viewed Gra's message with mixed feelings. If the very gods feared the thing that she had spoken of, what business had a mere mortal pursuing it? On the other hand he had never been to the mainland and had long wished to travel. While Lorsk was a fine rich land, the real centers of culture and wisdom lay eastward: Sederado with its philosophers, Torrutseish with its wizards, and who knew what other ancient cities?

Kuros said sourly: 'If we were fools enough to believe that harridan —'

Vakar interrupted: 'Brother, since you always seem so eager to discredit warnings against the Gorgons, could you have a motive other than simple skepticism?'

'What do you mean, sir?'

'Such as – let's say a little present from King Zeluud?'

Kuros jumped up, reaching for his knife. 'Are you calling me traitor?' he yelled. 'I'll carve the word on your liver ...'

Ryn the magician reached up to seize Kuros' arms while King Zhabutir laid a hand on Vakar's shoulder as the latter, too, started to rise. When they had pacified the furious Kuros he sat down, snarling:

'All that effeminate bastard does is to stir up trouble and enmity amongst us. He hates me because he knows if the gods hadn't fumbled, I should be heir and not he. If we followed the sensible mainland custom of primogeniture ...'

Before Vakar could think of a crushing reply, Ryn spoke: 'My lords, let's sink our present differences until the matter of the foreign threat be resolved. Whatever you think of Gra or Söl, I've had confirmation of their tale.'

'What?' said the king.

'Last night I dreamt I stood before the gods of Poseidonis: Lyr and Tandyla and Okma and the rest. As usual I asked if they had advice for Lorsk.'

'What did they say?' asked Kuros.

'Nothing; but it was the manner of their saying it. They turned away their eyes and faces as if ashamed of their silence. And I recalled where I'd seen that expression. Many decades ago, when I was a young fellow studying magic in mighty Torrutseish —'

'Gods, he's off on another of those!' muttered Kuros.

'— and one of my friends, an Ogugian youth named Joathio, got excited at a bullfight and made indiscreet remarks about the city prefect. Next day (though the remarks had been nothing dreadful) he disappeared. I asked after him at the headquarters of the municipal troop, and those tough soldiers turned away from me with that same expression. Later I found Joathio's head on a spike over the main gate. Not a pretty sight for one still young and soft of soul, heh-heh.

'I therefore infer something's impending in the world of the gods, unfavorable to us, against which our own gods are for some reason forbidden to warn us. In view of Söl's news it could well be a Gorgonian invasion. Therefore let's send Prince Vakar on his quest. If he fails —'

'Which he will,' put in Kuros.

'— no harm will be done, whereas if he succeeds he may save us from an unknown doom.'

King Zhabutir said: 'But the gods – how can we oppose them?'

Vakar said: 'It were cowardly to give up before the first has even begun, merely because we might face odds. If the gods fear something they can't be all-powerful.'

'Atheist!' sneered Kuros. 'When do you go? While I can't understand sending Vakar Zhu on a supernatural quest, Gra did name you and not me.'

'Tomorrow.'

'As soon as that? You'll miss the games of the vernal equinox, but that'll be small loss as you've never won a prize.'

'Anything to get away from your brags and boasts,' said Vakar.

Kuros had always boasted his superiority in sport: He could out-run, out-jump, and out-wrestle his brother. He had also annoyed Vakar by stressing the sobriquet 'Zhu' which meant, not exactly 'fool' or 'deaf one,' but 'one who lacks supernatural perceptions.' For Vakar had the unenviable distinction of completely lacking normal powers of telepathy, prescience, or spirit communication. Not even did the gods visit him in dreams.

'When you return,' said Kuros, 'you'll have thought up such a fine assortment of lies about your adventures that I, who must depend upon my known accomplishments, shall be quite outclassed.'

'Am I a dog, that you call me a liar?' began Vakar with heat, but his father interrupted.

'Now, boys,' said King Zhabutir in his vague way, then to Ryn: 'Are you sure she meant Vakar? It does seem a challenge to the gods to send the heir to the throne on a wild chase for who-knows-what.'

Ryn said: 'There's no doubt. Say your farewells and sharpen your bronze tonight, Prince.'

'Whither am I bound?' asked Vakar. 'Your lady consultant was as vague in her directions as my brother is about the paternity of his wives' children.'

'You —' began Kuros, but Ryn interrupted the outburst:

'I know of nothing in Poseidonis answering Gra's description. I advise you to go to lordly Torrutseish, where the greatest wizards of the world make their dwelling.'

'Do you know any of these wizards?' inquired Vakar.

'I haven't been there for decades, but I recall that Sarrar and Nichok and Vrilya and Kurtevan were preëminent.'

'How many shall I take with me? A troop of soldiery and – let's say – a mere dozen or so of servants?'

A faint smile played about the corners of Ryn's old mouth. 'You shall take one – possibly two persons with you. One body-servant, let's say, and one interpreter —'

'I have the interpreter for him,' chuckled Kuros. 'A fellow named Sret with the most marvelous gift of tongues —'

'What?' cried Vakar in honest amazement. 'No bodyguard? No women? By Tandyla's third eye!'

'Not one. For your kind of search you'll go farther and faster without a private army.'

'Who'll know my rank?'

'Nobody, unless you tell them, and usually you'd better not. Princes have been known to fetch fine ransoms.'

Kuros threw back his head and laughed loudly while the king looked ineffectually anxious. Vakar glared from one to the other, his knuckles itching for a good smash into his brother's fine teeth. Then he pulled himself together and smiled wryly, saying:

'If the hero Vrir in the epic can run all over the world alone, I can do likewise. I go to procure a beggar's rags, suitably verminous. Think kindly of me when I'm gone.'

'I always think kindly of you when you're gone,' said Kuros. 'Only you're not gone enough.'

'It's time we were in bed,' said King Zhabutir, rising.

The others bid their respects to the king and departed, Vakar towards his chambers where his mistress Bili awaited him. He dreaded telling her of his plan, for he disliked her scenes. He would not be altogether displeased to be leaving her, for not only was she ten years his senior and fast fattening, but also her late husband had with good reason referred to her as 'Bili the Birdbrained.' Moreover he would have to take a wife or two one of these days when matches with the daughters of rich and powerful Pusadian lords could be organized, and such matters were more easily arranged without the complication of a concubine already at home.

He shouted: 'Get out!' and kicked at one of the royal goats who had somehow wandered into the castle.

'Prince Vakar!' said a low voice from the shadows.

Vakar whirled, clapping a hand to his hip where his sword-hilt would have been had he been armed. It was Söl the spy.

'Well?' said Vakar.

'I – I couldn't speak out in council meeting, but I must tell you that …'

'That what?'

'You guarantee my safety?'

'You shall be safe though you tell me I'm the son of a sow and a sea-demon.'

'Your brother is in league with the Gorgons —'

'Are you mad?'

'By no means. There's proof. Go ask – *urk!*'

Söl jerked as if he had been stung. The man half-turned and Vakar saw something sticking in his back. Söl gasped:

'They – he – I die! Go tell ...'

He folded up upon the stone flooring, joint by joint. Before Vakar could have counted ten the spy was huddled motionless at his feet.

Vakar stooped and pulled the dagger from Söl's back. A quick examination showed the spy to be dead, and also that the dagger had been thrown so that the point had stuck in the muscle covering the man's right shoulder-blade: a mere flesh-wound. Holding the dagger, Vakar moved quickly down the corridor in the direction from which the weapon had come, his moccasins making no sound. He neither saw nor heard anyone and presently turned back, cursing himself for not having run after the assassin the instant Söl fell.

He returned to the victim whose eyes now stared sightlessly up, reflecting tiny highlights from the nearest lamp. Vakar held the dagger close to the lamp and saw that the bronzen blade was overlain with a coating of some black gummy substance, covering the pointward half of the blade. This stuff was in turn coated by a faint film of blood for a half-inch from the point.

Vakar, his blood freezing, pondered his predicament. Could Kuros be playing so deadly a double game? Somebody had shut Söl's mouth just as he had been about to reveal matters of moment. If Söl were right, what could Vakar do? Accuse Kuros publicly? His woolly-headed father would scoff and his brother would ask whether he, Vakar, hadn't murdered Söl and then invented this wild tale to cover the fact. Whatever the proof Söl had spoken of, Vakar had no access to it now.

At last Vakar wiped the dagger-point – lightly, so as not to remove the substance under the blood – on the edge of Söl's kilt and tiptoed away. As he entered his outer chamber he heard Bili's voice:

'Is that you, my lord and love?'

'Aye. Don't get up.'

He picked up the lighted lamp from the table and held it close to the row of daggers and axes and swords that hung upon the wall. He took down one of the daggers and tried the murder-weapon in the sheath. He had to go through most of the collection to find a sheath that fitted.

'What are you doing?' came the voice of Bili, whose curiosity must have been aroused by the snick of blades in their sheaths.

'Nothing. I shall be along presently.'

'Well, come to bed! I'm tired of waiting.'

Vakar sighed, wondering how often he had heard that. Much as he esteemed Bili's lectual accomplishments, he sometimes wished she would occasionally think of something else. He replaced the dagger-sheaths on their racks, hid in a chest the dagger in whose sheath he had placed the murder weapon, and went into the bedchamber.

III

The Sirenian Sea

Before dawn Vakar was awakened by a knock on his door and a voice: 'Prince Vakar! There's been a murder!'

It was the captain of the castle guard. His noise partly awakened Bili, who stirred and reached out. Vakar eluded her embrace, tumbled out of bed, and pulled on some clothes.

They were all standing around the body of Söl, even that fisherman whom Kuros (normally more rank-conscious than Vakar) claimed as a personal friend to be entertained at the castle. King Zhabutir said:

'Terrible! Do – do you know anything about this, Vakar?'

'Not a thing,' said Vakar, and looked hard at Kuros. 'You, brother?'

'Nor I,' said Kuros blandly.

Vakar stared into his brother's eyes as if in hope of seeing through them into the brain behind, but could make nothing of the man's expression. He turned away, saying:

'Perhaps Ryn can make something of this. I have to collect my gear for departure.'

He went back to his chambers, but instead of packing at once he took down the murder-knife from the wall-rack, hid it in his shirt, and went down into the courtyard. The East was pale with the coming dawn and the wind whipped Vakar's cloak. A dozen swine lay in a mud-wallow, huddled for warmth, chins resting on each other's bristly bodies. An old boar grunted and showed his tusks. Vakar kicked him out of the way and grabbed a half-grown shoat, which burst into frantic struggles and squeals.

With a quick look around Vakar drew the murder-dagger from his shirt. He clamped his teeth upon the sheath, drew the blade, and pricked the pig's rump with the point to a depth of a quarter-inch. Then he released the animal, which raced across the court. Half-way across it began to slow down. Before it reached the far side its legs gave way under it, and it lay twitching for a few seconds before it died.

Vakar stared thoughtfully at the dagger as he sheathed it and hid it in his shirt. If the venom worked so fast upon a beast notoriously resistant to poison, there was no doubt of what it would do to a man. He started to return to his chambers, then paused as another thought struck him. It would not do to have this poisoned porker fed to the castle's dogs, or even more so to have it unknowingly fried up for the royal breakfast. Vakar walked over to the pig, picked it up, and carried it to the outer gate. There the usual pair of guards leaned on their zaghnals or dagger-halberds: pole-arms with knife-like triangular bronze blades.

'Which of you is junior?' he said. When that question had been answered he handed the shoat to the startled young man, saying:

'Get a shovel from the tool-house and take this pig outside the city and bury it: deeply, so no dog or hyena shall dig it up. And don't take it home for your wife to cook unless you wish a sudden death.'

At that instant Drozo, King Zhabutir's treasurer, appeared at the gate on his way to work. Vakar went with him to pick up a supply of trade-metal. Drozo gave him gold rings and silver torcs and copper slugs shaped like little ax-heads, then handed him a semicircular piece of bronze, saying:

'If you get to Kernê and are pressed for funds, go to Senator Amastan with this. It's half a broken medallion whereof he has the other half, and will therefore identify you.'

Vakar went back to his room. Bili called from the bed-chamber:

'Aren't you coming back to bed, Vakar? It's early —'

'No,' said Vakar shortly, and began rummaging through his possessions.

He took down one dagger for which he had rigged a harness of two narrow strips so that the sheath was positioned in front of his chest. He switched this harness to the sheath that now housed the poisoned dagger, took off his fine linen shirt, strapped the harness around his torso, and donned the shirt again.

Then he began collecting garments and weapons. He assembled his winged helmet of solid gold with the lining of purple cloth; his jazerine cuirass of gold-washed bronzen scales; his cloak of the finest white wool with a collar of sable. He looked over his collection of bronze swords: slender rapiers, heavy cut-and-thrust longswords, short leaf-shaped barbarian broadswords, and a double-curved sapara from far Thamuzeira, where screaming men and women were flayed on the altars of Miluk. He picked the best rapier, the one with the gold-inlaid blade, the hilt of sharkskin and silver with a ruby pommel, and the scabbard of embossed leather with a golden chape at the end …

At this point it occurred to Vakar that while he would no doubt make a glittering spectacle in all this gaudery, it would be useless to pretend that he was but a simple traveller of no consequence. In fact he would need a bodyguard to keep the first robber lord who saw him from swooping down with his troop to seize this finery.

One by one he returned the pieces to their chests and pegs and assembled a quite different outfit. As the rapier would be too light to be effective against armor he chose a plain but serviceable longsword; a plain bronze helm with a lining of sponge; a simple jack of stiff-tanned cowhide with bronze reinforcings; and his stout bronze buckler with the repoussé pattern of lunes: work of the black Tartarean smiths. Nobody in Lorsk could duplicate it.

He was pulling on a pair of piebald boots of shaggy winter horse-hide when Fual, his personal slave, came in. Fual was an Aremorian of Kerys who had been seized by Foworian slavers and sold in Gadaira. He was a slender man, more so even than Vakar, with the light skin of the more northerly peoples and a touch of red in his hair that suggested the blood of the barbarous Galatha. He looked at Vakar from large melancholy eyes and clucked.

'… and why didn't you call me, sir? It isn't proper for one of your rank to work for himself.

'Like Lord Naz in the poem,' grinned Vakar:

'Slavishly swinking,   weary and worn …

'If it makes you unhappy you may complete the job.'

They were stuffing extra clothing into a goatskin bag when Bili, scantily wrapped in a deerskin blanket, appeared in the doorway, looking at Vakar from brown bovine eyes. She said:

'My lord, as this will be the last time —'

'Don't bother me now!' said Vakar.

He finished packing and told Fual: 'Get your gear too.'

'Are you taking *me*, sir?'

'And why not? Get along with you. But remember: You shall steal nothing except on my direct order!'

Fual, who had been a professional thief before his enslavement, departed looking thoughtful. It now occurred to Vakar that once they touched the mainland Fual could easily run away. He must try to learn more of what went on the mercurial Aremorian's mind; Fual's attitude towards him might make the difference between life and death.

A snuffling from the bedroom attracted Vakar's attention. Bili huddled sobbing under the blankets.

'Now, now,' he said, patting her awkwardly. 'You'll find another lover.'

'But I don't wish —'

'You'd better, because there's no knowing when I shall return.'

'At least you might …' She rolled over, throwing off her blankets, and slid her plump hands up his arms.

'Oh, well,' sighed Prince Vakar.

They paused as they topped the pass to look out over the irrigated plain on which stood sunny Amferé. The spires of the city shone distantly in the afternoon sun on the edge of the blue Sirenian Sea. The capital of Zhysk was laid out as a miniature of mighty Torrutseish, with the same circular outer wall, the same sea-canal running diametrically through it, and the same circular harbor of concentric rings of land and water at the center.

Vakar twisted on his saddle-pad to look back at his convoy of two chariots, one carrying Fual and the interpreter Sret, the other the baggage. They were all splashed with mud from fording streams swollen by the melting of the snow on the higher peaks. Vakar rode horseback instead of in a chariot because, in a day when equitation was a daring novelty, it was also one of the few physical activities wherein he excelled. This was not entirely to his own credit, but was due in some measure to the fact that the average Pusadian, standing six to six-and-a-half feet, was too heavy for the small horses of the age. Though Vakar was small for a Lorskan, his boots cleared the ground by a scant two feet.

'Shall we be there by sundown?' he said to the nearest charioteer, who replied:

'Whatever your highness pleases.'

Vakar started down the slope, slowly, for without stirrups not even an accomplished rider can gallop downhill without the risk of being tossed over his mount's head. Behind him the bronze tires of the vehicles ground through the gravel and squished in the mud. Vakar smiled wryly at the reply, reflecting that if he asked them if the tide would obey him they would no doubt say the same thing.

They drew up to the walls of Amferé at sunset, to wait in line behind an ox-cart piled with farm produce for the last-minute rush before the gates were closed. The people were lighter in coloring than those of Lorsk, lending support to the legend that a party of Atlanteans had settled Zhysk some centuries back.

When Vakar identified himself, showing his seal-ring, the guard waved him through, for there was peace at the moment between Zhysk and Lorsk. Vakar rode for the citadel at the center of the city, meaning to sponge on the King of Zhysk. The citadel comprised an island surrounded by a broad ring of water. The palace and other public buildings stood on the island, and the outer boundary of the ring formed the harbor, instead of three concentric rings as in Torrutseish.

When Vakar arrived at the bridge across the oversized moat (a bridge that had been the wonder of all Poseidonis when built, as the continent had never seen a bridge longer than the length of a single log) he found that the guards had already stretched a chain across the approach for the night. A guard told him in broad Zhyskan dialect:

'King Shvo's not here. He's gone to Azaret with all his people for the summer. Who's calling?'

'Prince Vakar of Lorsk.'

The guard seemed unimpressed, and Vakar got the impression that the fellow judged him a liar. He tugged his mustache in thought, then asked:

'Is his minister Peshas here?'

'Why, didn't ye know? Peshas lost his head for conspiracy two months gone. Eh, ye could see it on its spike from here, rotting away day by day, but they've taken it down to make room for another.'

'Who is the minister then?'

'Himself has a new one, Lord Mir, but he's gone home for the night.'

Under these circumstances it would be more trouble than it was worth to try to talk his way in. Vakar asked:

'Where's the best inn?'

'Try Nyeron's. Three blocks north, turn right, go till ye see a little alley but don't go in there; bear left ...'

After some wandering Vakar found Nyeron's inn. Nyeron, speaking with a strong Hesperian accent, said that he could put up Vakar and his party for six ounces of copper a night.

'Very well,' said Vakar and dug into his scrip for a fistful of copper, wondering why Nyeron had looked surprised for a flicker of an eyelid.

After the usual period of weighing and checking they found a small celt of just over six ounces.

'Take it and never mind the change,' said Vakar, then turned to one of the charioteers. 'Take this and buy a meal for all of us for Nyeron to cook, and also fodder. Fual, help with the horses. Sret ...'

He paused to notice that Sret was speaking in Hesperian to Nyeron, who replied with a flood of that tongue, in the dialect of Meropia. It seemed that Sret, a small man with a long ape-like upper lip, had once lived in Meropia and that he and Nyeron had acquaintances in common. Although he had never visited the Hesperides, Vakar had a fair acquaintance with their language by virtue of having had an Ogugian nurse. However, being tired from his day's ride, he said impatiently in his own tongue:

'Sret! Haul in the baggage and see that nobody steals it until we're ready to eat. And not then, either.'

Sret went out to obey while Nyeron shouted for his daughter to fetch a wash-basin and a towel. A handsome wench appeared lugging a wooden bowl and a ewer, in one door and out another that led into the dormitory. Vakar followed her with an appreciative eye. Nyeron remarked:

'A fine piece of flesh, no? If the gentleman wishes, she shall be at his disposal ...'

'I've had all the riding I can manage in the last ten days,' said Vakar. 'Perhaps when I've rested ...'

He went back to the dormitory for the first turn at the wash-basin and found Fual beside him. Vakar, scrubbing the grime off his hands with a brush of pigskin with the bristles on, said:

'How are we doing, Fual?'

'Oh, very fine, sir. Except ...'

'Except what?'

'You know it's unusual for one of your rank to stop at a vulgar inn?'

'I know, but fortune compels. What else?'

'Perhaps my lord will excuse my saying he hasn't had much experience with inns?'

'That I haven't. What have I done wrong?'

'You could have got lodging for three ounces a night, or at most four, if you'd bargained sharply.'

'Why the boar-begotten thief! Am I a dog? I'll knock his teeth —'

'My lord! It wouldn't become your dignity, not to mention that the magistrates would take a poor view of the act, this being not your own demesne. Next time let me haggle, for my dignity doesn't matter.'

'Very well; with your background I can see you'd make a perfect merchant.'

Vakar handed over the washing-facilities. By the time the last of the party had washed, the water and towel were foul indeed. They ate from wooden bowls with the dispatch and silence of tired and hungry men, washing down great masses of roast pork and barley-bread with gulps of the green wine of Zhysk and paying no heed to a noisy party of merchants clustered at the other end of the long table.

When they turned in, however, Vakar found that the chatter of the merchants kept him awake. They seemed to be making an all-night party of it, with a flute-girl and all the trimmings. When the flute-girl was not tweetling the men were engaged in some game of chance with loud boasts, threats, and accusations.

Vakar stood it for a couple of hours until his slow temper reached a boil. Then he climbed out of bed and knocked aside the curtain separating the dormitory from the front chamber of the inn.

'Stop that racket!' he roared, 'before I beat your heads in!'

The noise stopped as four pairs of eyes turned upon him. The stoutest merchant said:

'And who are you, my good man?'

'I'm Prince Vakar of Lorsk, and when I say shut up —'

'And I'm the Queen of Ogugia. If you foreigners don't like it here, go back —'

'Swine!' yelled Vakar, looking for something to throw, but Nyeron, cudgel in hand, intervened:

'No fighting here! If you must brawl, go outside.'

'Gladly,' said Vagar. 'Wait while I fetch my sword —'

'Oh, it's to be swords?' said the stout merchant. 'Then you must wait while

I send home for mine. As it's drunk the blood of several Gorgonian pirates it shouldn't find a Lorskan popinjay —'

'What's that?' said Vakar. 'Who are you, really?' His initial burst of rage had subsided enough for his ever-lively curiosity to come into play, and he realized that he was making himself look foolish.

'I'm Mateng of Po, owner of three ships, as you'd know if you weren't an ignorant —'

'Wait,' said Vakar. 'Are any of your ships leaving shortly for the mainland?'

'Yes. The *Dyra* sails for Gadaira tomorrow if the wind holds.'

'Isn't Gadaira the nearest mainland port to Torrutseish?'

'It is.'

'How much —' Vakar started to say, then checked himself. He stuck his head back into the dormitory and called: 'Fual! Wake up; come out and haggle for me!'

Next morning Vakar was collecting his crew to ride to the docks when he found that Sret was missing. Back in the inn he found the interpreter chatting with Nyeron.

'Come along!' said Vakar.

'Yes sir,' said Sret, and as he started out called back over his shoulder in Hesperian: 'Farewell; I shall see you again sooner than you think!'

Then he came. They rattled down to the harbor where Vakar stopped at the temple of Lyr to sacrifice a lamb to the sea-god. While he did not take his gods too seriously (as they never visited him) he thought it just as well to be on the safe side. Then by questioning all and sundry he located the *Dyra*. Mateng was ordering the stowing of a cargo of copper ingots, bison-hides, and mammoth-ivory.

'Waste no time in getting home!' Vakar told the charioteers, who clattered off leading the horse he had ridden. Vakar sauntered up to the edge of the quay and stepped aboard the ship, trying not to show his excitement. Fual and Sret staggered after under their loads of gear and food for the trip.

Mateng called: 'Ruaz! Here's your passenger! He's all paid up, so take good care of him.'

'A prince, eh?' said Captain Ruaz, laughing through his beard. 'Well, keep out of the way, your sublime highness, if you don't want an ingot dropped on your toe.'

He bustled about directing his men until, after a long wait, they got the last goods stowed and the hatches closed and cast off. The crew manned four sweeps which they worked standing up, maneuvering the ship out from its quay. They plodded around the annular harbor to the main canal, Vakar craning his neck this way and that to see all he could of Amferé from the water.

As they entered the canal they picked up speed, for a slight current added its impetus to the force of the oars. Soon they passed through the outer city wall, where a great bronze gate stood ready to swing shut across the channel to keep out hostile ships. Then down the canal half a mile to the sea.

At the first roll of the *Dyra* in the oceanic swell, Sret curled up in the scuppers with a groan.

'What ails him?' said Vakar.

'Seasickness, sir,' said Fual. 'If you don't suffer a touch also you'll be lucky.'

'Like what happened to Zormé in the poem?

'With eyeballs aching   and hurting head,
Sunk in the scuppers   the hero huddled
Loathing life   and desiring death?

'I'm not so badly off as that yet.'

Fual turned away with a knowing look. After a few minutes of tossing, Vakar did experience a slight headache and queasiness of stomach, but not wishing to lose face he stood proudly at the rail as if nothing was wrong. The four sailors hauled in the oars, lowered the steering-paddles until they dipped into the water, and hoisted the single square scarlet-and-white striped sail. The west wind sent the *Dyra* plunging toward the Hesperides. Vakar now saw the reason for the high stern, as wave after wave loomed up behind and seemed about to swamp them, only to boost them forward and up and slide harmlessly underneath.

He staggered to the poop where Ruaz held the lever that operated the yoke that connected the two steering-paddles, and asked: 'What happens when you wish to sail back from the mainland to Amferé and the wind is against you? Do you row?'

'You wait and pray to your favorite sea-god. In this sea the wind blows from the west four days out of five, so you must wait for the fifth day. I've sat in port at Sederado a month awaiting a fair wind.'

'That sounds tedious. What if some other sea-captain is praying for the wind to blow in the opposite direction?'

Ruaz's shoulders and eyebrows went up in a great shrug. Vakar looked past the poop towards Amferé, now fast dropping out of sight behind the bulge of the ocean. He felt a lump rise in his throat and wiped away a tear. Then for a long time he stared at the water. Though normally nervous and impatient, quickly bored by inactivity, he found that he could watch the soothing sight of the endless series of crests riding by.

But something nagged him, filling him with a vague feeling of incongruity and unease. In the late afternoon they skirted a mountainous coast.

'Meropia,' said Captain Ruaz.

By nightfall Sret had recovered enough to eat. Afterwards Vakar, though monstrously sleepy, got little sleep because of the moonlight, the motion, and the ship-noises. Next day they left Meropia behind in the afternoon and sailed eastward over the empty sea. Ruaz explained:

'We don't see other ships because we're the first out of Amferé after the winter layup. We're taking a chance on a late storm to get higher prices in Gadaira before the competition arrives.'

Vakar wondered at his continuing unease until the sight of Sret chatting with Ruaz gave him a clue. He remembered Sret's saying to Nyeron he'd be back sooner than expected. Why? Did he think that Vakar would lose heart and turn back, or get killed in a brawl? Or …

Vakar felt like kicking himself for not having seen it sooner. Kuros, acting in concordance with the Gorgons, could have sent Sret along to murder him and then go home with a story of how his master had been eaten by a monster. Sret had spoken to Nyeron in Hesperian in ignorance of the fact that Vakar knew that tongue. Vagar fingered his hilt and glanced narrowly to where Sret huddled under his cloak, the hood pulled up over his head, swapping jokes with the captain. He thought of walking up to the fellow and striking off his head. Still, he might be wrong in his suspicions, and at best the killing would be embarrassing to explain.

Vakar wondered whether to take Fual into his confidence. He asked:

'Fual, who *is* Sret? I never knew him before this journey.'

Fual shrugged. 'I think he's part Lotri, but I never knew him either.'

If true, that made it unlikely that both Sret and Fual were in on the plot. After the evening meal Vakar told Fual that they should keep watch-and-watch through the night in case of foul play. Fual looked startled and produced a handsome silver-inlaid dagger.

'Ha!' said Vakar. 'Where did you get that? You stole it at Nyeron's! I ought to beat you … But perhaps 'tis a lucky theft for once. Go to sleep while I take the first watch.'

Shortly before midnight Vakar was aroused by Fual's shaking him. The valet whispered:

'You were right, sir. They're gathered aft, whispering.'

Vakar rolled over and peered aft from the bow where he and Fual lay. Below the lower edge of the sail he could see the whispering knot of men in the light of the just-risen gibbous moon.

He slowly drew his sword and whispered to Fual: 'Get your knife ready. Keep close to me and cover my back.'

His shield was still in the duffelbag, but for fighting on an unsteady deck one needed a free hand to grab things.

'You – you're going to attack six men?' quavered Fual.

'Lyr's barnacles! Should I wait for them to cut my throat?'

'But six —'

'Our only hope is to rush them. If it makes you any happier I'm frightened too, but I prefer a small chance to none.'

Fual's teeth chattered. Vakar inched caterpillarlike along the deck aft hoping to get close enough to overhear before the crew noticed him. As he neared the mast he found that he could make out the separate figures. Sret was talking in low tones to Ruaz, who turned a leaf-shaped broadsword this way and that so that the moon glimmered dully upon it. Sret was saying:

'... not an experienced fighter, though he's been in brushes with hill-robbers. But he's young and no giant; one quick rush while he sleeps ...'

'Come on,' breathed Vakar, rolling to his feet.

IV

Queen Porfia

Vakar ducked under the lower yard and ran towards the group. With a shout the sailors leaped apart, drawing knives. Vakar bore down upon the nearest, feinted once, and ran the man through. The man's scream pierced the rising clamor. As Vakar stepped back to pull out his blade he glanced over his shoulder. Fual had hardly finished ducking under the sail.

Damn the coward! thought Vakar, setting his teeth. As his victim fell he faced Ruaz, Sret, and two sailors, plus one other on the poop steering. Sret and Ruaz were shouting:

'Forward! Kill him! Get in close! Rush him!'

Vakar leaped over the body on deck, slashing right and left. His sword clanged against Ruaz's blade and bit flesh and bone, and then he was through them. As he whirled to face them again, his back to the poop, he saw that they were all still on their feet. As Fual finally came closer, a sailor turned and closed with him rather than face the sword. Now the twain were staggering about in a deadly waltz, each gripping the other's wrist.

The three facing Vakar closed, Ruaz in the middle. Vakar cut and thrust at the captain, who parried while Sret and the other sailor closed in from the sides. Vakar, wishing he had a light rapier against these agile unarmored foes, had to leap back until he backed into the high step up to the poop and almost fell.

They came on. Vakar slashed wildly, only his superior length of blade keeping them from finishing him. He could not quite reach them, for if he moved far enough towards any one the others would get him in the back. They moved on the swaying deck with catlike ease while he reeled and staggered. One got close enough to send a stab home, but the point failed to pierce Vakar's leather jack.

A shout came from behind: the steersman encouraging his mates. Vakar wondered what a ship would do without a man at the helm. He leaped back up on to the poop, turning as he did so, and swung a mighty blow at the sailor. The sharp bronze sheared through the man's neck. The head thumped to the deck, rolled off the poop, and continued its bloody course forward towards the mast while the spouting body collapsed beneath the steering-yoke.

Vakar turned to face his three antagonists on the main deck, but as they confronted each other the *Dyra* slewed to starboard and heeled far to port so that water poured over the port rail.

Vakar found himself sliding down the steep deck towards the black water. He threw up his free hand and snatched at the night air for support – and to his infinite relief caught a mast-stay. As the ship continued to heel, Vakar found his feet dangling over the water while he gripped the stay in a death-grasp.

He glanced forward in time to see a figure that he took for Sret go over the side into the smother of foam while the other, sprawling or sitting on the deck, snatched at the ropes and each other for purchase.

As the wind spilled out of the sail the *Dyra* began to right herself. When his feet were firmly on the slanting deck again, Vakar let go his stay to creep forward on knees and knuckles. Captain Ruaz was also on all fours, grouping for his sword. Vakar rose as he neared the captain and brought his sword down on his head. Down went Ruaz.

One sailor clung to the rail, which was just emerging from the water. Vakar struck at the gripping hand, missed, and struck again. This time the edge hit home and the seaman disappeared.

Up forward Fual lay upon the deck, holding the mast with his arms while his antagonist, the remaining sailor, clutched Fual's legs to keep from going over the side with the roll of the ship. Only a few heart-beats had elapsed since the ship had started to right herself and roll in the opposite direction. Vakar ran forward and, as the sailor rose crying a word that might have meant 'mercy', he struck. The man threw up an arm, yelped as the blade bit into the bone, and an instant later collapsed with a split skull.

Fual started to rise, then clutched the mast as the ship rolled in the other direction. Vakar, staggering over to the starboard rail, cried:

'How do you straighten this damned thing out?'

'The steering-lever,' said Fual. 'You – you keep the ship's – that is —'

Without waiting for more explicit directions, Vakar, the next time the ship righted herself, bounded aft and seized the lever-arm. He hung on until the wind caught the sail and the *Dyra* began to pick up way on her former course. When she was straightened out and running free again, Vakar examined the steering-mechanism. He experimented so that the ship yawed wildly until he got the hang of steering. Fual said:

'My lord, I've never seen anything like the way you slew those four men! Just one – two – three – four, like that!'

'Luck,' growled Vakar. 'Must we always sail exactly with the wind?'

'No, I think one can sail at a small angle to it, or sailors would never reach home.'

'I wish I knew whither we were headed. What land did Ruaz expect to sight next?'

'I don't know, sir. I believe Eruthea and Ogugia and Elusion lie somewhere ahead of us.'

'In what order?'

'That I don't know.'

'I once met the present Queen of Ogugia; a gangling child, but she'd be a grown woman now.'

'Has Ogugia a king, sir?'

'Had; Porfia married a Lord Vancho, who was said to have been an amiable nonentity. He died of some pox, and as the Hesperian throne descends in the female line she'd still be queen.'

'What sort of place is it?'

'Ogugia? I know little, save that it's called the Isle of Philosophers. I've always wished to ask those sages some simple questions, say about the origin of life and the immortality of soul and so on. Oh, Fual! Since you're no more mariner than I, throw these bodies over-board.'

'Including this one without his head, sir?' said Fual with such a pronounced grimace of distaste that Vakar could see it in the moonlight.

'Especially that one. They clutter the deck.'

Fual went to work, first stripping each corpse. When he had finished he came back to the poop with Ruaz's broadsword, which he had found in the scuppers, saying:

'May I carry this, sir? If we're to meet such perils we can't be too well armed.'

'Surely, surely.' Vakar turned the helm over to Fual while he straightened the kinks out of his own sword and smoothed down the nicks in the blade with his pocket-hone.

Towards morning Vakar sighted another land ahead and said: 'Let's follow this coast around to the right until we come to a port.'

'What will you do with the ship, sir?'

'I hadn't thought.' Vakar looked around. 'If somebody sees the blood they'll make trouble. Clean it up, will you?'

'And then what?' said Fual, hunting for rags.

'How does one sell a ship?'

'One finds a merchant who wishes to buy. Unless somebody recognizes it as belonging to Mateng of Po.'

'How could we disguise it? When you finish with the blood, see if you can remove that image of Lyr at the stern.'

Thus about noon a somewhat altered *Dyra* came in sight of a harbor full of tubby merchantmen and rakish fifty-oared war-galleys, with a fair city lying behind it. Vakar said:

'How do we steer this ship into the harbor without the wind at our backs?'

'I think one lowers the sail and rows in.'

'And how – oh, I see! One unties that rope that runs from the upper what-ever-you-call-it, that long stick, and lowers it until it rests upon the bottom one.'

He meant the upper and lower yards, for the ship had yards at both the top and bottom edges of the sail. A tackle of ropes confined the sail and kept it from spilling over the deck when lowered. Vakar steered the ship as far into the port as it would go. Then Fual unhitched the halyard, but, as the upper yard and the sail were heavier that he, they sank down into their tackle hoisting the little Aremorian into the air. The spectacle so doubled Vakar up with mirth that, despite Fual's yells, it was some time before he came forward to pull his servant back to the deck.

They got out the sweeps and pushed the ship shoreward. It was a long row for only two oars, and Vakar, thought his hands were hard from weapon-practice, had begun to develop blisters before they reached the shore. Along the waterfront men were unloading ships and hauling their cargoes away in ox-drawn sledges and truckle-carts. As the *Dyra* neared the quay a small knot of loafers gathered to gaup: dark men smaller than those of Poseidonis. Vakar said:

'Get ready to leap ashore with the stern-rope.'

As they drifted against the quay, Vakar sprang ashore with the painter and belayed the rope to one of the row of posts, while Fual did likewise astern. Vakar caught the eye of the nearest loafer and called in Hesperian:

'What place in this?'

'Sederado, the capital of Ogugia.'

Vakar said to Fual: 'Let's hope Queen Porfia remembers me ... I know! As we can't drag this whole cargo with us, I might jog her memory with a portion of it and dispose her to help us on the next leg of our journey. Ho, you people! I wish four strong porters to carry a load to the palace. Fual, pick the four and make an arrangement with them for their wage. You with the nose! Is copper mined in Ogugia?'

'Yes,' said the man addressed.

'Do you have mammoths or bison?'

'No mammoths, though there are a few bison in the royal park.'

Vakar turned back to Fual. 'Ivory is the thing she'll best appreciate. Help me get these hatch-covers off.'

In a few minutes Vakar had his porters lined up, each with a great curling mammoth-tusk over one shoulder. He was about to order them to march when he noticed that the people on the quay were staring seaward.

Vakar saw another ship drawing up to the adjacent wharfage-space: a low black thirty-oared galley, much larger than the *Dyra* with a crew of a dozen besides the rowers and three passengers. The ship had a beak of bronze jutting out at the waterline forward, and (like all ships) a pair of eyes painted on the bow so that, sailors believed, she could see her way. No device or insigne, like the mer-maid of Ogugia or the octopus of Gorgonia, variegated her plain brown sail, nor did any pennant or banderole betray her origin.

One of the passengers was a man of medium height with a small round cap perched on his shaven poll, a small pointed gray beard, and a loose robe to his ankles. The other two, who wore no clothes, were not really human. One was a pigmy about four feet high with huge membranous ears like those of an elephant in miniature, and covered all over with short golden-brown fur. The other was eight feet tall with a low-browed apish countenance and coarse black hair all over. He carried a great brass-bound club over one stooping shoulder while his other arm embraced a large wooden chest with bronze clamps.

'By all the gods, what are those?' said Vakar. 'Some kind of satyrs? The large one looks like the giant in the *Lay of Zormé*:

> 'Grimly glowering and fearsomely fanged
> The monster menaced the vulnerable virgin …

'Eh?'

Fual said: 'The larger I don't know, but the smaller is a Coranian.'

'A what?'

'A native of the northern isle of Corania. It's said they can hear any word uttered for miles around.'

The second ship tied up as their own had done, and its people climbed ashore and set out in various directions. Vakar said:

'We can't wait around all day; I'm for the palace. You stay here to dispose of the stuff …'

Just then the shaven-headed man pushed through the spectators towards Vakar. After him came the giant ape-man and the Coranian.

'You are for the palace, sir?' said the man in strongly accented Hesperian. 'Perhaps you will permit me to go with you, for my errand takes me thither also and I am not familiar with Sederado. And while I have never met you, something tells me I ought to know you. My name is Qasigan.'

'And whom have I the honor of addressing?' said Qasigan, smiling pleasantly as he fell into step beside Vakar. His leathery skin was even darker than Vakar's, and his broad head bore a round blunt-featured face. He stooped slightly and shuffled rather than walked.

'My name is Vakar.'

Vakar happened to be looking at the man's face as he spoke, and observed the pleasant smile vanish and flicker back again.

'Not Prince Vakar of Lorsk!' said the man.

Vakar tended to take a dour and suspicious view of untried strangers – especially queer-looking ones who travelled about in their own war-galleys with inhuman assistants and showed an egregious interest in his identity. He shook his head.

'Merely a relative. And what, sir, do you know of Lorsk?'

'Who does not know the world's greatest source of copper?'

'Indeed. Where do you come from?'

'Tegrazen, a small city on the mainland south of Kernê.'

'You have unusual servitors. The first, I understand, is a Coranian?'

'That is correct. His name is Yok.'

'And the other?' said Vakar.

'That is Nji, from Blackland. The Blacks caught him young, tamed him, and sold him. He can speak a few words, for he is not the great ape of Blackland – the gorilla – but another and rarer kind, intermediate between apes and men.'

Vakar fell into a wary silence until they arrived at the palace. He gauped like a yokel at the rows of gleaming marble columns and the gilded roof, for this was the first two-storey building that he had ever seen.

He sent in the four tusks with word that Vakar of Lorsk would like an audience. After a half-hour's wait he was ushered in, leaving Qasigan staring pensively after him.

'Prince Vakar!' cried Queen Porfia, stepping down from her audience-throne and advancing upon him. She kissed him vigorously. 'I thank you for your splendid gift, but you need not shower me with wealth to assure your welcome! Did you think I had forgotten when we won the dance-contest in Amferé ten years ago? What brings you so far from the bison-swarming plains of windy Lorsk?'

Porfia, Vakar thought, had certainly developed into a splendid-looking woman. Though she was not large, her proud carriage gave her a deceptive look of tallness. Lucky Vancho! He said:

'I am on my way to mighty Torrutseish, madam, and could not pass by Ogugia without renewing so pleasant an acquaintance.'

She looked at him keenly from emerald-green eyes. 'Now how, I wonder, does it happen that you and one servant put into the harbor of Sederado navigating a small merchant-ship all by yourselves in most thwart tyronic fashion? Are you running away from Lorsk to become a corsair? Perhaps to sail under the octopus banner of the accursed Gorgons?'

'You seem to have learned a lot in a short time.'

'Oh, I watch my kingdom's commerce, and was getting a report on you while you waited. Well, what happened? Was all the ship's company but you washed overboard, or snatched by a kraken?'

Vakar hesitated, then gave in to his instant liking for Porfia and told the story of Sret's treachery.

'So,' he concluded, 'being as you have said no barnacled mariners, we propose to sell this ship and continue eastward on the next merchantman that passes that way.'

'How much cargo have you?'

'By Tandyla's third eye, I do not know!'

'Well then. Elbien!' A man came in and Porfia told him: 'Go to the waterfront, board Prince Vakar's ship, and reckon up the value of the cargo.' As the man bowed and left she turned back to Vakar. 'I will give you your ship's fair value in trade-metal. If Mateng squeals we will remind him that as owner he is responsible for the murderous attack upon you. And what do you know of that odd fish who came in with you? The one who arrived in his private galley?'

'He claims to be Qasigan of Tegrazen, but beyond that I know no more than you, Queen. He is certainly as peculiar as a flying pig, though courteous enough.'

'So? The description of him sounds like one of the Gorgonian race, though that proves nothing because Tegrazen lies near the Gorgades on the mainland and the people of those parts are much mixed. But tell me how things go in Lorsk: the land of warriors, heroes, and athletes, with hearts of bronze and heads of ivory?'

Vakar laughed and plunged into small-talk. A man of few friends, he felt that at last he had found someone who spoke his language. They were chattering away some time later when Porfia said:

'By Heroë's eight teats, I have spent the whole morning on you, sir, and others await me. You shall stay at the palace, and we will have a feast tonight. You shall meet my minister Garal and my lover Thiegos.'

'Your —' Vakar checked himself, wondering why he felt a sudden pang of annoyance. It was none of his affair if the Queen of Ogugia kept a dozen lovers; but the feeling persisted.

She appeared not to notice. 'And I think I will have this Master Qasigan too if I like him. He seems like a man of position, and we should at least get some rare tales of far lands.'

'Queen,' said Vakar, 'I told Qasigan my name but denied being the scion of Lorsk, and should therefore prefer to be known simply as Master Vakar, a simple gentleman, while that fellow in the long shirt is about.'

'It shall be done. Dweros! Take Pr – Master Vakar to the second guest-chamber in the right wing and provide for his comfort.'

Vakar saw no more of Porfia until evening, but spent a lazy day sleeping, being washed and perfumed, and reading a Hesperian translation of the Fragments of Lontang in the library while his dirty clothes were being washed and dried. As the writing of the time was largely pictographic, the written languages of Ogugia and Lorsk differed much less than their spoken tongues. However, the symbols for abstract ideas differed widely. Vakar asked a dignified-looking oldster copying a roll of papyrus in the corner:

'Can you tell me what this means, my man? This skull-and-crescent thing?'

'That, sir, signifies "mortality". It combines the skull, which symbolizes death, with the inverted crescent, which represents the abstract aspect of the moon, to wit: time. Therefore the meaning of the passage is:

'Though germinate generations of mortal man
In thousands of thousands while in dwellings divine
A god grows his eye-teeth, yet time taketh all:
Even the gods so glorious must march at the last
Down the dim dusty road to death the destroyer.'

'Is Lontang trying to tell us that even the gods must die?'

'Yes. His theory was that the gods are created by the belief of men in them, and that puissant though they be, in time men will forsake them for others and forget them, and they will fade away and vanish.'

Vakar said: 'You seem a knowledgeable man in such matters. May I ask your name?'

'I am Rethilio, a poor philosopher of Sederado. And you ...?'

'I am Vakar of Lorsk.'

'Curious,' mused the man. 'I have heard your name ... I know! Last night I dreamt I witnessed an assembly of the gods. I recognized many of ours, such as Asterio, and some of those of other nations like your Okma. They seemed to be rushing about in agitated fashion, as if dancing a funeral-dance, and I heard them ejaculate "Vakar Lorska"!'

Vakar shuddered. 'As I never dream of the gods I can shed no light on this matter.'

'Are you remaining here long, Prince?'

'Only a few days. But I should like to return to Ogugia some day to study its famed philosophies.'

Too late Vakar realized that he should have at once denied his principate; by failing to do so he had confirmed Rethilio's guess as to his true identity. Rethilio said:

'Many of my colleagues believe that if only kings would study philosophy, or the people would choose philosophers as their kings, the world would be a less sorry place. In practice, however, kings seem to lack either time or inclination.'

'Perhaps I can combine the two.'

'A laudable ambition, though broad. The gods grant that you achieve it.'

'I see no difficulty. I have many ambitions and, I trust, many years to fulfill them.'

'What are these ambitions, sir?' said Rethilio.

'Well ...' Vakar frowned. 'To be a good king when my time comes; to master philosophy; to see far places and strange peoples; to know loyal and interesting friends; to enjoy the pleasures of wine, women, and song ...'

He stopped as Rethilio threw up his hands in mock horror. 'You should have been twins, Prince!'

'I am – or rather my brother Kuros is my twin. What do you mean, though?'

'No man can compress all that into one lifetime. Now it seems life is endless and you can sample all experience while attaining preëminence in any careers that suit your fancy. As time passes you will discover you must make a choice here and a choice there, each choice cutting you off from some of these many enticing possibilities. Of course there is the hypothesis of the school of Kurno, that the soul not only survives the body but is subsequently reincarnated in another, and thus a man undergoes many existences.'

'I do not see how that helps if one cannot remember one's previous lives,' said Vakar. 'And if that be so, how about the gods? Are their souls likewise reincarnated?'

They were at it hammer and tongs when Dweros appeared to tell Vakar that his clothes were ready.

'I hope I shall see you again before I leave,' he told Rethilio.

'If you are here tomorrow at this time we may meet. Good-day, sir.'

V

The Serpent Throne

The banquet-hall was smaller than that of the castle at Mneset, but of more refined workmanship, with plastered walls on which were painted scenes from the myths of Ogugia. Vakar was particularly taken by the picture of the seduction of an eight-breasted woman by a bull-headed man of egregious masculinity.

He met the plump minister Garal and his wife, the latter a pleasant but nondescript woman of middle age; and Thiegos, a tall clean-shaven young man wearing splended pearl earrings, who looked down a long nose and said:

'So you are from Lorsk? I wonder how you endure the winds and fogs. I could never put up with them!'

Though not pleased by this comment, Vakar was amused when a few minutes later Qasigan came in and Thiegos said to him: 'So you are from the South? I wonder how you endure the heat and the flies. I could never abide them!'

Another youth came in whom Thiegos introduced as his friend Abeggu of Tokalet, who had come from far Gamphasantia to Sederado to study philosophy under Rethilio. The newcomer was a tall slender fellow, very dark and quiet. When he spoke it was with an almost unintelligible accent. Vakar asked the conventional question:

'How do you find these northerly lands?'

'Very interesting, sir, and very different from my home. We have no such towering stone buildings or lavish use of metal.'

'Still, I envy you,' said Vakar. 'I have met Rethilio and wish I had time to study under the philosophers of Ogugia. What have you learned?'

'He is discoursing on the origin of the world-egg from the coiture of eternal time and infinite space ...'

Vakar would have liked to hear more, for philosophy had always fascinated him though it was little cultivated among the palaestral nations of Poseidonis. But Queen Porfia sat down and signalled to the servitors to pass a dry wine for an apertif. She poured a libation from her golden beaker on to the floor and said a grace to the gods, then drank.

Vakar was doing likewise when a startled exclamation from Garal's wife drew his attention across the ivory tables. Where Qasigan's golden plate had lain there now stood a plate-sized tortoise, peering about dimly with beady eyes. Qasigan laughed at the success of his feat of thaumaturgy.

'It is quite harmless,' he said. 'A mere illusion: It bites nobody and is housebroken. Are you not, tortoise?'

The tortoise nodded, and those around the tables clapped their hands. Vakar drank deeply and looked again. Where the tortoise had been he saw only the snub-nosed magician making passes over his plate, though from their comments he inferred that his fellow-diners still saw the reptile. He was about to boast of his ability (which he had long been aware of) to see through magical illusions when stimulated by drink, but forebore. He still harbored suspicions of Qasigan and thought it imprudent to give the fellow any advantage.

He looked to where Porfia sat in her chair of pretence. This was a most unusual throne, carved from some olive-colored stone in the form of a huge serpent. The head and neck of the snake formed one arm-rest and a loop of its body the other. The rest of it was wound back and forth to form the back and seat down to the ground.

'It is unusual,' said Porfia, whose pale flesh showed through the sheer sea-green robe she wore. 'It was brought from Lake Tritonis, where such serpents are sacred, in the time of my grandfather. They say it was carried across the Desert of Gwedulia slung between two curious beasts used in those parts, taller than horses and having great humps upon their backs. The legend is that it is a real serpent paralyzed by enchantment, and —'

'Of course,' broke in Thiegos, 'we as a civilized people do not believe such silly tales.' He dug at the carving with a thumbnail. 'See for yourself, Master Vakar. This artistic monstrosity is nothing but stone.'

Vakar touched the arm of the chair, which certainly felt like good solid chert.

Thiegos continued: 'Still, my dear, you would do well to drop it into Sed-erado harbor and get another, not for superstitious but for esthetic reasons. What is to eat tonight?'

Ogugian custom called for a circle of chairs with a small table in front of each. Servitors placed the food on golden plates in front of each of the small tables. Vakar thought the stuffed grouse excellent, but found the bread pecu-liar. He asked:

'What sort of bread is this, pray?'

Thiegos said: 'You Pusadians would not know. It is made from a new kind of grain called wheat which was brought from the mainland in the queen's father's time.' He turned to Porfia, saying: 'Really, madam, you must sell your cook before we all turn into swine from eating garbage!'

The wine was strong stuff, even better than that of Zhysk. Vakar drank deep and said:

'I beg to differ, sir. I find Ogugia's food the most delicious, its wine the headiest, and its queen the most beautiful —'

'You speak a fine speech, but you do not deceive anyone,' said Thiegos, who had also been drinking hard. 'You seek by flattery to wheedle favors from Porfia. Now, so long as these comprise such matters as trade-metal or ships or slaves I do not care. Should you however seek those of a more intim-ate kind, you must deal with me, for I —'

'Thiegos!' cried Porfia. 'You have already become a pig, if manners are any indication.'

'At least,' said Thiegos, 'I know how to eat and drink in civilized fashion, instead of tearing my meat like a famished lion and swilling my wine in great gulps.' He looked down his nose at Vakar, who colored, realizing that by Ogugian standards his provincial table-manners left much to be desired. 'So I am merely warning this mustachioed barbarian —'

'*Shut up!*' cried Porfia, half rising out of the serpent throne, green eyes blazing and oval face flushed.

Vakar said in a tone of deadly calm: 'He merely wishes to set himself up as palace pimp, do you not, Siegos?' He gave the fancyman's name the Lorskan mispronunciation on purpose to vex him.

'Boar-begotten bastard!' shouted Thiegos. 'I will cut off your —'

'Down, both of you!' cried Garal with unexpected force. 'Or I will have in the guards to whip you through the streets with leaded scorpions. Slaves, clear away these remnants!'

The servitors took away the plates and brought more wine. Abeggu of Tokalet looked shocked and bewildered; evidently he was unused to royalty with its hair down. Vakar, realizing that he was getting drunk, pulled himself together and said:

'Can one of you explain this?'

He pointed to the seduction-scene on the wall. Garal explained:

'Why, that illustrates the third book of *The Golden Age,* and represents the forest-god Asterio about to engender the first human pair on the earth-goddess Heroé. In the original it goes:

'Painting with passion the slavering satyr

Supine on the sward hurled helpless Heroé ...'

Thiegos interrupted: 'You cannot do it justice without singing it,' and he burst into a fine clear tenor:

'The rose-colored robe by the dawn-goddess dighted

He savagely seized and tore from her trunk ...

'Curse it, even I cannot perform properly without accompaniment. Shall we get in the flute-girl?'

'I do not think that will be necessary,' said Qasigan. 'I have here a small instrument wherewith I while away empty hours.'

He produced a tootle-pipe out of his bosom and played an experimental run. 'Now, sir, how does this tune of your go? Ah, yes, I can manage. Sing!'

With the pipe ululating, Thiegos stood up and roared out the rest of the story of the Creation. When he finished, Vakar said:

'Sir, you may be a pimp and several other things I will not shock our hostess by mentioning, but you have the finest voice I have ever heard. I wish I could do as well.'

'That is nothing,' said Thiegos, staggering back to his seat. 'The song does have a certain crude barbaric vigor, but now we are more refined. For instance, I at least do not take all this mythology serious – *uk!*'

An attack of hiccups ended the speech. Porfia called upon Vakar:

'Now, sir, contribute your part! What can you do?'

'I can tell you what I cannot do,' said Vakar, counting on his fingers. 'Once I thought I could sing, but now I have heard Thiegos I know I can only caw like a carrion-crow. I can dance when sober as the queen remembers, but just now I am not sober. I know a few stories, but not the sort a gentleman would repeat in such company —'

'Forget you are a gentleman, old man, old man,' giggled Garal. 'I have heard livelier tales from the lips of the queen herself than any you are likely to know.'

'Very well; do any of you know the tale of the hunchback and the fisherman's wife? No? It seems that ...'

They all laughed heartily; in fact Garal's wife got into a fit of hysterics and had to be pounded on the back. Vakar told a couple more, and then Queen Porfia said:

'You claim you once thought you could sing; let us hear this crow's voice!'

'But really, Queen —'

'No, I insist. Master Qasigan shall accompany you.'

'Then do not say I failed to warn you. Qasigan, it goes da de-de da de-de ...'

When the tune had been straightened out Vakar gave them the *Song of Vrir*:

'Vrir the Victorious rode to the river

His scabbard of silver shining in sunlight ...'

When he had finished, Porfia clapped, crying: 'Magnificent! While I do not understand Lorskan, you sing even better than Thiegos.'

'I have heard no singing,' growled Thiegos, who had got over his hiccups, 'only the croaking of bullfrogs.'

'What do you think?' said Porfia to Garal. 'Vakar is the better, is he not?'

'They are both very good,' said the minister with the adroitness of the practiced politician, and turned to Qasigan. 'Pray, play us one of the tunes of your native country.'

Qasigan played a wailing tune. Thiegos said: 'By Asterio's arse, that sounds like the tune of our dance to the moon goddess!'

'How would you know, since men are strictly forbidden near when the maidens dance it?' said Porfia.

'You would be surprised. Here, Porfia, you are the best dancer in Ogugia; dance it for us! Qasigan can play.'

'It would be blasphemous ...' said the queen, but the others shouted her down.

At last she stood up and, with Qasigan playing, began a slinking dance. Being unsteady from the wines she repeatedly stepped on the hem of her thin trailing robe until she burst out:

'Curse this thing! How can I ...'

She unfastened the robe, slipped out of it, and threw it across the serpent throne.

'Move those damned tables out of the way,' she said, and continued her dance naked save for her jewelled sandals.

Vakar found the room swimming in a delightful fog. It seemed that the flames of the wall-lamps swayed in time to the weird music, and that the frescoes came alive so that the bull-headed god appeared to get on with his protogenic project.

Vakar felt an urge to leap up and seize the swaying white figure of Porfia in imitation of Asterio, for though small she had a form that practically demanded rape of any passing male. But at that moment the queen tripped and fell across Garal's knees. The minister raised a hand as if to spank the royal rump, but reconsidered in time. The sight sent Vakar into such a convulsion of laughter that he could hardly keep his seat.

'That is enough of that!' said Porfia, reeling back to her throne, where she struggled to don the robe and got wonderfully tangled in its folds until Thiegos came over to help. 'Who knows something else?'

'We have a game in Tegrazen,' said Qasigan, 'called "Going to Kernê." A number of stools are set in a circle, the number being one less than that of the persons present. Music is played and the persons march around the chairs. The music is stopped suddenly and all try to sit down, but one fails and is counted out. Then one chair is removed and the march repeated until there are but two players and one chair left, and whichever of these gains the chair wins. Now, suppose I play while the rest of you march, for I am a little old for such athletics.'

'A childish sort of game,' said Thiegos. 'I fear we shall be bored —'

'Oh, you sneer at everything!' cried Porfia. 'Vakar, Garal, move that chair back to the wall. Master Qasigan, sit here in the center and tootle. Great gods, look at him!' she pointed to Abeggu of Tokalet, who had quietly curled up in a corner and passed out. 'Wake him up, somebody.'

Vakar said: 'How any man with blood in his veins could sleep through the spectacle we have just witnessed ...'

'It means nothing to him,' said Thiegos. 'They go naked all the time in Gamphasantia, he tells me. Ho, Lazybones, wake up!'

He kicked the sleeping man. When Abeggu had been aroused and briefed on the game they began marching unsteadily around the circle. When the music stopped all plumped on to the seats except Garal's wife, who being fat was slow on her feet. She laughed and went over to the wall to sit while Vakar lugged another stool out of the circle.

'Begin again!' said Qasigan.

His music became more and more exotic. The whole room seemed to Vakar to writhe in time with the tune. He wondered what was wrong, for he had been prudently holding down his consumption of wine since his quarrel with Thiegos.

The music stopped and Thiegos this time was left standing.

'Oh, well,' said the queen's lover, 'I do not find these antics very amusing anyway,' and went over to sit by Garal's wife. Out went another chair.

At the next halt, Abeggu of Tokalet was out.

This time the music seemed to go right through Prince Vakar, to make his teeth and eyeballs ache. The lamps darkened; at least he could not see clearly. The music shook him as a dog shakes a rat ...

Then it stopped. Vakar took a quick look and lurched towards a dark shape that he fuzzily identified as Queen Porfia's imported serpent chair, which as a seat of office was the only one in the room with arms and a back.

He half-spun and fell into its stone embrace just ahead of Porfia herself, who landed lushly in his lap with a playful squeal that changed to a shriek of terror.

Vakar echoed the scream with an animal noise, half grunt and half shout, as he realized in one horror-struck flash that he was sitting on the coils of a giant live snake. There was an explosive hiss as the head and neck reared up and back to stare down at the two human beings, its forked tongue flicking. At the same instant a loop, thicker than Vagar's thigh, whipped around both of them, preventing them from rising.

Vakar vaguely heard screams and the sound of running feet as the coil tightened. His ribs creaked; it was like being squeezed to death by a live tree-trunk. He had no sword and his left arm was pinned between Porfia and the snake; his right was still free.

Vakar frantically ripped open his shirt and pulled out the envenomed dagger that had slain Söl. With all his strength he drove it into the scaly hide, again and again …

The snake hissed louder, but the pressure of the coil relaxed an instant. With a tremendous effort Vakar freed his other arm. The snake's entire body was writhing convulsively around him. He got a foot against the coil in front and pushed. The coil gave, and he and Porfia were out of the monster's embrace. Vakar half-dragged the queen across the room out of harm's way, then looked back at the expiring snake.

They were alone in the room.

Vagar put away his dagger and held the queen in his arms until she stopped trembling. She put her face up for him to kiss, but when he would have gone on with a full course of lovemaking she pushed him away.

'Not now,' she said. 'Is the monster dead?'

Vakar stepped forward to see, then jumped back as the scaly body twitched. 'It still moves! What does that mean? We do not have these creatures in Poseidonis.'

'They die as a frog swallows a worm, by inches, but I do not think this one will harm us any more. Evidently the legend at which Thiegos sneered is no empty fable. And speaking of Thiegos, what a fine pack of poltroons I am served by! Not one stayed to help, save you.'

'Do not give me too much credit, madam. I was caught in the same scaly embrace as yourself, and could not have fled were I never so timorous. But why should our cold-blooded friend here come to life just as we sat upon him? Do you suppose our extra weight was more than he could bear, and he showed his displeasure by awakening from his sleep of centuries?'

'No, for I have often cossetted in that same chair with that craven Thiegos. There is malevolent magic in this, Vakar, and we must solve the riddle before the clues are scattered by the winds of time. But where *is* everybody? Elbien! Dweros!'

No answer. She led Vakar about the palace, which proved entirely empty except for a trembling knot of guards in the front courtyard who pointed their spears at Porfia and Vakar as they approached.

'What is that?' she said. 'Do you not know your own queen?'

A man in a cuirass of gilded scales stepped out and said: 'You are no ghost, madam?'

'Of course not, Gwantho!'

'May I touch you to make sure?'

'Of all the impertinent nonsense ... Very well, here!'

She held out a hand with a regal gesture. The officer took it and kissed it, then said to the men:

'She is real, boys. Your pardon, Queen, but the clamor of those that fled the palace so perturbed my men that but for me they would have bolted likewise.'

'It would have gone hard with them if they had. Next time you hear I am in danger you might try to help instead of thinking of nought but your own hides. Now back to your posts!'

As the guards slunk off, Porfia said to Vakar: 'That was Gwantho, the legate of the commandant of the city garrison. Are there no brave men outside the epics and legends? The runagates must have spread terror through the palace as they fled. What do you make of it?'

'I suspect our queer friend Qasigan,' said Vakar judiciously. 'On the other hand he is a stranger, as is Abeggu of Tokalet, while Garal and Thiegos, being among your familiars, might harbor some hidden rankling resentment.'

'I doubt that last. Neither is of royal blood and therefore neither could cherish regal ambitions.'

Vakar smiled. 'That is no sure barrier. How do you suppose most dynasties were founded in the first place?'

'Well, neither have I quarreled with either lately – unless you count my refusal to follow Garal's counsel to wed Shvo Zhyska.'

'He so advised you? Hang the hyena! I know Shvo well, being his cousin. He is as grasping as a Kernean and as perfidious as an Aremorian.'

'I am not likely to follow Garal in this matter. But we are not even sure the serpent came to life by human agency, instead of in the course of the natural termination of the enchantment that bound it ... Fetch your sword and cloak while I likewise dress for the street.'

'Where are we going?'

'In such perplexities I consult a wise-woman nearby. Hasten, and meet me here.'

Vakar went. When he returned with the hood of his cloak pulled up over his helmet he found a very different Porfia with peasant's cowhide boots showing under her short street-dress, a hood pulled over her head likewise, and a scarf masking her face below the eyes.

Porfia led Vakar out the front entrance, where he took a torch from a bracket. She guided him into the stinking tangle of alleys west of the plaza in front of the palace, where not even the starlight penetrated.

Porfia made a sharp turn and stopped to rap with a peculiar knock on a door. They waited, and the door opened with a creak of the door-post in its well-worn sockets.

They were ushered in by a small bent black figure whose only visible feature was a great beak of a nose sticking out from under her cowl. Inside, a single rush-candle lent its wan illumination to a small cluttered room with a musty smell. A piece of papyrus on which were drawn figures and glyphs lay on a three-legged table with one leg crudely mended.

The witch mumbled something and rolled up the papyrus. Porfia said:

'Master Vakar, this is my old friend Charsela. I need not tell her who you are, for she will have already discovered that by her occult arts.'

The witch raised her head so that Vakar could see the gleam of great dark eyes on either side of the beak.

'Now do you know,' quavered the crone, 'I cannot tell you one thing about this young man? It is as if a wall against all occult influence had been built around him at birth. I can see that he is a Pusadian, probably of high rank, and that he is by nature a quiet scholarly fellow forced by his surroundings to assume the airs of a rough predacious adventurer. That much, however, any wise person could have inferred by looking at him with the eye of understanding. But come, child, tell me what troubles you this time. Another philtre to keep that sneering scapegrace true?'

'No, no,' said Porfia hastily, and went on to recount the strange tale of the serpent throne.

'Ha,' said Charsela and got out a small copper bowl which she filled with water and placed on the table.

She lit a second rushlight, placed it in a small metal holder, and stood the holder on the table. She rummaged in the litter until she found a small phial from which she dropped one drop of liquid into the water. Vakar, looking at the bowl, had an impression of swirling iridescence as the drop spread over the surface. Charsela put away the phial and sat down on the side of the table opposite the flame, so that she could see the reflection of the flame on the water.

Charsela sat so long that Vakar, standing with his back to the door, shifted his position slightly, causing his sword to clink. Porfia frowned at him. Somewhere under the junk a mouse rustled; at least Vakar hoped that it was a mouse. He shifted his gaze from the motionless wise-woman to a large spider spinning a web on the ceiling. At last the witch's thin voice came:

'It is strange – I can see figures, but all is dim and confused. There is some mighty magic involved in this, mark my word. I will try some more ...'

She put another drop from the phial into the bowl and fell silent again. Vakar was watching her sunken face in the rushlight when the door burst open behind him with a crash.

Vakar saw the witch and Porfia jerk their heads up to stare past him, and started to turn his own head then a terrific blow clanged down upon his helm and sent him sprawling forward.

He fell against the table, which overturned with a clatter as the bowl and the rushlight struck the floor. Charsela and Porfia both shrieked.

Finding himself on hands and knees with his head spinning, Vakar by a desperate effort sprang to his feet, whirled, and drew his sword all at once. He got the blade out just in time to parry another overhand cut at his head. By the light of the remaining candle he saw that three men had burst into the room, all masked.

VI

The Black Galley

Vakar thrust at the nearest, the one whose cut he had just parried. As the man stepped back his foot slipped on the wet floor where the water from the upset bowl had run around the table and made the worn planking slippery. Before he could recover, Vakar drove his blade past the fellow's awkward attempt at a parry, deep into the folds of the man's clothing. He felt his point pierce meat.

'Get her out, Charsela!' yelled Vakar, not daring to turn his head.

The man whom he had stabbed fell back with a gasp, clutching his side with his free hand. Behind him Vakar became dimly aware of a yammering from the witch and an expostulation from Porfia, and the sound of a back door opening and banging shut again. Meantime he was engaged with the other two, who were stumbling around among the junk and trying to get at him from two sides. Blades clanged as the two bravoes drove Vakar, fighting a desperate defensive, back into a corner. With a shield and the advantage of left handedness he might have handled them, but he had no shield and did not dare stoop for the witch's stool.

Instead he reached into his shirt and pulled out the poisoned dagger that had already saved his life once that night. The poison, he thought, must have pretty well worn off by now, but at least it might furnish a diversion. He threw it at the shorter of the two men.

The man tried to dodge. The knife struck him anyway, but buttfirst, so that it clanged harmlessly to the floor. The man's attention had however been distracted, and even the other man let his eyes flicker from Vakar to the flying dagger.

Instantly Vakar threw himself forward, and his ferocious *passado* went through the throat of the tall assassin. At that instant he felt a heavy blow and the sting of a cut on his right arm. The shorter man, recovering from his attempt to duck the knife, had thrown a back-hand slash at the Lorskan.

As Vakar, withdrawing his point from the tall man, half-turned to face his remaining assailant, that one skipped back out of reach before Vakar could get set for a blow. The tall man dropped his sword, clutched at his throat, gave a gurgling cough, and began to sink to the floor. The man whom Vakar had first wounded was hobbling towards the door, but now the unhurt man turned, knocked the wounded one aside, and dashed out.

Vakar leaped over the body on the floor and made for the wounded man, meaning to finish him with a quick thrust. The wounded man had been knocked down by the one who fled and was now just getting up, crying: 'Quarter!'

The man's mask had come off in the fracas, and just before he sent the blade home Vakar jerked to a halt at the sight of a familiar face. A closer look showed that the man was Abeggu of Tokalet, the foreign friend of Thiegos at the rowdy supper-party at the palace.

'Lyr's barnacles!' cried Vakar, holding his sword poised. 'What are you doing here? It will take uncommon eloquence to talk yourself out of this!'

The man stammered in his thick accent: 'Th-thiegos told me I w-was to help thwart a plot against the queen. He never – never told me you were involved, and when I found out, it was too late to ask for explanations.'

'Thiegos?' said Vakar, and bent to jerk the scarf from the face of the dead man.

Sure enough, the corpse was that of Thiegos, Queen Porfia's paramour.

Prince Vakar whistled. Either Thiegos had been in on the serpent-throne scheme, or had been smitten with jealousy of Vakar Zhu because of the latter's attention to the queen and had gathered a couple of friends to do the traveller in. Luckily they had not known that Vakar wore a helmet under his cowl, or he would have been choosing his next incarnation by now.

He looked at his wounded arm. The bloodstain was still spreading and the arm was hard to move. The hut was empty; Charsela must have pushed Porfia out the back door.

'Well,' said Vakar, 'this is the first time a man has tried to kill me because of my singing! What else do you know of this attentat?'

'N-nothing, sir. I am ashamed to admit that when the snake came to life I fled with the rest. Thiegos and I went to my lodgings near the palace to drink a skin of wine to steady our nerves and collect our wits. Then Thiegos left me to return to the palace. A little later, just as I was going to sleep, he came back with another man, saying for me to come quickly with my sword.' Abeggu gulped.

'Go on.'

'I – I do not know how to use the thing properly, as we Gamphasants are a peaceful people. I bought it merely as an ornament. When we entered here they pushed me forward to take the first shock; a fine friend *he* was! This is all most confusing and unethical; I hope the people back in Tokalet never hear of it. Was there in sooth a plot against the queen?'

'Not unless your friend Thiegos was hatching one. I am probably foolish to let you go, but I cannot butcher one who comes from the rim of the world to seek philosophy. Go, but if you cross my path again ...'

Vakar made a jabbing motion, and Abeggu, still bent over with pain, hurried out.

Vakar looked out the door after him, but except for the wounded Gamphasant nobody was in sight. If any neighbors had heard the clash of arms they had prudently kept their curiosity in check.

Should he go back to the palace? Much as he liked Porfia, he was not sure that when she learned that he had slain her lover she would not, in a transport of emotion, have him dispatched out of hand. She might regret the action later, but that would not help him if his head were already rotting on a spike on the palace wall.

No, a quick departure would be more prudent. He took a last look at the corpse, recovered his dagger, and hurried out in his turn.

Down at the waterfront of Sederado he found the *Dyra* with Fual asleep with his back against the mast and his broadsword in his hand. Fual awoke and scrambled up as Vakar approached, saying:

'I hope it's all right about those men who came aboard the ship during the day, my lord. They pawed all through the cargo, saying they were sent by the queen, and there were too many for me to stop. I don't think they stole much.'

'It's all right,' said Vakar. 'We're putting to sea at once. Help me tie up this arm and cast off.'

'You're hurt, sir?' Fual hurried to fetch out one of the cleaner rags for a bandage. The cut proved about three inches long but not deep.

Vakar silenced the valet's questions, and presently they were laboriously rowing the *Dyra* out into the seaway. They got their ropes fouled up in hoisting the sail, and the ship took some water before they get her straightened out to eastward, with Vakar steering as best he could with one arm and Fual bailing water out of the hold with a dipper. Vakar said:

'I didn't see Qasigan's black galley at its place on the waterfront. Has it gone?'

'Yes, sir. Earlier in the night a party appeared on the wharf and boarded the black ship in haste. I recognized the ape-man by his stature even in the dark. There was some delay while the captain sent men ashore to drag his rowers out of the stews, and then they pushed off and disappeared out into the bay. What happened at the palace?'

Vakar briefed Fual on their situation, adding: 'If I remember the teaching old Ryn beat into me as a boy, we pass another one or two of these islands and come to the mainland of Euskeria. What do they speak there?'

'Euskerian, sir; a complicated tongue, though I know a few words from the time I spent in Gadaria waiting to be sold.'

'There should be a law compelling all men to speak the same language, as the myths say they once did. Too bad we couldn't have cut off Sret's head and kept it alive to interpret for us, as the head of Brang was kept in the legend. Teach me what you know of Euskerian.'

During the rest of the night Vakar's arm bothered him so that he got little sleep. The next day the Ogugian coast faded away to port, and later another great island loomed up ahead. They coasted along this until, towards evening, Vakar noticed an unpleasantly hazy look in the sky and an ominous increase in the size of the swells that marched down upon them from astern. He said:

'If this were Lorsk, I should guess a storm were brewing.'

'Then, sir, shouldn't we run into some sheltered cove until it blows over?'

'I daresay, save that being so green at seafaring we should doubtless run our little ship upon the rocks.'

The night passed like the previous one except that Vakar suffered a touch of seasickness from the continuous pitching. His arm ached worse than ever, though he changed the bandage and cleaned the wound. The wind backed to the south so that it was all they could do to keep the *Dyra* from being blown on to the dark shore to port.

With the coming of a gray dawn, Fual glanced astern and cried: 'Sir, look around! It's the black galley!'

Vakar froze. A galley was crawling upon their wake like a giant insect, a small square sail swaying upon its mast and its oars rising and falling irregularly in the swells. Vakar hoped that it was not Qasigan's ship, but as the minutes passed and the galley neared he saw that Fual had been right. He could even make out the figure of Nji the ape-man in the bow. He assumed that their intentions were hostile, and presently the ape-man confirmed his guess by producing a bow twice normal size and sending a huge arrow streaking across the swells, to plunk into the water a few feet away. Qasigan and the little Yok were standing in the bow with Nji.

'They mean us to stop, sir,' said Fual.

'I know that, fool!' fumed Vakar, straining his eyes towards the ever-nearing galley.

He wondered how they had traced him. This must be that strong magic spoken of by Charsela. Was Qasigan then the author of the bizarre episode of the serpent throne?

Why should this strange man try to hound Vakar Zhu to his death? Who would benefit by his removal? His brother, perhaps. Who else? He, Vakar, was trying to thwart the impending aggression of the Gorgons against Lorsk by seeing the thing that the gods most feared. Therefore either the gods, or the Gorgons, or both, might be after him.

'Sir,' said Fual, 'if a mighty magician pursues us, shouldn't we give up now, before we inflame him further by our futile efforts to flee?'

'You rabbit! The chase was hardly begun, and I know he couldn't cast a deadly spell at this distance, from a tossing deck, in this stormy weather. A spell requires quiet and solitude.'

'I'm still afraid, sir,' mumbled Fual. 'Do something to save me!'

Vakar muttered a curse upon his servant's timidity and searched his memory for what he had heard of the Gorgons. It was said that their wizards had the power to freeze anybody within a few paces into a rigid paralysis, by some means called a 'medusa,' though Vakar did not know what a medusa was. In dealing with Gorgons, then, the thing to do was to keep away from them. As for the gods ...

Vakar rolled an eye towards the lowering sky and shook a fist. If it's war you want, he thought, you shall have it!

At that instant thunder rolled, away to the north. The wind, which had veered back to the west, blew harder. Rain began to slant across the deck.

A voice came thinly across the waves: 'Prince Vakar! Heave to!'

Vakar called to Fual: 'Come back here and take cover!'

Vakar himself crouched down in the lee of the single high step up to the poop, holding the steering-lever at arm's length. In this position he was shielded by the sheer of the high stern.

Another arrow whipped by, close enough for its screech to be heard over the roar of the wind, and drove its bone point into the deck. Vakar said:

'So long as we keep down they can't reach us —'

'Beg pardon, sir!' said Fual, who had snatched a look aft. 'They're drawing abreast!'

'Oh.' If they did that, the pair on the *Dyra* would no longer be protected, and Qasigan could have them either shot down or sunk by ramming. As Qasigan had called Vakar 'Prince,' the man had evidently not been fooled by Vakar's denial.

Vakar took a look around, shielding his eyes from the rain with his hand. Sure enough, the dark nose of the pursuing ship was creeping up to the *Dyra's* port quarter.

Vakar felt of his sword. He had no illusions of being able to leap aboard the galley and clean it out single handed, even with Fual's dubious help. For though he downed one or two sailors, he could hardly dompt the weapons of the rest, the ape-man's club, and Qasigan's Gorgonian magic all at the same time.

Closer came the bow of the galley, its bronze ram-spur bursting clear of the water each time the ship pitched. Vakar shifted his steering-lever a little to starboard, sending the *Dyra* plunging off to southward, away from the shore, though at that angle the merchant-man heeled dangerously with a horrible combination of pitch and roll. The galley swung its stem to starboard to follow.

The wind waxed further and the rain became an opaque level-blowing mass, mixed with spray from the wave-tops. The *Dyra* rolled her port rail under and dipped the corner of her sail into the crests. Vakar was sure that she would capsize.

'Help me!' he shouted, and he and Fual strained at the steering-lever until the ship swung back on a straight down-wind course. The mast-stays thrummed and the slender yards whipped dangerously, but at least the ship stayed on an even keel.

Vakar said: 'You may let go … Take another look for the galley'.

Fual tried but reported back: 'I can't, my lord.'

'Can't what?'

'Can't see. It's like thrusting your face into a waterfall.'

Vakar fared no better. Clinging to the yoke they held the ship on her course, though Vakar expected momentarily to hear the galley's ram crunch through their stern. When the squall abated, Vakar left the helm to take another look.

There was no galley.

Vakar's heart leaped up with the thought that their pursuers had swamped and drowned. But another look showed the big black craft still afloat in the distance and making for shore. Peculiar bursts of spray rising up from the galley's deck puzzled Vakar until he realized that they were caused by the sailors of the galley bailing for dear life.

Fual asked: 'Why did they leave us?'

'Couldn't take the blow. With her low freeboard the galley is even less suited to rough water than we are, and her skipper decided to call it quits and lie up in a cove.'

'The gods be praised! It's like in that poem when your hero Vrir was beset on all sides, and – how does it go, sir?'

Vakar declaimed:

'Down to the deck livid with lightnings,
Scaly and seaweed-clad, Lyr thrust his trident.
Where the spear struck rose there a rufous
Ring-fence of fire, helping the hero …'

The galley became invisible with rain, distance, and the loom of the shore. Vakar held his course, the ache in his right arm running through him. In wrestling with the helm he had started his wound bleeding again. Soaked and wretched, he wondered if even the forlorn chance of saving Lorsk from the Gorgons was worth his present misery.

Wind and rain continued all day, though never with the severity of that first squall that had all but sunk both the *Dyra* and her pursuer. The wind moderated but veered to the north so that Vakar had to hold the ship at an uncomfortable angle to the wind to avoid being swept south out to sea. During the night he got only a few nightmarish moments of sleep and faced the dawn feeling feverish and light-headed. His arm hurt so that every time it was touched or jarred he had to set his teeth to keep from yelling.

The rain petered out and the wind turned colder. The cloud cover thinned until Vakar had an occasional glimpse of the sun. He took a good look around the horizon – and stopped, his jaw sagging in horror. A couple of miles aft the galley's small sail swayed upon its mast.

Vakar was overwhelmed with despair. With Qasigan's magical powers tracking him down, how could he ever shake off the fellow? He was in no condition to stand and fight.

He pulled himself wearily together. Somewhere over the horizon ahead lay the mainland, and from what he had heard it also projected eastward to the South of him in the peninsula of Dzen. Therefore if he angled off to the right, the way the wind was now blowing, he should fetch up against the mainland. He would be taking a terrific chance, for out of sight of land an overcast that hid sun and stars would leave him utterly lost, and if the wind swung round to the east he would be blown out to sea without knowing it. On the other hand the ship would sail faster and with less of this torturous rolling …

Vakar pulled his steering-lever to the left so that the *Dyra* swung to starboard. The galley followed.

As the hours passed, the island sank out of sight and the galley drew closer, though the water was still too rough for the latter to use her oars efficiently.

'Ah me!' said Fual. 'We shall never see our homes and friends again, for this time we are truly lost.'

'Shut up!' said Vakar. Fual wept quietly.

In the afternoon another coast appeared ahead. As they drew nearer, Vakar saw a wooded hilly region with a hint of towering blue mountains in the distance. He wondered if this were the Atlantean range of sinister repute. Behind him the galley was almost within bow-shot again.

'What do you plan now, sir?' said Fual.

Vakar shook his head. 'I don't know; I seem no longer able to think.'

'Let me feel your forehead,' said Fual, and then: 'No wonder! You're a sick man, my lord. I must get you ashore and put a cow-dung poultice on that wound to draw out the poison —'

'If I can get ashore I'll take a chance on the wound.'

Close came the shore and closer came the galley. Fual cried:

'Breakers ahead! We shall be wrecked!'

'I know it. Get our gear together and prepare to leap off the bow when we touch.'

'Too late! They'll ram us before we can reach the beach!'

'Do as I say!' roared Vakar, straining his eyes ahead.

A glance back showed that the galley was overhauling them faster than they were nearing the strand. Vakar gripped his steering-lever as if he could thus squeeze an extra knot out of the *Dyra*.

Behind, the galley gained; Vakar heard the coxswain exhorting his rowers. Ahead a line of rocks showed between waves, a score of paces short of the beach. As the combers toppled over they struck these rocks and sent up great fountains of spray, then continued on to the beach with diminished force. If he could guide the little ship between these rocks they might escape, but if he struck one they would drown like mice …

Crash! Vakar staggered as the galley's bow struck the stern of the *Dyra*. Fual tumbled to the deck, then rolled over and sat up with a despairing shriek. Under the whistle of the wind, the roar of the breakers, and the shouts of the men on the galley, Vakar fancied he heard the gurgle of water rushing into the *Dyra*.

He recovered his balance and looked ahead. They were headed straight for one of the needles of rock. Vakar heaved on the yoke to swerve the *Dyra*, which heeled and scrapped past the obstacle with timbers groaning and crackling. The change in the slope of the deck told Vakar that the ship was settling by the stern. The galley had withdrawn its beak and was backing water furiously to keep off the rocks.

'Get ready!' Vakar screamed to Fual, who blubbered with terror.

Then the deck jerked back under him as the ship struck the beach. Vakar staggered forward and stopped himself by grabbing the mast. He ducked under the lower yard to find that Fual had already tumbled off the bow into knee-deep water and was splashing ashore, leaving the bag containing their possessions on the deck.

With a curse that should have struck the Aremorian dead, Vakar threw the bag ashore and dropped off the bow himself, the pain of his arm shooting through him like red-hot bronze. He picked up the bag with his good arm and caught up with Fual, to whom he handed the bag, and then hit him across the face with the back of his hand.

'That'll teach you to abandon your master!' he said. 'Now march!'

Staggering, Vakar led the way straight inland up the grassy side of a knoll that rose from the inner edge of the beach. At the top he looked back. The galley was still standing off the rocks while the *Dyra* lay heeled over on the edge of the sand, her sail flapping and water pouring in and out of her great wounds. As the galley did not appear to possess a ship's boat to send a search-party ashore, Vakar felt secure for the time being – until Qasigan found a safer landing-place and took up his pursuit ashore.

Vakar led the weeping Fual down the back slope of the knoll until he was out of sight of the sea, then turned to the left and walked parallel to the beach.

They had tramped for an hour or so when a sound brought them up short:

a fierce barking and snarling as of the dog that guarded the gates of the hells. They went forward cautiously, hands on swords, and over the next rise found a wild-looking shepherd clad in sheep-skins tied haphazard about his person. In one hand he grasped a wooden club with stone spikes set in the thick end, while the other clutched the leash of a great dog, which strained to get at the travellers. The sheep huddled baaing in the background.

Vakar held out his hands. The shepherd shouted.

'What does he say?' asked Vakar.

'To go away or he'd loose the dog on us.'

'A hospitable fellow. Ask where there's a settlement.'

Fual spoke in broken Euskerian. After several repetitions, the shepherd waved his club, saying:

'Sendeu.'

'That's a village,' explained Fual.

'Tell him there's a wrecked ship back that way, and he's welcome to it.'

Vakar began a detour around the surly shepherd and his flock. As they passed out of sight the man was gathering his sheep to drive them south along the coast.

Vakar's arm hurt with an agony he had never known before. He muttered:

'I'll never sneer at others' sicknesses again, Fual ...'

Then the universe went into a whirling dance and Vakar lost track of what was happening.

VII

The Satyr of Sendeu

Vakar Zhu awoke to the sounds of domestic bustle. He was lying on a rough bed in the corner of a log hut that seemed, at the moment, to be entirely full of children and dogs.

The cabin had a door at one end partly closed by a leather curtain, and no windows. On the walls hung the family's tools: a fishing-spear barbed with sharks' teeth, hoes made from large clamshells, wooden sickles set with flint blades along their concave edges, and so on. Animal noises from beyond the wall opposite the door told Vakar that this wall was a partition bisecting the cabin, the other half being used for livestock. At one side of the room a husky-looking peasant girl was working a small loom whose clack-clack furnished a rhythm under the barking of the dogs and the cries of the children. A sweaty smell overhung the scene.

Fual was sitting on the dirt floor beside him. Vakar raised his head, discovering that he was weak as water.

'Where am I?' he said.

'You're yourself again, my lord? The gods be praised! You're in the hut of Juten, a peasant of Sendeu.'

'How did I get here?'

'You walked, sir, but you were out of your head. We stopped at the first likely-looking hut, and you told Juten you were emperor of the world and he should order out your chariotry to attack the Gorgons. He didn't understand, of course, and after much struggle with the language I explained to him that you were a traveller who had taken sick and needed to lie up a few days. He was suspicious and unfriendly, but when I paid him out of your scrip the finally let us in.' Fual looked around the hut with lifted lip. 'Hardly people of our class, sir, but it was the best I could do.'

'How long ago was this?'

'The day before yesterday.' Fual felt Vakar's forehead. 'The fever has left you. Would you like some soup?'

'By all means. I'm hungry as a spring bear.'

Vakar moved his right arm, wincing. Still, it was better than it had been. Fual brought the broth in a gourd bowl.

As the day wore on Vakar met Juten's wife, a very pregnant woman with lined peasant features. She began speaking to him while going about her chores, undeterred by the fact that they had only a dozen words in common, so the rest of the day Vakar was subjected to a continuous spate of chatter. From its general tone he guessed that he was not missing anything by lack of understanding.

The people were tall light-haired round-headed Atlanteans, who never bathed to judge by their looks and smell. The girl who ran the loom was Juten's eldest daughter. Vakar never did get the names of all the children straight, but a little girl of six named Atsé took a fancy to him. When he pointed at things and asked their names she told him, making a game of it and finding his mistakes a great joke. By nightfall he had a fair household vocabulary.

Then Juten came in, thickset and stooped with dirt worked deeply into the cracks of his skin. He gave Vakar a noncommittal look and spoke in broken Hesperian:

'Lord better now?'

'Yes, thank you.'

Supper was a huge loaf of barley-bread, milk, and a strange golden fruit called an 'orange'. Juten pointed apologetically to a jug in the corner:

'Beer not good yet.'

Next day Vakar, now well enough to move around, continued his fraternization with Atsé. He encouraged her to talk, stopping her every few words for an explanation. She got bored and went out, but then a rainstorm drove her in again.

'What do you do for fun?' he asked, shaving the three days' stubble from his chin with his bronze razor.

'I play with the others and I visit the tailed lady.'

'The what?'

'The lady with the tail. She lives in the hills over that way.' Atségestured eastward. 'I call her with this.'

She produced a tiny whistle tied around her neck with a string of grass and blew on it. Vakar, hearing nothing, asked:

'How can she hear you when that thing makes no noise?'

'Oh, but it does! A magical noise that she alone can hear.'

Vakar tried blowing on it himself, with no result save that the two dogs who happened to be in the hut both howled. Later, when Atsé had gone out again, Vakar asked Juten's wife about the tailed woman.

'She told you that?' cried the woman. 'I will tan her hide! She knows she should not ...'

'Why? Many children make up imaginary playmates —'

'Imaginary! Would that she were! This is a satyr of Atlantis who has settled near here and entices the children into stealing our food and taking it to her secretly. The men have hunted her with dogs, but her magic baffles them.'

Vakar, who had understood only about half of what the woman had said, dropped the subject of the satyr to take a snooze. That evening, after supper, Juten mumbled something about a village meeting and went out into the sunset. Vakar dozed until aroused by Fual's shaking him.

'My lord!' said the valet. 'We must flee or they'll murder us!'

'Huh? What are you talking about?'

'I spied upon the village meeting, which was called to discuss us. Egon, the headman, urged that we be killed and persuaded the others.'

'Lyr's barnacles! Why?'

'From what I could understand, they seemed to think that all foreigners are evil, and that we have wealth on our persons which the village could use. Moreover their witch-doctor said he could insure a year's prosperity by sacrificing us to their gods. They sacrifice people with torture, and the shaman claimed his gods had appeared to him in a vision to demand our lives. Juten and one or two others wished to spare us, but were outvoted.'

'What's their scheme?'

'They'll wait until we're asleep and rush in. They dare not attack us openly for fear of our swords.'

Vakar glanced to where Juten's wife sat placidly in the doorway, milling barley with a hand-quern. He thoughtfully twirled his mustache. Feeling sure that she would not have understood the conversation in Lorskan he said:

'Is all our gear in the bag?'

'Nearly, sir. I'll pack the rest now.'

Vakar got up, stretched, and put on his cloak. He bent over the children's beds until he located Atsé, whose single garment was wadded up to make a pillow. Vakar explored gently until he found the tiny whistle and withdrew it. He did not like robbing a child, but had little choice. He dropped the whistle into his scrip and said to Juten's wife:

'Your pardon, madam, but we are going out for a walk.'

'Are you strong enough, sir?' she said, rising to make way for the pair of them.

'I think so, thank you.'

Vakar led the way, Fual following with the bag on his back. Vakar walked toward the corner of the hut. Just before he reached it the woman called after him:

'Sir, why are you carrying your belongings? Are you leaving us?'

Pretending not to hear, Vakar swung rapidly around the corner of the house and headed eastward between it and the next hut. They passed a couple of store-sheds, detoured a pig-pen and a paddock containing horses, and strode through a plowed field, their boots sinking into the mud and coming out with sucking noises. Vakar felt a little weak and his arm was sore, but otherwise he seemed to be active again. He asked:

'This is the first I've seen of the neighborhood since recovering my senses. Can you lead the way?'

'No, sir. Except for a few glimpses of the main street of the village I know hardly more about it than you. Where are you taking us?'

Vakar told about the female satyr, adding: 'I know not whether she's real or a peasant superstition, but I brought the child's whistle along to try. She might conceivably help us, being of the third class of friends.'

'What's that?'

'There's your friend, and your friend's friend, and your enemy's enemy. She seems to be of the last kind.'

He blew experimentally, whereupon there was an outburst of barking from the village.

'For the gods' sake, my lord, don't do that!' said Fual. 'There must be some sound emitted by that thing, even though we mortal men can't hear it. You'll have all those devils on our trail.' He glared back at the village and muttered Aremorian curses upon the Sendevians.

They tramped in silence until they passed out of the fields and entered the zone of wild grass and scrubby forest. The stars came out though the moon, being past full, had not risen. Somewhere in the hills a lion roared. They were stumbling their way up a draw between two of the smaller foothills of the Atlantean Mountains when Fual said:

'Sir, listen!'

Vakar halted and heard, far behind them, a murmur of voices and a chorus of barking. Looking back he saw a tiny glimmer as of a swarm of fireflies. That would be the men of the village setting out with dogs and torches to hunt them down.

'Oh, hurry!' said Fual, teeth chattering.

Vakar hurried. One or two peasants he would have faced, but if all the able-bodied males of Sendeu caught him, emboldened by numbers, stone axes and wooden rakes and pitchforks would do him in as surely if not so quickly as whetted bronze.

He blew on the whistle again. Nothing happened.

They stumbled on, pausing betimes for breath. Each time the sounds of pursuit became louder. When the moon rose, Vakar straightened out their course towards the east, where, he hoped, the more rugged terrain would give them a better chance of escape.

Fual said: 'Sir, why did you bring me on this terrible journey, where we spend all our time fleeing from one dire doom after another? You could have left me to serve your brother —'

'Shut up,' said Vakar, gasping for breath.

He looked back down the valley they were now traversing and plainly saw the swarm of torches at the lower end. He raised the whistle to his lips, but Fual cried:

'Oh, pray don't blow that again! It only draws the dogs faster.'

'They'll track us by smell in any case, and it's our last —'

Fual sank to his knees, weeping, and kissed Vakar's hand, but Vakar pushed him roughly back.

'I shall blow, and if it doesn't work, look to your sword. I'm too tired to run further, and we can at least take a few of these sons of sows with us.'

Ignoring Fual's prayers, Vakar blew. The torches came closer and the barking became louder. Vakar was feeling his edge when a voice spoke in Euskerian:

'Who are you, and what do you wish?'

Vakar saw nobody, but replied: 'We are two travellers whom the villagers of Sendeu seek to murder. We thought you might give us sanctuary.'

'You do not look or speak like peasants. Could you do me a favor in return?'

'What favor?' said Vakar, with a lively memory of legends where in people offered some petitioner anything he asked and lived to regret their impulsiveness.

'I wish help in getting back to my native land.'

'We will do our best.'

'Come then; but if this is a trap you shall be sorry.'

There was a movement in the shrubbery on the hillside, and Vakar started towards the fugitive spot of pallor. His rest had given him strength to pull himself up the hillside. The three of them – Vakar, Fual, and their half-seen guide – crossed the crest of the ridge as the dogs and torches streamed past below. At the point where the fugitives turned off, the dogs halted and milled.

Vakar whispered: 'Will they not follow our scent?'

'No, for I cast a spell upon them. But come, for these spells are short-lived.'

An hour later Vakar followed the satyr into a cave on a hillside whose mouth was cunningly hidden by vegetation. The being rummaged in the darkness. Vakar saw the shower of sparks caused by striking flint against pyrites, and presently a rush-light glimmered.

'I do not use fire myself,' said their rescuer, 'but when my lovers used to come from the village I found they liked to see what they were doing, so I laid in a store of these things.'

Vakar looked. The satyr was a young female, naked, about five feet tall and quite human except for the horse-like tail, snub nose, slanting eyes, and pointed ears. He asked:

'Have you a name?'

'Tiraafa.'

'I am Vakar and he is Fual, my servant. What is this about human lovers, Tiraafa?' Vakar found the habits of the near-human species fascinating.

'With us,' said Tiraafa, 'one must have love, much more than among you cold and passionless humans. Since there are no others of my kind here-abouts I encouraged the lustier young men of the village to visit me. Of course the love of a man is a limp and feeble thing compared to that of a satyr, but it was all I could do.'

'Why are there no others of your kind?' said Fual. 'I always understood satyrs dwelt in Atlantis.'

'They do, but not of my tribe. I come from the Saturides, far to the north, having been seized by Foworian slavers. I was sold in Gadaira, but escaped and fled into the mountains. When I found a tribe of satyrs they thought, because I was a stranger who spoke a dialect different from theirs, that I must be a spy sent against them by the human beings. They drove me off with sticks and stones – and here I am.'

'You wish to return to the Satyr Isles?'

'Oh, yes! Could you help me?' She seized his wrist imploringly.

Fual, cheerful again, said: 'Have no fear, Tiraafa. My lord can arrange anything.'

'Maybe,' grunted Vakar. 'What ended your relations with Sendeu?'

'The maidens of the village complained to their fathers, who forbade their sons to visit me. No longer having the food they brought, I had to steal or persuade the children to bring me some, and the headman swore to kill me.'

'We have had our troubles with Egon too,' said Vakar. 'A right friendly fellow. But as we seem safe for the moment, let us get some sleep and plan our next move in the morning.'

'As you wish,' said Tiraafa. 'However, I have had no love for months, and expect as part of the price of your rescue —'

She began sliding her hands up his arms towards his neck in a way that reminded Vakar of Bili.

'Not me, little one,' said Vakar. 'I am a sick man. Begin with Fual, and in another day I may be able to help out. Fual, the lady wishes love; attend to it.'

And Vakar, not waiting to see how Fual took this unusual command, curled up in his cloak and dropped off to sleep.

'As I see it,' said Vakar as he shared Tiraafa's meager breakfast next morning, 'we must all head north to Gadaira, where I can put Tiraafa on a ship for her native land while we proceed up the Baitis to Torrutseish. How far to Gadaira, Tiraafa?'

As satyrs seemed to have no notion of measurement she was unable to answer his query. By questioning her closely about her erratic course from Gadaira to Sendeu, however, Vakar got the impression that the distance was somewhere between one and three hundred miles.

'Too far to walk,' he said, 'especially in a country where the peasantry sacrifice strangers to their gods. Whose horses are those I saw in the paddock last night?'

Tiraafa replied: 'They belong to the village, which really means Egon as he and his relatives control the village. They rear these creatures not to use themselves but to sell in Gadaira.'

'Do they not plow with them?'

'What is plowing?'

It transpired that neither Tiraafa nor the Sendevians had ever seen a plow. Vakar said:

'If we could steal these horses we should both provide ourselves with transportation and express our love for Headman Egon. They could not follow us, and we could sell those we did not need in Gadaira.'

'Why are you going to Torrutseish?' asked Tiraafa.

'To seek the advice of the world's greatest magicians. Do you know which of them is the best?'

'Not much, but when I was captive in Gadaira I heard the name of Kurtevan. All of us satyrs are magicians of a sort, and such news gets around among the brotherhood.'

Prince Vakar peered out of his hiding-place. The twelve horses were pegged out in the meadow, and the youth who guarded them sat with his back to a tree, wrapped in his black Euskerian mantle, with his long copper-headed spear across his legs. With this (probably the only metal weapon in the village) the horse-herd could stand off a prowling lion long enough for his yells to fetch help. Vakar looked at the young man coldly, with neither hatred nor sympathy. He knew that many self-sufficient peasant communities looked upon city-folk as legitimate prey, for their only contact with cities was when the latter sent tax-gathering parties among them, and from the point of view of the villages these were mere plundering expeditions for which they got nothing in return. But while he realized that the Sendevians' attack on him was not due to sheer malevolence, he would not on that account spare them if they got in his way.

Tiraafa peered around her tree and called softly: 'Olik!'

The young man sprang up, gripping his spear, then laughed. 'Tiraafa! According to my orders I ought to slay you.'

'You would not do that! I loved you the best of all.'

'Did you really?'

'Try me and see.'

'By the gods, I will!'

Olik leaned his spear against his tree and started for Tiraafa with the lust-light in his eyes. His expression changed to amazement as Vakar leaped out of the bushes and ran full-tilt at him. Vakar saw his victim begin to turn and fill his lungs to shout just as Vakar's sword slid between his ribs up to the hilt.

Vakar, sheathing his blade, said: 'Can either of you ride?'

Tiraafa and Fual, looking apprehensive, shook their heads.

'Well then, as it looks as though these beasts have never been ridden either, you both start from the same point.'

Vakar walked out into the field, where the horses had laid back their ears and were tugging on their tethering-ropes and rolling their eyes at the sight of strangers and the smell of blood. He selected the one who seemed the least disturbed, gentled it down, and began twisting its tethering-rope into a bridle.

Several days later, riding bareback, they halted in sight of Gadaira. Vakar, looking toward the forest of masts and yards that could be seen over the low roofs, said:

'Fual, before we take our little sweetheart into the city, one of us must go ahead and buy her clothes, or the first slaver who sees her will seize her. And as you're a better bargainer than I, you are elected.'

'Please, sir, then may I walk? I'm so stiff and sore from falling off this accursed animal that the thought of solid ground under my feet seems like a dream of heaven.'

'Suit yourself. And while you're about it, inquire for a reliable sea-captain sailing northward.'

An hour later Fual was back with a gray woolen dress and a black Euskerian cloak with a hood. The dress concealed Tiraafa's tail and the hood her ears. Fual said:

'I learned that Captain Therlas sails for Kerys in three or four days with a cargo of cork and copper, and that he is said to be a man of his word.' The little Aremorian hesitated, then burst out: 'My lord, why don't you set me free? I'm as anxious to see my home again as she is, and I could keep an eye upon her until Therlas dropped her off on her wild islands.'

'I didn't know you so wished to leave me,' said Vakar. 'Have I treated you badly?'

'No – at least not so badly as most masters – but there is nothing like freedom and one's home.'

Vakar pondered. The appeal did touch him, as he was not unsympathetic for an aristocrat and the ex-thief was at best an indifferent servant. On the other hand Vakar was appalled by the prospect of finding a reliable new slave in this strange city, even though he did need someone with more thews and guts than his sensitive valet.

'I'll tell you,' he said at last. 'I won't free you now, because I badly need your help and I think Tiraafa can take care of herself. But when we win back to Lorsk with our mission accomplished I'll not only free you but also provide you with the means of getting home.'

Fual muttered a downcast 'Thank you, sir,' and turned his attention to other matters.

They found lodgings and sold eight of the twelve horses, keeping the four strongest for their own use. Vakar took a variety of trade-goods in exchange for the animals: little ingots of silver stamped with the cartouche of King Asizhen of Tartessia; packets of rare spices from beyond Kheru and Thamuzeira in the Far East; and for small change the ordinary celt-shaped slugs and neck-rings of copper. Fual, looking with undisguised hostility at the horses, suggested:

'At least, sir, you might buy a chariot so we could continue our journey in comfort ...'

'No. Chariots are all right for cities, but we may be going where there are only foot-tracks for roads.'

When the time came they escorted Tiraafa to the docks and saw her aboard ship with provisions for the journey. She kissed them fiercely, saying:

'I shall always remember you, for as human beings go you are quite fair lovers. I hope Captain Therlas will equal you in this regard.'

On an impulse Vakar pressed a fistful of trade-copper into Tiraafa's hands and helped her aboard. Fual wept and Vakar waved as the ship cast off, and then they turned away to the four horses hitched to one of the waterfront posts. Vakar vaulted on to his new saddle-pad and clamped his knees on the barrel of the beast, which under his expert training had become quite manageable. Fual tried to imitate his master, but leaped too hard and fell off his mount into the mud on the other side, whereat Vakar roared. He was still laughing when he glanced out to sea, and the laugh died as if cut off by an ax.

'Fual,' he said, 'mount at once. Qasigan's galley is coming into the harbor.'

A few seconds later the four horses were headed away from the waterfront through the streets of Gadaira at a reckless gallop.

VIII

The Towers of Torrutseish

A hundred and sixty miles up the Baitis lay mighty Torrutseish, the capital of the Tartessian Empire and the world's largest city, known by many names in different places and ages. In Vakar's time it was so old that its origin was lost in the mists of myth.

In the days of Vakar Lorska, the king of Tartessia had extended his sway over most of the Euskerian nations: the Turdetanians, the Turdulians, and even the Phaiaxians who were not Euskerians at all. The city of Torrutseish, preëminent among all the cities of the world for its magic, stood on an island where the Baitis forked and rejoined itself again. Prince Vakar approached it up the river road, leading his two spare horses and followed by Fual (who kept his seat by gripping a fistful of his mount's mane.) To their left the broad Baitis bore swarms of dugouts, rafts of inflated skins, and other fresh-water craft.

Vakar sighted the walls and towers of the metropolis as he came around a bend. The outer wall was circular like that of Amferé but on a vaster scale. Like the lofty towers that rose behind it, it was built of red, white, and black stones arranged in bands and patterns to give a dazzling mosaic effect. The bright blue Euskerian sun flashed on the gilding of dome and spire and tourelle, and flags bearing the owl of Tartessia flapped lazily in the faint breeze.

Vakar thrilled at the sight of buildings of three or even four stories, though he would have enjoyed it more if he had not felt obliged to look back down the river every few minutes to see if the sinister black galley were rowing up behind him. For the Baitis was fully navigable thus far, and Vakar was sure that with his supernatural methods of tracking, his enemy would soon be breasting the current in pursuit.

When he had passed the inspection of the guards at the city gate and had found quarters, Vakar asked where the house of Kurtevan the magician was to be found.

'You wish to see Kurtevan? In person?' said the innkeeper, his jaw sagging so that Vakar could see the fragments of the leek that he had been chewing.

'Why, yes. What is so peculiar about that?'

'Nothing, nothing, save that Kurtevan does not cultivate the custom of common men like us. He is the principal thaumaturge to King Asizhen.'

Vakar raised his bushy eyebrows 'That is interesting, but I too am not without some small importance in my own land. Where can I find his house?'

The innkeeper told him, and as soon as he had washed and rested Vakar set out with Fual in the direction indicated. They got lost amid the crooked streets of one of the older sections of the city, and asked a potter, who sat in his stall slowly revolving his tournette:

'Could you tell us where to find the house of Kurtevan the magician?'

The man gave them an alarmed glance and began turning the tournette rapidly, so that the piece grew under his fingers like magic. Thinking that perhaps the fellow had not understook his broken Euskerian, Vakar laid a hand on his arm, saying:

'I asked you where to find the house of Kurtevan, friend. Do you not know, or did you not understand me?'

The man muttered: 'I understood you, but not wishing you ill I forebore to answer, for prudent men do not disturb the great archimage without good cause.'

'My cause is my own affair,' said Vakar in some irritation. 'Now will you answer a civil question of not?'

The Tartessian sighed and gave directions.

'Anyone would think,' said Vakar as he set out in the direction indicated, 'we were asking the way to the seven hells.'

'Perhaps we are, sir,' said Fual.

The house of Kurtevan turned out to be a tall tower of red stone in the midst of a courtyard surrounded by a wall. With the handle of his dagger Vakar struck the copper gong that hung beside the gate. As the sound of the gong died away the gate opened with a loud creak.

Vakar stepped in, took one look at the gate-keeper – and involuntarily stepped back, treading on Fual's toe.

'Oi!' said Fual. 'What —'

Then he too caught sight of the gatekeeper, gasped, and turned to flee, but Vakar caught his clothing and dragged him inside. The gatekeeper pushed the gate shut and stood silently facing them. He was silent for the good reason that he had no head.

The gatekeeper was the headless body of a tall swarthy man, dressed in a breech-clout only, whose neck stopped halfway up. Skin and a sparse growth of dark curly hair grew over the stump, except for a couple of obscene-looking irregular openings that presumably represented the thing's windpipe and gullet. A single eye stared out of its chest at the base of its neck. Its broad bare chest rose and fell slowly. A large curved bronze sword was thrust through its girdle.

Vakar looked blankly at this unusual ostiary, wondering how to communicate with one who lacked ears. Still, the thing must have heard the gong. Vakar cleared his throat uncertainly and spoke:

'My name is Vakar, and I should like to see Kurtevan.'

The acephalus beckoned and led the way to the base of the tower. Here it unlocked the door with a large bronze key and opened it, motioning Vakar to enter.

Fual muttered: 'Perhaps I should stay outside, sir. They seem all too willing to admit us to this suburb of hell ...'

'Come along,' snapped Vakar, nervously cracking his knuckle-joints.

He stepped inside. The setting sun shot a golden shaft through the wall-slit on the west side of the tower, almost horizontally across the room in which Vakar found himself. As his eyes adapted to the gloom he made out a lot of furniture gleaming with gold and precious stones, but the gleam was muted by quantities of dust and cobwebs.

Evidently, Vakar thought, headless servants did not make neat housekeepers.

He stood in a great circular room that took in the whole of the first floor of the tower, except for a spiral stone staircase that wound up to the floor above and down to some subterranean compartment below. There was nobody in the room; no sound save the frantic buzzing of a fly caught in one of the many spiderwebs. Overhead a grid of heavy wooden beams crossed the stonework from one side to the other, supporting a floor of planks. Vakar tried in vain to see through the cracks in the planks.

'Let's try the next floor,' he whispered.

Holding his scabbard, Vakar tiptoed over to the stair, followed by Fual wearing a stricken look. Up he went, though a stair to him was still a somewhat mysterious newfangled contrivance. Nothing barred his way as he came up the curving stair to the second floor. Here, however, he halted as his swift-darting glance caught the outlines of a man.

The man was sitting cross-legged on a low taboret with his eyes closed. He was a spare individual with the face of an aged hawk, and wrapped from head to foot in the typical black Euskerian mantle. The cloak was however made of some shiny fabric that Vakar had never seen. The man's hands lay limply in his lap. Before him stood a small tripod supporting a copper dish, in which burned a little heap of something. A thin blue column of smoke arose steadily from the smolder. Vakar caught a whiff of a strange smell as he stalked towards the still figure.

Vakar froze as the man moved, though the movement was the slightest: a minute raising of his head and the opening of his eyes to slits. Vakar had an uncomfortable feeling that if the eyes opened all the way the results might be unfortunate.

The man spoke in perfect Hesperian: 'Hail, Prince Vakar Zhu of Lorsk; Vakar the son of Zhabutir.'

'Greetings,' said Vakar without wasting breath asking Kurtevan how he knew his name.

'You have come to me to seek that which the gods most fear.'

'True.'

'You are also fleeing from one Qasigan, a Gorgonian priest of Entigta —'

'A Gorgon?' said Vakar sharply.

'Yes; did you not know?'

'I guessed but was not sure.'

'Very well, there shall be no charge for that bit of information. However, for the other matter, what are you prepared to pay for this powerful agency?'

Vakar, who had expected this question, named a figure in ounces of gold that amounted to about half the total value of his trade-goods.

The old man's hooded eyes opened a tiny crack further. 'That is ridiculous. Am I a village witch peddling spurious love-philtres?'

Vakar raised his bid; and again, until he was offering all his wealth except barely enough to get him back to Lorsk.

Kurtevan smiled thinly. 'I am merely playing with you, Vakar Zhu. I know the contents of that scrip down to the last packet of spice, and had you thrice that amount it would not suffice me. I am chief thaumaturge by appointment to King Asizhen, and have no need to cultivate common magical practice.'

Vakar stood silently, frowning and pulling his mustache. After a few seconds the wizard spoke again:

'Howsoever, if you cannot pay my price in gold and silver and spice, it is possible that you could recompense me in services. For I am in need of that which trade-goods cannot buy.'

'Yes?' said Vakar.

'As all men know, I am the leading wonder-worker of Torrutseish and receive the king's exclusive custom in the field of thaumaturgy. That, however, is but half the practice of magic, the other half comprising the divinatory arts. Now the leading seer of the city, one Nichok, receives the king's patronage for oracles and prophecies and visions. I would add that art to my own practice.'

Vakar nodded.

'I have composed a beautiful method of doing so, except that it requires the help of a strong man of more than common hardihood. Briefly, it is this: my rival Nichok lies most of the time in a trance while his soul goes forth to explore the world in space and time. If I could possess myself of his body while he is in one of these trances, I could seal it against the reëntry of his soul, and by threatening to destroy this body I could force Nichok's soul to divine for me as long as I wished.'

'You wish me to steal this body for you?'

'Precisely.'

'Why me?' said Vakar warily.

'Because the men of Torrutseish are so imbued with fear of us of the magical profession that none would dare let himself be involved in such a *coup-de-main*. Moreover your slave has, I believe, some authentic knowledge of the theory and practice of larceny and could help you.'

'Suppose that fear is well founded?'

'It is, to a degree. But this task, while admittedly dangerous, is by no means hopeless. Were I Nichok I could give you the precise odds on your success. As it is I can tell you that they are no worse than pursuing a wounded lion into its lair. As your friend Qasigan will not arrive in Torrutseish before tomorrow night, you have ample time.'

Vakar stood silently until Kurtevan spoke again: 'There is no likelihood of my reducing my demand, young man, so make up your mind. Either make this attempt or go elsewhere for means to thwart the Gorgons.'

Mention of the Gorgons gave Vakar the extra push needed to make up his mind. If Qasigan were indeed a Gorgon, then Söl's story of the Gorgons' impending descent upon his homeland was true.

'I will try,' he said. 'What must we do?'

'First you must wait until dark and go to the tower of Nichok. It is much like this one but smaller, and across the city – I will give you a map.'

'How do I get in?'

'There is a secret entrance that even Nichok does not know.'

'How is that?'

'For the simple reason that I built his present tower, and sold it to him when I erected this edifice fifty years ago. Now, when you have entered his tower by the secret entrance, you will find a trapdoor, and underneath the trapdoor a ladder leading down to the underground chamber where lies the body of Nichok. My arts tell me he is not lying completely unprotected; he has summoned a guardian from some other plane of existence, though its precise nature I cannot ascertain.'

'Hmm. How shall I cope with this guardian? An armed man I can take a chance with, but some ten-armed demon from another universe ... What am I supposed to do when I cut at the creature and my sword goes through it like smoke?'

'Do not let that concern you. Things from other worlds and planes, if they would dwell in our world, must obey the laws thereof. Therefore if this guardian is sufficiently materialized on this dimension to harm you, by the same token it must be equally vulnerable to your attack.'

'Well, if Nichok's soul is wandering about, how do you know it is not eavesdropping on us now?'

The wizard smiled. 'Every dog is invincible on its home ground. For one thing all openings in my tower are sealed with the juice of rue, garlic, asafetida, and other spirit-repellants. But come; it will be another hour before full darkness, and you must be hungry. Sup with me and then set out upon your task.'

Kurtevan clapped his hands. The headless servitor appeared and set out two stools and a low table. At least *a* headless servant appeared; Vakar realized that without faces to go by it was almost impossible to tell whether this were the same gatekeeper or not. He said:

'You have unusual servants, Master Kurtevan. Do you find them more obedient without heads? What *is* the creature?'

'A gift from the lord of Belem. Do you know Awoqqas?'

'I have heard sinister rumors of the land of Belem, that is all.'

'King Awoqqas has found a method of reanimating a freshly decapitated corpse by constraining a certain type of spirit of the air to animate it. If the operation is performed carefully so that the body is prevented from bleeding to death, the wound can be healed and a servant created who is more docile than any whole man. Its only disadvantage compared to a whole man, like yours, is that with that single eye in his chest it cannot look up or around. Awoqqas has a whole army of these izzuneg, as they are called in the language of Belem, and if your travels should take you thither I am sure you could persuade him to convert your slave to an izzuni.'

'An interesting idea,' said Vakar, 'but I must take Fual's feelings into account. Being very sensitive he might not like the loss of his head.'

'Ahem. You see,' continued Kurtevan, 'there are three schools of thought regarding the location of the intelligence: that it resides in the head, or in the heart, or in the liver. Now Awoqqas appears to have proved the first-named correct. Lacking a brain, there is no likelihood that the memories and thought-patterns that the acephalus had as a whole human being will be reanimated along with the rest of the organism, and perhaps interfere with the control of the body by the sylph ...'

The thin old wizard became almost animated as he discussed magical theory. Vakar, despite Kurtevan's callous disregard for other human beings, became so absorbed that he almost forgot the peril ahead of him. Fual continued to quake. But when the food arrived, Vakar said:

'I trust you will not deem me unduly suspicious, but do you swear by your magical powers that this food contains nothing harmful – no drug or enchantment that might affect us at any time?'

Kurtevan smiled crookedly. 'Old Ryn taught you well. Of course even the most wholesome food can be harmful if eaten in abnormal quantities —'

'No quibbling, please. Do you swear?' For Vakar knew that if a magician swore falsely by his magical powers these powers would at once leave him.

'I swear,' said Kurtevan, and addressed himself to his plate. 'Does this convince you?'

The tower of Nichok stood black against the stars. Although Kurtevan had said that it was smaller than his present keep, it loomed larger in the darkness. Vakar and Fual leaned against the wall surrounding the tower, listening. They had left their cloaks and satchel at Kurtevan's so as not to be encumbered more than was necessary.

Something moved around inside the wall, though the sound was not that of human footsteps. There was a curious shuffle and a scaly rattle about the sound, and something breathed with a hiss that was almost a whistle.

A light showed in the distance.

'The watch!' said Fual, convulsively gripping Vakar's arm.

'Well, don't twist my arm off. Remember what he told us.'

In accordance with Kurtevan's instructions, both men put their backs to the wall and froze to immobility. The wizard had thrown a glamor over them so that so long as they remained still the watch would simply not notice them; they were for practical purposes invisible.

The watch – a group of eight citizens holding torches and with staves and zaghnals over their shoulders – tramped past. Vakar caught a muttered comment about the price of onions, and the group swung by, never looking towards Vakar and Fual. When the watch had passed out of sight, Vakar led Fual silently back to the place where they had been listening.

'Six paces from the gate,' he breathed, 'and two feet from the wall ... Fual, your feet are smaller than mine, more like those of a Euskerian. Put them one behind the other ...'

Vakar marked the spot with his toe and began digging in the dirt with his fingers. When the ground proved too hard he attacked it with the blade of his knife, going round and round in an increasing spiral from the spot where he had started, and also deeper and deeper.

Once the blade struck something. Vakar scrabbled eagerly, but it turned out to be a mere stone, not the bronze ring he sought.

On the other side of the wall the peculiar footsteps came and went again.

Then the blade struck another obstacle. This time it was the ring, rough with corrosion. Vakar, wishing he had a shovel, cleared away the dirt around it; then grasped it with both hands and heaved. It stuck fast.

He cleared away more of the dirt from the stone slab in which the ring was set and motioned Fual to hook as many fingers as possible into the ring also. Both heaved, and with a loud scraping and grinding the ring rose. As the slab tilted up on one edge, dirt showered into the hole, about two feet square, that yawned beneath it. Vakar pulled the stone up until it stuck in a nearly vertical position.

'Come on,' he whispered, lowering himself into the hole.

IX

Death by Fire

They had to crawl through a mere burrow. Vakar's knees were sore and he was sure that the tunnel had taken them clear to the other side of Nichok's lot when he rammed his head into the end of the tunnel.

He felt around overhead until he located the contours of the stone slab that topped this end of the tunnel. Gathering his forces he heaved. Inch by inch the stone rose. A wan light wafted into the tunnel.

Vakar thrust his head up through the opening. A single oil lamp feebly illuminated a great round room like that which comprised the ground floor of Kurtevan's tower. A massive timber door was bolted on the inside.

Vakar climbed out, tiptoed over to the door, and listened. Through he thought he could hear those peculiar footsteps again, the door was too thick to be sure. He began hunting for the trapdoor which Kurtevan had told him led to the underground chamber where the rival wizard lay. It was not hard to find, for a bronze ring like that of the first slab was stapled to its upper surface. He bent and heaved upon the bronzen ring. This slab came up easily, revealing a square hole and the upper end of a ladder.

'Fual,' he said, 'get your sword ready … What ails you?'

The little man was kneeling with tears running down his face. 'Don't make me go down there, my lord! I had rather die! I'll not go though you torture me!'

'Damned spineless coward!' hissed Vakar, and hit Fual with the back of his hand, which merely made the Aremorian weep harder. 'I don't see how you could have ever worked up the courage to steal anything when you were a thief!'

In his nervous fury Vakar could have killed the valet, save that he feared making a lot of noise and knew that he would need the fellow's help with Nichok's body later.

At this point even Prince Vakar's grim resolution nearly failed him. What if he went quietly away and returned home to say that he had failed in his search? Perhaps he could find another magician. Or he need not go home at all, but could hire out as a mercenary soldier in one of the mainland kingdoms, and to the seven hells with Lorsk …

Then he caught Fual's eye, and pride of caste stiffened his sinews. It would never do to let a slave see him quail before peril. He started down into the hole.

He descended rapidly, anxious to get the worst over. The ladder led down into another chamber, smaller than that above, and like it lit by a single lamp. This lamp stood on one end of a large bier of black marble, on which lay a pallet and on the pallet, supine, a man. The light of the lamp fell upon the man's upturned face and cast deep shadows across the hollows of his eyes and cheeks. The rest of his body, except for his sandalled feet, was wrapped in a black mantle.

The man lay quietly, only an occasional movement of his chest betraying the fact that he was alive. However, there should be something else in the room. In fact Vakar, though little given to fancies and premonitions, was sure there was something else. Something, he felt, was watching him. He could neither see it nor hear it, but the faint smell in the stagnant air was not simply that of an unventilated crypt.

Gripping his scabbard lest it clank, Vakar tiptoed toward the bier. He was about to mount the single step around the black block to look into Nichok's face when a noise caused him to start back.

Something stirred in the shadows on the far side of the bier. As Vakar watched, the thing unfolded and rose on many limbs until its stalked eyes looked across Nichok's body into those of Vakar Zhu.

It was an enormous crab.

The crab began to scuttle with horrifying speed around the bier. Before Vakar could move it was coming at him from his right. As he leaped back, sidling around the bier in his turn to keep the obstacle between them, the crab swung round and with a sweep of a huge chela knocked the ladder down. It fell with a loud clatter. Sweating with terror, Vakar realized that this was no mere crab, but an intelligent being.

The crab came at Vakar again, its claws rasping on the stone floor. Vakar dodged around the bier; the crab stopped and began circling the bier in the opposite direction. Vakar perforce reversed too.

How in the names of all the gods, he wondered, was he to get out of this? They could go on circling the stone block until one or the other collapsed from exhaustion, and he knew which that would be …

No, they would not circle indefinitely; the crab had other ideas. Leg by leg it began climbing *over* the bier. Delicately it raised its feet so that its claws did not touch Nichok's body or the lamp, and stood swaying, balanced, its stalked eyes looking down into those of Vakar. The small forked antennae between the eye-stalks quivered and the many pairs of mandibles opened and shut, emitting a froth of bubbles.

The thing started to topple towards Vakar, who whirled and snatched at the ladder in the forlorn hope of getting it back in position and bolting up it. He had it partly raised when he heard the sharp sound of the crab's eight claws striking the floor behind him, and then the ladder was snatched out of his grasp. As he turned he heard the wood crunch under the grip of the great chelae that could snip off his head as easily as he could pinch off the head of a daisy.

The crab flung the ladder across the room and scuttled towards Vakar, chelae spread and opened. Vakar, backing towards a corner, drew and cut at the monster as it came within reach, but the sharp bronze bounced back from the hard shell without even scratching it. When Kurtevan had spoken of the guardian demon's vulnerability he had not mentioned the possibility of its having this loricated form.

Vakar felt the wall at his back. The chelae started to close in upon him.

In that last instant before he was cut to bits like a paper-doll scissored by an angry child, a picture crossed Vakar's mind. It was of himself as a boy playing on one of the royal estates on the coast of Lorsk along the western margins of Poseidonis, in the Bay of Kort. He was talking to an old fisherman who held a vainly struggling crab from behind with one horny hand and said:

'Eh, lad, keep your thumb on the belly of him and your fingers on the back, and he can't reach around to nip ye ...'

With that Vakar knew what he had to do. As the chelae closed in he threw himself forward and down. He hit the floor beneath the crab's mandibles and rolled frantically under the creature's belly, which cleared the floor by about two feet. As the chelae closed on the empty air with a double snap, Vakar rose to his feet.

He was now behind the crab, which swivelled its eye-stalks back towards him and began to turn to face him again. Vakar leaped to the creature's broad hard-shelled back. With his free hand he seized one of the forked antennae, then pulled it back and held it like a rein, standing balaced with legs spread and knees bent on his unusual mount.

The crab circled, its chelae waving wildly and their great pincer-jaws snapping as it strove to reach back to grasp its foe, but the joints of its armor did not permit it that much flexibility.

Vakar swung his sword, with a silent prayer to the gods of Lorsk that his edge should prove true, and slashed at one of the eye-stalks; then at the other. Blue blood bubbled as the blinded crab clattered sideways across the room – and blundered into the stone bier.

The impact threw Vakar off its back, breaking his grip on the antenna. He scrambled to his feet, ignoring the painful knock that he had received against the bier, and dodged away from the chelae. The crab set off in the opposite direction until it crashed into the wall. Then it crept slowly sideways, the hinder end of its shell scraping against the stone, until it reached the nearest corner. There it crouched, its chelae raised and spread defensively.

Moving quietly, Vakar picked up the sword he had dropped, sheathed it, and replaced the ladder. One of the rungs had been broken out of it when the crab seized it, and one of the uprights had been cracked by the pinch of the chelae. Vakar looked at it dubiously and then went to fetch the body of Nichok. He heaved the man up over his shoulder, staggered to the ladder, and began to climb. An ominous cracking came from the weakened upright, and he could feel the thing begin to give and turn under his hand and feet. Wouldn't it be just fine if it broke and dumped him down again into the trance-chamber with the crab for company and no way out?

He heaved his way up. Just as the ladder seemed about to give completely he heard Fual's voice:

'Hold, my lord! I'll pull him up.'

Fual reached down and got hold of Nichok. With much grunting and heaving they manhandled the body up through the hole. Vakar followed as quickly as he could. When he gained the surface above he sat down with his feet dangling into the hole.

'Just a minute,' he said.

He sat having a quiet case of the shakes while Fual whispered: 'Let's hurry, sir; that thing outside is still prowling around … When the crab came at you I was so sure you were a dead man I couldn't watch any longer; but when I looked around again you were putting up the ladder.'

Vakar gave a last glance down into the hole. Though no sentimentalist he felt a little sorry for the crab, crouching in darkness and waiting for the succor of a master who never came.

A few minutes later they were outside Nichok's grounds, having issued forth by the same tunnel. They pushed down the hinged slab and held Nichok between them, one of his arms around each neck as if they were taking him home from a drunken party. As they staggered along, Vakar limping from his fall from the crab's back, they sang a lusty Lorskan drinking-song:

> 'With foam-bubbling beer   and soul-warming wine,
> We drink to the deities   who brought us these boons;
> Glory to the gods   and well-being to warriors …'

*

Kurtevan was bent over a heap of yellowed manuscripts, shuffling them back and forth and tracing out their lines of cryptic glyphs with a long fingernail, when Vakar and Fual staggered up the stairs into his living-room with Nichok's body between them. They let the body slip to the ground, and Vakar said:

'Here you are.'

Kurtevan raised his heavy lids a little. 'Good.'

Fual went over to Vakar's scrip and began checking its contents under the contemptuous glance of the thaumaturge. He laid out the rings of gold and the ingots of silver, the copper torcs and celts, and the packets of spice in neat rows on a stool to facilitate counting. Vakar said:

'Well, sir magician, what is the thing the gods most fear?'

Kurtevan finished what he was reading, then rolled up the manuscripts and dropped them into a chest beside his taboret. He raised his head and said:

'The thing the gods most fear is the Ring of the Tritons.'

'What is that?'

'A finger-ring of curious gray metal that is neither tin nor silver nor lead, and why the gods should fear it I cannot tell you. This ring is on the finger of the king of the Tritons, one Ximenon, whom you will find on the island of Menê in Lake Tritonis, in the land Tritonia, which lies south of the Thrinaxian Sea. Now you have all the information you need, pray leave me, for I have strenuous magical works to perform.'

Vakar digested this speech with astonishment. 'You mean – you do not have this thing here?'

'Of course not. Now go.'

'I will be eternally cursed – of all the barefaced swindles —'

'That is enough, young man. I do not tolerate insolence, and I have not swindled you. If you remember our conversation, I did not make you any definite promise in return for your help in the matter of Nichok. You said you were seeking the object; very well, I have done what I could to help you by telling you where and what it is.'

The fact that the wizard's statement was literally true did nothing to check Vakar's rising anger. He felt the blood rushing to his face as he shouted:

'Oh, is that so? You asked me how much I would pay for the thing itself, and if you —'

'Silence! Get out!'

'After I have taken my payment out of your hide —'

Vakar reached for his sword and took a stride towards Kurtevan. The wizard merely opened his eyes all the way and stared into those of Vakar.

'You,' said the thaumaturge in a low voice, 'are unable to move. You are rooted to the spot …'

To his horror, Vakar found that as he advanced he met more and more resistance, as if he were wading in cold honey. By exerting all his strength he just barely made his next step and got his sword a few inches out of the scabbard. His eyes bulged and his muscles quivered with the strain. He was vaguely aware of Fual, crouched over their trade-goods, gaping with an idiotic stare as if he, too, were ensorcelled. Meanwhile the wizard also seemed to strain.

'You are no spiritual weakling,' grunted Kurtevan, 'but you shall see that your will in no way compares with mine. Stand still while I make preparations for your disposal.'

Kurtevan reached behind him and threw a powder into the brazier on the little tripod, which thereupon smoldered and smoked heavily. He picked a staff from the floor beside him and drew lines on the floor with it. Then he began an incantation in an arcane tongue.

Vakar strained like a dog on a leach. Sweat ran down his forehead as with a mighty effort he dragged his right foot a further inch along the floor and pulled his sword a finger's breadth more from the scabbard. Beyond that he could not go; he could not even turn his head or force his tongue to speak.

A shimmer appeared in the air over the diagram that Kurtevan had drawn. As the recondite syllables rolled on, the shimmer grew to a rosy brightness. A spindle-shaped mass of flame swayed and rippled in mid-air. Sometimes it looked vaguely man-like; again it reminded Vakar of a writhing reptile. He could feel its heat on his face and hands.

Kurtevan paused in his incantation to say: 'A fire-spirit makes an admirable means of disposing of garbage. It is unfortunate that you will not be able to appreciate the full effectiveness of the method – Ho, stay where you are!' he barked suddenly at the flame, raising his staff. 'They are dangerous, like captive lions, and must be treated with firmness. You should have departed when I first commanded you, foolish boy. The responsibility is entirely yours.'

Kurtevan began speaking to the flame again in an unknown tongue, evidently giving it orders for the disposal of Vakar and Fual. Vakar strained at his invisible bonds with the strength of a madman.

Then, just as Kurtevan was reaching the climax of his conjuration, Vakar saw a movement out of the corner of his eye. Something flew through the air and struck the wizard in the chest, to fall lightly to the floor.

Kurtevan stopped, his mouth open to show his blackened teeth. Then his head jerked back and forward in a tremendous sneeze.

As he opened his mouth for a second sneeze, the flame left its diagram and swooped upon the wizard. Vakar heard a single frightful scream as the body of the sorcerer disappeared in a mass of flame. Then the flame soared up and up until it licked the ceiling. It washed over the beams and the planks of the floor of the third storey, so that they began to blaze fiercely.

The main fire left the smoking body of Kurtevan, now nothing but a twisted black mass of char. The fire-being drew itself up to the ceiling, oozed through the widening cracks between the blazing boards, and disappeared, leaving a roaring fire in its wake.

At the instant of Kurtevan's death-scream Vakar had found himself able to move again. A glance showed that Fual was sweeping their trade-goods into the scrip. Vakar slammed his sword back into the scabbard, bounded forward even before the fire-elemental had entirely disappeared, dug both arms into the open chest beside the burning taboret, and scooped up the mass of manuscripts piled there in. Some of them were beginning to burn at the edges and corners. Vakar held the papyrus in one arm and batted out the flames with the other as he turned for the exit.

He ran down the spiral stairs, Fual behind him. As they raced across the ground-floor chamber, a thunderous crackling above told them that the third-storey floor was giving way. Vakar could see the firelight through the cracks between the planks overhead. They rushed out.

In the yard Vakar stumbled over the acephalus lying limp. Evidently on Kurtevan's death the spirit that animated it had fled. They burst through the gate and ran in the direction of their lodgings just as people began to put their heads out to see what was up. Somebody banged a gong to turn out the neighborhood with buckets. Vakar doubled around several corners in case anybody should follow them, while behind him flame and sparks erupted out of the top of the tower of Kurtevan the magician.

Fual said: 'Sir, these Euskerian wizards are not really gentlemen, or they would be served by proper human retinues and not by these acephali and crabs and such spooks. Why did you pause to gather up that stuff? Are you planning to become a magus yourself?'

'Not I. But I hated to see that arcane knowledge perish, and these sheets should fetch a pretty price among Kurtevan's colleagues, which will give us the means to reach Tritonia ... Damnation, where are we?'

When Fual's sense of direction had straightened them out, Vakar continued: 'I'm sorry about poor Nichok, but it's too late to drag him back to his dwelling now ... What did you throw at Kurtevan?'

'Our rarest spice, sir. It's from the Farthest East, beyond fabled Thamuzeira. The merchant who sold it to us called it "pepper".'

X

Lake Tritonis

A month later Prince Vakar and Fual arrived in Huperea, the capital of Phaiaxia. They had followed a trade-route that ran up the River Baitis, overland to the headwaters of the Anthemius, and down the latter stream to its issuance into the Thrinaxian Sea. They had had minor adventures: a narrow escape from a lion; another from a wild bull; another from a war-party of Laistrugonian savages. At last they had entered Phaiaxia, a peaceful smiling land where the language (unlike Euskerian) was closely related to Hesperian, so that after a few days of learning new inflectional endings Vakar could make a stab at it.

Where the Anthemius widened out into the Thrinaxian Sea stood Huperea: a spacious city of well-built houses instead of the usual combination of stockaded castle surrounded by a huddle of huts. Vakar had no trouble getting through the gates and rode down a broad street flanked by houses in front of which flowers grew in neat patterns around painted marble statues of gods and heroes. Feeling at peace with the world, Vakar sang as he rode:

'In the red sunrise   stood Vrir the Victorious,
On a cletch of cadavers,   splattered with scarlet,
Declaiming defiance   in tones triumphant ...

'Don't you have poetry in Kerys?' he asked Fual suddenly.

'Yes, my lord, but it's quite different from that of Lorsk. Rhymed triolets instead of this rhythmic alliterative verse with split lines. But I never went in for that sort of thing; I was too busy trying to steal the wherewithal for tomorrow's meal.'

'That's your misfortune, for I find that verse provides one of the cheapest and most harmless of life's major pleasures. But here's somebody who can perhaps give us directions.'

Vakar pulled up in front of a house where a stocky man sat naked on a bench and worked with adze and saw on a bed-frame. He shouted:

'Ho there, my good man, where can I find lodgings for myself and my servant in Huperea?'

The man looked up and replied: 'Strangers, if you seek a public inn like those of Torrutseish, know that there is none such here. Our custom is to lodge travellers among the citizens of the town, each in accordance with his rank. For three days you will be entertained without cost, except that you shall tell us freely of the land whence you come and of the world outside of Phaiaxia. After that you must be on your way, unless a pressing reason prevents.'

'An interesting custom,' said Vakar. 'What is its purpose?'

'Thus we receive warning of dangers gathering against us, and also learn of markets affording rich opportunities for our merchants. Now, if you will tell me your name and station, I will make arrangements.'

The lack of servility in the man's manner suggested to Vakar that the fellow was no slave, as he had supposed, but a citizen of standing. Since his entertainment would be proportioned to his status, Vakar saw no reason to minimize the latter. He said:

'I am Vakar the son of Zhabutir, heir to the throne of Lorsk in Poseidonis.'

The man wagged his full beard sagely. 'I have heard of Poseidonis and Lorsk, though no Phaiaxian has ever travelled so far west. Stranger, it is proper that you should lodge with me.'

The man picked up his cloak, threw it around him, fastened it with an ornate golden pin, and turned to call a servant to take the animals. Vakar was at first taken aback, wondering if the man disbelieved him. Then a horrid thought struck him. He said:

'May I ask who you are, sir?'

'Did you not know? I am Nausithion.' As Vakar continued to look blank the man added: 'King of Phaiaxia.'

Vakar felt his face reddening as he began to stammer apologies for his condescending tone, but King Nausithion said:

'Tush, tush, you are not the first to make such a mistake. We are a merchant kingdom and make no great parade of rank and precedence as do the

Euskerians. And since I am the most skilled carpenter in Huperea, I prefer to make my own bed rather than to hire it done. But come in. You will wish warm baths and change of raiment, and tonight you shall tell your story to the leading lords of Phaiaxia. We believe that a man who can sing as I heard you do cannot be altogether evil.'

Vakar found that he was enjoying himself among these hearty hedonists more than any time since the party at Queen Porfia's palace. He had cautiously watched his host's methods of eating and drinking so as not to commit any gaffes like those at Sederado. Here, for instance, it was customary and proper to convey one's meat to one's mouth on the point of one's dagger ...

The bard Damodox was singing, to the twang of his lyre, a lay about the lusts of the Phaiaxian gods: what happened to Aphradexa, the goddess of love and beauty, when her husband Hephastes learned of her tryst with the war-god. Vakar had been told that Damodox was the winner of last year's singing-contest, an event as important in Phaiaxia as athletic meets were in Lorsk. The paintings on the walls were the most vivid and realistic that Vakar had ever seen, and the repoussé patterns on the silver plates and beakers were of an incredible delicacy and perfection.

When the bard finished, Vakar said: 'Master Damodox, you certainly have a fine voice. Mine cannot compare with it, even though at home I too am considered something of a singer.'

The bard smiled. 'I am sure that if you had spent as many years in practice as I, you would far surpass me. But such tricks are no credit to a lord like yourself, as they show he has been neglecting his proper business of war and statecraft.'

'Are you sure your gods do not mind your speaking so frankly of their pecadilloes?'

'No, no, our gods are a jolly lot who relish a good joke. As a matter of fact, Aphradexa visited me only last night. She had a message for you from one of your western gods: Akima or some such name.'

'Okma,' said Vakar. 'Say on.'

'It is hard to remember exactly – you know dreams – but I think this Pusadian god was trying to warn you against a danger that has pursued you many miles, and that will soon catch up with you if you do not hasten.'

'Oho! I will bear your warning in mind.'

Vakar turned his attention back to his wine. Although he still felt that he had lost his heart to Ogugia, he thought that if he should ever have to leave Lorsk for good, and if Ogugia were forbidden to him because of the death of Thiegos, Phaiaxia would be the country for him. While they did not practice philosophy, they certainly lived well. He liked them and they seemed to like him, which for Vakar Zhu was a sufficiently unusual experience for him to treasure it. Could he get a dispensation from King Nausithion, marry some handsome Phaiaxian wench, and settle down here, and to the seven hells with windy Lorsk?

Then he thought of Porfia, and resolved not to commit himself irrevocably to anything until he had investigated his standing in that direction further.

He jerked out of his reverie with the realization that the king was speaking to him: 'And whither are you bound after you leave here, my lord?'

'Tritonia. That lies south of here, does it not?'

'Southeast, rather. What is your purpose?'

If he had not been heated by the sweet wine of the banquet Vakar might have been more cautious, but as it was he told openly about his quest for the Ring of the Tritons.

The king and the other lords nodded, the former saying: 'I have heard of that ring. It will take uncommon force, guile, or persuasiveness to get it away from King Ximenon.'

'What,' said Vakar, 'is its precise nature? How does it differ from any other ring?'

A Phaiaxian lord said: 'It is said to be a powerful specific against magic of all kinds, and to have been cut by a coppersmith of Tartaros from a fallen star in the possession of the lord of Belem.'

'Which,' added Nausithion, 'means it might as well be on the moon, for nobody leaves Belem alive. Tritonia is bad enough ...'

'What is hazardous about Tritonia?' asked Vakar.

'The situation there is peculiar. There are two dominant peoples in Tritonia, the Amazons who live on the island of Kherronex in Lake Tritonis, and the Tritons who live on the island of Menê. The subject tribes live around the lake on the mainland. Now the Tritons and the Amazons are the men and women of what was once a single nation. In my father's time they had a great war with the Atlanteans to the southwest of here, which so depleted their supply of fighting-men that their king armed their women and defeated the Atlanteans. Then however the women, being the more numerous, conspired against the men, and rose against them in one night, stripping them of their arms and reducing them to subjugation.

'This condition endured for several years, with the women ruling and the men doing all the work, not only in field and meadow but in house and hearth as well. At last the men revolted and fled to the island of Menê, where they armed themselves and stood off the women. So now there is war between them, and when a stranger arrives in Tritonia both sides try to capture him – or her – to take to one island or the other. If the visitor is of the sex of that island, they enroll him in their army; if not, they amuse themselves carnally with the newcomer until the latter's powers are exhausted.'

'A visit to Tritonia sounds strenuous,' said Vakar. 'If the men catch you, you are in for a lifetime of fighting, whereas if the women catch you – but what other nations lie near Phaiaxia?'

Nausithion began counting them off on his fingers: 'To the east, along the shores of the Thrinaxian Sea, live the Laistrugonian savages who, alas, are not in the least charmed by our sweet songs. In fact their raids have so galled us that we have had to place ourselves under the protection of the king of Tartessia. South of the Laistrugonians lies Tritonia, the land of lakes, where men ride striped horses. East of Tritonia one comes to the Pelasgian Sea, which gives our merchants access to Kheru and Thamuzeira and other far-eastern lands.

'Southeast of Tritonia dwell many curious peoples: the Atarantians who curse the sun daily, instead of praying to it as do most folk, and who refuse to tell their names for fear a stranger should acquire magical power over them; the Garamantians who have no institution of marriage, but couple promiscuously at any time or place like beasts; and many others. Some paint themselves red all over; some dress their hair in outlandish fashion. Among some, at a wedding-feast the bride entertains all the male guests in a manner that among most nations is reserved for the groom alone.

'South of Tritonia lies the dreaded land of Belem, and beyond that forbidding mountain-range the Desert of Gwedulia. There dwell only wild beasts and wilder men: the camel-riding Gwedulians who live by herding and robbery.'

Vakar nodded understandingly, for of all kinds of men the nomadic herdsman, hardly, truculent, and predatory, was the most feared in his world. Nausithion continued:

'West of Belem the Desert of Gwedulia sends north an arm called the Tamenruft, separating Belem from Gamphasantia. The Gamphasentians are said to be a peaceful folk with a high standard of ethics – so high in fact that it is unsafe to visit them, for normal mortals find their standards too lofty to adhere to for any length of time. North of them and west of us rises another mountain-range called Atlantis. West of Gamphasantia lies the free city of Kernê, whose merchants are so sharp that ours cannot compete with them, and south of Kernê is Tartaros with its black craftsmen.'

Vakar asked: 'What is south of the Desert of Gwedulia?'

'None knows; perhaps the traveller comes to the edge of the world-disk of which the philosophers tell, and finds the stair leading down to the seven hells. But that is all we know; now tell us of Poseidonis.'

Vakar had started an account of the glories of Lorsk (which with patriotic pride he unconsciously exaggerated) when a man came in and said: 'My lord King, there are strangers outside who wish to speak to you.'

Nausithion swallowed a mass of roast pork to make himself understood. 'What sort of strangers?'

'Very odd strangers, sir. They drove up in a chariot. One is a giant who looks like a Laistrugonian but uglier; one is a pigmy with enormous ears ...'

Vakar said: 'Excuse me, King, but I feel unwell. May I withdraw for a moment?'

'Certainly ... Ho, that is the way to the kitchen!'

Vakar plunged through the door and shouted: 'Fual!'

'Yes sir?' The Aremorian looked up from where he was eating.

'Qasigan has caught up with us. Get our gear and meet me in front, but don't go through the banquet-hall.'

'You mean to leave?' wailed Fual. 'Oh, sir, these are the first people since Sederado who have shown us the respect due our rank —'

'Don't be a bigger fool than you can help. Where are the beasts?'

A few minutes later Vakar led the four horses around the house to the front. Fual came after him. At the corner Vakar paused to peer around in time to see the shaggy back of Nji the ape-man disappear into the king's mansion.

'Hold the horses,' commanded Vakar.

He picked up a stone and walked towards the chariot hitched to the post in front of the king's residence. Several servants of the Phaiaxian lords clustered there, throwing knucklebones. Vakar strode around them, bent over the near wheel of the chariot, and with one blow of the stone knocked out the pin that held the wheel to the axle.

'Here, you help me!' he said, and such was his tone of assurance that two of the nearer gamblers got up and came over. 'Grasp the edge of the chariot and lift.'

The chariot was a heavy northern model with old-fashioned leather-tired solid wheels and a frame of elm and ash. The frame rose as the servants lifted. Vakar pulled off the wheel and rolled it ahead of him like a hoop to the corner of the house where Fual waited.

'Help me tie this on this horse,' he said.

The servants stared after Vakar but showed no inclination to interfere. A laugh ran through the group as they evidently took the act for a practical joke and went back to their game.

'Now,' said Vakar, 'to Tritonia, and fast!'

Off they went. Not this time would he settle down in fair Phaiaxia, forgetting his duty to his land and his dynasty.

'I can't tell whether it's a man or a woman,' muttered Vakar, lying on his belly under a bush. 'It looks more like a reptile with a man's shape.'

He peered around the hill at the figure that sat the oddest horse that Vakar had ever seen: a creature entirely covered with black and white stripes. Behind him, up the draw, Fual held their own horses in a clump of acacias.

They had ridden across Tritonia, where the people wore fringed buckskin kilts and goatskin cloaks with the hair dyed vermillion, to the shores of Lake Tritonis.

Vakar wriggled back out of sight of the immobile rider and told Fual: 'The thing seems to be covered all over with scales, with a pair of enormous feathers sticking out of the top of its head. I'm sure King Nausithion didn't describe any race of reptile-men in his account of the peoples of Tritonia.'

'He might have omitted to mention them,' said Fual with a shudder. 'I remember hearing the Tritons worshipped a snake-god named Drax. And who knows …?'

Vakar said: 'The only way to settle the question is to capture the thing. Luckily the shrubbery is dense. I'll circle around and come upon the creature from the far side while you creep out —'

'Me? No, my lord! The idea turns my bones to water —'

Vakar caught Fual's shirt in both fists and thrust an angry face into that of the Aremorian.

'You,' he said, 'shall do as you're told. When you've given me time to approach from the other side you shall make some small noise to distract the thing's attention, and I'll do the rest. Be ready to rush in and help subdue it.'

He was more than ordinarily exasperated by Fual, who still bore the marks of the beating Vakar had given him when the latter learned that his servant had stolen one of Nausithion's silver plates in Huperea.

A quarter-hour later Vakar crouched close by the rider. He had laid aside his scabbard so as not to be encumbered in the kind of attack that he had in mind. Through a tiny gap in the leaves he saw that the scaly skin was a cleverly made armor of reptile hide, covering the entire rider except the face. The rider carried a long lance and a small round shield of hide.

Though Vakar waited and waited, no distracting sound came from the direction of the draw. The striped horse snorted and stamped and Vakar feared that it smelled him.

At last he could wait no longer. He gathered his feet under him and sprang towards the sentry. The striped animal snorted again, rolling an eye towards Vakar, and shied away. Its rider turned too and began to swing the lance down to level.

Vakar left the ground in a long leap, caught the rider about the upper body as he struck it, and both tumbled to the turf on the far side in a tangle of thrashing limbs. Vakar, recovering first from the fall, slammed his fist into his victim's jaw. The slight body relaxed long enough for Vakar to roll it over and twist its arms behind its back.

'Fual!' he roared.

'Here, sir —'

'Where in the seven hells have you been?'

'I – I was just going to make the noise, my lord – but it took me so long to work up my courage —'

'I'll deal with you later; meanwhile lively with that strap!'

Vakar indicated the wrists of the rider, which Fual bound. The rider began to struggle until Vakar belted it across the face with his fist.

'Now we'll see about its sex,' he said.

The reptile-skin armor opened down one side and was kept closed by a series of thong ties. Vakar fumbled with the unfamiliar knots, then impatiently sawed the garment open with his dagger and pulled the front of it away from the wearer's chest. There was no questioning its femininity.

'Not bad for a warrior maiden,' said Vakar, then spoke in Phaiaxian: 'You! Do you understand me?'

'If you speak slowly,' said the Amazon in a dialect of the same language.

'I wish to make contact with the Tritons, and you shall guide me to their camp.'

'Then what will happen to me?'

'You may do as you like, once the Tritons are in sight. Come along.'

With her hands still tied and Fual holding the striped horse, Vakar boosted the Amazon back on to her mount. She sat glowering at him with her torso bare to the waist. Vakar handed the shield and lance to Fual, put his own baldric back on, mounted, and drew his sword.

'Which way?' he asked, grasping the Amazon's bridle.

The Amazon jerked her head westward, so Vakar set off along the trail in that direction. After they had ridden for some time he turned his head to ask:

'What do you call these horses with the giddy color-scheme?'

She glared silently until he hefted his sword in a meaningful manner, then sullenly answered: 'Zebras.'

'And what that shield made of? The hide of some great beast?'

'A rhinoceros. A beast with a horn on its nose.'

'Oh. I saw one of those on my ride thither, like a giant pig. And what do those feathers come from?'

'A bird called an ostrich, found in the Desert of Gwedulia.'

'A bird with such feathers must overshadow the earth with its wings like a thundercloud when it flies.'

'Ha, it does not fly at all! It runs like a horse, and stands as tall as you and your mount together.'

'How about your armor?'

'That is from the great serpents found in the swamps around Lake Tritonis.'

'Truly Tritonia must be a land of many strange beasts. Yesterday I saw three beasts like our Pusadian mammoth, but hairless – *Hé!*'

Everything happened at once. They had come around a hill to see a group of Amazons trotting towards them along a side-road leading up from the lake, which showed blue through notches in the dusty olive-green landscape. The captive Amazon leaned forwards and dug her heels into the zebra's ribs. The animal bounded, tearing the bridle out of Vakar's grasp. The Amazon shrieked something and galloped towards her fellows.

Vakar slashed at her as she went by him. Though he struck to kill he struck too late; the blade whistled through empty air.

He leaned forward in his turn and galloped. As the Amazons came up to the main road, Vakar and Fual and the spare horses thundered past, going in the same direction as before. A glance showed Vakar that his ex-captive, hampered by her bound arms, had fallen off her zebra. Vakar hoped that she had broken her neck.

Vakar's animals had been travelling all day and so were too tired to keep ahead of their fresh pursuers. Little by little the Amazons gained. Vakar thanked the gods of Lorsk that none of them carried bows; no doubt the scrubby trees of this dry country did not provide good wood for bow-staves.

Still the long slender lances came closer through the clouds of dust. A determined thrust would get through Vakar's leather jack, and even if it did not they would kill Fual and take the spare mounts and the baggage. There were five of them, too many for Vakar to wheel and charge into the midst of them.

A few more paces and they would be up …

The pursuers reined in with high feminine cries. Ahead of them appeared a score of riders clad in similar snakeskin armor, with crests of zebra-tail instead of ostrich-plumes. The Amazons galloped off. Vakar was tempted to do likewise, but reason told him that the panting horses would not get very far, and besides these were probably the Tritons whom he wished to reach.

As they came up he called: 'The gods be with you!'

They surrounded him, long lances levelled, and one said: 'Who are you?'

'Vakar of Lorsk, on my way to visit your king.'

'Indeed? Our king does not admit every passing vagabond to his intimacy. You shall enter our service at the bottom and work your way up, if you the guts. Seize him, men.'

XI

The Tritonian Ring

They took away Vakar's sword and knife, but missed the poisoned dagger in his shirt. They tied his and Fual's hands, while one rummaged through Vakar's scrip and exclaimed with delight over the wealth therein.

'Come along,' said the leader.

Vakar rode slowly in the midst of them, with spear-points poised to prod him should he make a break.

'Am I a dog?' he growled. 'I am a prince in my own country, and if you do not treat me as such it will be the worse for you.'

The leader leaned over and slapped Vakar's face with his gauntleted hand.

'Shut up,' he said. 'What you may be in another country means nothing to us.'

Vaker's face became suffused with blood and he gritted his teeth. He rode silently fuming until they came to the shores of the lake, where a permanent fortified camp was set up. On the lakeward side of the camp a jetty had been built out into the water, and to this was secured a big shallow-draft galley-barge.

The leader of the Tritons placed his hand against Vakar's shoulder and gave a sharp push. Vakar fell off his horse into the dirt, giving his shoulder a painful bruise. Fual followed his master into the muck, and the Tritons laughed loudly.

While Vakar was struggling into a sitting position a kick in the ribs knocked him over again, sick and dizzy with pain.

'Get up, lazybones!' said the officer. 'And get aboard.'

Vakar hobbled down the slope to the barge while the Tritons made off with his horses and property. He and Fual were prodded aboard, and the boat was cast off and rowed out into the lake. Vakar huddled in the bow, too despondent to pay heed to his surroundings until Fual beside him exclaimed:

'Sir! Prince Vakar! Look at that!'

Something was floating beside the barge: a thing like a great rough-barked log, except that logs do not keep up with galleys by swimming with an undulant motion. Vakar gulped and said to the nearest Triton:

'What is that? One of your great serpents?'

'That is a crocodile,' said the man. 'The serpents keep to the swamps. The abundance of crocodiles accounts for the fact that although we live on the water, no Triton can swim, for if you fell overboard that fellow yonder would have you before you could yell for a rope. So think not to escape from Menê by swimming.'

Another Triton said: 'It would be fun to lower him by a rope and then snatch him out when the crocodile snapped at him.'

'Amusing, but it would probably cost us a recruit. Do you not value unlimited commerce with women more highly?'

Vakar mulled over this exchange. The last remark no doubt referred to the Tritons' hopes of winning their war and reducing the Amazons to the status of housewives whence they had risen. It gave him an idea of how to approach King Ximenon. After all he had helped to negotiate the treaty with Zhysk last year. If he was not overly likeable, his dour reserve gave some folk a trust in his impartiality that they might not otherwise have.

When an hour later they tied up at a similar pier on the island of Menê, the Tritons hustled Vakar and Fual ashore. A small fortified city, also called Menê, stood tangent to the shorefront. The Tritons conducted Vakar to a stockade, thrust him inside, removed his bonds, and left him. Fual they took elsewhere.

Vakar stretched his cramped arms and looked around. There were about a score of men of various tribes and races, from a stout ebony-skinned fellow from Blackland to a towering fair-haired Atlantean. Most wore ragged clothing and straggly beards.

'Good day,' said Vakar.

The men looked at him and at each other, and began to sidle towards him. Soon they were all around him, grinning. One of them professed much interest in his clothing, pinching it and saying:

'A gentleman, eh?'

Another gave Vakar a sharp push, which made him stagger against another, who pushed him back. Prince Vakar had never been hazed in his life, so this treatment bewildered and infuriated him. At the next push he shouted: 'I'll show you swine!' and hit the pusher in the face.

He never had a chance to see how effective his blow had been, because they all jumped on him at once. They caught his arms, and blows rained upon him ...

Vakar came to an indefinite time later, lying in a corner of the stockade. He tried to move and groaned. His body seemed to be one vast bruise. He inched up into a sitting position and found that he was nursing a swollen nose, a split lip, a pair of black eyes, and a few loose teeth. They must have stamped on him.

He peered through swollen lids at the others, who huddled on the far side of the enclosure around some game of chance. For the time being they ignored him. He chewed his bruised lips with hatred. If he had thought that he could get away with it he would have planned to wait until they were all asleep and then to murder the whole lot with his poisoned dagger. As it was he could only huddle miserably and wait for his hurts to heal. He thought of using the dagger on himself; what had he to look forward to save a life of deepening misery and degredation?

The sun was low when the gate of the stockade opened and a man stepped in with two buckets, one full of water and the other of a repellant-looking barley-porridge. The men crowded around the buckets, scooping up water and mush with their hands. A couple of fights broke out. Vakar, though hungry, felt that he had no stomach for such rugged competition in his present state. The turmoil around the buckets subsided as the men stilled their most acute pangs of hunger.

'Here, stranger,' said a voice, and Vakar looked up from his broodings to see the Black standing over him with an outstretched fist.

Vakar held out his cupped hands and received a gob of mush. The Negro said:

'You did not look as though you could get any for yourself. Next time the boys want a little fun with you, do not be a fool.'

Vakar said: 'Thank you,' and fell to eating.

The following morning the same man came in, this time with an apronfull of pieces of stale bread. Vakar hobbled over and snatched up a piece that rolled to his feet out of the scrimmage. He turned back towards his solitary place to eat it when a long arm came over his shoulder and tore the bread from his grasp.

He whirled. The tall blond Atlantean who had taken his bread was already turning away and beginning to eat it, confident in his superior size. He was the biggest man in the enclosure, and Vakar had inferred that he was the unofficial leader.

Vakar saw red. His hand darted inside his shirt and came out with the dagger. A second later he had buried the blade in the Atlantean's broad back. The Atlantean gave a strangled noise, jerked away, and collapsed.

The rest of the men chattered excitedly in a dozen languages. They looked at Vakar, standing over the dead man with the dripping dagger, with more respect than they had shown before. One said:

'Quick, hide that thing! They will be here any minute!'

It sounded like good advice. Vakar wiped the dagger on the Atlantean's leather kilt, took off the harness under his shirt, sheathed the blade, dug a hole in the dirt with his fingers, buried the weapon, and stamped the earth into place over it.

He had hardly done so when a pair of Tritons entered. When they saw the corpse one of them shouted:

'What happened? Who did this? You there, speak!'

The man addressed said: 'I do not know. I was relieving myself with my back to the rest, and heard a scuffle, and when I looked around he was dead.'

The Triton asked the same questions of the others, but got similar answers: 'I was throwing knucklebones and was not watching ...' 'I was taking a snooze ...'

'Line up,' said the Triton and passed down the line searching the men's scanty clothing. He finally said: 'We could torture you, but you would tell so many lies it would not be worthwhile. Off you go to drill. Lively, now. Ho, you!'

Vakar saw that the Triton was addressing him.

'You looked battered. Have they roughed you up?'

Vakar, who had been limping towards the gate, said: 'I fell.'

'Well, you need not drill today.'

'I am Prince Vakar of Lorsk, and I wish to speak to your king.'

'Shut up before I change my mind about the drill,' said the Triton, following the recruits out.

Vakar found an uncontaminated spot and sat down wearily. After a while a couple of slaves came in and dragged out the Atlantean. The day wore on until Vakar became so restless with boredom that he wished that he had gone to drill despite his hurts.

In the afternoon the men came in again to loaf, gamble, or chatter until the evening meal. Vakar wondered how some of them seemed able to do nothing indefinitely without going mad.

The next day he felt better and was taken to drill. He found that the men were being taught the rudiments of marching and handling a spear. As an experienced rider and swordsman he was told off to supervise some of the others. He asked the drillmaster to be allowed to see the king, and was told:

'One more of those silly requests, young man, and you shall be beaten. Now shut up and get back to work.'

After about the tenth day Vakar lost track of the time he spent in the stockade. He learned that life among these unwilling soldiers was on a lower level than he had ever known to exist; no self-respecting savage would live like that. Dirt was ubiquitous and perversations were rampant. The only kindly gesture he ever saw was from the Black on the first day. When he had murdered the Atlantean the men had protected him not because they liked him, but because they hated him less than they did the Tritons. For their own protection they recognized one iron law: death to tattle-tales. It was lucky for Vakar that he had not complained about his hazing.

For the rest he found little among them but stupidity and mutual hatred. They seemed for a while to have been willing to take him as their leader, since he had killed the old, but when he did nothing to confirm his title they turned to a swarthy, thick-thewed Atarantian who had gouged out a man's eye in one of the daily fights.

So long as Vakar wore his dagger nobody molested him. When he had somewhat recovered from the despair induced by his beating, he engaged some of his fellow inmates in conversation, picking up what information he could about the peoples and customs of the surrounding regions and a few words of their languages. In line with the scheme that he was concocting he asked what the Tritons deemed their most sacred oath.

'They swear by the horns of Aumon,' a small Pharusian told him. 'That is some sheep-headed fertility-god of theirs. While they break all other oaths, that one holds them. Though why any right-minded people should choose such a stupid and timid beast ...'

Before a month had elapsed, a day came when the Tritons announced that as the men were now well enough trained, they would be moved elsewhere. But instead of sending Vakar off with the rest, one of them told him:

'You shall see the king after all. Step lively, and bear yourself respectfully in his presence.'

'What am I supposed to do? Kiss his butt, or bang my head on the floor?'

'No insolence! You shall kneel until he tells you to rise, that is all.'

Vakar was conducted back to the waterfront of the city of Menê and aboard a large red galley. On the poop, in a chair of pretence, sat the man whom he had come to see: King Ximenon, big, stout, clean-shaven, in bright shimmery robes, with a golden wreath on his curly graying hair. Beside him stood a man in gilded snakeskin armor, and a pet cheetah lay purring at the king's feet. On the middle finger of his left hand, Vakar saw, he wore a broad plain ring of dull-gray metal.

The Ring of the Tritons.

'Well?' said the king.

Vakar gathered his forces. 'Have they told you who I am, King?'

'Something about your being a prince in some far-western land, but that means nothing to us. We cannot prove you are not lying. Get to your business, or by the fangs of Drax it will go hard with you.'

Vakar suppressed an urge to make pointed remarks about his unroyal reception in Tritonia. Back in Lorsk his sharp tongue was always getting him into trouble, but now that it was a matter of life and death he found that he could control it. He said:

'All I wish to suggest is that I may be able to end your war with the Amazons.'

The king's porcine eyes glittered with interest. 'So? Some new weapon or stratagem? I listen.'

'Not exactly, sir, but I think I could negotiate a treaty of peace with them.'

The king leaned forward with an impatient motion. 'Peace? On what terms? Have you reason to think these doxies are ready to surrender?'

'Not at all.'

'Then are you proposing that *we* give up? I will have you flayed —'

'No, sir. I had in mind a half-and-half arrangement, whereby each should respect the rights of the other. It might not give you all you would like, but at least thereafter you could strive with them as men and women should strive, on a well-padded bed …'

Vakar gave King Ximenon another quarter-hour of argument, with an eloquence that he had not known he possessed. He depicted the beauties of cohabitation until the king, squirming with concupiscence, said:

'A splendid idea! We should have tried it sooner, but after the bloodshed and bitterness between us no one on either side would make the first move. As an outsider you are in a position of advantage. Queen Aramnê is a fine-looking woman; could you arrange for me to wed her as part of the peace-settlement?'

'I can try.'

'If you can do that along with the rest you can practically name your own reward.'

'I have already chosen it, my lord.'

'Huh? What then?'

'The Tritonian Ring.'

'What? Are you mad?' shouted the king, looking at the dull circlet on his finger. 'I will have you —'

At that instance the man who stood beside the king's chair leaned over and spoke in the king's ear. They muttered back and forth, and the king said to Vakar:

'Your price is impossible. We will instead give you all the gold you can carry.'

'No, sir.'

The king roared and threatened and haggled, and still Vakar held out. Finally Ximenon said:

'If you had not caught us at a time when prolonged continence has driven us nearly mad ... But so be it. If you can put this treaty through you shall have the ring.'

'Do you swear by the horns of Aumon?'

The king looked startled. 'You have been inquiring into our customs, I see. Very well. I swear by the holy horns of Aumon that if you negotiate this treaty with the Amazons successfully, without impairing our masculine rights to equal treatment, and get me Queen Aramnê to wife, I will give you the Ring of the Tritons. You are a witness, Sphaxas,' he said to the man beside him, and again to Vakar: 'Does that satisfy you? Good. How soon can you set forth for Kherronex?'

XII

The Horns of Aumon

Queen Aramnê was indeed an impressive-looking woman, as tall as Vakar, with a broad-shouldered mannish figure clad in a loose short tunic that left one small breast bare. She sat in a chair of pretence on her galley-barge, the torchlight gleaming on and pearls in her diadem, and rested her chin on one capable fist. Vakar guessed her age as the middle thirties. She said:

'Your words are persuasive, Prince Vakar. In fact, a party among us has been urging that we take the initiative in such negotiations. However, before I make my decision, we will undertake a divination to aid us. Zoutha, proceed!'

There was a burst of activity among the attendant Amazons. Some set up a small stand with a copper bowl on it while others dragged in a naked man whom they forced to his knees in front of the bowl. There was nothing to indicate what sort of man he was and Vakar thought it injudicious to ask.

An elderly woman who seemed to be high priestess or head sibyl prayed, and then the man's head was forced down while Zoutha, the old woman, cut his throat so that his blood poured into the bowl. When the man's throat stopped gushing the Amazons threw the limp body over the side, where the crocodiles soon carried it off.

Zoutha stared into the bowl a long time. She dipped a finger into the blood and tasted it, and said:

'Queen, a thing will almost come to pass.'

'Is that all?' said Aramnê.

'That is all.'

The queen said to Vakar: 'I have almost decided to accede to your proposal – with a few minor reservations. I will give you my counter-offer on the morrow.'

For the next few days Vakar shuttled back and forth between Menê and Kherronex while King Ximenon and Queen Aramnê bargained over the final terms of the treaty: what rights each sex should have in the reunited Tritonian state, the marriage contract between the king and the queen, and other details.

At last all was settled. The royal galleys of the two sovreigns should meet in the lake midway between the islands. To show mutual trust, Queen Aramnê should come aboard the king's galley for the signing of the contract; then the king should board hers for the wedding ceremony and the feast to follow.

The ships met. A dinghy brought the queen across the short stretch of the glassy lake between them. The red ball of the sun was just touching the smooth blue horizon when Aramnê, followed by a small guard of Amazons, clambered up the side of the king's galley.

Sphaxas, Ximenon's minister, spread a big sheet of brown papyrus on a table on the deck and read the terms. The king and queen swore by Aumon and Drax and all the other gods of Tritonia to abide by the terms of the treaty and called down an endless concatenation of dooms and disasters upon their own heads should they fail. Finally (as neither could write) they impressed their seals upon the papyrus and exchanged a kiss as a pledge of amity. Then they turned, the tall woman and the grossly massive man, towards the companionway, laughing at some private joke. Sphaxas followed. Before they put foot over the side the queen turned her head back and said:

'You shall come too, Prince Vakar. What would the celebration be without the man who did the most to bring it about?'

Vakar followed, grinning. Impatient as he was to get his ring and begone, he saw no harm in one good binge. The gods knew that he had suffered enough in that stinking pen, living on stale bread and barley-porridge.

On the queen's ship a priest of Aumon performed the marriage ceremony. The king cut the throat of a white lamb and let the blood trickle on the altar. He dipped a finger in the blood and marked a symbol on the queen's forehead, and she did likewise to him. All sang a paean to the gods of Tritonia, after which there was much familiar back-slapping and lewd jests. Vakar, feeling thoroughly pleased with himself, said:

'And now, King, how about my ring?'

King Ximenon grinned broadly and pulled the ring off his finger. 'Here,' he said, dropping it into Vakar's palm.

'And now,' continued the king, 'there is one other small matter we must attend to before proceeding with the feast. Seize him!'

Before Vakar knew what was happening, muscular hands gripped his arms. His mouth fell open in bewilderment as the king stepped forward and wrenched the ring out of his hand.

'I will borrow this,' said the king, slipping it back upon his finger. 'Strip him for sacrifice.'

'Ho!' said Vakar. 'Are you mad? What are you doing?'

Ximenon replied: 'We are about to sacrifice you to Drax.'

'But why, in the name of Lyr's barnacles?'

'For two reasons: First, old Drax has not had much attention from us lately. Curiously, since I came into possession of the ring, not one god has visited me in slumber. Secondly, I have sworn by the horns of Aumon to give you the ring. But I have not sworn to respect your life and liberty afterwards, and I cannot let so valuable a talisman leave the kingdom.'

'Well, take the damned thing!' cried Vakar, sweating, as the guards peeled off the gaudy Tritonian raiment that had been lent him for the occasion.

'No, for your giving it to me under duress would not be a true legal gift. On the other hand when you die, having no legal heirs in Tritonia, your property falls to the throne. Therefore the only way I can legally fulfill my oath and retain the ring at the same time is to kill you.'

'Queen Aramnê!' shouted Vakar. 'Can you do nothing about this?'

The queen smiled frostily. 'It is your misfortune, but I fully agree with my consort. We planned this stroke just now on the king's barge, while you were gauping at the flute-girls. And why should you complain? Better men than you have died upon our altars to insure our land's fertility.'

'Strumpet!' screamed Vakar, straining in the grip of the guards. 'Was my nocturnal performance then insufficient, that you turn me over to this treacherous hyena?'

He went on to shout intimate details an imaginary liason with the queen on Kherronex. At least, he thought, he might stir up jealous dissention between his two murderers, and escape in the turmoil or at any rate spoil their pleasure.

The king put on a sardonic smile, saying: 'If you had been wise you would have kept your mouth shut and gained a quick death. Now, for slandering the queen, you must receive additional punishment. Flog him.'

'How many strokes, my lord?' said a voice behind Vakar.

'Until I tell you to stop.'

The first stars were coming out as Vakar's wrists were bound and hoisted above his head, so that he half-dangled with only his toes on the deck. He had sometimes wondered what he would do if flogged, and had firmly resolved not to give his tormentors the satisfaction of seeing him weep or hearing him scream.

But when the whip whistled behind him and struck across his bare back, sending a white-hot sheet of pain shooting through his torso, he found it much harder to bear than he had ever imagined. The first blow he took in silence, and the second, but the third brought a grunt out of him, and the fourth a yell. By the tenth he was screaming like all the others, and felt warm blood trickling down his back.

Swish – crack! Swish – crack! He jerked and screeched with each blow, though hating himself for doing so. The pain filled his whole universe. He would do anything – anything—

Then a vestige of his natural craft asserted itself. With a terrible effort he stopped screaming and relaxed, letting his legs bend, his head loll, and his eyes close.

After a few more lashes came a pause. A voice said: 'The wretch has swooned. What now, sir?'

'Wake him up,' said the king.

The rope that held Vakar's wrists was let run so that he fell at full length on the blood-spattered deck. He continued to play dead, even when a heavy boot slammed into his ribs and when a gout of cold water splashed over his head.

The queen said: 'Let us waste no more time on him; I am hungry. Sacrifice him now.'

'Very well,' came the voice of the king. 'Drag him over to the altar. You shall do the honors, Sphaxas.'

Vakar felt his wrists being untied. He was dragged across the deck to the small altar on which the lamb had been sacrificed for the wedding. Watching through slitted lids, Vakar saw the minister draw the broad knife and try the edge with his thumb, while the king stood nearby, leaning back against the rail.

Vakar relaxed as completely as possible, so that the Tritons had more trouble dragging him than they otherwise would have. When they got him to the altar they asked another of their number to help them hoist him across it, for by Tritonian standards Vakar was a big man.

Then came the moment when the grips on his arms were relaxed while the Tritons braced their feet and shifted their hands to lift him. In that second, Vakar came to life with the suddenness of a levin-bolt.

With a mighty twist and jerk he broke the loose grips upon his arms, got his feet under him, and dealt the nearest Triton a punch in the belly that doubled the man up in a spasm of gasps and coughs. There was a shout from those watching:

'Watch out!' 'Seize him!' 'He is —'

Hands reached out from all sides, but before they could fasten on to his naked hide, slippery with sweat and blood, Vakar burst through them. He brushed past Sphaxas, standing open-mouthed with the sacrificial knife in his hand, and as he passed dealt the minister a buffet below the ear that stretched his length upon the deck.

Now one man stood between Vakar and the rail: King Ximenon, three paces away. Vakar strained forward, leaning as if he were starting a hundred-yard sprint, and smote the back with the balls of his feet while the hands of the closing Tritons snatched at his bloody back. At the first break Ximenon had reached for the silver-shafted palstave thrust through his girdle, and as Vakar bounded forward the bronze hatchet-head whipped up and back for a skull-shattering blow.

Vakar left the deck in a diving leap and, as the palstave started down, struck the upper part of the king's body head-first with outstretched arms. The stubble on the king's chin rasped his ear as he caught the king around the neck, and his momentum bore the king back against the crotch-high rail. Down and back went the king's torso and up flew his feet. In deadly embrace the two men tumbled over the rail into the dark water below.

The Lorskan let go as soon as they struck the water. With his eyes open under water he saw the cloud of bubbles that represented King Ximenon, the weedy bottom of the queen's ship beyond, and the king's tomahawk gyrating down into the blackness beneath. As his head broke the water he was aware of a strangled shout from the floundering king through the bedlam that had broken out upon the deck a few feet over his head.

Vakar took a deep breath, dove, and seized a sandalled foot that lashed out from the swirl of robes. He pulled it downward. The king came with it, eyes popping and mouth emitting bubbles. Vakar remembered that Tritons could not swim. Even if Ximenon were an exception, the fact that he was fully clothed and weighted with gold and jewels, while Vakar was nude, gave the latter an advantage. As the king started to rise towards the surface, arms and legs jerking wildly, Vakar pulled him under again.

Then Vakar felt a movement of the water behind him: the fluid pushed sharply at him as if displaced by the passage of a large body. A glance over his shoulder saw an immense crocodile, a forty-footer, bearing down upon them from the murk.

Vakar let go the king to use his arms for swimming just as the crocodile arrived with a tigerish rush. The great jaws gaped and clomped on the still struggling king. A hide of horny leather brushed past Vakar, tumbling him over in the water and lacerating him with its projections. He had a brief impression of the great serrated tail undulating lazily as it propelled the monster past him.

Vakar came to the surface again. As he shook the water out of his eyes and ears he perceived that he was now somewhat further from the galley, on which people rushed about madly, some yelling for bows, some for spears, and some for oars.

A bowshot away lay the king's galley. Vakar struck out for it, simultaneously trying to think up some specious story.

He swam as he had never swum before, ears straining to hear the first splash of the oars of the queen's galley behind him. He was over halfway to the king's ship when he heard it. At the same time an arrow plunked into the water nearby.

He plowed on. Another arrow came closer. The king's ship was near now; a row of expectant faces lined the rail. Someone called:

'What in Drax's name goes on over there?'

'A rope!' yelled Vakar.

The oars of the king's ship moved too, gently so as not to run Vakar down. A rope slapped across his tortured back. He grabbed it but was too exhausted to climb. At last they dropped a bight for him to wriggle into and hauled him up. He gasped:

'They slew the king! It was all a plot to get him into their hands. They cut the throats of the king and Sphaxas and all the other Tritons, and would have cut mine had I not dived over the side.'

Exclamations of horror and amazement burst from the Tritons crowing round. An officer of the galley said:

'How do we know you are not lying?'

'Look at my back! Does that look like a fake?'

The captain of the galley roared: 'I knew there was some such trick in the offing! Bend the oars; we will sink them before they slip away in the darkness! Stroke! Stroke!'

The galley moved with increasing speed in a path that curved towards the other ship. As the king's barge bore down, the oars of the queen's ship, which had been idle for some minutes, began to move again. But the king's ship was going too fast for the other to dodge. As the former neared its target, a chorus of screams burst from the queen's barge. In the dusk Vakar could see the

Amazons running about, waving arms, and shrieking at the approaching ship.

Crash!

The ram of the king's ship crunched through the side of the other as if it had been papyrus. With a terrible clatter and roar of breaking timbers and a thin screaming of women, the queen's barge broke up into a floating tangle of boards, ropes, oars, gilded ornaments, bright hangings, and thrashing human limbs. The king's ship plowed through the mass and out the other side, ropes trailing from her ram.

As the king's galley turned and headed back towards Menê, Vakar caught sight of a couple of moving objects on the dark surface of Lake Tritonis: crocodiles swimming towards the wreck. He felt a little badly about having caused the deaths of all those Amazons of lesser degree, who might not had anything to do with the attempt to murder him. Vakar disliked killing women on grounds of waste not, want not. But then, he consoled himself, they were probably all as perfidious as their queen. And what else could he have done?

Though his experience had been exhausting, Vakar Zhu turned his mind immediately to his next step. The Tritonian Ring was gone for good in the belly of a crocodile, but the thing from which it had been cut, the 'fallen star' (whatever that was) lay to the south in the realm of Belem. And if one ring had been made from it, another could be.

He must persuade the Tritons to give him back his property and be on his way – quickly, before somebody suggested that the death of King Ximenon had been his fault and they dealt with him accordingly.

Drax said: 'The wretch has departed from amongst the Tritonians and is now riding south, with his manservant, towards Belem. While I cannot foresee events to happen in the neighborhood of Niowat, for reasons you know, I fear that his journey concerns the Tahakh.'

The gods all shuddered. Entigta gurgled: 'Somebody must warn King Awo-qqas and set him against this man, or it will be too late.' The squid-god spoke to Immut, the god of death of Belem. 'Cousin, will you see to the matter?'

Drax glared round the circle and hissed: 'I think there has been too much warning – to the wrong party.' He looked hard at the Pusadian gods. 'Are you sure none of you has been dropping a quiet word here and there to forewarn this Vakar of the doom intended for him?'

Lyr and Okma and the rest looked innocent, and Vakar Lorska cantered across the parklands south of Lake Tritonis.

They crossed wide grassy plains seeing immense herds of gazelles, antelopes, buffalo, ostriches, zebras, elephants, and other game. They skirted Lake Tashorin where crocodiles lay in wait in the shallows and herds of hippopotami bellowed and splashed, and finally rode up the dark defiles that led into the rocky range of Belem.

For several days after the Tritons had released him, Vakar had been in his gloomiest mood, seldom speaking save to snarl at Fual, and brooding on his own insufficiencies. Besides the tenderness of his healing back there was the feeling of defilement and degredation at having been flogged like a mere slave.

Then as the scenery became more somber Vakar cheered up. He said: 'We were lucky to get away from that treacherous crew so easily. You know, Fual, it occurs to me that it must hurt you to be flogged just as much as it does me!'

'And why shouldn't it, my lord?'

'No reason; I've simply never considered the matter. You must hate me for the times I've beaten you. Do you? Be honest.'

'N-no, sir. Save when you lose your lordly temper you're not a hard master to serve. Most slaves get far more beatings than I.'

'Well, I apologize for any beatings I've given you in excess of your deserts.' Then Vakar amused himself by singing an old Lorskan lay, *The Death of Zormé*:

'Heaped up in hills⠀⠀⠀⠀lay Bruthonian bodies
When a hailstorm of hits⠀⠀⠀⠀felled the far-famed one ...

'There goes another!' He pointed to where a goatherd bounded barefoot from rock to rock, his vermillion-dyed goatskin cloak flapping, until he disappeared. 'Why should they all run from us as from a pair of fiends? We're not such fearsome fellows.'

'I can't imagine,' said Fual, 'but I wish you'd never brought me to these dreadful lands of violence and sorcery. Ah, could I but see the gray towers of Kerys and the silver beaches of Aremoria once again before I die!'

The valet wept great tears. Vakar, with a snort of impatience said:

'Do you think I revel in sleeping on the ground and dodging death from wild beasts and wilder men? I'd rather settle down in some civilized city to the study of literature and philosophy, but I don't complain at every step. Having put our hands to the plow we must finish the furrow.' He paused. 'However, in view of Belem's unsavory reputation, you'd better get out my shield.'

With the bronze buckler slung against his back Vakar felt better, though the sparse inhabitants of this barren land continued to flee from the sight of him.

'Why no houses?' he said. 'I never heard the Belemians lived in the open like wild beasts.'

Fual shrugged, but when Vakar began another song the Aremorian pointed and said: 'Isn't that a house, sir?'

Vakar guided his horse in the direction indicated. The structure was a round hut of stones, roughly chinked with mud, which blended into the stony landscape. It had once possessed a roof of wood and thatch, but this had been burned off.

Vakar dismounted and kicked a skull that lay near the threshold of the hut, saying: 'That was a child. There must have been war hereabouts. Since we can't get to Niowat tonight, this place will do.'

As Fual set up the cooking-pot he said: 'We haven't seen any of Awoqqas' headless servants, my lord. Let's hope we never do.' He struck sparks from his flint and pyrites to start the fire. 'Material dangers we've surmounted, but this is the home of the blackest magic in the world.'

All was peaceful as they ate their frugal meal, watching the long shadows climb up those cliff-faces that were still illuminated. A hyena gave its gruesome laugh somewhere in the hills. Vakar said:

'Look at the horses.'

The four animals were tugging at their tethers, rolling their eyes, and swinging their ears this way and that. Both men peered about and up and down, and Vakar's uneasy gaze caught a movement among the rocks. There was a shrill yell and—

'Great gods!' yelped Fual. 'Look at them!'

Scores of men popped into view and rushed down the steep slopes, bounding from rock to rock and screeching. Some wore goat-skins, some were naked, and all were hairy and filthy. They carried clubs, stones, and boomerangs, and as they came closer the stones and throw-sticks began to whizz through the air.

'To horse!' cried Vakar, vaulting on to his own animal.

A stone clanged against the shield at Vakar's back as Fual scrambled on to his own mount with his usual awkwardness. A thump behind Vakar and a neigh told him that another missile had struck one of the horses. With a quick glance to see that his cavalcade was in order, Vakar set off at a canter along the winding track to the south, hoping that his beast would not stumble in the twilight.

'Now,' said Fual mournfully, 'we have lost not only that good meal I was preparing for you, my lord, but also our only cooking-pot.'

Vakar shrugged. 'You can steal another.'

'Why did they attack us?'

'I don't know; maybe they're cannibals. They kept yelling a word like '*Ullimen, ullimen*' which as I remember means 'lords' or 'gentlemen.' But if they considered us aristocrats, why should they mob us? This part of the world must be stark mad.'

Vakar led the way southward until darkness forced them to halt again. They snatched a cold meal and an uneasy sleep, watching alternately as usual, and took off before dawn.

The mountains became ever steeper and rockier and grimmer-looking.

The morning was well advanced when they entered a prodigiously long, deep, and narrow defile that wound south and up into the very heart of the Belemian Mountains. They rode on and on, winding between the rough steep skirts of the slopes on either side, the rocks sometimes brushing against their legs, the hooffalls echoing loudly. After a long ride they pulled up for a breather.

'This seems to go on forev — What's that?' said Vakar, whose ears had picked up the echo of the sound of many men moving. 'Are some more of our unwashed friends coming to greet us?'

He set his horse in motion at a walk, peering ahead. The sounds grew louder. After an interminable time the source of the sounds came in sight, and both Vakar and Fual gave an involuntary cry of astonishment and horror.

The noise came from a group of twenty-odd izzuneg – the headless zombies that served Lord Awoqqas. These were dog-trotting three abreast down the road, carrying copper-headed spears. Behind them a pair of men rode small horses, like sheep-dogs herding their flock. These men shouted and pointed at the travellers, and the izzuneg broke into a run, their spears raised and their single pectoral eyes staring blankly ahead.

XIII

The Kingdom of the Headless

Vakar wheeled his horse and started back down the defile. As he turned he saw that Fual had already done so, and was going at a reckless gallop, though the little Aremorian was usually afraid of anything faster than an easy canter. Vakar could hear the slap of the bare feet of the izzuneg on the trail behind him. A glance back showed that he was gaining on the pursuers, and after a few more bends in the defile they were out of sight. Vakar kept on at an easier pace as Fual called back:

'Do they wish to kill us too, sir?'

'I know not. How can you judge the expression on a man's face when he has no face? But that charge looked hostile. It seems we are not welcome in Belem.'

'What shall we do now, sir? Try to find another road to Niowat?'

'I'm cursed if I know. If somebody in this accursed land would only stand still long enough to talk to him ...'

They rode on until Vakar began to look for the lower end of the defile. And then—

They came around a bend in the road and almost ran headlong into another group of izzuneg with a single mounted man behind them. Again the horseman pointed and shouted, and the headless ones rushed.

Vakar and Fual whirled again and galloped up the trail down which they had just come. Behind him Vakar heard Fual's wail:

'We're lost! We're caught between two armies!'

'Not yet lost,' grunted Vakar. 'Keep your eye peeled for a place to climb.'

He remembered Kurtevan's remark that the izzuneg could not look around or up, and the sides of the defile, while steep, were not unscalable. After several minutes of hard riding he sighted a suitable place. With a warning cry to Fual he thrust down upon his horse's back with his hands and threw himself into a crouch, his feet on the saddle-pad. Then before he could lose his balance he leaped up and to the side.

He landed on a ledge six feet above the roadway, skinned a knee, and then went bounding and scrambling up the hillside, sending down a small landslide of rocks and pebbles. Fual panted and clawed after him. Below them the horses trotted a few paces further, then stopped to eat the scanty herbage.

'Hurry up there,' gritted Vakar. 'And no noise!'

They clambered on up but had not yet reached the top of the slope when Vakar heard the sound of the approaching enemy. The horses snorted and ran off to southward, but in a few minutes were back again. Vakar said:

'Flatten out on this ledge and keep still.'

The horses snorted and whinnied as the two groups of izzuneg converged. The animals collected in a solid group, rolling their eyes and showing their teeth. The headless ones trotted from either hand and met right below Vakar, milling witlessly and accidentally pricking each other with their pikes. As they brushed against the horses, these lashed out with teeth and hooves. One headless one was hurled flat and lay still.

The horsemen shouted back and forth over the neck-stumps of their strange force, carrying on a conversation in which Vakar could sense astonishment and frustration. Finally one of them dismounted, gave his bridle to an izzuni to hold, and pushed through the crowd toward the horses. He reached for the bridle of Vakar's own horse.

Watching from his ledge, Vakar felt red rage rise within him. It was bad enough to be attacked and chased by everybody whom one saw in this wretched country; to be stranded afoot and destitute would be worse. And the disparity in numbers would not much matter if he made use of his altitude ...

'Come on,' he muttered and rose to his feet. He seized the nearest stone of convenient size and sent it crashing down the slope; then another and another. Fual joined him.

The rocks bounded and plowed into the milling mass below. Some struck other rocks and started them too rolling down. Horses screamed; the three men with heads yelled and pointed to where Vakar and Fual, working like demons, were hurling every stone within reach. The bigger stones plunged in among the izzuneg, who did nothing to avoid them, with a sound of snapping spear-shafts and breaking bones. Several of the creatures were down. The man who had tried to take Vakar's horses in tow started to push his way back out of the crowd towards his own horse.

Vakar found a precariously perched boulder as tall as himself. He called to Fual, and both put their shoulders against it and heaved. It gave a little with a deep grinding sound, then rolled down the hill after the others. The ground shook with the vibration of its passage, and as it went it started more stones rolling until the entire hillside below Vakar and Fual came loose with a thunderous roar and slid down upon the enemy. Vakar was reminded of a pailful of gravel being poured upon a disturbed anthill.

When the slide stopped, the mass of izzuneg was nearly buried along with the officer who had dismounted. Limbs and spears stuck up here and there among the rocks, and all four of Vakar's horses were more or less buried. At the north end of the slide the izzuni to whom the dead officer had given his reins still stood holding the horse, while at the other end the remaining two mounted men still sat their horses.

As Vakar started down the hill, these two leaped off their animals and began climbing up towards him.

'Come on, Fual, your sword!' said Vakar, unslinging his buckler.

He leaped down upon the first of the two. The man bore a small shield of hide and brandished a copper battle-adze, while his fellow swarmed up behind him with a stone-headed casse-tête.

As the man and the adze swung his awkward weapon, Vakar slammed his shield into his face. The adze clanked against the thin bronze, and Vakar made a low deep thrust with his sword under both shields. The blade ripped into the man's belly, and he screamed and fell backwards in a tangle of his own guts.

Vakar started for the other, the one with the club, but a stone thrown by Fual flew past his head and struck the man in the chest. The man turned and bounded down the slope that he had just climbed. At the bottom he took off in a great leap that landed him on the back of his pony, and seconds later he streaked out of sight up the gorge to southward.

While the sound of his hooves still drummed in his ears, the Lorskan turned towards the remaining izzuni. The creature had not moved, and did not move even when Vakar climbed over the landslide and faced it. The single eye looked calmly out of its chest as Vakar approached.

'Can you hear me?' said Vakar to the thing in his rudimentary Belemian. Nothing happened.

'Let go that bridle.' Still no action.

'Well then, don't!' cried Vakar, and drove his bloody sword into the creature's chest.

The body swayed and collapsed. Vakar snatched at the bridle and caught the horse before it had time to shy away. He tethered it and went back to the rock-slide.

Three of his horses were dead and the remaining one had a broken leg. Vakar cut its throat and then chased the remaining horse, the one belonging to the officer he had killed, until he had backed it up against the rock slide and caught its reins. With both animals secured he went back to the slide. A few of the projecting members of the izzuneg still twitched, but none seemed dangerous. The corpses of the whole men, he noted, were well-dressed in turbans and knee-length tunics of fine wool with elaborate girdles of woven leather set with semi-precious stones. They also had golden rings in their ears and on their fingers (which Fual promptly took) and were evidently men of substance by the standards of these mountains.

Vakar and Fual sweated for an hour moving the rocks that had half buried their horses so that they could get at their belongings. With his sword Vakar cut a haunch off one of the dead horses for food, and by main force they pulled and pushed the live horse at the north end of the slide over the rocks to the south end. Fual said:

'My lord, aren't you going to give up this mad enterprise *now?*'

'And have Kuros taunt me for cowardice? Never! Get on your nag and we'll go on to Niowat.'

Vakar did not like his new mount, for it was smaller and, being unused to him and his style of riding, skittish and recalcitrant.

'All the same,' grumbled Fual, 'there's a word for a man who attacks a hostile kingdom single-handed, and it isn't "brave."'

Vakar grinned. Though tired, he was proud of having come through one more trial. He said:

'That's all right; some of the greatest heroes have been mad too. As in *The Madness of Vrir*:

'Foaming with fury   he hurled the hatchet
At his helpless helpmeet,   whose brains bespattered
The wattled walls;   a dreadful deed ...'

Fual shuddered but said no more.

Next day a man rode out of the mountains ahead of them and held up an empty hand in a gesture of peace. Vakar let him approach but kept his hand near his hilt. The man spoke a little Tritoninan and Vakar a few words of Belemian, so that with effort enough they managed to make themselves mutually understood. The man said:

'I am Lord Shagarnin, and I have been sent by King Awoqqas to welcome you to our land and guide you to Niowat.'

'That is kind of Awoqqas,' said Vakar. 'Were those his servants who gave us such a boisterous reception yesterday?'

'Yes, but that was an error. The gods had warned Awoqqas that a certain Vakar Lorska was approaching from Tritonia, and that the interests of gods and men required that he be destroyed. You are not he, are you?'

'No, I am Thiegos of Sederado,' said Vakar, giving the first name that popped into his head.

'That is what the king thought when report was brought to him of what a mighty magician you are, for the gods had specifically described Vakar as an ordinary man of no fearsome powers. So when the lone survivor of this unfortunate attack told how you flew straight up in the air on bat's wings and hurled a mountain upon your attackers by your spells, he thought there must be some mistake. He hopes you will pardon his fault and accept his hospitality.'

'I shall be glad to do so,' said Vakar.

He understood what had happened: The surviving officer had galloped back to Niowat and, to avoid blame for the disaster, had told a highly colored tale of the battle. Vakar was not sure that Shagarnin or the king would be taken in by his denial of his identity; this looked like an effort to lure him to destruction. Having failed to kill him by brute force they would now try guile. His previous narrow escapes had made Vakar suspicious almost to the point of mania. He said:

'This is the most remarkable land I have seen in my travels. For example, the day before yesterday we were also attacked, but by savages with heads.'

'That is unfortunate,' said Shagarnin, eyes opening in something like fear. 'It must have been some of our commoners. The disorderly beasts attack the better sort of people whenever they catch one or two alone, so that it is unsafe to travel away from Niowat without an escort. We shall have to send a detachment to wipe out this band.'

'Why do your commoners attack you?'

'Because the fools do not wish King Awoqqas to make izzuneg of them. As if such filth had rights!' Shagarnin spat.

'Does he plan to make your whole commonality into these – izzuneg?' asked Vakar, keeping the astonishment out of his voice.

'Yes; it is his great plan. For our king is the world's greatest magician and has learned that izzuneg make ideal subjects: docile, tireless, fearless, orderly, with no subversive thoughts of their own. He has even found it possible to breed them, though the children have heads like normal folk. Come back in a few years and you shall see an ideal kingdom: The *ullimen*, that is to say us, ruling a completely headless subject population, and everybody orderly and happy.'

'It is an astounding idea,' said Vakar.

'I am glad you think so. Meanwhile we have trouble rounding up our subjects for decapitation. As if heads did the rabble any good! And since the making of an izzuni requires a mighty spell, this great design cannot be accomplished all at once. Our poor king labors day and night, so that we who love him fear for his health.'

Vakar nodded sympathetically. 'The rabble never know what is good for them, do they? I think I understand, however, why that mob attacked us.'

'I am glad. But, Lord Thiegos, what is your purpose here?'

'I travel for pleasure.'

Shagarnin looked at Vakar curiously. 'I cannot imagine travelling for pleasure; but perhaps in your country things are different.'

Vakar shrugged. 'I understand Awoqqas owns a fallen star?'

'The Tahakh. Yes, he does, but you will have to ask him about it.'

As they neared Niowat, Vakar saw more of the round stone huts, but few people. Those whom he did see darted into huts or behind rocks with the speed of a lizard fleeing into a crack in the wall. Once he saw a little group of filthy faces peering around a hut with an expression of such concentrated hatred as to make him shudder. As they rode higher up the road they passed substantial stone houses which Vakar took for those of the aristocracy.

'Here is the palace,' said Shagarnin.

Vakar did not at first see what the Belemian meant. Then he observed a hole in the side of a craggy hill that dominated Niowat. A bridge of logs with a straw paving crossed a deep ditch in front of this opening. Several izzuneg stood about the entrance with spears.

As the party trotted over the bridge, the hooves of the horses sounded like muffled drums. They dismounted, and an izzuni led the horses away. Shagarnin parleyed with a whole man inside the entrance to the tunnel, then said: 'Come.'

He led them through a maze of tunnels. Vakar whistled: If the palace was a rabbit-warren of holes dug out of the inside of the hill, Awoqqas had spared no trouble to make it a handsome warren. The walls were plastered and painted with geometrical patterns outlined with nails of gold and silver; no representations of living beings as in Ogugia and Phaiaxia. Every few feet a yellow oil-flame danced on top of a great copper torchère. Vakar passed an izzuni lugging a copper kettle along the corridor and pouring oil into the lamps as he went. Vakar tried to remember the turns and cross-tunnels, but soon gave up, saying in Lorskan to Fual:

'I hope we shan't have to leave in a hurry, because we should never get out without a guide.'

After much winding and waiting and passing of passwords and pushing through massive doors ornamented with gold and precious stones, Shagarnin led them into a room where several izzuneg stood guard. The nobleman said:

'Take off your weapons and hand them to this izzuni.'

As this was a standard regulation for visitors to royalty, Vakar complied. Another izzuni opened a door on the far side and Shagarnin said:

'The king! Prostrate yourselves in adoration.'

Coming from Lorsk with its free-and-easy manners, Vakar did not like prostrating himself for any mortal and would have even been choosy about which gods he so honored. However, not wishing to become an izzuni over a matter of protocol he did as he was bid until a squeaky voice said:

'Rise. Shagarnin, show our visitor's slave to the chamber they will occupy, so that he shall prepare it for his master. You – what did you say your name was?'

'Thiegos of Sederado,' replied Vakar.

'Fiegos, remain where you are and be quiet, for I am about to perform a divination.'

Vakar looked around. The man speaking to him sat on a throne cut in the stone of the side of the chamber, six steps above the floor-level. He wore many-colored robes of that shimmery stuff called silk, which Kurtevan had also worn, and which Vakar had been told came from the land of Sericana beyond the sunrise. Awoqqas was a slim yellow-skinned balding man with deep lines in his careworn face – commonplace-looking enough except for his size. He was, Vakar judged, less than five feet tall.

In a flash of insight Vakar realized why Awoqqas sat upon a throne six feet up, and why he was beheading the entire commonality of his kingdom. He could not bear to be smaller than his subjects, and therefore was employing this drastic method of reducing their stature so that they should no longer look down upon him in any sense of the phrase.

Not wishing to give Awoqqas any unwholesome ideas, Vakar deliberately slouched to subtract a couple of inches from his own stature.

Awoqqas was staring at a cleared space on the stone floor in front of his throne. On the edges of this space two small oil-lamps with copper reflectors burned and, as Vakar watched, an izzuni came in and extinguished the torchères, leaving the chamber illuminated only by the two little lamps on the floor.

The space lit by the lamps, Vakar saw, was marked with a large and complex pentacle. Awoqqas extended his arms towards it, fingers pointing, and muttered a spell in a language that the Lorskan did not know. Gradually the pentacle faded from sight as a phantasm appeared on the illuminated space. The phantasm was a reproduction in miniature of a stretch of sandy desert, across which flowed a mass of riders. These riders bestrode tall humped animals that Vakar recognized from descriptions as camels, but like the rest of the scene they were in miniature, man and camel together standing no more than a span in height. The men wore shroud-like black cloths that were fastened to their heads by head-bands and fell away in folds to cover most of their bodies, and the lower parts of their faces were concealed by veils. They carried long spears. Their number seemed endless; as some passed out of sight on one side of the phantasm, others came into view on the other.

King Awoqqas spoke a word and the phantasm vanished. As the izzuni came in again and relit the torchères, the king said:

'You have seen the army of the Gwedulians marching westward along the southerly borders of my land. I though they might turn north to attack us; but they are continuing west. I suspect they mean to cross the Tamenruft to assail Gamphasantia.'

Vakar said: 'Do you mean to warn the Gamphasantians, King?'

'Nay. I have nothing to do with them; I do not wish to antagonize the Gwedulians; and it would do no good, for the Gamphasants pay no heed to outside advice.'

'Are they a civilized people?'

'One might say so; they have a capital city and raise their food by farming. In other respects they are very odd. But tell me what you are doing here, Master Fiegos?'

'I am travelling for pleasure, to see places far and strange before settling down. For instance, I have heard of the – ah – unusual customs of Belem, and of your talisman, the Tahakh, and should like to see these marvels with my own eyes.'

Awoqqas nodded. 'It is proper that the barbarous and disorderly outer lands should send men to learn our superior ways. Perhaps some day they will all be as orderly as we. You have seen the izzuneg, and tomorrow I will have you shown the fallen star. There is a fascinating story of how it got into my possession after it originally fell in Tartaros. But – you are something of a magician yourself, are you not?'

Vakar made a modest gesture. 'Not compared to you, my lord King.'

Awoqqas nodded with the ghost of a smile. 'That is the spirit I like. Most travellers are insufferable braggarts and disorderly to boot. But I cannot continue this audience because I must be about my great work.'

'Making more izzuneg?'

'Precisely. It is the greatest feat of thaumaturgy in the history of magic. By it I not only reduce my subjects to order; I please Immut, the god of death and the greatest of all the gods. Now, you may watch me eat as a mark of special favor.' The king clapped his hands.

'Is this the usual time of dining in Belem?' asked Vakar.

'*My* usual time is whenever I hunger. As I remain underground nearly all the time, the revolutions of the heavenly bodies mean little to me save as their astrological aspects affect my magical operations.' As an izzuni came in with a tray of food and drink, the king added: 'Shall I have you served also?'

'Pray excuse me. My stomach has been upset, and I am fasting to let it settle.' Vakar's real reason for declining the offer was fear of poison.

The king ate for a few minutes, then said: 'Perhaps you would like livelier entertainment,' and to the izzuneg: 'Send in Rezzâra and a musician.'

As the headless servant went out, Vakar asked: 'How do you control those beings? How can they hear you without ears?'

'They do not hear with material ears. When you speak to one your thoughts are perceived directly by the sylph animating it. The sylph will, however, obey only me or one whom I have expressly delegated to command it; otherwise a fearful disorder would ensue. Ah, here is our most accomplished dancer. Dance for the visitor, Rezzâra!'

Two people had come in: a small Belemian with a tootle-pipe and a woman. The latter was young and voluptuously formed – a fact that was patent at once, for she wore nothing but an assortment of rings, bracelets, anklets, and pendants of jewels and amber beads suspended from ears, neck, and waist. This gaudery clattered and clicked as she moved.

The little man sat cross-legged on the floor and began playing a wailing tune that reminded Vakar of the music that Qasigan had played in Sederado when he had brought the serpent to life. Vakar braced himself for some such marvel, but all that happened was that Rezzâra went into a sensuous dance. She sank to her knees before him, leaning back and looking up through half-closed lids, her arms writhing like serpents. Had he been alone with her …

As it was he had to sit with the blood pounding in his ears while Rezzâra strove by all the arts known to the dancing-girl to stimulate him to madness. She had a trick of making her breasts jiggle while all the rest of her remained immobile. He could feel his face flushing and was not displeased when Rezzâra finished her act with a prostration in front of Awoqqas and ran out, her ornaments jingling. Her accompanist followed.

'A splendid performance,' said Vakar sincerely.

'Yes, she too is among the wonders of Belem. Now I must return to my labors. You shall hear when it is convenient for you to be shown the Tahakh.'

'Thank you, sir,' said Vakar, making his belly-flop.

An izzuni at the door handed Vakar back his sword and guided him through the maze of tunnels to a chamber lined with gay-colored cloths that concealed the cold rough rock behind them. There was a substantial bed with a kind of canopy over it, a couple of stools, and a niche in the wall in which stood an ivory carving of an ugly Belemian god. Fual, who had been sitting on one of the stools, rose and indicated a tray of food and a jug of wine.

'Now where,' said Vakar, 'did you get those?'

'I stole them from the king's kitchen while the chief cook's back was turned. As the under-cooks are all headless they presented no problem. Let me pour you some of this wine. Sour stuff, but better than water.'

Vakar sat down upon the edge of the bed saying: 'I could use a little, after my interview with the wizard-king.'

'How did it go, sir?' said Fual, handing his master a brimming silver cup.

'I thought I'd seen everything, but —'

A knock interrupted. Vakar called: 'Come in!'

The golden rivets of the door glittered as it swung inward to reveal Rezzâra the dancer, who said: 'Send your servant away, my lord Thiegos. I would speak to you alone.'

XIV

The Naked Puritans

Fual looked alarmed, but Vakar hitched his sword around and said: 'Go on, Fual. What is it, Rezzâra?'

Fual went out. Vakar tensed himself, but reflected that at least he need not worry about her whisking a dagger from her clothing. Any weapon that could be concealed in her costume would be too small for anything but cleaning fingernails.

She waited until the door closed, then said: 'Lord, when do you plan to go?'

'I had not planned. Why?'

'Take me with you! I can stay here no longer.'

'Huh? What is this?' Vakar's suspicions were at once alert.

'I hate King Awoqqas and I love you.'

'*What?* By Tandyla's third eye, this is sudden!'

She blinked her large dark eyes at him. 'I cannot endure that fiend, with his fanatical notions of order, and I burned with passion for you from the moment I saw you. Oh, take me! You shall never regret it!'

'An interesting idea,' said Vakar dryly, sipping his wine, 'but how should I carry it out?'

'You are a man. You can overcome obstacles. What are you really here for?'

'To see the sights.'

'I do not believe that. You wish to steal the Tahakh.'

'The Tahakh is certainly valuable. Would you like some wine?'

'No! All I wish is for you to crush me in your strong arms and cover my eager body with your burning kisses.' She writhed at him.

'You are nothing if not explicit, Rezzâra. But —'

'Do you seek the Tahakh? Do you?' She grasped his wrist in both her hands and shook him.

'I have come a long way to see it.'

'If I show it to you, to do with as you wish, will you take me?'

'If I can,' he said, stroking his mustache.

She stepped over to the niche in the wall and lifted out the ugly ivory image. Behind it Vakar glimpsed something dark.

'There,' she said. 'Take it yourself, but be careful not to get it near me. Its touch is said to make women barren.'

'Hm.' Vakar advanced cautiously and looked into the niche. There lay what looked like a stone: about the size of two fists, a dark brown that was almost black, and rough and pitted on its irregular surface.

He extended a finger. When nothing happened he continued to advance his finger until it touched the stone. It felt colder than he would have expected. He grasped it and lifted it out with a grunt of surprise. It must weigh well over ten pounds.

He turned the thing over and found a place where tools had worked upon it: evidently to saw or chisel off the small piece from which the smith of Tartaros had made the Ring of the Tritons. He gazed at it in wonder. So this was what a star looked like up close? He would have expected something bigger. He asked:

'Are you sure this is the Tahakh?'

'Quite sure.'

'Why does Awoqqas leave it in such an accessible place? One would think to find it in an underground chamber guarded by an army of izzuneg and a couple of dragons.'

'He is a man of strange quirks. Perhaps he thought if it were left practically in the open nobody would notice it. But let us talk of other matters, my lord.'

She lay back on the bed, stretching luxuriously. 'You will soon realize you have never known what joy life can hold. Come kiss me!'

She held up her arms. Well, thought Vakar, why not? Life did not go on forever, and in this career of adventure into which he had been pitched it was likely to be even shorter than otherwise. He laid down the Tahakh, lifted his sword-belt off over his head and laid baldric and scabbard beside the fallen star, and picked up the silver wine-cup for one more swallow.

He stood by the bed, holding the cup in his hand and looking down at Rezzâra's sleek olive-skinned form, from which the jewels winked up, adorning without concealing. He realized that these ornaments represented enough of an asset to take a traveller a long way ...

And then the wine-cup dropped from Vakar's limp fingers as a horrifying change took place before his eyes. The girl's head faded from view, leaving her nothing but a female izzuni.

'Rezzâra!' he called sharply.

A faint voice – Rezzâra's, but barely audible, sounding inside his skull, replied: 'Come, my love, let us take our fill of passion ... I burn for you ...'

He leaned over and passed his hand through the air where her head had been. It met no resistance. He could not quite force himself to touch the downy neck-stump. Again that tiny voice sounded in his head, like the cry of a distant bird flying off into the sunset:

'So – you know? Do not blame me, stranger, for I am but a wandering sylph, constrained by Awoqqas' will. He cast a glamor upon this body to beguile you. If you wish, you may still …'

The suggestion was never completed, for a sound over Vakar's head caused him to look up and then to jerk frantically back as a great net detached itself from the canopy. It fell down upon the bed and was drawn tight over Rezzâra's body. One of the ropes brushed Vakar's hair as he leaped, and at that instant the door flew open.

In rushed a squad of izzuneg, unarmed, with hands outspread to clutch, and behind them came the little king.

Vakar stooped for his sword. His right hand snatched up the scabbard while his left touched the Tahakh. He rose, whirling to face the intruders with both objects, and hardly knowing what he did he hurled the heavy stone over the izzuneg at Awoqqas, then drew his sword just as the izzuneg reached him. There was no time for thrusting. Sidestepping, he struck right and left, slicing open torsos and reaching arms. The izzuneg, spraying blood, came on anyway. Hands clamped upon his arms …

The grip of the hands relaxed. All the izzuneg, with a faint exhalation of breath, slumped to the floor in a tangle of bare brown bodies. Looking across the shambles, Vakar saw the king lying near the door with his head staved in. And in his mind the thin voice of the sylph that had animated Rezzâra sounded:

'The spell is broken and we are all free … Thank you, stranger, and farewell …'

Vakar stood staring stupidly, his mind wandering, until Fual burst in, crying: 'What's happened, my lord? I was in the kitchens, where this king ordered me to go, when all the headless ones fell dead! Isn't that the king, dead too? And who's that on the bed? Have you cut off her head? I should not have thought that of you, sir …'

'She never had any, poor thing,' said Vakar slowly. 'She was an izzuni like the others, but Awoqqas put a spell upon her to make her look like a whole woman. Thinking me a great wizard he sent me into the room containing the Tahakh with the intention that I should touch it and lose my magical powers. Then Rezzâra should lure me on to the bed. The door has a spy-hole, and the king meant to watch me through it and drop the net over us both, as in that myth about the goddess Aphradexa that fellow sang of in Huperea. Then Awoqqas would rush in to secure me, no doubt to turn us into izzuneg. But I'm no wizard, and the wine showed me Rezzâra's true shape.'

Fual's teeth chattered. 'What now, sir?'

'Collect our stuff and get out.'

Fual leaned over the body of Rezzâra, cut the ropes of the net with his dagger, and started stripping the carcass of its ornaments. The bodies began to stink of decay with unnatural rapidity. He said over his shoulder:

'My lord, whither now?'

'Since the smiths of Tartaros seem to know how to make things of this star-stuff, I thought we should go there.'

'To Blackland? But they *eat* people!' wailed the Aremorian.

'Not all of them, and we're too lean to be appetizing. Roll the Tahakh up in our blanket.'

A few minutes later they were walking the corridors, Vakar prowling in the lead with buckler before him and sword out, Fual clumping behind. Here and there they passed the sprawled corpse of an izzuni. Once a whole man brushed past them and ran down the corridor, his sandals slapping. Vakar gazed after him, then whirled as another charged around a corner.

'Halt there!' cried Vakar, stepping in front of the man. He recognized the fellow as his acquaintance Shagarnin, who had guided them to Niowat. The Belemian tried to dodge past, but Vakar held his arms out. 'How do you get out of here?'

The man breathed heavily and his face was distorted with fear. 'Izzuneg all dead,' he gasped. 'The commoners are up in disorder and are tearing all the *ullimen* to bits! Let me go – they will kill me – they will kill me —'

'Stand still!' shouted Vakar. 'Tell me how to get out of here or I will rob the commoners of that pleasure!'

'Go the way I just came – turn right, then left, then go straight ...'

'Where are our horses?'

'Paddock off to the right as you come out the entrance, but the rabble will be there. Let me go ...'

'Why not come with us? You would have some chance to save your worthless life.'

'No – I am afraid – they will kill me —' Shagarnin ducked under Vakar's arm and raced down the corridor as his predecessor had done.

'Hurry,' said Vakar, setting a pace that Fual with his burdens could scarcely follow.

As they neared the entrance to the tunnel-palace Vakar became conscious of a buzzing sound as of an overturned beehive. When the tunnel entrance came in sight he was struck by the red glow around it. It would, he reflected, be just about sunset.

But the glow was not sunset, though the sun had already set behind the peaks. The redness was the light of the fires that were burning the houses of all the *ullimen* of Belem. Here and there in the city below the palace lay little groups of bodies of both sexes and all ages, stripped and mutilated, while a crowd of several hundred commoners danced shrieking around the burning houses. In one place Vakar saw a group gathered about an aristocrat whom they had tied to a tree and were skinning alive; another group was torturing a young girl with fire. The stench of rotting izzuneg combined noisomely with that of burning human flesh.

'Let's go quickly,' said Vakar, and led the way to the paddock, where lay another clump of dead izzuneg.

An outburst of yells from the mob below caused Fual to look back: 'They've seen us, sir! They're coming this way!'

'Well, help me catch these damned animals!' snarled Vakar.

Presently they had rounded up three of the least skittish, bridled them (the Belemians rode bareback) and lashed their load to one. The screams of the approaching mob grew louder.

'Our only chance is to go through them at full speed,' said Vakar. 'Ready?'

He slapped his horse's rump with the flat of his sword, and the animal started as if bitten and bounded out of the paddock. The commoners were swarming all around the entrance to the palace; some were pushing into the tunnels while a group of others was coming towards the paddock. The yells redoubled in volume. A stone struck Vakar's shield with a clank and another glanced off his helmet.

The horse tried to leap over the side of the path, but Vakar hauled it back with a brutal jerk, knowing that if they tried to gallop down the steep hillside they would surely be unhorsed. He forced the animal right at the screeching savages, who tumbled out of the way as he leaned forward, howling like a demon himself and cutting right and left. He looked one of them in the face: a face covered with dirt and matted hair, out of which a pair of bloodshot eyes glared insanely. He struck at it and felt the blade bite into the skull; felt his horse stumble on the body and jerked the reins to bring the beast's head up ...

They pounded across the echoing bridge and down the main street of Nio-wat, skimming through the scattered crowds, and then they were out of town. Behind them the yells of the commoners died away, and the flames of the burning houses vanished around the bends in the road.

Vakar said to Fual: 'I've never been for pampering the commoners, but neither is there any sense to oppressing them to madness. Cutting off all their heads forsooth! No wonder they wished to flay Awoqqas and his nobles. The only sad thing is that they will in their stupid fury have destroyed all the amenities of civilized life in Belem, so that there will remain nothing but wretched savages, unable to rise from their own filth ...'

They were riding towards Lake Kokutos, the chief body of water in Gamph-santia, having retraced part of their route from Tritonia to Belem and then turned off westward at Lake Tashorin, skirting around the northern end of the Tamenruft. The tropical midsummer sun glared down cruelly upon them from a cloudless sky.

Fual said: 'Let's hope these next people won't be even worse company. The strange nations have been getting worse and worse ever since we left Phaiaxia.

Ah, that was a fine land! Are you sure about these Gamphasantians? They're said to be unfriendly to strangers.'

'I'm not worried. I met one in Sederado who seemed decent enough even if he did try to murder me, and if I can warn them of the attack by the Gwedulians I should earn their gratitude.'

Fual shuddered. 'If the Gwedulians haven't got there before us. Why not go straight home, sir? We have that lump of star-metal ...'

'Because I'm minded to have this lump made into rings and things, and the smiths of Tartaros are the only men who can do it. Are you thinking of that promise of freedom I made you?'

'Y-yes, sir,' said Fual, mopping his forehead.

'Don't worry; I keep my word ... These Gamphasants keep good-looking fields, don't they?'

They had left the sands of the Tamenruft behind them and were cutting into the meadowlands of Gamphasantia. Vakar sweated in the August heat, though he had stripped down to mantle and loincloth. In the middle distance a tall naked brown man hoed his patch with a stone-bladed hoe. Ahead a hamlet of mud huts took form out of the haze.

'*Hé!*' cried Vakar.

As they entered the hamlet, people rushed out of the huts and surrounded the three ponies in a jabbering mass. All were tall and slender with curly black hair and narrow aquiline features, and all were nude and burnt nearly black by the sun. Dogs ran barking around the edges of the crowd.

'Stand back!' shouted Vakar, drawing his sword. He repeated the warning in all the languages he knew. 'Get away from those animals!'

When they paid no attention he whacked one with the flat to clear a path. With an outburst of yells the mass closed in. Before he could strike again, Vakar felt himself seized in a dozen places and ignominiously hauled from his horse. Out of the corner of his eye he saw Fual being likewise dismounted. He gritted his teeth in rage; what a fool he was!

The Gamphasants hauled Vakar to his feet and wrenched the sword out of his hand, but did not strike him. A wrinkled leathery-looking man with a white beard and a melon-like potbelly stepped in front of Vakar and spoke to him.

Vakar shook his head. 'I don't understand.'

The oldster repeated his inquiry in other languages and finally in broken Hesperian:

'Who are you?'

'Vakar of Lorsk.'

'Where is Lorsk?'

Vakar tried to explain, but gave up with a vague gesture towards the northwest.

'You come with us.'

The old man gestured, and a couple of younger ones slipped a noose over Vakar's head and another over that of Fual. These nooses formed part of a single rawhide rope whose ends were held by several husky Gamphasants. Under the old man's direction these now started along the road towards Tokalet, dragging the travellers with them. Others led the horses. Vakar, masking his fury, asked the old man why they were being so treated.

'Foreigners no live in Gamphasantia,' was the reply.

'You mean you will kill us?'

'Oh, no! Gamphasants good people; no take life. But you no live.'

'But how —'

'Is other ways,' chuckled the patriarch.

Vakar wondered if that meant that they would toss Fual and himself into a cell to die of starvation, thereby achieving their end without personally slaying their guests. He tried to tell the old man about the Gwedulians, but the latter either had never heard of the desert raiders or did not care about them. They walked all day until Vakar's feet were sore, spent the night in another mud-hut village, and the next day set out with another escort. Thus they were passed from village to village until they came to Tokalet.

Tokalet, on the marge of sparkling Lake Kokutos, was a sprawling unwalled town, essentially a mud-hut village on a larger scale. Vakar shambled down a broad street in his noose, eyeing blank walls of sun-baked brick. Few of the folk were abroad in the heat of the day, and those few looked stolidly at the prisoners.

Vakar was dragged into some sort of official building. He listened uncomprehendingly to a colloquy between the leader of his present escort and a man who sat on a stool in a room, and then was stripped and shoved into a cell with a massive wooden door, closed by a large bolt on the outside. The door slammed shut, the bolt shot home, and they were left in semidarkness.

The door had a small opening at eye-level with wooden bars; a similar opening served as a window on the opposite side of the cell.

'Well, sir, now you have got us in a fix!' said Fual. 'If you'd only —'

'Shut up!' snapped Vakar, cocking a fist.

But then he relaxed. Their energy had better be put to uses other than fighting each other, and he had resolved not to hit Fual any more over petty irritations. He prowled around, scratching at the soft bricks with his thumbnails and wondering how long it would take to claw one's way through the wall. The window gave a restricted view across the main street of Tokalet. All that could be seen was another mud-brick wall opposite, and occasionally the head of a passing pedestrian. (The Gamphasants seemed neither to ride nor to use chariots, and Vakar had seen no metal among them.) The window also revealed that the wall was at least two feet thick.

At the other opening, that through the door, Vakar started back with a grunt of surprise. Another cell stood opposite this one, and through the grille in its door a fearful face looked into Vakar's. It was huge, ape-like, and subhuman, and at the same time vaguely familiar.

'Ha!' said Vakar. 'Look at that!'

Fual got up from where he crouched and looked, raising himself on tiptoe. He said:

'My lord, I think that's the ape-man we saw in Sederado, or another just like him.'

Vakar called: 'Nji!'

A low roar answered.

'Nji!' he said again, then in Hesperian: 'Do you understand me?'

Another roar, and the thump of huge fists against the door. Vakar tried various languages, but nothing worked, and he finally gave up.

Vakar Zhu had seen enough nudity in his life not to be impressed by it, but he still found the sight of the nation's highest court meeting in that state incongruous. It was the morning after his arrival in Tokalet.

His interpreter said in Hesperian: 'You are accused of being a foreigner. What have you to say to that?'

'Of course I am a foreigner! How can I help where I was born?'

'You may not be able to help where you were born,' said the judge through the interpreter, 'but you can help coming to Gamphasantia, where it is illegal for outlanders to trespass.'

'Why is that?'

'The Gamphasants are a virtuous people, and fear that commerce with barbarian nations would corrupt our purity.'

'But I did not know about your silly law!'

'Ignorance of the law is no excuse. You could have inquired among the neighboring nations before you so rashly invaded our forbidden land. We will therefore stipulate you are a foreigner. Next, you are accused of carrying weapons in Gamphasantia. What do you say?'

'Of course I carried a sword! All travellers are permitted to in civilized countries.'

'Not in Gamphasantia, which is the only truly civilized country. As no Gamphasant ever takes life, there is no reason why anybody should go armed, save when a farmer in an outlying region is allowed a spear to drive off lions. We agree, then, that you are guilty of carrying this murderous implement I have here before me. Next, you are accused of wearing clothes. What say you?'

Vakar tugged at his hair. 'Do not tell me that too is illegal! Why can you not let folk do as they please?'

'If such a shocking anarchistic suggestion were followed we could never maintain our standard of ethics. Clothes are worn for three reasons: warmth, vanity, and false modesty. Gamphasantia is warm enough to make them unnecessary, and vanity is such an obvious sin that we need not discuss it. As for the third motive, found in some barbarous nations, the gods made the human body pure and holy in all its parts, and it is therefore an insult to them to cover any part as if it were shameful. We will therefore agree that you have worn clothes. But we are just people. If you object to this trial or the conduct thereof, speak before sentence is passed.'

Vakar cried: 'I do indeed have something to say! I could have skirted your country, but chose to enter it instead to warn you of a deadly danger.'

'What is that?'

'Do you know of the Gwedulians?'

'A barbarous tribe, I believe, who live far to the east around Lake Lynxama. What about them?'

'A great army of Gwedulians is nearing Gamphasantia across the Tamen-ruft on camels, to assail and plunder you.'

'How do you know this?'

Vakar told of his séance in the throne room of King Awoqqas. The judged pulled his scanty beard and said:

'It might or might be true, but it makes little difference.'

'Little difference! The difference between life and death!'

'No; you do not understand us. We deem it unethical to oppose aggression by force; why, we might cause the death of one of these Gwedulians! If they come, we shall show them there is nothing worth stealing – no gold or jewels or fine raiment or such gewgaws – except food which they might have for the asking. Then we shall courteously ask them to leave, confident that, faced by our greatness of soul, they will do so.'

'Oh, is that so? Judge, the usual wont of such robbers is to kill first and discuss ethics afterwards. If you do not —'

'The gods will take care of us. Once previously raiders came out of the eastern deserts, and before they reached our land a sandstorm overwhelmed them and killed the lot. Another time an army of Gorgons marched up the Kokuton River to attack us, and a plague smote them in the marshes so only a few fled back to the Gorgades. However, we cannot continue this interesting discussion because I have other cases to judge. I find you guilty and sentence you both to be placed in the arena this afternoon with the ape-man Nji, and then that will happen which will happen. Take them away.'

'Ha!' shouted Vakar. 'You speak so virtuously of never taking life, but if you shove me into a pit with that monster it is the same thing —'

The attendants dragged Vakar, still shouting, out of the courtroom and back to his cell.

XV

The Arena of Tokalet

'Hells!' growled Vakar as the big bolt slammed home again. 'This time it looks as though they had us.'

Fual said: 'Oh, my lord, say not that, or I shall die of despair even before the ape rends us! You've gotten us out of worse fixes …'

'That was mostly luck, and any man who presses his luck too far will at last run out of it.' Vakar kicked the wall, hurting his toes. 'Ow! If this were a civilized country the door would have a bronze lock to which you might steal the key, but I have no idea of what to do about that great stupid bolt.'

They settled down to a despondent wait, but before they had sat staring for long Vakar heard the bolt drawn back. In came a young Gamphasant.

'Master Vakar!' said this one in Hesperian. 'Do you not know me? Abeggu the son of Mishegdi, in Sederado?'

'I am glad to see you,' said Vakar. 'I did not know you without your clothes. What brings you here?'

'Hearing two foreigners were to be tried today I came to watch and recognized you. I tried to catch your eye, but you were otherwise occupied.'

'You find us in a sad state indeed, friend Abeggu. What is your tale? How goes it with you?'

'Far from well.'

'How so?' asked Vakar.

'My travels unsettled many of the ideas with which I started out, and when I returned home I imprudently went around telling people how much better things were done abroad. As any such talk is frightful heresy to a Gamphasant, I was ostracized, and for months nobody would have anything to do with me. If my family had not let me have access to their food-stores I should have starved. Now, though folk are beginning to ease up, they still look down upon me as one corrupted by foreign notions. But what brings you to this doom?'

Vakar outlined his travels since leaving Sederado, adding: 'What happened in Sederado after Thiegos' body was found?'

'I do not know, for like you I went into hiding and fled at the first chance after my wound healed.'

A rumble came from the cell across the corridor. Vakar said: 'That thing across the way looks like the giant servant of Qasigan, that wizard who tried to kill Porfia and me —'

'It is indeed Nji! Not many days ago Qasigan and his ape-man came to Gamphasantia in a chariot. They were not stopped when they first appeared, as you were, because they raced through the villages and because the peasants were afraid of the chariot, most of them never having seen a wheeled vehicle. However, as they entered Tokalet their was was blocked by an ox-drawn sledge and the people seized them. The ape-man slew three with his club before they threw a net over him. It was intended to expose them in the arena to the attentions of a lion we kept for the purpose, but the next day there was a great hole in the wall of this cell and the wizard was gone, no doubt with the aid of his magic. You can see where the wall has been closed up with new bricks.

'When the ape-man was thrust into the arena, he wrenched the door out of its sockets and broke the lion's back with it. Then it was decided that as Nji was more beast than man, it would be more just to keep him as the national executioner in place of the lion he had slain.'

Vakar said: 'Why do you kill people in this unusual manner? For such a peaceful people it seems like a bloodthirsty amusement, watching men eaten by lions.'

'It is no amusement! We are required to attend as a salutary moral lesson. Since our principles forbid us to kill undesirables ourselves, our only alternative is to let a beast do it.'

'Quibbling!' said Vakar. 'If you force a man into a pit with a lion you are as responsible for his death as if you had sworded him personally.'

'True. We Gamphasants, being an honest folk, admit it, but what can we do? Our ethical standards must be maintained at all costs, or at least so think most of my people.'

'What happened to Qasigan's other servant, the one with the ears?'

'I visited Qasigan in his cell – did I understand you to say he had tried to kill you and the queen?'

'Yes; he brought the serpent throne to life with his damned piping. But go on.'

'I did not know that and supposed him merely an old acquaintance. Besides I do not often get a chance to converse with foreigners, and after my travels I find my own folk dull.

'Qasigan told me he had been following you – he did not say why – with the aid of this Coranian, whose ears served not only to hear sounds of the usual sort but also to hear men's unspoken thoughts – even though the men were miles away. Thus so long as he followed you closely enough Yok could always tell what direction you were in. You left Huperea at such a clip that for a while you were out of Yok's range, but the King of Phaiaxia had told Qasigan you were bound for Tritonia —'

'Curse the old rattlepate!' cried Vakar, but then remembered that he had no cause to blame Nausithion, whom he had not sworn to secrecy. Abeggu continued:

'They had a hard time getting to Tritonia. First you stole a wheel from their chariot, which took them many days to replace, and then the vehicle kept breaking down and getting stuck. Qasigan may be a mighty magician, but he is no wainwright. In Tritonia the Amazons captured this odd trio and took them to Kherronex. The warrior women had just chosen a new queen to replace the old, who had died in some confused sea-battle wherein the king of the Tritons had also perished. Now, the Amazons extend the ultimate in female hospitality to any male they catch. Nji performed nobly, serving the queen herself; Qasigan begged off on grounds of loss of his magical powers; but poor little Yok succumbed under the strain of so much love-making and died.'

'I can see how he might. What then?'

'Without the Coranian, Qasigan lost the trail, as nobody among the Amazons knew whither you had gone. Therefore he escaped from the Amazons by magical means and started homeward.'

'How did he do that?'

The Gamphasant's melancholy face lit up with a rare smile. 'He cast upon them the illusion that an army of lovers came to visit them: tall beautiful men with great – ah – thews. These phantoms told the Amazons they loved them but would not consummate their love until Qasigan were safely ashore on the mainland, and so he set out for our land.'

Vakar grinned. 'I imagine the girls were in a rare rage when their promised gallants faded away. Go on.'

'Well, Qasigan came hither as I have told you. When I saw him he was in a gloomy state, fearing that even should he escape his present predicament and win back to the Gorgades, King Zeluud would take off his head because of his failure.

'However, let us concern ourselves with methods of saving you, for I have no wall-shattering magic like that of Qasigan. I have a plan, though. If when you enter the arena you take three paces straight out from the door and dig in the sand, you will find two broadswords. These I brought back from my travels, but I had to hide them or the magistrates would have had them thrown into Lake Kokutos.'

'Why are you helping us?' asked Vakar.

'Because you once spared my life in Sederado when, by your principles, you were entitled to take it.'

'If we beat Nji, what then?'

'It will give us time to plan something else while the consuls send men to catch another lion. This is a hard land to escape from, being flat treeless country with few places to hide; and horses are not tamed here.'

Vakar mentioned the impending attack of the Gwedulians. Abeggu shook his head, saying:

'The judge's action is what I should have expected. Even if he had wished to defend the land by force, what could he have done? The folk have no weapons and would not know how to use them if they had, for they have been taught weapons are accursed things.'

'Could you not appeal to the king?'

'We have no king. There is a hereditary senate of big landowners – my father is a senator, which is how I could travel – and every year the people elect two consuls. As these consuls are men of conventional Gamphasantian outlook, it would do no good to appeal to them.'

Vakar said: 'I believe some free cities like Kernê are governed like that. Judging from your people, the masses are not enough aware of their own interests for the scheme to work.'

Abeggu shrugged. 'It might work if they could all read, and if papyrus were so common every family could own a scroll containing the wisdom of the race. But here writing is deemed an evil foreign innovation, and all knowledge is handed down by word of mouth. However, I must go now to bury those swords, or it will be too late.'

He called to the jailer, who came with his assistants to unbar the door. Vakar, watching Abeggu's departing back, said:

'It's nice to know we have one friend in this hog-wallow of a country. Cheer up, Fual; we're not dead yet ... Yes?'

The jailer had placed his face against the grille and was saying: 'What is this?'

Vakar took a look. The fellow had the Tahakh in one hand and held Abeggu's arm with the other. Using the latter as interpreter the jailer explained:

'We have burned your clothes and thrown your weapons into the lake, and your other possessions we have placed in the common store, but we do not know what to do with this. What is it?'

'Tell him,' said Vakar, 'it is a talisman – you know, a good-luck piece.'

The jailer went off, staring at the heavy blackish mass, and Abeggu departed likewise. Then Vakar had to put up with Fual's nervous chatter. One minute the little man was boasting of what such puissant heroes as they would do to the monster; the next he was giving garrulous tongue to abysmal despair:

'... last night I dreamed of a goat that ate three blue apples while reciting poetry, which undoubtedly means we shall be slain, sir. Ah, why didn't you let me go when I asked you in Gadaira? Never shall I see the golden spires of the Temple of Cuval in Kerys again ...'

Vakar was tempted to cuff his man about to silence him, but forebore, thinking how sorry he would be if he did and then Fual did die in the arena after all.

Under the blazing tropical sun the sand of the arena glared whitely in Vakar's eyes. He put a bare foot upon it, then hopped back with a yelp.

'That's hot!' he said.

'Out you go,' said the jailer behind him. 'Or must we push you?'

'Come, Fual,' said Vakar, setting his teeth against the heat of the sand. 'We should have toughened ourselves by walking barefoot on hot coals like the devil-dancers of Dzen.'

A door opened in the far end of the arena and Nji slouched in with the same old brass-bound club over his shoulder. Vakar took three paces quickly and started to dig.

'Help me, ass!' he snarled at Fual as his sifting fingers met nothing solid.

Nji swaggered closer. Vakar was too busy scrabbling in the sand to notice the elliptical plan of the arena, the tiers of mud-brick benches, and the silent brown crowd.

'Ha!' His fingers struck metal. An instant later he and Fual were on their feet facing the ape-man, each with a broadsword in hand. A murmur of surprise came from the spectators.

'Remember,' said Vakar, 'our only hope is a headlong attack. If we run in under his club quickly enough, one of us at least may get home before he knocks our brains out. Ready?'

Vakar tensed for a dash. Nji took hold of his club with both hairy hands and opened his great mouth.

'Go!' cried Vakar, sprinting.

Nji gave a roar and charged – but not at Vakar. He ran at an angle, in pursuit of Fual, who in a spasm of panic had dropped his sword and run towards the side of the arena, apparently with the idea of climbing up among the spectators.

Vakar struck at the ape-man as the latter lumbered past him but missed; then doubled, leaning for the turn and cursing his servant's cowardice under his breath. Fual had almost reached the wall when Nji caught up with him and brought the club down in a mighty blow. Fual's skull crunched and his brains spattered. And at the same instant Vakar came up behind Nji.

With no time for a survey of the towering hairy back, Vakar bent and struck a powerful backhand draw-cut at the monster's leg just above the heel, then sprang back just as Nji started to turn. As the creature put weight on his hamstrung leg the member buckled under him. He fell with a ground-shaking thump. Vakar sprang in again to slash at the ape-man's throat. The great teeth snapped and an arm caught Vakar's ankle and hurled him to the ground, almost dislocating the attached leg.

Vakar rolled over in an effort to twist free, but the bone-crushing grip held fast. Feeling his foot being drawn towards the ape-man, Vakar looked and saw that the creature was about to stuff the appendage into his gaping mouth. The Lorskan doubled and twisted, planting his other foot against Nji's chest to give him a purchase and, getting a grip on Nji's shoulder-hair with his free hand, hacked at the hairy hand that held his ankle.

Nji screamed shrilly and let go the ankle, but instantly caught Vakar's right arm in one hand and his hair with the other. This time the monster began to pull Vakar's head towards his jaws while it scratched and kicked at his body with its great splay feet.

Vakar grasped Nji's thick throat with his right hand, not to choke the ape-man (a task far beyond his strength) but to hold off the slavering fangs that wanted to tear off his face. Meanwhile his left arm was furiously driving the sword into Nji's chest and belly. Again and again he stabbed, but the ape-man's immense strength seemed undiminished.

Though the muscles on Vakar's lean arms stood out like iron rods, little by little his right arm bent as the ape-man drew him nearer. Blood and spittle ran over his gripping hand, and the creature's foul breath blasted into his face. The tusks gaped closer.

At last he drove the sword into the gaping mouth itself, and up through the crimson palate – and up – and up …

Nji relaxed with a shudder as the bronzen point broached his brain. For an instant Vakar, battered and worn, lay panting on the baking sand, his blood and that of the ape-man running over his skin in big red drops. The front of Nji's body was covered with wounds any of which would have killed a man.

Then Vakar staggered to his feet. He was covered with blood and dirt and some of his hair had been pulled out. His ankle was swollen and discolored where Nji had wrenched it, and the scratches from Nji's toe-nails on his belly and legs stung like a swarm of hornets. When a glance showed him that Fual was patently beyond help, he turned towards the exit.

He found himself facing a crowd of Gamphasants with nets and ropes in their hands. For an instant he considered trying to cut his way through, but gave up that idea. Though he killed two or three, the rest would overpower him and then things would only go harder with him. A similar crowd had issued from the other entrance, the one through which Nji had come.

'All right,' he said in his rudimentary Gamphasantian. 'I will come quietly.'

The jailer, scowling, asked: 'Where did you get that sword?'

Vakar smiled. 'The gods visited me in dreamland and told me where to dig. Does this make me the official executioner?'

'No. Nji was made executioner because he was more beast than man, and the Gamphasants, being a just people, do not punish dumb brutes for breaking laws beyond their comprehension. You, however, are not only a man but also an intelligent one, and must therefore pay the full penalty as soon as we can get another lion.'

Vakar limped back to his cell feeling forlorn. Poor Fual would never see the silver beaches of Aremoria again. The little fellow may have been a snob, a coward, and a thief, but he had been faithful in his lachrymose and unreliable way. Vakar would keenly miss a man to tote his burdens and listen to his jokes and songs. He regretted the beatings he had given Fual because of the latter's incurable thievery; for all his faults Fual had saved his life in Torrutseish, which counted for more than a bookkeeper's balance of virtues and vices.

The tears were running freely down Vakar's own face when his cell door opened and in came Abeggu lugging a ewer and a towel. The Gamphasant said:

'You did a great deed, and I am sorry your servant was slain. I cannot spend much time with you for I think I am suspected of having a hand in this affair. I asked my father if he would intercede to free you, but he said he had got in enough trouble by letting me travel abroad contrary to the traditions of the Gamphasants, and would do nothing.'

'I hope,' said Vakar, 'you can think of something before the next lion arrives.'

'I will try, but I am not hopeful.'

'How about a tool to dig through the wall?'

'No good. The jailer comes into your cell every day, and since Qasigan's escape one of his assistants walks continuously around the outside of the prison. But we shall see.'

And off he went, leaving Vakar feeling let down. He thought some bitter thoughts about fair-weather friends; but then he reflected that Abeggu had already saved his life once at some risk, and he had no reason to expect the man to do it over and over.

In the morning Vakar was awakened by a distant murmur. Still stiff and sore from the previous day's ape-handling, he called the jailer:

'Ho there, Nakkul! What is happening?'

The prison seemed deserted. Vakar went to his window but could see nothing. The murmur grew and the heads of several Gamphasants shot past Vakar's window, going at a run. Now Vakar could distinguish shrieks of pain and terror.

If anyone were here to bet with, he thought, I'd wager ten to one the Gwedulians have come. And then the bolt of his cell door thudded back and the door creaked open. Abeggu, standing in the doorway, cried:

'The Gwedulians are slaying us! Flee while you can!'

'Good of you to remember me,' said Vakar, hurrying out.

'The consuls went forth unarmed to welcome them, and these fiends slew them with javelins ...'

In the jailer's office Vakar paused to glance around on the slim chance that some of his belongings might still be there. It was no easy thing to flee forth in a strange country without clothes, arms, or trade-goods. He saw none of these, but in one corner lay a dark lumpish thing: the Tahakh. He snatched it up by the knob at one end and turned down the short corridor that led out.

At that instant a Gwedulian stepped into the entrance, a few paces away. The intruder wore the usual head-cloak and face-veil. On his left arm was strapped a small round ostrich-hide buckler that left his left hand free, and in both hands he carried a long copper-headed spear. Before he could do more than stare at the newcomer Vakar heard a shriek beside him and saw that the Gwedulian had thrust his spear deep into the brown belly of Abeggu, who seized the shaft with both hands.

Vakar took three long steps forward, swinging the Tahakh down, back, and up in a circle at the end of his straight left arm. The Gwedulian tugged on his spear, but Abeggu still gripped it. Then the Gwedulian released the shaft with his right hand to fumble for a hatchet in the girdle of his breech-clout. Before he could pull the shaft free the Tahakh descended on his head with a crunch. Down went the Gwedulian.

Vakar looked back at Abeggu, who lay huddled against the wall of the corridor, still clutching the spear-shaft, though the Gwedulian's tug had pulled the head out of the wound.

'Can you walk?' asked Vakar.

'No. I am dying. Go quickly.'

'Oh, come along! I will help you,' said Vakar, though in his heart he knew that men seldom recovered from a deep abdominal stab.

'No, go. It will do you no good to drag me, for I shall be dead soon, and you will merely get yourself killed if you try.'

Muttering, Vakar tore the head-cloak and veil off the dead Gwedulian and put them on. Under them the nomad was a lean dark man, physically much like the Gamphasants, with his head shaved except for a scalp-lock. Vakar also took the man's sandals, but left the corpse its breech-clout, feeling squeamish about putting so foul a garment against his own skin. He appropriated the buckler, the ax with the head of polished stone, and the spear. Then he took Abeggu by the arm and tried to drag him down the corridor, but the man shrieked, crying:

'Go on, fool! You can do nothing for me!'

Vakar gave up and hurried out the door, feeling a mixture of guilt at leaving Abeggu and relief at not having to haul the wounded man to safety.

In front of the entrance knelt the Gwedulian's dromedary. Vakar glanced up and down the street. Gamphasantian corpses lay here and there, and other Gwedulians rode hither and thither in pursuit of live victims, riding them down with their lances or hurling javelins into their backs. A swirl of pursuers and pursued raced past Vakar while the camel sat placidly chewing its cud. A hundred paces up-street a knot of dismounted Gwedulians was raping a woman *seriatim*.

Vakar approached the camel in gingerly fashion. The beast looked at Vakar from under long eyelashes, its jaw moving with a rotary motion. A wooden frame fitted over the hump on its back, with a foot-long piece of wood sticking up in front. A kind of blanket was fastened over and under this frame, and from the sides of this saddle hung a quirt, a quiver of flint-tipped javelins, a large goatskin booty-bag, and smaller bags containing food and water.

Vakar gathered up his meager booty and climbed on to the camel's back, trying to assume the Gwedulians' posture. The Tahakh and the ax he dropped into the large bag. But how to make the creature go? Several commands produced no result; he knew no Gwedulian. Finally he unhooked the quirt and struck the camel on the rump. Nothing happened, so he punched the beast with his fist.

The camel's hindquarters rose with such suddenness that Vakar was pitched off its back on to his head in the roadway. He saw stars and wondered for an instant if his neck were broken. When he rolled over and got to his feet the camel was standing beside him, still chewing. Its legs were hobbled with a tackle of braided rawhide to keep it from running away.

Now how should he mount the creature without a ladder? He tried speaking to it and tapping it here and there with the whip, hoping to persuade it to kneel again, but the camel stood masticating while the wrack of conquest and massacre swirled past it.

At last Vakar untied the hobble, planted the Gwedulian spear in the ground, and hauled himself up hand over hand, kicking and straining. He took hold of the spear and whacked the camel with the whip, whereupon it grunted and started up with a jerk that nearly unseated him for the second time. He found that a camel did not trot: it paced, jerking its rider from side to side until Vakar thought he would fly to pieces. In his present bruised and battered state the motion was torture. He clung to the post in front of the saddle, and by sawing on the reins got his mount headed out of Tokalet.

The sounds of massacre died away behind Vakar as the camel racked along the road that followed the shore of Lake Kokutos southward.

XVI

The Wizard of Gbu

Vakar Zhu rode along the margin of Lake Kokutos seldom seeing a living person. Sometimes he passed through a village, but it was either deserted or Gamphasant corpses lay about, showing that the Gwedulians had arrived before the inhabitants had time to flee. In the stifling heat the bodies became noisome in a few hours, so that Vakar learned to detour such settlements.

The few live Gamphasants he saw fled screaming at the sight of his head-cloak. Bands of camel-riding Gwedulians paid him no heed save to call an occasional hail. When he came upon a group of them in a sacked village he stopped to watch them manage their camels. When he rode on he at least knew the tongue clicks used to make the animals kneel and rise.

When the food in the Gwedulian's provision-bag ran low, Vakar killed an abandoned cow and, using the copper head of his lance and his stone ax, cut the more accessible portions of the meat into narrow strips across the grain. After hours of sweaty work he hung a hundred pounds of these strips on the camel's saddle to dry. Thereafter until the beef was jerked at the end of the following day he rode amidst an opaque cloud of buzzing flies and blessed the voluminous head-cloak for keeping most of them off his person. He would have preferred a nice compact pig, but the Gamphasants did not seem to keep them. In fact he had not seen a pig, barring the big wild tuskers of the inland savannas, since leaving Phaiaxia. When the beef was dried he scraped the flies' eggs off it with his nails and stowed it in his bags.

Vakar had always been accustomed to travelling with a lavish equipage of spare clothes, toilet-articles, weapons, and trade-metal, and one or more menials to carry the stuff. Now that the Gamphasants had stripped him down to fundamentals he learned that one can live on a much simpler level, with practically no worldly goods save a supply of food or means for getting it. He never learned to like it, though. He missed Fual keenly.

Because of the terror incited by his costume he had less trouble on this leg of his journey with men than with his mount. Though a tame and tireless beast, able to eat anything in the plant line, it was also stupid and unresponsive, quite apt unless watched to stop short in the middle of a morning's run, fold its long legs (pitching Vakar over its head) and settle down to a placid session of cud-chewing.

By painful experiment Vakar mastered the art of camelitation. To make the camel go one waved the whip where the animal could see it; to stop it one pulled the reins and hit the beast over the head with the butt of the whip. Its racking pace was hard enough; its walk was worse, bouncing less but jerking the rider back and forth and from side to side in a labyrinthine pattern; while its gallop was impossible to endure for any time.

Vakar missed Fual and somberly pondered on the bloodshed that had dogged his track. Surely the gods had it in for him. Nearly everybody who had been friendly to him – Queen Aramnê, Fual, and Abeggu of Tokalet – had come to a violent end. What curse lay upon him? He was not a bloodthirsty man, but one who only asked to be allowed to go about his business in peace …

As Vakar neared the southwest end of Lake Kokutos the farms thinned out and the signs of Gwedulian violence ended. Vakar took off the stifling face-veil and stopped the camel within earshot of a goatherd who did not seem to have heard of the invasion, for he did not run away. With their few words in common and much sign-language Vakar learned that beyond the end of the lake a track continued across the sandy wastes to the Oasis of Kiliessa, and beyond that one came to the Akheron River which flowed to the sea. The goatherd had never heard of Tartaros and its black craftsmen, but Vakar was sure that he could find that region once he reached the Western Ocean.

Two days later Vakar rode over a rise into sight of the Oasis of Kiliessa. A glance showed human beings moving among the palms. Tired of hearing no voices but the yap of jackals, the laugh of hyenas, and the gargling groans and grunts of his camel, he rode rapidly down the slope with a hail on his lips.

As he neared the oasis there was a stir of activity and mounted figures came out towards him: three men on asses, beating their beasts along. As they came nearer the leading rider nocked an arrow and let fly just as he passed the camel. The shaft grazed Vakar's face, tearing a two-inch gash in his cheek at the edge of his beard.

Vakar was so caught by surprise that he did not even try to dodge the arrow, but then he moved quickly. The second and third men each held a bundle of javelins in one hand and poised a single such dart in the other as they came closer. The second man's javelin struck the saddle-frame. Vakar, holding the saddle-post with one hand, leaned over and drove his lance into the third man just as the latter threw. The javelin went wild and the man's ass continued its rocking gallop, the man clawing at the spear so that the shaft was wrenched out of Vakar's hand.

Vakar turned the camel around, slipped the ostrich-hide buckler over his forearm, and started back towards his assailants, pulling Gwedulian javelins out of their quiver. The first two attackers had turned also. As they came close again each loosed a missile as Vakar threw two in quick succession. Vakar caught the arrow with his shield; the other foe's javelin struck the camel. One of Vakar's javelins missed while the other struck the archer's donkey, which bucked with such violence that it pitched its rider off into the sand.

The man whom Vakar had speared had now fallen off his ass. The remaining rider took to flight, galloping off into the desert. The archer got up and started to run. The Lorskan followed him, throwing flint-headed javelins until the man collapsed with five of the things sticking in his back. Then Vakar knelt his camel, walked over to the man, and brained him with the stone ax.

Vakar took stock. The man he had speared lay dying with bloody froth running from his mouth. The wounded ass was disappearing over the sky-line, while the unwounded one had fallen to nibbling on a desert shrub. Vakar examined the camel and found the stone-pointed javelin stuck into the shoulder-muscle. He pulled the dart out; the camel bled a little but chewed its cud without appearing to notice the wound.

Vakar picked up his spear and cautionsly approached the palm-trees. The other human occupants of the oasis comprised twelve naked Negroes: nine men and three women, fastened together by means of a set of wooden yokes strung together like a chain. One named Yoju spoke some Hesperian, the universal trading-language of the coasts of the Western Sea. Yoju explained:

'We are from between the Rivers Akheron and Stoux, but inland from that land you call Tartaros. The chief of the Abiku (may his wives bear scorpions) enslaved us and sold us to these traders, who were taking us to Kernê. We hope your lordship will not slay us.'

Vakar asked: 'Why did the traders attack me?'

'Because they greatly fear Gwedulians, who slay all who come across their path. Thinking you a scout for a party of raiders, they thought their only chance was to kill you before you could fetch your fellows.'

More useless bloodshed! Vakar leaned upon his spear in thought. He could use a couple of stout slaves and would have had no great compunction about so employing these people. But as a practical matter he could not use all of them, for being afoot they would slow him to a walk. They would be of little use chained, and if he unshackled them they would likely murder him in his sleep and flee. Even if Vakar had been willing to butcher all but one of the Negroes in cold blood (which he was not) that one might still stave in his skull with a stone some night.

'What,' he asked, 'would you do if you had your choice?'

'Return to our homes!'

'Then hear me. I am no Gwedulian, but a traveler on his way to Tartaros. I am minded to free you. Have you enough food to take you back to settled country?'

'Yes.'

'In addition I need a servant to accompany me to Tartaros. If *you*' (he indicated Yoju) 'would like to ride home instead of walking, you may come with me, earning your food and fare. If I release you and carry you as far as Tartaros, will you swear by your gods to serve me faithfully until I find the man I am seeking there?'

The man swore. Vakar freed the Negroes, stripped the corpses, and rounded up the unwounded ass. He found that he had acquired a good woolen tunic to cover his nakedness, several gold rings and a fistful of copper torcs, and a bronze sword: a two-foot chopper with a double-curved blade like a Thamuzeiran sapara.

As his own wound had begun to sting abominably, he looked at his reflection in the water of the oasis. The luxuriance of his beard, now all matted on one side with dried blood, startled him. He thrust his face into the water to wash away some of the blood and dirt, and pinned the edges of the wound together with a small golden pin that he had found among the effects of the dead traders.

One of the Negroes spoke to Yoju, who translated: 'He says that as whites go you are a good man, and if you ever come to his village you need not fear being eaten.'

'That is kind of him,' said Vakar dryly. 'If you are ready we will set out.'

He mounted the camel and signalled it to rise. Yoju mounted the ass and together they started southward. The remaining Negroes waved after them.

Twenty days later Vakar arrived at Tegrazen, at the mouth of the Akheron, and once again heard the boom of the surf. The town was formidably walled against a possible Gorgon raid. The language was similar to Gamphasantian and Belemian, but many of the people spoke Hesperian. The houses were mixed: some of the mud-brick Gamphasantian style, some stone Kernean-type dwellings, and some beehive thatched huts like those of the Negroes to the south. The population was equally mixed: tall brown Lixitans, bullet-headed yellow-skinned renegade Gorgons, bearded Kerneans, Tartarean blacks, and all intermediate shades.

Vakar thrust through the teeming tangle, towing his camel. The town boasted an inn where Vakar took a place on a bench with his back to the wall. (He had made a habit of doing so ever since his experience in the house of the Ogugian witch Charsela.) The innkeeper set down big blackjacks of tarred leather and filled them with barley-beer from a gourd bottle. Vakar was setting down his mug when he observed a curious expression in the eyes of Yoju.

'What is it?' he asked.

Yoju pointed. Vakar craned his neck and saw, on the end of the bench, a man dressed as a Kernean trader, a horny-skinned fellow with a full black beard speckled with gray – but the man was less than two feet tall. This midget was drinking barley-beer too, but out of a child's cup.

When the innkeeper came to refill Vakar's blackjack, the latter jerked a thumb, saying: 'What on earth is that?'

'Him? That is Yamma of Kernê. When his accident happened he did not dare return home, but settled in Tegrazen as a dealer in metals. Would you like to know him? He is a friendly little fellow.'

'I should indeed,' said Vakar.

The innkeeper picked up the midget by the slack of his tunic and set him down upon the table in front of Vakar, saying: 'Here is a traveller named Vakar Lorska, Yamma, who would like to know you. Tell him the story of your life: tell him what happened to you when you told that witch-doctor he was full of ordure.'

'I should think it was obvious,' said Yamma.

'What witch-doctor is this?' asked Vakar.

'Fekata of Gbu, the greatest smith of Tartaros. If I had known who he was and had not been drunk I should have been more careful.'

'Tell me more of Fekata. He sounds like the man I seek.'

'It is said he can pull down a star from heaven with his tongs and hammer it into shape on his anvil. He is headman of Gbu, in the middle of the peninsula of Tartaros, halfway to the Abiku country. When you find him, spit in his soup for me, though he will probably turn you into a scorpion for your trouble.'

Gbu was, like all Tartarean towns, a cluster of beehive huts, whence came the barking of dogs, the yelling of children, the tinkle of the bells hung round the necks of a Kernean trader's asses, and the buzz and clang and clatter made by the craftsmen of Tartaros as they plied their trades. Vakar threaded his way among the stalls of woodcarvers, bead-drillers, jewel-polishers, shield-makers, and goldsmiths until he found the premises of Fekata, Headman of Gbu, smith, and wizard.

Fekata had his smithy in an open shed alongside the clump of huts that served him and his wives for a home. A fresh leopard-skin hung at the back, drying in the sun. A young Negro tended the furnace, while in the middle of the shed Fekata himself hammered a bronze ax-head into shape with a stone-headed sledge-hammer. He was a middle-aged Negro of about Vakar's height, but much broader, with a prominent potbelly and the most massive and muscular arms that Vakar had ever seen. One eye was blinded by a cataract, and a short grizzle of gray wool covered Fekata's head.

As Vakar approached, the smith looked up and stopped hammering. The buzz of flies became audible in the quiet. Vakar identified himself and asked:

'Are you he who made a ring from the metal of a fallen star?'

'That is true, and if I ever catch the blackguard who swindled me out of my price on that job ...'

'What happened?'

'Oh, it was long ago, though I, Fekata of Gbu, do not forget such things. There was a beggarly trader from Tritonia, one Ximenon, who had been in the Abiku country when the thing fell with a great flash and roar and buried itself, and he had tracked it to the spot and dug it up. He promised me enough ivory and gold to break the back of that camel of yours if I would make him a ring of the metal of the star. I did, though it took a crocodile's lifetime to learn how to work the stuff. Then when he had the ring he started off on his ass as jaunty as you please. "Ho," said I, "where is my price?" "Come to Tritonia when I have made myself king and I will pay you," said he, and away he galloped. I threw a curse after him that should have shriveled him to a centipede – not knowing then that the star-metal was a protection against all magical assaults. Later I heard he had become king of the Tritons by the help of this ring, but I did not see fit to travel halfway across the world on the slim chance that Ximenon would honor his promise. What do you know of this?'

'King Ximenon is dead, if that pleases you,' said Vakar. 'As for the fallen star, is this it?' He produced the Tahakh.

Fekata's eyes popped. 'That is it! Where did you get it? Did you steal it from Ximenon?'

'No, from another king: Awoqqas of Belem. How he got it I do not know, though I should guess Ximenon gave it to him in return for help in making himself king of the Tritons. Could you make more rings from it?'

Fekata turned the lump over in his huge hands, his good eye gleaming. 'For what price?'

'I have several ounces of gold, and some copper ...'

'Pff! I, Fekata of Gbu, have little need of gold and copper. I make enough from my regular work to keep myself and my six wives and twenty-three children in food and drink. But to work on a new metal ... I will tell you. I will make one article for you – one only – from this piece, and in payment you shall give me the rest of the piece. How is that?'

'What? Why you damned black swindler —'

The smith shot out a hand and gripped Vakar's arm. The great fingers sank in and in, and Fekata pulled and twisted until Vakar thought his arm would come off. Though a wiry and well-muscled man he was like a child in the hands of this giant.

'Now,' said the smith in a deadly-soft voice, 'what was that again?'

'I said I thought your price was a little high,' grunted Vakar, 'but perhaps we can agree.'

The crushing grip relaxed. Vakar, massaging his arm and inwardly cursing the cross-grained temper that got him into these tiffs, said: 'Will you agree before witnesses to make one article, anything I demand, in return for the rest of the star?'

'I agree.' Fekata spoke in his own tongue to the youth, who trotted off.

'What did you say?' asked Vakar.

'I told my son to fetch the heads of the Ukpe, our secret society, to act as witnesses.'

In time four men with ostrich-feather headdresses and faces painted with stripes and circles, wrapped in buckskin blankets and an immense dignity, showed up. Vakar and Fekata repeated their engagement before these. Fekata asked:

'Now, how big a ring do you wish?'

'Who said a ring? I will have a sword-blade, made to my measurements.'

The smith stared blankly; then his face became distorted with rage until Vakar feared the fellow might spatter his brains with a hammer-blow. But then Fekata's expression changed again and he burst into a roar of laughter, slapping his paunch.

'You damned whites!' he bellowed. 'How can an honest craftsman make a living with you rascals cheating him? But I will make your sword. I, Fekata of Gbu, keep my word, and the biggest sword an insect like you could swing will take less than half the star. Give me that thing. Angwo, fetch a few of your brothers; we shall need all the lungs we can get on the blow-pipes. You see, Vakar, the trick in working the star-metal is that it must be forged at a bright-red heat where copper or bronze would shatter, and with a hammer of double the normal weight ...'

XVII

The Grip of the Octopus

Vakar bid farewell to Yoju and rode back to Tegrazen, where he found little Yamma of Kernê drinking barley-beer in the same tavern. Yamma was telling the story of his life to a shaven man with the yellowish skin of a Gorgon.

'Hail,' squeaked Yamma as Vakar sat down. 'You are that fellow who was on his way to see Fekata, are you not? Did you spit in his soup?'

'No; he and I did a bit of business.'

'It is always like that! Nobody will take up the cause of poor Yamma, who is now too small to fight his own battles.'

'You know what Fekata looks like,' said Vakar. 'I should want a small army at my back before I crossed him. But who is your friend?'

'Wessul, late of the Kingdom of Gorgonia.'

'Why late?'

Wessul spoke: 'A slight difference of opinion with my captain, which developed into an exchange of knife-thrusts. He wished to demote me from mate to ordinary seaman, claiming I was too popular with his wife. I left him holding his spilt guts in both hands and weeping into them as he waited to die, and came away, for Gorgonian law is hard in such cases.' The Gorgon sighed. 'Now I am out in the great world with nobody to order me about, and I do not mind telling you gentlemen it is a lost and lonesome feeling. Worst of all I shall miss the great raid.'

'What raid?' said Vakar sharply.

'Have you not heard? The mainland has been buzzing with it. King Zeluud has gathered all the forces of Gorgonia and its tributaries for an assault upon some northern land.'

'What land?'

'He is not saying, though some rumors name Euskeria, some Poseidonis, and some far Aremoria.'

'When will he sail?'

'He may have done so already for all I – ho, where are you going?'

'Kernê,' Vakar flung back. 'Innkeeper! The scot, quickly.'

Five days later Vakar jounced into Kernê, haggard from hard riding with mere snatches of sleep. He led the weary camel along the waterfront where the great stone warehouses looked down upon the picket-fence of masts and spars. Men of all nations and colors jostled him; horses and asses shied from the smell of camel and their owners cursed him in many languages. Vakar, sunk in thought, paid them no heed. It was time, he thought, to make use of his connections.

He inquired until he learned where Senator Amastan dwelt and presented himself at the door, giving his name as Prince Vakar of Lorsk. After a long wait a eunuch beckoned him in.

Even after all his travels Vakar found the ostentatious wealth of this house overpowering, with palms standing in pots of solid gold. Amastan was a big stout man with rings on all his pudgy fingers. He smelled strongly of perfume, wore multicolored silken robes, and said:

'Welcome, Prince Vakar. Have you brought the other half of Drozo's medal?'

'No. The damned Gamphasants stripped me to the skin.'

'Indeed?' Amastan tapped the fingers of one hand on the palm of the other. 'That may be true. But – ah – we really must have some means of identification, you know.'

'Hells!' blazed Vakar, then controlled his impatience, remembering that to Amastan he was just a wild-looking sun-baked wanderer. 'Find somebody who knows Lorsk and I will answer his questions till Poseidonis sinks beneath the Western Sea. Meanwhile, assuming that I am who I say I am, I should think my credit would be good.'

'The credit of the heir to the throne of Lorsk would certainly be good,' murmured Amastan, and turned to a scribe. 'Fetch Suri. Prince – ah – Vakar, what do you wish with me?'

'I want to get to Amferé, quickly.'

'Well, if you have the fare, ships still leave for Amferé every few days, though this is near the end of the trading-season.'

'Too slow! I am likely to be stuck in Sederado a month waiting for a fair wind. Do you know about the Gorgons' raid?'

'We have heard of their collecting an armament, but not of their having yet put to sea.'

'Well,' said Vakar, 'I must get home to warn my people.'

'What can we do? Though we have some passable magicians, I know of none who can give you fair winds all the way.'

Vakar made a rude comment as to what Kernê could do with its sailing merchantmen. 'I want a galley! One of your precious battleships. Lorsk will pay you well for the service.'

'Ah, but unfortunately the Free City must keep its navy close to home while the Gorgon threat overhangs us. Much as we hate to let a good profit go, I fear we can do nothing for you.'

Vakar argued some more but got nowhere. When the mariner Suri came in, the Lorskan said:

'Oh, never mind the inquisition, as you will not make a deal in any case. Perhaps you know a captain sailing for Amferé soon who will not cut my throat as soon as we are out of sight of Kernê?'

Suri said: 'Jerro of Elusion sails in two days; it is his last trip of the year.'

Vakar found Jerro's ship, engaged passage, sold his camel, got a much-needed haircut – and then waited three days for an easterly wind. They coasted along the south shore of the peninsula of Dzen. Then, as the wind turned southerly enough to carry them north towards Meropia, Jerro headed in that direction across the blue Sirenian Sea.

The wind held fair, keeping the sail taut and creaking on its yards as one blue crest after another heaved against the high stern and slid underneath. For a day and a night they drove northward, and then a sailor cried:

'Ships aft! A whole fleet!'

Vakar's heart sank, for the horizon was pricked by a score of mastheads, and every minute the number grew. Soon the low black hulls of a great fleet of war-galleys could be seen.

Another sailor cried: 'It is the fleet of the Gorgons!' and fell to praying to his Hesperian gods. Jerro cursed.

Vakar said to Jerro: 'What do you mean to do?'

'To run as long as I can. You might as well be dead as a Gorgon's galley-slave. If they are in haste they may not stop for us.'

All the sailors were now weeping and praying, crying out the names of their women and homes. Vakar kicked the gunwales in frustration. He toyed nervously with his hilt, realizing that if the Gorgons sent a ship after them there was little that he, the captain, and four terrified sailors could do.

The fleet of galleys came closer, crawling across the smooth sea like a swarm of centipedes from under a flat stone. All their sails bore the octopus of Gorgonia, a symbol which ignorant landsmen sometimes thought to represent a human head with snakes for hair – which it did somewhat resemble. One galley detached itself from the rest and angled towards Jerro's ship.

Vakar interrupted his fuming to say: 'If we are taken alive, pray say I am Thiegos of Sederado.'

'Aye-aye,' said Jerro. 'But what in the seven hells is that?'

Vakar looked. On the forward deck of the galley stood a man in the garb of a Gorgonian priest. He held one end of a golden chain, the other end of which was linked to a golden collar that encircled the neck of a creature whose like Vakar had never seen. It was a little smaller than a man and vaguely human in shape. It had a tail, pointed ears, and a hooked beak, and was covered all over with reptilian scales, something like a Triton in his snakeskin armor. It squatted on the deck like a dog.

'That must be a medusa,' said Vakar.

'A what?'

'Creatures said to have strange powers of fascination, though I see nothing fascinating about that overgrown lizard. Watch out, there!'

The approaching galley swerved to avoid running down the little merchant-man. Somebody shouted across the water. Jerro shifted his steering-yoke to send the ship angling away from the galley, but a sailor in the bow of the latter threw a grapnel over the rail of the merchantman. Several sailors pulling on the rope began to draw the two vessels together.

Vakar leaped to the rail of the merchantman, drawing from his girdle the curved sword-knife that he had taken from the Kernean at Kiliessa, to chop the grapnel-rope. Before he could complete the action, the priest on the galley pointed at him and spoke to the medusa. The latter reared up against the rail of its own ship, extended its scaly neck, opened its beak, and gave a terrific screaming hiss, like steam escaping from a hundred cauldrons.

In mid-stride Vakar's muscles froze to stony rigidity. His momentum toppled him forward so that his head struck the rail. He saw a flash of light and then nothing.

When he regained consciousness he was already lying aboard the galley, still in his rigid statuesque posture, gripping the bronze sword in his fist, on the poop in front of a chair of pretence in which a bearded man sat wearing a bronze helmet inlaid with gold and crested with ibis plumes. This man was examining Vakar's sword of star-metal, turning it over, squinting along the blade, and swishing the air with it. He said to another Gorgon:

'Strip the others and set them to the oars when they recover. This one, however, seems to be something else. He looks like a Pusadian but is clad like a Kernean and carries a sword like nothing I have ever seen. We will save him to show to the king.'

'Aye-aye, Admiral,' said the other man, and pushed Vakar's body over to the rail out of the way.

Vakar found himself facing the gunwale a few inches from his face. Since he could move neither his neck nor his eyes he was forced to stare at the weathered wood by the hour as the ship plowed on. His paralysis had not diminished his capacity for discomfort, and after a few hours of lying on the heaving deck his body was one vast ache. He could barely breathe, and his mind ran in futile circles trying to figure what course he should have followed instead of the one he had.

The sun rose to the meridian, though Vakar was fortunate in that the awning over the poop shaded him as well as the admiral. The sun went down. Vakar, suffering torments of thirst, lay where he was. The Gorgons must be in haste, he thought, for otherwise they would not have driven their rowers to make the two-day jump straight across the Sirenian Sea with no chance for the crews to sleep. No doubt they wished to get their great raid over before the storms of winter set in.

Towards morning Vakar's paralysis wore off sufficiently for him to blink and swallow. His mouth tasted foul and his eyeballs were dry and scratchy.

When the sun came up again there was much trampling and talking behind him, though he could not follow much of what was said. At length a change in the motion of the galley told him that they were drawing into a quiet cove. They stopped with a lurch as the galley's bow grated on the stand, and there were sounds of men running about. Hands seized Vakar's body and half-carried, half-dragged it over the rail of the bow and down to the beach. As the sailors carrying Vakar turned him this way and that, his rigid eyeballs took in a wooden shore that looked like that of one of the Hesperides.

The men carried him shoulder-high down the beach, past the noses of more galleys. They hoisted him up over the bow of another beached ship, the largest of all. He was carried along the catwalk between the rowers' benches to the poop. Here he was stood upright leaning against the rail, facing a dark paunchy man who sat on a chair like that on the other ship but more ornate. The admiral, who had followed Vakar, told the paunchy man of Vakar's capture. The paunchy man said:

'The effect should have begun to wear off. You there, can you speak?'

With a great effort Vakar forced his vocal organs to say: 'Y-yes.'

'Who are you then?'

'Th-thiegos of Sed-sederado.'

'A Hesperian, eh? Well ...'

Just then another man thrust his way forward. Although Vakar could not yet turn his head or eyes, he was able to see that this was his old acquaintance Qasigan.

'King!' said Qasigan. 'This is no Hesperian or Kernean, but our main quarry himself: Prince Vakar of Lorsk! I know him despite the whiskers.'

The paunchy man, thus identified as King Zeluud, gave an exclamation. 'Let us slay him quickly, then, and go on with the rest of our mission. Khashel, take this sword. Lean the body of the prisoner so that his neck lies across the rail, and strike off his head.'

'N-no!' murmured Vakar, but they paid no attention.

The man addressed as 'Khashel' seized Vakar's body and pulled it inboard so that Vakar's neck lay across the rail. He spit on his hands, spread his feet, and grasped Vakar's own iron longsword, the one Fekata had made for him, in both hands for a full-strength downward cut. He extended the blade in front of him and made a half-swing, sighting on the neck and checking the sword before it reached its target. He lowered the blade so that it just touched Vakar's skin, then raised it high above his head …

The instant the blade touched Vakar's neck, before Khashel raised it for the definitive blow, the paralysis departed from Vakar's muscles. Suddenly relaxing, he fell into a huddle against the gunwale. Khashel's blow, descending with terrific force, drove the blade into the rail where Vakar's neck had just been.

Khashel, eyes popping, tugged the hilt as Vakar rose to his feet, still clutching the curved Kernean weapon he had in his hand when the medusa had petrified him. Khashel still had both hands on the hilt of Vakar's longsword when the Lorskan stepped forward, bringing his arm around in a backhand cut that laid the bronze blade across Khashel's throat below his short beard.

As Khashel slumped into the scuppers, blood streaming from his severed throat, Vakar hurled his bloody blade at King Zeluud, who ducked. In the same movement Vakar seized the hilt of the longsword, yanked it out of the split rail, and vaulted over the side.

He lit with a splash in waist-deep water. As an uproar arose on the ship he bounded shoreward, half falling as a wave tripped him, then sprinted across the beach, ignoring the stares of Gorgonian soldiery scattered about taking their ease. He plunged dripping into the woods and raced up the slope, away from the sea, dodging trees, until pounding heart and panting breath forced him to slow down. After him came sounds of turmoil: shouts, trumpet-blasts, and the clatter of armament as the Gorgons rushed about like a disturbed ant-city and organized a pursuit.

Vakar continued straight inland for a while, then angled to the right to lose his pursuers. Bushes scratched at his bare shanks as he fled. Up and up he climbed.

A patch of blue sky ahead drew him to a ledge of rock on the hillside from which he could look out over the treetops at the shore below and the Sirenian Sea beyond. Here he collapsed, drinking in air in great gasps, and lay while beetles ran over his unprotesting limbs.

When his vision had cleared he sat up and looked towards the landing-place of the Gorgons. Their search-parties should still be streaming inland. Should he climb a tree? Would they have hounds? Could medusas follow a trail like a dog, or locate him by occult means?

Then he realized that the scene was not what he expected. Trumpet-blasts, thin with distance, were recalling the searchers to the ships, and the Gorgons were swarming up over the bows of the beached galleys, some of which were pushing off.

Raising his eyes, Vakar saw why. Out in the Sirenian Sea lay another huge fleet, crawling towards the Gorgonian armada. This, Vakar guessed, must be the united navies of the Hesperides. He cracked his knuckle-joints with nervous anticipation. Was he to have an arena-seat at the greatest naval battle of history?

But as time passed the new fleet halted while the Gorgons, instead of sallying out to meet them, rowed off to Vakar's right parallel to the shore and away from the Hesperians. Vakar got up and climbed until he found a better lookout. Thence he could see that the shore curved around northeastward to his right, and beyond a wide stretch of sea, on the horizon, he could see the blue loom of another land-mass to the Northwest. If he were on Ogugia that would be Meropia; if on Meropia, the continent of Poseidonis.

The Gorgonian fleet was swinging northward to pass through this wide strait, the Hesperians following at a respectful distance. Evidently the Gorgons were not heading for Amferé, to march through Zhysk to attack Lorsk. Then what? North on the coast of Poseidonis lay the smaller Zhyskan city of Azaret, after which there was not a decent harbor until one came to Diöprepé, a mere village in rocky Lotör. As there was nothing in Lotör worth stealing, what then? Did the Gorgons mean to fall upon Avalon, or the Saturides, or fare even farther north to Aremoria or the coasts of wild Ierarné?

If they did land at Azaret, Lorsk would have little to fear, for the road thence to Lorsk led through lofty mountains where a resolute squad might hold up an army.

Vakar Zhu watched for over an hour while the Gorgonian fleet, growing smaller and smaller, crept away northward. Then, seeing that the sun was near its apex, he turned back towards the beach.

Several days later Prince Vakar trudged into Sederado – for, as he had soon learned, he was on Ogugia. He had lived by stealing from farmers and now was looking for means of subsistence with no assets save the naked sword thrust through his girdle. He felt that he could relax as far as the Gorgons were concerned, as they evidently did not mean to assault Lorsk. Queen Porfia might still have it in for him because of Thiegos, but he hoped that between his beard and the prominent scar across his left cheek he would pass unrecognized.

What had he to offer? Though rated a scholar in Mneset, a provincial princeling like himself could hardly capitalize on his modest learning in the City of Philosophers. On the other hand, while no great warrior or athlete at home, being bigger than most Ogugians he might be valued for his modest attainments in those lines here.

He found his way to the barracks of the Royal Guard, Ogugia's only professional, permanent force of fighting-men, for like the other Hesperian nations the Ogugians put most of their trust in their navy. Most of the Guard were foreigners, because the native Ogugians were more concerned with philosophy and their creature comforts than with martial glory.

Viahes, the commandant of the garrison, asked: 'Who are you, and where do you come from, and what do you want?'

'I am Znur, a Lorskan.' Vakar had given some thought to his alias; it would not have done to call himself Thiegos of Sederado again. 'I have been travelling for months on the mainland, which explains the sunburn and the garb. Now I seek a livelihood, and thought the Guard might use me.'

'What can you do?'

'Ride, and use this.' Vakar touched the sword.

'Let me see that. Look at it, Gwantho. What is it?'

Vakar replied: 'Something I got in Tartaros. The black smiths have a magical method of treating bronze.'

'How did you get to Ogugia, with all ships hugging their harbors for fear of the Gorgons?'

'The Gorgons brought me.'

'What?' cried Gwantho, Viahes' legate. 'Are you a spy for them?'

'Not at all. They caught me, but I escaped when their fleet stopped on your shore to rest men and take on water.'

'It could be,' said Viahes. 'We will have one of our Lorskan troopers question you in his own language to see if you are genuine, and then if you can demonstrate your skills we will take you on at three pounds of copper a month plus food and quarters. We will issue you a shield, helmet, and spear which you shall pay for at one-and-a-half pounds a month for six months.'

'That is agreeable to me,' said Vakar.

'Fine. You may have a chance to show your skills this afternoon, when the queen will make a short inspection.' Viahes flashed a grin at his legate.

While Vakar was wondering how to get past the Queen's inspection without recognition, the Lorskan trooper came in: Riazh of Lezôtr, who looked sharply at Vakar and said:

'I'm sure I've seen you.'

'Maybe. Though I'm of Mneset I've often passed through Lezôtr. I usually stop at Alezu's inn.'

'He is a Lorskan,' said Riazh to the officers in Hesperian. 'I should know that affected accent they use in the capital anywhere.'

The guardsmen were lined up with helmets and spear-points gleaming from their morning's polish. Vakar, whose arms had not yet been issued to him, stood to one side as Queen Porfia walked down the line – not exactly lurking, but trying to keep out of the queen's immediate range of interest. As she came close he felt his blood run faster; what a woman! Fantasies crossed his mind, of sweeping Porfia up in his arms, covering her with kisses, and bearing her off to the nearest couch. But much as he esteemed the Queen of Ogugia, Vakar valued his head still more and so kept quiet.

The queen finished her inspection, pudgy Garal jerking along in her wake, and turned away. Viahes said something to the queen, then called: 'You there! You with the hatchet-face, whatever your name is, Znur!'

'Who, me?' said Vakar in a meek voice.

'Yes, you. Since you claim to be an expert rider, you shall show your skill by riding Thandolo.'

'A horse?' said Vakar, realizing that the queen and Minister Garal were looking at him with that same expression of puzzled near-recognition that he had seen earlier on the face of Riazh.

'And what a horse! Here he comes.'

Two grooms were dragging in a big black stallion who rolled his eyes ominously. Vakar, with an inaudible little sigh, walked towards the animal, pulling up his long Kernean jelab through his girdle.

Thandolo wore a bridle but no saddle-pad, not even the girth just back of the forelegs with which the Hesperians equipped their horses. He made a set of teeth at Vakar as the latter came close.

'Behave yourself!' barked Vakar, and cuffed the animal's nose, jerking his hand away in time to avoid a riposte with equine incisors. 'Give me the reins,' he said.

He got a firm grip on the reins and vaulted aboard. As he came down he clamped his knees on the beast's barrel and got a fistful of mane in his free hand just as Thandolo bucked.

Vakar clung with all his might, hauling on the reins to bring the angry animal's head up. It seemed to have a mouth of iron. Up came its back in another stiff-legged buck-jump. Vakar felt his knees slip a little on the glossy hide, but as the beast came down he dug his toes between Thandolo's forelegs and body to keep from flying off at the top of each jump. Up – down; up – down; Vakar vaguely realized that he was yelling Lorskan curses and beating the horse with the slack of the reins. Up – down. The watching guards, Commandant Viahes, and Queen Porfia fled past in saw-toothed jerks …

Then Vakar missed his timing by a fraction of a second and felt the horse's barrel slide out from between his legs. He saw the ground come at him with a circular motion, and landed on his left hip with jarring force.

Thandolo trotted off shaking his head while the grooms began the weary business of rounding him up. Vakar got shakily to his feet. No doubt the grinning Viahes had cooked this stunt up to have a laugh at his expense. While Vakar had never seen anything very funny in jokes on himself, he would not have minded so much if the commandant had not arranged that he be disgraced in front of Queen Porfia. He thought of challenging Viahes to a fight, but then told himself not to be silly. He was unarmed, and lame and battered from his fall, and Viahes would probably order his troopers to fill the Lorskan full of spears at the first hostile move.

His only course was to hobble out (since he had evidently flunked the test) with such dignity as he could muster. Perhaps he could work as a longshoreman …

He was limping towards the gates when Viahes' bellow came after him: 'Ho there, Znur! Where are you going?'

As Vakar looked back blankly the commandant bawled: 'Come back! What is the matter with you?'

Vakar walked back to where Viahes stood with fists on hips, wondering if he were to be offered another chance. 'Well, sir?' he said.

'Why were you running away? You are the best rider in Ogugia!'

'What?'

'Of course! No man has ever stayed on Thandolo's back for more than three heart-beats!'

'We can use men like you,' said a familiar female voice, and there was Porfia: green eyes, black hair, and figure to drive men to madness.

'Did you hear that?' cried Viahes heartily. 'Now get back to barracks, where Gwantho will give you your arms.'

Vakar bowed and departed. He was thoughtfully shining his new helmet until he could see his narrow, scarred face in it when a man came in. Vakar recognized Dweros, one of Porfia's lackeys.

Dweros said: 'Prince Vakar, the queen asks that you come with me to the palace.'

XVIII

The Philosophy of Sederado

Vakar looked up narrowly. So she had recognized him! Was she trying to lure him to his death? If she were, wouldn't she more likely have sent a squad of soldiers to seize him?

He pulled his mustache in perplexity. Strike down Dweros and flee? This time he had no ship waiting, and on such an island it was only a matter of time before he was hunted down …

He made his decision, told Dweros: 'Wait here,' and a few minutes later was back with his magical sword (in a borrowed scabbard) at his side. Now let somebody try to disarm him!

He followed Dweros through the streets, scowling somberly. At the palace gates he saw no sign of ambush: only the usual bored-looking guards leaning on the helves of their zaghnals, and the thin traffic of petitioners and officials going in and out. Inside, Dweros led him through the anteroom ahead of his turn, so that he was conscious of sour looks from those who waited. He tensed as Dweros pushed the curtains aside, ready to whip out the star-sword …

And Porfia's arms were around his neck and she was pressing her lips to his. Then she thrust him back, saying:

'Well! By Heroë's eight teats, when I kiss a man, he does not usually stand like a statue with his hand on his sword!'

Vakar smiled, his eyes darting around the chamber, ready to seize Porfia for a hostage if need be. He said:

'Excuse my caution, dear madam, but I thought you might have cause to kiss me with sharpened bronze.'

'So that is why you skulk about my kingdom under a false name with that bush on your face! Why should I kill you?'

'Thiegos,' he said dryly.

'Oh, him! I was disturbed by his taking-off, true, but you did the only thing you could. Anyway I had ceased to love the cowardly jackanapes, with his airs and his sneers.'

'Well then?' said Vakar, making a movement towards Porfia and raising his arms.

She held out a hand. 'Not until you are cleaned up. Elbien! Take Prince Vakar ...'

In the chamber he had occupied on his first visit he found a fine Ogugian tunic laid out: a knee-length garment of sky-blue linen embroidered with sea-monsters. There was also a razor, with which he removed the beard, leaving the luxuriant mustache. In the silver mirror the pallor of his newly-exposed jaw contrasted oddly with the swartness of the rest of his face, which bore a lean, worn look, like an old and oft-whetted knife-blade.

He dined alone with a radiant Porfia. When she saw him she said: 'I wonder I knew you, you look so much older.'

'Oh, is that so? The things I have experienced in the last seven months would age a god.'

'Where did you get that great scar?'

'I forgot to duck.' He entertained her with a slightly censored account of his adventures. She commented:

'I always thought those Pusadian epics to be mere barbarous bombast, but here we have such an adventurer-hero in the flesh.'

'I am neither hero nor adventurer, but a quiet bookish fellow who would like to settle down in Sederado and study philosophy. In all these fights and flights I have never known that mad joy of battle of which the epics speak. Before the combat I am frightened, during it I am confused, and after it I am weary and disgusted.'

'Well, if that is what you can do when you are frightened, confused, and disgusted, I hate to think of the slaughter you would wreak if you really took to the trade. Are you sure King Awoqqas tried to net you before the headless woman's temptations had time to take effect?'

'Quite sure, madam, though I do not claim any special virtue. I have merely been fleeing my ill-wishers for the past few months too fast for dalliance.' Vakar thought it more tactful to say nothing about Tiraafa the satyr. 'But now that we are being frank, who is the lucky successor to Thiegos?'

As he spoke, Vakar tried to keep the glitter of interest out of his eyes and the pant of passion out of his voice. He could not look at Porfia without feeling the blood rush to his face. Though he had as a matter of course been introduced to the arts of love early, he had never met a woman who affected him like this.

She said: 'In truth I have the same tale to tell as you. For seven months I have slept in a cold bed; I have forsworn all light loves and resolved to hold myself inviolate until I find another consort, as Garal has been plaguing me to do. But I will not have that grasping Shvo; I will have none of your Pusadian polygamy.'

Vakar nodded sympathetically. Though in Poseidonis the male ruled the roost absolutely, his detachment enabled him to appreciate a different point of view. Porfia continued:

'Besides, it is time I produced some heirs, lest I die and leave my cousins to fight for the throne and rend the kingdom in their struggles.'

'Can you?'

'Surely. I bore a girl to Vancho who died, poor thing. Thiegos was my only other. But enough of me. Tell me of your plans. You will be off to Lorsk on the first ship, I suppose?'

'That depends. What have you heard of the Gorgon fleet?'

'When our combined Hesperian fleets broke off following them they were still headed north.'

The servants had taken away the food. They faced each other across a single small table supporting a jug of wine. Porfia sat on a new carven chair of pretence, replacing the serpent throne, while Vakar sat on an ivory stool. The flames of the lamps made little highlights in her green eyes.

'Then,' he said, 'they cannot intend to attack Lorsk, and I need not hasten home.' He set down his goblet and stretched. 'Do not worry about having to keep me, Porfia darling. I will send home for funds to live on while I study philosophy under your Ogugian masters and tame that stallion Thandolo.'

'Really?' She gave him an eager smile.

'Yes.' He rose and stepped around the table and took her hands and gently raised her from her throne.

With an easy fluid motion their arms went around each other and their lips met. After a while he sat down on the chair of pretence and pulled her down upon his lap, marvelling again at her lightness. Vakar rapped the oak of the chair with his knuckles, saying:

'Let us hope this chair does not act in the uncanny manner of the other, the last time you sat in my lap.'

Porfia giggled. They kissed. Vakar slid one hand over her shoulder and down inside the thin robe, but she snatched it out and gave it a slight slap.

'No,' she said. 'I told you I had forsworn light loves, and that includes you, Vakar dear, even though those big black eyes of yours almost turn my will to water.'

'Who said light? I, madam, am heir to the throne of Lorsk, and do hereby most solemnly propose myself as your consort and wedded spouse.'

'Oho! That sheds another light upon the matter. But what should we do when you are King of Lorsk? Where should we dwell?'

'Let us ford that stream when we come to it. Perhaps we can spend our summers in Lorsk and our winters here.'

'And how if we return to one of our kingdoms to find our regents have seized the throne in our absence?'

'That is a matter of choosing reliable surrogates. But think of the advantages: The bronze and brawn of Lorsk wedded to the philosophy and fleet of Ogugia! Who would dare molest such a combination?'

'You bring weighty arguments to the conference table, sir. But we should take into account one other slight matter.'

'Yes?'

'Whether our personal natures are such as to ensure the growth and endurance of love and affection between us.'

'Do we not love already? I, at least, burn for you with white-hot passion.'

'I speak of the other kind of love, not mere carnal lust, which for all its delights both of us know for a sly deceiver. Oh, I know you would give me a tumultuary time beneath the drugget; but how about the long pull, when teeth decay and skins wrinkle and sag and tempers grow short?'

'I have thought of that too,' said Vakar, who had not considered the matter at all until that moment. 'Do you wish a quiet reliable husband, who would rather chase obscure tomes than lustful wenches, but who can if need be prove an adequate man of his hands?'

'You make it sound wonderful, sir. Could I but be sure ...'

'Wait to be sure of anything and you will find yourself looking out through the sides of a funerary urn, your quest unaccomplished. As it says in *The Death of Zormé*:

'Death distrained all,   the primly prudent
And roistering reckless,   the grimly grasping
And squandering spendall,   with divine disdain
Of dealing just deserts ...'

He drew Porfia's face to his and kissed her some more. This time she did not object as he slid his hand over her shoulder, but pressed his hand against her with her own. After a while she gently disengaged herself and rose to her feet. As Vakar looked up, his bushy brows making a question, she held out a hand.

'Come,' she said.

He stood up, picked her up as if she were a kitten, and carried her in the direction that she indicated.

Next morning, with a fistful of copper celts borrowed from the Ogugian treasury in his scrip, Vakar Zhu threaded his way through the streets of Sederado, gaily whistling a Lorskan lyric, until he found the house of Rethilio. Porfia had offered to send a lackey to fetch the owner of the house, but such was Vakar's respect for philosophy that he preferred to go in person. Besides he was curious to see how a philosopher lived.

Like other Hesperian residences, Rethilio's house was built around a court, presenting a blank brick wall to the other world. A porter let Vakar in and presently the philosopher himself appeared, saying:

'Why, I know you! I met you some months ago ... Let me see, you are ...'

Vakar identified himself.

'Of course!' said Rethilio. 'And what can I do for you, sir?'

'As I am likely to be in Sederado for an indefinite time, I should like to study your philosophy.'

'Admirable! Do you wish to enrol in my regular afternoon class, or do you prefer special tutoring? The latter is more costly, but I suppose a prince would not care about that.'

'This prince does,' said Vakar, whose periods of destitution in the course of his wanderings had wonderfully sharpened his appreciation of the value of trade-metal. 'However, as I wish to cram as much as possible into a short time, I will undertake both.'

The philosopher seemed delighted, and presently Vakar was listening ecstatically to Rethilio's theory of the world-egg. When the philosopher had brought his pupil up to date on the main points of his course, he began asking him about his travels and the peoples he had seen. Vakar in his turn asked about the Gorgons.

'Their origin,' said Rethilio, 'is lost in the mists of myth. An ancient race, and in many ways a strange and evil one. The story – and let him believe who will – is that thousands of years ago the Gorgades were inhabited only by medusas, who then were a civilized folk themselves, with cities.'

'Those reptiles civilized?' said Vakar.

'Yes, it is said that they are really as intelligent as men. In that day the present Gorgons were a nation of naked savages dwelling along the shores of Tartaros, barely come to full manhood from their apish ancestry. Well, the medusas, being not over-fond of toil, were wont to raid the mainland for slaves, until there dwelt in the islands several times as many Gorgon slaves as reptilian masters. And a hard servitude that was, for the medusas tortured their slaves for pleasure and ate them for food.

'An aristocracy of wizards ruled the medusas, and would no doubt have continued to do so to this day had not the president of this sorcerous senate been even lazier than most medusas. Not satisfied with compelling his human slaves to carry him about, dress and disrobe him, and put the very food (he preferred roast young woman) into his scaly mandibles, he became too indolent even to perform his own magical spells and taught a trusted slave his principal cantrips.'

'I think I know what is coming next,' put in Vakar.

'Quite so. The upshot was that the slaves rose and overthrew the masters, slaying all but a few. These they kept to be slaves in their turn, but, learning from their predecessors' error, they take care to rear each new medusa in solitude, allowing it to learn no more than is absolutely necessary for it to fulfill its functions. And their chief function is to hiss at those enemies whom their masters point out to them, striking them with paralysis.'

Vakar sat rapt through the afternoon lecture. At its close he could hardly tear himself away – until he thought of Porfia. He grinned with pure happiness.

He was bidding farewell to the philosopher when the porter announced: 'Master, a man to see you. He says he is Ryn of Mneset.'

Vakar gave a violent start as Rethilio said: 'Show him in. I have heard of – what is the matter, Prince? Do you know him?'

'All too well. He is our court wizard, who sent me on this chase.'

The hunched figure of Ryn scuttled in. 'Well, well!' he cackled. 'They told me I should find you here. So our young savior, instead of rushing home, is learning how to split a hair and cut blocks with a razor! Hail, Master Rethilio. I arrive just in time, before he becomes so entangled in your sophistical cobwebs that nothing will extricate him.'

'Now look here,' said Rethilio, 'you may be the deadliest spell-caster in Poseidonis, but that gives you no license to contemn the divine art of philosophy, which is to your dark sorceries as day is to night.'

'Who is insulting whom now? At least my magic accomplishes some practical good, as when by the help of the witch Gra I learned this lad was in Sederado. Come, Vakar, we can talk on our way to that gilded cage of yours. Farewell, Rethilio; I will tell the Lorskans you are the finest quibbler among the Ogugians, who are the greatest quibblers on earth!'

As they walked towards the palace Vakar asked: 'Why don't you like Rethilio?'

'Pff! I dislike him not, but I know his kind. They spend the morning combing their beards to present a specious appearance of wisdom, and in the afternoon they haul in gold with hoes by lecturing on the worthlessness of wealth. His world-egg theory is no worse than the others, to wit: utterly worthless, for no man knows how man and the universe originated. But now to more weighty matters: What are you doing here instead of hastening back to Lorsk in her hour of peril?'

'I stopped here because I saw the Gorgon fleet sail off to northward, having no intention of landing in Zhysk. I see no reason why I shouldn't settle here, wed Queen Porfia, and become a real scholar and not a brainless Lorskan bison-hunter.'

'Oh, so you'd marry her green-eyed majesty! At least your taste in women is good. Does she know of this?'

'Knows and approves. So you may tell my loving family —'

'Young fool! Don't you know what the Gorgons are up to? They're sailing around the north end of Poseidonis, around Lotör, to come at us from the west!'

'Oh!'

'Yes, oh. They thought to surprise us by the maneuver, and would have save that one of our lords, Kalesh of Andr, happened to make a pilgrimage to the temple of Three-eyed Tandyla in Lotör and heard a rumor among the Lotris. He scouted the coast and saw the Gorgon fleet creeping along upon the sky-line, and posted home as fast as his nag could bear him. Now, what's this magical whatnot you were supposed to run down? Have you found it?'

Vakar told his tale and showed the sword of star-metal.

'Ah!' said Ryn. 'This all ties in together. Now I know what the gods most fear and why.'

'What is it?'

'Before I took ship across the Sirenian Sea, I stopped in King Shvo's library in Amferé. You know Shvo's a fanatical collector: of land, wealth, women, records, anything he can lay hands on. I suppose you know he's been trying to collect your pretty little Porfia?'

'What? Just let him try —'

'Easy, easy. Bear it in mind and be careful, for if he knows of your intentions he might bribe somebody to poison your wine. Watch that fat Garal; he's less harmless than he looks. In this case, however, Shvo's greed stood us in good stead, for amidst that warehouse full of junk he calls a library I found a tattered old papyrus from a ruined temple in Parsk that bore the legend of Kumiö.'

'What's that?'

'It's a legend referred to in Oma's *Commentary*, of which only a fragment survives and which is itself so old it can no longer be dated. But here was the original, or at least a copy of a copy of a copy of the original.'

'What did it say?' asked Vakar.

'It tells how a thief and blasphemer named Kumiö found a fallen star as your friend Ximenon did. He broke off a piece and wore it around his neck as an amulet, gradually discovering it rendered him proof against all supernatural influences. Witches could not cast spells upon him; demons could not harm him; even the gods could neither touch him nor communicate with him.

'Now, Kumiö lived in what is now the Bay of Kort, west of Lorsk. There stood the capital of the Kingdom of Kort, the great city Klâto with its towers of scarlet and black. The people were wont to rely for protection of their goods on spells and talismans they bought from the magicians, but with the advent of Kumiö and his amulet all was changed. A chest kept closed by the mightiest spell would easily open to Kumiö once he had touched it with his piece of star. He even got into the king's zenana, guarded by a three-headed fiend of anthropophagous tastes who nevertheless could not come near him, and revelled among the king's concubines for six days and fled before the king learned of his visit. And thus the first locks and bolts were invented, to keep out the light-fingered Kumiö.

'In time the gods took counsel, for it occurred to them that if knowledge of this metal became widespread, all men would seek to carry a bit of it, and then the gods would be unable to communicate with men, who would forget the gods and cease to worship them, which for a god is virtual death.'

Vakar said: 'Rethilio was explaining the Fragments of Lontang along those lines.'

'So,' continued Ryn, 'the gods decided to do away with Kumiö. First they tried to take him off by sickness, but he was proof against plagues from any but natural causes. Then they incited another thief to steal his piece of metal, but the thief relied upon a spell of invisibility he bought from a wizard, and Kumiö saw him coming and knifed him. I won't tell you all the things they tried; but at last, growing desperate, they sank the whole Kingdom of Kort beneath the waters of the Western Ocean. Thus Kumiö was drowned along with all the other Kortians save a handful of survivors.'

'Is this true?'

'Who knows? Probably not in all details. But it gives us the reason for the gods' fearing star-metal.'

'What is the stuff? Is it found on the earth's surface?'

Ryn shrugged his uneven shoulders. 'How should I know? Of the five known metals, gold and silver are found in their native state, tin and lead are extracted from rocks, and copper occurs both ways. How do we know what other kinds of metal lurk in the rocks, could we but extract them? But nobody has yet so obtained star-metal.'

Vakar mused: 'I see how the sword broke that spell the medusa put upon me, when the fellow who meant to cut my head off touched my neck with the blade first, as you do to aim your stroke. Now that we know how it works, what shall we do with it?'

'That will transpire at the proper time; I've never known Gra's prescience to fail. Meantime you must hasten back with me before the seas wax too boisterous.'

'Hells!' Vakar kicked a clod. 'Why should I, when I've just found what I really want? What's there in Lorsk save a perpetual bicker with my brother? Why can't you take the sword —'

'There's the kingdom to which you're heir. Your father is unwell, and if you're not there at the time ... I leave the inference to you.'

Vacillating, undecided, Vakar marched gloomily back to the palace. He sent a footman in to interrupt an audience the queen was giving, and told her the news.

'No!' cried Porfia, a hand to her throat. 'You shall not go! Our nuptials are in six days, and having found the one man to share my throne I will not let him be slain in some petty brawl on the edges of the world ...'

Her tone nettled Vakar enough to make him say: 'Consort or none, dear madam, I shall make my own decisions. After all I have my duty to my people as you have yours.'

After further argument she said: 'Let us take counsel with Charsela. Will you abide by her advice?'

'I will take her counsel into full account,' said Vakar carefully, 'if you will let me send for Rethilio likewise.'

'I see where I shall have to feed all the seers and sages of Sederado,' said Porfia, 'for the dinner-hour draws nigh.'

'Huh!' said Ryn. 'As if my advice were not so good as that of that hairsplitter! He will wish you to stay here, so he can continue to milk the treasury of Lorsk by his lectures.'

The old she-wizard arrived first, saying: 'It is the young gallant who saved the queen and me! Though you did leave my house in a gory mess. And this if I mistake not is the great Ryn of Mneset?'

'Yes, yes,' gruffed Ryn. 'How is the love-potion business?'

'Poorly, your honor, for the maggots of philosophy have so far addled the brains of the people that they have little thought for love. I of course except our royal protectors here, who obviously have thought for little else at the moment.'

Rethilio arrived, gravely greeting those present. Queen Porfia led them to a dark little chamber in the midst of the palace, lighted by a single lamp. Charsela filled her cauldron and went into her trance. After a long while she said:

'If Prince Vakar returns to Lorsk he will suffer great loss, but will not long regret it.'

Porfia cried: 'Do not go, my love! She means you will lose your life!'

'While I do not hold my life cheaply,' replied Vakar, 'yet after the perils I have lately escaped I am not to be deterred from returning home by fear of a doubtful oraculation. What do you think, Rethilio?'

The philosopher said: 'Most men possess an inner voice that informs them what is the righteous course to pursue. Some attribute this to a guardian spirit, some to a favorite god, and some to the soul of the man himself. Which is right I know not, but you disobey this voice at your peril, for it will have its revenge upon you. Thus if you steal despite the prohibitions of the voice, it will cause you to stumble when the watchman is chasing you and so bring you to justice.'

'Then,' said Vakar, 'I will return to Lorsk forthwith. What transport is available, Ryn?'

'A galley of the navy of Zhysk awaits at the waterfront. We can be off tomorrow.'

'So be it. We shall – why, Porfia!' Vakar started to rise.

For the Queen of Ogugia had dissolved in tears. She rose, saying between sobs: 'I will have my servants bring you dinner, but pray excuse me. I wish to be alone – no, Vakar, you shall remain here to entertain our guests. Later you may come to me.'

Vakar unhappily watched Porfia depart, fingering his mustache and wishing that he were better able to cope with such emotional crises. While he stood indecisive the servants brought in food and wine. Over the tables Ryn said to Rethilio:

'I owe you an apology; I had not thought you would give such disinterested advice.'

'Oh, I claim no special virtue for it,' said Rethilio blandly, breaking open his loaf of bread. 'My livelihood depends upon my reputation for impartiality, and what would it profit me to urge the prince to remain in hope of collecting fees from him, if he then became bored and sought other amusements, leaving me with tarnished repute?'

'You wrong me, sir philosopher,' said Vakar. 'I would not leave you from boredom, but only if I learned of a philosopher more profound than yourself, for to me the pursuit of ultimate truth is the world's most fascinating pastime.'

'Well, let us hope we shall all live for you to resume it. Master Ryn, it occurs to me that you too had better take up philosophy.'

'Why?'

'Because if the knowledge of star-metal and its properties diffuses widely, so that all men take to carrying fragments of the material, your profession would wither away to nought.'

'A point I had not thought of. However, I am too old to learn a new bag of tricks and shall not live to see this change. Perhaps my successors, now young sprigs in the magical lycea of Torrutseish, will improve their art to counter the anti-magical qualities of the stuff.'

Charsela spoke in her hollow voice: 'There is more to it than that. The star-metal will some day cast the very gods from their thrones, for with it men will be cut off from their gods, as to benefits, punishments, and mere communication.'

'Then no more gods?' said Rethilio.

'No; there will be gods, but mere ineffectual wraiths, kept in being by their priests to enable these priests to live without toil on the offerings of the credulous. I have seen it in my visions.'

'And then,' said Vakar, 'all men would be like me, who have never conversed with the smallest godlet. Which might not be a bad thing.'

Later, Porfia clung to him with a violence that made his ribs creak, alternating spells of passion such as he had never known from a woman with periods of tempestuous tears.

'I shall never see you again!' she wailed. 'I know Charsela meant you will be slain!'

'Oh, come, love. She did not say so, and we all have our time —'

'Nonsense! That is one of those philosophers' arguments, sounding impressive and meaning nothing. I love you to madness and cannot give you up. You know I am no blushing virgin, but never have I known a man so to stir me ...'

He gave her passion for passion, but stubbornly refused even to defer his sailing for a day or two. She was still asleep when he stole from the palace with Ryn before dawn. As the Zhyskan galley creaked and crawled out of Sederado Harbor, Vakar leaned on the after rail, staring somberly back at the graceful city, pink in the sunrise. Ryn at his elbow said:

'Cheer up, my boy. Just think of me; you may have loved and lost, but with my hump I never —'

'Shut your mouth, you old fool! No, I don't really mean that. But if I'm killed on this expedition I'll haunt you to your urn.'

XIX

The Bay of Kort

At the grim craggy walls of Mneset, Vakar reined up as the guards crossed their halberds and said: 'I'm Prince Vakar! Let me through, fools!'

'What's that?' said one of the guards. 'Everybody knows Prince Vakar went a-travelling over the earth and fell off the edge.'

'He do look something like the prince,' said the other. 'Who can identify you, sir?'

'Oh, hells!' growled Vakar.

He had ridden on ahead of Ryn in his impatience to learn how things went in Lorsk, and now he had to sit his panting mount until Ryn's chariot rattled up. Then the guards were profuse with apologies to which Vakar paid little heed as he spurred for the castle.

The first person of rank he met there was the chamberlain, whom he asked: 'Where is everybody? Where are my father and brother?'

'The king lies sick, sir, and Prince Kuros has gone to the Bay of Kort with the army.'

Vakar went quickly to his father's chambers. King Zhabutir lay on his bed, surrounded by servants and adherents and looking blankly up. Vakar pushed through them and said:

'Hail, Father.'

The king's eyes looked out of their sunken sockets. He said faintly:

'Oh, Vakar. Where did you come from, dear boy? Have you been away? I haven't seen you lately.'

Vakar exchanged glances with the people who crowded the room, and it seemed to him that they looked at him with pity. The king continued:

'How did get that great scar on your face, son? Cut yourself shaving?'

Then Ryn came in and steered Vakar out by his elbow. The old wizard said:

'He's been like this for a month, gradually sinking until now he seldom talks sense.'

'Shouldn't I stay until he either mends or dies?'

'Nay. He might go any time and again he might last months more, while the army fights the Gorgons. We must set out for the Bay of Kort now, trusting to luck he'll still be alive when we return.'

'Shouldn't I stop to sacrifice to Lyr and Okma, then, for bringing me through so many perils?'

'Not now. After all this time they can wait a few days.'

Vakar went to his chambers feeling shaken, for though he had never been very close to his father the loss of a near relative is sobering. He armed himself with his jazerine cuirass of gilded bronze scales, his second-best helmet (not the solid gold one, which was too soft) and a bronze shield like that he had started his journey with. He kept the sword of star-metal, which in odd moments he had honed down to razor sharpness. Then he and Ryn set out for the Bay of Kort, where the Gorgonian fleet was expected.

Four days later they reached the pass through the hills around the bay, where from a bend in the road they could see the whole bay and the crescent of flatland between it and the hills spread out below like a dinner-plate. The cool autumnal wind whipped their cloaks. In the foreground lay the Lorskan camp.

'Lyr's barnacles!' cried Vakar.

The Gorgon fleet was already drawn up along the beach in a line miles long, hundreds of vessels great and small with sails furled, oars shipped, and bows resting on the strand. The Gorgonian army had disembarked and was drawing up in a great rectangular mass, in regular ranks with big wood-and-leather shields and helms in exact alignment, bristling with spears, while clumps of archers gathered on the flanks. Over each unit floated its vexilla, hanging from a gilded cross-yard.

A half-mile inland from the Gorgonian array, the forces of Lorsk were strung out in loose aggregations, each group comprising the followers of some lord or high officer.

'The damned fool!' croaked Ryn. 'He told me he meant to attack while they were disembarking! A good enough plan, but it's gone somehow awry. Having failed to catch them with their kilts wet, he should withdraw into the hills to ambush and block them, meanwhile harrassing them with cavalry, of which they have none. On the plain that Gorgonian meat-grinder will make short work of our gallant individualists.'

'We have an advantage of numbers.'

'That'll avail us little. The headstrong fool ...'

'Perhaps he's planned it that way,' said Vakar, and told Ryn of the words of the dying Söl.

'Ye gods! Why haven't you told me before?'

'I left Mneset in such a rush I had no time, and so much happened later that it slipped my mind.'

Ryn muttered something about the dynasty's ending in a litter of halfwits, then said: 'Let's get on to the battle.'

'It'll take us an hour,' said Vakar, but started his horse down the slope. Ryn's chariot bumped behind.

As Vakar rode he saw the course of the battle like a game played on a table-top. The shrill Lorskan trumpets rang out and the horsemen and light chariots moved out to harrass the foe, dashing up to within a few feet of them to discharge bows or cast javelins, then wheeling away. A few such skirmishers swirled around the ends of the Gorgonian line, but the archers drove them off with flights of bone-tipped arrows.

Others galloped towards the ships drawn up along the beach beyond the ends of the Gorgonian army. As they came, these ships pushed off. Vakar saw the Lorskans catch one still beached. There was a scurrying of little figures and a twinkle of weapons in the sunlight, and then smoke rose from the ship as the Lorskans set it afire.

Now the deeper tones of the Gorgonian trumpets answered those of Lorsk. Vakar saw a ripple of motion go through the Gorgonian array as the phalanx began to advance. The Lorskan chariots and horses bolted back through the gaps in their own force to the rear, and the towering kilted Lorskan foot-soldiers loped forward under their bison banners, yelling and whirling their weapons.

Then Vakar could see clearly no more, for he had reached the level of the plain. Now the battle was a dark writhing line of figures on the horizon, the plan and progress of the battle being hidden from view by the backs of the rearmost Lorskans and by the clouds of dust that now arose.

'I halt here!' called Ryn. 'I'll cast a few spells; you go on and see what you can do.'

Vakar rode forward, skirting the Lorskan camp whence camp-followers yelled unintelligibly at him. The roar of battle strengthened until he could make out individual shrieks. Behind the main battle-front the Lorskan cavalry and chariotry stood awaiting orders. As Vakar approached he glimpsed the faces of foot-sholdiers, first a few, then here, there, and everywhere. That meant that they were facing the wrong way – were running away. Had the battle been lost already?

The fleeing foot zigzagged between the horses and chariots and ran past Vakar through the grass towards the hills: first one or two, then hundreds, most without weapons. Now the cavalry and chariots too began to move retrograde, sweeping past Vakar and overtaking and passing the infantry. Once Vakar glimpsed his brother Kuros, riding rearwards with the rest. Kuros would naturally be among the first to flee, knowing that his men would soon follow his example and that his secret pact with King Zeluud would thereby be carried out. It was a full-fledged rout.

Vakar caught one foot-soldier by his crest. The chin-strap kept the helmet from coming off, and the jerk nearly broke the man's neck.

'What's happened?' roared Vakar into the dazed man's face.

'Magic!' gasped the man. 'They had creatures like great lizards in front of their line, and as we closed with them the lizards hissed at us and our men fell as if struck by thunderbolts. Let me go! What can mere men do against such magic?'

Vakar released the man, who resumed his flight. The bulk of the Lorskan army had now swept past Vakar, who almost wept with rage. Never in the memory of man had the proud men of Lorsk suffered such a disgraceful defeat. After the Lorskans came the Gorgons under their swaying octopus banners, the sun gleaming on their cuirasses. Most of them had dropped their heavy shields of wood and bull's hide to run faster after their foes. In their pursuit they had abandoned their rigid rectilinear formation so that they now surged forward in a great irregular and scattered mass. From his height Vakar could see over the heads of the Gorgons the bodies of thousands of Lorskans lying stiff and stark in the grass. Off to his right King Zeluud stood in the Gorgons' only chariot, trotting at the head of his men.

Vakar drew his sword and put his horse towards one of the gaps in the Gorgonian line. The Gorgons stared at the single horseman hurling himself into their midst. One or two took a few steps in Vakar's direction, but he went past them like a whirlwind. A plumed Gorgonian helmet appeared in front of him. The Gorgon swung a battle-ax, but before he could strike, Vakar drove his sword into the man's face. He felt the crunch of thin bones and wrenched his point out as the man fell. Then he was through the hostile array and pulled up to look around.

Back towards the hills he now saw the backs of the Gorgon mass, still running after the Lorskans. Their officers urged them on with hoarse shouts; nobody bothered with the lone horseman whose mount had evidently gone mad and carried him willy-nilly through the army.

Between Vakar and the sea the victims of the medusa attack lay in long rows, in stiffly unnatural positions like statues toppled from their pedestals. Their heads lay towards the sea, for when the screams of the medusas had petrified them in mid-charge their momentum had caused nearly all of them to fall forward.

Between Vakar and the fallen Lorskans he saw what he sought: the medusas and their attendant priests of Entigta. There were nine reptiles, each on a leash. At the start of the battle the priests had been spaced evenly along the Gorgonian front, but now that their part was over they were gathering in a single group in the middle of their line, a few hundred feet to Vakar's right as he faced the sea. Half a dozen of them had congregated there already, and the remaining three were walking towards this group.

Vakar spurred his horse and cantered in a wide curve that brought him up to the last of the priests from behind. Before he reached the Gorgon, the priest, aroused by hoof-beats behind him, looked around. The priest pointed at Vakar and spoke to the medusa, which opened its beak and hissed.

The horse shied, and Vakar felt a vibration run through him, but gripping the magical sword he plunged at the pair. So long as he gripped the hilt, the contact between his hand and the tang of the blade protected him. A downright slash sank into the medusa's scaly head and then he was past, sparing only a glance back to see the reptile writhing in the dust.

Then he was on the second. A sweeping backhand cut shore through the snaky neck and sent the medusa's head flying.

He swept past the clump of priests and rode towards the remaining individual who had not yet reached them. His swing missed a vital spot and sheared off one of the medusa's ears; he jerked his horse around in a tight circle and came back. This time another head flew off.

'Prince Vakar!' cried the priest, and Vakar recognized Qasigan.

But now he had no time to settle old scores with mere men. He rode at the remaining six priests who stood in a group and watched uncertainly. At the last minute they grasped what he was doing. There was a flurry of movement as they tried to form a circle around the medusas, drawing knives from their belts to defend their beasts with their lives. Then Vakar crashed squarely into the group. There were screams of men and medusas as bones crushed under the horse's hooves and Vakar's sword flashed down on shaven polls and scaly crania.

Then he was through and wheeling to charge back, blood spraying from his sword as he whirled it, yelling wordlessly. Crash! A sharp pain in his leg told him that one of them had gotten home with a knife, but he kept on, slashing and thrusting ...

And he was chasing one surviving medusa over the grass. The reptile went in buck-jumps like a rabbit, the golden chain attached to its collar leaping and snaking behind it. Vakar rode it down and left it writhing with its entrails oozing out. Four priests, including Qasigan, were running for their ships, hiking up their robes to give their legs free play.

Back towards the hills the Gorgonian army still receded in pursuit of the Lorskans. Vakar knew that the road up to the pass would get jammed and the Gorgons would have a holiday massacre. And now what? The sword that had destroyed the medusas would also revive the fallen Lorskans, whom the Gorgons had not taken time to bind or slay.

Down at the waterfront, among the beaks of the beached ships, men were pointing at Vakar and shouting, but seemed undecided what to do. Most of them were mere unarmed servants.

Vakar rode down to one end of the windrows of stricken Lorskans and turned back. Holding his horse's mane with his shield-hand he leaned down as he passed the bodies and slapped them on faces and hands with the flat of his blade. As he did so they lost their rigidity and scrambled up. Vakar shouted:

'Get up! Get in formation! Pick up your arms!'

There seemed to be no end to the process. He had to keep looping back to touch men whom he had missed, hundreds and hundreds of them. It was as tiring as a battle. But the crowd of recovered Lorskans grew and grew. For want of other guidance they obeyed him. Down at the shore the Gorgonian galleys, alarmed by the springing to life of an army of corpses, were putting to sea.

Time passed. Vakar's arm ached. Only a few-score more bodies to go ... Vakar speeded up, careless of slicing off an occasional nose or ear. And then they were all on their feet. He rode back to the middle of the line and waved the sword, shouting:

'Get in line and follow me! The magical powers of the Gorgons have been destroyed. We can take them in the rear and wipe them out!'

He harangued them and got them into motion across the plain at a fast mile-eating walk: tall bearded Lorskan yeomen with their miscellany of weapons. As they neared the edge of the coastal plain, Vakar could see what was happening ahead. Many of the Gorgons had abandoned the pursuit to sack the Lorskan camp, where they were amusing themselves by butchering the cooks and sutlers and raping the women. The rest had caught the fugitives funnelling into the road leading up to the pass and had fallen upon them with spear and sword. The slaughter of the mixed mass of Lorskan soldiers and camp-followers had been terrific, checked only by the fact that the front ranks became so jammed up that they had no room to swing a weapon.

As Vakar neared the Gorgon rear with his force he could see Gorgonian officers rushing around trying to get their men faced about to receive the new attack. Vakar, judging the distance, yelled: 'Charge!'

Forward they went at a run with deep roars, stumbling over bodies. They plunged through the camp, sweeping the plunderers before them and trampling them down, and then the lines met with a crash and a crush that lifted men off their feet and snapped the shafts and spears and halberds. Weapons rose and fell like flails. Behind the Gorgonian array the Lorskan fugitives picked up courage and instead of trying frantically to elbow their way up the road or to scale the steep hillsides to safety, some turned back, picked up discarded weapons, and plunged into the fight. As most of the Gorgons now lacked shields, their advantage in equipment was neutralized.

Howls of dismay rose from the Gorgons as they realized that they were trapped. Vakar, caught in the melée, hewed at every plumecrested head he saw until he could scarcely swing his blade. A spear-point gashed his leg again; another drove through the chest of the already wounded horse. With a scream the animal died, but such was the press that it could not fall, but gradually subsided on to a struggling knot of fighters. Vakar, exhausted, dragged himself clear and then was knocked over and buried under a welter of bodies.

He dragged himself out from under the pile of wounded and dead, battered and bruised and covered with his own and others' blood, to find that the Gorgons had been split into several small groups being ground to nothing. In the midst of the largest knot rose King Zeluud's chariot. The horses had been killed and the king stood in the vehicle, swinging over his followers' heads with a long two-handed sword at any Lorskan who tried to break through to reach him. Vakar began to push through the press towards the chariot. The Gorgons around the chariot fought like fiends until a huge Lorskan burst through to climb up behind the king, seize him by the neck, and drag him over the side. King Zeluud disappeared.

Now the Gorgons began to lose heart. Some cast down their arms and cried for quarter. Most of these the infuriated Lorskans struck down without mercy, but Vakar managed to save a few from slaughter. There was much about Gorgonia that he wished to know, and dead men could tell him nothing.

The sounds of battle died away, leaving several thousand Lorskans leaning on the shafts of their weapons and panting. Those who had the breath to do so raised the shout of victory. Some cut the throats of the Gorgon wounded; others dragged their own wounded out from the piles of dead to see if they looked salvageable or whether they too should, as an act of mercy, have their throats cut. The ground was carpeted with bodies and severed members and with helmets, shields, swords, spears, daggers, axes, maces, halberds, trumpets, and all the other paraphernalia of war. Tattered battle-standards lay among the litter, some so bloodstained that the bison of Lorsk could hardly be distinguished from the octopus of Gorgonia.

Where the ground could be seen it was dark red-brown with blood. Clouds of flies were settling upon the cadavers, and vultures circled expectantly overhead.

Vakar Zhu sheathed his blade and tied up his leg-wounds with strips of cloth from the garments of fallen men. He found Lord Kalesh (he who had brought word of the Gorgons' circumnavigation to Lorsk) astride a blood-spattered horse. Vakar put Kalesh in charge of the army with instructions to secure any Gorgonian ships that had not gotten away, and to camp on the plain that night. Then he borrowed Kalesh's horse and set off up the steep road for Mneset. At the top he picked up Ryn with his chariot. Vakar slid off his horse, saying:

'Mind you if I ride with you? These wounds in my legs will heal faster.'

'Get in, get in.'

They creaked slowly homeward, learning that nearly evedybody they met thought that the Lorskans had lost the battle, such word having been spread throughout the land by the early fugitives.

Nine days later they reached Mneset in a drizzle with several hundred men trailing behind them. They found the gate shut and signs of preparations for a seige. Vakar shouted:

'Ho there! Open for Prince Vakar! The Gorgons are beaten!'

An armed man stuck his head over the wall. 'What's that, sir?'

'I said, the Gorgons are beaten. Open up!'

'Just a minute, my lord.' The man disappeared, but others appeared in his place, looking down silently and fingering their bows and spears.

Vakar fidgeted with impatience. The stragglers from the army came seeping along the road, afoot and on the backs of horses and mules, until a crowd of them was gathered in a semicircle around the gate.

Vakar fumed: 'I don't know what ails those fellows. They've had plenty of time to open.'

He shouted, but without effect; the armed men on the wall stared down silently. After a while the head of his brother Kuros appeared, saying:

'What's this lying tale of the Gorgons' being beaten?'

'Lying!' cried Vakar. 'Come out here, coward, and I'll show you what's a lie!'

'What? No man speaks to a king like that and lives!'

'King?' yelled Vakar. 'What do you mean, king?'

'Just what I said. The old man died while you were gone, first naming me his successor. He agreed it was high time we dropped the absurd old custom of ultimogeniture.'

It took Vakar a few seconds to gather his wits after this shattering news. Finally he said:

'That's illegal and unconstitutional, and you know it. Even if it's true, which I have only your worthless word for, the king may not change the succession without the Council's approval.'

'Well, I'm king in any case, with several thousand soldiers to make it stick. What are you going to do about it?'

'Murderer! Traitor! Usurper!' screamed Vakar, foaming in his rage. 'You slew Söl the spy when he'd have revealed how you'd sold Lorsk to the Gorgon king! You tried to destroy your own army at Kort by fleeing as the battle started, and now you've seized the throne after no doubt hurrying our poor father into his next incarnation by smothering him with a pillow! Come out here with your sword, now, and we'll settle the succession man to man!'

'Do I look stupid?' replied Kuros. 'Here!'

As he spoke, Kuros snatched a bow from a man beside him, nocked an arrow, and let fly. Vakar ducked as the missile whizzed past, missing him by inches and piercing the foot of one of the spectators, who yelped. The stragglers scattered in all directions, the wounded man limping after them with the arrow in his foot. As Kuros reached for another arrow, Vakar cracked his whip, wheeled the chariot around, and drove back out of range, snarling:

'I'll back-track and pick up the rest of the army! I'll take Mneset by storm and hang that traitor from the gate-towers until he rots ...'

Ryn shook his head, clawing at his goatish beard. 'That would be hard on the city, no matter who won.' Vakar leaned against the side of the chariot, staring somberly into space. The stragglers stood about in little clumps, looking from Vakar to Kuros, who stood on the wall with his second arrow nocked but not drawn, waiting to see what Vakar would do. Ryn added softly:

'And is that what you really want? Think now.'

Vakar straightened up with a laugh. 'Now I see what Charsela was driving at! And I also know what Rethilio meant when he said I should have to make a choice of destinies; I couldn't encompass them all in one lifetime. Why should I fight that oaf for a drafty old castle and the right to boss a mob of yokels when I have a much pleasanter berth awaiting me in Ogugia?'

'Why indeed?'

'I'm no conqueror, but a quiet fellow who asks only to be let alone to acquire true scholarship. Say farewell to Bili for me and lend me some trade-metal. I'm for Sederado!'

Vakar filled his scrip and, his legs now healed, vaulted on to Kalesh's horse. He raised his voice to the stragglers and the men on the wall:

'You have all seen and heard what has happened here. If you wonder why I'm not pressing the fight against my brother, 'tis for two reasons: first, I'm not so avid of the duties of kingship as he seems to be, and second, our land has suffered enough of late without plunging it into civil war. I'm going into exile, without renouncing any claim to the throne. If at some future date you tire of the rule of a murderer and traitor ... Well, we'll let that take care of itself when the time comes. Farewell!'

Vakar waved, threw an ironical salute to Kuros, and galloped off towards Lezôtr, singing:

> 'Vrir the Victorious   rode to the river,
> His scabbard of silver   shining in sunlight ...'

*

The gods, gathered in their place of assembly, all yammered at Drax: 'Fool! Why told you us not that the center of this malign influence would shift to Tartaros, Vakar Lorska being but one minor link in the chain of causation ...'

Drax writhed uncomfortably. 'Pray be patient, divinities. I gave you all that my science had revealed to me. Perhaps all is not yet lost. By speeding the sinking of the western regions we can submerge not only Poseidonis but Tartaros as well.'

'What matters it,' said Lyr, 'whether we perish by the spread of the star-metal or by the extermination of our worshippers? Why could you not leave well enough alone? If we had not caused Entigta to stir up his Gorgons, the Tahakh would still be a mere lump of meteoric iron, a harmless curiosity in the hands of Awoqqas of Belem.'

'No doubt all this was fated from the beginning,' said Okma.

This started a furious argument over free-will versus predestination, in the course of which Asterio, the bull-headed forest-god of Ogugia, pulled Entigta's tentacles cruelly.

But Vakar of Lorsk rode happily towards Amferé to take the last ship of the season for Sederado.

THE STRONGER SPELL

Dimly seen through an autumnal drizzle that made the cobble-stones of its waterfront glow in the fading light, the city of Kernê – ancient, bustling, colorful, and wicked – brooded over the waters of the Western Ocean. The flying-fish flags of the city stirred in sopping folds from poles atop the watchtowers along the walls, where sentries paced and peered through the murk.

Along broad Ocean Street, as the waterfront was called, few folk moved in the dusk, and water gurgled in the gutters. Most of the tubby roundships that carried Kernê's commerce and the slender galleys that protected it from the corsairs of the Gorgon Isles had been laid up for the season, hauled out of water into sheds along the beach south of the waterfront proper. Hence few ships were using the quays and piers of Ocean Street except the usual scuttle of fishing craft, and most of these were sitting out the storm.

A two-horse chariot came by plop-plop, its bronze tires banging harshly on the cobbles and its driver braced against the pull of the half-wild horses. The passenger was muffled to the eyes against the wet, but lights from the houses caught the golden trimmings of the vehicle and told that he must be one of the oligarchy of merchant princes.

Suar Peial, hugging a couple of bulky objects under his cloak, strode along the street paying little heed to the questionable characters who peered out of doorways and alleys. These took in Suar's stature and the slender scabbard visible below the cloak, and went off to look for easier pickings.

A noise from an alley attracted Suar's attention. A man with his back to an angle in the wall was defending himself by kicks and the blows of some sort of club against an attack by five others. The looks of these latter, as tattered as the falling leaves of the cork oaks that lined Kernê's avenues, told Suar that they were typical thieves of the quarter.

A sensible man on the Kernean waterfront would walk swiftly away pretending that he had seen or heard nothing amiss. But if Suar had been sensible he would not have been in Kernê in the first place. He would have been home in Zhysk across the Sirenian Sea; he might even have been king of Zhysk. As it was, the lone man was due to go down under the clubs and swords of his attackers in a matter of a few heart-beats. Even had he been twice as big and much better armed, he could not face five ways at once. If his cowardly assailants had been willing to risk a hard knock or two in closing they would already have had him down.

Suar shucked off the cloak, made a bundle of the cloak and the objects that he had been carrying, drew his slim bronze rapier, and started for the scene. As he went he picked his first opponent: the one with the cudgel. Of the others, two carried short bronze broadswords and the remaining two knives. With shield or armor Suar would have had little to fear from the club, but lacking defenses he feared to fence with it lest a wild swing snap his thirty-inch blade.

The man with the club turned at the sound of Suar's approach and sprang back. The other four backed away from their victim also, their attitude bespeaking imminent flight. Then he of the club said:

'There is but one. Slay him too!'

He stepped forward himself, swinging the bludgeon. Suar did not try to parry; instead his long knobby arms and legs shot out in a lunge that sent the point through the club-man's arm. Suar bounced back, trying to recover before the club arrived. He did not quite succeed. Although the blow went weak and awry because of the wound in the thief's arm, the wood still grazed Suar's scalp, scraped his right ear, and bounced off his right shoulder: a painful knock but not a disabling one. Then the club clattered to the ground as the man's grip failed.

As the man stood there, holding his wounded arm and staring stupidly, Suar's sword flicked out again like a serpent's tongue and the point pierced the thief's broad chest. The club-man, coughing a curse, folded up into the mud of the alley. As the others began to close in upon Suar, the latter shot a thrust at the nearest swordsman, who gave ground, then engaged one of the knife-wielders. The man tried to grab the blade with his free hand, but Suar avoided the clutch and thrust him through the body.

All this had taken as much time as an unhurried man would require to breathe thrice. At that instant a sharp sound drew the glances of all. The original victim had stepped up behind his nearest assailant and brought the club-thing down upon the latter's head with a mighty blow.

Then there were three thieves lying in the mud and two others fleeing. One of those lying in the alley still moved and groaned.

Suar looked at the man whom he had rescued. He could not make out much in the dim light save that the man wore the tartan trousers and the sweeping mustache of the northeasterly barbarians. The man stood back, gripping his club-thing as if still doubtful of Suar's intentions.

'You may put that away, fellow,' said Suar, straightening his blade. 'No robber am I, but a mere poetaster.'

'Who are you then?' asked the shorter man. Like Suar he spoke the bastard Hesperian of the ports of the Western Ocean, but with a strange spitting accent.

'I am Suar Peial of Amferé, by trade a singer of sweet songs. And you, good sir?'

The man made some curious sounds in his throat, as if he were imitating the growl of a dog.

'What said you?' asked Suar.

'I said my name was Ghw Gleokh. I suppose I should thank you for rescuing me.'

'Your eloquence overwhelms me. Are you a stranger?'

'That I am,' said Ghw Gleokh. 'Help me bind up these cuts.' As Suar bandaged Ghw's two slight wounds the latter inquired: 'Could you tell me where in Kernê one can buy a drop of wine wherewith to wash down one's bread?'

Suar said: 'I was on my way to Derende's tavern to ply my trade. I have no objection to your coming along.'

As he spoke, Suar wiped his blade on the clothing of the nearest corpse, sheathed it, and turned away. He picked up his cloak and the bundles wrapped therein and resumed his course. Ghw Gleokh trotted after him with the broadsword of the dead swordsman, for he had none of his own.

Suar walked steadily to Derende's tavern and shouldered his way around the leather curtain that served as a door. He had to duck to avoid hitting his head on the top of the door-frame, for he came from Poseidonis across the western seas where six and a half feet was not unusual stature. A central hearth-fire crackled and snapped, its glow picking out faces bearded and faces bare and its smoke forming a blue pall that crept sluggishly out the hole in the roof. It was a small fire, for Kernê never got really cold.

Suar threaded his way among the crowded benches, nodded to a couple of acquaintances, and eased his bundles on to Derende's serving counter. One was a battered old lyre; the other a provision-bag of coarse sacking which smelled strongly of sea-food, even above the many odors of the inn.

'Oh, it's the poet,' said Derende, pushing his huge paunch up against the other side of the counter. 'Well, vagabond?'

'Well indeed, mine host!' cried Suar. 'I bring you, to cook for my supper, the very queen of sea-creatures; the pearl among fish. Behold!'

He loosened the draw-string of the provision-bag and dumped out upon the counter a very large octopus. Ghw, who had been crowding behind him to see, leaped back with a hoarse cry.

'Gods!' he cried. 'That is the world's monster for fair! Are you sure it is dead?'

'Quite sure,' said Suar, grinning.

'No doubt you stole it from some poor fisherman,' growled Derende.

'How the world misjudges an artist!' said Suar. 'If I told you I had gotten it honestly you wouldn't believe me, so why should I argue? In any case, cook it up properly with olive-oil and a few greens, and serve it up with a skin of the best green wine of Zhysk.'

Derende began to gather up the octopus. 'The greens and the oil you may have in return for your croaking, but any wine you will have to pay for.'

'Alas! I had some trade-metal earlier today, but I got into a game of knuck-lebones. If you would let me have credit until I have sung and passed my scrip ...'

Derende shook his head. 'In that case barley-beer will do for the likes of you.'

'Lyr's barnacles!' exclaimed Suar. 'How do you expect me to sing on that bilgewater?' He gestured towards the rest of the room. 'You don't suppose all these people have crowded in here for love of your bitter beer and sour face, do you? They came to hear me. Who fills your stinking hovel night after night?'

'You heard me,' said Derende. 'Beer it shall be, or take your squawk else-where. I'll get in a girl; some bouncing bosomy wench who'll not only sing 'em but also —'

Ghw Gleokh stepped up and laid on the counter a small copper wedge, shaped like an ax-head in miniature and stamped with the flying-fish of Kernê.

'Here,' he said in his weird accent. 'Give us a sack of wine.'

'That's more the spirit,' said Suar. 'Master Derende, you old tub of lard, have you seen my friend Midawan the smith?'

'Not tonight,' said Derende, lugging out a leather bottle and a couple of tarred leather drinking-jacks.

'He'll be in later, no doubt,' said Suar. 'What's news?'

Derende replied: 'The Senate has hired a new wizard, a Tartessian named Barik.'

'What happened to the old one?'

'They had him impaled because of that sandstorm.'

'What is this?' asked Ghw with interest.

Derende explained: 'He conjured up a sandstorm to overwhelm a camel-raid of desert-dwelling Lixitans, but by misdirection buried a score of our own warriors instead. What news have you, Suar?'

'Oh, young Okkozen, the son of Bulkajmi the Consul, was arrested for driving his chariot recklessly while drunk. Because of his connections the magistrate let him off with an admonition. And Geddel the trader has been murdered in the Atlantean Mountains by a witch whom he tried to cheat out of her price for death-charms.' Suar turned to his companion. 'Good Ghw, let's find a seat, if we have to pitch one of these greasy Kerneans out on his arse. You shall share my beautiful octopus while I in return munch a piece of your bread.'

'The bread you may have, because of my debt to you,' said Ghw sourly, 'but red-hot sword-blades would not force me to eat a piece of that hideous sea-monster.'

'The bigger fool you.' Suar, looking over the heads of the throng, pointed. 'I see a bench as vacant as my purse. Come on.'

The bench was one of two flanking a corner table. Two men occupied the bench opposite with their backs against the wall, black cloaks drawn up over their heads. At first Suar took them for Euskerians because of the cloaks, but as he sat down he became aware of an indefinable alienness about them. The younger and larger one, with the pimples, ate bread and cheese while the older and smaller did not eat but inhaled the pungent smoke that rose from a tiny brazier on the table in front of him. They paid no attention to the new arrivals.

Suar rolled up his cloak and stuffed it under the bench, revealing that under it he wore the striped kilt of Poseidonis and an old shirt of what had been fine-grade wool, now much patched and mended. He pushed in to the wallward end of the bench, facing the small black-clad stranger, while Ghw likewise disposed of his cloak and took the other end. Suar poured out mugs of wine while Ghw went to work with his knife on the loaf of barley-bread he carried, now slightly soggy from the rain. Presently they were both munching and gulping. Suar, his mouth full, asked:

'My dear old comrade, what's that curious thing with which you were smiting the thieves, like Zormé belaboring the Bruthonians? It looks like nothing I ever saw.'

Ghw, a short man with reddish hair and arms of simian length, gave his companion a blank stare. 'That is something I do not discuss,' he growled.

Suar shrugged. 'Be a louse, then.' He twanged the strings of his lyre and spoke to the small man across the table:

'Your pardon, sir, but that smoke does not impress me as a very nourishing diet. If you would like a piece of the finest octopus salad in Kernê, I shall be pleased to spare you a portion when it arrives, for the monster is too large for even my ample capacity.'

The man looked up at last, his pupils mere dots in the flickering glow of the rush-light that stood in a little bronze holder in the middle of the table. He said:

'Your intentions are meritorious, for which you shall receive credit in the ledgers of the gods. But know, mortal, that when the soul is properly fed the body takes care of itself.'

'Mortal yourself,' said Suar. 'It appears, then, that I shall have to eat the whole thing —'

'Not so,' said a new voice. 'I have brought it over to share it with you.'

A dark man of medium height and enormous brawn, with somewhat Negroid hair and features, stood at the end of the table holding a great wooden platter on which was heaped up a pile of steaming pieces of cooked octopus. 'Move that light, old giraffe, and change places with this red-haired one.'

He slid the platter down the table, pulled up a stool, and planked down a slab of cheese, a half-loaf of bread, and a bag of jujubes as his contribution to the meal.

'No,' said Suar. 'This red-haired one is my friend, by virtue of my having just saved his life.' Suar gave a slightly inflated account of the battle in the alley, adding: 'His name is Ghw Gleokh, if you will believe it. If you can't say it, just clear your throat and you will come close enough. I should guess he hails from one of the barbarous and bloody Keltic tribes. Is that right, Ghw?'

'All but the part about our being barbarians. I am a Galathan. Who is this man?'

'My old friend Midawan the armorer,' said Suar. 'He eats bronze spear-heads for breakfast, and comes from Tegrazen, to the south, which is on the borders of Blackland. Though of partly Black descent he swears he has never tasted human flesh. I twit him about it when he vexes me.'

'Some day you will twit me once too often,' said Midawan, sitting down on the stool at the end of the table, 'and I'll tie that swan's neck of yours in a knot. Here, Galathan, have a tentacle!'

'Take that slimy sea-creature away!' said Ghw. 'Is there no such thing as an honest roast in Kernê?'

'Certainly,' said Suar, 'for the rich. We common folk deem ourselves lucky to taste one on the Feast of Korb. It was not so in my homeland, where we gorged on bison steaks every day. And speaking of hunting, is that mysterious bronze bar of yours some sort of weapon or hunting-implement?'

Ghw Gleokh had now drunk enough wine to have mellowed. He belched loudly and said:

'You might say so; you might say so. It is in fact a magical tool of the highest power. When properly used neither man nor beast can stand before it.'

At this point the larger and younger of the cloaked men across the table spoke: 'Ha, hear the barbarian brag!'

Ghw stiffened. 'Sir, I do not know you, but I do not let riffraff speak to me in that manner.'

'As to that,' said the cloaked one, 'I am Qahura, apprentice magician, and this is my master Semkaf. We come from the city of Typhon in the land of Setesh, whose magic is as far beyond yours as yours is beyond the mud-pies of children.'

'Quiet, fool,' muttered the older magician, the one identified as Semkaf.

'But master, it is not meet that these savages should taunt and flout us. They must be taught a lesson.'

'If there is any teaching to be done,' said Ghw loudly, 'I shall do it. I am an initiate druid of the Galatha, known to all, whereas I have never heard of your Typhon and doubt it exists.'

Qahura said: 'Indeed it exists, as you would learn soon enough did you visit us and were flayed upon our sacrificial altars. Typhon rises in black and purple from the mystic margins of the Sea of Thesh, amid the towering pyramidal tombs of kings who resigned in splendor over Setesh when mighty Torrutseish was but a village and golden Kernê but a vacant stretch of beach. No man living knows the full tale of Typhon's history, or the convolutions of its streets and secret passageways, or the hoarded treasure of its kings, or the hidden powers of its wizards. As for you,' sneered the apprentice, 'if you are a druid, where are your white robe and crown of mistletoe? What are doing in Kernê?'

'Oh, that, my bombastic young friend, is a matter of tribal politics. Our arch-druid died suddenly and some were evil-minded enough to say I had stabbed him.'

Qahura said: 'His vaunted druidic magic was evidently not able to turn knife-blades. Can you do anything besides read the weather signs?'

'All that you can do, I can do, and much besides. For instance, would you see the heroes of the Galatha?'

Without awaiting an answer Ghw swept his hand back and forth across the table, muttering a spell. At once a score of little figures, about the size of a man's thumb, appeared on the table, some afoot, some mounted, and some in scythe-wheeled chariots. Some wore barbarian trews while others were naked and painted in bizarre patterns. They darted about, their cries sounding in Suar's ears like the buzzing of gnats. A couple began to fight, lunging and slashing with swords the size of splinters.

'Ha!' said Qahura. 'Dainty little mannikins, but one of the sacred cats of Setesh would make short work of them.'

He cast a spell in his turn, whereupon a large yellow cat appeared upon the table. It pounced on a miniature Galathan and began to worry it like a mouse. With a gesture Ghw swept the other heroes into nothingness, but the cat continued to bait its victim.

'All that you can do I can do, and better,' said Ghw. 'If you conjure up a familiar in the form of a cat, I will fetch one in that of a wolf, and we shall see —'

'Gentlemen!' said Suar, laying a hand on Ghw's arm. 'Before this competition works up to lions and mammoths, consider that Derende's tavern is no place for fights between such creatures. They would squash us and the other customers like bugs in their struggles. Moreover I haven't yet sung my songs and passed my wallet. I urge that you wait until the weather clears and repair to an open field outside the walls, and then have at each other with your entire demonic retinues. The Kerneans would love the sport.'

'There is something in what you say, poet,' said Qahura. 'Still, let it be understood that we of Setesh have the utmost contempt for any spells that this unfrocked druid could bring into action. For my master Semkaf commands the great serpent Apepis itself, which could swallow Master Ghw and all his minions at one gulp.'

'I fear it not,' said Ghw, reaching under the bench. 'Here is the strongest spell of all. I have but to point it at you or any of your monsters and they will fall dead as though blasted by a levin-bolt.'

He held up the object with which he had been defending himself against the robbers: a two-foot bronze tube open at one end and closed at the other, and fastened by bronze straps to a piece of carved wood extending beyond the closed end and terminating in a squared-off butt.

The elder Seteshan roused himself from his stupor again. 'That is interesting, Galathan,' he said. 'While I am all Qahura says and more, never have I seen a wand like that. How does it work?'

Ghw took a big gulp of wine, hiccupped, and fumbled in his scrip. He brought out a fistful of a dark granular substance and poured it down the open end of the tube.

'One inserts this magical powder thus,' he said. 'Then one drops this leaden ball, molded to fit loosely into the tube, down upon the powder – thus. One thrusts down a wad of rag to hold the ball in place – thus. One sprinkles a little of the powder in at this small hole – thus. Then one lights the powder with any convenient flame, and with a mighty flash and thunderclap the ball is driven through any object standing in the way. Fear not; I value the stuff too highly to waste it in mere demonstration before a pair of degenerate mountebanks.'

'Why didn't you use it on the thieves?' asked Suar.

'Because it was not charged, and even if it had been I had no fire wherewith to set it off.'

The pin-points of Semkaf's eyes stared unwinkingly at the contraption. 'And what,' he purred, 'is the composition of the powder?'

Ghw wagged his head with drunken solemnity. 'That you shall never learn from me! It was confided to me by our lamented archdruid just before his mischance. When he lay dying from the cut he had unwittingly given himself he bequeathed to me the device and all its secrets.'

Midawan the smith, who hitherto had been too busy eating to take part in the conversation, spoke up: 'I don't like your magical device, stranger. With power enough behind that ball it would pierce my strongest shield or breastplate. Then where would my trade be? At the bottom of the ocean.'

'High time, too,' said Suar. 'With these improvements in armor the fine old art of fence is dying out. Now that men fight laden like lobsters with bronze plates and scales, they prefer to the rapier these clumsy broadswords to batter through the foe's defense. Mere wood-cutter's strokes, chop-chop.'

'Times change, and one must change with them,' said Midawan.

'True, but that also applies to you,' said Suar. 'So you had better start working up a line of bronze lanterns and mirrors against the day when these things will have swept armor off the battlefield.'

Semkaf leaned forward towards Ghw Gleokh. 'I wish your device, mortal. Give it to me.'

'Why, you insolent knave!' replied Ghw. 'Are you mad? Among the Galatha we slay men for less.'

'Gentlemen!' said Suar. 'Not here, pray! Or at least wait until I finish giving them the *Song of Vrir* and have collected my bounty. I'll rend your hearts with emotion …' He hastily tuned his lyre.

Semkaf said: 'What are your songs to me? I have no mortal emotions. I wish —'

'So you're like these greedy Kernean swine?' said Suar. 'No appreciation of the arts; all they care for is trade-metal. Anyway the device will do you no good without the formula for the powder.'

'I can learn that through my arts at my leisure,' said Semkaf. 'Come, friend Ghw, I offer you in return that which is of the very highest value to you.'

'And what is that, buffoon?' said Ghw.

'Only your life.'

Ghw spat across the table, and followed this gesture by picking up his blackjack and throwing the lees of his wine into the Seteshan's face. 'That for you!'

Semkaf wiped his narrow face with the edge of his cloak and turned his hawk-like head towards his apprentice, murmuring: 'These savages weary me. Slay them, Qahura.'

Qahura wetted a finger in the spilt wine, drew a symbol on the table, and began to incant. Before the first sentence in the unknown tongue had rolled out, however, Ghw Gleokh raised the tube device in his right hand and set the wooden stock against his shoulder, so that the open end of the tube pointed towards Qahura's chest. With his left hand he picked up the rush-light and applied the flame to the little hole in the top of the tube.

There was a fizz, and a plume of yellow flame and sparks shot up from the hole. Almost instantly the room rocked to the crash of a tremendous explosion. Flame and smoke vomited out from the open end of the tube, hiding Qahura from view.

While the room still rang with the echoes of the report, every other face in the tavern turned towards Suar's table. Then there were hoarse yells and the clatter of overturning tables and benches as the rest of the customers fought to get out, trampling one another in their panic. The cat conjured up by Qahura had vanished at the instant of the explosion. Suar coughed at the smell of burnt sulfur.

As the smoke cleared, Qahura, his eyelids drooping and his mouth hanging slackly open, fell forward across the table and lay with his smoke-blackened face in the spilt wine. Over his body Semkaf and Ghw stared at one another. Ghw had dropped the tube and snatched up the broadsword that he had taken from the thief, but now he seemed to be struggling in the grip of some strange paralysis. Suar tried to rise, but found that he had gotten his legs entangled with the bench and with his cloak and his rapier.

'I underestimated you,' said Semkaf, slipping a ring of reptilian form off his finger and making mystical motions with it. '*Antif maa-yb, 'oth-m-hru, Apepite!*'

Suar became aware of a horrid reptilian stench and the dry slither of scales. He saw nothing, but on his right hand Midawan the smith recoiled as from an unseen contact and Ghw Gleokh screamed an unearthly shriek. Something caught hold of the Galathan and dragged him off his bench to the floor. Suar, still trying to gain his feet, was astonished to observe that the ex-druid's right arm had vanished up to the shoulder.

The other customers had now nearly all crowded out through every aperture in the building.

Midawan in one hulking motion drew a big broad knife from his belt and vaulted over the table diagonally from where he sat at the end, coming down almost in Suar's lap in the place where Ghw had sat. As he alighted his right arm lashed out and drove the knife into Semkaf's chest, cutting into the middle of another sentence of anathema and sorcerous doom.

On the floor, Ghw was undergoing strange convulsions, as if some immense and invisible snake were squeezing him to death. His body bent and thrashed; blood spurted and bones cracked like sticks.

Suar got untangled from his gear, stepped back over the bench, and started for the door. He and Midawan were the last persons in the room except for the three magicians. As Suar ran for the door, trailing his cloak and hugging his precious lyre, he paused to look back.

Semkaf now lay forward face-down across the table like his apprentice beside him. On the floor Ghw Gleokh, bloody and distorted, had ceased to flop and writhe. He lay quietly, but now his head and most of his other arm had also vanished. In that last glance Suar saw the zone of invisibility slip down until only the lower half of Ghw's body and his legs were visible. Just as if one were watching a frog being swallowed head-first by an invisible snake ...

Outside, Suar and Midawan raced three blocks through the wet along Ocean Street before stopping to breathe. Suar asked:

'Why did you kill Semkaf? It wasn't really our quarrel.'

'Didn't you hear him tell Qahura to slay the lot of us? These he-witches are not nice in dealing out their dooms.'

'How were you able to do it when Ghw was not?'

'I really do not know. I suppose because I was careful not to look him in the eye, and perhaps he was weak from the effects of that drug he was inhaling; the rose-of-death if I know the smell.'

'But now his private fiend is loose without a master to banish it back to its own world!'

Midawan shrugged. 'Those things usually go back of their own accord, I'm told. If we hear that Apepis is still slithering around town tomorrow we can go off to visit my cousins in Tegrazen. Besides, Semkaf would have learned the secrets of the thunder-tube, and if the thing had come into general use that would have been bad for my trade.'

Suar Peial became aware that Midawan was carrying the tube-device in question. As he spoke, the smith threw the thing gyrating far out into the bay. Suar heard a faint splash as it struck the water invisibly in the dark.

'*Hé!*' said Suar. 'If you didn't want it, I could have sold the bronze for the price of several meals. As I had no chance to sing tonight, Lyr only knows when I shall eat again, let alone drink a skin of wine or bounce a wench.'

'Such things are better out of reach,' said Midawan. 'And I can stake you to a meal or two. Not that it really worries me, you understand. We should have to improve our craft, no doubt; but no magical toy like that will ever put us out of business. Aye, never shall the armorer's proud trade perish!'

THE OWL AND THE APE

Jarra was always promising to complete Gezun Lorska's education for him and never getting around to it. This was one of the times:

'… so if you'll come into the garden after the supper-hour, Gezun, I'll show you some of the singular things one of Father's sailors taught me …'

Gezun said: 'Meseems I've heard all that before.' He grasped her wrist. 'I suspect that what you really yearn for, my lass —'

'My goodness, Gezun!' she said. 'Aren't you strong! Are you *sure* you're only fourteen?'

'Quite certain.' (Actually, he thought that his fourteenth birthday was yet some days off. In the year since he had been sold to Sancheth Sar he had somewhat lost track of time, and moreover the calendar used here in Gadaira differed from that of his native Lorsk. Still, her question had cogency, for a fourteen-year-old Pusadian like Gezun might well be as tall as a mature Euskerian.)

'As I was saying,' he continued, 'I'm a peaceable wight, and don't like to slay folk save those who wantonly offend me. But I take not teasing kindly, and am minded to drag you back into this fabulous garden of yours —'

'Not *now!*' she squeaked. 'Mother's hanging out the —'

'*Gezun! Gezun Lorska!*' came the familiar caw of Sancheth Sar. 'Boy! Hither, forthwith!'

Gezun dropped Jarra's wrist. 'Run along, Jarra; this is men's business.'

He stuck his thumbs into the belt of his kilt and ambled around to the front of Sancheth's house, fast enough to avoid serious trouble with his owner but not so fast as to give the old wizard exaggerated ideas of his submissiveness. He was secretly grateful to Sancheth for rescuing him from what might, as a result of his own youthful ignorance, have developed into an embarrassing situation. What if Jarra had said 'Yes'?

'You take long enough, you young bull-mammoth,' said Sancheth Sar, leaning on his stick and glaring down his hawk's nose. Though in former years the sorcerer had stood a good span taller than Gezun did now, age had bowed him until the difference was no longer great.

'Yessir sorrysir.'

'When you apologize, speak distinctly and run not all your words together; else the whole effect be lost.' The sorcerer blew his nose upon his mystic robe and continued: 'Where was I? Ah, yes, the auction.'

'What auction, Master?'

'Why, lout, the auction of Dauskezh Van, what else? But I forget; I've not avised you thereof. Dauskezh, wishing to retire from active practice of the sorcerous and thaumaturgic arts, has —'

'Who's Dauskezh Van?'

'Such ignorance! He's the greatest, the wisest, the profoundest magician ever to practice in the Tartessian Empire. But now, despite all that longevity and rejuvenation spells can do, age claims him for its hoary own. Where was I?'

'You were telling me about the auction.'

'So I was. Well, wishing to retire from practice and spend the balance of his life in peace, he's selling off all his magical talismans, tokens, sigils, relics, and other accessories. I was to have departed to wend my way to his cave on Tadhik Mountain in rocky Dzen beginning on the morrow, but now that Nikurteu has sent this cursed tisick upon me I must remain at home to nurse my infirmities.' He sneezed.

'You mean you wish *me* to go to Dzen in your stead?' cried Gezun, torn between excitement and apprehension.

'With admirable promptitude you grasp my meaning ere I've formulated it in words. Aye, boy, the task is yours to dare and do.'

'What do you wish me to seek to buy? Anything that seems good?'

'By no means! But one particular item, namely: the Hordhun Manuscript.'

'What's that?' said Gezun.

'As the name implies, a set of waxen sheets with pictographs inscribed thereon.'

'I mean, what's in it?'

'Spells.'

'What sort of spells?'

'Curse you for a nosey quidnunc! But then, perhaps indeed you ought to know, that you shall watch well where you place those monstrous feet of yours. As you're no doubt aware, your land of Poseidonis is slowly, in the course of many earthquakes, sinking beneath the waters of the Western Sea.'

'So I've heard. It's said that one can take a boat in the harbor of Amferé on a calm day and through the water see the ruins of former edifices, once on dry land but now paving the harbor-bottom.'

'Just so. My reckonings show that in three thousand years there'll be nought left of Pusâd save chains of islands, now the tops of mountains.'

'What difference does it make what happens thousands of years hence?'

'To you none, stripling, but kings must take a view that's longer than the span of their own petty lifetimes – at least if they'd rise above the level of mere crowned beasts – and it is with kings I'd deal. The Hordhun Manuscript, 'tis rumored, harbors spells of such puissance that they'll either halt or speed this continental settling. With that in my hands, do you see in what an advantageous site I'd be respecting the Pusadian kinglets?'

'I see. Do these spells really work?'

'That I know not; but even if they don't, they'll furnish a lever wherewith the pry open the bulging coffers of Lorsk and Parsk and the rest.'

'Then I saddle up Dostaen tomorrow, ride to Dauskezh's cave, and out-bid our rivals when this work comes up?'

'Yes, but it's not quite so simple. For this auction entails two unique attributes. First, you'll not see the faces of your fellow-bidders, because 'tis one of Dauskezh's crotchets to make all who'd attend his auction wear masks resembling the visages of animals.'

'Do I don such a mask here?' Gezun had an unpleasant mental picture of himself wearing the head of a leopard or an ibex and jogging through Gadaira on his mule, to the uproarious mirth of his fellow-striplings.

'Nay; Dauskezh will furnish them on your arrival, assigning to each the semblance of the beast his hoary fancy thinks that bidder most in soul and character resembles. And that fact provides you with your only clue to the second difficulty, to wit: that neither will the items to be sold be openly displayed, but be identified by number merely.'

'What japery! How shall I know the Hordhun Manuscript when it's offered?'

''Tis the conceit of Dauskezh that a true magician can perceive without being told; and in sooth, were I there, I'd no doubt contrive to make head against his quillets. Lacking such skills, you must devise another means. Now, there's no doubt that Nikurteu Balya, may the gods blast his leprous soul, is also bent upon procurement of this manuscript. And if you rate the wizards of Tartessia in order of intelligence, Dauskezh stands first, myself second, and Nikurteu third. It follows that of all who come in masks to this event, Nikurteu'll be the most sagacious. Therefore you should know him by his mask, which I presume will be that of an owl since that bird is universally conceded to be the wisest of the brute kingdom. And when you perceive that he displays unwonted interest in some item, you may infer that that's the manuscript in question, and bid the limit.'

'But,' said Gezun Lorska, 'what's to hinder this same Nikurteu from casting on me some baneful spell that shall strike me immobile or speechless till the bidding be completed?'

'Oh, a trifle, a trifle that had slipped my old mind. I'll put on you a counter-spell that should endure till your return, so that such unnatural assaults shall rebound and recoil upon the sender.'

'Why not lend me the ring of star-metal?'

Gezun indicated the band of metal, like silver but duller, that encircled the finger of Sancheth Sar. What the metal was none knew, save that it was harder than the toughest bronze, and was said to have come from a stone that fell from the sky. The stone itself had passed through many hands – those of

King Awoqqas of Belem and Prince Vakar of Lorsk among others – and the material was so effective as a repellant for all sorts of spells and spirits, that Gezun's master had to doff it before he could undertake any magical operation himself.

'Heh-heh, and have you defy my commands with impunity, you young coystril? Not likely!' said Sancheth.

'Huh. You don't care what becomes of me, it seems, but only for your art. Some day I'll slay myself in sheer despite.'

'Oh, come now ... I'll tell you. You've been a good boy, though betimes exasperating; in recognition whereof I'll make you a bargain. I have another of these rings, raped from the same sky-stone, and if you procure this manuscript despite all perils, I'll give you this spare ring to keep.'

Gezun Lorska grinned under his mop of black Pusadian curls. 'I'll fetch your zany writing, Master, or perish in the trying! You'll faithfully feed my beasts whilst I'm gone?'

'Aye; though I know not why I submit to having my house turned into a menagerie. Go now, fetch our supper, for your tomorrow commences ere dawn.'

Gezun rode his mule a week down the coast, and then for three days into the deep defiles and gloomy mountains of the haunted peninsula of Dzen, with plenty of time to think.

He wondered, for instance, at his master's plan to extort treasure from the kinglets of Poseidonis by means of the Hordhun Manuscript and its alleged spells. These kinglets included his own former sovereign, Vuar the Capricious of Lorsk. Now, whither lay this primary duty, towards King Vuar or towards Sancheth Sar? This was his first real chance to ponder such problems since his purchase from the pack of Aremorian pirates a year before. Ever since he had been kidnapped while exploring his family's estate on the supposedly safe western shores of Lorsk he had lived in too constant a ferment of sudden terrors and new experience to have time to think.

He was hazy as to what rights a slave had. If he ran away but was recaptured before leaving the confines of the Tartessian Empire, he knew he'd be forcibly returned to Sancheth's custody, minus an ear as a reminder. On the other hand if he crossed the Sirenian Sea to Poseidonis he would, he thought, be safe; and once in Lorsk his family's influence could interpose an army between him and any pursuers.

Unfortunately there lay that somber sea between himself and home, and passage would not easily be arranged for a fourteen-year-old boy with a slave-brand on his hand.

And how eager was he to escape, really? To him enslavement was one of the normal risks of life, and he would no more have thought of attacking the institution as a whole merely because it had caught him in its toils than he would have thought of proposing a law against dying.

All things considered, he had gotten off rather well. Sancheth had not inflicted on him any mutilation besides the pirates' brand, and had, in his erratic and absent-minded way, treated him kindly enough, so that Gezun had become warily fond of the old man. Or as fond as any adolescent normally becomes of an adult master. His real friends were those of his own age in Gadaira, whom he dominated partly by a certain amiable ingenuity in plotting forays against the common enemy, the adult world; partly by the glamor of his magical apprenticeship; and partly by sheer size.

If he continued to work with reasonable fidelity for this strange master, he thought, he might even look forward to stepping into the wizard's shoes some day. Such a career might well provide more fun and glory than life as a petty lordling on the bison-swarming plains of windy Lorsk. Perhaps he could set up headquarters in lordly Torrutseish, whence Sancheth had originally come. Maybe he could win a daughter of the king of Tartessia to concubine; become vizier, or even king himself ...

Another thought made him grin: He certainly wouldn't leave Gadaira until he had had a showdown with Jarra on that matter of completing his education.

When the mountains of Dzen had grown so tall that they seemed to lean over and glower down upon him, Gezun came to Mount Tadhik and the cave of Dauskezh Van, which opened out into a natural amphitheater among the crags. A small almost-human being came up and took Gezun's mule and led it to where other beasts of burden were tethered, then returned to Gezun. It laid a finger on its lips and led him into the mouth of the cave, picking up a small copper oil-lamp whose flame cast a meager yellow glow into the dark.

'You were almost too late,' it whispered, tugging Gezun along the rocky corridor. 'Wait here.'

It disappeared into a side-cave or room and came out again with a curious object: a hollow head-mask in the form of a lamb's head. Gezun remembered his master's warning about Dauskezh's custom of making the bidders don masks that symbolized their respective natures, and felt anger stir within him.

'Why you —' he began, but just then the creature popped the object over his head and tied it in place with a draw-string before he could avert the event.

Gezun's anger subsided and he allowed himself a chuckle. Let them think him a lamb; the reputation of being a simpleton might be an asset to a man – provided he were not one in fact.

Then the being led him swiftly further back into the labyrinth of caves where Dauskezh made his home. Here and there the little lamp showed where the wizard and his helpers had improved the natural formations for their own conveniences, enlarging a minor vug to serve as a storage space or shoring up a precarious bit of cave-roof with planks and props. Then they entered a large cavern lit by several lamps, in which were gathered Gezun's fellow-bidders, seated on the swept stone floor in concentric crescents and wrapped in the black mantles of the Euskerian peoples.

As the being pushed Gezun into a vacant place in the last row, most of the heads of the earlier arrivals turned towards him, exhibiting, not human faces, but more animal-masks. Through the eye-holes in his mask he saw a horse, a lion, an aurochs, a fallow-deer, a rhinoceros, a badger – even one grotesque simulacrum in minature of a mammoth's head, complete with curling tusks and dangling trunk.

By the lamplight he could discern along the walls row after row of dim-lit painting of animals, executed in a lively and life-like though archaic style. There were mammoths and bison and the giant deer now found only in savage Ierarné. This, then, must be one of the caves of which the legends of Poseidonis told, where his forebears had lived scores of centuries earlier, before the gods had taught men the copper-smelting art – before the short sharpbrowed Euskerians had driven the Pusadians across the Sirenian Sea and made all of Tartessia theirs. His people, though individually larger than the Euskerians by the length of a foot, had been too much absorbed in their art, their songs, their totemistic religion, and their intertribal feuds to resist these taciturn and tenacious newcomers, who swarmed into the land like hornets, bringing a new and deadly sting: the bow and arrow.

Now the Pusadians on their sea-girt land painted new pictures and dreamed dreams of returning to their homeland. The animals on the wall reminded Gezun that he was a Pusadian too, and that his real name was Döpueng Shysh, not this servile cognomen his master had imposed upon him as easier for Euskerian vocal organs to pronounce than the vowels of Poseidonis. Gezun wondered whether he could, by taking Sancheth's place and becoming the greatest wizard in the Tartessian Empire, expedite this homecoming before all of Poseidonis sank beneath the Western Sea.

But right now he had to pick Nikurteu Balya out of the crowd without a face to go by. Sancheth had hinted that Nikurteu, for his sagacity, might be honored with an owl's head. Gezun, however, knew a lot about animals. He had kept as a pet practically everything short of a bison, both home in Poseidonis and here in Tartessia, and had given Sancheth a terrific turn by producing a pair of snakes at supper. Unknown on Poseidonis, these reptiles had fascinated Gezun's artistic eye by their grace, and fortunately they were not of a venomous species.

Gezun knew that the owl, for all its sage appearance, was no more intelligent than any other bird – if anything rather less so.

He peered through the crowd, picking out a leopard, a hyena, a bear, a wolverine, a wild ass, and a monkey. He had also had to do with monkeys, and knew something of their trickiness and resource. It seemed to him that if Dauskezh were as wise as he was alleged to be, and were going to choose an animal to symbolize the character of Nikurteu, he could hardly select a more suitable symbol than the monkey.

Well, he'd be taking a chance either way, so he might as well take it his way as another's. The ape it should be.

Leather curtains rustled and Dauskezh Van came in. He was even older than Sancheth Sar, and in the dim light he seemed to Gezun to be already dead and reanimated by some not altogether successful witchery.

'Bids on One,' whispered Dauskezh.

'Fourteen nasses of gold,' responded a wizard with the head of a chamois.

'Fifteen,' said a beaver.

'Sixteen,' said the owl.

Gezun Lorska felt an urge to jump to the conclusion that the owl was Nikurteu after all, and begin bidding against him. He restrained himself, bearing in mind that he had reached his decision dispassionately, uninfluenced by the excitement of the moment, and had better stick to it.

Item Number One went to the chamois and Two came up. It was a very dull business, and Gezun almost fell asleep when a bid on Number Twenty-three from the direction of the monkey brought him sharply out of his doze.

'Twelve nasses,' said the monkey.

'Fifteen,' said Gezun, heart pounding.

'Twenty.'

'Twenty-five,' said Gezun, thankful now that Sancheth had forced him to learn simple sums.

They went on up in jumps of five until they neared fifty, Sancheth's limit. It was a formidable price; not only for Sancheth, but also, apparently, for his rival, for the monkey-head began slowing down as they neared it.

'Forty-eight,' said the monkey.

'Forty-nine,' said Gezun.

'Forty-nine and a half.'

'Fifty.'

Now Gezun waited, feeling as though his heart would burst through his chest. All the monkey had to do was add another fraction of a nas, no matter how small, and take the item …

'Sold!' croaked Dauskezh. 'Item Number Twenty-four …'

Gezun relaxed, letting his breath out – then caught it again as another fear fingered his windpipe. Suppose he had been mistaken and the ape was not Nikurteu after all? Or suppose Number Twenty-three were not the Hordhun Manuscript?

It would all come out in due time. If he had gone astray he could at best expect a beating from Sancheth – not that he held Sancheth's beatings in much awe, for the old wizard no longer had the strength even to raise a welt on Gezun's tough hide. More serious was the prospect of having Sancheth cast upon him some bothersome curse, like muteness or inability to touch water – but then, he now carried a protective spell from Sancheth himself, and by the time it wore off, the sorcerer would have simmered down and forgotten his costly error.

Item Thirty proved the last of the lot. The near-human thing touched Gezun and beckoned while the others kept their places. Gezun inferred that under Dauskezh's quaint rules the bidders were allowed to depart at intervals only, so as not to see each other's faces. He, being the last to arrive, would go first.

So it proved. The being stopped Gezun at the anteroom, took the lamb's head from him, and handed him a cylindrical package wrapped in lambskin and tied with a string of esparto grass. In return Gezun handed over the entire contents of the bag of golden rings and wedges which Sancheth had sent with him. The being weighed the gold with care before letting Gezun go.

Once free, Gezun wasted no time but rode off on Dostaen at once, chewing a great chunk of barley-bread from his scrip.

The sun was sending a last red ray through a notch in the mountains of Dzen, and Gezun Lorska was lolling on his mule and humming a song of Poseidonis, when two men sprang out from behind the rocks. One, who carried a big bronze sword, seized Dostaen's bridle; the other made at Gezun with a hunting-spear.

As the man with the spear drew it back for a stab, Gezun tumbled off his mule's back, so that the bronze spearhead darted like a snake's tongue through the empty space where Gezun had just been. He scrambled to his feet on the leeward side of the mule and made off up the nearest slope as fast as he could.

Gezun's ear caught a fragment of speech between the men: something like '... you hold the mule whilst I ...' A glance showed the spearman coming after him, bounding with great leaps from rock to rock, his black cloak flapping like bat's wings. Though more agile than the man, Gezun had a horrid feeling that the fellow would run him down in the long run. And he had nothing but a modest bronze knife to fight with.

He ran on anyway. The slope narrowed to a tongue of land as Gezun neared the summit of a small hill which on the far side dropped away in sheer precipices. A quick look showed no way down on that side. He was cornered.

The panting breaths of the pursuer came louder and louder to Gezun's ears; any second the man would appear. The knife would be of little use. So would his sandals. His only other possessions at the moment were the Hordhun Manuscript (if such it was), his kilt, and the broad leather belt that held the kilt in place. His cloak he had shed at the start of the chase. The bronze buckle on the end of the belt might prove useful …

A jumble of rocks lay about the hilltop; one nearly the size of his head and of curious elongated shape, like an enlarged fingerbone. Gezun whipped off his belt, letting his kilt fall; made a loop of his belt, and slipped the loop over the narrow place in the middle of the stone.

When the spearman topped the rise, Gezun rushed at him, screeching in hope of disconcerting him. First he threw the rolled-up kilt at the man's face. The man dodged, but his attention was distracted long enough for Gezun to step in close, whirling the stone around his head on the end of the belt-loop. The spearman was scarcely taller than he was, and the slope gave Gezun some slight advantage.

The stone struck the side of the man's head with a solid sound of crunching bone, and the man fell sidewise across his dropped spear. Gezun made sure the fellow was dead by cutting his throat; then pondered. He could not press his luck too far. The other man, he was sure, would recognize him the minute he appeared, and would be ready to meet him with sword and rolled-up cloak. Craft was indicated.

Gezun Lorska therefore donned the dead man's clothes, pulling the black mantle over his head as these Euskerians did at night. Then, picking up the spear, he swaggered back down the slope. The sun had disappeared.

The swordsman, still holding the mule, looked up as Gezun approached and said: 'Did you get it?'

'Uh-huh,' grunted Gezun, striving to imitate with his changing voice the deeper accents of his victim. When he was close he said:

'Take it.'

But as the swordsman tucked his sword under his left arm and put out his right hand, what Gezun laid on the hand was not the Hordhun Manuscript, but the freshly-severed head of the spearman, which he had been carrying under the cloak.

The swordsman gave a cry of horror and dropped the head with a thud. Gezun whipped up the spear and plunged the point into his foe's thick body. When his young muscles failed to drive it very far in on the first thrust, he shoved on the shaft with all his might, pushing the man back from him.

The man dropped his sword with a clatter and tried to recover it, but another push by Gezun forced him off-balance and he fell. He tried to wrestle the spear-shaft out of his body, but Gezun kept pushing it in. Then he tried to reach Gezun, who was now at the far end of the spear and beyond reach. At last the man threw himself away from Gezun, tearing the spear-shaft out of his grasp.

Gezun danced back as the man rounded on him and pulled the spear out of his side, hobbled back to where he had dropped his sword, picked it up too, and set out after Gezun with a weapon in each hand. Gezun ran – not uphill this time, but down. Behind him the man plowed through the scrub and scrambled over the rocks, cursing by his various gods in a gasping undertone.

The chase went on until Gezun realized that the gasping breath and the muttered curses were no longer keeping up with him. He looked back and saw a dark shape sprawled on the hillside among the boulders.

He scouted cautiously towards it. The man was lying and holding his side, but as Gezun approached he sat up and hurled the spear at him. It was a bad throw, for the spear slewed sidewise in the air and the shaft hit Gezun on the forearm he threw up to ward it off – a bruising knock but not crippling. Gezun picked up the spear and backed as the man tried to rush with his sword. Lacking the strength to make it, the fellow sank down again among the rocks.

Gezun sat down on a boulder and waited warily for the man to weaken further. Darkness deepened; the evening star appeared. The gasping breath became a rattle and then stopped. Gezun rose, bounded around behind the man, and drove the spear into his back to make sure he was dead. He looted the corpse with swift efficiency and found his way back up to the road, where Dostaen placidly munched the scanty herbage.

A few minutes later, wearing his own clothes and carrying the Hordhun Manuscript and the weapons of his late attackers, he sat out again on the way to Gadaira.

'Gezun! Gezun Lorska!' cried a voice.

Gezun recognized it. 'Jarra!' he shouted. 'What on earth are you doing here?' In his excitement his voice slid up into the high boy's range.

She hopped down to the road and caught his leg. 'Oh, right joyful am I that you came! My father brought me on a trading-trip down the coast, and a pack of knaves set upon us and scattered the caravan, though I think my father got away safe. Will you take me back to Gadaira?'

'What think you? Here, catch my hand and hop up behind.'

'Won't you dismount a minute first? So weary am I of wandering these forsaken hills, and you can't go much further tonight in any case.'

'I'll go far enough to put a healthy distance betwixt me and the ghosts of those I sped!'

'You've been manslaying?'

'Merely in self-defense. There were six, but I drove Dostaen at full gallop into the ruck, slew two at the first onset, and put the rest to rout.'

'Marvellous! You shall tell me all about it; but meanwhile dismount. Have you aught to eat? I'm so weak of starvation that without a bite I fear I can go no further.'

'Oh, very well.' Gezun vaulted off. 'But for all these things there is a price, as says the philosopher Goishek.'

Laughing she put her face up to be kissed. Although the light was too dim to discern her features clearly, her Euskerian eyebrows, like a pair of little black sickles, showed against the lighter tone of her skin. She melted into his arms and he felt her ripening young body against his. He kissed her frantically, his pulse pounding.

'There's a place – nearby —' she gasped, 'where – your education might —'

Somewhere an owl hooted. The sound touched off a train of thought in Gezun's mind, even while he was kissing Jarra. The owl is really a stupid creature, he remembered, for all his appearance of wisdom. Was he playing the owl by any chance?

It was odd that when he had seen Jarra eleven days ago she had said nothing of any such trip. It was odder that Jarra's father, the merchant Berota, a patriarch with strong ideas of the place of women in society, should take his daughter with him on such a commercial foray. And the rocky peninsula of Dzen, haunted by demons and their depraved worshipers, was no profitable field for trade. Perhaps it was more than a coincidence that the type of education which Jarra proposed to give him was precisely that guaranteed to dissolve and cancel the spell that Sancheth had cast upon him to ward off Nikurteu's maleficent magic.

As he hesitated, torn between prudence and passion, the owl hooted again. With that he thrust her to arms' length, looking at her through narrowed eyes.

'What's the name of my mother?' he demanded abruptly.

'Why Gezun, as if I should know that ...'

'Then be damned to demon-land!' he shouted, vaulting back on the mule. 'May all your brats be stillborn! May Dyosizh smite your tenderest parts with an itch! May the teeth rot in your head!'

He trotted off into the night, knowing that the real Jarra knew the names of his parents perfectly well. Hadn't he spent hours telling her of his life in Lorsk?

A glance back showed Jarra standing quietly by the road. As he watched, her features changed into something not quite human, and peals of shrill aged laughter came after him. He spat and wiped his mouth with his mantle.

'Thinks he can befool me with his shape-changing sprites, eh!' he mused. 'Me, *me*? Döpueng Shysh of Lorsk, the future king of Tartessia?'

He gestured with the spear against the unresisting night air.

The heart of Gezun Lorska beat high as he rode into Gadaira in the early morning. At the edge of town he dismounted to lead Dostaen the rest of the way, for the narrow streets did not encourage cantering, and anyway Gezun's bottom was sore from days of hard riding.

He paused at the little bridge over the Arrang to watch a gang of workmen digging a foundation for a house. It would be a fine house, judging from the size and depth of the excavation. They had dug a trench from the house-hole down to the edge of the little river, and now were laying semicylindrical tiles in the trench to carry off the wastes of the house.

Gezun filed the idea away for his own future use. He became lost in contemplation, thinking of the fine palace he would build when he was king, until a voice behind him roused him:

'Daydreaming, Gezun? You'll never attain the style of magician by that road!'

It was Nikurteu Balya, riding past on his fine black horse. With a laugh Gezun's master's rival rode on and disappeared.

Gezun pulled himself together and trudged the small remaining distance to Sancheth Sar's house. Sancheth himself hurried to the door at the sound of his approach.

'What news?' creaked the old wizard.

'Success, Master!'

'*Haulae!* Glorious! You're a fine lad, as I've always said!' Years fell away from Sancheth as he waved his stick, did a little dance-step, and thumped Gezun affectionately on the back. 'Tell me all about it.'

'Here's the manuscript,' said Gezun, handing it over. 'But before I begin, wasn't there a certain other bargain between us?'

'You mean the ring? Here, take mine; I'll use the other.'

Sancheth Sar slipped the ring of sky-metal off and handed it to Gezun, who experimented till he found a finger that it fitted comfortably.

'And now to your tale – wup! What's this?'

As Gezun watched with increasing alarm, Sancheth's eyes widened, the corners of his mouth turned down, and his fingers began to shake.

'Listen,' he said in a voice like one of Gezun's pet snakes in a rage: '"To my esteemed colleague, Sancheth Sar, from his admirer Nikurteu Balya. Your servant bore himself nobly on the mission whereon you sent him. Nevertheless it is written in the Book of Geratun that he who assigns to a boy a task properly appertaining to a man shall rue the day he did so. For Gezun shrewdly surmised which item of the auction was the Hordhun Manuscript and overbid me; he bravely fought and slew two servants I sent to waylay him; he resisted with inhuman self-control the advances of a sprite I sent to entice him from the path of rectitude in the form of his sweetling. Yet when he entered Gadaira did he stop to watch four men digging a hole in the ground – four men whom I, knowing that no boy can resist the spectacle of an excavation, had hired for the purpose. And so bemused became he that it was no tough task to take the Hordhun Manuscript from his scrip and substitute this commiseratory screed. Farewell!"'

'You!' screamed Sancheth, and his eyes were like those of a hungry eagle. 'You bawbling oaf! You imperceiverant hilding! You incondite loon! I'll cast upon you an itch that shall leave you no peace for —'

'Forget not this, Master!' cried Gezun, backing toward the door and holding out the clenched hand that bore the ring of star-metal. 'You can't enchant me!'

'But that protects you not from more mundane chastisement!' yelled Sancheth, and went for Gezun with his stick.

And thus it came to pass that the citizens of Gadaira were treated to the diverting if not uplifting spectacle of Gezun Lorska running full-tilt down the main street, while behind him came the town's senior sorcerer, Sancheth Sar, making a speed that none would have expected in a wizard of his centuries, and cleaving the air with his mystic walking-stick.

THE EYE OF TANDYLA

This is a story about a man who stole the jewel from an idol's eye – but not the one you're thinking of. *That* story was told eighty-odd years ago by Wilkie Collins.

But the present story began much longer ago than that – 'So long, that mountain have arisen since, with cities on their flanks.' It began on the sinking continent of Poseidonis, in the kingdom of Lorsk, in the capital city of Mneset, in the royal palace of King Vuar the Capricious, and in the apartment of that palace tenanted by Derezong Tâsh, the king's sorcerer.

On this particular afternoon Derezong sat in his library reading the Collected Fragments of Lontang and drinking the green wine of Zhysk. He was at peace with himself and the world, for nobody had tried to murder him for ten whole days, by natural means or otherwise. When tired of puzzling out the cryptic glyphs, Derezong would gaze over the rim of his goblet at his demon-screen, on which the great Shuazid (before King Vuar took a capricious dislike to him) had depicted Derezong's entire stable of demons, from the fearful Fernazot down to the slightest sprite that submitted to his summons.

One wondered, on seeing Derezong, why even a sprite should bother. For Derezong Tâsh was a chubby little man (little for a Lorskan, that is) with white hair framing a round youthful face.

On this occasion Derezong planned, when drunk enough, to heave his pudgy form out of the reading-chair and totter in to dinner with his apprentice, Zhamel Se. Four of Derezong's sons should serve the food as a precaution against Derezong's ill-wishers, and Zhamel should taste it first as a further precaution. After they had consumed a few more jars of wine, Derezong would choose three of his prettiest concubines and stagger off to bed. A harmless program, one would have said. In fact Derezong had already, in his mind, chosen the three, though he had not yet decided upon the order in which he proposed to enjoy them.

And then the knock upon the door and the high voice of King Vuar's most insolent page: 'My lord sorcerer, the king will see you forthwith!'

'What about?' grumbled Derezong.

'Do I know where the storks go in winter? Am I privy to the secrets of the living dead of Sedö? Has the North Wind confided to me what lies beyond the ramparts of the Riphai?'

'I suppose not.' Derezong yawned, rose, and toddled throneward. He glanced back over his shoulders as he went, misliking to walk through the halls of the palace without Zhamel to guard his back against a sudden stab.

The lamplight gleamed upon King Vuar's glabrous pate, and the king looked up at Derezong from under his hedge of heavy brows. He sat upon his throne in the audience chamber, and over his head upon the wall was fastened the hunting-horn of King Vuar's ancestor, King Zhabutir. On the secondary throne sat the king's favorite concubine Ilepro, from Lotör: a dumpy middle-aged Lotri, hairy and toothy. What the king saw in her … Perhaps in middle age he had become bored with beauty and sought spice from its antithesis. Or perhaps after the High Chief of Lotör, Konesp, had practically forced his widowed sister upon the king after Ilepro's husband had died of a hunting-accident, the monarch had fallen truly in love with her.

Or perhaps the hand of the wizard-priests of Lotör was to be discerned behind these outré events. Sorcery or its equivalent would be needed to account for King Vuar's designating Ilepro's young son by her Lotri husband as his heir, if indeed he had done so as rumor whispered. (Derezong was thankful that the youth was not present, though that quartet of Lotri women, swathed in their superfluous furs, squatted around the feet of Ilepro.)

Derezong was sure there was something here that he did not understand, and that he would not like any better when he did understand, and that he would not like any better when he did understand it. Despite the present peace-treaty between Lotör and Lorsk, he doubted that the Lotris had forgotten the harrying that King Vuar had inflicted upon them in retaliation for their raids.

After his preliminary prostration, Derezong observed something else that had escaped his original notice: that on a small table in front of the throne, which usually bore a vase of flowers, there now reposed a silver plate, and on the plate the head of the chief minister, wearing that witlessly blank expression that heads are wont to fall into when separated from their proper bodies.

Evidently King Vuar was not in his jolliest mood.

'Yes, King?' said Derezong, his eyes swivelling nervously from the head of the late minister to that of his sovereign.

King Vuar said: 'Good my lord, my concubine Ilepro, whom I think you know, has a desire that you alone can satisfy.'

'Yes, Sire?' Jumping to a wrong conclusion, Derezong goggled like a bull-frog in spring. For one thing, King Vuar was not at all noted for generosity in sharing his women, and for another thing, of all the royal harem, Derezong had the least desire to share Ilepro.

The king said: 'She wishes that jewel that forms the third eye of the goddess Tandyla. You know that temple in Lotör?'

'Yes, Sire.' Although he retained his blandest smile, Derezong's heart sank to the vicinity of his knees. This was going to prove even less entertaining than intimacy with Ilepro.

'This small-souled huckster,' said Vuar, indicating the head, 'said, when I put the proposal to him, that the gem could not be bought, wherefore I caused his length to be lessened. This hasty act I now regret, for it transpires that he was right. Therefore our only remaining course is to steal the thing.'

'Y-yes, Sire.'

The king rested his long chin upon his first and his agate eyes saw distant things. The lamplight gleamed upon the ring of gray metal on his finger, a ring made from the heart of a falling star, and of such might as a magic-repellant that not even the sendings of the wizards of Lotör had power to harm its wearer. Kings had worn these rings ever since the time of Vakar the Great. He continued:

'We can either essay to seize it openly, which would mean war, or by stealth. Now, although I will go to some trouble to gratify the whims of Ile-pro, my plans do not include a Lotrian war – at least not until all other expedients have been attempted. You, therefore, are hereby commissioned to go to Lotör and obtain this jewel.'

'Yes indeed, Sire,' said Derezong with a heartiness that was, to say the least, a bit forced. Any thoughts of protest that he might have entertained had some minutes since been banished by the sight of the unlucky minister's head.

'Of course,' said Vuar in tones of friendly consideration, 'should you feel your own powers inadequate, I'm sure the king of Zhysk will lend me his wizard to assist you …'

'Never, Sire!' cried Derezong, drawing himself up to his full five-five. 'That bungling beetlehead, so far from helping, would be but an anchor-stone about my neck!'

King Vuar smiled a lupine smile, though Derezong could not preceive the reason, 'So be it, then.'

Back in his own quarters Derezong Tâsh rang for his assistant. After the third ring Zhamel Se sauntered in, balancing his big bronze sword by the pommel on his palm.

'Some day,' said Derezong, 'you'll amputate some poor wight's toe showing off that trick, and I only hope it will be yours. We leave tomorrow on a mission.'

Zhamel grasped his sword securely by the hilt and grinned down upon his employer. 'Good! Whither?'

Derezong told him.

'Better yet! Action! Excitement!' Zhamel swished the air with his sword. 'Since you put the geas upon the queen's mother we have sat in these apartments like barnacles on a pile, doing nought to earn King Vuar's bounty.'

'What's wrong with that? I plague none and nobody plagues me. And now with winter coming on we must journey forth to the ends of rocky Lotör to try to lift this worthless bauble the king's sack of a favorite has set her silly heart upon.'

'I wonder why?' said Zhamel. 'Since she's Lotri by birth you'd think she'd wish to ward her land's religious symbols instead of raping them away for her own adornment.'

'One never knows. Our own women are unpredictable enough, and as for Lotris … But let's to the task of planning our course and equipage.'

That night Derezong took only one concubine to bed with him.

They rode east to fertile Zhysk on the shores of the Sirenian Sea, and in the capital city of Amferé sought out Derezong's friend Goshap Tuzh the lapidary, from whom they solicited information to forearm them against adversity.

'This jewel,' said Goshap, 'is about the size of a small fist, egg-shaped, without facets, and of dark purple hue. When seen from one end it displays rays like a sapphire, but seven instead of six. It forms the pupil of the central eye of the statue of Tandyla, being held in place by leaden prongs. As to what other means, natural or otherwise, the priests of Tandyla employ to guard their treasure I know not, save that they are both effective and unpleasing. Twenty-three attempts have been made to pilfer the stone in the last five centuries, all terminating fatally for the thieves. The last time I, Goshap Tuzh, saw the body of the thief …'

As Goshap told the manner in which the unsuccessful thief had been used, Zhemal gagged and Derezong looked into his wine with an expression of distaste, as if some many-legged creeping thing swam therein – although he and his assistant were by no means the softest characters in a hard age.

'Its properties?' said Derezong Tàsh.

'Considerable, though perhaps overrated by distant rumor. It is the world's most sovereign antidemonic, repelling even the dread Tr'lang himself, of all demons the deadliest.'

'Is it even stronger than King Vuar's ring of star-metal?'

'Much. However, for our old friendship, let me advise you to change your name and take service with some less exacting liege lord. There's no profit in seeking to snatch this Eye.'

Derezong ran his fingers through his silky-white hair and beard. 'True, he ever wounds me by his brutally voiced suspicions of my competence, but to relinquish such luxe as I enjoy were not so simple. Where else can I obtain such priceless books and enrapturing women for the asking? Nay, save when he becomes seized of these whimsies, King Vuar's a very good master indeed.'

'But that's my point. When do you know his notorious caprice may not be turned against you?'

'I know not; betimes I think it must be easier to serve a barbarian king.

Barbarians, being wrapped in a mummy-cloth of custom and ritual, are more predictable.'

'Then why not flee? Across the Sirenian Sea lies lordly Torrutseish, where one of your worth would soon rise —'

'You forget,' said Derezong, 'King Vuar holds hostages: my not inconsiderable family of fourteen concubines, twelve sons, nine daughters, and several squalling grandchildren. And for them I must stick it out, though the Western Sea swallow the entire land of Poseidonis as is predicted in the prophecies.'

Goshap shrugged. 'That's your affair. I do but imply that you are one of these awkward intermediates: too tub-like ever to make a prow swordsman, and unable to attain the highest grade of magical adeptry because you'll not forswear the delights of your zenana.'

'Thank you, good Goshap,' said Derezong, sipping the green wine. 'Howsoever, I live, not to attain preëminence in some austere disciplinary regimen, but to enjoy life. And now who's a reliable apothecary in Amferé from whom I can obtain a packet of syr-powder of highest grade and purity?'

'Dualor can furnish you. What semblance do you propose to cast upon yourselves?'

'I thought we'd go as a pair of traders from Kernê. So, if you hear of such a couple traversing Lotör accompanied by vast uproar and vociferation, don't fail to show the due surprise.'

Derezong bought his syr-powder with wedges of gold bearing the stamp of King Vuar, then returned to their inn where he drew his pentacles and cast his powder and recited the Incantation of the Nines. At the end both he and Zhamel were lying helpless on the floor, with their appearance changed to that of a pair of dark hawk-nosed fellows in the fluttery garb of Kernê, with rings in their ears.

When they recovered their strength they rode forth, and for days rode through farmlands and pasturelands and deserts and forests and mountains. Nothing of note befell them. At last they wound their way among the rocky hills of Lotör.

As they stopped for one night Derezong said: 'By my reckoning and according to what passersby have told us, the temple should lie not more than one day's journey ahead. Hence it were time to try whether we can effect our mission by surrogate instead of in our own vulnerable persons.' And he began drawing pentacles in the dirt.

'You mean to call up Feranzot?' asked Zhamel Se.

'The same.'

Zhamel shuddered. 'Some day you'll leave an angle of a pentacle unclosed, and that will be the end of us.'

'No doubt, but to assail this stronghold of chthonian powers by any but the mightiest means were an even surer passport to extinction. So light the rushes and begin.'

'I can fancy nothing riskier than dealing with Feranzot,' grumbled Zhamel, 'save perhaps invoking the terrible Tr'lang himself.' But he did as he was bid.

They went through the Incantation of Br'tong, as reconstructed by Derezong from the Fragments of Lontang, and the dark shape of Feranzot appeared outside the main pentacle, wavering and rippling. Derezong felt the heat of his body sucked forth by the cold of the daev, and suffered the overwhelming depression the thing's presence engendered. Zhamel, for all his thews, cowered.

'What would you?' whispered Feranzot.

Derezong gathered his weakened forces and replied: 'You shall steal the jewel in the middle eye of the statute of the goddess Tandyla in the nearby temple thereof and render it to me.'

'I cannot.'

'And why not?'

'First, because the priests of Tandyla have traced around their temple a circle of such puissance that no sending or semblance or spirit, save the great Tr'lang, can cross it. Second, because the Eye itself is surrounded by an aura of such baleful influence that not I, nor any other of my kind, not even Tr'lang himself, can exert a purchase upon it on this plane. May I return to my own dimension now?'

'Depart, depart, depart … Well, Zhamel, it looks as though we should be compelled to essay this undelightsome task ourselves.'

Next day they continued their ride. The hills became mountains of uncommon ruggedness, and the road a mere trail cut into cliffs of excessive steepness. The horses, more accustomed to the bison-swarming plains of windy Lorsk, misliked the new topography, and rubbed their riders' legs painfully against the cliffside in their endeavor to keep away from the edge.

Little sun penetrated these gorges of black rock, which began to darken almost immediately after noon. Then the sky clouded over and the rocks became shiny with cold mist. The trail crossed the gorge by a spidery bridge suspended from ropes. The horses balked.

'Not that I blame them,' said Derezong, dismounting. 'By the red-hot talons of Vrazh, it takes the thought of my fairest concubine to nerve *me* to cross!'

When led in line with Zhamel belaboring their rumps from the rear, the animals crossed though unwillingly. Derezong, towing them, took one brief look over the side of the bridge at the white thread of water foaming far below and decided not to do that again. Feet and hooves resounded hollowly on the planking and echoed from the cliffsides, and the wind played with the ropes as with the strings of a great harp.

On the other side of the gorge the road continued its winding upward way.

They passed another pair, a man and a woman, riding down the trail, and had to back around a bend to find a place with room enough to pass. The man and the woman went by looking somberly at the ground, barely acknowledging with a grunt the cheerful greeting that Derezong tossed at them.

Then the road turned sharply into a great cleft in the cliff, wherein their hooffalls echoed thrice as loud as life and they could scarcely see to pick their way. The bottom of the cleft sloped upward, so that in time they came out upon an area of tumbled stones with a few dwarfed trees. The road ran dimly on through the stones until it ended in a flight of steps, which in turn led up to the Temple of Tandyla itself. Of this temple of ill repute the travellers could see only the lower parts, for the upper ones disappeared into the cloud floor. What they could see of it was all black and shiny and rising to sharp peaks.

Derezong remembered the unpleasant attributes ascribed to the goddess, and the even more disagreeable habits credited to her priests. It was said, for instance, that the worship of Tandyla, surely a sinister enough figure in the Pusadian pantheon, was a mere blind to cover dark rites concerning the demon Tr'lang, who in elder days had been a god in his own right. That was before the towering Lorskans, driven from the mainland by the conquering Euskerians, had swarmed across the Sirenian Sea to Poseidonis, before that land had begun its ominous subsidence.

Derezong assured himself that gods and demons alike were not usually so formidable as their priests, from base motives of gain, tried to make them out. Also, that wild tales of the habits of priests usually turned out to be at least somewhat exaggerated. Although he did not fully believe his own assurances, they would have to suffice for want of better.

In front of the half-hidden temple, Derezong pulled up, dismounted, and with Zhamel's help weighted down the reins of their beasts with heavy stones to hinder them from straying. As they started for the steps Zhamel cried:

'Master!'

'What is't?'

'Look upon us!'

Derezong looked and saw that the semblance of traders from Kernê, in jelabs and kaffiyehs, had vanished, and that they were again King Vuar's court magician and his apprentice, plain for all to see. They must have stepped across that line that Feranzot had warned them of.

Derezong took a sharp look at the entrance, and half-hidden in the inadequate light he saw two men flanking the doorway. His eye caught the gleam of polished bronze. But if these doorkeepers had observed the change in the looks of the visitors they gave no sign.

Derezong drove his short legs up the shiny black steps. The guards came into full view, thick-bodied Lotris with beetling brows. Men said they were akin to the savages of Ierarné in the far Northeast, who knew no horse-taming and fought with sharpened stone. These stood staring straight ahead, each facing the other like statues. Derezong and Zhamel passed between them.

They found themselves in a vestibule where a pair of young Lotri girls said: 'Your boots and swords, sirs.'

Derezong lifted off his baldric and handed it to the nearest, scabbard and all, then pulled off his boots and stood barefoot with the grass he had stuffed into them to keep them from chafing sticking out from between his toes. He was glad to feel the second sword hanging down his back inside his shirt.

A low remark passed between Zhamel and one of the girls – a girl who, Derezong observed, was not bad-looking for a Lotri in a plump moon-faced way.

'Come on,' said Derezong, and led the way into the naos of the temple.

It was much like other temples: a big rectangular room smelling of incense, with a third of the area partitioned off by a railing, behind which rose the huge black squat statue of Tandyla. The smooth basalt of which it was carved reflected feebly the high-lights from the few lamps, and up at the top, where its head disappeared into the shadows, a point of purple light showed where the jewel in its forehead caught the rays.

A couple of Lotris knelt before the railing, mumbling prayers. A priest appeared from the shadows on one side, waddled across the naos behind the railing ... Derezong half expected the priest to turn on him with a demand that he and Zhamel follow him into the sanctum of the high priest, but the priest kept on walking and disappeared into the darkness on the other side.

Derezong and his companion advanced, a slow step at a time, towards the railing. As they neared it the two Lotris completed their devotions and rose. One of them dropped something that jingled into a large tub-like receptacle behind the railing, and the two squat figures walked quickly out.

For the moment Derezong and Zhamel were entirely alone in the big room, though in the silence they could hear faint motions and voices from other parts of the temple. Derezong brought out his container of syr-powder and sprinkled it while racing through the Incantation of Ansuan. When he finished, there stood between himself and Zhamel a replica of himself.

Derezong climbed over the railing and trotted on the tips of his plump toes around behind the statue. Here in the shadows he could see doors in the walls. The statue sat with its back almost but not quite touching the wall behind it, so that an active man, by bracing his back against the statue and his feet against the wall, could lever himself up. Though Derezong was 'active' only in a qualified sense, he slipped into the gap and squirmed into a snugly-fitting fold in the goddess' stone draperies. Here he lay, hardly breathing, until he heard Zhamel's footfalls die away.

The plan was that Zhamel should walk out of the temple, accompanied by the double of Derezong. The guards, believing that the temple was now deserted of visitors, would relax. Derezong would steal the stone; Zhamel should raise a haro outside, urging the guards to 'Come quickly!' and while their attention was thus distracted Derezong would rush out.

Derezong waited a while longer. The soft footsteps of another priest padded past and a door closed. Somewhere a Lotri girl laughed.

Derezong began to worm his way up between the statue and the wall. It was hard going for one of his girth, and sweat ran out from under his cap of fisher-fur and down his face. Still no interruption.

He arrived on a level with the shoulder and squirmed out on to that projection, holding the right ear for safety. The slick stone was cold under his bare feet. By craning his neck he could see the ill-favored face of the goddess in profile and by stretching he could just reach the jewel in her forehead.

Derezong took out of his tunic a small bronze pry-bar he had brought along for this purpose. With it he began to pry up the leaden prongs that held the gem in place; carefully lest he mar the stone or cause it to fall to the floor below. Every few pries he tested it with his finger. Soon it felt loose.

The temple was quiet.

Around the clock he went with his little bar prying. Then the stone came out, rubbing gently against the smooth inner surfaces of the bent-out leaden prongs. Derezong reached for the inside of his tunic, to hide the stone and the bar. But the two objects proved too much for his pudgy fingers to handle at once. The bar came loose and fell with a loud *ping-ping* down the front of the statute, bouncing from breast to belly to lap, to end with a sonorous clank on the stone floor in front of the image.

Derezong froze rigid. Seconds passed and nothing happened. Surely the guards had heard ...

But still there was silence.

Derezong secured the jewel in his tunic and squirmed back over the shoulder to the darkness behind the statue. Little by little he slid down the space between statue and wall. He reached the floor. Still no noise save an occasional faint sound such as might have been made by the temple servants preparing dinner for their masters. He waited for the diversion promised by Zhamel.

He waited and waited. From somewhere came the screech of a man in the last agonies.

At last, giving up, Derezong hurried around the hip of the statue. He scooped up the pry-bar with one quick motion, climbed back over the railing, and tiptoed toward the exit.

There stood the guards with swords out, ready for him.

Derezong reached back over his shoulder and pulled out his second sword. In a real fight he knew he would have little hope against a hardened and experienced sword-fighter, let alone two. His one slim chance lay in bursting through them by a sudden berserk attack and keeping on running.

He expected such adroit and skillful warriors to separate and come at him from opposite sides. Instead one of them stepped forward and took an awkward swipe at him. Derezong parried with a clash of bronze and struck back. *Clang! Clang!* went the blades, and then his foe staggered back, dropped his sword with a clatter, clutched both hands to his chest, and folded up in a heap on the floor. Derezong was astonished; he could have sworn he had not gotten home.

Then the other man was upon him. At the second clash of blades, that of the guard spun out of his hand, to fall ringingly to the stone pave. The guard leaped back, turned, and ran, disappearing through one of the many ambient doors.

Derezong glanced at his sword, wondering if he had not known his own strength all this time. The whole exchange had taken perhaps ten seconds, and so far as he could tell in the dim light no blood besmeared his blade. He was tempted to test the deadness of the fallen guard by poking him, but lacked both time and ruthlessness to do so. Instead, he ran out of the vestibule and looked for Zhamel and the double of himself.

No sign of either. The four horses were still tethered a score of paces from the steps of the temple. The stones were sharp under Derezong's bare and unhardened soles.

Derezong hesitated, but only for a flash. He was in a way fond of Zhamel, and his assistant's brawn had gotten him out of trouble about as often as Zhamel's lack of insight had gotten them into it. On the other hand, to plunge back into the temple in search of his erratic aide would be rash to the point of madness. And he did have definite orders from the king.

He sheathed his sword, scrambled on to the back of his horse, and cantered off, leading the other three beasts by their bridles.

During the ride down the narrow cleft, Derezong had time to think, and the more he thought the less he liked what he thought. The behavior of the guards was inexplicable on any grounds but their being drunk or crazy, and he did not believe either. Their failure to attack him simultaneously; their failure to note the fall of the pry-bar; the ease with which he, an indifferent swordsman, had bested them; the fact that one fell down without being touched; their failure to yell for help …

Unless they planned it that way. The whole thing had been too easy to account for by any other hypothesis. Maybe they *wanted* him to steal the accursed bauble.

At the lower end of the cleft, where the road turned out on to the side of the cliff forming the main gorge, he pulled up, dismounted, and tied the animals, keeping an ear cocked for the sound of pursuers echoing down the cleft. He took out the Eye of Tandyla and looked at it. Yes, when seen end-on it showed the rayed effect promised by Goshap Tuzh. Otherwise it exhibited no special odd or unnatural properties. So far.

Derezong set it carefully on the ground and backed away from it to see it from a greater distance. As he backed, the stone moved slightly and started to roll towards him.

At first he thought he had not laid it down on a level enough place, and leaped to seize it before it should roll over the edge into the gulf. He put it back and heaped a little barrier of pebbles and dust around it. Now it should not roll!

But when he backed again it did, right over his little rampart. Derezong began anew to sweat, and not, this time, from physical exertion. The stone rolled toward him, faster and faster. He tried to dodge by shrinking into a recess in the cliff-wall. The stone swerved and came to rest at the toe of one of his bare feet, like a pet animal asking for a pat on the head.

He scooped out a small hole, laid the gem in it, placed a large stone over the hole, and walked away. The large stone shook and the purple egg appeared, pushing aside the pebbles in its path as if it were being pulled out from under the rock by an invisible cord. It rolled to his feet again and stopped.

Derezong picked up the stone and looked at it again. It did not seem to have been scratched. He remembered the urgency with which Chief Konesp was said to have pressed his sister upon King Vuar, and the fact that the demand for the stone originated with this same Ilepro.

With a sudden burst of emotion Derezong threw the stone from him, towards the far side of the gorge.

By all calculation the gem should have followed a curved path, arching downward to shatter against the opposite cliff. Instead it slowed in mid-flight over the gorge, looped back, and flew into the hand that had just thrown it.

Derezong did not doubt that the priests of Tandyla had laid a subtle trap for King Vuar in the form of this jewel. What it would do to the king and to the kingdom of Lorsk if Derezong carried out his mission, he had no idea. So far as he knew it was merely an antidemonic, and therefore should protect Vuar instead of harming him. Nevertheless he was sure something unpleasant was planned, of which he was less than eager to be the agency. He placed the gem on a flat rock, found a stone the size of his head, raised it in both hands, and brought it down upon the jewel …

Or so he intended. On the way down the stone struck a projecting shelf of rock, and a second later Derezong was capering about like a devil-dancer of Dzen, sucking his mashed fingers and cursing the priests of Tandyla in the names of the most fearful demons in his repertory. The stone lay unharmed.

For, Derezong reasoned, these priests must have put upon the gem not only a following-spell, but also the Incantation of Duzhateng, so that every effort on the part of Derezong to destroy the object would redound to his own damage. If he essayed some more elaborate scheme of destruction he would probably end up with a broken leg. The Incantation of Duzhateng could be lifted only by a complicated spell for which Derezong did not have the materials, which included some very odd and repellant substances indeed.

Now Derezong knew that there was only one way in which he could both neutralize these spells and secure the jewel so that it should plague him no more, and that was to put it back in the hole in the forehead of the statue of Tandyla and hammer down the leaden prongs that held it in its setting. Which task, however, promised to present more difficulties than the original theft. For if the priests of Tandyla had meant Derezong to steal the object, they might show greater acumen in thwarting his attempt to return it than they had in guarding it in the first place.

One could but try. Derezong put the jewel into his tunic, mounted his horse (leaving the other three still tethered) and rode back up the echoing cleft. When he came out upon the little plateau upon which squatted the temple of Tandyla he saw that he had indeed been forestalled. Around the entrance to the temple now stood a double row of guards, the bronze scales of their cuirasses glimmering faintly in the fading light. The front rank carried shields of mammoth-hide and big bronze swords, while those in the rear bore long pikes which they held in both hands and thrust between the men of the front rank. They thus presented a formidable hedge to any attacker, who had first to get past the spear-points and then deal with the swords.

One possibility was to gallop at them in the hope that one or two directly in one's way would flinch aside, opening a path by which one could burst through the serried line. Then one could ride on into the temple and perhaps get the gem back into place before being caught up with. If not, there would be a great smash, some battered guards, a wounded horse, and a thoroughly skewered and sliced sorcerer all tangled in a kicking heap.

Derezong hesitated, then thought of his precious manuscripts and adorable concubines awaiting him in King Vuar's palace, which he could never safely enter again unless he brought either the gem or an acceptable excuse for not having it. He kicked his mount into motion.

As the animal cantered toward the line, the spear-points got closer and larger and sharper-looking, and Derezong saw that the guards were not going to flinch aside and obligingly let him through. Then a figure came out of the temple and ran down the steps to the rear of the guards. It wore a priest's robe, but just before the shock of impact Derezong recognized the rugged features of Zhamel Se.

Derezong hauled on his reins, and the horse (who had not much cared for the looks of the spear-points either) skidded to a halt with its nose a scant span from the nearest point. Derezong, living in a stirrupless age, slid forward until he bestrode the animal's neck. Clutching its mane with his left hand he felt for the gem with his right.

'Zhamel!' he called. 'Catch!'

He threw. Zhamel leaped high and caught the stone before it had time to loop back.

'Now put it back!' cried Derezong.

'*What?* Are you mad?'

'Put it back, speedily, and secure it!'

Zhamel, trained to obey commands no matter how bizarre, dashed back into the temple, albeit wagging his head as if in sorrow for his master's loss of sanity. Derezong untangled himself from his horse's mane and pulled the beast back out of reach of the spears. Under their lacquered helmets the heads of the guards turned this way and that in evident perplexity. Derezong surmised that they had been given one simple order, to keep him out, and that they had not been told how to cope with fraternization between the stranger and one of their own priests.

As the guards did not seem to be coming after him, Derezong sat on his horse, eyes on the portal. He'd give Zhamel a fair chance to accomplish his mission and escape, though he thought little of the youth's chances. If Zhamel tried to push or cut his way through the guards they would make mincemeat of him, unarmored as he was. And he, Derezong, would have to find and train another assistant, who would probably prove as unsatisfactory as his predecessor. Still, Derezong could not leave the boy utterly to his fate.

Then Zhamel ran down the steps carrying a long pike of the kind held by the rear-rank guards. Holding this pike level he ran at the guards as though he were about to spear one in the back. Derezong, knowing that such a scheme would not work, shut his eyes.

But just before he reached the guards, Zhamel dug the point of the pike into the ground and pole-vaulted. Up he went, legs jerking and dangling like those of a man being hanged, over the lacquered helmets and the bronze swords and the mammoth-hide shields. He came down in front of the guards, breaking one of their pikes with a loud snap, rolled to his feet, and ran towards Derezong. The latter had already turned his horse around.

As Zhamel caught hold of the edge of the saddle-pad, an uproar arose behind them as priests ran out of the temple, shouting. Derezong drummed with his bare heels on the stallion's ribs and set off at a canter, Zhamel swinging along in great leaps beside him. They wended their way down the cleft while the sound of hooves wafted after them.

Derezong wasted no breath in questions while picking his way down the trail. At the bottom, where the cleft ended on one side of the great gorge, they halted for Zhamel to mount his own horse, then continued on as fast as they dared. The echoes of the pursuers' hooves came down the cleft with a deafening clatter.

'My poor feet!' groaned Zhamel.

At the suspension-bridge the horses balked again, but Derezong mercilessly pricked and slapped his mount with his sword until the beast trotted out upon the swaying walkway. The cold wind hummed through the ropes and the daylight was almost gone.

At the far end, with a great sigh of relief, Derezong looked back. Down the cliffside road came a line of pursuers, riding at reckless speed. He said:

'Had I but time and materials, I'd cast a spell on yonder bridge that should make it look as if it were broken and dangling useless.'

'What's wrong with making it broken and useless in very truth?' cried Zhamel, pulling his horse up against the cliffside and hoisting himself so that he stood upon his saddle.

He swung his sword (his second, the first having been left in the temple) at the cables. As the first of the pursuers reached the far side of the bridge, the structure sagged and fell away with a great swish of ropes and clatter of planks. The men from the temple set up an outcry, and an arrow whizzed across the gap to shatter against the rock. Derezong and Zhamel resumed their journey.

A fortnight later they sat in the garden back of the shop of Goshap Tuzh the lapidiary in sunny Amferé. Zhamel told his part of the tale:

'... so on my way out this little Lotri cast her orbs upon me once again. Now, thought I, there'll be time in plenty to perform the Master's work and make myself agreeable in this quarter as well —'

'Young cullion!' growled Derezong into his wine.

'— so I followed her. And all was going most agreeably when who should come in but one of these chinless wonders in cowl and robe, and went for me with a knife. I tried to fend the fellow off, and fear that in the fracas his neck got broke. So, knowing there might be trouble, I borrowed his habit and sallied forth therein, to find that Master, horses, and Master's double had all gone.'

'And how time had flown!' said Derezong in sarcastic tones. 'I trust at least that the young Lotri has cause to remember this episode with pleasure. The double no doubt, being a mere thing of shadow and not a rational being, walked straight out and vanished when it crossed the magical barrier erected by the priests.'

'And,' continued Zhamel, 'there were priests and guards rushing about chittering like a pack of monkeys. I rushed about as if I were one of them, saw them range the guards around the portal, and then the Master returned and threw me the stone. I grasped the situation, swarmed up the statue, popped Tandyla's third eye back into its socket, and hammered the prongs in upon it with the pommel of my dagger. Then I fetched a pike from the armory, pausing but to knock senseless a couple of Lotris who sought to detain me for interrogation, and you know the rest.'

Derezong rounded out the story and said: 'Good Goshap, perhance you can advise our next course, for I fear that should we present ourselves before King Vuar in proper persons, without the gem, he'd have our heads set tastefully on silver platters ere we finished our explanation. No doubt remorse would afterwards overwhelm him, but that wouldn't help us.'

'Since he holds you in despite, why not leave him, as I've urged before?' said Goshap.

Derezong shrugged. 'Others, alas, show like lack of appreciation, and would prove no easier masters. For example had these priests of Tandyla confided in my ability to perform a simple task like carrying their gemstone from Lotör to Lorsk, their plot would doubtless have borne its intended fruit. But fearing lest I should lose or sell it on the way, they put a supernumerary spell upon it —'

'How could they, when the stone has anti-magical properties?'

'Its antimagical properties comprise simple antidemonism, whereas the following-spell and the Incantation of Duzhateng are sympathetic magic, nor sorcerous. At any rate, they caused it to follow me hither and thither, thus arousing my already awakened suspicions to the fever-pitch.' He sighed and took a pull on the green wine. 'What this sorry world needs is more confidence. But say on, Goshap.'

'Well then, why not write him a letter setting forth the circumstances? I'll lend you a slave to convey it to Lorsk in advance of your persons, so that when you arrive King Vuar's wrath shall have subsided.'

Derezong pondered. 'Sage though I deem your suggestion, it faces one insurmountable obstacle. Namely: That of all the men at the court of Lorsk, but six can read; and among these King Vuar is not numbered, whereas of the six at least five are among my enemies, who'd like nought better than to see me tumbled from my place. And should the task of reading my missive to the king devolve on one of these, you can fancy how he'd distort my harmless pictographs to my discredit. Could we trick old Vuar into thinking we'd performed our task, as by passing off on him a stone similar to that he expects of us? Know you of such?'

'Now there,' said Goshap, 'is a proposal indeed. Let me cogitate … Last year, when the bony specter of want came upon the land, King Daiör placed his best crown in pawn to the Temple of Lyr, for treasure wherewith to still the clamorings of his people. Now this crown bears at its apex a purple starsapphire of wondrous size and fineness, said to have been shaped by the gods before the Creation for their own enjoyment, and being in magnitude and hue not unlike that which forms the Eye of Tandyla. And the gem has never been redeemed, wherefore the priests of Lyr have set the crown on exhibition, thereby mulcting the curious of further offerings. But as to how this well-guarded gem shall be transferred from this crown to your possession, don't ask me, and in truth I had liefer know nought of the matter.'

*

Next day Derezong Tâsh cast upon himself and Zhamel the likeness of Atlantes, from the misty mainland mountain range of Atlantis, far to the east across the Sirenian Sea, where it was said in Poseidonis that there were men with snakes for legs and others with no heads but faces in their chests. Zhamel grumbled:

'What are we, magicians or thieves? Perhaps if we succeed in this, the king of Tartessia across the Sirenian Sea has some bauble he specially fancies, that we could rob him of.'

Derezong did not argue the point, but led the way to the square fronted by the Temple of Lyr. They strode up to the temple with the Atlantean swagger, and in to where the crown lay upon a cushion on a table with a lamp to illuminate it and two seven-foot Lorskans to guard it, one with a drawn sword and the other with a nocked arrow. The guards looked down over their great black beards at the gangling red-haired Atlanteans in their blue cloaks and armlets of orichalc who pointed and jabbered as they saw the crown. And then the shorter Atlantean, that was Derezong beneath the illusion, wandered out, leaving the other to gape.

Scarcely had the shorter Atlas passed the portal than he gave a loud squawk. The guards, looking that way, saw his head in profile, projecting past the edge of the doorway and looking upward as though his body were being bent backward, while a pair of hands gripped his throat.

The guards, not knowing that Derezong was strangling himself, rushed to the portal. As they neared it the head of the assailed Atlantean disappeared from view, and they arrived to find Derezong in his proper form strolling up to the entrance. All the while behind them the powerful fingers of Zhamel pried loose the stone from King Daiör's crown.

'Is aught amiss, sirs?' said Derezong to the guards, who stared about wildly as Zhamel came out of the temple behind them. As he did so he also dropped his Atlantean disguise and became another Lorskan like the guards, though not quite so tall and bushy-bearded.

'If you seek an Atlas,' said Derezong in answer to their questions, 'I saw two such issue from your fane and slink off into yonder alley with furtive gait. Perhaps it behooves you to see whether they have committed some depredation in your hallowed precincts?'

As the guards rushed back into the temple to see, Derezong and his assistant made off briskly in the opposite direction. Zhamel muttered:

'At least let's hope we shall not have to return this jewel to the place whence we obtained it!'

Derezong and Zhamel reached Mneset late at night, but had not even finished greeting their loving concubines when a messenger informed Derezong that the king wanted him at once.

Derezong found King Vuar in the audience room, evidently fresh-risen from his bed, for he wore nothing but his crown and a bearskin wrapped about his bony body. Ilepro was there too, clad with like informality, and with her were her ever-present Lotrian quartet.

'You have it?' said King Vuar, lifting a bushy brow that boded no good for a negative answer.

'Here, Sire,' said Derezong, heaving himself up off the floor and advancing with the jewel from the crown of King Daiör.

King Vuar took it in his finger-tips and looked at it in the light of the single lamp. Derezong wondered if the king would think to count the rays to see if there were six or seven; but he reassured himself with the thought that King Vuar was notoriously weak in higher mathematics. The king extended the jewel towards Ilepro.

'Here, madam,' he said. 'And let us hope that with this transaction ends your incessant plaint.'

'My lord is as generous as the sun,' said Ilepro in her thick Lotrian accent. ''Tis true I have a little more to say, but not for servile ears.' She spoke in Lotrian to her four attendants, who scuttled out.

'Well?' said the king.

Ilepro stared into the sapphire and made a motion with her free hand, meanwhile reciting something in her native tongue. Although she went too fast for Derezong to understand, he caught a word, several times repeated, that shook him to the core. The word was 'Tr'lang'.

'Sire!' he cried. 'I fear this northern witch is up to no good —'

'What?' roared King Vuar. 'You vilipend my favorite, and before my very optics? I'll have your head —'

'But Sire! King! Look!'

The king broke into his tirade long enough to look, and never resumed it. For the flame of the lamp had shrunk to a bare spark. Cold eddies stirred the air of the room, in the midst of which the gloom thickened into shadow and the shadow into substance. At first it seemed a shapeless darkness, a sable fog, but then a pair of glowing points appeared, like eyes, at twice the height of a man.

Derezong's mind sought for exorcisms while his tongue clove to the roof of his mouth with terror. For his own Feranzot was but a kitten compared to this, and no pentacle protected him.

The eyes grew plainer, and lower down horny talons threw back faint high-lights from the feeble flame of the lamp. The cold in the room was as if an iceberg had walked in, and Derezong smelt an odor as of burning feathers.

Ilepro pointed at the king and cried something in her own language. Derezong thought he saw fangs as a great mouth opened and Tr'lang swept forward towards Ilepro. She held the jewel in front of her, as if to ward off the daev. But it paid no attention. As the blackness settled around her she gave a piercing scream.

The door now flew open again and the four Lotri women rushed back in. Ilepro's screams continued, diminuendo, with a curious effect of distance, as if Tr'lang were dragging her far away. All that could be seen was a dwindling shapeless shape of shadow in the middle of the floor.

The foremost of the Lotris cried 'Ilepro!' and sprang towards the shape, shedding wraps with one hand while tugging out a great bronze sword with the other. As the other three did likewise, Derezong realized that they were not women at all, but burly male Lotris given a superficially feminine look by shaving their beards and padding their clothes in appropriate places.

The first of the four swung his sword through the place where the shape of Tr'lang had been, but without meeting resistance other than that of air. Then he turned toward the king and Derezong.

'Take these alive!' he said in Lotrian. 'They shall stand surety for our safe departure.'

The four moved forward, their swords ready and their free hands spread to clutch like the talons of the just-departed demon. Then the opposite door opened and in came Zhamel with an armful of swords. Two he tossed to Derezong and King Vuar, who caught them by the hilts; the third he gripped in his own large fist as he took his place beside the other two.

'Too late,' said another Lotri. 'To slay them and run's our only chance.'

Suiting the deed of the declaration he rushed upon the three Lorskans. *Clang! Clang!* went the swords as the seven men slashed and parried in the gloom. King Vuar had whirled his bearskin around his left arm for a shield and fought naked save for his crown. While the Lorskans had an advantage of reach, they were handicapped by the king's age and Derezong's embonpoint and mediocrity of swordsmanship.

Though Derezong cut and thrust nobly, he found himself pushed back towards a corner, and felt the sting of a flesh-wound in the shoulder. And whatever the ignorant might think of a wizard's powers, it was quite impossible to fight physically for one's life and cast a spell at the same time.

The king bellowed for help, but no answer came, for in these inner chambers the thick stone walls and hangings deadened sound before it reached the outer rooms of the palace where King Vuar's guards had their stations. Like the others he, too, was driven back until the three were fighting shoulder to shoulder in the corner. A blade hit Derezong's head flatsides and made him dizzy, while a metallic sound told that another blow had gotten home on the king's crown, and a yelp from Zhamel revealed that he also had been hurt.

Derezong found himself fast tiring. Each breath was a labor, and the hilt was slippery in his aching fingers. Soon they'd beat down his guard and finish him, unless he found some more indirect shift by which to make head against them.

He threw his sword, not at the Lotri in front of him, but at the little lamp that flickered on the table. The lamp flew off with a clatter and went out as Derezong dropped on all fours and crept after his sword. Behind him in the darkness he could hear the footsteps and the hard breathing of men, afraid to strike for fear of smiting a friend and afraid to speak lest they reveal themselves to a foe.

Derezong felt along the wall until he came to the hunting-horn of King Zhabutir. Wrenching the relic from the wall, he filled his lungs and blew a tremendous blast.

The blast of the horn resounded deafeningly in the confined space. Derezong moved, lest one of the Lotris locate him by sound and cut him down in the dark, and blew again. With loud trampings and clankings the guards of King Vuar approached. The door burst open and in they came with weapons ready and torches high.

'Take them!' said King Vuar, pointing at the Lotris.

One of the Lotris tried to resist, but a guardsman's sword sheared the hand from his arm as he swung. The Lotri screamed and sank to the floor to bleed to death. The others were subdued with little trouble.

'Now,' said the king, 'I can give you the boon of a quick death, or I can turn you over to the tormentors for a slower and much more interesting one. If you confess your plans and purposes in full, you shall be permitted the former alternative.'

The Lotris exchanged glances and kept silence.

'Speak!' said Vuar.

Still no reply.

'Fetch the tormentors,' said Vuar.

A quarter-hour later the tormentors and their instruments were ready. Vuar pointed to one stripped Lotri, saying:

'Start on that one. He seems to be the leader.'

Derezong wrinkled his nose in disgust as the room filled with the stench of burning flesh. After the tormentors' instruments had sizzled against the tissues of the quivering victim for some time, the Lotri suddenly shrieked.

'I'll speak!' he sobbed. When allowed to sit up, he said: 'Know, King, that I am Urkil, the spouse of Ilepro. The others are gentlemen of the court of Ilepro's brother Konesp, High Chief of Lotör.'

'Gentlemen!' snorted King Vuar.

'As my brother-in-law has no sons of his own, he and I concocted this scheme for bringing his kingdom and your under the eventual rule of my son Pendetr. This magician of yours was to steal the Eye of Tandyla so that, when Ilepro conjured up the daev Tr'lang, the monster should not assail her as she'd be protected by the gem's powers; it should, instead, dispose of you. For we knew no lesser creature of the outer dimensions could assail you whilst you wear the ring of star-metal. Then she'd proclaim the child Pendetr king, as you've already named him heir, with herself as regent till he comes of age. But the antisorcellarious virtues of this jewel are evidently not what they once were, for Tr'lang engulfed my wife though she thrust the gem in his maw.'

'You have spoken well and frankly,' said King Vuar, 'though I question the morality of turning your wife over to me as my concubine, yourself being not only alive but present here in disguise. However, the customs of the Lotris are not ours. Lead them out, guards, and take off their head.'

'One more word, King,' said Urkil. 'For myself I care little, now that my beloved Ilepro's gone. But I ask that you make not the child Pendetr suffer for his father's faulty schemes.'

'So he can plot revenge when he grows up? Be not absurd. Now off with you and with your heads.' The king turned to Derezong, who was mopping at his fleshwound. 'What is the cause of the failure of the Eye of Tandyla?'

Derezong, in fear and trembling, told the true tale of their foray into Lotör and their subsequent theft of the sapphire in Amferé.

'Aha!' said King Vuar. 'So that's what we get for not counting the rays seen in the stone!'

He paused to pick up the jewel from where it lay upon the floor, and the quaking Derezong foresaw his own severance, like that which the Lotris were even now experiencing. Then Vuar smiled thinly.

'A fortunate failure, it seems,' said the king. 'I am indebted to you both, first for your shrewdness in penetrating the plans of the Lotris to usurp the throne of Lorsk, second for fighting beside me to such good purpose tonight.

'Howsoever, we have here a situation fraught with some slight embarrassment. For King Daiör is a good friend of mine, which friendship I would not willingly forego. And even though I should return this gem to him with explanation and apology, the fact that my servants purloined it in the first place would not sit well with him. My command to you, therefore, is to return at once to Amferé —'

'Oh, *no!*' cried Derezong, the words escaping involuntarily from him.

'— return to Amferé,' continued the king as if he had not heard, 'and smuggle the jewel back into its original position in the crown of the king of Zhysk, without letting anyone know that you are involved either in the disappearance of the stone or in its eventual restoration. For such accomplished rogues as you and your apprentice have shown yourselves to be, this slight feat will pose no serious obstacle. And so goodnight, my lord sorcerer.'

King Vuar threw his bearskin about him and tramped off to his apartments, leaving Derezong and Zhamel staring at one another.

If you've enjoyed these books and would
like to read more, you'll find literally thousands
of classic Science Fiction & Fantasy titles
through the **SF Gateway**

✴

*For the new home of
Science Fiction & Fantasy . . .*

✴

*For the most comprehensive collection
of classic SF on the internet . . .*

✴

Visit the SF Gateway

www.sfgateway.com

L. Sprague de Camp (1907–2000)

Lyon Sprague de Camp was born in 1907 and died in 2000. During a writing career that spanned seven decades, he wrote over a hundred books in the areas of science fiction, fantasy, historical fiction, non-fiction and biography. Although arguably best known for his continuation of Robert E. Howard's Conan stories, de Camp was an important figure in the formative period of modern SF, alongside the likes of Isaac Asimov and Robert A. Heinlein, and was a winner of the Hugo, World Fantasy Life Achievement and SFWA Grand Master awards.